Ronnie Darwin was My Uncle

by

Paul Crampton

Pen Press Publishers Ltd

© Paul Crampton 2006

All rights reserved

No part of this publication may be reproduced,
stored in a retrieval system, or transmitted
in any form or by any means, without
the prior permission in writing of the publisher,
nor be otherwise circulated in any form of binding or cover other than that in
which it is published and without a similar condition including this condition
being imposed on the subsequent purchaser.

First published in Great Britain by
Pen Press Publishers Ltd
The Old School Road
39 Chesham Road
Brighton BN2 1NB

ISBN: 1-905203-99-3
ISBN13: 9-781905203994

Printed and bound in the UK

A catalogue record of this book is available from
the British Library

Cover design by Jacqueline Abromeit

For Chris.

ABOUT THE AUTHOR

Paul Crampton comes from Canterbury – a place where he still lives, and from which he continues to draw inspiration. Paul is now a full timer writer of both fictional and non-fiction works, as well as keeping busy running a small on-line, second-hand bookselling business. As far as his non-fiction books are concerned, eleven titles have been produced to date, with a twelfth due this year, being *'Canterbury's Lost Heritage'*, published by *Alan Sutton*. This will be out at almost the same time as *'Ronnie Darwin was my Uncle'*. Paul's first novel *'Strangers in Focus'*, also published by *Pen Press*, came out in 2005, to an enthusiastic response.

Recording The Past

08:59 on a Monday morning, was by far the most daunting and depressing time of the whole week, thought Dave Darwin with dread, as the seconds counted down to the time when the telephone switchboard opened up.

'*Stand by your beds*!' yelled someone keenly, from the opposite end of the office, almost as if that person relished the prospect.

Dave watched the second hand jerking round to the hour, and just knew that of all the people in his immediate block of four desks, his own phone would be the first to ring.

'*We're open for business*!' enthused the same motivated madman from the far end, as an unseen button was pressed to start the day's business going.

Within seconds, as predicted or rather feared, Dave's telephone warbled into life, much to the amusement of his three closest colleagues.

'Good morning, Telecom Customer Relations, Dave Darwin speaking, how may I help you?' he announced, in a cheerful and welcoming tone that did little to give away his true feelings.

As the agitated voice on the other end launched into the inevitable tirade, Dave's head sank into his right hand, while holding the loathed telephone receiver with his left. This was the first complaint of the new week, and he knew from bitter experience that it would be the first of many.

God, I hate Monday mornings, I hate working for Telecom and most of all I hate these bloody people who phone me with their petty complaints, Dave groaned to himself, as he tried to block out the sound of the squawking woman who had called him. He also speculated as to what her actual complaint would be, once she'd finally stopped shouting: the line was crackly, the last bill was too high, the telephone engineer who installed my phone left a coffee cup ring on the bird's eye maple veneered sideboard; it was bound to be something like that!

Dave had heard it all over the years, and inevitably, had become very cynical.

He had to assume that these customers –he was no longer allowed to call them subscribers – must save up their petty whinges all weekend, just to phone first thing on the Monday morning and remind him of what a crappy job he had. Why can't they just leave me alone and get a life, he thought, as he began to make sympathetic noises in response to the woman's complaint.

In spite of his initial feelings, once Dave had got over the psychological barrier of actually picking up the receiver and saying his opening greeting, most of the time, he quickly formed a relationship with the caller and did all he could to help them with their problem.

As he despatched that first caller with a promise of immediate help, Dave pressed the pause button and looked over at the three other people who shared that block of four desks with him. These were his closest colleagues, in both senses of the word; they were his fellow Telecom sufferers.

There was Monica next to him: tall, willowy, well dressed, and with her left clip-on earring removed so that it wouldn't clatter on the telephone receiver. She had an assertive manner and liked to take control. Considered by many to be beautiful, in a pattern book sort of way, she was pleasant, yet utterly spoiled by both parents and boyfriends alike. A lover of gossip and potential management material, Dave concluded, with a resigned sigh.

Opposite her, plump, shell-suited Tiffany never seemed to let life get her down. The almost permanent smile on her face came through in her voice, and endeared her to many of the more regular telephone complainants. Of all of them, she seemed to mind Monday mornings the least. Gossipy and almost completely devoid of any conscience, Tiffany preferred to live her life permanently set at the mental age of 16.

Next to Tiffany, and opposite Dave, was Tim: a recent Telecom recruit and a man he had now got to know very well, and yet in many ways, not know at all. His classical features, accentuated by a Roman nose and receding temples, made him resemble a study of the young Napoleon, although a rather dishevelled one. Tim hated everything about this job too. He was the proverbial square peg, and this was one of the reasons why he was also Dave's best work friend. Tim would regularly remark that all these people really wanted were the £10.00 compensation payments: 'Good morning, Telecom customer relations, Tim Cross speaking, your cheque is in the post', was Tim's all too often quoted Monday morning joke.

This was indeed a typical start to the working week and there was little let up. It therefore came as no surprise to Dave that, when he released the pause button, his telephone rang straightaway. For him though, there were two things that would make this particular Monday different from all the others. The first was his dreaded annual appraisal interview: a school-like process, where line managers assessed every aspect of an individual staff's work for the last year. Dave was due to be 'assessed' at eleven o'clock by his new manager, Darryl Giles. The other factor was much more unexpected, and did not become apparent until mid-morning, when he began to notice the customers' unusual reaction to his opening telephone greeting.

The telephone call he took at 10:25 was typical: 'Good morning, Telecom Customer Relations, Dave Darwin speaking, how may I help you?'

'Dave *Darwin* eh, any relation?'

'*Yes* actually, Ronnie Darwin was my uncle!'

After the sixth telephone call of that morning to attract the same response to his friend's greeting, Tim could stand it no longer, and leant over to laugh at him.

'Oh Dave, why are you assuming they mean your *Uncle* Ronnie?' he mocked, good-humouredly. 'They could be referring to *Charles* Darwin!'

'*Ha*, that's where you are wrong my bookish buddy,' Dave responded, with his arms folded and a haughty expression on his face. 'I doubt that *any* of them have even heard of that weirdy beardy. No; they're saying it because, my *dear* Timothy, another clip from one of Ronnie's old shows was repeated on the television at the weekend – *you* wouldn't have seen it, of course – and these people are merely grateful for a chance to communicate with a member of the same talented family!' He was clearly joking, but his obvious admiration for the talents of his beloved uncle was absolutely genuine.

It came as no surprise to Dave that Tim had missed the TV show in question. His friend cared little for television, although like almost everyone else, he owned a set. However, few programmes would ever attract his attention, if there were the preferred alternative of a good book to be read. Tim was an educated man in an academic sense, but he also had all the implied limitations that invariably seemed to go with it. As an example, he knew what existentialism was, but could not boil an egg to save his life. Unlike Dave himself, who'd left school after his O levels, Tim had taken a batch of A levels, and then gone on to university. He'd also recently taken an Open University degree in philosophy, claiming that he welcomed both the stretching of his mind, and the letters he was confident would be placed after his name. In fact, Dave often thought that in an ideal world, Tim would have much preferred to remain in a perpetual state of learning, shielded by academia from the realities of life, many of which he seemed to struggle with. Tim had joined the company only in the last few years, a decision that was motivated purely and simply by dire financial necessity.

Dave, on the other hand, had now put in 16 years with Telecom – murderers do less time, Tim would often say – and was now on the maximum salary for his grade. Unlike his learned friend, Dave had hated school and anything remotely to do with it. Consequently, he had escaped at the first opportunity and quickly turned to Telecom; attracted, as much by the pretty young women in the glossy prospectus, as the fact his father was a well-paid Telecom engineer. Over the intervening years, he had developed many domestic skills, more through necessity than desire and, much to Tim's envy and admiration, was currently way beyond the egg boiling stage.

Despite some reservations, there was a great deal that Dave both admired and envied about Tim Cross. He had a young family – a boy and a girl – a talent for music, and a casual confidence when dealing with customers and colleagues alike. And yet, he also had a certain vulnerability that was not obvious at first. This was something that Dave had been picking up as their friendship deepened and consolidated.

The two men had become close friends in the short time that they'd worked together and, despite their different educational backgrounds, they shared many things in common, not the least of which was a daft sense of humour. The origins of Tim's familial funny bone were unknown, but Dave had inherited it from Ronnie, his father's younger brother. In fact, he'd first used this skill for comedy at school, where, as a chubby boy, it had become a useful tool to ward off the inevitable bullies. The younger David had reasoned that it was better they laugh at you for your impersonation of the Spanish master, than because of your spots or fat bottom. Dave also used his talent for humour in the work environment; it was the only thing that had kept him going all these years. In this respect, he had Tim as an ally, so now there was a pair of jokers in the pack. Having said that, Tim's humour was different from Dave's, and clearly gave away his bookish nature. He had once joked about the ironic 'sartorial elegance' of the man who cleaned the Telecom House toilets, and who sometimes wore a bow tie. Dave had laughed heartily at the comment, but when he got home that night, had looked up the word 'sartorial' in the dictionary. Between them, they had also invented a series of secret catchphrases that were verbal responses to certain things said or done in the office by other people. For example, if anyone else made a slightly rude or risqué remark, Tim and Dave would respond in unison with: 'another teacake vicar?' They would then both giggle like schoolboys, with other people's puzzled looks only making it all the funnier.

As 11:00 came round, Dave sunk his head into his hands again and let out a deep despairing sigh. It was time for his appraisal interview, and even the thought of not having to field any telephone calls for a while couldn't make up for that daunting prospect.

'I wonder what *this* year's trendy buzz word will be?' he asked, of any of his immediate colleagues who cared to listen.

'I hear '*motivational*' is very popular at the moment,' Tim responded, with a disapproving expression, whilst hitting the pause button on his phone.

'He'd better not bloody well try *that* one on me, the *bastard*!' Dave furrowed his brows, and then slowly slid off his chair back.

'*Oo*, another teacake vicar!' retorted Tim, with liberal amounts of mock shock.

'Yeah, I suppose I *asked* for that!' Dave conceded. 'But *still*, being put under the spotlight like that ... I *hate* it!'

Tim stared over at his friend without the least bit of envy.

'Anyway, good luck, matey. Just imagine him with no trousers on; they say it helps,' he smiled, hoping to lift Dave's spirits a little.

'It always works for *me*', joked Tiffany, looking across from her monitor.

With another resigned sigh and a slightly nervous chuckle, Dave slunk over to the glass-fronted interview room, like a schoolboy having been caught smoking, and with the prospect of a caning being an absolute certainty. Seeing that his new boss had already taken up position in that small multi-purpose side room – known as the goldfish bowl, for obvious reasons – he knocked rhythmically on the door and then entered.

'Ah Dave, *come* in, *sit* down; nice to finally be able to touch base with you!' remarked Darryl Giles, without looking up, but making a beckoning gesture.

Dave sat in the armless chair, on the opposite side of the small desk, whilst his new manager flicked through what he assumed to be his appraisal document. My God, he seems so young, Dave thought, as he studied the man who would soon be judging him. It also struck him that his new boss certainly didn't look like the sort of person that Telecom usually favoured as a manager, with his gelled hair, oval metal-framed glasses, and gold stud in his left ear. However, the general assumption in the wider office was that he must have something that the anonymous senior bosses liked. What *was* it exactly, Dave pondered, as he continued to sit there, and why is the bastard keeping me waiting? He soon speculated that it must be some sort of modern managerial controlling technique to make the senior person appear more important.

The young manager finally looked up from the document and smiled broadly, revealing a mouthful of variously cream-coloured capped teeth.

'Sorry to keep you waiting Dave! *Anyway*, I'm Darryl Giles, the new *ACRE*,' he announced, raising himself off the chair and extending a hand, on which a half-sovereign ring was prominently displayed.

'ACRE?' queried a puzzled-looking Dave, as he returned the greeting.

'Didn't you read my welcoming *Handshake Memo*?' Darryl said with a disappointed frown. '*Oh* well! You see, err, Dave ...one of the benefits of this new job was that I got to choose my own title. It translates to Area Customer Relations Executive!' he revealed proudly. 'So what do you think?'

'It's very *you*!' Dave remarked, with a wry smile. At the same time, he thought that perhaps Cretinous Upstart New to Telecom might be a more appropriate title.

'*Anyway* Dave – call me Darryl by the way – I've been looking through your appraisal and I like what I see,' he remarked, quickly flicking through the document in question. 'Very impressive, *especially* the customer feedback surveys. There are plenty of *Kisses* here Dave, well done!'

'What in the name of all that's sane are *Kisses*?' Dave enquired incredulously, his mouth gaping open.

'Oh Dave, Dave, *Dave*!' despaired Darryl, with a weary shake of the head, and his eyes tightly shut. 'You *obviously* don't read your *Weekly Inspirational Notes do* you? A 'Kiss' is a Key Indicator of Subscriber Satisfaction, and your feedbacks are *full* of them! Listen to this: 'kind', 'reliable', 'empathetic' – *that's* a good one – and of course, 'patient'; you're a very good *Kisser* Dave!' he added, seemingly oblivious to the obvious double meaning.

'But I thought we weren't allowed to call them *subscribers* any more, only *customers*?' Dave commented with a barely concealed smirk.

'Yes I *know*, but *Kics* sounds so *negative*, don't you think?' he asked in all sincerity, his head cocked to one side.

Dave struggled in vain to suppress a snigger, by pretending to study the wilting potted plant in the corner.

Unfortunately, his new boss noticed the gesture.

'I'm picking up some cynicism here Dave,' Darryl remarked, with a disappointed frown on his face. He then quickly re-examined the appraisement documents. 'Umm, *that* could be one of the reasons why you're the second lowest call taker in the group!'

'Look, I'm here to help the customers with their problems and sometimes that takes *time*, especially if you take pride in doing it *properly*,' Dave reasoned, in defensive mode. 'So I may not sing the company song as loud as you *want* me to, but that doesn't make me any less effective at my job!'

Darryl Giles did not respond straightaway, but sat there calmly looking down, with his hands knitted together on the desk. He then slowly looked up, and studied his junior through narrowed eyes.

'I'm picking up some negative vibes here, Dave. All I'm saying is that your existing skills can be enhanced with a little coaching from *me*! *Yes*, be patient with the customers, but be prompt as well; *shorten* those telephone calls. *Yes*, be empathetic, but don't forget to be *efficient*. Monica and Tiffany give away *far* less compensation payments than you! And as for being reliable, reliable is *good*, but so is a little ruthlessness. If they complain that their extension phone isn't working properly, sell them a second one *and* repair the first! You may well be kind to the customers Dave, but I need you to be keener on the company as well!'

'*Look*, I cannot change who or what I am, and I'm *sorry*, but I've no intention of trying,' Dave declared, with a defensive fold of his arms.

Darryl ignored the comment, and merely adopted a well-practised serene posture, coupled with a forced corporate smile.

'Listen Dave, I'm soon going to be organising a voluntary, motivational paint-balling weekend. I think it would be *good* for you!' he proposed, reinforcing his words with a slow nod.

Having passed through phases of both cynicism and defensiveness, Dave now began to look and sound angry. 'I'd sooner eat my own scrotum,' he responded dismissively, and haughtily studied the fire extinguisher on the rear wall.

'I *urge* you to reconsider and I feel, quite honestly, that you should…that you *need* to attend,' Darryl pressed, with a hint of ominous menace in his voice. 'I'll turn you into a team player *yet* Dave, and you'll *thank* me for it!'

'If it's voluntary, then I will *not* volunteer!' barked Dave obstinately, as he restored his direct gaze in Darryl's direction. 'Unlike *some* people, I've got a *life* you know, and my weekends are my *own*, okay?'

'I'm picking up no small amount of hostility here Dave, I just want you to be delighted to work for Telecom and then…'.

'Can't you *speak* properly?' interrupted Dave loudly, as he rose from his seat. 'Have you ever tried *listening* to yourself? One minute you're saying I'm doing a good job, the next, you're spouting all these bloody trendy American clichés and making up ridiculous anachronisms to try and prove that I'm *not*! *Tell* me, *please* ... am I doing a good job or not, *eh*?'

For the first time in the whole interview, it was Darryl Giles who began to look defensive, and it was he who now broke eye contact with his challenger.

'Yes you *are* doing a good job Dave; I wouldn't want to be *without* you in my team,' he conceded, with a slight shrug. 'But I'm just a little disappointed with your attitude.'

'I'll learn to live with it, and I'm perfectly capable of doing my job without your Customer Relations Aggravating Prattle, if you get my meaning!'

A defeated Darryl desperately struggled to think of something appropriately corporate to say in response to the outburst, but it was too late. With a slam of the door, a seething Dave left the interview room, but he felt no particular sense of victory. He knew full well that, one way or another, he would be made to pay for challenging the *Stated Telecom Doctrine*, or the 'STD', as it was known by some.

'Who the *hell* does that prat Giles think he is!' barked Dave, as he dropped heavily into the chair by his own desk.

'Mmm, *that* went well then,' grinned Tim in Tiffany's direction.

'Yeah, but he's *right* though... Darryl Giles *is* a prat!' she confirmed, with a dismissive tut, above her packet of crisps.

'I *like* him,' added Monica, without looking away from her computer screen. 'Such expensive clothes ... nice shoes as well!'

As Tiffany chortled quietly to herself in response to their colleague's comment, the two male friends exchanged knowing glances. No words were necessary.

Dave then glanced up at the office clock and his mood became a lot more positive.

'Thank *God* we've booked the afternoon off, Timothy my man ... have you got your camera with you?' he enquired, before re-booting his computer.

'Yep ... I can't wait to get out of here *myself*!' Tim agreed, with a much-relieved sigh.

Humour was not the two friends only escape from Telecom. Often, they would build up flexi-time hours and take a long lunch break, or even use annual leave for an afternoon off together, as would be the case that Monday. These excursions, usually organised by Dave, followed the same pattern, giving away his love for routine. Having escaped the tyranny of Telecom, the pair could be found wandering in and around Canterbury, with camera bags slung over their respective shoulders, either photographing something specific, or just looking for pictorial inspiration.

Photography was something that Tim had encouraged Dave to take up, and once he'd given it a try, the man was completely hooked. Dave had long wanted a medium to help preserve the memory of those things that meant something to him, be it a threatened place or person. He often wished that there had been more old photographs, taken in his formative years, to reinforce those early memories of Uncle Ronnie, and those cherished childhood places - like Oakenden Nursery, his paternal grandparents smallholding - which were lost forever. Ronnie had used a camera to record things every so often, but it had been Tim who'd really got Dave inspired; specifically, with his black and white photographs of one of the recently closed Kent collieries. And it was one particular enlarged image that had commanded his attention. This depicted the ghostly, stilled winding gear of the abandoned mineshaft, silhouetted against a dark, stormy sky. After seeing that print, it was only a matter of persuading his wife Sheila to allow him to spend the necessary amount in order to get properly set up with a decent camera, and all the photographic paraphernalia that went with it.

The Telecom twosome's cameras may have been the same type, but their preferred subject matter was very different. Tim was always on the look out for that indefinably interesting shot: an odd pattern in brickwork, the long winter shadow cast by an old street lamp against the road surface; the dishevelled man of indeterminate age in the doorway, holding a large bottle of strong cider. Dave, on the other hand, had a more documentary approach, a passion for recording the past. He loved photographing old buildings or even modern buildings, as long as they were under threat of demolition. He also enjoyed picturing the passing of the seasons, as mirrored by the trees and plants around him. This botanical interest had been inherited from Grandad Darwin, his parental grandfather and a major influence on his life. That Monday afternoon, the skeletal trees were of particular interest, but here and there beneath the bare hedges in the more rural parts of the city, the basal leaves of alexanders and cow parsley were already evident; very early reminders that spring was on the way.

The planning policy in Canterbury was changing almost as fast as the passing of the seasons. Industrially based businesses were now being encouraged to leave the city, in order to make way for the more lucrative option of middle class housing. Consequently, there were a lot of threatened industrial buildings in the vicinity, and Dave would often drag Tim along to these unglamorous sites, and this particular occasion was no exception. Dave had taken his friend to an old garage complex in North Lane that was to be cleared for a dense sheltered housing scheme. This was the place where his father had once bought the regular weekly three gallons of four-star, and also been given double Green Shield stamps. He couldn't bear the thought that something so fondly remembered from his past, be swept away without some sort of record being made.

Dave Darwin often thought about the past, and could never let things go. He still had all his old Dinky toys and Ladybird books at home; it was a foible that Sheila tolerated and his stepson, Julian, ridiculed. His mind was as crammed-full as their spare room with cherished images that he didn't ever want to forget. At least, now that Dave had his camera, he could create some sort of backup record.

The old garage, which had been out of use for some time, proved to be a compelling subject, and Dave made sure that he pictured every elevation of the derelict and boarded-up buildings. Tim was quite happy too, as he had found the dried stalks and seed heads of a buddleia sprouting from the base of a long since abandoned petrol pump, and was trying to line up the most artistic shot.

Dave looked over at Tim, crouching in front of the ranks of rusty petrol pumps, and his mind wandered back over 30 years to the early 60s. As a young boy, he had often accompanied his father to the garage, but hadn't he also come here once with his beloved Uncle Ronnie?

*

'Don't open your presents just yet old chap,' his father said, from above his after-lunch cup of tea. 'Your Uncle Ronnie will be here in a moment'.

'*Yes* David,' his mother added, as she came in from the kitchen, 'he's driving here for the first time, in his *own car*!'

Young David didn't mind in the least, delaying that much-anticipated moment, for he was exceptionally happy that day. It was his fifth birthday, and for once, his parents were turning their attention towards him and not his little sister Lucy. But best of all, his Uncle Ronnie was coming to see him in his very first car, and he was also going to stay to tea with them all.

Ronnie was his favourite uncle, his funny uncle, and at eighteen years' old, his father's junior by some ten years. To David's young perception, that ten year gap seemed so much wider. He loved his father dearly, but he was a man who wore cardigans, who regularly told him off and nearly always seemed to prefer Lucy to him. So despite their occasional jokes together, David's love for his father was slightly qualified. Uncle Ronnie, on the other hand, liked *The Shadows* and *Fireball XL5*, just as David did. What is more, he had not long since bought something his mother called a 'bachelor pad' in Herne Bay, and was now living on his own, having just moved out of the tied cottage at Rothermead where Nanna and Grandad Darwin still resided.

Ronnie was not the only one to have relocated; in fact, everyone in the family seemed to have moved house recently. Only Nanna and Grandad Maybury, his mother's parents, were still in the same house where they'd always been. The first people to start the trend were his Grandparents Darwin, who had moved from the Tankerton based Oakenden Nursery to Rothermead Farm, near Sittingbourne. Ronnie went with them, but within months, had obtained his own place in Herne Bay. And then, just before Christmas, David's own immediate family, who had previously lived at Tankerton, next door to Nanna and Grandad Darwin's smallholding, moved back to Canterbury. The Cathedral city was where Len and Meg had originally set up home at the very beginning of their married life. They had now been in their new house for about three months.

A car horn sounded rhythmically outside; it was a pattern that the whole family recognised.

'*Uncle Ronnie*!' shouted both David and Lucy, the latter having just woken up from her nap, and they each ran out to greet him.

'*Don't run into the road you two*!' their father warned, as he and Meg followed them through the open front door.

Seeing his niece and nephew bearing down on him, Ronnie crouched down and threw open his arms.

'Alright then Dave,' he enthused, as he picked him up. 'Alright curly top', he added, ruffling Lucy's hair as she keenly clung to his left leg.

'Settled *in* alright then Len?' he asked of his older brother, adjusting his hold of David so that the two men could shake hands.

'Yes thanks,' replied Len, with a warm smile. 'And I must say: it's *much* more handy for work!'

'*Hello* Ronnie love,' greeted Meg, leaning forward to kiss his cheek. 'Put David down if he's too heavy for you!'

'No, he's *fine*, aren't you mate?' Ronnie replied, as his nephew gripped on happily. '*Come* on then Dave, show us your new house.'

'Alright then,' David agreed happily, for although this was his uncle's second visit, the family were barely unpacked when he first came over.

As they went back up the front garden path, David could not have been happier. Uncle Ronnie was the only person ever to call him 'Dave' and what is more, the only person to pick him up now. His parents never did that anymore, claiming that he was 'a ton weight', whatever *that* was. Being in Ronnie's arms, the five-year-old felt that, this time, he had really triumphed over Lucy, his sibling rival, who was still clinging to their uncle's leg beneath him.

Once inside the house, the family all gathered in the front room. Almost straightaway, Ronnie put David down and went over to speak to Len and Meg in a low, conspiratorial-sounding voice.

'But you've only just passed your test,' Meg remarked at her normal volume, clearly responding to the preceding whispers.

'No, I think it'll be alright Meg,' interjected his father, before plunging his hands into the pockets of his cardigan. 'You *know* Ronnie will be careful, and there are *still* three or four hours until we have tea.'

David's dad broke away from the huddle, walked over towards him and then knelt down, in order to talk to him at eye level.

'Your uncle says that your present is over in his new Herne Bay flat, and that you can go back there with him now and get it. Would you *like* that?' he asked, with a warm, expectant smile.

'Oh yes *please*!' enthused David, jumping up and down on the spot.

'*Come* on then,' responded his father, with a wink, before straightening himself up again, and then taking his hand.

Meg picked up Lucy and they all walked back out to the car together.

'*I* wanna go *too* Mummy!' the small girl pouted as she squirmed to get down.

David looked back at his sister with anxious eyes, and for one brief moment, he thought that they might let her. But he needn't have fretted.

'Not this time Lucy; this is your *brother's* birthday treat,' Meg explained in soft, soothing tones. 'Besides, you're *far* too young at the moment!'

The birthday boy resumed his journey to the car with an air of triumph, but he tried his best not to let it show.

As Ronnie held the passenger door open for David to clamber in, Len walked up and down the newly acquired car, and carefully examined it with an air of expertise that he did not possess.

'Ford Consul?' he asked, having already read the badge on the front of the car.

'That's right Len; what you would call a jelly mould,' Ronnie smiled, with a wink in Meg's direction.

'HP?' asked the older brother, with raised eyebrows, already suspecting he knew the answer.

Ronnie chuckled but did not answer the question.

'Don't worry folks, I'll look after the birthday boy, and have him back in good time for tea!' he vowed cheerily, before getting into the driver's position.

Young David waved through the back window, as his uncle negotiated a rapid three point turn; after which, the car accelerated away down Westgate Court Avenue, and probably a lot faster than his mother would have liked. The family all waved back, and then turned to go in as the late 1950's Ford disappeared round the bend.

As soon as the vehicle was out of sight from the house, Ronnie slowed down and held up his left hand.

'*Scar brothers*!' he shouted, with a broad grin in his nephew's direction.

David did the same and also yelled '*Scar brothers*!'

They then banged their left hands together and gripped tightly. This was a ritual the two of them had only begun to perform fairly recently. Moreover, not only was it carried out in secret, but also David and Ronnie alone knew exactly what its significance was. They both chuckled and then were able to resume the journey.

Uncle Ronnie drove confidently, perhaps a little too fast like most young men, but still carefully fed the steering wheel around corners, which gave away his novice status. However, David noticed nothing wrong; on the contrary, everything seemed fine. Uncle Ronnie's car may have been secondhand and possess a funny smell, but it was clearly better than his father's three-wheeled Bond. At least he wouldn't be embarrassed if his friends saw him now, the five-year-old concluded.

'What did you get for your birthday then, Dave?' Ronnie asked, as they sped round the Westgate Towers, like a hairpin bend at Silverstone.

'I haven't opened them yet; I'm waiting until later when *you* can be there to see me,' David replied, as he clung to the edges of the car seat.

Although he said nothing in response, a contentedly grinning Ronnie was obviously very touched by this gesture.

Before long, the car was passing through the village of Sturry and approaching the railway line. To David's delight, he saw the level crossing gates being closed a few yards in front of them. They were now the first in a short queue of cars that was rapidly forming behind.

'*Come* on Dave,' Ronnie said quickly scrambling out of the car, ' we may not get another chance.'

David followed suit and was lifted into his uncle's arms once again, as they stood hard against the level crossing gates. Peering in the Canterbury direction, the pair soon saw the belching smoke, and heard the rhythmic pounding of an approaching coast-bound express train. The faded green locomotive was soon upon them and whistled loudly as it roared through the small village station, adjacent to the crossing. Although David was excited by the spectacle, he was also rather alarmed and so gripped on to his uncle tightly.

'There it goes,' Ronnie remarked, with a sad twinge to his voice. 'By this time next week, the electric trains will be working on this line like all the others, and that old locomotive will probably be sent to the scrap yard'.

As they hurried back to the car, David pondered on the thought that such a magnificent, yet frightening train could be there one day and then gone forever the next. The concept disturbed him and he didn't know why. All he was sure of, at that moment, was that he would try and hold on to the memory of the steam engine, as by this time next week, this would be all that was left.

After an uneventful, yet speedy journey, they were soon driving along Herne Bay seafront. The town was now the sedate and exclusive off-season domain for the local population, at least for the next few months, and there were few people about, even in the middle of a Saturday afternoon. Before long, Ronnie pulled up alongside a regency, three-storey terrace, set back a few yards from the seafront road. The cream-coloured, stuccoed façade was arranged in a series of large, semi-circular, bay windows that encompassed all three floors.

Dizzy with anticipation, David followed his uncle along the front path, and then up the steep flight of stone steps to the shared front door. Once inside the lofty, echoing hallway, David looked around him and thought it strange that you had to go up somebody else's stairs to get to the flat. After Ronnie had unlocked the heavy panelled door of his second-floor 'bachelor pad', the small boy peered inside and was immediately struck by its vastness: the big main room, the tall ceiling and the pair of huge bay windows that overlooked the bandstand, with the pier beyond it to the left. The main room's contents seemed rather familiar to him, and so they should. David's parents had donated some of their old furniture to get Ronnie started, having bought a lot of new items for the recent house move to Canterbury.

David sat on the familiar sagging sofa and looked around him, sipping an orange squash. He noted that not everything in the flat was familiar to him after all, such as the bottles standing in line on the ex-Darwin family sideboard. Some were full; others were half full of a liquid, which was the colour of tea with no milk in it. The lad knew it was alcohol, as he had seen it on the television. He was also aware of the fact that people drank it, and it then made them act funny. No wonder Uncle Ronnie told so many jokes, he determined wisely; he's got a lot of alcohol. David's parents did not have bottles on their new sideboard; they preferred tea, hot tea with milk in it.

'*Hey Dave, you don't mind if your present is not wrapped do you?*' an unseen Ronnie shouted from the next room.

'Na' replied David, knowing full well that he could safely use slang or talk badly in Uncle Ronnie's presence, without ever being told off.

As he put his empty squash glass down, his attention was soon drawn to a magazine that was lying on that familiar small coffee table: the one with the spindly legs. He could see it was called *Playboy*; in fact, David was the third-best reader in his class. Spreading the magazine on his lap, he began to turn the pages methodically. He already knew what little girls looked like; he had often seen his sister in the bathroom, as their mother was drying her. But these were pictures of ladies, bare ladies, and he soon felt a strange sensation in his shorts. This rather puzzled him, as it does all young boys when they experience their first erection. He thought that it might mean he wanted a wee and did not associate it with the pictures at all. Nevertheless, the impact of those images, on those well-thumbed glossy pages, was another impressionable memory from that day, which he carefully stored away in his mind.

'*Shut your eyes,*' bellowed his uncle, coming back into the room and holding his unwrapped gift. Ronnie froze for a moment when he saw the small boy, sitting upright with his eyes tightly shut and a copy of *Playboy* open on his lap. Quickly shrugging off the shock, he put his gift on the coffee table, causing the spindly-legged structure to wobble under its not inconsiderable weight.

'Okay mate, you can open your eyes *now*,' his uncle announced cheerily.

David was delighted; it was the crane that had been one of Ronnie's favourite childhood toys, and one that he himself had long coveted. Better still, it was now sporting a new coat of red paint. The toy crane was made of metal, not plastic like many of his other toys at home, and it had rubber wheels and two handles protruding from the side: one that pulled a string to make the hook go up and down, and another to raise and lower the jib at the front.

'Oh *thanks* Uncle Ronnie; this is the *best*!' the birthday boy enthused, beaming up at him from the sagging sofa.

'Well, it's only right that you should have it Dave,' Ronnie said sitting down beside him.

'When *my* mum gave it to me – that's your Nanna Darwin by the way – *I* was five too; she also told me that it was a present that only *special* little boys should have!' Ronnie revealed, before getting in closer, as if he were about to share a confidence. 'Apparently, *another* special little boy owned it before *me*, but I'm afraid I don't know who *he* was!'

'Could it have been my dad?' posed David, as he slowly turned the handle that raised the hook.

'*No* mate; Len never cared much for the crane,' his uncle explained with a down-turned mouth and solemn shake of the head. '*His* pride and joy was a massive old jigsaw that had once belonged to our Uncle James, when *he* was a boy!'

David beamed from ear to ear, as he peered up at him. 'Oh I can't *wait* to tell my mum and dad about the story of the crane, and the little boy who had it before you!'

'Yes, but you'd better not tell your mum and dad about *this*,' Ronnie said, with a crooked grimace, as he removed the magazine from his nephew's lap.

David was happy to comply, and nodded vigorously in agreement. He loved having secrets with his uncle, like the scar brothers' ritual for example, and that time recently, when Ronnie had spent the day with them in Canterbury just before Christmas, and only a short time after they had moved in to Westgate Court Avenue. Officially, the eighteen-year-old had come down from Rothermead to go flat hunting, but he'd confided in David that he was going in for a talent competition at the Marlowe Theatre. For the act, he told him that he'd planned to tell a few jokes; maybe even sing a Cliff Richard song to demonstrate his versatility. However, on the afternoon of the contest, his uncle had not gone. Instead, David found him crying in the shed, when he went to explore the bottom of their new Canterbury garden. He had never seen a grownup cry before and thought it even more puzzling, as Ronnie had been very lively and joking only that very morning. David had put his hand on his uncle's shaking shoulder and offered him his handkerchief. He hadn't told his parents about that incident; it was one of their secrets.

In no time at all, the birthday visit to his uncle's new flat was over and before very long, they were driving back over the level crossing in Sturry. This time, there was no green locomotive to frighten him. Perhaps it had already gone to the scrapyard, pondered David sadly, as the car cruised through the small Kentish village.

'Oh blimey, I've just noticed, I'd better get some petrol!' Ronnie suddenly announced, and with a sense of urgency. 'D'you know anywhere *around* here Dave?'

David realised that, before very long, they would be approaching the northern outskirts of Canterbury, and he had a sudden flash of inspiration.

'*Yes* Uncle Ronnie, there's a filling station in North Lane, near the Westgate Towers!' he announced triumphantly. 'Dad's been going there ever since we moved to Canterbury; you get given Green Shield stamps there too!'

Having successfully guided his uncle to the garage he had in mind, David sat there, with the crane in his lap, and watched the white-coated attendant putting petrol into the car, whilst his uncle went over to the garage to pay. And then, to his delight, Ronnie re-emerged, not only with his trading stamps, but also brandishing two Crunchies that, as it turned out, was Ronnie's favourite chocolate bar, as well as his own. They made a mutual pact to eat them there and then, before their tea and not let on back at home. That additional sweet, chocolatey secret just about made the day perfect, and David knew it would be one that he'd never ever forget.

*

'All done?' Tim enquired, brushing the dirt from his knee. 'Have you recorded your precious doomed building for posterior?'

'Erm, just another couple of shots of the frontage to finish the film off,' Dave replied, still partly lost in his cherished memories of the past. 'You see; we may not *get* another chance!' he added, unconsciously paraphrasing his beloved uncle.

Having finally completed the photographic record, he carefully rewound the spent film in his camera, as Tim tutted playfully, and then they both headed for 'The Olde City', where real ale was the cheapest in Canterbury. Going to the pub was an integral part of those escapee afternoons, and on the days when the weather was poor, it became the main event. Tim enjoyed this part of the schedule so much that if the day turned out to be fine, he would almost look disappointed.

The friends were soon pushing their way up the main pedestrianised street, where shivering shoppers and the occasional hardy winter tourist vied for space.

About two thirds of the way through their journey, Dave suddenly paused at a side street.

'*Look* Tim, I wouldn't mind taking some city-scapes from the top of the multistorey car park, as we're in the vicinity,' he said pointing southwards. 'But don't worry mate, we can go to the *pub* that way; I promise you won't miss *very* many drinking minutes!'

Oh if you *must*!' Tim responded in mock fatalistic tones.

Tim was familiar with the multistorey, but this was the first time he had actually 'looked' at it from a photographic point of view. The low winter sun, hitting the brutalist concrete of the car park's staircase towers, caused the textured surface to glow brightly. At the same time, the stark towers were casting long, crisp geometric shadows across the adjacent road surface.

Having reloaded his camera and recorded a number of external images of the structure itself, the two friends ascended to the top deck, being the fifth level of the car park. Dave approached the edge above Gravel Walk and then cast his eyes around the modernist cityscape that was spread out before him. On their last lunchtime drinking session, he had explained to Tim that enemy bombs had devastated this, the southeast quadrant of the city, in 1942; it was all part of the research for his latest book. The brave city fathers of the immediate post-war years had seized this opportunity to build a new Canterbury in the current modernist styles of the period, clearly inspired by the London Festival Exhibition and developments in other blitzed cities, such as Coventry.

'Look at *this* Tim; everything you can see before you: they're going to pull it *all* down in the next few years and, *no doubt*, build something in a hideous pastiche of older styles, just to please the tourists *and* those big shopping chains,' Dave said all-too-obviously getting on his metaphorical soapbox.

Tim stood there in amazement, and not a little amusement, as Dave passionately waved his arms about and pointed at one flat-roofed building or another, in order to reinforce what he was saying.

'And at the same time, you can be *sure* that they'll squeeze in *much* more square footage of retail space to increase their revenues. It'll be a *disaster* and believe me ... I'll *really* be having my say at those public consultation meetings in the near future!' Dave vowed, tub-thumping with fervent passion.

Tim chuckled as a result of his friend's earnest diatribe. 'Don't waste your energy on matters you can't *resolve* Dave,' he answered, in calm, measured tones. '*Remember*, everything happens for a reason and *none* of us can cheat fate.'

'Oh I disagree!' Dave intervened, his camera, and the reason for their diversion, now completely forgotten. 'We have the power as individuals to use our votes to effect change, and our voices to *demand* change. '

'Only if it's *destined* for that change to take place!' pleaded Tim, clearly drawing on his recent open university studies. '*Come* on Dave, politics are a complete waste of time, and so are the bloody politicians. Everything is pre-ordained; we may as well just accept what happens. '

'No, you're *wrong* Tim, there's too much historical evidence of individuals who, through their sheer strength of will and determination, have brought about changes for the better; sometimes against terrific odds.'

'Only because it was their *destiny* to achieve whatever they had,' his friend countered, taking Dave's place on top of the soapbox. 'Rather than wasting your time and efforts trying to *change* things, the secret is to use that intellectual capacity to work out *why* that change had taken place. If we understand why something has happened ... you know the *reason* for the change ... we will *all* be more at peace with the world, *and* ourselves!'

As with many assertive discussions that had occurred before, they eventually agreed to differ on the subject and go off to the pub instead. That was the beauty of the friendship between Dave and Tim. They may have disagreed with each other on a number of topics, but they still enjoyed the argument and never fell out because of it.

The 'Olde City' was only a few hundred yards from the multi-storey car park and they were within its welcoming walls in a matter of minutes. Tim appreciated a good real ale; in fact, he liked any beer at all. The problem was that he rarely had enough money to pay for his round. Dave felt pity for his friend as he watched him carefully counting the change in his pocket, but recognised that Tim genuinely hoped to have enough money for at least one round. This happened each and every time, but it was never a source of frustration for Dave. He did not mind standing the bloke a few drinks; after all, he did earn more money than Tim, and didn't have two young children to support, or a wife who only worked part-time.

Tim Cross could get through a pint very quickly, and Dave was always fascinated by his friend's apparent ability to open his throat, and then literally pour the beer down without seeming to gulp.

'Don't you ever *taste* the bitter as it's going down mate?' Dave asked, having just got in the first round.

'*Sort* of I suppose, but surely that's not the *point*, is it?' Tim replied, with a quizzical expression on his face. 'That's like saying you own a car because you like the smell of the upholstery. The car's there to get you from A to B, and the alcohol, my friend, is *exactly* the same!'

Dave listened with much interest. 'So, in your analogy, 'A' is normality…'.

'Hideous, *horrible* normality, 'Tim stared down at his now empty pint glass.

'*Indeed*!' Dave chuckled. 'And 'B' is *what* ... being pissed?'

'Yes, being pissed, as you so eloquently put it, my dear Dave; that wonderful chemical change in the body that makes life seem…well…oh *fuck it*; let's have another pint!' Tim suggested, thinking better of continuing with the explanation.

Dave finished his own drink and then stood up.

'I'll get 'em *in* then mate,' Dave said, and reached for the empty glasses.

By 02:30, even Dave's money had run out, and so the pair proceeded to the usual third stage in these escapee afternoons, and headed for the cathedral. There were few tourists around during the winter months and that was exactly the way Dave Darwin preferred it. The fact remained that most Canterbury people liked it this way too, except, of course, the ones who owned gift shops, or ran cafes and restaurants. Another benefit of the winter was that locals were mostly rid of those people who pushed those irritating peddler's barrows up and down the pedestrianised main street. These street traders had a tendency to cluster around important junctions selling lighters, silly string, stink bombs and exploding caps, and preventing easy passage by busy people in their lunch hours,. Dave concluded that those French school children, who now came to the city in seemingly ever more disorganised hordes, appeared to be more interested in these trashy items than they did the principal building of the Church of England. They seemed to care little for his beloved cathedral, with its thousand years of history, and he sadly concluded that once the channel tunnel was open, it would surely be ten times worse.

Dave dismissed all thoughts of these latter-day pilgrims, as he and Tim passed through the Christ Church Gate, crossed the south precincts and then headed for the cathedral's entrance porch, with its crumbling victorian statues, all depicting past archbishops. These figures had been placed in long vacant medieval niches, almost as an afterthought. However, the inferior stone used in their creation made them deteriorate prematurely and, therefore, look far older than they actually were.

Once inside this venerable building, the two friends hurried along the north side of its lofty perpendicular nave, as usual, and made for the stone steps that led down into the crypt. Having descended into the cool, subterranean darkness, they kept to the usual ritual and made for the Chapel of the Holy Innocents, with its romanesque arches and grotesquely carved capitals. Dave knew a lot about the cathedral, much of which he had learnt from his father. He particularly liked this little chapel because of its remoteness and the fact it had changed little since being built in the early twelfth century. Tim liked it for the atmosphere and, more especially, the solitude it offered. Indeed, on that particular winter's afternoon with the light outside already fading, there was an uncanny sense of calm in the chapel. Even the crypt's familiar smell of musty, damp stone seemed stronger than usual.

'Do you think we are finally feeling the presence of God?' Dave mused, as he pushed open the low half-door that led into the chapel.

'*Probably* not,' Tim said, condescendingly patting him on the back.

'But there's … there's an uncanny vibe here today; I'm *sure* of it!' Dave insisted, staring back at him in earnest.

'*Come* on Dave, it's *much* more likely to be the real ale,' Tim scoffed, with a weary shake of the head.

They both smiled and then sat silently for a few minutes on the hard wooden chairs, which were, as always, carefully positioned between the two massive round pillars that supported the low vaulted ceiling of the chapel.

Dave and Tim were practising agnostics, in the sense that they both thought about and discussed religion with each other, unlike their work colleagues, Tiffany and Monica who, if pressed, assumed an agnostic position, but never gave the matter another thought. The Chapel of the Holy Innocents had become a regular venue for these 'deep' spiritual discussions. These were the occasions when the joking, if not altogether ceasing, then died down quite considerably. Dave would always approach any religious debate with the idea, or rather hope, that God, in the broadly accepted Christian sense, probably did exist. Tim however, preferred to argue from the perspective that there was no God, only a vague and indefinable cosmic force that controlled our destiny. After a lengthy debate, they would always reach the same stalemate and then sit once more in silence. During this time, Dave would always study his surroundings and envy the faith of those men who, years before, had erected those massive round pillars, carved the monsters on the capitals and assembled those perfectly round arches, all in praise of their God. He also envied the faith of his wife Sheila who, as a cradle catholic, happily accepted the existence of God, as well as saints, the pope and transubstantiation, without a moment's thought. Ironically, in this non-thinking sense, she was much more like his so-called agnostic friends back in the office, than she was him. None of them could understand his pain, his struggle, and his doubts concerning all matters religious.

Having exhausted the inevitable debate about God, Dave and Tim turned to other matters of mutual interest, in particular the problems with their respective marriages.

It was Tim who started the ball rolling.

'Do you *know* Dave, Alison seems to be using *any* excuse to avoid sleeping with me these days!' he gravely admitted, quite happy to speak in the frankest of terms to his companion.

'Are you sure you're not just misreading the situation?' Dave said, with a look of concern. 'After all, we *both* know that it's never like it is in the films, especially after that first flush of being in love has passed!'

'No, it's *more* than that,' his friend clarified, with an emphatic shake of the head. 'She seems to find the whole idea repugnant. And *another* thing: she's now talking about wanting a career again, and one in *teaching* as well!'

'I suppose it's good money, and you *do* get those nice long holidays,' said Dave, as he tried to home in on the more positive aspects.

'Yes, but you've got to train for *years* first!' Tim retorted, with an air of frustration. 'Why does she want to go into teaching when it means giving up her part time job *and* spending several years at college, when we're struggling for money as it is! Don't misunderstand me, I see nothing wrong with the actual *concept* of teaching, and given a different set of circumstances, I'd like to have followed that path myself.'

Dave nodded and then smiled empathically.

'Yes I can see that ... given your skills ... the idea of forever being able to absorb, and then impart knowledge would seem very appealing,' he asserted with a friendly chuckle.

'Oh indeed it *does*!' Tim said. 'But then *I* gave up the idea of becoming a professional musician to be more responsible to my family; to join bloody Telecom and earn some steady money. It's just not *fair*!'

Dave felt sympathy for his work colleague and fellow photographer, but quietly doubted that he had ever seriously considered making a living out of playing the drums, however good he was. Indeed, Dave would be the first to admit that Tim *was* a very accomplished musician, but he also knew that the life of a gigging musician would have imposed impossible limits on him: it would have taken him away from his books, as well as that potent but inexpensive home brew, both of which he absorbed every evening.

'At the end of the day Dave, I think I might have to go along with this teacher training idea,' Tim said stoically, with a long and loud sigh. 'You see, Alison seems so dissatisfied, almost *bored* with her life these days. Worse than *that* though, she appears to be weary, not only with her life in general, but also with *me* as well!' he revealed unhappily. 'D'you know, she's recently started going out of an evening, with some newly acquired female friends, and to be *quite* honest, I'm totally *fed up* with being stuck at home, looking after the *children* most of the time. I can't even have a *beer* until they're settled down for the night!'

'But she still enjoys her part-time job though, doesn't she?' Dave asked, rather concerned by what he'd heard so far.

'More than *that* my friend, she *cherishes* her two mornings a week as library receptionist, but she seems to want more, a *lot* more. And there's *another* thing to consider ... her parents won't be able to look after the children all the time, if she went back to college, so we would have to pay for a child minder', Tim explained, pausing to chuckle in wistful fashion, and then fixing his friend with a penetrating stare. 'At least you won't have *that* problem,' he said, slapping Dave on the knee.

'Err ... no, I suppose not', Dave responded, with very mixed feelings.

This was a reference to a very sensitive confidence that he had shared with Tim quite early on. Dave had confessed to him that he had a low sperm count, according to several hospital tests, and was unlikely ever to be able to father a child. Ironically, he would have gladly endured the Cross family's money problems and regular rows to have had a couple of kids like them. And it was no mere assumption of Dave's that Tim and Alison were having rows; by the evidence of his own eyes, they were having some bad ones. On more than one occasion recently, Tim had come to work with either a black eye or scratches on his face, and no one, least of all Dave, believed his unlikely explanation of having walked into the airing cupboard door while he was drunk, or other similar sitcom type excuses.

Tim wasn't alone in experiencing trouble at home. Dave had also been having some concerns about his own marriage, and these were ones that he'd recently begun to voice to his friend and confidante.

'Well, if it's any comfort to you, you're not alone in the old strife department, Timothy my man; things between Sheila and I are *still* not very good these days!' he lamented, whilst staring down at the flag-stoned floor between his knees.

'I don't know why you two married in the *first* place,' remarked Tim, clearly keener to make a judgement, than ask for specific reasons. However, after a short pause, he changed his mind.

'So *come* on then, why *did* you then ... *marry* her that is?' he added, with a blatancy that no one else could get away with.

Dave looked up at his friend with a sideways smile.

'I suppose you may as *well* know the whole gruesome story; after all, Monica and Tiffany already do,' he began, before grimacing over at an eagerly attentive Tim. 'As you're already aware, Sheila is my *second* wife, but there was someone else between her and my first wife Vivien ... a very *special* someone else as it happened!'

'*Really*? You dark horse you!' Tim remarked folding his arms in Les Dawson fashion. 'Anyone *I* know?'

'No mate ... her name was Chloe and she worked in our office. Effectively, you replaced her when she left!' Dave said, in a manner which indicated that the memory was still rather painful to him. '*Oh* Tim, we were *so* much in love with each other; we were even going to set up home together. *She* was the reason I actually left Vivien; I was preparing the ground for an exciting new future with Chloe!'

'*Uh-oh*, I get the ominous feeling that you're about to tell me how it all went horribly wrong,' Tim suggested, with an exaggerated wince.

'Well of *course* I am mate; I'd be *married* to her by now otherwise, *wouldn't* I!' Dave exclaimed, slightly exasperated, before giving out a stoic chuckle. 'The thing is, I told her about my…umm ... problem with fertility ... you see, I didn't want to keep it from her, and I rather naively thought that, given our feelings for each other, we could have transcended the ... err ... complication.'

'But Chloe *couldn't*?' his friend said, now showing more sympathy than he had before this moment.

'No, she couldn't!' Dave confirmed, with a weary shake of the head. 'It turned out that she wanted *children* more than she wanted *me*. Consequently, she couldn't go through with her marital split, and was persuaded by her husband to stay with *him*!'

'*So*, you married Sheila on the rebound then!' Tim stated disapprovingly, having jumped to the inevitable conclusion.

Dave frowned, and puckered his mouth up.

'I wouldn't have put it *quite* like that!' he defended, somewhat awkwardly, and a little taken aback. But at the same time, he couldn't help wondering to himself whether Tim was actually right?

It was certainly true that not many months had passed between Dave and Chloe parting company, and the time when he married Sheila: another work colleague and good friend, but had he really settled for second best? There was no question of the fact that he had been in love with Chloe, but Dave was also very fond of Sheila as well. Physically, the two women were very different: Chloe was tall and slim with a convex face, whereas Sheila was short and voluptuous with a concave face. Characterwise, they were much like chalk and cheese too – no one could have been sweeter than Chloe – but at the end of the day, he was on his own, and so was Sheila. She also had a young son from her first marriage: a ready-made family for him. It had seemed like the ideal opportunity to seize hold of, and so he did, with both hands. However, three years into the marriage and Dave was now having serious doubts that he had, in fact, made the right decision for all the right reasons.

'How are you getting along with Julian these days?' Tim asked, almost as if he had been picking up his friend's train of thought.

'Don't ask!' was the short, and yet utterly revealing retort.

Sheila's teenage son Julian had been the subject of one of Dave's previous, and more bitter diatribes, so Tim thought he would be on safer ground if they talked about photography. He was pleased that he'd encouraged his friend to take it up, but had been rather surprised, if not a little jealous, at the success he was having with the medium. During the previous year, Dave had seen a local book of his own photographs published: a slim volume that showed the affect that rapid rural housing expansion, and bypass-building, were having on the trees and buildings of the northeast Kent area.

'Photography? *Yes*, I've got a few little projects on the go!' Dave said, his spirits immediately lifting with the change of subject. 'As I think I bored you with *before*, I'm working on a pictorial book about Canterbury in wartime, but I'm also trying to learn about *glamour* photography ... you know, to broaden my horizons a little!'

'*Glamour* photography? *Ha*, you'll *never* be able to persuade anyone to get their kit off for *you*!' Tim scoffed, in a mocking manner that was only partly playful.

'Already *have* mate,' Dave retorted haughtily. '*And* we've already had a photographic session together too!'

Tim's jaw nearly hit the chapel floor.

'You jammy *bastard* Dave; anyone *I* know?' he asked, for the second time that afternoon; his eyebrows raised as high as was humanly possible. 'And *please*, make it someone I *know* this time.'

'You *do* know her actually,' Dave smiled and left a dramatic pause. ' ... it's Cordelia Cavendish actually!'

The girl in question worked in another department in Telecom House, and everyone, including Sheila, liked her, largely due to her warm and engaging personality. She was tall, dark, and magnificently statuesque: the sort of confident girl that instantly turned all men's heads.

Dave knew the appealing middle class Cordelia far better than Tim did, but it was the latter who really fancied her. Consequently, the news had quite an impact on him.

'How the *hell* did you get *her* to pose for you?' he asked in a mock sulky voice. 'Did she get *all* her kit off and if so, can I see the pictures?'

Dave laughed as loudly as he felt comfortable doing, given their surroundings, and decided to answer the first question first.

'Cordelia and I attended that three-day work development course last month, at a hotel just outside Maidstone ... *you* remember ... it was the first of Darryl Giles' so-called *initiatives*,' he explained to a now very attentive Tim. 'We teamed up every evening in the bar to escape the other Telecom bores, who only wanted to talk about their jobs. Inevitably, our conversation came round to photography, on the strength of my recently published book, and also to Cordelia's sideline ... the job she had trained for and wants to take up full-time one day... as a make-up artist for professional photo shoots. So .... we were talking ... in a quite matter-of-*fact* way ... about glamour photography, and when I expressed an interest in the area, Cordelia happily volunteered to act as a model for me. I...I couldn't *believe* it!' Dave chuckled again. 'The shoot took place at my house the very next week, and to my surprise, I got no opposition from Sheila whatsoever!'

'*Yes* Dave, but did how far did the curvy Cordelia *go*?' questioned a frustrated Tim; his knuckles clenched white in anticipation.

'In what way do you *mean*?' Dave asked calmly, knowing full well what Tim was getting at.

'Tits out?' Tim sneered smuttily.

'Yes, there *were* some topless shots,' Dave teased, ' ... but no, you *can't* see the pictures I'm afraid ...I promised Cordelia that it was just between her and me.'

As Tim pouted like a schoolboy who had been denied a comic, Dave felt immensely smug and superior, having just described his recent exploits behind the camera. His clever friend may have got A levels, and a BA honours degree in philosophy, but he hadn't seen Cordelia practically naked.

Tim soon recovered from his disappointment, but was keen to stick to the same subject.

'So, has the lovely Miss Cavendish been the *only* subject of your lustful lens, or have you taken any *other* glamour shots you've not *told me about*?' his envious companion asked, with the merest hint of hurt.

'*No* mate, she's been the only one so far,' Dave said, with a slow shake of the head.

It was then he remembered the photographs that he'd taken in his back garden, during the previous summer. Surely *they* couldn't be considered as glamour shots, he thought, as his mind wandered back to the day in question.

*

It had been a warm midsummer Saturday afternoon and Dave and Sheila had just returned home from a long circular walk through the local woodland. They arrived to find Julian and his girlfriend, Amanda-Jayne, sunbathing on the lawn in the back garden. She had just turned 16 at the time, although Julian was a few months older. After the usual pleasantries, Sheila went inside to fix some cold drinks, whilst Dave stayed in the garden. He'd noticed that his lupins were finally in flower and had decided to photograph the herbaceous border whilst it looked so lovely. Both youngsters propped themselves up on their elbows, and watched him with amused interest. But before very long, Julian got up and went inside alone to talk to his mother.

'Another whispering session I suppose,' Amanda-Jayne observed, with an astuteness that rather surprised Dave.

'I wouldn't be surprised!' he said, for seeing Julian go into the house after Sheila, he had thought the same thing.

Still feeling rather amazed at the coincidence of he and the teenage girl making the same observation, Dave continued to picture the flowering border, but without the same enthusiasm. Having taken three or four close up botanical photographs, he then lined up a shot that included Amanda-Jayne, lying on the lawn in front of a clump of achillea 'Cloth of Gold' in full flower. Seeing the approach of the camera, the sixteen-year-old sat up and then smiled. Dave took the picture he'd planned, and then snapped one of her alone. She giggled in response and proceeded to strike a series of exaggerated poses, to which Dave reacted in like manner by impersonating David Bailey. But it was the very last shot of her he took that stilled his play-acting. Amanda-Jayne knelt upright on the rug and, not so much smiling as pouting, looked at him with her head on one side. She then arched her back and dropped her arms behind her. Dave's throat went dry, but he somehow managed to focus the shot and then 'clonk'; the image was captured. Amanda-Jayne beamed brightly and resumed her sunbathing. Not long afterwards, Sheila re-emerged holding a tray of cold drinks, with Julian trailing obediently behind her.

Dave did not experience the full impact of that last photograph until his pictures had been developed a few days later. And there she was, Amanda-Jayne, barely sixteen-years-old and striking the pose of an adult model. Her black one piece swimming costume was stretched tightly over her body, and it was a woman's body too, despite her petiteness. The taut black material seemed to emphasise her pubic mound and small breasts. Dave was completely and utterly transfixed. It was that day at Uncle Ronnie's flat, on his fifth birthday, all over again, and although there was no stirring in the shorts this time, he certainly experienced a feeling of desire. But he also felt shame as well, for she was just about young enough to be his daughter; there being a twenty-year gap in their respective ages. Dave removed that particular photo from the pack, before either Sheila or Julian went through them, and hid it in the dust-wrapper of one of his old Ladybird books.

*

'No ... I've not taken *any* other glamour pictures,' he re-affirmed, to a slightly disappointed Tim. That photograph of Amanda-Jayne was to remain Dave's guilty little secret, and even his best friend could not be a party to it.

The January afternoon was short and the limited available daylight in the Chapel of the Holy Innocents was fading rapidly. An approaching footfall prompted the pair into silence once more, as a cathedral verger entered the chapel to light the candle on its small rudimentary altar. He eyed both Dave and Tim in such a way that it made them both think that he'd overheard everything they'd said in the last hour or so. Dave was especially glad that his thoughts could not have been read, for if God did exist, then the almighty would surely have a pretty dim view of him right now.

They waited until the verger had done his rounds, and the diminishing footfalls had once more given way to silence, before either of them spoke again.

'He stares at us every time!' grumbled a disgruntled Tim. 'Perhaps he thinks we're a couple of gay blokes who have come in here for a quiet cuddle!'

'Perhaps we should hold hands next time, eh?' Dave proposed, with a sideways grin. 'Then again, perhaps not!'

'Yeah, perhaps not!' Tim said, with a nod and a grimace.

The increasing gloom of the late afternoon seemed to strengthen the musty smell of ancient stone, and that uncanny sense of peace and calm. The effects of the real ale had worn off by now, although Dave realised he could still feel that special vibe. He also concluded that this was no place to have been thinking about Amanda-Jayne's nubile young body, and imagined his name being written down in some celestial book under the heading: 'irredeemable sinner'.

Tim and Dave reluctantly left the further darkening crypt and once more passed through the cathedral nave that, by comparison, still seemed bright, even though the sun was almost down. A few elderly people were gathering for a service, and behind them in the choir, someone was playing random phrases on the cathedral organ as if they were practising for a later performance.

The air outside had a seasonal chill to it and cold misty rain fell almost reluctantly to the ground. Tim turned the collar of his jacket up, and then forced his hands into the small pockets.

'What are you reading at the moment?' he asked, as they re-crossed the south precincts with their heads down, and teeth gritted.

'The Ian Carr biography of Miles Davis,' Dave replied; invoking the name of the black trumpeter they both admired above all others. 'And *you*?'

'*Well*,' Tim announced, with a wry grin, 'I'm trying to get through *The Origin of Species* by that Darwin fellow, and I don't mean *Ronnie* Darwin either!'

He mentioned this to wind Dave up over all the Darwin-name comments from that morning, but he also happened to be reading it for his own pleasure.

As for Ronnie, Dave had more than once remarked, to his un-appreciative colleague, that he reminded him of his beloved uncle. Tim, on the other hand, would have preferred a comparison to the famous bearded anthropologist. Indeed, had he wanted to be compared to the infamous Ronnie Darwin, it would have been more appropriate for him to have found a copy of *Lolita* to read instead, if the rumours he'd heard about Dave's late uncle were true.

In the Buttermarket just beyond Christchurch Gate, the two friends parted company. Tim would be driving home, despite his lunchtime consumption, but as he always claimed in his defence, the affect of the alcohol had more than worn off after a few hours in the cathedral. Fortunately, Dave would be getting a lift home with Sheila, who always preferred to drive in any case, so he only had a ten minute, half-mile walk in front of him, in order to get back to the Telecom House car park.

On the wet stone sets of the Buttermarket, Dave passed a small group of cold, damp, yet stalwart Japanese tourists who were taking photographs of the surrounding buildings. He smiled at their determination and conceded that not all tourists were a pain in the arse after all.

As he walked, huddled and head down, through the wet lanes of his native city, Dave ruminated on his immediate future, partly inspired by his rumbling stomach: what were they going to have for dinner that evening? And would Julian be bringing Amanda-Jayne along? Another thing: how could he spend more time alone with Sheila, without Julian's seemingly constant presence? Indeed, given the present situation, would his wife actually welcome more time alone with him? If circumstances had turned out differently, what would his Uncle Ronnie be doing now? And, of course, there was the one perennial concern that ran through everyone's mind in early January: what would this brand-new year bring; will 1991 be as bland and uninspiring as the previous year?

Halfway way along St Margaret's Street, Dave passed a shivering huddled figure in a darkened doorway, and noticed him from the corner of his eye.

'Spare any change mate?' came the feeble pathetic voice from the gloom.

Dave usually steered well clear of vagrants, but this time, something made him stop. He felt in his trouser pocket. There was still a pound coin left from lunchtime, so he approached the crouched figure, who held out a filthy hand to receive the alms. Dave caught a glimpse of the man's face and was shocked to see that he was probably no older than either himself or Tim. In his other hand, he gripped on to what appeared to be a bottle of supermarket sherry.

'*Cheers* my friend, go careful now,' came the pathetic voice, from what sounded like an educated man.

'And you too,' responded Dave, before hurrying away. How did someone end up like *that*, he wondered? Tim and I may have our troubles, but God willing, we'll never be like him!

The cathedral clock, sounding the three-quarter hour, echoed back from the centre of town. The freezing rain began to come down a little harder now, as he left St Margaret's Street and the vagrant behind him. Quickening his pace, Dave once more thought about his evening meal, and the man in the doorway was entirely forgotten for the moment.

That night, with his belly full and his bed warm, Dave recalled fragments from the day: there was 'Farmer' Giles with his anachronisms, the customers with their angst, Tim with his alcohol and that poor huddled figure, his meagre alms. But it was that recollection of Ronnie at the old filling station that Dave smiled about as he slowly drifted off to sleep. Those happy childhood memories more than compensated for Sheila's indifference to his sexual advances, as she had joined him in bed some twenty minutes after him, having worked late on some Telecom business she'd brought home.

Much later on, all those twilight thoughts in his mind coalesced into one, to produce a disturbing dream: a distorted memory of the eventful, or rather fateful summer of 1969, when Dave was twelve and his beloved Uncle Ronnie was in trouble. However, the nightmare had begun almost normally:

.........By now, Dave was really exhausted, but he had to keep going; he was barely halfway there yet. There was no way he could possibly miss it; everybody said it was going to be Ronnie's finest performance. Wearily, Dave climbed the rickety stile and dropped into the second of the two cherry orchards on his route. The wet grass was much longer here and the fruit trees, closer together. And, the nearer he got to the village green, the steeper the ground became. It all combined to slow his progress, and also make running impossible, even if he did have the stamina.

A sudden breeze got up and carried the voices of the crowd, who were obviously already gathering on the green, which was, unfortunately, still many yards ahead of him. Their chanting could now just be made out: *Ro-nnie, Ro-nnie, Ro-nnie*, and this served to spur Dave on. If only his legs didn't feel so heavy! The breeze quickly became much stronger and the lower branches of the dew-soaked cherry trees began to sway violently in the air, spraying him in both water and clouds of pink-white blossom petals. Dave ducked and dived to avoid the whipping boughs, but could not miss the one that suddenly came at him from the left and promptly knocked him hard on to his back. Dazed, Dave rolled over and slowly got on to his hands and knees. It was then that he noticed the many perfect, white mushrooms growing amongst the long wet grass. He keenly began to gather them up. There would surely be enough for everyone to have fried mushrooms for breakfast that morning, he thought happily.

The chanting of the crowd once more carried on the breeze, but was now more clearly heard: *Ro-nnie, Ro-nnie, Ro-nnie*. What the hell was he doing? He didn't have time to pick mushrooms; he had to get to the green before the performance began. Once more, Dave resumed the fight through the long wet grass and swaying sodden branches, until the chanting could be discerned much more loudly. Finally, there it was in front of him: the five-bar gate that gave access onto Rothermead Green. He'd made it!

Dave climbed the gate and, still panting heavily, staggered onto the green beyond. His eyes immediately focused on the old derelict windmill: the conical tar-black, brick tower that had long since parted with its top-most cap and sweeping sails, but was beautiful nonetheless. And there too was Uncle Ronnie, many feet above him, and standing perfectly still, almost to attention, on the flat circular roof of the abandoned mill tower. The loftily perched, motionless figure suddenly raised his arms in the air and the chanting resumed: *Ro-nnie, Ro-nnie, Ro-nnie.* Dave began to push his way through the tightly packed crowd, which was now at least twenty people deep, and arranged in a semicircle around the front of the mill. As they chanted, the crowd swayed from left to right, just like the branches in the cherry orchard. Dave found himself being jostled from one side to the other, but he pressed on. Somewhere in the crowd were his father and grandfather, and he had to find them; he had to let them know that he'd made it. As soon as that thought entered his head, there they suddenly were in front of him; he'd have recognised the back of Grandad Darwin's head anywhere. Dave approached his family members and slipped in between them. He looked up at his grandfather to the right, who winked and smiled sweetly at him. He then peered up to the left and at his father Len, who glared back at him impassively.

High above, Ronnie began to perform his regular comedy routine. Everyone in the crowd around them laughed heartily, and Dave laughed too.

'It's not funny!' growled his father, as he scowled down at him.

'But it *is* funny,' Dave pleaded in earnest. 'It's hilarious; it has to be Ronnie's finest performance without doubt!'

He then looked to his grandfather to see if he was enjoying the show, but the old boy was no longer there.

'Grandad Darwin has had to leave us!' remarked his father, in a low emotionless monotone, from the alarmed boy's left.

The crowd's laughter intensified as Ronnie's act gradually reached its climax. Eventually, the much expected and meticulously rehearsed finale was performed, as a man in a gorilla costume chased Ronnie round the edge at the top of the mill. Everyone went wild, laughing loudly and clapping enthusiastically.

'It's *not funny*,' repeated his father crossly, but his words were drowned out by the clamour of the appreciative crowd.

Before long, the performance was all over. Ronnie stood on the very edge and once more, threw up his arms in triumph. The huge crowd chanted his name in wild appreciation: *Ro-nnie, Ro-nnie, Ro-nnie.* Len averted his upward gaze from the jubilant performer and reached down to touch his son on the shoulder. Dave looked up in response and noticed tears streaming down his father's face.

'What if things had been turned round the other way?' his father asked cryptically, and then slowly pointed up to Ronnie.

Dave looked back up at his uncle, and also saw the man in the gorilla suit, who was standing just behind him. But there was something wrong: it now looked like a real gorilla. With an almighty roar, the beast surged forward and pushed his uncle hard in the back. As Ronnie teetered on the brink, the crowd fell silent; in fact, no sound could be heard whatsoever. And then, as Ronnie lost control and began to fall forward, he let out a long piercing scream. Dave's hapless uncle hurtled right towards the family group, which once more included Grandad Darwin.

'We'll all be killed,' Dave panicked, as Ronnie's screaming face rapidly bore down on them.

Dave screamed too, as he suddenly sat up in bed; the beads of sweat already forming on his brow. Unfortunately for him, he had woken up Sheila as well.

'For Christ's *sake* Dave, what the *hell's* going on?' she barked in a groggy voice, invoking heaven and Hades in the same sentence.

'Oh, oh dear, I'm ... I'm so *sorry* love,' Dave panted in obvious distress.

Sheila peered at the digital display of the radio alarm clock.

'Oh *no*, it's four in the morning,' she snapped crossly. 'We have to be *up* in less than two hours!'

'Yes, I'm *sorry*, but I've just had a terrible nightmare,' whispered Dave, as he tried to settle down again. 'In fact, it's left me feeling rather unsettled and a little frightened; do you…do you mind if I cuddle up?'

'I keep *telling* you ... there's a time and place for *everything*, now bloody well let me *sleep*!' Sheila snarled, as she rolled over in a violent movement, taking most of the duvet with her.

Dave lay back, cold, scared and wide awake, as the minutes on the radio alarm clock display slowly blinked their way towards dawn.

Family Life?

Dave unlocked the door of their Ford Escort and plonked himself down into the passenger seat, emitting a deep, satisfied sigh in the process. Ah, Friday evening at last, he thought, before shutting his eyes and pushing his head back on to the rest.

Five o'clock on a Friday was his favourite time of all, because it meant that the long working week was finally over. For two days, there would be no more Telecom, and no more moaning minnies on the phone blaming him personally for all their life's troubles. The best thing of all was that for those two brief days, he would be free of 'Telecom speak': those American clichés the office staff were all now required to memorise, in order that they become better 'Customer Champions' and, therefore of course, better people.

For the first time since before Christmas, Dave was feeling optimistic. It had a lot to do with the beautiful spring evening and the fact that he and Sheila could now drive home in the light. And then, of course, there was also a party of sorts to look forward to that weekend: the Cross family were coming over for Sunday lunch.

Tim, Alison, Sheila and Dave were no strangers to socialising together, but had always made a rather uneasy quartet. Sheila did not really like Tim, and the only reason that Dave could give for this was that he stood up to her. Dave also got the impression that Alison was none too keen on *him* either. Nor did the wives have anything in common. As a result of all this mutual antipathy, the conversation could sometimes be somewhat strained. All in all, it seemed that there wasn't too much to look forward to after all, except for the fact that the two of 'them blokes' could really enjoy being in each other's company. Indeed, Tim was the only Telecom person Dave wanted to socialise with outside of work by a long chalk, and he knew his friend felt the same way.

It was Dave who had suggested Sunday lunch, as his best work mate had been very down in the dumps recently. This was largely owing to the fact that Tim's marriage to Alison was under enormous strain, as revealed to Dave in a number of their confidential crypt conversations. He had reasoned that a meal together might give them a chance to function as a couple again, and not bicker so much because they were in company. Dave had also managed to persuade Sheila to talk to Alison about careers and establish whether or not this teacher training idea was what she *really* wanted. Lunch on Sunday was the only condition under which Alison had agreed to attend, because it meant she could bring along their two young children, Henry and Phillipa. Sheila, for her part, would only concede to the gathering if Dave cooked the meal; a term to which he had willingly agreed.

Dave looked across the Telecom House car park and at the neat ranks of cars that were progressively thinning, as other equally optimistic people cast off their Telecom shackles and headed home for the weekend. He would be off too shortly, just as soon as Sheila finally left the building. It was five minutes past now and Dave was beginning to hope that she hadn't volunteered to stay on and run an errand for her department head, as was increasingly the case these days. Ah no, think optimistic thoughts, he thought to himself, before studying his surroundings once again. There were daffodils bordering the planted islands in the car park; their cream and yellow heads not quite yet obscured by the municipal shrubs that had been allowed to sprawl unchecked for years. Beyond the tarmac, and along the edge of the railway embankment, the fresh green leaves of the hawthorn hedge still managed to poke through the dark and dominant branches of the Leyland cypresses that had been planted to supersede it. At last, spring seemed to be here and very soon the garden would be full of flowering bulbs, anticipated Dave optimistically. This was a new season, a new beginning and therefore, it was the appropriate time to put the past, and all their troubles, behind them. He looked at his watch and was perturbed to see that it was now ten past five. Sadly, there was still no sign of his wife.

Things had not been going well for Dave and Sheila in recent months. He had tried to tell Tim that in the crypt, back in January, but only some of the angst had come out on that occasion. However, the problem was not only with Dave and Sheila, but also involved Dave, Sheila *and* Julian. As a relatively recently married couple, Dave had wanted to spend at least some time with Sheila alone, but from his point of view, the boy always seemed to be there. And it wasn't as if Julian was a dependant toddler anymore; the umbilical cord had been cut some 16 years before. Tim had not unreasonably argued that if you marry a woman with a child, then you are taking them both on. Dave understood this perfectly well; he even welcomed it, but then surely, he had reasoned, this commitment must run both ways, and perhaps even three ways.

Dave remembered back to nearly four years before, when he and Sheila first discussed the possibility of getting married. This was plan number two, as her parents' traditional catholic attitude to 'original sin' had ruled out any possibility of them merely living together. Almost straightaway, Sheila had taken Julian on one side to consult him about it. Very soon however, it became clear that her son had already considered the possibility that his mother might want to marry this strange man who now regularly stayed for weekends at their house; this odd bloke who seemed obsessed with photography, gardening, Dinky toys and Ladybird books. Indeed, the boy had not only been thinking about it, but was also ready with a list of conditions. If they both agreed to his terms, Julian had told his mother, then he would condescend to allow her to wed this Dave Darwin, this weird man with the famous dead uncle. Sheila had agreed to these conditions without qualification, and then presented them to Dave as a fait accompli. He could remember the exact wording even now:

Number one: Julian did not want to be disciplined, or in any way be told off by Dave. He was not his father and would never be considered as such. This led very neatly on to the second condition. *Number two*: he did not want to be adopted by Dave and would not take his name. He was Julian Bishop and he did not want the name of a pervert, the name of a Darwin.

Dave had felt somewhat alarmed and rather upset when Sheila recounted that second condition to him, and was forced to wonder: what did that little shit, that twelve-year-old upstart, mean by 'pervert'? Had Sheila's pious parents briefed him on poor old Ronnie's decline and fall? At the end of the day though, despite these negative feelings against him, Dave's desire not to be alone was more powerful than his anger at Julian's conditions, and he, therefore, endorsed Sheila's acceptance of them. Only later, did he really begin to resent the fact that the spotty teenage son of his future wife had besmirched the sacred memory of his beloved Uncle Ronnie. And it wasn't as if Julian's real father was still around muddying the waters. The squaddy known as Alan Bishop had left Sheila when his son was barely two years' old; he didn't even remember his natural father. Since then, Alan hadn't made any attempt to contact either Sheila or Julian so his presence, or non-presence, was not an issue and any objections that had been raised against Sheila's prospective second husband were aimed at Dave alone. Thus, the formal part of their relationship, their engagement, started on that sort of footing. Julian had made it clear that he did not want to be 'taken on', as Tim had put it, and deliberately excluded himself from the future family scenario, or rather, the one naively envisaged by his quasi-stepfather. But why then, wondered Dave, was he the one who was currently feeling excluded?

It hadn't always been like that though, and Dave could recall a time when he and Sheila were actually happy, a time when marriage was not yet on the agenda. It had been during that first year of their going out together; of their courtship – as his father might put it – when they each had separate houses and, for much of the time, separate lives. Although the loss of Chloe was still very raw, the ever pragmatic Dave decided not to dwell on what could never be, and focus instead on his family, his hobbies, and his new Telecom girlfriend; a policy that had resulted in some magical weekends. They took it in turns to play host to each other, either eating in, or going out to their favourite pasta parlour in Canterbury. Dave especially looked forward to those weekends when Sheila would come to him at his small terraced house, in the St Radigund's part of the city, not least because her parents would have Julian with them for those particular times. Dave would come home, with his bulging bag of supermarket provisions, feeling almost as excited as he had with the anticipation of those childhood weekends at Rothermead. Following a quick bath and shave, he would put on an appropriate LP, and then wander into the kitchen to prepare the dinner. Having dropped Julian off, Sheila would arrive, hungry for both the meal and for him. Free from the loneliness of the week, the demands of a teenage son, or the horrors of Telecom, Dave and Sheila would then enjoy a blissful and carefree night, of food, music, wine and lovemaking. By comparison to his first marriage, this was really living, and as a result, Dave imagined himself to be in love. The weekends at Sheila's house were almost as good, as far as he was concerned, although the presence of Julian restricted the more spontaneous moments of sexual enjoyment. Nonetheless, Dave came away from her house on a Sunday morning, feeling contentedly happy, and as he waited for the bus to go over to his grandparents' house in Herne Bay, would often wish for it to be like that all of the week. However, it was the very fact that they limited it to weekends, and created those eagerly anticipated oases of optimism and overindulgence that kept their relationship fresh, and made it feel so special. As soon as thoughts of co-habitation and, later, marriage were exchanged between them, the magic seemed to evaporate in an instant, and the problems, especially with regard to Julian, began to make themselves known.

Dave leaned over to the driver's side of the car and put his keys in the ignition to start up the radio. The car clock blinked into life: it was now 05:20.

'*Come* on, *come* on', barked Dave crossly, and out loud. 'Where the hell *is* she?'

Their car was now one of only four left in the car park. At that moment, Monica strode confidently over to her four-wheel drive and, with a dainty wave in his direction, climbed aboard, revved the engine up and roared away. And then there were three. Sadly, Dave's earlier sense of optimism had now all but vanished, and he once more pondered on his feelings of exclusion.

Julian's set of pre-nuptial conditions had made it plain that once Dave and Sheila were married, they would not be able to function as a normal family. This is exactly what had happened, and was still happening. As far as Julian was concerned, he and Sheila, mother and son, were already a family, and he didn't need Dave. Then again, perhaps neither of them did, Dave thought unhappily, as he fumed alone in the car. It then occurred to him with sickly succinctness that that must be the reason; that was why he was being excluded. He had long been unhappy about the closeness of the relationship between Julian and Sheila. They were always talking together and laughing in a huddle: their 'whispering sessions' as Amanda-Jayne had so shrewdly put it. Sometimes if he came into a room where the other two were in close conference, he would become aware that the conversation between them had suddenly stopped. Was this really the case, or was he just being paranoid? Should he have tackled Sheila about it, each time it happened? Sadly, for a long time he had chosen to ignore it; he had decided to say nothing.

Dave was all too aware of the uneasy alliance between himself and his wife's son. The pre-nuptial agreement had clearly stated that he was not allowed to discipline Julian. Therefore, if Dave had a grievance, or felt that Julian was out of line, he had no other choice but to go to Sheila and expect her to act as an arbitrator, effectively a go-between. If his wife then felt that the grievance warranted some attention, she would approach her son and sort it out. On the other hand, Julian never seemed to complain via Sheila, about him – unless of course, that was what the whispering sessions were all about. In actual fact, Dave tried very hard to give Julian nothing to complain about and so, the arbitration process was largely one-way. This system had worked quite well for three years or so and therefore, Dave did not want to push his luck by complaining to Sheila about the so-called whispering sessions, or anything else that might upset that balance. However, on some more recent occasions when Julian was really pissing him off, Dave had gone to Sheila as arbiter, and laid it on a bit thick, sometimes rather too thickly. He would then derive some sadistic pleasure in watching, from a safe distance of course, as Sheila punished Julian, usually with her tongue. Naturally enough, the teenage boy had begun to resent even this indirect discipline that, all too obviously, originated from Dave.

Things finally came to a head during the Christmas period. In fact, several things occurred that not only upset the balance – the uneasy alliance between the males of the household – but also put Dave firmly on the losing side. They were only small seemingly insignificant incidents, as these things often are, but they tipped the scales ever so slightly; forming a crack in the dam and letting through a trickle that might one day turn into a flood.

The first of these pivotal moments happened on one of those rare occasions when only Dave and Julian were at home together. Sheila had popped out to do an errand for her parents, who lived locally, when Julian suddenly announced that he wanted to make a snack for himself. The sixteen-year-old had recently decided to give his personality a bohemian edge by becoming a vegetarian; it was a decision that Dave had supported, even if it did push up the weekly shopping bill. The only problem was that, as a result of the change in diet, the lad was almost permanently hungry. At Julian's insistence, Sheila had purchased large catering packs of instant mash potato, which enabled his voracious appetite to be satisfied with minimal delay. And so, on the afternoon in question, when he had wanted to make a snack, Julian understandably reached for the instant mash. Dave happened to be in the kitchen at the time, making a chilli con carne for the 'immoral' meat eaters of the household, and had dared to suggest that Julian might like to boil up some pasta, as an alternative option, and one more likely to satisfy and sustain his chronic hunger. The 'starving' teenager seemed to agree, and did just that. Later, when Sheila came home, Julian quickly took her to one side. Dave thought that it might be just another whispering session, but soon learnt that Julian had gone to her as arbitrator of a grievance he had with him. Later on, Sheila judged that it had been unreasonable of Dave to tell Julian that he couldn't make some instant mash as a snack, because after all, this was what she had bought it for. Dave desperately tried to explain what he had actually said and also gave his reasons why. Sheila listened, thought for a moment, and then ruled that she did not accept his version of the incident. She had also made it quite clear that there was nothing he could say to change her mind. As a result, a smirking Julian had certainly got his revenge for Dave 'laying it on a bit thick' in his own recent arbitration appeals.

The next incident was just two days later, on the last Saturday before Christmas, and Amanda-Jayne had come round to help decorate the tree. Her mother never bothered to get one any more, and it was a seasonal ritual she greatly missed. There had been some talk about Amanda-Jayne and Julian getting engaged now that she was 16, but so far, nothing had happened. On the contrary, he seemed to be seeing less of her, and therefore, this Saturday afternoon visit had been the first in a while. As it was to turn out, Dave would have good reason to be glad she was there; he would have a much-needed ally in another dispute involving Julian.

Dave had just brought the decorations down from the loft when Sheila, who was going through the Christmas nuts and sweets she had amassed, realised that they hadn't got any chocolates. She decided to nip out and rectify the matter, right there and then – 'while there was still some left to buy' – and so asked everyone what they would like her to get. Dave had opted for *Cadbury's Roses*, whereas Julian decided that he would prefer *Quality Street*. Dave then argued that *Roses* were more preferable as they were all chocolate covered and, besides which, the plain *Quality Street* toffees pulled his fillings out. Sheila left for the shop and, at the very last moment, Julian decided to go with her.

Dave had then found himself alone with Amanda-Jayne. She looked at him and smiled, with her head slightly on one side, and straightaway, Dave thought about that day in the garden last summer. She was taller now and her hair longer, but she still had the same elfin features, the same slender form, and that same sweet nature. However, Dave could not relate the Amanda-Jayne standing there in front of him, with the one in that secret photograph: the picture that had shown a young seductress in a tight black swimming costume; that forbidden fantasy figure who had become detached from reality. The Amanda-Jayne with him now was a real person; she was the girl who was always kind to him; she was the daughter he never had; the one who delighted in helping him decorate the Christmas tree.

They had sat on the floor together in contented silence, untangling the line of fairy lights from the box he had brought down from the loft. After a while, they began to talk about his work and her school; it had been an easy, natural conversation, and he hadn't felt the need to watch what he was saying lest it be the wrong thing. Inevitably, she asked him about his various hobbies, and photography in particular. Dave was always happy to explain what he was doing in that respect, as Sheila rarely showed an interest.

'Well, my publisher has asked me to work on a second pictorial book ... this one will be on the Canterbury blitz,' he proudly told her, picking pieces of detached tinsel from his jeans.

'Oh *do* sign me a copy when it comes out, *would* you?' Amanda-Jayne asked with an enthusiasm that for a moment made him feel like a real author, as opposed to a mere compiler and caption writer.

'Of course I'd be *delighted*,' he was happy to respond. 'I'm also trying to expand my photographic horizons by getting into other areas, such as portrait work and ... err ... glamour!'

'*Glamour*? Gosh, how *interesting*!' Amanda-Jayne gushed, smoothing down the skirts of the venerable Christmas tree fairy. 'Have you *taken* any yet?'

'Yes I *have* actually ... a girl from work called Cordelia agreed to pose for me, so that I could get some practice,' he replied, both surprised and delighted that she was showing so much interest in his activities.

'Oh David, could I *see* the pictures ... would you mind?' she pleaded, widening the size of her eyes, as she looked up at him.

Dave stared back into Amanda-Jayne's large expectant eyes and remembered his promise to Cordelia, as well as the fact he had already forbidden Tim from seeing them. But then again, how could he deny her?

'Yes, of *course* you can see them, but please bear in mind that they *are* my first attempt,' he qualified modestly, and then immediately went upstairs to fetch the album.

Before long, Amanda-Jayne was sitting on the settee with the album across her knees, carefully turning the pictures over one by one.

'What a pretty girl Cordelia is,' she said innocently, gazing up at him with a sweet smile. 'And what a good figure she's got!'

'She's not *really* a model, just a friend from Telecom,' Dave said feeling slightly uncomfortable, as image after image of a semi-naked or erotically-clad Cordelia flashed past his eyes.

'Ah you *see*, it's your photography that makes all the difference, David,' Amanda-Jayne reached over to pat the top of his down-turned hand. 'You make her *look* like a model. Oh, these are *great* pictures!'

'You're *very* kind!' he remarked, with an embarrassed half-chuckle.

Having studied the final shot, she shut the album and smiled up at him again.

'Oh, you are *so* clever David ... I'll bet you could even make *me* look glamorous!' she said handing the book back to him.

As Amanda-Jayne laughed, her eyes sparkled more than any Christmas tree lights possibly could. With his heart rate suddenly quickening, Dave looked at her closely and for the first time, he saw a woman, sitting there next to him on the settee. Of course, he knew that he would love to photograph her in the same way he had captured Cordelia, but was quick to realise that he could no longer undertake such a session objectively.

'Oh no Amanda-Jayne, I *couldn't* improve on what nature has already done,' he responded diplomatically, in answer to her question.

'David, you are so *sweet* to say that,' she gushed, grabbing his hand again. She was the only one to call him David these days.

With the album returned to the safety of the spare room, the two of them had resumed decorating the tree. Dave admired the fact that she carefully placed each glass bauble and plastic icicle just so, evenly covering the stiff needle-clad branches. As they completed the process, they contentedly went on to talk about music, both in general, and more specifically. Amanda-Jayne proudly announced that she was singing in a school's performance of Mozart's 'Great' Mass in C Minor. By an amazing coincidence, Dave had recently bought a CD of the piece. She was thrilled and he soon found himself promising to do a tape of it for her.

After a short pause, his young companion looked over at him with a serious countenance.

'Sheila *will* buy *Quality Street* you know ... Julian will make sure of it ... that's why he's *gone* with her!' she predicted, with a piteous countenance.

Her words had uncannily echoed Dave's own thoughts on the subject, and ones he'd not dared to express out loud. He said nothing in response, and was still hoping that Sheila would remember that he didn't like all those hard toffees with no chocolate on them: the ones that benefited the dentist far more than they did him.

Just as the last bauble had been placed on the final bare branch, the front door slammed and in marched Julian, proudly holding out in front of him, a large tin of *Quality Street*. He placed it in the centre of the coffee table and then, smiling smugly, strode out of the room in triumph, no doubt to rejoin Sheila who was unpacking other provisions in the kitchen. Dave peered at Amanda-Jayne, who again stared back at him with a look of pity. It was all too evident, to both of them, that Julian could not have been more proud of that tin, than if he had been parading Dave's severed head around on a silver platter.

Beginning to lose his temper, Dave stormed into the kitchen and stood in front of Julian.

Do you *mind*, I want to speak to your mother alone', he announced starkly, barely able to contain his rage.

Julian stood his ground and stared at him insolently, half smiling, half leering. A few feet away, Sheila continued to unpack the shopping, disregarding them both.

Deftly side-stepping Julian, Dave approached his seemingly indifferent wife.

'Why did you buy *Quality Street*? You *know* I can't eat them!' he protested, finally daring to confront Sheila.

The short, stocky woman stopped unpacking and slowly turned her head towards him.

'*Please* don't exaggerate Dave ... you *know* you can eat the soft ones,'she retorted wearily, with deliberately slow blinks of her eyes. 'Or if you prefer, you don't have to have any *at all*,' came the cutting coda, before she returned to her unpacking and putting-away duties.

Without looking back at Julian, whom he assumed must be gloating, Dave returned to the lounge feeling somewhat bewildered. No one followed him. Seeing his rapidly developing sense of distress, Amanda-Jayne immediately approached Dave and then engaged him in a huge emphatic embrace. He willingly hugged her back and also gently kissed the top of her head. The kiss was genuinely fatherly in its emotion, or rather, largely so.

'*I* would have preferred *Roses too*,' she softly whispered, close to his ear.

The voice on the car radio detailed the news headlines and then predicted the weekend's weather. Dave, no longer lost in thoughts of the recent past, looked at his watch and sighed in deep frustration. It had gone past 05:30, and there was still no sign of Sheila. As the last vestiges of his optimistic mood evaporated, a miserable Dave gazed out of the window, and surveyed his immediate surroundings. Now, even those cheering early signs of spring seemed less obvious, and he could no longer see the daffodils for the municipal shrubs that covered them, nor could he any more enjoy the erupting hawthorn hedge for the leylandii that smothered it. It wasn't long before he realised that such self-indulgent brooding was getting him nowhere, and he pulled himself up shortly. Dave speculated that the only way out of this problem was to change things at home, and he recognised that an early priority had to be the redressing of the balance with Julian, or else the arbiter may never listen to any of his grievances in the future. Somehow, that ever-widening crack in the dam had to be sealed, or he would surely drown.

Dave jumped as the driver's side door suddenly opened. '*Sorry* I'm late,' Sheila announced cheerfully, as if nothing was out of the ordinary, 'Mr Goodhew wanted to consult *me* over the quarterly stats!'

'*Well*, now that you're *finally* here, let's get home,' an irritated Dave retorted, as he snatched the seatbelt and then yanked it across his chest.

'*Okay, okay* ... calm down!' tutted his wife, with a condescending smile, before starting up the engine. And then, realising that her husband's chagrin wasn't entirely unjustified, she attempted to offer him a more benevolent attitude.

'You'll be *pleased* to know that I've got all the ingredients for your friends' lunch on Sunday,' she added, with a characteristically slow blink.

'They're *your* friends as well,' Dave countered, in a much calmer manner.

'*Hardly*!' Sheila scoffed, with a sardonic chuckle. 'However, I must say, it will be nice to have Sunday lunch cooked for me and, after all, you *do* make a fabulous lasagne'.

High praise indeed, Dave thought, as their car began to roll forward.

Their long-delayed departure left just two vehicles in the car park: the mini driven by his wife's manager, John Goodhew, that portly swoop-haired bachelor who still lived with his elderly mother, and the XRI, owned by Dave's boss, that – in his own words – prat Darryl Giles.

Sheila glanced over at the glumly silent Dave's still-brooding face, and realised she still had some ground to make up.

'By the *way*, I've also bought lamb chump steaks for dinner tonight,' she announced, as the car paused at the junction onto the city's ring road.

'Oh *fabulous*; I *love* lamb steaks,' Dave smiled, suddenly much happier at last. That's a good sign, he re-assured himself; she's bought one of my favourite dinners. Perhaps things aren't so bad after all.

'Yes, we *all* do,' Sheila added, as she accelerated along the dual carriageway, 'Julian asked me to get them to celebrate his return to meat eating!'

Dave could not reply, and merely castigated himself for ever daring to think that he was up there somewhere in the pecking order. Feeling utterly wretched, he stared out of the car window, and as they flashed past the school playing fields, he miserably imagined he could see Julian playing football with his severed head.

As soon as they reached home, at the end of a close in the outlying village of Wellbourne – which was less than three miles away from Telecom House – Dave helped Sheila carry the shopping into the house from the car's boot. It was as he was putting the lamb chump steaks in the fridge, that he noticed one of them was larger than the other two, and mentally earmarked it for himself.

Leaving Sheila to finish unpacking, Dave went into the hall to turn off the answerphone, and to check for messages. Finding none, he sat at the foot of the stairs to undo his shoe laces. It was then that a familiar voice boomed out from the lounge: '*And my mother-in-law is less evolved than most, she can peel bananas with her feet*!' came the jovial baritone-pitched delivery.

A startled Dave jumped to his feet. My God, that was Uncle Ronnie's voice, he realised with alarm, but how is that possible?

A loud chorus of teenage laughter, also emanating from the lounge, suddenly jolted him back to reality. Dave went through to find Julian, and three of his male friends, watching his video recording of Ronnie Darwin's appearance on *The Lulu Show* from the spring of 1969. It had been included in a compilation programme screened over Christmas, entitled 'Fallen Heroes'. The four youths were sprawled all over the room, feet up on the coffee table, legs up on the sofa, and with dirty plates casually discarded everywhere. The unmistakable blueish

39

pall of cigarette smoke hung in the air, while on the TV screen a man in a gorilla costume was chasing Dave's immaculately dressed uncle around the stage.

*

Rain lashed against the steamed-up windows of the coach as it slowed at yet another set of traffic lights. It was now getting dark and people, illuminated by the harsh light of anonymous shop windows, hurried along the wet pavements outside. Although soaked to the skin, they were at least making more progress than the passengers in that miserable coach, now firmly embedded in a long queue of traffic. David couldn't understand why his father had not taken them up on the train instead. It would have been a lot quicker and much more fun for him. Besides, Lucy wouldn't have been sick at Blackheath because of that horrid selfish man on the coach with his Russian cigarettes. However, on the plus side, they had been given the afternoon off school and better still, they were travelling up to London to see *The Lulu Show* being recorded. The Darwin family were going to be part of the audience: the people who laughed and clapped on the telly, no matter how bad the joke was, but you never actually saw them. Best of all was the fact that Uncle Ronnie was going to be the star guest on the show; it was going to be his first TV appearance since winning *Opportunity Knocks* last year.

What a year it had been, David thought, as he gave up trying to look out of the window, and sank back in the seat. His voice had broken, men were going to travel to the moon, his brother Eddie had been potty trained and his own uncle had become famous. Apparently, young girls his own age now thought that Ronnie Darwin was dishy, whatever that meant. In any case, it had certainly earned the twelve-year-old some favour at school, and he needed all the help he could get, his rapidly spreading acne having recently taken over from his fat bottom as the main object of ridicule.

The plodding coach finally passed through the barrier at Television Centre and having disembarked, they were all ushered into a reception area, before being taken to the studio. Photographs of famous TV stars hung on the wall: David Nixon, Dick Emery, Peggy Mount, Jack Warner, but not his uncle, well, not yet anyway. Then, as if on cue, the left-hand pair of lift doors opened and out stepped his Uncle Ronnie. Dave immediately marvelled at how good looking he was, in his 'show-biz' suit. His uncle's hair was also much longer now, and its straightness contrasted well with the curliness of his sideburns. The schoolboy knew that his parents would *never* let him have his hair that long and Grandad Maybury, who was very anti anything 1960's, would have him down the barber's, before you could say George Harrison.

A murmur rippled through the assembled party as people began to recognise who Ronnie was. David felt so proud as he came over to speak to the family group.

'*Hello* you lot .. alright then Dave ... alright curly top, good journey up Len?' Ronnie said, ruffling both children's hair, and addressing his brother.

'Well, the M2 was very busy ... I've *always* said that they should have built it with three lanes in the *first* place!' David's father remarked, with a shake of the head. 'And then when you get to the outskirts of London ... it's stop start, stop start.'

'Yes, and I was sick on the coach,' Lucy added sulkily. 'I had to do it in the carrier bag mum brought the sandwiches in, and there was a lot and…'

'Yes, *thank* you Lucy!' interrupted Meg, with a polite, but slightly awestruck smile in her brother-in-law's direction. 'Are you at all nervous Ronnie?' she added, in a half-whisper.

Her brother-in-law leant in close to her.

'I'm terrified, but don't let *on* Meg ... it's not good for my image!' he joked, in hushed tones. Ronnie then acknowledged a wave from the crowd, before turning towards David. 'How would you like to come up and see my dressing room?' he said, with a discreet wink.

'Oh *yes please*!' David enthused, before beaming up at his parents.

Meg was a little irritated that Ronnie had not asked them first, but after David's delighted response, she had no choice but to allow him to go. Len, however, seemed unconcerned, although perhaps a little jealous.

'Don't worry,' Ronnie reassured turning to David's mother, 'I'll make sure he's brought down to the studio in plenty of time for the start of the show.'

'Be good then,' instructed mother to son, as the crowd began to be ushered through the double doors at the far left.

Dave waved goodbye to his little sister, who gave a half-hearted response. Lucy did not seem to want to go, or appear to be at all concerned that she hadn't been asked. The poor child still felt a little queasy and was glad of her mother's arm to cling on to.

Uncle and nephew stepped into the still-waiting lift, and turned back round just in time to see the remaining Darwins ushered out of the reception area, before the doors slid shut. They only had three floors to travel, and the lift seemed to get there in an instant, but there was just enough time for Ronnie and David to perform the secret 'scar brothers' ritual. Soon, they were walking down a long narrow corridor, with numerous closed doors on either side.

David had missed his uncle over the previous months, especially as his baby brother Eddie was now so lively; with the inevitable result that his parents' attention had once more been taken away from him and focused on yet another troublesome new sibling. But Ronnie's career was rapidly taking off, and he'd had to spend more time in London. Sadly, this meant that his family at both Rothermead and Canterbury now saw far less of him. David also missed visiting the flat in Herne Bay, where his uncle had practised some of his comedy material on him. In particular, he loved the joke about the mother in law and the bananas.

Equally, David missed those trips out in the ever-changing succession of Ronnie's secondhand cars, to those familiar places: Reculver Towers, Dreamland at Margate and the local off-licence that stocked his uncle's favourite malt, which was apparently some sort of whisky, and where the owner always gave David a free Crunchie bar. He always wondered if Ronnie actually ever drank it; he'd never be there when he did, and yet they regularly went out together to get some more. Above all though, David especially missed his uncle suddenly turning up at Rothermead Farm, invariably late on Saturday afternoon or early evening, on those weekends when they all went up to stay with Nanna and Grandad Darwin. It was some consolation, though that ten-year-old Lucy had been some comfort to him. She too was feeling squeezed out at home, and had become an ally in those days when Eddie did nothing but cry and demand this drink or that toy. She may have played too roughly with David's Dinky models and chipped paint off his Thunderbird Two, but even allowing for that, he was very glad of her companionship.

The BBC corridor with the numerous doors was indeed a very long one. En route to the dressing room, a man walked past them, whom Uncle Ronnie cheerily acknowledged. Briefly looking behind him, David could have sworn it was the person who played Dr Who on the television, but he didn't dare say anything. Finally the pair came to a door, on which a handwritten label proudly exclaimed 'Ronnie Darwin'. David was a little disappointed, as there was no star on the door, just like in the films, but assumed that his uncle would very soon acquire one; how could he not? He followed Ronnie inside and was surprised to find that a young woman was already in there waiting for them. Even to his young eyes, she was stunningly beautiful, and had long straight blonde hair that cascaded over the puffed sleeves of a white mini dress. Her unstockinged legs were crossed as she perched on a high steel-legged stool. The girl reminded David of Mary Hopkin, one of Uncle Ronnie's rivals from *Opportunity Knocks*, although less moon-faced and with a large yet elegant nose that was perfectly framed by her centre parted hair.

His uncle and the beautiful young woman kissed on the lips in greeting. Ronnie then turned to David and beamed. 'I'd like you to meet Katie.... my girlfriend,' he announced, with equal measures of pride and bashfulness.

'Delighted to finally *meet* you,' Katie said, holding out a long slim arm from which numerous gold bangles hung.

'Hello!' David replied, in utter awe. At the same time though, he felt spotty and awkward, as well as profoundly regretful that his mother had made him wear his school uniform, even if it was the only smart outfit he possessed. And yet David was pleased that his uncle had felt able to introduce him to Katie. There had certainly been no mention of a girlfriend at home or at Rothermead. In all his twelve years, he had never been in the presence of such a lovely girl.

David watched with interest as Ronnie poured a glass of whisky and ginger ale and two more of ginger ale only. The alcoholic drink was passed to Katie, while he and his uncle had the ginger ale.

'Here's to success,' Ronnie proposed, holding his glass aloft.

Both David and Katie responded with a loud '*cheers*' and everyone drained their glasses in one go.

His uncle then pulled back the sleeve of his jacket, and quickly examined his watch.

'Anyway Dave ... better get you back before your mother starts fretting,' he declared, taking the empty glass from his nephew's grasp.

As Ronnie got up to go, he paused to kiss Katie lingeringly on the lips. David noticed that his uncle was caressing the exposed, upper part of her leg as he did so. David wished for all the world that he and Ronnie could have changed places in that moment. The young voyeur's pubescent hormones began to surge and he turned to hide his embarrassment. However, neither of the adults noticed, and within a minute, he and Ronnie were passing back down that same corridor, and then descending in the same speeding lift. All too soon, he found himself back in the reception area, which was now empty with the exception of a young bespectacled woman holding a clipboard.

'Felicity, can you take my nephew to studio C please,' his uncle requested, with a sideways smile and a wink in the young lady's direction.

'Right *away* Ronnie!' she responded, breaking into a broad beam.

His uncle then waved at David, just as the lift doors closed to envelop him. The twelve-year-old trotted obediently behind Felicity, as she led him along another corridor. As David caught the young woman up, and walked alongside, he studied her discreetly from the corner of his eye, and decided that she looked strangely familiar.

'Are you one of those pretty girl dancers on television ... *you* know, the *Young Generation*?' he asked, having finally plucked up courage.

'*My*, what a flatterer,' Felicity responded, looking across at him from above her glasses. 'You're *just* like your uncle!' At the end of that particular ground-floor corridor, she pushed open a pair of doors that had a circular window set in each of them.

The television studio was buzzing with excitement as David was shown to his seat. He sat next to his mother who smiled at him and then proceeded to smooth his hair down. 'Did you have your uncle to yourself?' she whispered, knowing how special he considered their time together to be.

'Yes Mum, I *did*,' he responded, with a bright smile, before covering his mouth with his right hand, and adding: 'apart from his girlfriend Katie.' David murmured that last bit very quietly to himself, so technically, he had not actually told a fib. Although Ronnie hadn't specifically said that Katie was a secret, he hadn't mentioned her to anyone else in the family either. There had always been confidences between nephew and uncle, and he was certainly not going to let him down now by giving too much away.

Although David had just convinced himself that he hadn't actually lied to his mother, he was nonetheless grateful when, at that moment, the opening music started up and the lights dimmed to hide his flushing cheeks. In the dark, David allowed himself to dwell on the beautiful image of Katie sitting on that stool, with her long legs crossed, and waiting for more of Ronnie's caresses.

*

'Looks like your Uncle Ronnie has fallen out with his girlfriend,' Julian hooted, as the image of the well-dressed comedian once more darted across the TV screen, with the gorilla still in hot pursuit.

Dave smiled too, but his reaction was more out of affection, as he recalled that this was the well-rehearsed finale to Ronnie's act. His uncle would tell some jokes based on the works and reputation of Charles Darwin, especially the theory of evolution and the origin of man, and would then claim to be the great man's descendant. The gorilla, having been offended by some of his remarks, would burst on to the stage, chase Ronnie about for a while before carrying him off stage over its shoulder. Dave had run through this scenario a couple of times with Ronnie over at the Herne Bay flat and had always acted the part of the gorilla, even though he couldn't actually take his uncle's full weight.

On hearing Julian's comment, the other lads noticed that Dave was in the room.

'Hello Mr Darwin,' one of them blurted out, with insincere courtesy.

'Would you like a toffee?' asked another, followed by muffled sniggers from the assembled gathering.

It was immediately obvious to Dave that Julian had been rubbishing him in front of his friends. More to the point, he began to wonder what all those louts were doing in his lounge in any case, and watching his precious tape too? Not only that, but they also had their feet on the furniture and, no doubt, had been eating his food all day. He wanted to watch the six o'clock news, he always did; it was part of his regular routine. Dave liked a routine; it made him feel comfortable, and watching the early evening news helped him unwind from work. Julian knew this all too well, and was deliberately preventing it, or at least that was how it seemed to him. He badly wanted to confront Julian about it, or rather, appeal to the arbiter, but what good would that do, he reasoned to himself. Since the events of last Christmas, he could no longer guarantee receiving any support from Sheila in these matters.

Dave stepped on a dirty plate by the settee, and the discarded cutlery jangled loudly as a result, which caused him to jump back in alarm. This produced more gruff sniggers from the unwelcome hoard of lounge invaders.

'Perhaps the gorilla is not Ronnie Darwin's girlfriend *after* all, but his mother instead,' one particular acne-encrusted youth proposed. 'Perhaps she's carrying him back to the jungle for being such a *dirty old man*!'

The laughter was no longer concealed, but a sneering Julian wasn't joining in anymore.

'Oh that Ronnie Darwin really splits my sides,' he remarked, with obvious venomous sarcasm, and holding his stomach with mock laughter whilst staring up insolently at Dave from his sprawling settee-bound position.

That's really done it this time, raged an inwardly fuming Dave. Being teased by those crass layabouts was one thing, but when they sullied the memory of his uncle, then they'd gone way too far. At that moment, he came close to slapping Julian, but just did not have it in his nature to lash out physically. His only recourse was to run and tell Sheila in the vain hope that she might intervene on his behalf. Dave left the room to a chorus of gorilla noises and more hoarse teenage laughter.

On entering the kitchen, he found Sheila peeling potatoes at the sink. Dave wanted to tell her what a little bastard her son was; that he had prevented him from seeing the news and much more seriously, that he had been ridiculing his Uncle Ronnie. He also wanted to tell her to choose between himself and Julian, because he could no longer stay in the same house as that little shit. Unfortunately, the hapless husband realised that there was little point; he knew exactly what Sheila's answer would be, whom she would choose, and it wouldn't be Dave Darwin.

Sadly, it had been many months since Sheila had been prepared to even listen to his grievances, let alone arbitrate in his favour. So he had little faith that she would ever again support him in any matters of conflict with her son. Dave had been emasculated by the conditions Julian had set when he and Sheila had got engaged, and the current hopeless state of affairs was a legacy of those terms, as well as Dave's own feeble agreement to them. Effectively, the marriage had started at the beginning of its own end. What was there left to say that could do any good?

'*Sheila*, they've been smoking in the lounge,' he complained, in the manner of a schoolboy informant. It was the only thing he could muster: a pathetic childish whinge that made him balk at his own petty inadequacy.

'*Have* they now,' Sheila responded, before drying her hands, and then marching through to find her son.

Dave was taken aback by her positive response, and began to tell himself that his words weren't so limp after all, especially if it meant that Julian would be getting a damned good telling-off.

His wife returned seconds later, a lit cigarette in her hand.

'*Thanks* for that Dave,' she remarked, before blowing a long plume of smoke in his direction. 'I'd forgot to buy any today and had completely run out by mid-afternoon.'

'When…when did you start *smoking* again?' Dave asked in disappointed disbelief, his jaw gaping widely.

'Oh, they *all* smoke at the managers' meetings ... I just slipped back into the habit,' she stated shamelessly, and with a dismissive shrug, before taking another long exhibitionist drag.

Turning away in disgust, Dave wondered if they all stuck cucumbers up their arses at managers' meetings, whether Sheila would do the same just to fit in; to be one of the power set. He sat down at the kitchen table and shook his head in despair. This would not do at all, he pondered dejectedly; something had to be done to restore that balance in his favour. The crack in the wall of the dam had widened again, and he was up to his knees in floodwater.

'*Listen* Sheila,' Dave said, after a few minutes brooding, 'it's been *ages* since we spent any time alone together, just you and me. Why don't we go for a walk tomorrow, and then lunch at the Duck Inn afterwards?'

Sheila said nothing straight away, but was clearly thinking about the proposal, as she placed the three chump steaks in the frying pan.

'Yes, that would be quite *nice*,' she replied at long last, before stubbing out her cigarette butt on the impromptu saucer ashtray, 'but if Julian *wants* to come along too, he can *come*. After all, we *are* supposed to be a family; it really *is* about time you *realised* that!'

For Dave, that comment went beyond irony and way beyond his ability to respond to it in any meaningful way whatsoever. And so he said nothing and imagined Julian at the Duck Inn, eating his boiled severed head, with a side order of garlic mushrooms and instant mash. What more could he say or do? At that moment, Dave wished he were back at work taking calls, and that was really saying something!

The pleasant smell of the frying lamb steaks shook him out of his downward spiral and he went over to Sheila and watched her tease the meat with a wooden spatula. Almost straightaway, he became aware of callous, gruff voices in the hall and realised that Julian's friends were finally leaving. Perhaps something could be rescued of the weekend after all, Dave speculated, desperately trying to buoy himself up; at least the lounge had now been liberated.

The front door slammed, shaking every utensil in the kitchen, and in walked a smiling Julian. Completely ignoring the close presence of Dave, he went over to Sheila, slipped an arm round her waist, from behind, and then peered over her left shoulder to better study the contents of the frying pan.

'Can I have *that* one?' he asked, pointing at the largest of the chump steaks.

'Yes of *course* you can, darling,' came Sheila's all too obvious reply, as she manoeuvred round to kiss him.

A defeated Dave turned away from the intimately involved couple, and slouched over to the crockery cupboard.

'I suppose I'd better lay the dining room table,' he announced in dejected fashion, before throwing open the door. '*Here* ... where have all the large dinner plates gone?' he asked, in a deliberately loud voice, already knowing the answer.

Sheila spun round, looked at Dave, and then turned to glare at Julian.

'That's you and your pals, *isn't* it? ... leaving your dirty plates in the lounge again. I've *told* you so many times before,'she crossly berated. 'Now go and *get* them please Julian, and wash them up straightaway; *all* of them mind. Dinner's in five minutes, so you'd better get on with it!'

'Yes mum,' conceded the sixteen-year-old, as he sloped off, making sure to sneer in Dave's direction, as he passed him.

Sheila returned to her frying pan, and also turned down the heat beneath the boiling potatoes, the matter already forgotten as far as she was concerned. However, as her husband rifled through the cutlery drawer, he couldn't help but smile to himself. Julian getting told off was only a small consolation, but it clearly showed how bad things had become for the incident to have cheered Dave up so much.

The following morning was a gloriously sunny spring Saturday, so the Duck Inn walk went ahead as planned, despite Dave's almost total lack of enthusiasm. However, all of that suddenly changed when Julian asked Sheila if Amanda-Jayne could come along too. Dave had volunteered to drive, which meant limiting himself to a couple of pints, but that now seemed unimportant, compared to the happy thought of seeing his young ally again.

As he turned the car into the road where Amanda-Jayne lived with her divorced mother, they could already see her waiting on the pavement by the front gate of her house. The sixteen-year-old girl jumped and waved as the vehicle approached her, and she only appeared to calm down when Dave pulled up, and then got out to let her in on the driver's side.

'*Hello* David, long time no see,' she smiled, before kissing him on the cheek.

'Hello there Amanda-Jayne,' he responded, happily accepting her demonstrative gesture of greeting.

It was a daughterly kiss, yet he felt the warmth and moistness of her lips react throughout his nervous system. It had indeed been a long time since Dave last set eyes on her. In fact the previous occasion was when she came up to help decorate the Christmas tree and had been so sweet and supportive to him.

A few miles into the journey, as the car bumped over the familiar level crossing at Sturry, Dave became aware of a heated conversation from the back seat; not exactly raised voices, but more like loud whispers. What was going on, he speculated; were Amanda-Jayne and Julian having a row?

It soon became apparent that his wife had noticed too.

'*Alright* back there you two?' Sheila challenged, before turning to peer between the front seats.

'Yeah, *sure* Mum,' came her son's none too convincing response.

Amanda-Jayne said nothing, but a little later in the journey, Dave caught sight of her in the rearview mirror, and she did not look at all happy.

The second half of the journey was deathly quiet, and an uneasy atmosphere seemed to pervade the car. As a result, Dave felt quite relieved as they finally parked in the lane alongside the beer garden. The circular walk – planned meticulously by Dave – would take about an hour and bring them back to the Duck Inn, in plenty of time to grab a good table and order the food. Sniffing the warm springtime air, Dave speculated to himself that it might even be warm enough to sit outside for the pub lunch. As always, he had brought his camera to record the realisation of the new season; the one that he, and most other people, associated with a sense of optimism. The hawthorn blossom was just coming out along the many hedgerows, and those damp ditches along the Marshside Road were crowded with pink ladysmock. Every so often, Dave paused to picture the eruption of all this joyous natural beauty, and despite recent events, he couldn't help himself but feel strangely positive about the future.

Sadly though, Sheila cared little for the simple things that meant so much to her husband. A tree was a tree as far as she was concerned: in the summer, it had leaves and in the winter, it didn't. In fact, she accepted the wonders of nature in the same unthinking way in which she accepted God. Therefore, on that brightest of spring Saturdays, she marched on ahead – with Julian keeping pace by her side – heedless of the hawthorn, blind to the bluebells, and oblivious to those early ox-eye daisies. Usually, his wife's dismissive attitude to his gasps of wonderment was a source of annoyance for Dave. However, today was different, for he had the company of a kindred spirit. He was delighted that Amanda-Jayne was taking an interest in what he was photographing, and she was even asking him the names of the wild flowers they encountered. It was the very thing that he had done on those fondly remembered country walks with Grandad Darwin and Uncle Ronnie at Rothermead, all those years ago.

At one particular point along the Marshside Road, there was a slight bend in the hedge-lined lane, and Sheila and Julian, who had marched on ahead, were now out of view. Amanda-Jayne was the first to notice this, and took the opportunity to quickly grab onto Dave's arm.

'Julian broke up with me in the car just now,' she announced, gazing at him with large, vulnerable eyes. 'He only invited me *here* today to announce that we weren't going out anymore.'

'How…how do you *feel* about that?' enquired a suddenly crest-fallen Dave.

'I'll miss our time together, that is, not with Julian, but with *you*,' she replied, and then kissed him once more on the cheek; it was a slightly warmer, wetter and more lingering kiss than before.

'I'll miss you *too* Amanda-Jayne!' he said, surprised by the surge of emotion he suddenly felt at the prospect of the teenager no longer being around.

'Perhaps we'll bump into each other in the town… *soon*,' she added, squeezing his hand, and staring at him intently with those same wide eyes.

Unable to speak, Dave nodded in agreement, before they walked on again in glum silence. Which of the Amanda-Jaynes from the recent past was *this*, he wondered, as his head spun: the supportive daughter who helped him decorate the Christmas tree, or the young seductress of that secret summer photograph?

Dave felt a bewildered confusion as the lines between the two images of her blurred, and something new emerged; something neither one thing or the other. It was similar to when blue watercolour runs into a recently applied yellow pigment, to form a small area of green along the edges.

The Marshside Road now straightened and ran parallel to a water channel, the North Stream, which had once marked the shoreline of Kent, in the days when Thanet existed as an island in its own right. As the quiet couple continued to walk along, they passed a series of little brick bridges that spanned the North Stream and linked the ancient Kentish shoreline with the reclaimed farmland of more recent centuries. Amanda-Jayne ran on ahead and stood on one of those little drover's bridges, before turning back to face him. The sun behind her shone through the purple and pink cheesecloth material of her full length skirt and highlighted her tiny white panties. As she stood there, her legs apart in a casual pose, she pulled the elasticated top of her gypsy blouse over her shoulders to reveal her finely crafted collarbones.

'Take my *picture* David,' she earnestly entreated, almost pleading. 'You won't *forget* me then!'

'Oh, there's *no* possibility of *tha*t!' Dave responded, in hushed tones she couldn't have possibly heard, as he trembled to adjust the focus of his camera.

Briefly, he looked along the road and saw that Sheila and Julian had about-turned and were now heading back towards them. We may not get another chance, he quickly decided, and with a clonk, the image of Amanda-Jayne was captured. The picture having been taken, she ran off the bridge, quickly grabbed hold of his hand, and the pair went on to join the others. Dave's mind was reeling all the time now, as he saw those blues running into the yellows and that patch of green growing ever larger. It was a bright green, as awesome as the new spring foliage on the hawthorn trees. As the colours coalesced, one clear question formed in his head: was he falling in love with Amanda-Jayne or merely overcome by her beauty, and his own lust?

At the end of the circular walk, the Duck Inn once more came into view. It was a charming country pub, and one that managed to completely avoid all the usual chocolate-box clichés. Originally, the premises had been much smaller, just the middle property in a terrace of three, with a village shop on one side and a cottage on the other. And then, over the last few decades, the Duck Inn first absorbed the shop premises and eventually the cottage. It was in this condition when Chris Jones took over as landlord in the mid 1970s. This amiable ginger bearded giant knew Dave well, as he had been drinking there on and off throughout Chris' entire tenure. Each and every one of his girlfriends, and wives, had been brought here. For Dave, the Duck Inn was a reliable unchanging constant in an everchanging world and best of all, it served hand drawn 'Favershams Ale'. The homemade pub food they provided there had also grown in reputation over the years, so on fine days, and especially at weekends, it always paid to get there early.

Everyone agreed that the weather was warm enough to sit out for the first time this year, so a food order was quickly made and a four-seater picnic bench secured in the pub garden. The North Stream flowed through the garden too and today, it played host to a family of newly hatched ducklings. Amanda-Jayne cooed at the obedient little brown balls of fluff, as they followed their mother past the prospective diners, and then disappeared under the bridge that spanned the lane. Julian sneered at such sentimentality and was soon chastised by his mother who had, by now, noticed that all was not well with the young couple. She therefore accepted that Dave holding hands with Amanda-Jayne was an attempt by him to compensate for Julian's indifference towards her.

What a wonderful day this was turning out to be, Dave thought, as they all sat in the warm spring sunshine. The Favershams ale, which was smooth and as perfumed as a Kentish hop garden, was going down very well. Better still, Amanda-Jayne was hanging on to every word he said and squeezing his arm when he told a joke. Sheila and Julian both smoked before the lunch was ready, and even *that* didn't bother him. At last, one of Chris' daughters brought out their food order, accompanied by many enthusiastic noises from the participants. He always had the same thing: bean and pepper hotpot, topped with chunks of home cured ham and garlic bread. In addition, he always had to have a side order of four sausages with a dollop of whole grain mustard. Sheila had the same as her husband but her hotpot was topped with sausage chunks. Julian had a steak torpedo sandwich with chips, and Amanda-Jayne, a tuna baked potato with salad. What could possibly be better, Dave decided, as he unwrapped his paper serviette from around the cutlery. Besides, Julian always shut up when he was eating and now his sulking ensured that he was quiet even when he was not stuffing his face.

Life usually ensured that, while bad days always felt like they might drag on endlessly, the good ones always seemed to end far too soon. This fact was not lost on Dave when, later that day, they dropped Amanda-Jayne back at home, and he wondered when he would next see her again, if at all. Bumping into someone couldn't be relied upon, even in a place as small as Canterbury and he couldn't believe that she had really implied that they should actually arrange to 'bump into each other'. Then again, perhaps Julian would change his mind; after all, he and Amanda-Jayne had been going out for two years. As much as it now pained Dave to imagine that sweet sixteen-year-old being with someone as unworthy as his wife's troublesome son, at least it would guarantee her continued presence in his own life.

For all Julian's faults, Dave had to admit that he was very good with children and young kids especially seemed drawn to him. So, he had no worries about what to do with the two young Cross children when Tim's family arrived for Sunday lunch. As far as the food was concerned, lasagne had been his first choice, because it could be made in advance freeing him up to go and talk to his guests while it was in the oven. He could not understand why Sheila always insisted on doing a roast on such occasions, as nice as it was. She missed all the social interaction, by constantly having to dash to and from the kitchen, but on the other hand, perhaps that was the whole point?

Dave was determined that his family, or rather, the disparate members of his household, would give as positive an image as possible, for the benefit of the Cross family, who were definitely going through their share of angst at the moment. If that meant his biting his tongue or not rising to the bait, then he could do that, certainly for one day. Perhaps he could even try to *like* Alison; after all, merely disliking someone because you perceived they disliked *you*, was no basis on which to solely judge a person, he rightly reasoned.

The Cross family had been there for over half an hour before Tim began to warm up, and become the man Dave knew when he *wasn't* with Alison. It was strange how some people had separate work and home personalities, and Tim was certainly one of them. Nevertheless, a few glasses of wine later and he was beginning to make jokes again. However, it was clearly evident that Sheila was struggling with Alison: a woman who was wont to give one or two word answers to questions, and who hardly ever asked any of her own. It was at this stage in the proceedings that Dave decided to take a drastic, if unwise, step. With clandestine care, he put vodka in Alison's next glass of wine to loosen her up a bit. She would be having a big meal that would soon soak it all up; so he told himself that it could do no real harm. Dave also knew that she played the oboe, so he put on a CD of Vaughan Williams' Oboe Concerto to make her feel more at home.

'Are you familiar with this piece Alison?' he asked, as part of his predetermined effort to be nice to the monosyllabic spouse of his best friend.

'Don't *know* it, but it sounds rather plodding and derivative!' she said unsmilingly, without making eye contact with him.

What the hell did she mean by *that*, pondered a very irritated Dave; you just can't bloody well *please* some people!

After only one movement of the concerto, he put on some contemporary jazz to please himself and, more especially, Tim.

Ironically, it was Alison whose foot was soon tapping along to the irregular beat.

'*Ah*, now this is *much* more to my taste,' she responded approvingly, before taking a large draught of the 'fortified' wine.

Tim immediately scowled at his wife.

'You never *used* to like improvised music,' he challenged unhappily, with a hurt, childlike expression.

'Maybe *not*, but it reminds me of an impromptu concert I saw recently at the feminist jazz workshop in Cliftonville,' Alison smiled, as she took another mouthful of her drink. 'D'you know, they actually asked me to jam along on my oboe!'

A thus far silent Sheila now thought she saw an opportunity to contribute to the conversation, in a positive way.

'Perhaps you *and* Tim could go and play there *together* as part of the workshop,' she suggested, with well-meaning intent, if not a little naively.

Alison immediately glared at her hostess as if she'd just broken wind.

'For goodness sake, it's a *feminist* workshop,' she retorted with an accompanying laugh that was almost derisive. 'Tim would be barred on account of his penis!'

As the haughty female guest turned her head away dismissively, Sheila tightened her mouth and narrowed her eyes, determined she was now completely done with making any further attempts to draw Alison out. Dave, on the other hand, was delighted that the spiked drink was beginning to have an affect, and got up to fix another round. Unfortunately, the rapidly stupefying Tim was already helping himself between rounds, and had just uncorked another bottle of red wine. However, as his mate tottered away, Dave was able to work more magic with the vodka bottle.

Tim, who had been thinking about his wife's last comment, now had a reply in readiness:

'I don't know *what* that wife of mine is on about, but I've *never* tried playing the drums with my penis!' he loudly said, at Alison's expense, before slumping back into his seat.

'No mate, you'd need to get a phallic cymbal for that!' Dave retorted, unable to help but join in as he handed refilled wine glasses to the women, making sure that Sheila got the normal one.

'Then, I could *beat* myself off,' Tim added, with the emphasis of a 70s stand-up comedian, whose act relied heavily on sexual puns.

Dave and Tim both then howled like schoolboys as a result of the funny, if not slightly infantile exchange.

Sheila smiled politely, but Alison showed no such grace at her husband's smutty humour.

'It always gets back to what's in your trousers with you, *doesn't* it!' she dismissed scornfully, before drinking deeply from her glass.

Straightaway, Tim sat forward angrily, red wine slopping down his trousers in the process.

'Listen love, *you* were the first one to mention knobs, although I'm surprised you can still remember what one *is*!' he retorted, with an aggression that Dave had not witnessed before.

'*Huh*, I can't remember the last time you weren't too drunk to *get it up*!' Alison snarled back, matching his threatening posture.

Thank goodness the children are upstairs with Julian, thought Dave, as he and Sheila exchanged ominous glances.

'Umm, *ah*, shall we all go through to the dining room for lunch then?' he suggested, in an effort to break up the row.

Without verbally responding to the suggestion, Alison picked up her drink and followed the Darwins through; although Tim hung back in order to pour himself another glass of claret first.

'Don't worry mate, there's wine on the table,' Dave called back to his friend, as he hovered in the dining room doorway.

With everyone finally gathered in the dining room, Dave served the adults at the table, but the children were allowed to take their meals upstairs and watch a video in Julian's room.

As everyone began eating, the dinner table conversation was awkward, sparse and humourless, and there were no words of praise for Dave's culinary efforts, not even from Sheila. Undaunted, Dave pushed aside the half-finished drinks that his guests had brought through, and poured out some fresh wine into clean glasses.

Again, without a word of thanks, Alison made a grab for her new glass, and took a big glug.

'Ish thish the shame wine we had in the lounge?' she asked, now clearly slurring some of her words.

'I *think* so,' replied Sheila somewhat coldly, before picking up and then examining the bottle in question. 'Yes it is: Sainsbury's Reserve Claret.'

'*Oh,* but it tastes different,' An unbelieving Alison reached for, and then sniffed the half-drained glass she'd originally brought through with her.

This was all too much for a still-fuming Tim.

'For fuck's *sake* woman, if you don't want it, *I'll* drink it' he barked, leaning over in order to snatch the half-full glass from her.

He knocked it back in one, spluttered, and then laughed with his head thrown back.

'There's *vodka* in this you silly bitch,' her husband derided, without thinking about how it might have got there.

Sheila, who had been monitoring the bizarre exchange, turned to her husband with eyes narrowed.

'Dave?' she asked, looking to him for an explanation.

Dave just didn't know what to say; he couldn't find the words to confirm, deny, or even explain how vodka happened to have found its way into Alison's drink.

Looking at the struggling Dave, Tim in spite of his advanced state of inebriation, quickly realised what must have happened, and now tried to redeem himself.

'Actually, it was *me* who put it in your drink, my dear; I wanted to bring out your *charming* side,' he declared, with sarcastic emphasis on the last two words.

Alison wasn't a stupid person, and strongly suspected that her husband was covering up for Dave. Whether Tim was responsible for the Mickey Finn, or for just taking the mickey, she no longer cared; either way, she rapidly judged him in need of assertive censure. In an act of spontaneous rage, fuelled by her alcoholic intake, Alison threw her entire plateful of dinner at her husband. The plate broke across his forehead and he fell to the floor amidst splatters of pasta, cheese sauce and tomato. A shocked Sheila and a distressed Dave rushed to help him back on to his chair, and as they propped him up, it became immediately obvious that a badly stunned Tim had a large bleeding gash across his forehead. Just at the moment when Sheila was on her way to get something to deal with the wound, Alison stood up suddenly, swayed and then vomited copiously all over the dinner table.

Between them, Dave and a stony-faced Sheila managed to clean up both of their guests. Afterwards, she volunteered to drive the Cross family home, having drunk the least amount of wine. She also stated, in no uncertain terms, that Tim would just have to jolly well collect his battered vehicle the following day; assuming that he was sober enough to do so by that time.

As the two children were brought downstairs by Julian, Henry took one look at his semi-comatose parents, who were both waiting in the hall below.

'Oh *no*, not *again*!' was all that the small boy had to say on the subject.

While Sheila was gone, Dave had the equally unpleasant ordeal of clearing up the dining room table, and whilst doing so, he unhappily reflected on the disastrous dinner party. All his hopes for the gathering to be a healing one for Tim and Alison had come to nothing. On the contrary, Dave considered his foolish venture with the vodka to have made matters between the bickering Cross couple, infinitely worse.

That night, Dave and Sheila sat exhausted on the sofa in the lounge, sipping coffee, and munching chocolate biscuits, whilst staring zombie-like at the television.

During one particularly dull advert break, she turned to her half-asleep husband.

'Dave, *did* you put vodka in Alison's drink?' she asked, in a non-challenging manner.

'We both clearly heard Tim say that *he* had done it', Dave replied, without taking his half-closed eyes off the flickering screen.

'Fair enough!' said Sheila, with a slight shrug.

Pilgrimage

Dave replaced the receiver of the bedside telephone and, still sitting on the edge of the duvet, leant forward and rubbed his furrowed forehead.

'*Who was that on the phone?*' Sheila bellowed from downstairs.

Dave sat up straight again and then sighed deeply.

'*Hold on, I'll come down and tell you*!' he replied, before slowly getting to his feet. Dave didn't want to have to shout back down to her from the bedroom, so decided not to change out of his work clothes just then but go and find his wife instead. In any case, he concluded that he probably wouldn't have been able to make himself heard above all the music emanating from Julian's room.

Some of the stuff his quasi-stepson played quite appealed to Dave and even reminded him of the late 1960s, early 1970s album bands he himself had listened to at Julian's age. On one particular occasion recently, Dave had told him as much, in an effort to find some sort of common ground between them; something they could discuss face-to-face without having to go through Sheila. However, his encouraging comments had not been welcomed. In fact, the music he had reported as liking was never played again, as if an old fart like him appreciating it had somehow tainted it. Instead, Julian moved on towards louder, harder-edged American bands, the assumption being that Dave could not possibly like that sort of stuff. The temptation to knock on the door and say to his quasi-stepson how much he liked *Metallica* was overwhelming, in other words, to damn it by praising it and, once more, force Julian on to something else. But he resisted the notion, and decided that it was a trick he would save for another day. Dave concluded that, some time soon, he might even play Julian some early 1970s *Black Sabbath*, just to prove that there was nothing new under the sun, or rather, nothing that he hadn't been grooving to since well before Julian was born.

Dave found Sheila in the dining room, her numerous Telecom files open all over the table.

'Are you *still* working on that presentation?' he asked, with a face contorted in horror at the sight of work related paperwork in his sanctuary.

'Just refining my approach,' she replied, with controlled irritation, before looking up at him. 'You *know* that getting a manager's job is important to me Dave. I would have expected you to be more supportive.'

'I *am*, honestly,' he defended, holding his hands out to the side. 'It's just that we get precious little time alone together as it *is*!'

Sheila just looked at him sideways with narrowed unsmiling eyes, and then reached for her fag packet and lit a cigarette, knowing full well that it usually made him leave the room. However, her husband realised that this was probably what she was trying to achieve, so instead, pulled out a dining room chair and sat at the table directly opposite her.

Dave studied her closely as she feverishly flicked through the photocopied pages.

'That was Nanna Darwin on the phone just now,' he remarked, after about a minute's silence.

Sheila looked irritated at being interrupted.

'*What*?' she barked, throwing her pen down.

'You *asked me* who it was on the phone, and I'm *telling you* that it was Nanna Darwin!' he retorted in calm, measured tones.

'Yes I *did*, didn't I? ... I'm *sorry* Dave,' Sheila chuckled wearily. 'It's just this sodding presentation, it's not going at *all* well.' Feeling defeated by the task, she supported her head in her left hand, and then stared at the smoke curling up from her lit cigarette.

Straightaway, Dave got up, walked round and stood behind her, placing his supportive hands on her shoulders. In response, she immediately extinguished the offending cigarette for him without being asked to. He then leant over her shoulder and looked at the pages on the table in front of her.

'*May* I?' he asked, before reaching for her notes.

'*Huh*, go *ahead*!' Sheila replied, with a dismissive hand gesture.

He quickly scanned through the basic plan of her speech.

'There's a *lot* of detail for you to read out here,' Dave observed, knowing that he would neither want to give this presentation himself, nor have it presented to him.

'*Yes*, but it's *all* got to be covered,' Sheila despaired, with another emphatic hand movement.

Dave took a deep breath.

'This is just as a *suggestion*,' he began tentatively, 'but why don't you sum up the main points verbally, perhaps supported by some acetates on an overhead projector, and then *afterwards*, distribute handouts showing all the minute picky details for the hardcore Telecom anoraks to wank over *later*.'

'Yes…*yes*, that's a *brilliant* idea Dave, thanks *ever* so much,' Sheila beamed, reaching up to squeeze the hand that was once more resting on her shoulder. 'But now that I know where I'm going with this, I can do it later. *Meanwhile*, you and Julian must be hungry; I'll get dinner', she added, before beginning to stand up.

Straightaway, Dave barred her way with his arm and gently pushed her back into the chair.

'*I'll* get the dinner, you stay and finish that,' he insisted, before kissing her on the top of the head. 'After all, I *think* I can just about manage cheese omelette and salad. It won't take me a moment.'

Sheila smiled gratefully and resumed her work, as Dave made for the kitchen.

'Oh, would you like garlic bread with it?' he shouted, from just beyond the hall doorway.

'*Lovely*', came the concise yet enthusiastic response from the dining room.

This was the first meal Dave had prepared since that disastrous Sunday lunch with Alison and Tim, the weekend before last, but as he walked into the kitchen, he tried to block the fact from his mind, with only partial success.

Dave chopped the salad vegetables and thought about the telephone call from Nanna Darwin, still concerned by how down in the dumps she had sounded. By the tone of her voice, he was sure that Nanna was still worried about Grandad Darwin's health; in fact the whole family shared her concern. The old boy still worked too hard in the garden, but at the end of the day, it was obvious to all that he thoroughly enjoyed it, so no one had yet tackled him on the subject. However, Dave was glad she had invited them over for lunch on Saturday, as he would then be able to more accurately gauge how they were both really feeling; neither grandparent was comfortable using the phone, and they never sounded like themselves. Dave had accepted the invitation without consulting Sheila, but there shouldn't be a problem, for as far as he was aware: the day was quite free of any other pre-arranged commitments.

When his grandparents finally retired from Rothermead in 1976, and had decided to buy a bungalow on the northeast Kent coast, Grandad had made up his mind that he wanted a place with a sizeable plot. They both settled for just such a property in the village of Beltinge, on the outskirts of Herne Bay. This, he sub-divided into a vegetable garden, herbaceous borders and so on. Given the old boy's dedication and experience, the results were magnificent, but it was all so much work to maintain. Then six months ago, Nanna noticed that his usual hearty appetite had diminished and she began to wonder if her cooking no longer appealed to him. Her fears turned out to be unfounded, and Grandad was happy to reassure her that her dinners were as good as they had ever been. However, after much coaxing, he did finally admit to having been troubled recently with some stomach pains. Her husband never usually complained about being ill, even when he was evidently very poorly, and hated anything to do with doctors, or worst still, hospitals. Nevertheless, the fact that he had mentioned the pains at all, given his notorious reticence, caused Nanna much concern, and a fortnight ago, she had finally managed to persuade him to go down to the surgery. Initially, the worry was that his plastic aorta – inserted five years ago during a life saving operation – was playing up, but the doctor had quickly ruled that out. However, to get to the bottom of the problem, Grandad had been sent for tests and a scan at Canterbury Hospital.

As he spread garlic butter onto the baguette slices, Dave thought of those early days at Oakenden Nursery, before he was five, and recalled that Grandad Darwin had always suffered with his stomach as far back as he could remember. And was it not excessive stomach acid that had forced Grandad to give up pipe smoking back then? Dave tried to reassure himself that, perhaps, the latest problem was nothing more than a recurrence of that old trouble. In any case, the test results were due any day now, so he would probably find out soon enough, if not at lunch on Saturday.

As soon as Sheila had cleared her files away, Dave laid the table for dinner, and then Julian came downstairs straight away, his food radar having activated.

'Thanks for your help with the presentation,' an appreciative Sheila smiled as she sat down. 'I don't know why you don't go for a manager's position *yourself*, you've got the knowledge *and* the organisational skills.'

'Perhaps, but I haven't got your people skills; I just can't be ruthless, and I'm *far* too scared of the likes of Monica and Tiffany to attempt to *manage* them!' he shrugged, helping himself to salad.

'Ah, but that's just a lack of training. I'm *sure* you could achieve it,' she responded encouragingly, before biting into her garlic bread.

Dave smiled, but thought to himself that he would rather be boiled in oil than go through the Telecom indoctrination process. It was all right for Sheila though, he concluded; she was a natural!

The conversation having lapsed, they both watched Julian piling up his plate. Dave did not mind today, as he'd made plenty in anticipation.

'If you want some instant mash with that, you know where the packet is', he remarked, before winking at Sheila, to reassure her that he wasn't having a serious pop at her son.

Luckily, Dave was currently in her good books.

'Yes, and there's a big shovel in the shed if that serving spoon's too small,' she added, before bursting into laughter.

Dave laughed too, and even Julian joined in. What a rare family moment, he reflected; if only it could always be like this!

'Err, good ... garlic bread!' Julian commented, through a packed mouthful.

'*Dave* made it!' Sheila exclaimed, before smiling across the table at her husband.

Julian looked up at his quasi-stepfather, and forced a smile.

'*Yeah*, it's nice!' he conceded, before returning to his plate.

With everyone in apparent upbeat mood, Dave quickly judged the moment right to resurrect the subject of Nanna Darwin's telephone call.

'Oh, by the way, I'm sure you'll all be pleased to know that we're going over to Beltinge for lunch on Saturday,' he announced, trying to put a strong positive emphasis on the news.

Straightaway, Julian beamed with delight.

'*Brilliant*!' he responded, loading another excessive forkfull.

Dave was pleased at the positive reaction to his announcement from the unpredictable sixteen-year-old. He knew the lad liked his Grandparents Darwin, not least because they always showered him with gifts, including large quantities of chocolate. Julian didn't seem to mind that Nanna Darwin obtained it from the 'food woman': a regular and legally dubious participant at local boot fairs, who somehow managed to obtain goods with recently expired sell-by dates, which she then sold on at huge discounts.

Unfortunately, unlike her son, Sheila was not happy.

'But I've arranged to go into work on Saturday morning to help with the installation order backlog,' she bemoaned unhappily. 'You should have asked me *first*!'

So much for family harmony, thought Dave, as his head dipped dejectedly.

Sheila looked first at Dave, and then towards Julian. She too had appreciated the happy atmosphere at table that evening, and didn't want to be the architect of its destruction.

'*Look*, I can see how much you…umm ... *both* want to go, so how about this? I'll work until 11:30, which will still give us more than enough time to get over to Beltinge, okay?' she proposed, her eyes held wide in expectation of a positive response to her compromise proposal.

'Thanks love; I'm *ever* so grateful,' Dave happily conceded, and almost ingratiatingly. 'Do you know though, I could even go in to work *with* you!'

Sheila dropped her fork, with a loud clatter, having listened to his suggestion.

'*What*, am I *hearing* right ... Dave Darwin volunteering to go into work on a *Saturday*?' she gulped, with the same reassuring wink he had previously given, to indicate her words as being a joke, rather than a jibe.

'*No*, no, *not* to do overtime,' Dave played along with the tease. 'But it *will* give me the opportunity to use that new personal computer in my office. I want to type up some research notes that I'm going to need for my next local history book.'

Julian seemed pleased by the agreed arrangements too.

'So, I'll meet you both at the car by 11:30. You see, I'll be in town too, seeing my new *girlfriend*!' he announced, with a rather smug countenance.

'Oh *really*, what's her *name* then love?' asked his mother, with equal measures of surprise and interest.

'Her name is Daphne, but my friends call her Duvet!'

59

Julian and Dave smiled at each other knowingly.

Sheila however, looked rather puzzled.

'Is that because her real name is rather old-fashioned sounding?' she asked, with innocent interest.

'No, it's because she's easy to spread on the bed!' her chortling son replied.

Dave nearly choked on his mouthful of omelette, as he tried to suppress a schoolboy snigger, and immediately received a withering look of chastisement from his wife for encouraging the teenager.

Sheila then glared at the lad himself.

'Well, I hope you take precautions,' she advised in a responsibly parental, if not strictly catholic way.

'Yes of *course*,' responded a calm, wide-eyed Julian, 'I'm going to tie my feet to the bedposts, so I don't fall in!'

Both husband and son laughed again, whilst Sheila looked on disapprovingly. Dave was tempted to tackle her about papal edicts and condoms, but didn't want to spoil the moment. Julian and he so rarely laughed together and even then, it was usually on the sixteen-year-old's terms, and concerning something that he had initiated. His own so-called funny comments only rarely made Julian laugh, even if he did find them funny. Perhaps it was more of the 'not wanting to like the same things as that old fart' syndrome. But at the end of the day, the television clip of Uncle Ronnie hadn't made Julian laugh either, recalled Dave with a resigned sigh, so at least he was in good company.

The most disquieting thing of all was that, despite the jokes concerning condoms and casual sex, the mention of a new girlfriend meant that Amanda-Jayne was now definitely off the scene, and that fact wasn't lost on Dave. For him, she had become an ally and friend, as well as a clandestine object of desire, albeit on a different plain. What a pity she wouldn't be coming round any more, he thought, and at the same time, just couldn't imagine that anyone dubbed 'Duvet' would ever replace Amanda-Jayne in his affections.

When the Saturday morning in question finally came, Julian begged a ride into Canterbury with Dave and Sheila. Arriving at the Telecom House car park, he pointed out that 'Duvet' was there already, waiting for him. Dave was interested to note that she was a plumpish girl, with huge breasts and long ginger hair that hung down in ringlets. What is more, she wore hippy-style clothes and a threequarter-length skirt that didn't quite hide her black Doctor Marten boots. Sheila didn't bother to hide how horrified she was at the girl's appearance, and very nearly crossed herself. Following cautious nods of greeting from the two adults, they all went their separate ways, with a promise to meet back at the car 11:30 sharp.

Dave hated going into his office at the best of times, but this was a Saturday, and therefore, the sense of dread was magnified as he climbed the empty staircase.

At least there would be no Tim, Monica or Tiffany to distract him, he thought, as he used his pass card to activate the door on the fifth floor. Best of all though, there would be no complaining phone calls coming in. Sheila and the other overtime idiots were way below him on another floor, so he concluded that he wouldn't be disturbed by them either. As he plodded through the deserted canteen, on his way to the Customer Relations office, Dave reminded himself that the only reason he was here at all was that his publisher no longer accepted photo captions in conventionally typed script, and that today was a good opportunity to work on the office's new personal computer, or more specifically, its word processing facilities. It was the only one so far, but they had been promised that, before very long, all their desk terminals would have 'WordStar' installed.

By 11:00, Dave was getting on quite well and estimated that, with any luck, he would be able to get the job done in time. It was then that the telephone on his desk rang, and immediately wiped the smile from his face. It could only be Sheila, he thought, trying to quell a rising tide of panic; no one else knows I'm here! Having assumed that, he hoped she was not ringing to say she would be delayed. With the greatest of reluctance, he answered the loathed instrument, and found that it was indeed Sheila.

'Hello Dave, look *here*, I have a Mr Haynes on the line,' she began, with officious efficiency. 'There has been a delay in the installation of his telephone extension, due to lack of parts, and Telecom have missed the agreed contractual date. Would you please talk to him about a compensation payment?'

Dave was absolutely incensed.

'But...but I'm not meant to *be* here,' he said angrily. 'I have to finish the captions.'

'*I* know you're there and so does everyone *else* now', retorted Sheila, quite unmoved by his reaction. '*Come* on, it won't take you long, besides which, it will look good for Telecom if we can get it sorted out today.'

Look good for *you*, thought a fuming Dave, but he reluctantly agreed to take the call. Nevertheless, he was pissed off; very pissed off. It was quite clear that Sheila had put Telecom before him again. However, having quickly got rid of the unwelcome customer with a promised maximum payment, he was just about able to finish his captions, get them saved to disk, and also printed out. This was just as well, for Dave vowed, right there and then, that he would never again be going into the office on a Saturday for any reason, and end up taking calls for Sheila.

In the car over to Herne Bay, Dave was quiet. After all, it was not easy to talk when you were biting your tongue so hard. There was also the fact that he did not want to make a scene about that call, and risk spoiling the day, so reluctantly had let it go.

No trains delayed them at the Sturry level crossing, so the journey was quick and they were turning into Gainsborough Drive, at Beltinge, with five minutes to spare. Grandad Darwin was in the front garden, tending the borders, and as the car pulled up, he laid aside his hoe and waved enthusiastically. Then, as everyone alighted, the old boy greeted Dave with his usual demonstrative bear hug. In fact, he greeted both Sheila and Julian in this way as well.

Dave was so pleased to see him, as always wearing his standard garden 'uniform' of Wellington boots, old waistcoat and that beloved battered trilby. And then there was that familiar smell of coal tar soap; so very much part of Grandad Darwin's essence. The aroma transported Dave back to his earliest recollections, which were not so much memories, as a sense of happiness, coupled with a feeling of safety. But there was something different about his grandfather today as well, he thought, as the old boy slapped him on the back. His tanned, rosy cheeks seemed somehow more hollow than before, and his old gardening trousers hung off him loosely. There was no doubt in Dave's mind: Grandad had lost weight.

Nanna Darwin was soon out of the bungalow to join them all in the front garden. After a brief round of greetings, which included a peck on the cheek for everyone, she turned towards Sheila.

'I simply *must* show you my new electric sewing machine!' beamed Nanna with enthusiasm. 'You'll *love* it; I made this jacket and skirt yesterday, in a matter of *hours*!' She twirled around to show off her beautifully tailored and stitched, matching two-piece outfit, made with some bizarrely patterned material.

'Oh *yes*, it's…umm, it's *very* well made!' Sheila responded, with a careful choice of words.

Dave was quick to agree.

'A testament to your tailoring skills Nanna,' he added, not daring to look at Julian, who was desperately trying to suppress his sniggers.

Grandad clearly enjoyed seeing his wife so praised, and took the words at face value.

'She's a clever Nanna alright!' he commented, placing his muscular arm round her shoulders.

Whilst everyone agreed how professional the work looked, no one had the heart to tell her that her choice of material, no doubt acquired at a local boot fair, made her look like a 1970s settee.

As the women went inside to look at the sewing machine, Dave followed Grandad Darwin round to the back garden, keen to see what he had been up to since their last visit. Julian was eager to go with them too; he was genuinely fond of the old boy and actually called him 'Grandad' as well. Dave was delighted that he held Grandad Darwin in such high regard, but felt saddened that the teenager's feelings did not extend to his mother's father, Grandad Maybury, who, because of a series of strokes, was now a shambling shadow of a man who dribbled and slurred his words. Moreover, his other grandfather was still so grief stricken at the death of Nanna Maybury, now some 15 years ago, that he talked about little else. Julian just couldn't imagine the cheerful, joking man whom Dave had known as a boy, and who had now gone forever.

With the side gate open, the beautiful back garden – the best part of a third of an acre – now opened up before them. In the 15 or so years that Nanna and Grandad Darwin had been retired and resident in the Beltinge bungalow, a verdant floral paradise had been created by both of them, but especially by him. It was a process that was still on-going, though now entirely concentrated on the finer horticultural details. Having crossed the lawn, they approached the gravel path that led to the pond area and then, the vegetable garden. The beginning of the route was framed by the two faithful cherry trees that Grandad had put in shortly after moving there, and Dave was thrilled to see that both were now in full blossom.

'What do *they* remind you of my old Dave?' asked Grandad Darwin, gesturing towards the pinky-white floriferous mass.

'Oh, Rothermead *Farm* of course ... they always *do*!' his grandson smiled, with a slow reflective sigh.

The old boy stared up into the branches and watched the many assembled bees manically circling and drinking the cherry blossom nectar.

'Do you remember those early morning walks we took through the orchards to collect mushrooms?' he asked, once more throwing his arm round his grandson's shoulders.

'How could I forget,' Dave replied straightaway. 'Those weekends on the farm were the happiest days of my childhood by *far*!'

Having released his grip, Grandad went lumbering down the path and beckoned both Dave and a quiet Julian to follow. As he did so, Dave watched his grandfather ahead of him, and realised that there hadn't been any mention of tests or doctors, so far. He was happy to infer from this that they'd either heard nothing, or, if they had, that there was nothing to worry about.

Grandad stopped by the ornamental pond area, where Nanna regularly overfed the goldfish, and it was immediately obvious to both visitors that the old boy had been very busy of late. A new wooden trellis and metal arch now divided the pond area from the vegetable garden beyond.

'*Wow*, did you do all this yourself Grandad?' Dave asked, upon seeing the massive upright posts that supported the whole structure.

'Of *course*,' replied his grandfather, and then flexed his right arm whilst slapping the bicep muscle that still bulged beneath his brown wrinkled skin. This was something he had always done: his strong man act, and yet it had always seemed at odds with his gentle passive nature. The expression 'he wouldn't hurt a fly' could have been specially written for Grandad Darwin.

He pointed to the bottom half of the newly constructed trellis, which was already crowded with foliage, from recently planted rambler roses, clematis and honeysuckle. All had been grown in his greenhouse, no doubt, from cuttings 'acquired' on those occasional coach trips to the various big houses, stately homes and gardens.

'Nanna always disowns me when I'm liberating my cuttings,' he remarked with a wry smile and a wink.

His grandparents had always referred to each other as 'Nanna' and 'Grandad', probably ever since Dave was born; a time when they would have first inherited those titles. Sometimes, he would call her 'the Nanna', an endearing idiosyncrasy that sometimes extended itself to 'the Dave', 'the Lucy' or 'the Len'.

Grandad Darwin bent to tuck in a honeysuckle tendril that was trying to find something to entwine around, and his face contorted with pain.

'Are you alright?' Dave enquired with concern, placing a hand on his grandfather's back.

'Yes, me old boy, just hunger pains,' he replied, with a dismissive smile, before straightening himself up slowly.

Dave nodded in acceptance of the explanation, but immediately wondered, if his 'no news, is good news' assumption had been somewhat premature.

They all wandered through the new arch and into the vegetable garden beyond, having first managed, with some difficulty, to prise Julian away from the well-stocked pond. The early salad crops were already well under way, and both Dave and Julian were allowed to pull and eat some of the swollen radishes. This was something that Dave had done as a small boy, and ever since, preferred his radishes with a bit of soil left on them. Across the rest of the well-manured beds, there was much evidence of other crops in various stages of development, including rows of young cabbage plants, the faint haze of recently-germinated carrot seeds, and neat rows of potato mounds, out of which, the earliest spuds were already sprouting. The runner bean supports were still bare, but a greenhouse that was crammed full of seedlings, all itching to be planted out, more than made up for that. Also under glass, the young tomato plants were just getting underway, and as he slid the greenhouse door back, Dave could already detect the unmistakably evocative aroma of tomato plant foliage; a delight that reached its height in mid summer, especially on a warm day, after a good watering. The whole of his grandfather's productive patch reminded him of the old, walled vegetable garden at Rothermead, which, funnily enough, had been laid out in very much the same way as here in Beltinge. The main difference was that now, being on his own land, and him being his own boss, Grandad could grow and then harvest all the produce for his table, as opposed to that of his former paymaster at the 'big house'.

Having thoroughly inspected the whole kitchen garden, the trio returned to the bungalow via a different route and entered the large conservatory that extended along the back of the property. As usual at this time of year, it was crowded with a vast array of seed trays and cuttings, for which there had been no room left in the greenhouse. There was also a strong and familiar smell of curry wafting out from the adjacent kitchen.

Grandad keenly sniffed the air like an over-sized Bisto kid.

'Mm, I think I know what *we're* having for dinner today!' he remarked, with eyebrows raised.

'Oh *good*,' responded Julian hungrily, 'I *love* Nanna Darwin's curries!'

Dave loved them too; they were like no other he'd ever had, although they were not strictly 'curry', but more like an English stew made from mince, with curry powder added in varying quantities. This rather random approach meant that sometimes, you got a real 'hottie', as Grandad often put it.

Everyone met up again in the dining room, just as the lunch was being brought in, although in this household, as Grandad Darwin had already demonstrated, midday meals were referred to as 'dinner', whatever they consisted of, and evening meals, always called 'tea'.

'I see my curry radar is working as well as usual,' beamed Nanna Darwin, as the men walked in.

Sheila was close behind her, with a huge, steaming dish of mashed potato.

'And wash your hands before you sit down please,' she instructed, looking at both her husband and son.

Having obediently completed his ablutions, Dave sat down at the table that both his father and Uncle Ronnie had eaten at when they were boys. No doubt, they had enjoyed 'curry' here on many occasions too, he pondered. Nanna began to ladle out the mixture, to which she added spoonfuls of the buttery mash. Dave waited eagerly for Grandad Darwin's musical 'Oh lovely', when his loaded plate was handed to him, but it never came; the old boy didn't say it. He felt such disappointment at that long cherished ritual being broken. It was only a small thing, but to Dave, it seemed to matter; it was something missing from the usual routine. As the meal began, there was little dinner table conversation, but what there was, largely consisted of polite enquiries about gardening and Telecom, although Dave tried to quash the latter in favour of the former, much to Sheila's barely disguised irritation.

Halfway through the meal, Dave looked across the table at his beloved grandparents. There was Nanna with her home-tailored outfit, bifocal glasses and neatly set grey hair. She did this herself every morning with a device resembling a medieval article of torture, which could be heated on the rings of the stove. And then there was Grandad with his bronzed bald head, as usual scarred and scabbed from the various knocks he got in the garden, and most times,at the very moment he had taken his hat off. Normally, when Grandad Darwin ate one of Nanna's curries, small beads of perspiration would appear on his pate, but not today it would seem. Dave soon realised that this was not because of the relative mildness of the curry, but rather because his grandfather wasn't eating much. Nanna Darwin had also noticed, and was looking concerned, but she knew not to say anything from bitter experience. In the past, if Grandad ever left some of his dinner– usually as a result of her having overloaded his plate – she would always think that he hadn't enjoyed it. As a result, he would somehow force it all down and then have violent indigestion for the rest of the afternoon.

Something was wrong, Dave thought with alarm, why isn't he tucking in as usual? He noticed that Sheila was looking uncomfortable as well, and almost deliberately trying *not* to look at Grandad Darwin.

Soon, the dinner plates were cleared away, and they were all empty except for Grandad's. The old boy was all too aware that his barely-touched meal had been noticed, and he tried to make light of it.

'I'm afraid you've overloaded me again the Nanna,' he admitted, in a slightly bashful manner, as he passed his plate back to her.

So much for hunger pains, concluded a troubled Dave; there's definitely something wrong here!

To follow, a cold pudding was offered: a wonderfully old-fashioned confection consisting of tinned fruit, jelly and ice cream. Grandad Darwin politely declined, and so did Sheila. Dave said that he was full, but this was more of a gesture of solidarity to his grandfather, than the true state of his stomach.

It was likely that Nanna realised this, and also sought to make light of the situation.

'Well if you two boys have had enough, then you can both get up,' she remarked, before slowly pushing her chair back, '*Oh,* and Grandad, you can show Dave your new church pictures!'

Before their hostess could get fully to her feet, Sheila intervened.

'Sit down Nanna,' she instructed, quickly standing up herself. '*I'll* bring the pudding through, and then begin the washing up; I'll be *happy* to!'

'Oh, are you *sure* dear, *thank* you,' Nanna responded, before looking towards Dave. 'That's a good wife you've got there my boy!' she added, with an appreciative smile.

Her grandson grinned back in response to her comment, but said nothing in reply.

Contented to remain at the table, Nanna now turned to Julian, who was still sitting down in anticipation of his dessert.

'*So* then, tell me about your latest girlfriend dear,' she requested, as the other adults went their separate ways.

On hearing the question, Dave hoped that the lad wasn't going to be too frank about Daphne, or rather 'Duvet', and he judged that Sheila was also thinking the same thing, seeing the way she was hovering in the kitchen doorway.

Unable to hear the hushed conversation that ensued, Dave followed Grandad Darwin through to the spare room, at the front of the bungalow, which also doubled as his studio. Pen and ink drawing was a lifelong passion of his, second only to gardening and he was keen to show his grandson the series of pictures he'd recently begun, depicting Kentish churches. The old boy had completed six so far, all in fast ink, over which, he had applied a watercolour wash and other embellishments. These finished works were based on his own pencil sketches, made over the years, and supplemented by Dave's photographs, which had been captured on their more recent country walks.

'Oh *Grandad*, these are really good,' Dave commented beaming, as he examined the picture of Wickhambreaux Church. 'How many of these are you planning to do?'

'Well, I'm just going to keep on and finish as many as I can,' he replied, in suddenly quite sombre tones. 'The Nanna is absolutely *insistent* that I take it easy in the garden, so I'll be spending more time in here.'

Dave put his arm around the old man's shoulders.

'We *all* want you to take it easy in the garden, Grandad; you ain't no spring chicken any more!' he joked, with warm affection.

'*Good old* Dave,' chuckled his grandfather, before returning the demonstrative gesture. 'And don't you worry about *me*; there's plenty of life left in the old Grandad yet!'

Dave knew from as far back as he could remember, that Grandad Darwin habitually took a nap, his 'forty winks', in the early afternoon. So, after they had all regrouped in the front room, and enjoyed a pot of tea together, Dave made his excuses and got up to leave. As usual, Nanna and Grandad Darwin came out to the front of the bungalow in order to see them off. A long-practised family tradition was for all of the parties concerned to wave until the departing car was out of sight. Consequently, everyone dutifully waved as they started back up Gainsborough Drive. Dave waved out of the driver's side window and, at the same time, looked at his grandparents through the rearview mirror. At that moment, Grandad suddenly leapt into the air and clicked his heels together, just as he had done when Dave was a boy. His grandson tooted the car horn to acknowledge the familiar gesture, but noticed that Nanna was gently telling her husband off for having done it.

As they drove through the main part of Beltinge, Sheila asked Dave to pull over by the small village supermarket. She then gave Julian a short verbal list of groceries for him to pop in and purchase, and as these included toffees for the journey and chocolate biscuits for home, he willingly went.

As soon as Julian had entered the shop, Sheila turned to Dave and quite unexpectedly, reached out to hold his hand.

'I'm afraid I've got some bad news for you,' she said, with a tenderness he hadn't experienced in a long time.

'What…what *is* it?' he retorted in alarm, his stomach churning ominously.

As his wife regarded him with uncharacteristically doleful eyes, Dave listened in chilled silence as she informed him of what Nanna Darwin had told her, back at the bungalow before lunch. Grandad Darwin's test results had not been good: they'd discovered a massive tumour in his stomach. Worst of all though, it was inoperable and untreatable; and there was no doubt about it.

'How…how long does he *have*?' stammered a bewildered Dave, as his breathing became more rapid.

Sheila slowly shrugged her shoulders.

'No-one can be *sure*,' she gently replied. 'Probably up to a year, at *best*! But the most important thing is *this* Dave: Grandad Darwin doesn't want *anyone* to refer to it. He just wants to carry on as normal, and for as long as he can…and we *all* have to respect that, okay?'

Dave nodded emphatically, his eyeballs darting from side to side.

'Of *course*', he replied, in a dry and trembling voice. He soon felt the emotion rise up within and the tears forming; there was no way he could stop them.

Sheila quickly unclicked her seatbelt, adjusted her position, and then flung both arms around his shoulders.

'I'm *so sorry* darling … I'm so sorry,' she said quietly, as he shook with grief.

'Why him, why *him*!' he lamented, in between tear sodden sobs. 'It's just not *fair*!'

'Shush now, we'll talk more later,' she whispered, before gently pushing him away from her. 'Julian will be back soon.'

Dave sniffed and nodded in agreement before wiping his face and then beginning the process of 'acting normal' again. However, he could not stop those images of the past flooding through his mind: Grandad at Oakenden Nursery, Grandad in his garden, Grandad on those many country walks, Grandad at Rothermead Farm; all those things that were as important to him as his Uncle Ronnie had been, but for different reasons.

A largely recovered Dave suddenly turned to Sheila.

'Let's go to Rothermead … let's go *now*!' he said, with eyebrows raised in keen expectation.

Sheila thought quickly; she had hoped to finalise the plans for her presentation that afternoon, even do a dummy run, but she could see the pain in his eyes, and had all-too-clearly heard the pleading in his voice.

'Yes, *why* not' she replied, forcing a smile. 'You're *always* going on about how wonderful it was up there, and now I'll be able to see for myself if it's true.' Sheila winked at him to confirm that she was teasing, and he smiled warmly in response.

Before very long, Julian returned with a bulging plastic carrier bag and scrambled into the back of the car. His mother strained her head round to look in the back.

'We are going up to Sittingbourne, to see where Nanna and Grandad Darwin used to live,' she announced to him, before facing forward again, and then doing-up her seatbelt.

'Yeah, brilliant,' replied Julian, in a matter-of-fact manner, as he opened the bag of toffees and offered them round.

Little was said as the car cleared the village, and then pulled on to the Thanet Way, heading in the direction of Faversham and the M2 motorway. At Brenley Corner roundabout, a few miles later, Dave left the dual carriageway in order to take the old A2 route, via Faversham town and the village of Teynham. In the 1960s, this was the route his family had always taken when they went up to Rothermead Farm for those cherished weekends away. Back then, of course, they would have come from the Canterbury direction, having also travelled along the old A2 in order to reach Brenley Corner.

At the designated roundabout, Dave steered on to the aforementioned A2 and once more joined the old familiar route to Rothermead. He immediately recalled that, in those bygone days, his father always allowed him to sit in the front passenger seat, as it greatly helped to ease his travel sickness.

*

.'Are you still feeling alright David?' his mother asked from the back seat.

'Yes thanks,' he replied, turning his head half round. 'And little Ollie is okay too!' David looked at the budgie in the cage on his lap, and smiled with satisfaction. Ollie always came with them to Rothermead and by now, was completely unperturbed by the 15 mile journey.

Both David and Lucy always looked forward to going to stay at Rothermead Farm for the weekend; it was like going on holiday. On the Friday afternoon in question, they would rush home from their respective schools, check the weekend bags their mum would have already packed for them, and then eagerly, if not a little impatiently, wait for their father to come home. Once he'd had a cup of tea and opened his mail, they'd be off to Rothermead, budgie and all.

Whilst it was David's job to look after Ollie during the trip, his little brother Eddie would be the responsibility of their mother; usually sleeping on her lap, in the back of the car, throughout the entire journey. Although he was very young, and didn't say much at the moment, neither Lucy nor David doubted that Eddie also very much enjoyed going up to stay at Rothermead Farm.

Of all the many weekends away, this particular one was going to be very special and therefore, the level of excitement in the car was increased as a result. *The Lulu Show*, on which Uncle Ronnie had appeared, and the one they had gone up to London to see being recorded, was going to be screened on the Saturday night on BBC1, after the usual episodes of *Doctor Who* and *Dixon of Dock Green*. Everyone was pleased that they would all be able to watch it together as a family, except of course for Ronnie himself, who would not be there with them. The young comedian was very busy, now that he was becoming famous, and had recently taken a flat in London to be closer to his work. Although Ronnie had still hung on to his old place on the Herne Bay seafront, he no longer came down to Kent as often as he used to.

David glanced at his watch and smiled; the journey was going well. The family would usually arrive at the farm cottage at about 06:00, by which time, Nanna Darwin had got the Rayburn lit and heated up nicely, ready for the baked potatoes. At ten minutes to the hour, the car was passing through the village of Teynham. By five to six, it was traversing the country lanes around the edge of Beckensfield. They would be there before long, he concluded excitedly.

The old village of Rothermead was soon before them. It consisted of little more than a large church, an old rectory, a few cottages, and, of course, the farm complex itself. However, most of the local population lived at Rothermead Green, which was situated a mile or so further along the lane, where the pub, school and village shop could be found.

The cherry orchards began to appear as soon as they had passed the old church; the one that Grandad Darwin loved to sketch. The spring blossom en masse was magnificent and quite overwhelming, for on their last trip to Rothermead exactly a fortnight before, there had been no evidence of even the odd petal having come out.

Barely two hundred yards further along the lane, and just before the double wrought-iron gates to the 'big house', David's dad took a right-hand turn onto the narrower metalled track that curved round to Rothermead Court Farm, to give it the full title. On the left, the track was bordered by the high hornbeam hedge that was twice yearly clipped by Grandad Darwin. David had helped him with this task on several occasions, during those longer school holiday stays, when he didn't go home with the rest of the family on the Sunday afternoon. Beyond the hedge were the grounds of the 'big house', or Rothermead Court House as it was properly called, where Grandad was the head gardener. This was his official title, although in truth, he was the only gardener, except that is, for the occasional drafting in of one of the farm labourers for some big task.

Having curved round the edge of the grounds to the 'big house', the farm track then veered off to the right, but the Darwins car went straight ahead and entered the outer courtyard area. To the left of this elongated space was the timber-framed seventeenth century north wing of the 'big house', which had originally been the main dwelling. However, it had long since been relegated to a secondary role by the addition of a Regency period south-facing wing, complete with grand entrance and a gravelled drive that led down to the wrought-iron gates, by the junction for the farm's access track. Effectively, this early nineteenth century re-ordering and expansion meant that what had once been the front of the house was now the back. Half of this older wing currently served as the cook's residence – a strange woman called Edwina Cohen– and the other half was empty, semi-derelict, and used for other non-residential purposes.

On the right-hand side of the outer courtyard were extensive stables, where her ladyship kept race horses and next to that, a long garage in which Lord Rothermead housed his Rolls Royce collection, and also where Grandad Darwin was allowed to keep his brand new red Ford Escort.

At the far end of this area was the early eighteenth century brick-built cottage where David's grandparents lived. In the 1950s, this had been divided into two dwellings by the almost arbitrary blocking up of some internal doors and the partitioning, literally in half, of the staircase. There was also a 1950s extension at the south end of the building to provide more rooms on both floors. The right-hand two thirds of the original cottage was the home of the stable's head groom, Ronald Carter, the only groom as it happened. The remaining left-hand third of the original building, plus the postwar extension, was allocated to the head gardener. The external proportions of the newer part were the same as those of the original Georgian cottage, but its garish red bricks and large metal-framed windows made it obvious which part was new, and which was old.

Len's mushroom-coloured Ford Escort pulled up alongside the kitchen door in the south-end wall of the cottage – David's father, grandfather and Uncle Ronnie had all bought new Fords at the same time, but whereas the older men had chosen Escorts, Ronnie went for the racier option of a Ford Capri. The car horn was sounded in the usual rhythmic pattern to indicate their arrival: toot, to-to-toot, toot, toot-toot. In almost immediate response, Grandad Darwin rushed out to greet them, fresh from his bath and change of clothes to a smart shirt, tie and waistcoat.

A beaming Len was the first to get out of the car, only to be immediately encircled by his father's powerful arms.

'Ah, *the Len*; good to *see* you again my boy,' Grandad Darwin enthused, before finally relaxing his grip. 'Good trip up?'

'Hello Dad; *yes*, the journey was as uneventful as usual,' responded his oldest son, before pulling the driver's seat forward, in order to release the vehicle's back seat passengers.

While he did this, Grandad Darwin, moved round the front of the car's hot, clicking bonnet, threw open the passenger-side door, and relieved a smiling David of the budgie's cage. With only one arm free, he nonetheless embraced his grandson in the same fervent manner as ever.

'Hello Grandad,' David said happily, inhaling that strong and familiar smell of coal-tar soap.

'*Alright* me old David,' responded his grandfather, tightening his grip briefly before releasing it.

With his left arm holding Ollie's cage aloft, and his right round his oldest grandson, Grandad Darwin crossed back to the driver's side of the car, and greeted Lucy in the same emphatic one-armed manner as he had her older brother. Meg was the last to get out, restricted as she was by the slowly rousing form of her youngest son. Eddie, having just woken up would usually be grouchy as a result, but now he smiled and extended his arms out for Grandad to pick him up, which he duly did with his free right arm. If it were not for the fact he was now carrying both Eddie and Ollie, the old boy would have also given Meg a greeting bear hug too. Thus loaded, Grandad led the family into the kitchen and thence through to the dining room, where Nanna Darwin was laying the table, and the Rayburn was radiating its heat. Both of these rooms – being part of the 1950s portion of their cottage – were filled with the aroma of baking potatoes from the old log-stoked range. For David, it was an eagerly anticipated sensory delight that never failed to reward him.

The twelve-year-old had always been fascinated by the arrangement of the cottage, and the contrast between the larger, taller, utilitarian rooms of the extension and the lower more fascinating, yet musty-smelling beamed rooms of the older part. It was David who suggested that the Rayburn had been put in the dining room, as opposed to the kitchen as normal, to allow it access into the old Georgian chimney breast, built into what would have been the end wall of the original cottage, prior to the construction of the extension.

Another thing that the children looked forward to was seeing and hearing Nanna's cuckoo clock, which was situated high up on the wall of the dining room, immediately opposite the Rayburn. She had purchased it many years before at a jumble sale, and the ever-resourceful Grandad Darwin had managed to get it going. The cuckoo would appear at every quarter hour, followed by the clang of a deep sounding bell. The effect heard being: 'cuckoo-dong'. On the hour, one would get the appropriate number of 'cuckoo-dongs'. However, in recent years, the cuckoo's bellows must have become punctured and now it was a very odd sounding contraption. The family's arrival, just before six o'clock, was partly in order for the children to hear the clock as it reached the hour. On that particular Friday, they were just in time, and everyone stood there gazing up in eager anticipation. Only Nanna continued what she had been doing at the Rayburn, which involved turning the potatoes in the hot oven, and then putting more logs into the firebox. However, even she smiled when the cuckoo finally struck: 'oo-dong', 'oo-dong', 'oo-dong', 'oo-dong', 'oo-dong', 'oo-dong', followed by peals of laughter from everyone including Eddie, who wasn't really sure what he was laughing at, but enjoyed the collective activity in any case. The cuckoo clock would be heard many more times over the weekend, but it would never be so funny as that first six o'clock strike.

There was one occasion during the previous visit, when David and Lucy were watching Nanna Darwin put the Yorkshire puddings into the Rayburn for Sunday dinner. The cuckoo clock started to strike noon, and both children had gazed up at it, as per normal. On the second 'oo-dong', David had started to count from three, and thus convinced his sister that the clock had actually struck thirteen.

With the weekend bags taken upstairs, and all young hands thoroughly washed, Nanna finally extracted the baked potatoes from the Rayburn and put one on each of the plates round the table. This was the signal that both adults and children were waiting for, and everyone eagerly sat down. In David's opinion, no other baked potatoes tasted quite like Nanna Darwin's. Whether it was the fact they had been cooked in an old range, or grown on the farm itself and stored in the darkness of one of Grandad's sheds, he could not firmly establish. The young lad further speculated that, perhaps, it was because the potatoes would be broken open and then spread with real butter, together with a scattering of ground black pepper – as opposed to the margarine and Pricerite pepper they normally had at home in Canterbury – which gave them that special taste. Without fail, the baked spuds would be served with thick crumbly slices of home-cured ham, with the addition of baked beans for the children and salad for the grown-ups. Taking everything into account: the mouth-watering home-prepared food, the smell of the cherry wood log fire of the Rayburn, and the hilarious 'oo-dongs'; it all contributed to transforming those Friday evening meals into lasting magical moments for the family, and for David in particular.

After all the plates had been comprehensively cleared, Nanna insisted that everyone move into the sittingroom whilst she quickly sorted out the table and then made some tea. The sittingroom was the only downstairs room of Nanna and Grandad Darwin's cottage that belonged to the older building phase. One entered it with a noticeable step down to a lower level. The ceiling was likewise low and also beamed, so that none of the adult males of the family could stand up straight in it. David was the first to follow his grandmother's instructions, and was soon happily soaking up the room's aged atmosphere. It was small and square, with a huge fireplace against its south wall that was back-to-back with the Rayburn in the adjacent room, and with which it shared the same chimneybreast. This economy of space allowed just enough room to fit in the three-piece suite and a few occasional tables. The sittingroom, in common with the two upstairs bedrooms from the older part of the house, had a unique musty, dusty smell that almost went beyond the normal olfactory sensation. However, the oddest thing of all, and the fact that fascinated David the most, was that this downstairs room stretched across only half the width of the building as a whole. A similar room, parallel to it, was actually part of the house belonging to the groom, Ron Carter, his wife Doreen, and daughter Samantha. When no one else was about, he would often put his ear to that wall, and see if he could pick up any sounds of the next-door family, but was never able to. It only went to prove that, either the Carters were very quiet, or that the internal wall in question was very thick indeed.

Gradually, family members drifted in to join David; the last one being his mother, who had defied Nanna Darwin's order and stayed to help her with the clearing away. Before long, Nanna came in with the tea and a huge box of broken biscuits: chocolates and creams, which was another much anticipated habitual treat, especially for the twelve-year-old. As soon as everyone had settled down, Grandad turned the telly on and they all watched *Dad's Army* and the *Stanley Baxter Show*. In between the two programmes, Eddie was taken upstairs to his cot in the old yellow bedroom. Soon it would be David and Lucy's turn to go up those stairs to bed, but they wouldn't think about that until they had to. In the meantime, the tea was hot and strong and the biscuits, delicious and plentiful. They both sat on the furry rug, in front of the fire, with their skin glowing red, but they were both far too contented to move away. The fire was too mesmerising and reassuring, unlike those scary stairs.

David was in charge of keeping the fire fuelled and every so often, he would select a log, cut from the farm's ancient fruit trees, and then throw it onto the existing embers, with the resultant shower of sparks. Of course, there would be no fire lit here in the summer months, and it was always greatly missed by both of the older children. Nevertheless, David and Lucy still sat on the furry rug, in front of an empty grate, in eager anticipation of one of the regular minor soot falls that, at least, provided a vague aromatic reminder of those fondly remembered winter comforts.

Inevitably, bedtime finally came and a sense of deep dread was felt by both of them; they would have to go up those stairs. Funnily enough, that long-sensed feeling had not diminished in David, even though he was about to enter his teenage years. It was also the reason why he and Lucy would always rather cross the outer courtyard in the dark to the outside toilet block – which was part of the stable complex – than go upstairs for a wee once the sun had gone down. Luckily, Grandad Darwin instinctively knew of their rarely spoken about fear of the cottage's staircase, and always accompanied them up to bed.

After the usual round of 'good nights' had been said, the old boy lifted the latch of the door to the stairwell in the far corner of the sitting room. As he opened it, the darkness from the void beyond almost poured into the room. He then reached into the gloom for the round Bakelite switch, and following a sharp, metallic clink that seemed to echo throughout the stairwell, a dim forty-watt bulb blinked into life. Every time, the small amount of electric light that resulted, attempted to fight a battle with the evil darkness, and it always lost. At the foot of the stairs, there was an immediate ninety-degree turn to the left, and then, as the staircase straightened, it became quite narrow and stayed as such all the way to the top. This was because the Darwins only possessed half of the original staircase, the other half being beyond the partition and within the groom's house to the right.

Another peculiar feature of that daunting stairwell was a huge hard lump that protruded out of the wall, half way up on the left. No one knew what it was or why it happened to be there, but the bulge had been wallpapered over time and time again, along with the rest of the wall. Every time Grandad went upstairs, he would pat the lump in the wall for luck; it was another small ritual that both David and his sister appreciated. No doubt, it was their grandfather's way of diverting their attention from the uncanny sense of dread that, perhaps, he could pick up as well.

At the top of that steep, scary staircase, was a small, square landing from which, a doorway opened out to the left. During the daytime, the children felt both reassured and urged on by the small amount of daylight that exuded from that doorway: it made the stairwell seem slightly less menacing. At night time however, there was no such crumb of comfort, and only more darkness awaited them at the top of the stairs.

As always, Grandad Darwin was the first to complete the climb, and both

David and Lucy held their breath as he groped beyond the doorframe to the left for the light switch. Luckily, the reassuring clonk came quickly, and the room beyond was illuminated at last. This was the bunk bedroom; this was where the two older children slept. As Grandad drew the curtains to the window that overlooked the cottage's narrow rear garden, David took his sister's hand, prior to beginning the trip to the bathroom for that final wee, and the teeth-cleaning ritual. Lucy refused to go there alone, ever since she had witnessed a small mouse scurrying across the lino whilst she was perched on the loo.

The journey to the bathroom was an interesting one that began by passing through the doorway in the wall, immediately opposite the rear window. The children were now in a narrow passage, with another door almost directly opposite. This was the small aforementioned yellow bedroom, situated at the front of the house, and overlooking the outer courtyard. Here was where their parents and Eddie all slept. The passage itself appeared to be partitioned off to the left, and David speculated that it probably once continued into what was now the Carter's house. Turning right in the passage, there was a step up into the 1950s extension and then, a few more yards of slightly wider passage on the higher level. At the far end, was a window, which overlooked the hard-standing area where the family car was parked, with the door to the bathroom on the left and Nanna and Grandad Darwin's bedroom to the right. If you cared to walk right through their grandparents' bedroom, you would come to another door, and a step back down into the bunk bedroom, which also signified a return to the older part of the house. Thus, one could do continuous circuits upstairs, if the fancy took you. Eddie had recently cottoned on to that idea, as soon as he could walk, but usually, the game would end in a fall and a howl of tears when he came to grief either on the step up in the passage, or the step down between bedrooms.

The children quickly cleaned their teeth, and used the loo in turn, whilst Grandad Darwin waited for them back in the bunk bedroom. Upon their return, via the passage route, they hastily slipped into their pyjamas; modesty was not a problem at Rothermead, as they both usually kept their pants on at night. David then quickly climbed the wooden stepladder up to the top bunk, whilst Lucy scrambled in below. The bunk beds were against the wall, on the other side of which was the spooky stairwell. Unfortunately, for David and Lucy, the dread they felt about the stairs, also extended into their bedroom, especially when it came to the time to try to get to sleep. It was weird; no other part of the house seemed to be affected. As a result, they both insisted on being tucked in really tight and then submerging completely beneath the bedclothes as soon as Grandad Darwin went back downstairs. Once there, strapped in tightly with Mr Brewster, his teddy bear, David tried to rationalise away this fear they both felt. He was vastly becoming a man, getting spots and alarming sproutings of body hair; soon he would be too old for teddy bears, he told himself. So why be afraid of a narrow staircase with a lump in the wall and a room at the top of it, containing some bunk beds and little else?

The irrational but no less palpable dread had begun when they were both much younger. Len and Meg often remarked that fears of this sort were commonplace in imaginative children, but neither David nor Lucy derived much comfort from the fact. More recently, the twelve-year-old realised that the fear could very well be connected to the fact that half of the staircase also existed in next-door's house. On several occasions, much earlier on, while playing in the bunk bed- room, they had both heard the sound of someone coming up the stairs, only for no one to appear through the door at the top, once the footsteps had completed the climb. David now knew that it must have been one of the Carters, probably tall lumbering Samantha, going up their half of the staircase on the other side of the partition. However, the logic of the explanation could not remove the terror that was now so deeply engrained in both David and Lucy, and sustained by feeding off each other's fears. Sometimes, he wondered if Sam next door had experienced similar feelings of fear when she was younger, or if the sense of dread was confined to the Darwin side of the stairwell partition, or even, to their own overly active imaginations. It was something he'd always been meaning to ask her, but had always been held back by a concern that the gangly eighteen-year-old might think him foolish.

The staircase apart, no amount of logic could explain away some of the other scary things that had happened over the years. One night, David woke from a deep sleep and thought he saw a clown's face staring at him at close quarters. On another occasion, Lucy screamed in the middle of the night because she had convinced herself she'd seen a hand and arm reaching down to her from the middle of the mattress above her head. Although he'd never voiced it to anyone, David wondered to himself if these experiences had actually been real, or were just nightmares. Perhaps they were merely bad dreams after all, but it all added to the cumulative dread and partly explained why it had perpetuated all these years. Nevertheless, everything else about coming to Rothermead: the farm, the food, the country walks, and the company of their grandparents, was so very wonderful that they still looked forward to each booked weekend visit, and both agreed it was well worth a little fear at bedtime.

David and Lucy always woke early when staying at Rothermead Farm; not just relieved that the night was over, but also both looking forward to what the weekend might offer. The adults, on the other hand, invariably took the opportunity of it being a non-working day to sleep in. However, once awake, the children were happy to stay in bed and work their way through the huge pile of *Look and Learn* magazines that Nanna Darwin had bought at a jumble sale several years before. Eventually, as the rest of the household stirred, washed, dressed and gradually wandered through the children's room on their way downstairs, the two bunk bed occupants quickly rose and did likewise.

Saturday morning breakfast was a help yourself affair consisting of tea and toast. The first person up, and it was usually Nanna Darwin, would put more logs in the Rayburn and revive the fading embers from the night before. She would then put the kettle on one of the hot plates and her hair rolling tongs on the other. The tea tasted different at Rothermead and the youngsters had long since worked out that it was because of the unpasteurised milk, which came straight from the farm's cold storage unit. A small churn would be delivered to each of the farm's tied cottages early every morning. The toast was wonderful too: thick doorsteps of Nanna's home made bread, toasted either on top of the Rayburn using a strange wire mesh device, or with the fire door open and a toasting fork. David always preferred the latter method, as it gave him a chance to use the beautiful brass toasting fork that Nanna and Grandad Darwin had brought with them from Oakenden. Grandad told him that it used to belong to his mother, and as he sat there in the vivid glow of the fire box embers, David would imagine Great-Gran Darwin toasting bread with it down in Hythe, as the Germans were shelling the coast from across the Channel. There was nothing quite like partly burnt toast topped with melting farmyard butter and Marmite, which was Grandad Darwin's special favourite. The older children preferred to spread liberal helpings of Nanna's homemade marmalade or strawberry jam on their toast. These concoctions had a tendency to ferment in the jar, Nanna's boozy jam as Grandad referred to it, but it was delicious despite those occasional lumps of mould.

For the rest of Saturday, the family would go out on a day trip in a convoy of Ford Escorts. And there would always be a picnic, eaten either outdoors if the weather was fine, or in the cars if it was not. If the latter were the case, then the vehicles would be parked side by side, to better enable cheese, tomatoes or hard-boiled eggs to be passed from one car to the other through the wound-down windows.

On the recent occasions that Uncle Ronnie had joined them for the weekends, he never seemed to want to go on the Saturday picnics anymore, preferring to stay on his own and read, or go for solitary walks. Len had a theory that this was because his brother must be sweet on the Carter girl next door, who was about seven years' younger than him and soon to do her A levels. David, on the other hand, could not imagine them being interested in each other, especially as Samantha seemed far too obsessed with horses to be bothered with anything else. The honourable Victoria Dutnell, Lord and Lady Rothermead's only daughter, and a redheaded curvaceous beauty, was much more his type, but at fifteen-years-old, she was far too young for him. However, David was privy to the secret about Katie and therefore knew with certainty that his father was completely and utterly wrong.

That particular Saturday's trip was to Sheerness and Minster, on the Isle of Sheppey, where some of Nanna Darwin's ancestors had come from. David always prayed there would be a ship in the Swale Estuary and that all the cars to and from the island would be halted whilst the bridge lifted to allow the vessel through. He got his wish on the return journey, when they were held up for 20 minutes. While they all waited in the line of traffic, and watched the funnels of the freighter glide beneath the concrete bridge towers, David suddenly remembered what day it was, and what would be happening that very evening: Uncle Ronnie was going to be on the telly. He looked at the red Ford Escort in front of them in the queue and, more specifically, at the two beloved figures within it. What a pity Ronnie won't be with us tonight to share in his triumph, he thought ruefully; it would mean so much to Nanna and Grandad to have him there. He would be the only member of the immediate family missing, although in a strange way, he would be with them after all, on the other side of the television screen.

Once they'd all arrived back at the farm, Meg assisted Nanna Darwin in the preparation of one of her famous curries, and Len fed the budgie before settling down to read the newspaper. Lucy meanwhile played with Eddie, and tried to discourage him from wanting to go upstairs to run round in dangerous circuits. David went back out with Grandad Darwin, who had a few weekend duties he had to carry out for the 'big house'. David was always fascinated by anything to do with the Dutnell family's house and garden. Sometimes, if Lord and Lady Rothermead were away, Grandad would even show him round the main rooms of the house itself, as part of his additional role as caretaker. However, they *were* at home that weekend, as was their youngest daughter Victoria, with a friend from school, so access to the 'big house' would be limited.

Grandad's first task necessitated a visit to the main greenhouse: an ancient lean-to structure some thirty or so yards long. It was built against the far side of a substantial wall, which began almost opposite the kitchen door of Nanna and Grandad Darwin's cottage and extended eastwards to within a few feet of the 'big house' itself. The greenhouse was divided into two halves: the one nearest the cottage end being for tender plants and the other, nearest the 'big house', exclusively for a massive mature grapevine. They entered the greenhouse at the cottage end by passing round the west end of the thirty-yard wall; their task being to close the fanlights as they passed through the glass structure. Beyond the halfway door, David marvelled at the branches of the old gnarled grape vine, which were all well covered in leaf but not, as yet, bearing any of those numerous, luscious bunches of grapes. However, he knew that the hand-thinning of those hanging bunches was one of Grandad Darwin's least favourite jobs, and he often told him as much as they passed through.

The pair eventually re-emerged at the 'big house' end of the long greenhouse, and glanced briefly over at the walled vegetable garden, which was beginning to look very verdant. And then, having passed through the arch in the wall, the two Darwin males found themselves staring into the three-sided inner courtyard of the Rothermead's residence, with the Regency south wing to the right, the older north wing on the left and the linking east wing, straight ahead of them. Grandad's second evening task was to check the boiler in the cavernous cellar that was situated beneath the east wing. However, the cellar could only be accessed from the main garden, on the east wing's opposite side, which would necessitate a walk right round to the left, in order to reach it via the long outer courtyard. Therefore, the Darwin duo walked by the 'front' of the old careworn north wing, and then turned right before passing through a secondary pair of iron gates – being less grand than the ones by the lane – that accessed the main garden of the 'big house'. After a few yards, they veered right again and found themselves on a path of crumbling bricks that cut across an area of shade-loving shrubs. Adjacent to the outer wall of the east wing – a curious mix of Regency and much older phases – was a short flight of worn stone steps that descended to a square brick-lined stairwell, from which a low gothic arched doorway gave access to the cellar complex. An excited David followed Grandad Darwin down the steps, and watched as he retrieved his bunch of 'big house' keys, and then proceeded to unlock the old studded wooden door at the bottom to the left. Having pushed it open, with a rusty, metallic creak, Grandad fumbled in the dark for the light switch.

Once his eyes had adjusted to the cellar's dimly lit interior, David looked around to reacquaint himself with the surroundings. He had been coming to Rothermead Farm now for about seven years, but this was only his third or fourth visit to the old cellar beneath the 'big house'. It was barrel vaulted, in lime-washed brick, and caked with the accumulated dust and cobwebs of countless years. The lower parts of the cellar walls were constructed of irregular stone blocks and narrow Tudor bricks, arranged in a haphazard fashion. Grandad Darwin had told him on a previous visit, that those lower courses of the cellar walls were all that was left of the original house that once stood on this site. Members of the Dutnell family, who were ancestors of the present Lord Rothermead, were said to have built it at around the time of Henry VIII, although an alternative, less-repeated tale, told of another family who had built the first Rothermead Court House, only to be usurped by the Dutnell family some years afterwards. Whatever the truth was, local historians agreed that the stone, used in the construction of the foundations, as well as other non-visible parts, had been taken from the ruins of an old castle at Tonford: a village just a few miles north of Rothermead. David tried to imagine what the original Tudor period 'big house' might have looked like, as he touched those old bricks and stones, and pondered on the many stories the old fabric could, no doubt, tell him.

Situated against the far left-hand wall of the cellar was the vast boiler that served the house above and which had to be kept going all year round. Grandad busied himself with that leviathan, whilst David wandered round this unfamiliar, yet fascinating territory. Straight ahead, as one entered the cellar, was another flight of stone steps that ascended to a firmly locked door, and gave access directly into the interior of the 'big house'. To the right, a low brick arch, with a dark passage beyond, led through to another cellar in which Lord Rothermead kept his vast wine collection. David was itching to go exploring but knew that the wine cellar was definitely out of bounds. With the Dutnell family at home, there was always the possibility that, at any moment, his Lordship might appear at the top of the internal flight of steps and come down to fetch a bottle of wine or two to accompany his evening meal.

When Grandad had finished putting coke in the boiler, from the dark, dusty pile that stood next to it, he ushered Dave back outside, and locked the old cellar door, before the pair climbed back up to the garden level. They then retraced their steps through the outer-courtyard, and returned to the smaller inner courtyard. Here, the quasi-caretaker opened an unlocked door that led into the semi-derelict part of the old north wing. The inside was poorly lit and there was only one bare fly-spotted bulb hanging from the plasterless ceiling. The glass in the windows had long gone and been replaced by sheets of rusting corrugated iron, which had been roughly nailed to the ancient, rotting window frames. The ground floor, now devoid of some internal walls, was currently in use as a woodshed and log store. The upper storey, on the other hand, had been converted into a studio, by one of Lord and Lady Rothermead's twin sons, Benedict, who was currently away, presumably at art college.

Grandad Darwin soon filled an old wicker basket with logs – a supply that was regularly topped up, as old cherry trees were either pruned or grubbed up as life expired – and then they made their way back to the cottage. On a number of occasions throughout their duties, David had wanted to ask Grandad if he was looking forward to seeing Ronnie on the television that evening, but realised that it was a silly question, with an obvious answer; one may as well enquire of the old boy if he was hungry for his dinner. As soon as the pair had passed by Grandad's toolshed, a structure that leant against the north side of the thirty-yard wall, they both began to detect the unmistakable aroma of Nanna's curry.

David's grandfather sniffed the air hungrily.

'I can feel my old bald head breaking out into a sweat already!' he enthused, as each of them quickened their pace towards the kitchen door.

All throughout the eagerly anticipated curry and mash dinner, with its accompanying 'oh lovely' superlatives, David kept on looking up at the old cuckoo clock. He wanted, or rather, he needed to make absolutely sure that they were not going to miss Uncle Ronnie's television appearance, scheduled for that very evening. Of course, there was no chance of that happening; his siblings, parents and grandparents would not want to miss it either, he concluded, and was soon reassured to notice that each of the adults were now constantly referring to their watches. In any case, with all those 'oo-dongs' every quarter hour, the boy comforted himself with the fact that the family could hardly *not* be aware of the time.

The hours passed slowly, as they always did when you watched the clock, but finally the appointed time approached and the whole family, including a sleepy Eddie, gathered round the television in the old dusty, musty sitting room. As *The Lulu Show* would be starting in half an hour's time, they all settled down to watch *Dixon of Dock Green*.

Only five minutes into the programme, it soon became obvious that no one could really concentrate on that old avuncular constable and, inevitably, the family lapsed into small talk to calm their nerves; a process kicked off by Len.

'I recently read that you can now get a machine that tapes television programmes,' he remarked, looking from one of his parents to the other.

Whereas Grand Darwin smiled and nodded with polite interest, Nanna stared back at him with her brows furrowed.

'Why would you need one of *those*?' she asked, with a slight air of condescension. 'Half the things they put on these days are repeats *anyway*!'

Everyone laughed, except David, who thought it was a jolly good idea.

'What a shame we don't have a television recording machine tonight,' he remarked, gazing up principally at his father. 'We could have recorded Uncle Ronnie and kept it *forever*!'

However, even if such a machine were possible, the twelve-year-old realised that his parents probably wouldn't get one for ages. They hadn't even acquired a stereo radiogram yet and he knew full well that all his school friends' parents had owned one for quite a while now.

Meg, who had been quietly pondering on the concept of the invention her husband had talked of, was now ready to add her two-pennyworth.

'No; I expect the television recorder will prove to be one of those impractical 'flash in the pan' ideas you see on *Tomorrow's World*, then never *hear* about again!' she said dismissively, but with a smile in the children's direction.

'Yes, you're right there,' Nanna Darwin reinforced, with a vigorous nod. 'Did you see *last* week's programme? They reckoned that before long, everyone will have a computer in their house!'

In response, the whole family laughed again, and even David found that particular Dr Who-type notion rather fanciful.

Of them all, perhaps Grandad Darwin laughed the loudest.

'Imagine all those whirring tapes, flashing lights and ticker tapes spewing out everywhere, whilst you're trying to have your dinner!' he observed, raking his fingernails across his bald pate.

Straightaway, Nanna gave him a playful poke.

'*Yes*, and it would be *me* who would have to clear it all up,' she commented, with a knowing nod in her daughter-in-law's direction.

At that moment, every family member jumped at the sound of the kitchen door being shut firmly.

A flustered Nanna Darwin leapt out of her chair.

'Oh, that could only be her ladyship', she said, quickly removing her apron and straightening her hair. 'She's got into a habit recently of popping in unannounced, if she wants any sewing or mending done.'

Her husband, however, appeared completely unfazed, and remained seated.

'Yes, one day I'll be sitting here in my vest and pants when she bursts in, and her Ladyship won't bloomin' well like *that*!' Grandad Darwin observed with a smile, before being shushed by his wife.

Len began to chuckle in response to the comment.

'You never know Grandad, perhaps that's what she's *hoping* for,' he added wryly; a comment that made his father hoot with laughter.

'*Will you two be quiet*, Lady Rothermead might hear!' Nanna scolded in a cross half-whisper, as she went to push open the door that led back up into the dining room.

David's father and grandfather looked at each other, mimicking the facial expressions of two naughty schoolboys who had just been told off. However, their play-acting was suddenly stilled, as everyone looked up in response to a loud gasp of shock coming from Nanna Darwin at the open doorway.

'*Ronnie*, oh my giddy aunt, you gave me the *fright* of my *life*! Why didn't you *say* you were coming down?' she cried, with her right hand on her chest, before embracing the unexpected visitor.

'It wouldn't have been a *surprise* if I had!' Ronnie countered, as he stepped down into the sittingroom immediately in front of her.

Everyone stood up spontaneously and happily gathered round the prodigal son in greeting. Both David and Lucy were far too big now, so Eddie, who had been allowed to stay up, had the privilege of being picked up by Uncle Ronnie. Nonetheless, the two older children clung to his lean form, gazing up at him adoringly.

'You came *after* all,' David choked, with tear-wetted eyes, as he looked up into his uncle's familiar face.

'How could I *not*; I *knew* you would all be here together tonight and I wanted to be part of it,' Ronnie said, looking around at everyone, but stroking his oldest nephew's head.

As the excited clamour died down, David wondered to himself where Katie was, and why Ronnie hadn't brought her along this evening. He was sure that everyone would love to meet her, but true to the scar brothers' code, he said nothing on the subject.

'*Dixon of Dock Green* is finishing', shouted Lucy excitedly. 'He's just said: *good night all*!'

Everyone offered Ronnie their seat, but he delighted the children by getting down on to the furry rug with them, which was ample compensation for Grandad Darwin not having put a match to the ready-made-up fire, so far that evening.

As the music for the Jack Warner programme reached its conclusion, David gently grabbed his uncle by the arm.

'Did you know that you can now get machines for recording what's on the television?' he asked, to a wide-eyed and attentively beaming Ronnie.

'Yes, but what would it sound like if it went wrong?' suggested the older of the two, before quickly following his comment by an impersonation of a voice slowing right down, then speeding up incredibly fast.

The laughter that followed was short-lived, as the rotating globe on the TV set that heralded the start of a new programme, made its sudden appearance.

'It's *starting*, it's *starting*,' Nanna Darwin gabbled above the rapidly diminishing laughter, as she straightened her hair once more.

'Lulu won't be able to *see* you Nanna,' commented Len, who was soon shushed by everyone except the laughing Ronnie.

'That's what *you* think!' she retorted, without taking her staring eyes off the flickering screen.

Recalling that wet evening, when most of them had travelled up to London to see the show being recorded, Lucy leant in close to her brother.

'Will I be able to hear myself clapping?' she asked, whilst the show's titles rolled, and the rousing but ritzy fanfare blared out.

As David woke on the Sunday morning, he became aware of a movement in the room and just caught sight of Grandad Darwin disappearing through the door into the dreaded stairwell, though not quite so dreaded in the daylight. The twelve-year-old sat up and marvelled at what a good night's sleep he had just experienced, and concluded that it was, perhaps, the best he'd ever had at Rothermead. Peering over the edge of the top bunk, he could see Lucy below and she was still sound asleep. Evidently, she had also enjoyed a peaceful night, and wasn't submerged beneath the blankets as usual. In fact, neither of them had minded going upstairs to bed quite so much last night. For some reason, the usual fear had all but disappeared. Nor did either of them feel the need to be tucked in so tightly, secure against the irrational fears of the stairs and their room. Having thought about this, David put it down to the fact that Uncle Ronnie had slept on the settee in the sittingroom last night, which was immediately below them at the foot of the stairs. He had clearly warded off whatever evil lurked there in the treads and risers.

Cheered on by the happy thought of Uncle Ronnie as an impromptu guardian angel, David slipped down the wooden steps of the top bunk and padded along the narrow passage to the bathroom. Once there, he quickly washed – what Grandad Darwin would call a 'lick and a promise' – dressed and fearlessly dashed downstairs. Having reached the sitting room, he could see that Ronnie's sheets and blankets were already folded in neat pile on the settee. Obviously, his uncle was up too, so David proceeded through into the dining room, where he found him.

'Morning Dave, me old matey,' Uncle Ronnie said as he knelt in front of the

Rayburn. 'We let it go out last night. *Huh* ... too busy watching me make a fool of myself on TV!' he added as a bashful aside.

'Oh I thought you were *brilliant*!' retorted David unashamedly, as he watched his uncle put lumps of tepid clinker into the metal kitchen bucket.

Ronnie peered up from his task and grinned.

'Ah, what would I *do* without my biggest fan,' he gratefully responded, with an accompanying wink. 'Oh, and by the way, I've also fed and watered your budgie.'

'*Thanks* Uncle Ronnie!' David said, glancing at the suspended cage in the corner, from which, the occasional high-pitched chirrup was emitting.

Still smiling, David pulled out a diningroom chair, and began to think about last night's broadcast. He had always liked the gorilla-chasing finale of his uncle's act, and thought that it came off particularly well on the TV. He also quite enjoyed that duet with Lulu, towards the end of the show. Uncle Ronnie had a good singing voice, but that song: the one about the windmills of your mind; even David had to admit that it was rubbish.

As soon as Ronnie had raked all the ash out, he set the fire with screwed up newspaper sheets and wood kindling.

As luck would have it, Grandad Darwin very soon emerged through the kitchen door, clutching a fresh basket of logs.

'Ah, right on *cue*, the Ronnie!' the old boy commented, as he deposited his load alongside the crouching figure of his youngest son. 'Ah, *good morning* the David!' he added, on straightening up, and seeing his oldest grandson.

'Morning Grandad,' he smiled in response, before turning his attention back to his busy uncle.

Ronnie slid the log-filled basket slightly further forward.

'*Thanks* for getting these Grandad,' he remarked, before pushing three or four of the dirty, dusty logs into the fire compartment on top of the kindling. He then lit a match and, having established that the fire had taken, shut the iron door and adjusted the vent.

Before the three Darwin males could turn their attention to any other morning task, the sound of the back door slamming made them all turn towards the entrance into the kitchen. Nanna soon appeared, unbuttoning her overcoat.

'Oh *thanks* for getting the Rayburn going Ronnie dear; I saw the chimney smoking as I came back up the outer courtyard!' she commented, before throwing her coat over the back of a vacant wooden seat.

Grandad looked at her with concern registered on his face.

'How *is* he this morning?' he asked, slowly approaching her.

'Oh he's *still* not right; at *this* rate, he'll *have* to retire before very long!' she responded, with a deep sigh and shake of the head.

'Who's *ill* then mum?' intervened a worried-looking Ronnie, as he joined David at the table.

'It's old Bill Blackett, you know, the farm foreman; he's recently been complaining about chest pains and breathlessness. Doreen, from next door, and I are taking it in turns to look after him,' Nanna sighed, as she looked at all three concerned faces in turn.

'Heavy smoker, isn't he?' asked Ronnie, in grave tones.

Nanna puckered her mouth and nodded vigorously.

'Roll-ups, all his *life* apparently!' she replied, giving a resigned hand gesture. Her husband also nodded his head slowly.

'It's not easy to give up either; I should *know*! I *still* miss the old pipe!' he admitted, with a look of fond remembrance for a habit long since quitted.

'*Maybe* Grandad, but your stomach acid problem isn't *nearly* as bad as it was!' countered Nanna, giving him a supportive smile, before looking back to Ronnie. '*Still*, we're hoping Bill recovers before the Dutnells notice that he's taken to his bed. Mind *you*, Ron Carter and Edwina Cohen can't fill in for him forever; they've got their *own* duties to perform!'

Grandad Darwin smiled broadly upon hearing that last comment.

'Isn't it *marvellous* how people rally round to help one another!' he remarked, with a tinge of emotion sounding in his voice. 'And you can tell Ron that *I* don't mind helping out on the farm until old Bill's better!'

'Oh no you *won't* Grandad,' she quickly retorted, before scurrying over to the rapidly warming Rayburn. 'You're *far* too busy as it *is* this time of year; not to mention all those extra unpaid jobs his lordship keeps finding for you!'

Nanna opened the firebox door, and peered in briefly, before slamming it shut again.

'*Listen*, it'll be a while before I can start cooking breakfast,' she said, looking back up at the males gathered round the table. 'Why don't you boys go out and gather some mushrooms, and we can add them to the rest of the fry up; you'll find an empty cardboard trug in the kitchen!'

Hearing the suggestion, Ronnie gazed back at his mother with a look of confusion.

'But you don't *get* mushrooms this time of year; late *summer* perhaps, autumn *definitely*, but certainly not spring!' he asserted, with absolute assurance.

'But you *do*!' countered David, sounding equally as sure of his facts as his uncle had. '*These* days, there are always *some* mushrooms in that first cherry orchard off the farm path!'

The young comedian seemed to remain unconvinced, that is until he caught Grandad Darwin's eye, or more specifically, his winking eye.

'Umm ... err ... *yes* Dave, come to think of it, perhaps you're right *after* all!' he admitted, clearly realising that there was more to this whole mushroom debate than he was aware.

'Come on then boys, chop-chop,' Nanna prompted, clapping her hands in the air. 'Off you go then, and let me get on!'

Grandad, Ronnie and David needed no further encouragement and soon had their coats and shoes on. Having said goodbye to Nanna, the trio walked through the kitchen, and out onto the hard-standing area between the cottage and the thirty-yard wall, where Len's mushroom-coloured Ford Escort was parked.

Before they'd gone more than a few steps away from the back door, Ronnie paused, and chewed the side of his index finger.

'I think I'll just pop back and quickly grab my camera', he said, before dashing back into the house. Within seconds, he was back, his trusty camera slung round his neck.

'There's *still* no one else up yet, so it looks like it'll be just us three, as per normal!' Ronnie exclaimed, as the trio proceeded to cross the outer courtyard.

'So where shall we *go* then?' David asked, as they drew level with the long garage, where Grandad Darwin kept his car.

'Lets go to the old windmill and back,' suggested his uncle, slapping him on the back. 'We can take in the cherry orchards en route, and see if we can find any of your magic springtime mushrooms!'

David was thrilled at the suggestion, and Grandad Darwin also nodded his approval. The old mill at Rothermead Green was a ruin; it had been for years, as were the four tumbledown cottages situated immediately in front of it. David was fascinated by the abandoned appearance of this group of old buildings, and he knew that his uncle was too.

As they left the farm cottage behind, there was just enough light to allow Ronnie to take pictures of David, Grandad and the dwelling itself, both separately and with them posed in front of it. By this time, a good column of whitish smoke, rising from the cottage's chimney, was reassurance that the Rayburn was heating up nicely, and each of them imagined Nanna bringing through the old frying pans, and then retrieving the home-made dripping from the fridge.

The party walked on through the outer courtyard, with the stables on the left and , the cook, Mrs Cohen's house to the right. Soon, a turn to the left put them on to the metalled farm track, which was a continuation of the one the Canterbury-based Darwins had driven along on Friday evening, to first access the farm. Once clear of all the out-buildings, the trio scrambled over a stile on the left of the track, which was situated opposite the old reed-choked pond, where a group of old quince trees grew.

Before they could get to the orchards, they first had to cross a small open field that currently contained sheep and adolescent lambs. There wouldn't be any mushrooms here, thought David, as he remembered a walk the three of them had done across this field several years ago, in January or February. At that time, lambs were being born all around them and the grass was strewn with afterbirth. It had been a very frank and early biology lesson for him.

This particular spring morning was crisp and bright. The short chewed grass glistened with dew and more ominously, splatters of fresh green sheep dung, which were to be avoided if at all possible. After about two hundred yards, they passed through a gate at the far end of the field and entered the first of the cherry orchards.

The grass was much longer and wetter now, but the mushroom hunt could finally begin. Grandad Darwin hung on to the cardboard trug he'd been carrying, as the group separated, although the threesome didn't move too far apart, so they could all continue heading roughly in the same direction. As soon as they began to encounter the old fruit trees, the ground started to rise gently, and would continue to do so all the way to Rothermead Green. The mushrooms began to come thick and fast now, and Ronnie soon realised that, not only were they all of the neat, small closed-cup variety, but also appeared to have already been cut from their roots, and merely scattered on the ground. It quickly dawned on him that either Nanna or Grandad must have come out here first thing, whilst performing their early-morning duties, and then distributed shop-bought mushrooms near the gate of the first orchard, for David's benefit and his delight in the old routine. A quick glance over to Grandad Darwin, and the receipt of another sly wink, confirmed his hypothesis.

Oblivious to the well-meaning deception, a happy David looked over at his Uncle Ronnie, who was gathering mushrooms only a few yards away from him, and wondered what other famous people did on a Sunday morning. I'll bet Lulu isn't out, scrambling for her own breakfast in long wet grass and with sheep poo on her shoes, he thought, with a contented smile. David also wondered what Katie did on a Sunday morning, and in particular, this Sunday morning. It then occurred to him that Ronnie still had not mentioned either Katie, or even the fact he had a girlfriend to any other family member. At the end of the day though, if his uncle didn't want it known, then he certainly wasn't going to let him down by blabbing; after all, Dave and Ronnie were 'scar brothers', who looked out for each other. Nevertheless, it seemed rather strange to him, especially as Uncle Ronnie and Katie seemed so close. David was in no doubt that if he had a gorgeous girlfriend, he'd want the whole world to know!

A quick hop over another stile and they were into a second cherry orchard. There was absolutely no sign of mushrooms here, and Ronnie noticed that the trug his father was carrying had been just big enough to contain all the mushrooms they'd found in that first orchard. Even so, he continued to pretend looking for them, very much for David's sake; a lad who seemed to have no clue as to the lengths his grandparents went to ensure his cherished mushroom-gathering ritual was sustained all year round.

In the second of the orchards, the trees were older, larger, more gnarled and their blossom-laden branches hung low towards the ground. Ronnie soon discovered that if you were not very careful when pretending to look for mushrooms, one of those dew-soaked branches would suddenly spring up and slap you square in the face. Unfortunately, this soon happened to Grandad Darwin, not once but twice, and on both occasions, it knocked his hat off as well. As a result, Ronnie was bent double with laughter, at the sight of his father standing there with an exaggerated silly grin on his face and his wet, bald head covered in white and pink blossom petals. In fact, with David looking on and laughing as much as he was, he managed to take several photographs of the bizarre spectacle. However, with the camera shaking so much with giggling, he wasn't at all sure that they would come out.

Having got over this amusing interlude, they all continued onwards and upwards. David soon realised that there were no more mushrooms to be had, but consoled himself with the fact that their one trug was quite full. But there was no point in turning back now, as they had nearly reached Rothermead Green. Ronnie was the first to see the top of the windmill, as it appeared briefly above the branches of the cherry trees. And then, as they got closer still, more of the ruined structure came into view. Rothermead Green Windmill was a tower mill, that is, a cone shaped brick structure, as opposed to the much more common smock mill type, which was largely timber-framed, weather-boarded and usually octagonal in shape. Sadly, the old structure had long since lost its wooden cap and sails, partly to a storm and partly through later concerns for safety. The remaining brick tower was still coated in the layer of black pitch that would have been applied when Grandad Darwin was David's age.

The three generations of the Darwin family finally reached the edge of the orchard and, having cleared the five-bar gate, found themselves on Rothermead Green. As the name implied, this was a large, undulating grassy area of wedge-like shape, circumnavigated by a gravelled track, and surrounded by houses and cottages of varying size, age and status. The gate from the orchard gave access to the sharp end of that massive wedge-shaped green. Immediately to the right, was the group of derelict buildings that so fascinated David and Ronnie, of which the mill was the centrepiece, and loomed up behind.

A few years before, an old farm labourer told Grandad Darwin that the old properties had once been part of Rothermead Farm. Three of the cottages on the site were tied dwellings for farm hands and their families; the fourth was the miller's house. In fact, Doreen Carter's father, 'Dusty' Daniels: a famous local character and part-time Baptist minister, had been the last miller in residence. Then, in the late 1920s, or early 1930s, with the arrival of the tractor, fewer labourers were needed on the land, and the cottages began to empty. At the same time, the then Lord Rothermead decided to expand his acreage of cherry orchards, at the expense of the cornfields, thus making the mill redundant as well. The farm still retained ownership of the empty properties, in case there was a change in labour requirements, but then the war came and the change never happened. Inevitably, the empty and unmaintained cottages had become increasingly more derelict, ruinous and overgrown. The remains of the mill's wooden cap were finally removed in the late 1940s.

Ronnie led the group over to the first pair of cottages, situated to the right of the mill.

'My God, they're *far* worse than I remember them,' he remarked, equally horrified and fascinated by the romantic scene of dereliction in front of them.

The two adjoining cottages in question were now little more than brick shells, but Ronnie was still able to estimate them to be of eighteenth century date. Vast buddleia and elder, having long since colonised the cottage's interior, now exceeded the height of the few remaining roof rafters. The elder was coming into flower and its branches could be seen spilling out of every glassless window and unbarred doorway.

Having finally broken his almost mesmeric study of the ruined buildings, Ronnie turned to Grandad Darwin.

'Have you ever sketched these old cottages Dad?' he asked, with keen interest, in between snapping off numerous photographs of the fascinating scene himself.

'Yes, shortly after we moved to Rothermead, and just after you got your first flat.' The old boy paused, and stared back up at the upper portions of the long-since derelict cottages.

'When I *first* came up here back in '62, you could still see the remains of a thatched roof,' he recalled, before lowering his head. The old boy then carefully scanned through the long-ago abandoned and overgrown gardens for the potential of any cuttings to be liberated.

The second pair of cottages to the left was of more recent date, probably early nineteenth-century, according to Ronnie, and the slate covered roof, although largely intact, nevertheless sported many small holes. Here, nature was also trying to soothe the wounds of abandonment and age, but unlike the first pair of cottages, the vegetation was all still growing externally. What once must have been a carefully trained and pruned climbing rose round one of the cottage doors, now arched above gutter level, with many of its unchecked branches hanging aimlessly in mid air. A mixture of ivy and wild honeysuckle had adhered to the brickwork and now mingled with the rose branches. Some of their tendrils were already penetrating the numerous holes in the roof. As before, a fascinated Ronnie captured it all on film.

Looming up behind the old cottages, the tower mill still looked impressive for all its years of dereliction, and this was the structure that now drew their collective attention.

'Have either of you ever been *inside* the mill?' David asked, as he scanned up and down its conical-shaped body.

Uncle Ronnie immediately shook his head.

'No, but I'd *love* to!' he replied, very much echoing his nephew's feelings.

Grandad Darwin responded in like manner.

'Me neither, but apparently, it's still safe to climb the interior,' he responded, with a slow nod of the head.

With eager anticipation, David studied the narrow gap between the two pairs of cottages, but couldn't see any easy way through the thick vegetation. In any case, he knew that they had to get back with the mushrooms for breakfast, and so did both of his older companions.

They retraced their steps on to the green and then paused to look back at the romantic scene. Ronnie, who had already been getting many detailed shots of both cottages and mill, took one last picture of the group of buildings together, and then a few more of Grandad Darwin and David on the green, with the derelict structures behind them. David also offered to take one of Ronnie with the same backdrop, and his suggestion was gratefully taken up.

As the threesome made their way back towards the orchard gate, Ronnie couldn't resist one last glance back.

'Imagine how picturesque it will look in the summer, with the roses, honeysuckle and buddleia in full flower', he remarked poetically. 'Let's vow to come back in June or July, all *three* of us, and revisit the old mill and cottages on another dawn walk gathering mushrooms!'

'We may not get the *chance*,' Grandad Darwin responded ominously. 'According to Ron Carter next door, Lord Rothermead has sold the site to a property developer. The whole lot could very well be demolished at any moment.'

'*Oh no!*' Ronnie bellowed in horror, as an equally taken-aback David looked on. 'Not the old windmill *as well*?'

'I'm afraid it seems that way,' Grandad Darwin confirmed, with a resigned shrug of the shoulders. 'Mind you, there's a *hell* of a stink about it locally. Nanna and I signed a petition to save the mill a few weeks ago – one that Doreen's sister, Elsa Rother, had organised – and that did *not* go down at *all* well in the 'big house'!'

David was the last over the five-bar gate back into the orchard. Perching on top, he too looked back at Rothermead Green, initially at all the neat little cottages further along, with their cars parked along the perimeter track and all those curtains still shut to the world. How many of those people watched *The Lulu Show* last night, he wondered? And of those, how many would have the first clue that Ronnie Darwin, comedian and singer, had been standing on their green not five minutes ago? And, how many of them would care, or even know, that the old mill might soon be pulled down? The genuine Rothermead Green folk, the ones born here, surely they would mind, he speculated? Those people who went to primary school on the other side of the green and wore the blazer badge depicting the windmill in happier times, wouldn't they want to rally round and take action to prevent its destruction? But what of the recent incomers; those people who owned the larger cottages and four-wheel drive vehicles? What of those more recent 'villagers' whom Grandad Darwin referred to as 'townies', and the ones who, no doubt, ate supermarket-bought mushrooms for breakfast: would they give a damn about the old mill?

David stared up at the old tower mill itself and wondered if this would be his last sight of that magnificent structure. Thank goodness for Uncle Ronnie's photographs, he thought, before wearily jumping off the gate to join his rapidly retreating relatives.

*

'Have you ever tasted mushrooms picked fresh from the orchards and then fried in home cured bacon fat?' asked Dave as the car cruised through Teynham. '*Ah, there's nothing quite like it to start the day!*'

'Sounds rather unhygienic to me,' Sheila said, from the passenger seat. 'I think I'll stick to those nice clean Sainsbury's ones, thank you very much!'

Julian, with a head full of *The Smiths*, and a mouthful of toffees, did not comment; his headphones rendering him oblivious to the conversation.

Soon Dave took a left turn along the country lane that skimmed the edge of the village of Beckensfield; an unimpressive community that was little more than a council estate tacked on to a few venerable houses and an unremarkable church. He was shocked to discover that the once leafy 'avoiding route' was now actually part of a greatly expanded Beckensfield. A vast new housing development was in the progress of being built on both sides of the widened and straightened lane; a place where once butterflies danced above the long grass of ancient meadows, and bees fertilised the blossom of many a Kentish fruit tree. Indigenous fauna and flora were now swept aside, and in their place: pattern book four and five bedroomed houses, which were being shoehorned into every available space; their low-maintenance gardens, a euphemism for lack of any significant size. Fluttering flags, and not butterflies, together with garish banners, proudly announced that show houses of the 'Churchill', 'Macmillan' and 'Baldwin' style, were now available for viewing.

'Fancy living in a detached 'Thatcher' with en suite facilities, double garage and waste disposal unit, eh?' Dave grimaced mockingly, as he sped past the orange-bricked scene of horror.

Sheila unwrapped a toffee and smiled.

'Yes, I wouldn't *mind* actually!' she replied in all seriousness. 'All the other Telecom managers have gone for such properties!'

It was another 'cucumber-up-the-arse' statement, but even leaving the work reference aside, Dave realised that, as a Tory voter like her parents, Sheila would not mind in the least, living in a property with such a name; it would carry absolutely no shame for her.

The hideous sprawl of ochre tile and brick came to an end as they left the new expanded village behind. Mercifully soon, they found themselves back onto a Kentish style country lane, with the occasional tuft of grass growing in the middle, as it meandered and descended towards the outskirts of Rothermead. To Dave, the old unspoilt village appeared to be exactly the same as it had in 1969, and the church looked just like it did in one of Grandad Darwin's recently-completed pen and ink works. However, beyond the church, the cherry orchard on the left had been grubbed up in favour of a field of oil seed rape, but thankfully, the one on the right was unchanged, and the cherry blossom was as glorious as he remembered it. With a quickened heart rate, Dave then set the indicators for the right-hand turn that would take the car on to the metalled track, which would lead to the farm and his grandparent's old cottage.

Half of him was looking forward to the pilgrimage, this nostalgic trip back into his own past, and the place where he had spent countless hours in the shadow of Grandad Darwin. However, his other half felt a surge of fear at the thought of what he was currently undertaking, and as the car completed the manoeuvre, he couldn't help but wonder: what if it had all changed? If that was the case, he might regret ever having returned! Sheila would always say: 'you can never go back' and as far as she was concerned, that phrase covered both people and places. Unlike Sheila though, Dave worshipped the past, particularly his own, and he was keenly aware of that fact. Now though, he was about to kneel before one of the most important shrines from his formative years. Many of the things that interested him in life were developed here at Rothermead Farm, and many of his life's values, learnt here also. Grandad Darwin had played a pivotal role in that development and, second only to Uncle Ronnie, helped to make him the man he was today. Of course, Dave wasn't expecting Rothermead to be exactly the same, to smell the baked potatoes as it were, but he hoped that there would be enough left to reinforce those cherished memories of the place and its people; enough to bolster his faith in himself and his values, and enough to give him the strength to face what he sensed was going to be an uncertain future.

The familiar farm track curved to the left, keeping in line with the same old hornbeam hedge that, apparently, had continued to be maintained by Grandad Darwin's successors. So far, so good, thought Dave, forcing a smile. However, as he drove into the outer courtyard area, what he could then see directly in front, made him realise that his initial reaction had been somewhat overly optimistic.

Not wanting to get too close to the old cottage as yet, Dave parked the car over by the old stable block to the right. Julian, who had been listening to his Walkman and sucking toffees, suddenly realised the vehicle had stopped and wearily got out with them. Straightaway, Dave could see that the stables were empty, and not just temporarily either, but seemingly permanently. Weeds now grew from cracks in the concrete surface of the stable yard; there was no evidence that a horse had been near the place for ages. At that moment, Dave regretted not having his camera with him. The decision to visit Rothermead Farm had been made on impulse, otherwise he would have definitely brought it along. The old stable block would have made a good photographic subject, he thought; and not only for being a derelict building, but also as a valued part of his own past. Perhaps her ladyship had become too old to manage the half dozen or so racers that used to be stabled and also grazed here? But then again, Dave quickly realised that he had no idea if either Lord or Lady Rothermead were still alive, and if so, how old they would be now. He hadn't even known, or had even thought to ask, how old they were back then. In any case, when Dave was a boy, the Dutnell family had seemed very old, but perhaps not quite as ancient as his grandparents, who were, after all, both still alive today.

Dave had already caught an ominous glimpse of Nanna and Grandad Darwin's old tied cottage as they pulled up. Now, he forced himself to look again, and then slowly led Sheila and Julian up towards the place with a heavy heart. The 1950s extension, well over half of his grandparents' house, had gone; it had been completely demolished. As they got closer, it became clear that the two tied cottages appeared to have been sold off and the original eighteenth century portion, restored to its pre-1950s state as a single dwelling. A brand new Range Rover was parked outside the much-altered property.

'Townies,' Dave mumbled quietly, very much echoing his grandfather's opinion of such people.

No one seemed to be about, despite the presence of the car, so he dared to go even closer. It soon became apparent that where the 1950s extension had once stood, there was now a small parterre garden; a trendy mix of flowers, herbs and vegetables, with a stainless steel obelisk at its centre. Some of the old courtyard metalling had also been broken up in the making of this 'garden'.

The south wall of the restored cottage was rendered over and painted cream, to hide the scars of the now-removed later addition. With a reluctant Sheila and Julian alongside, Dave stared long and hard at it, and tried to imagine how it would have looked, as internal walls, in his grandparent's time. Obviously, great effort had been made to remove all evidence that a 'modern' extension had ever existed, which made his task even harder. There were no visible scars of the three doorways that would have been knocked through this end wall in the 1950s, to access the new rooms of the extension: one downstairs and two upstairs. Where the Rayburn had once stood against the north wall of the dining room, there was now a wooden bench from which the current owner, presumably the driver of the four-wheeled vehicle, could survey his or her trendy designer plot. Having seen all this change, part of him was glad that he didn't have his camera; would he really have wanted to record all this?

Having got his bearings, Dave tried to explain how the place had looked when he was young, but Sheila's eyes soon glazed over and she seemed restless. As for Julian, standing there with his hands in his greatcoat pockets and that Walkman tssst tsssting away, Dave concluded that he wouldn't have noticed if he'd suddenly been transported away to another planet. They were both non-believers and did not understand this 'past' he so worshipped. Nor did either of them care that his sacred shrine had been desecrated. This was one of those occasions when Dave missed Amanda-Jayne the most, for she always seemed to take a genuine interest in the things that were important to him. As he saw it, they shared the same passions; they had the same beliefs. Amanda-Jayne would surely have loved this pilgrimage to Rothermead, Dave concluded with a heavy heart. What the hell was the matter with Julian? How could he have ditched such an angel for someone like 'Duvet'?

Unhappily Dave turned away from the much-changed scene. He consoled himself with the fact that, at least, the thirty-yard wall was still there, and that led him to wonder if the long lean-to greenhouse could still be found on the other side of it. To find out for sure, mainly for the sake of nostalgic curiosity, he realised that there was no choice but to go round and check. An approach from the cottage end of the wall was no longer possible, as the way was now blocked by the fenced-off parterre garden. So, he determined that they would have to walk towards the 'big house' and then go through the arch, in order to get round to the other side of the wall. Strictly speaking, this would be trespassing, but Dave quickly decided there was no need to worry Sheila with that fact. On the way, he was saddened to see that Grandad Darwin's tool shed, abutting the thirty-yard wall on this side of it, had been largely dismantled. All that remained were its end walls, and the void in between them was now in use as an open log store.

The visitors had only just passed the former tool shed, when they were approached and challenged by a short, middle-aged man who had hurried across the outer courtyard towards them. Almost immediately, Dave thought he recognised him, and it didn't take him long to work out that this was the young man Grandad had always referred to as 'Smiler', the stable lad who assisted Ron Carter.

'What are you folk doing a wandering around here? This is *private* property you know!' challenged the familiar face from the past.

Dave smiled a little nervously.

'Ah, hello there; we're on a pilgrimage, of sorts. I've brought my ... err ... family up here to see where my grandparents once lived,' he explained, in a polite manner. 'Their names were George and Elizabeth Darwin ... I'm Dave, or rather David: their oldest grandson!'

As soon as the name 'Darwin' was mentioned, their challenger began to beam, revealing a mouthful of discoloured teeth and, at the same time, confirmed to Dave that his initial identification had been correct.

'Oh, Mr Darwin, and Mrs Darwin too,' a still beaming Smiler remarked. 'I remember Mr and Mrs Darwin, oh dear *me* yes ... how *are* they these days?'

'Well, Nanna, that is, my *grandmother*: she's *very* well, but my grandfather...he's, *ah*, he's *not* so good these days...but he's keeping *cheerful*!' Dave said, experiencing a rollercoaster of emotions, in one short sentence.

A hitherto glum Sheila, now looked up at her husband, smiled piteously, and gave his arm a supportive squeeze.

The Rothermead retainer, however, was completely unaware of the ominous connotations implicit in Dave's words, and merely grinned in response.

'Well, give 'em the best from me, *won't* you!' he exclaimed, with a broad toothy grin.

Encouraged by the connection he'd made, but also wishing to change the subject, Dave pressed on.

So, err…my friend, what are you doing on the farm these days?' he asked, in a desperate attempt to extend the range of the conversation.

'Well Mr David Darwin, since the stables closed, I've become the gardener for the 'big house'!' Smiler boasted, stretching himself proudly.

'Good for *you*!' Dave replied, trying not to sound too condescending. At the same time, he couldn't help but notice that the title 'head gardener' had been dropped since Grandad Darwin's days.

'If you were after seeing Lord and Lady Rothermead, they're not *here* I'm afraid; they've gone to their place in France. Miss Victoria *is* at home, but she's not around at the moment either; she's out somewhere with her…with the farm manager!'

'No, *that's* alright, we've only really come to see the old place!'

'Well, as I *say*, there's no one at home, so you're welcome to look round the grounds of the 'big house' if you like?' proposed the man who was, seemingly, in charge of the entire establishment at that moment.

'Yes, *thanks*…umm, old chap,' Dave responded, neither remembering the man's real name, nor feeling comfortable referring to him as 'Smiler' to his face.

With a cheery wave, the successor to his grandfather then walked away in the direction from which he had come and muttered out loud to himself: 'Mr and Mrs Darwin, well I *never*!'

'Who was *that*?' Sheila asked, screwing up her face, as soon as the little man had disappeared from view.

'That was Smiler, he used to be the stable lad here, and he sometimes took the race horses out for exercise,' Dave replied, remembering the days when a much younger Smiler used to walk two or three steps behind the groom, Mr Carter, as he himself had done behind Grandad Darwin.

'*Huh*, judging by those teeth, his father *was* one of the horses,' Sheila retorted, with an unkindly grimace.

Trying to ignore the remark, Dave led his reluctant companions round to the other side of the old wall and was pleased to see that the lean-to greenhouse was still there. Moreover, the ancient grape vine inside appeared as though it was still being looked after, presumably by Smiler. However, the adjoining greenhouse, which used to be crowded with tender and exotic plants in his grandfather's day, and heady with the scent of geranium leaves, had gone completely. Only the peeling lime wash on the south face of the thirty-yard wall, together with a few rusty nails embedded in its mortar, gave any indication that the greenhouse had ever existed.

The surrounding walled vegetable garden also made a sorry sight; there was certainly little there to impress either Sheila or Julian, he sadly concluded. The beds that had once been crowded with well-tended, mouth-watering produce were now utterly abandoned and covered in nettles. However, here and there, huge clumps of fennel were still rising up defiantly; having seeded themselves around from the long neglected herb patch. There also appeared to be piles of weed-covered rubble, randomly scattered over the area. Crouching down to look closer, Dave began to wonder: was this the demolition material from his grandparents' cottage? Had his past been so carelessly razed, only to be ground into the dirt for good measure?

As Dave straightened himself up again, something caught his eye in the far corner of that desolate walled garden. Spurred on, he began to slowly stumble his way over to where hanging tendrils of ivy from the old walls, were partially obscuring the object of his quest. Neither Sheila nor her son made any attempt to follow him, nor had he expected them to. In fact, he saw his wife stare impatiently at her watch, whilst Julian paced round in slow, slovenly circles. Undaunted, Dave pressed on and, upon reaching the corner, he quickly happened upon his first discovery. What appeared to be six or seven rusty metal window frames were leaning against the wall in a stack. Almost straightaway, he was as sure as he could be that they must have been recovered from the demolished 1950s extension. He then turned his attention to the object that was right in the corner, and the one that had drawn him over there in the first place. Having pulled aside the curtain of ivy tendrils, he took a couple more steps forward, and then could not believe what he had found. It was dirty, rusty, and covered in the sort of organic debris that one might expect from it having spent years in the garden, but it was definitely an old Rayburn cooker. It had to be the one from his grandparents' dining room, he speculated excitedly; it certainly looked very much like it. Dave turned round to give the thumbs up sign to Sheila and Julian, but they were in close conference and appeared to have entirely forgotten him.

'Non-believers, *townies*!' he muttered, through clenched teeth.

Not at all discouraged by the lack of support, Dave turned back to the object of his quest, and crouched down reverently in front of it. He then tried to open the fire door, but it was rusted shut, and would not budge. However, the door of the hot oven finally yielded to his efforts, with a grating squeak. Inside, he noticed that there were some rusted implements, all liberally coated in spider's web, including a badly corroded toast-maker, and an old fire poker. But there was also something else in there, right at the back; something that had endured all those years of abandonment far better than the other contents evidently had. Dave reached further inside and, ignoring the spider that scampered over his knuckles, pulled out a brass toasting fork. To his utter delight, he could see that it was *the* brass toasting fork. There was no longer any doubt: this was Nanna and Grandad Darwin's Rayburn; the one from the demolished dining room, and the one responsible for those memorable Friday-night baked potatoes.

Normally, when someone goes on a pilgrimage, an offering is made at the shrine of the saint chosen for veneration. One then comes away with absolution or, perhaps, a blessing. However, as this particular pilgrimage had almost been a curse, Dave thought it only appropriate that things be reversed and that he take something away from the ruined fragments of this shrine. In any case, however he justified it, there was no way he was going to leave that precious toasting fork there. So, with his souvenir recovered, Dave picked his way back across the wasteland of a once well-tended vegetable garden, to rejoin a very bored-looking Sheila and Julian.

'Can we go *home* now?' pouted the latter, to no one in particular.

Straightaway, Dave was disappointed, both by the boy's attitude, and the fact that neither of them had asked about his regained family heirloom.

'Oh, I was hoping we could have walked up to Rothermead Green before heading back,' he said, looking somewhat crestfallen in the direction of his wife.

Sadly, Sheila had also run out of patience.

'We came here to see your grandparents' old cottage, *not* go for a walk, surely?' she said, with the deft skill of a prosecution counsel about to nail her witness.

'You're *right*, so let's compromise,' Dave reasoned, forcing a smile and doing his best to keep his cool. 'We'll *drive* up to Rothermead Green, have a quick look and then go home. How about that?'

Julian grimaced immediately.

'Oh *Mum*!' he bellyached, appealing directly to her, and completely ignoring Dave.

Sheila thought for a few seconds, and then puckered up her mouth, as she slowly shook her head.

Dave realised that even his compromise suggestion was about to be rubbished as well, so he didn't allow her the satisfaction of refusing his request verbally.

'*Never* mind, perhaps another day, eh?' the defeated pilgrim proposed, with a stoical smile, before making his way back to the arch in the thirty-yard wall. He didn't wait for a reply, but the faces being pulled, as he averted his gaze, had effectively rubbished that suggestion as well.

As the threesome slowly wandered back across the outer courtyard to the car, Dave realised that Rothermead couldn't possibly have lived up to expectations, as far as both Julian and Sheila were concerned. But they hadn't seen it in its heyday; they hadn't known the place when the walled gardens were in full production, and the stables, full of race-winners. Back then, it was a time when the farm was populated with such colourful characters as Bill Blackett, Ron Carter, and Edwina Cohen, as well as Dave's own beloved Grandad Darwin.

Having thought back to the late 1960s, and this time of year in particular, Dave began to remember the photographs that Ronnie had taken on that spring morning long ago, when he, Grandad Darwin and his late uncle had walked up to the green, through the cherry orchards, picking mushrooms on the way. He seemed to recall that, amongst others, Ronnie had taken many shots of those lovely old ruined cottages and that mill tower up there. As he stared down at the old toasting fork he was holding, Dave wondered what had ever become of those pictures his uncle had taken on that day towards the end of April 1969. He'd gone through his parents' and grandparents' family photograph collections on many occasions, and had even collated that mass of miscellaneous prints for them. If any of those pictures from that memorable Sunday morning walk had been amongst them, then he would have surely remembered; of that there was no doubt. Sadly, it seemed that the Rothermead Green pictures were nowhere to be found, and Dave was forced to conclude that, in all probability, Ronnie had never got round to having them developed.

Having unlocked the car to admit the eager-to-depart Sheila and Julian, Dave hovered by the open driver's door and stared over at the old north wing. He noticed that this once semi-derelict part of the 'big house' had very recently been extensively renovated. Had that been sold off as well, he wondered? Did Mrs Cohen still live in part of it? There were no curtains in the windows of her part – curtains that would surely have been twitching had she still been in residence – in fact, the whole of the newly restored wing seemed empty. As he finally clambered into the car himself, Dave pondered on the strange reversals in fortune that had taken place at Rothermead since he was here last. The once rundown farm properties: the north wing and former tied cottages, had now been 'restored' and sold off, or were waiting to be so. On the other hand, the once thriving kitchen garden and once busy stable block were now in a very rundown condition.

Dave started the engine and drove slowly forward in order to turn a circle by the former tied cottage. How he would have loved to have had enough courage to knock on the door and ask to see what was left of Nanna and Grandad Darwin's former home: the musty sittingroom and eerie staircase, the latter now presumably restored to its fullest width. And then there was upstairs; there was the room where he and Lucy had spent so many fearful nights, and across the narrow passage: the small yellow bedroom, in which there had been just enough room for a double bed. That had once briefly been Ronnie's room, but latterly, it was where Dave's parents had slept when they all stayed up here.

As the car pulled away, Dave stared in the rearview mirror, and took one last look at his grandparents' old place. For one brief moment, he thought he could see them both waving him goodbye. And didn't Grandad Darwin just click his heels before the image faded?

Amanda-Jayne

What a summer of changes this is turning out to be, Dave thought, as he slowly lifted up another clump of turf from his rapidly diminishing back garden lawn. Some of those changes had been bad; others not quite so bad, he pondered, before a painful twinge in his lower back forced him to straighten up again. At least his plants were as predictable and reliable as ever: the honeysuckle was reassuringly scented, the lupins faithfully bright and erect, and the buddleia unfailingly smothered in butterflies. In fact, the herbaceous borders were so successful that he was currently expanding them by eliminating much of the lawn; hence the painful backbreaking work today.

Sheila had wanted a small area of grass retained – somewhere to sit out on, when the fancy took her – and Dave was happy to comply, by leaving the patch where Amanda-Jayne had so alluringly sunbathed the previous summer. Of course, the teenager was no longer on the scene as a result of Julian ending his relationship with her earlier that spring. Dave had hoped that Julian might have rekindled his relationship with Amanda-Jayne, following his recent split with that bizarre creature Daphne, or 'Duvet', so named because of her alleged free attitude towards sex. Unfortunately though, Julian hadn't seemed interested in returning to her; no doubt guided by his mother's oft-quoted adage that a person can never go back. On the other hand, it could be that he was still too put out by the fact that 'Duvet' had not obliged for him, as her advance billing had promised, Dave speculated, as he wiped the sweat from his brow with a muddy hand.

Although Dave had often thought of Amanda-Jayne, and on occasions missed her, particularly on that springtime 'pilgrimage' to Rothermead Farm, he had not actually seen her since the April walk along the Marshside Road, when she had posed for him on the drover's bridge. That last ambiguous photograph had joined the earlier bathing costume picture in his secret hiding place, from where, shameful glances could be enjoyed – and often were – when no one was about.

However as time passed, that drover's bridge picture was becoming less ambiguous. Amanda-Jayne, the daughter, was no longer around to confuse the issue, thus allowing Amanda-Jayne, the young fantasy seductress, to dominate. The shift became more focused with each occasion that Dave clandestinely studied the images, rather like a pubescent schoolboy under the bedclothes at night, with a well-thumbed copy of *Health and Efficiency*.

The summer of changes was also affecting Dave's work life, or more specifically, the relationship with his work colleague and best friend, Tim Cross. In early June, and without warning, Darryl Giles had announced, with startlingly mock moroseness, that Tim had gone on long-term sick leave. Dave could not find out what was going on, and his boss was no help, insisting that it was a confidential personnel matter. Even Monica, who devoured gossip like most people do sweets, didn't have a clue as to why he was off, but at the end of the day, Dave suspected that it had something to do with Tim's deteriorating marriage. What made matters worse was that no one seemed to be answering Tim's home telephone. Dave had thought about phoning a lot more times than he had actually made the attempt, so fearful was he that his friend's wife Alison might answer it. And then, one morning at work, three weeks ago, Tim rang Dave out of the blue, to ask if they could go on a lunchtime excursion 'just like in the old days'. The friends agreed to meet on that very Thursday at noon and, to be on the safe side, Dave booked the afternoon off. Tim concluded the call by making it clear that there was no question of a walk or photo quest; he wanted to go straight to the pub and did not care which one. Dave suggested they meet in the 'Olde City' as usual, which had been the only part of the so-called excursion routine he was able to salvage.

Tim was already there in the pub when Dave had arrived at the agreed time. As soon as he had seen his much-missed friend, sitting there alone in a dingy corner, he'd been shocked by his appearance. Tim seemed to be even more dishevelled than usual: his eyes were dark and sunken, his teeth discoloured, and his clothes looked like he'd slept in them for the last couple of nights. Any recent encounter with either a hairbrush or razor had also apparently eluded him.

Tim, who was getting through his third pint, made his priorities clear as Dave sat down to join him.

'My turn to buy *you* a drink at long last,' he announced in greeting him, before sliding his chair back noisily. 'I've sold some books, so we can have a really *good* session!'

'Yeah…*great*…thanks,' Dave responded, trying to sound enthusiastic, but looking desperately worried. At that moment, he was glad that he'd taken the afternoon off. It certainly sounded as if his friend was on a bender and he knew it would be a struggle to keep up with him.

Having stood up, Tim drained the remains of his third pint in one ungulping draught and immediately went to the bar. He hadn't seemed to notice his work colleague's look of concern.

Dave's morose friend had seen off most of his fourth pint before he really felt like talking, and then he just cut straight to the chase.

'You may not be surprised to learn that Alison has finally left me!' he admitted, in an almost resigned and quite emotionless monotone. 'She's become involved with a group of *women*, through mutual acquaintances at teacher's training college. Huh, the unkinder of my musician friends refer to this group as the 'Thanet Lesbians'. *Apparently,* Alison's now living in a women's commune and has taken the children ... *m*y children ... with her.' Having completed this shocking revelation, he looked away from his drinking companion and lifted the nearly empty pint glass to his lips.

Although the news wasn't entirely unexpected, Dave nevertheless, felt an immediate tug of sadness.

'I don't know what to *say* Tim,' he said, in a sympathetic baritone, before reaching out to squeeze his friend's forearm.

Tim moved his arm away, and shrugged whilst contorting his mouth.

'There *is* nothing to say; just drink up and I'll get us another,' he dismissed in fatalistic tones, before slowly getting to his feet again.

Having got in the next round, Tim drank quickly, deeply and with little apparent pleasure. Moreover, he didn't seem to want to resume his rambling explanation to Dave, and the round was consumed in mutually miserable silence.

All that quickly changed, however, after Tim had tottered back to the table from yet another trip to the bar. Now it was he who made the demonstrative gesture, by gripping Dave's arm as he leant in close to him.

'D'you know; that poisonous bitch has insisted that our house be put on the market and expects *me* to show people round, while I'm still *living* there!' he said, with surprising clarity of speech, before lurching back in his chair. 'I may as *well* though I suppose, after all, I've nowhere *else* to go.'

Unlike his more hardened drinking buddy, Dave was feeling the affects of the alcohol, and beginning to have trouble thinking of things to say in response to this latest wretched announcement, without sounding too trite. On the other hand, as a true friend, he knew that this should have been his cue to offer Tim their spare room, but recognised there was no point, solely on the grounds that Sheila famously disliked his troublesome and troubled work colleague. Tim probably realised this and did not expect the offer. In fact, Sheila's long-held negative feelings towards Dave's best friend had deteriorated still further, following that disastrous dinner party between the Cross family and the Darwins back in the spring. Even to this day, Dave still felt terribly guilty about that occasion, and largely because his own ill-judged intervention had greatly contributed towards the unsuccessful outcome that Sunday. It then suddenly dawned on him, with a sickening surge in the pit of his stomach, that the lamentable lunch he'd organised, and also been instrumental in wrecking, might have finally pushed Alison into making the decision to leave her husband.

Dave had no choice but to ask Tim, by way of selfish reassurance if his fears were founded: 'Umm. *Listen* mate; was that Sunday dinner, we…err, *threw* for you, at all pivotal in the break-up of your marriage?' he asked, keen to absolve himself of any blame, and at the same time, feeling utterly wretched for doing so.

Much to Dave's relief, Tim laughed loudly in response to his question.

'*No* mate, not at all! In fact, that Sunday seemed like light relief, compared to *some* of the things I've had to put up with in the last few months,' he confessed, with a stoical, joyless chuckle.

Dave empathised greatly with his unfortunate friend's unenviable situation, and tried to imagine what *his* concerns and priorities would be, should he ever find himself in that same position. However, he had a pretty good idea what they would be, and it had a lot to do with the reasons why he'd married Sheila in the first place. In fact, a rather unsettled Dave had to sink another pint himself before summoning up the courage to ask the question that had been troubling him the most.

'Do you have any idea of where you're going to live after the house has been sold?' he enquired; solemn and beetle-browed, over the top of his pint glass.

'*Ah*, but I have no intention of letting it *be* sold,' Tim retorted, finally beginning to sound a little slurred, and wagging his finger to indicate a negative intention. 'Got a few things up my sleeve, *you* know; some tactics to put off prospective buyers like not flushing the lav after having a poo, *that* sort of thing,' he added, tapping his temple, and then winking in an exaggerated fashion to reinforce the point.

Dave couldn't help but smile at the notion.

'Having the misfortune to experience your obscene flatulence on *more* than one occasion, I would imagine that ploy might prove somewhat *effective*!' he smiled, whilst trying to dispel those unpleasant mental images that had suddenly become lodged in his mind.

Having been both welcomed and encouraged by his friend's abandoned sense of gravitas, Tim went on to loudly catalogue some of the other less savoury tactics he had already planned; much to the evident amusement of the rest of the pub.

Following the sixth pint, which, like all the others, Tim had insisted on paying for, he gradually clammed up again and seemed to have nothing more to say.

A rather muzzy-headed Dave glanced at his watch and realised that 'time' was about to be called.

'Do you fancy going to the cathedral, like we used to, and perhaps carry on the conversation in a calmer setting?' he suggested, finally breaking the long, morose silence.

'*No* thanks,' Tim said unambiguously, and without making eye contact.

Having left the pub, along with the last of the more hardened lunchtime clientele, the two friends stood awkwardly at the road junction, where their respective routes home would diverge. Dave felt profoundly affected by his companion's drunken, downcast state, and wanted to give him a hug in the Grandad Darwin manner, but he hesitated for too long, and the moment was lost.

The pair finally parted company at 03:30: Dave to go up to Telecom House car park and a long wait for Sheila; Tim to stagger to the bus station for the number eight to Margate. Their last words to each other had been a mutually mumbled promise to keep in touch.

Dave put his spade down and glanced at his watch. It was a few minutes after midday; no wonder he was beginning to feel hungry. Sheila had scheduled the Sunday dinner for early evening, which allowed her to work through the day on extracurricular Telecom work, and not to have to clear her papers off the diningroom table to make way for the meal. It also gave Dave a chance to finish his back garden transformation, before finally being able to relax with his dinner and the ubiquitous accompanying wine. Consequently, he now retired to the kitchen to make himself a sandwich for lunch: a snack he promptly took back outside with a cold drink.

Sitting on the pile of turves that he'd painstakingly and painfully lifted, Dave once more pondered on that midday meeting with Tim from several weeks before. He realised that not once throughout that lackadaisical lunchtime session, had Tim asked him about Sheila, and how their fragile marriage was faring. However, if he had, Dave could have truthfully reported that things between them were better, in that they hadn't got any worse. He was encouraged by the fact that Sheila had 'been there for him' when Grandad Darwin's terminal illness was announced; in fact, it had been the only consolation for him as a result of hearing that terrible news. Since then, he had also enjoyed a certain amount of qualified support from her, that is, so long as he didn't get too upset, too often. Dave certainly welcomed a quieter and more harmonious life at home, especially now that he had, not only the stress of Grandad Darwin's condition, but also the worry of Tim's alarming deterioration to cope with. Consequently, with equal measures of cause and affect, the futile rebellion he'd begun at Christmas had now been duly abandoned. As a result, they currently lived a sort of stalemate existence, carefully avoiding all areas of conflict. In actual fact, this was not at all hard for Dave, for his main source of conflict had been removed, at least for now. In the late spring, Julian had left home; or rather he had sort of left home. The, by now, seventeen-year-old and several friends – no doubt including some of the louts who had regularly taken over Dave's lounge – had decided to finish their year out by taking jobs on the channel ferries. To avoid travelling too far, they had also decided to share a rented flat in Dover. However, this did not prevent Julian from making regular trips back to Canterbury: his incoming journeys laden with dirty laundry; the outgoing ones with clean laundry and ample provisions, including several catering boxes of instant mash. Dave had often wondered if the town of Dover was completely devoid of either laundrettes or supermarkets. However, it was a thought he quietly kept to himself, thus avoiding potential conflict with his wife, and therefore allowing that fragile ceasefire to continue.

By the Sunday evening, Dave had dug over his newly extended borders and had also planted-out large drifts of herbaceous perennials. Just as he firmed the earth round the final monarda didyma, Sheila appeared on their small patio area.

'Dinner's ready Dave,' she announced, shielding her eyes from the lowering sun. 'Cor, you *have* worked hard today!'

Dave slowly straightened himself up and smiled.

'Do you *like* it then; not too much lawn taken?' he asked, reasonably positive of a favourable response from her.

'No, no, it's great; in fact, it's just right!' she said, with her arms firmly folded, scanning her eyes over the new planting.

As a result of his wife, not only passing comment, but also making it a decidedly positive one, Dave couldn't have been more delighted.

Hand-in-hand, they then went inside to enjoy lamb chump steaks of equal sizes, together with fresh vegetables and mash made from real potatoes. A fine bottle of the slightly more expensive Sainsbury's claret washed it all down nicely.

Later that evening, as Sheila relaxed with a cigarette, and Dave sipped slowly from a generously charged tumbler of whisky, they watched an old film on video together. It was neither so good that it demanded one's full attention, nor so bad that either of them felt compelled to get up and turn the thing off; in fact, it was almost a metaphor for the current state of their marriage.

Sheila stubbed out her fag, and then blew the last inhalation of smoke away from her husband before turning to face him.

'I ran into Amanda-Jayne yesterday,' she announced, in a matter-of-fact manner.

Dave instantly felt his heart rate quicken, and wanted to bombard her with questions about the meeting, but somehow managed to temper his enthusiasm.

'Oh *really*…err, where *was* this…and, umm, is she *alright*?' he enquired, feigning mild interest to hide his keener reaction to the news.

'It was in St. Dunstan's High Street; I was getting those butcher's sausages you like, and she walked past the shop on her way to getting some groceries for her mum,' Sheila responded, before drawing her legs up on to the settee.

He was now able to embroider the mental images of that Saturday afternoon encounter, but still needed to know more: was Amanda-Jayne's hair longer, what clothes had she been wearing; was she still as pretty as ever? However, Dave bottled all that up, and waited a full minute of casual TV watching before posing his next, carefully worded, enquiry.

'Did, erm, did Amanda-Jayne mention either of us?' he questioned cautiously, trying to appear as if he didn't care either way.

Sheila looked over at her husband impassively, and guilt immediately compelled him to wonder if he'd asked one question too many, and if she had now become suspicious of his motives. Fortunately, it quickly became apparent that it was the drink that his wife was more interested in, and she borrowed his tumbler for a quick sip of scotch before answering.

'*Yes*, Amanda-Jayne mentioned us *both*; she even said that she *missed* us, which was rather sweet,' Sheila replied, before leaning forward to retrieve her cigarette packet. 'Oh, *and* she asked about your photography: whether you were still taking loads of pictures, and I told her that you *were* still boring us all with your snaps!' she added, and then winked at him to emphasize the gentle teasing nature of her remark.

Dave smiled in response, and then glanced casually back towards the television screen, but his mind was now completely occupied with thoughts of Amanda-Jayne. She must be seventeen now, just like Julian, he speculated, and then reminded himself that a whole year had passed since he'd taken that first pivotal picture of the teenager in the back garden. As the alluring images became ever more engrained in his mind, Dave decided that the next time he needed to go up to the loo, he would sneak into the spare room, and then examine his secret photographic stash, if two small four-by-six prints could be described as such.

The one thing that never seemed to change for Dave was Telecom on a Monday morning. As soon as the phones opened at 08:30, one could guarantee that every single line in the office would warble into life, with some waste-of-space woman or miserable old man on the other end, whose cretinous complaint had been fermenting all weekend. However, he had already decided that those telephone customers who asked if he was any relation to the famous Darwin – and they couldn't possibly have meant Charles – would now be getting larger compensation payment offers. Leaving that dubious private payment policy aside, this particular Monday morning was made slightly brighter by the fact that Tim was back at work. Although his friend had the makings of a half decent beard and his hygiene regimen was still all too obviously rather lax, he nonetheless seemed to be in great spirits. They soon agreed that another outing was in order and both booked the Wednesday afternoon off without any problem. Evidently, Darryl Giles had decided that allowing Tim some leeway was appropriate under the circumstances, and so happily granted the short-notice request.

At around mid-morning, during a quieter moment with the telephones, Tim beckoned Dave over to his desk. In clandestine fashion, he undid the top of his flask and, winking at Dave, motioned for him to take a sniff at his 'coffee'. It became immediately obvious that Tim's beverage was heavily laced with whisky.

Great spirits indeed, thought Dave, as he slowly returned to his desk and flashing telephone instrument.

'*Please* mate, be careful; don't let old 'farmer' Giles catch you,' he warned, in a loud whisper over their shared desk partition.

'Don't worry, he'll never know,' Tim responded, patting his nose with an index finger. 'I've got *these*!' he added, without the discretion of a quietened voice. He then waved a packet of Trebor Mints in the air, spilling at least half the contents on his desk and computer terminal.

Monica and Tiffany exchanged glances and, with the former smirking knowingly and the latter trying not to giggle, they both kept a close watch on him from the safety of their respective desks. Things went quickly downhill from that moment onwards. Tim took few calls and, to a mixture of envy and shock from his three immediate work colleagues, actually told one customer to 'piss off'.

Without seeking permission to do so, Tim went home early that day, and by Tuesday morning, he was reported as being on sick leave again.

Wednesday morning came, and there was still no sign of Tim, but rather than cancel his booked afternoon leave, Dave decided to take it anyway. As it happened, a 1950s shopping development was being demolished just off the main street in Canterbury and he decided that it would be a good opportunity for him to record its passing. The doomed buildings were a flat-roofed, modernist development that had been constructed round the surviving tower of a blitzed medieval church. And, the postwar shopping scheme in question occupied an area that, according to some of Dave's old archive photographs, used to be a quiet, leafy churchyard.

The row of three-storey terraced shops, which he now headed for, would seem nothing special to the layman, but to Dave, they were part of his past; they were another section of his history that was being snatched away from him. He'd often come to these shops as a child, with his parents, and had a clear memory of each and every one of them: number one had been the baker's premises, who did a wonderful range of homemade cakes, and number two was the wool shop that always seemed to smell funny; it was only later that he realised the nylon-bloused proprietress had suffered from a bad case of BO. Number three, perhaps his favourite and most frequented of all, was a toyshop from where many of his Dinky models had originated. The shop unit at number four was the one that always seemed to be changing hands, but he was fairly sure that, at one time, it had been a fishmongers. Finally, number five, situated right in the corner, used to be a chemist's and had been of little interest to Dave as a boy, except, that is, for the weighing machine outside, which he used to like to stand on, but didn't feel it worth wasting a precious penny of his pocket money in order to activate it.

As he approached, Dave could see that the terrace of shops had already been stripped of any re-useable parts, including roof tiles, and a crane with a pincer-like attachment was about to start work on the actual demolition. He lined up his first shot, and captured it just as a swipe from the machine brought bricks tumbling to the ground with a loud crash and clouds of dust. In a strange, literal sense, the noise was enough to wake the dead, he thought: those long-departed citizens, who had suffered the ignominy of having shops instead of tombstones above their places of rest for the last thirty-five years, and would so again when the new, much larger, mock-Georgian development followed. He then took three paces back for his second shot and felt himself bump straight into someone. Dave quickly turned to apologise to the person and was surprised and delighted to discover that it was Amanda-Jayne.

'Hello David, I *knew* it would be you and was just on my way over to say *hi*, but you beat me to it!' she beamed, looking directly and deeply into his eyes.

They both laughed and then spontaneously hugged, before she kissed him on the cheek. Dave happily returned the gesture.

'It's lovely to *see* you, to bump into you as it were, you… you look *great*!' he rejoiced, unashamedly studying her from tip to toe.

Amanda Jayne seemed even taller than the last time they were together, and her dark hair was now not only shoulder length, but also tinted in a reddish henna hue. There was not a scrap of obvious make up on her flawless elfin-like face, and to his amazement, she appeared to be wearing the same long psychedelic skirt and gypsy-style top she'd had on during that last spring walk: the one when Julian had split up with her. Dave knew that outfit intimately, from many a furtive glance of that drover's bridge photograph, and much more, in the shameful secrecy of the spare room, over the last three months.

With the row of doomed shops now entirely forgotten, Dave, once more, smiled into her happy, welcoming face.

'So…so, what have you been up to in the last three months? Boyfriends *galore* I shouldn't wonder!' he suggested coyly, really hoping for an answer to his exclamation, rather than the question.

'Just school, and *no* boyfriends! My contemporaries: they all seem so… so *immature*!' she admitted, smiling with her eyes narrowed slightly. 'And *you* Dave?'

'Just work, and no boyfriends *either*!' he chuckled, with an accompanying wink, as he pointed at her playfully.

The resultant high-pitched ripples of laughter to the joke were a delight to his ears; they were something he hadn't realised he'd missed so much, until hearing them again at that moment.

With her face still registering mirth, Amanda-Jayne reached up and gently touched his left upper arm.

'Oh I *have* missed your sense of humour,' she remarked, by way of an unconscious coincidence.

After the laughter had died down, Dave's young companion stared deeply into his eyes, and then looked down as if deciding something. With the matter seemingly resolved in her mind, she restored her direct gaze.

'How are you going to spend your afternoon David?' came the intriguing enquiry.

Dave extended his bottom lip and then shrugged.

'Well, I just planned to wander round with my camera,' he responded, heedless as a section of 1950s masonry crashed to the ground. 'And what about you?'

Amanda-Jayne once more narrowed her eyes, as she gazed up at him.

'I'm just going to sneak off to my secret place, find a cool shady spot and then read all afternoon!' she declared in a soft, calm voice.

Dave was instantly intrigued by her comment as, no doubt, she had hoped he would be. The fact that she didn't have a book on her was entirely lost to him.

After a moments further thought, perhaps a deliberately teasing moment, Amanda-Jayne posed her well-timed question.

'Would you like to *see* my secret place? I can't think of *anyone* else I'd rather share it with,' she said, with her eyes widened again, accompanied by a broad beaming smile. 'And then I can talk to *you* rather than have to pop into Smith's for a paperback!'

'I…I'd be *honoured*, erm, *thank* you!' he responded, with tremulous enthusiasm, as a shot of adrenalin seeped through his stomach.

Having readily agreed to his young companion's surprising suggestion, Dave was further alarmed when she grabbed his arm, and clung to it as they walked off. He was also slightly embarrassed by the thought that one of his work colleagues might see him with this beautiful young girl on his arm. What might they think, or assume? Indeed, what would *her* friends think if they saw her with this old bloke? It was then that, with the inevitability of tumbling toast landing butter-side down, Dave saw a familiar face coming towards them along the crowded High Street. It was Chloe, of that there was no doubt, and it suddenly felt as if he had been phased into some sort of alternative reality: with Amanda-Jayne being on his arm, and the only woman he had, thus far, ever loved bearing down on them. And what is more, judging by the way her Laura Ashley dress extended out at the front, Chloe was pregnant. Dave's former lover noticed him only at the last second and not only looked shocked, but also flushed violently in the cheeks. However, it was far too late for her to take any avoiding action, so she smiled at him, and paused to exchange a polite, and yet hesitant greeting. Dave noticed Chloe glance over briefly at Amanda-Jayne, who was still clinging to his arm and had been grinning from the outset. The teenager, for her part, noted Dave glancing at Chloe's frontal bump, with more than the usual interest. However, neither woman made any verbal reference to the other. The brief encounter was ended by another exchange of pleasantries, before a relieved and blotchy-red Chloe hurried on her way.

As they parted, Dave mused on the fact that Chloe was finally getting what she had always wanted: a family. At the same time, he was both confused and surprised that seeing her again hadn't triggered any feelings of longing or regret. It then dawned on him that he must be over her; that all those once deep-rooted emotions must have receded. In fact, his strongest sense, at that moment, was one of genuine delight that Chloe's fondest wish was about to be fulfilled. Amanda-Jayne must have sensed his introspection, but to her credit, did not enquire about their meeting with the pretty, pregnant woman, and so the pair walked on in silence.

Having made about two hundred yards progress, Dave caught sight of their reflection in the plate glass window of a building society, as they passed by. For him, it was an unwelcome affirmation of the fact that he was certainly no oil painting. At six feet, four inches, he was just the same height as Uncle Ronnie had been, which counted on the plus side, but Dave had rather nondescript brown hair in common with his father, unlike Ronnie's jet black locks, and he was also beginning to go thin on top. Moreover, as was currently the case, he often carried a few pounds too much weight. And yet, for all that, a lovely woman such as Chloe had fallen in love with him. This thought led him to speculate that perhaps women were more evolved than men, and wondered what Charles Darwin would have said on the subject. It was true; women did seem to judge the whole person and take everything into account, when considering a potential partner. Having now decided to modify his initial rather negative self-analysis, Dave conceded that he did, in fact, have a few other things going for him, apart from his height. A number of women had told him that he had warm eyes and a kind, if not actually handsome, face. Others had considered him amusing, passionate and sensitive; in fact, they'd pointed out qualities that his Uncle Ronnie had also possessed in droves. Dave reasoned that, perhaps, this was why someone with Chloe's undoubted qualities, could consider spending the rest of her life with him. Now feeling very much better about himself, Dave looked at Amanda-Jayne, who, in response, smiled and squeezed his arm tighter. It then occurred to him that, maybe, the seventeen-year-old could see those same, so-called qualities in him that Chloe once had. Suddenly, he felt that his immediate future was open to endless possibilities. As they walked on, Dave decided to tell Amanda-Jayne about the woman they had just bumped into; the woman he was once going to marry.

Before very long, the pair turned away from the High Street, and found themselves in the narrower, more intimate environs of Stour Street. Almost straightaway, the tourist driven hubbub of the main drag, gave way to a scene of calm, and a byway occupied by only a few local people quietly going about their business. Having loosened her grip of his arm, Amanda-Jayne grabbed Dave's hand and then, after about fifty yards, led him into a dark passageway to the right, which passed beneath the first-floor jetty of a seventeenth century house. The pair quickly re-emerged into the sunlight again, behind the old dwelling, and then followed a path that ran between a miscellany of tall, ancient buildings, before reaching a little bridge that spanned the River Stour. Dave couldn't help but think of the Amanda-Jayne in that springtime photo, in which she was wearing the same clothes as today and standing on the little bridge off Marshside Road. But there she was, right next to him, and in the here and now too; it was as if his fantasy mannequin had come to life, but at the same time, Dave knew that she was also so much more than that.

After they had crossed the bridge, and taken a narrow riverside path to the left, Dave found himself in the familiar surroundings of the Greyfriars Gardens: the site of a former friary, through which one branch of the Stour slowly slithered. The surviving medieval chapel – which had been built by the hands of men who had known St Francis personally – still straddled this lesser-known branch of the river, and could now be seen before them. For hundreds of years, the river had approached that ancient structure in the sparkling sunlight, and then passed through its twin gothic arches, to plunge into the cold darkness of the building's undercroft. All too soon, it would then flow through two more gothic arches and so re-emerge back into the sunlight; there, once more, to reflect the sun and sky on its clear green surface. It was almost a metaphor for human existence itself, and a positive one too: it said that no matter how bad those dark episodes may seem at the time, the ones we all inevitably suffer from through life, things will almost always become much brighter and warmer before very long.

Halfway along the little path, Amanda-Jayne paused, and then squeezed his hand.

'*This* is my secret place,' she announced, in an emotionally charged half-whisper, before peering up to anxiously gauge his response.

'What a lovely, tranquil place!' breathed Dave, as he looked down into her grey-green eyes. 'Who'd have thought that we were only yards away from the city's clogged main artery,' he added, with a warm smile. In actual fact, he knew the garden and chapel very well, and had been here with Tim during a number of their earlier photographic expeditions. On one occasion, he'd even had a clandestine lunchtime meeting with Chloe in this secluded setting. However, he said nothing to his young companion; he didn't want to spoil her delight in sharing the place with him.

The ancient Franciscan chapel was partly obscured by the bulk of an old beech tree that grew close to the water's edge; its smooth-barked roots partly sitting on the river Stour's brick retaining wall, and also spreading dangerously close to the old building itself. Amanda-Jayne approached the tree and proceeded to sit on the grass that grew beneath those laterally-spreading roots. Dave noticed that she had chosen to sit with her back against the foot of the trunk, and with both legs slightly drawn up. Having first deposited his camera case on the grass close by, he joined her and then mimicked the same posture, whilst also getting as close to her as he could without actually making physical contact. He then watched, in dumb-struck awe, as she slowly hitched her skirt right up to expose the full length of her legs to the sun.

Amanda-Jayne let out a long, low moan of complete contentment.

'Oh *David*, isn't it just *lovely*,' she sighed, in a lazy half-whisper.

He leant forward and glanced over in her direction. Her full lips were parted slightly, her eyes were tightly shut, and as she slowly breathed in and out, her nostrils gently quivered with the rhythm.

'Yes, it certainly *is*!' he replied, quite overwhelmed by the close presence of his alluring young companion. You are so sweet and so lovely, he said over and over to himself as he watched her, quite unawares.

Enjoying the sun's warmth on her bare legs, Amanda-Jayne now slowly pulled her gypsy blouse off both shoulders. A thrill of sexual excitement coursed through his entire body, whilst, at the same time, a sudden breeze rustled the leaves of the beech tree above them. As a result of this, he noticed that her freshly exposed skin had begun to gently goose-bump. And then, as his eyes slowly scanned down her body, he rather shamefully found himself looking to see if she was wearing a bra. Her nipples had hardened in response to the breeze, pressing against the thin fabric of her blouse, and in so doing, effectively answered the question for him.

Without opening her eyes, or turning her head, the seventeen-year-old reached out to hold his hand.

'I've missed you *so* much David,' she confessed in a low, sleepy-sounding voice.

'I've missed you *too*,' he replied, with a restrained earnestness that only partly expressed his true feelings.

His young companion did not respond but, with her eyes still closed, smiled contentedly and then gave his hand a gentle squeeze.

Dave leant back against the trunk of the tree and shut his eyes as well, to better ponder on the predicament he now found himself in. Straightaway, a confusion of questions began to pose themselves in his mind: which version of Amanda-Jayne was this sitting next to him? Was it the daughter, or the young seductress? How did she regard *him*? Was he a substitute for the father she had not known since childhood, or a potential lover? Could it be that she *was* using her superior female evolution to see through his many flaws and the age difference, to consider him a possible partner and mate? Was she flaunting herself for his pleasure, or merely sunbathing?

The beech leaves once more rustled above their heads, as the river slowly slid by beneath them. The close presence of the water prompted him to remember the ambiguity between the two versions of her he had felt on that spring day at Marshside. The question that he'd begun to ask himself then, was perhaps even more pertinent now, and probably the most important of all those that currently swirled round his head: was she the substitute daughter, or the potential lover? Back then, he could sense that the two disparate versions of Amanda-Jayne had begun to coalesce in his mind. Right now, beneath the shade of that old beech tree, he could feel that process becoming complete. It was as if the calm, clear waters of the River Stour had absorbed equal amounts of the blue from the sky and the yellow of the sun, to make a vivid green: a new colour from the two primary contributors.

With his hand still encircled by hers, Dave slowly leant forward once more, and glanced over at his lovely young companion. Her eyes were still shut, and her breasts were gently rising and falling, as she slowly breathed through still parted lips. For one moment, he thought that she might be asleep, but she soon signalled her waking state by brushing off an ant that had begun to climb up the exposed skin of her upper thigh. Her legs parted slightly during the process, and he briefly caught sight of the soft downy hairs on either side of the gusset of her small, white panties. It was too much for him, and he again leant back against the tree's smooth bark, and desperately attempted to stem the rising tide of his own desires.

Having calmed down a little, Dave began to tell himself that he would be quite happy to love her as a daughter, if that was all that was on offer. They could continue what they already had: the walks, the talks about art, music and nature and the sharing of confidences. If he had to, he could ignore those primal urges that had been so abruptly re-awakened in him today; it would not be an easy process, but then again, he would still have those secret photographs for that purpose. All this only served to reiterate what he'd earlier already conceded: that men were not as evolved as women; they were too much aware of their need to reproduce. Man may be at the top of Charles Darwin's evolutionary tree, but we were still animals, differing from the major primates by only a few genes.

Dave sat there in quiet, yet troubled contemplation for a good five minutes, with no discernable sound coming from either Amanda-Jayne, or their immediate surroundings. Even the temperature of their respective clasped hands had adjusted to the same level, and he had to wiggle his fingers ever so slightly to remind himself that they were still in physical contact. Finally, he dared to open his eyes, and peer over at her. Oh, you are *so* lovely, he thought to himself again. Dave wanted to say it out loud, and then he wanted to tenderly touch her in ways that a father would not even contemplate with his daughter, but he had to be sure she would want that as well. Why could she not tell him, he wondered, or give him a definite and unambiguous sign? He dare not make a move now and spoil what they already had, unless he was absolutely sure of not being rejected. If he was slapped back, then he might lose Amanda-Jayne in any role, and that could not be allowed to happen. One way or the other, Dave had a curious feeling that she was destined to play a significant part in his future, but one clumsy, inept or inappropriate move on his part could put in jeopardy whatever it was he'd convinced himself the fates had in store for them both. Caution was clearly called for, and to recklessly act on those primal urges right there and then, could be to court disaster. Such bad handling on his part would bring them both only pain and humiliation, not to mention universal condemnation for him alone, especially given their age difference.

It was inevitable that Dave now began to think about his poor old Uncle Ronnie who, unwittingly, had found himself in a similar position. As a result, he had suffered not only much personal hurt, but also a great deal of very public humiliation and condemnation. The circumstances were different, but if he wasn't very careful, Dave realised that he could very well find himself suffering the same fate.

*

What's going *on* this morning? David wondered to himself, as he slowly poured milk on his Shreddies. He could feel that there was something wrong; the atmosphere in the kitchen was somehow different that morning. The twelve-year-old took the first mouthful of his cereal and then looked about him. Lucy seemed okay, as she worked her way through a pile of Rice Krispies almost as tall as herself, and Eddie was pleasantly absorbed with his bread and Marmite soldiers. However, their mother seemed preoccupied; being both silent and unsmiling as she held an un-drunk cup of rapidly cooling tea on the table in front of her. David also noticed that she was stealing regular, but unhappy glances at the door to the hall, which unusually was shut. Directly opposite him, his father's boiled egg sat there unattended and, no doubt, getting cold too. The top had been removed, but that was as far as he'd got with it, when the phone had rung. Dad's been in the hall now for about ten minutes, pondered David as he glanced, first at the kitchen clock, and then again in the direction of his mother's worried face. Something was definitely wrong.

The phone had rung late last night as well. It had woken David and he couldn't get back to sleep for the sound of his father's raised voice resounding up from the hallway below. Instead, he had strained hard to listen, but no actual words could be discerned, just a low mumbling sound with long, silent pauses and the occasional acoustic crescendo. Lying there, propped up on one elbow, David dearly hoped that none of his grandparents had been taken ill, but reasoned that there would have been no need for his father to speak in a raised voice if that was the case. No, the person his father had been talking to was in trouble, and had done something wrong. From bitter experience, he knew only too well what his father's cross voice sounded like.

The door from the hall suddenly opened and his ashen-faced father re-emerged. Both David and his mother looked towards him with anxious expressions. Unaware of anything out of the ordinary, Lucy continued to munch at her cereal, whilst little Eddie happily smeared Marmite round his face.

Len sat down dejectedly and pushed his abandoned egg to one side.

'That was Ronnie again,' he announced, in an ominously worried tone. 'He's in a *terrible* state. It seems the *papers* have got hold of it somehow.'

'Oh God, *no*!' his shocked-sounding wife responded, before placing a trembling hand over her mouth.

'Afraid so,' Len said, with an accompanying sigh. 'Ronnie suspects a leak in the Met; he says it's as corrupt as it's possible to *get*!'

David glanced at both his dejected-looking parents, and could no longer bear not knowing what was happening.

'What's the matter?' he asked, continuing to look rapidly from one adult to the other. '*What* have the papers got hold of?'

Before either of them could answer his question, the letterbox clattered at the far end of the hall. As usual, David rushed to get the paper for his father as he always did, but today in particular, he was spurred on by the fact that his weekly comic should also be inside.

However, to his considerable surprise, his dad leapt quickly from the table and physically intervened.

'No David, *David*,' he shouted, dragging the boy back by his jumper, in an uncharacteristically rough way. '*I'll* get it today!' he snapped, before dashing into the hall himself.

Lucy looked up briefly at her rapidly retreating father, before returning to her bowl, having remembered that her comic came on a different day to David's.

Her bewildered brother, on the other hand, reacted very differently and dropped back heavily into his seat.

'What's *happening*?' he moaned, suddenly feeling very frightened, as he looked to his mother for an explanation.

They briefly exchanged glances, before she turned away from him, got up from the table, and then put two slices of bread into the toaster. Having depressed the lever with the usual click, Meg sat back down and resumed stealing unhappy glances in the direction of the hall door as she'd done before. David's father soon came back with the folded paper and slumped down at the table, shifting it slightly on the lino, with a noisy squeak. His face was drained white, as he slowly unfolded the newspaper and then held it up in front of him. David's *Smash* comic slipped from the middle of the paper and fluttered to the floor, but as it did so, neither father nor son made any attempt to retrieve it.

Len stared at the front page in grim silence for a few seconds, before looking over at his wife.

'It's as bad as I'd feared!' he announced, in a grave monotone. 'Listen to *this*: Gorilla…'

'*Len, no*!' Meg intercepted, as she reached out and then roughly pushed the paper down on to the table.

Her husband carefully slid the crumpled tabloid out from under her flattened palm, and proceeded to straighten it out.

'I think the children have a *right* to know love!' he responded softly; even forcing a weak smile. 'After *all*, this may very well affect them too.'

By now, Lucy had stopped eating and was also anxiously gazing at both parents. David suddenly felt an awful sick feeling in his stomach, which was even worse than just before a visit to the dentist. The silence in the room was broken, only by Eddie's audible chewing of his soggy bread crusts.

Having given Meg's outstretched hand a squeeze, Len picked up the paper and resumed reading: '*Gorilla Gagman's Gymslip Gaff*'. He paused and then peered at his wife from the top of his eyes. '*Not* a very happy start, *is* it!' he remarked, with brows furrowed in evident concern.

The headline had already made Meg force a sharp intake of breath, but now, as she held a hanky to her mouth and shook her head in agreement with his comment, tears began to form in her eyes. At the same time, Lucy's bottom lip began to tremble at the sight of her mother's distress.

Undaunted, Len reverted his gaze back to the front page, and continued to read:

'*Rising star and comedian, Ronnie Darwin, fell dramatically to earth yesterday when it was revealed that his lover was not only a public schoolgirl, but also under age as well. Blonde beauty, Katie Townsend, 15, became a fan of the 1968 Opportunity Knocks overall winner when she was just 14, but she soon fell under the spell of ape-man comic Ronnie. Sun photographer, Johnny Hartman, secretly captured the pair leaving Darwin's new London flat last Saturday evening, bound for an unknown destination. A neighbour confirmed that leggy Katie had been staying there since Friday night. The affair came to light, when the beautiful Binningdene boarder asked to go home for the weekend, but rushed into the arms of rude Ronnie instead. Mother of three and divorcee, Vanessa Townsend 45, happened to call the school and finding her absent, contacted the police. Runaway Katie was subsequently tracked to the capital, due to the vigilance of railway ticket collector and Ronnie Darwin fan, Rashid Ali, who saw the dashing funny man meeting a girl in school uniform from an incoming train. 'I recognised him straightaway. He's the only one on telly who doesn't tell jokes about nig-nogs, or darkies' commented immigrant Ali. Our sources, concerned to preserve the moral standards of this great nation, contacted this paper so that we can bring you this shocking exclusive. For details of Ronnie Darwin's rapid rise to fame, see pages 4 and 5, blah, blah, blah*!'

An utterly despairing Len dropped the paper and once more looked to his wife in despair.

'The bloody fool, the bloody stupid young *fool*!' he declared, wearily rubbing his shaking forehead. 'What the hell was he *playing* at…I mean to say: a fifteen-year-old *schoolgirl*?'

Len expected no answer, as he swept the paper to one side, sending his egg and plate with it. Almost straightaway, Lucy began to cry, Eddie looked up at them all rather bemused, and the toast popped up unregarded. Meanwhile, David stared down at the soggy mess that was once his breakfast, and all he could think of was that alluring image of Katie, perched high atop the stool in

115

Ronnie's dressing room; his uncle's lips pressed against hers, and his hands caressing her smooth, exposed thigh.

Meg finally broke a period of what seemed like interminable silence, punctuated only by Lucy's sobs.

'Wha…what's Ronnie going to *do*? Where will he *go*?' she asked, with the beginnings of panic sounding in her voice.

Len shrugged in a matter-of-fact manner.

'Well, he *can't* stay at the London flat; Ronnie and I have already *talked* about that!' he replied, with an open hand gesture. 'Apparently, it's besieged by both TV *and* the press!' He stared solemnly into Meg's face before continuing his statement. 'That's why I've asked him to come down *here* to stay!'

His wife immediately looked alarmed at the prospect.

'But the *press*!' she interjected; once more reaching out, but this time, to grab at her husband's left arm.

'The press don't *know* about us, the *Canterbury* Darwins, just yet!' he responded, whilst gently easing her rather tightly gripped hand from his shirt sleeve. 'Besides which, *whatever* that stupid idiot has done, he's still my brother; he's family and he *needs* us!'

'Of *course* he is love,' Meg sighed, as she gradually calmed herself. 'I'm sorry; it's just that…'

'No need to apologise; these are trying times, but I fear they've only just begun, *especially* for poor Ronnie!' Len exclaimed, with a kindly smile, and a resigned sigh before reaching out a comforting hand to stroke Lucy's tear-streaked cheek.

As the fraught atmosphere began to ease, David started to look forward to the prospect of his uncle coming to stay with them.

'Will Uncle Ronnie be going over to the Herne Bay flat when he's down here?' he asked; hoping for another one of their familiar trips together.

His father immediately and emphatically shook his head.

'No, that place is *strictly* off limits,' he replied, in no uncertain terms, but offering no explanation as to why. 'But that *reminds* me,' he added cryptically, getting up from his chair. 'Ronnie has asked me to make some phone calls for him!' Len once more went into the hall and shut the door behind him as he did so.

David peered over at his mother, who seemed as equally perplexed as himself, about these phone calls that suddenly needed to be made. This is all very odd, he thought, before carrying his bowl to the sink.

Because of all that morning's upset, the twelve-year-old completely forgot the fact that it was the very first day of the long school summer holidays. From the kitchen window, he could see that the weather was warm and bright, but he just didn't want to go out to play. It also seemed that his father was now taking the day off work as well, as he was still secreted away in the hall, and the time at which he usually set off had long since passed.

As soon as he'd helped clear away the rest of the breakfast things, David retrieved his comic from the kitchen floor and went to sit by the front window in the lounge where he could peer through the net curtains for any signs of his Uncle Ronnie. At the same time, Len finally finished his mysterious telephone calls, and then shut himself in the kitchen with Meg for a confidential conference, from which the children were evidently excluded. As it happened, Lucy had already taken Eddie out into the back garden to play in the sunshine. Meanwhile, by the front room window, David maintained his quiet vigil, regularly glancing between the pages of his comic and the sloping roadway outside.

As David sat there, partly swathed in net curtain, he thought about the terrible facts his father had read from that newspaper article. At the same time, he also tried to remember every detail of the time he'd met Katie in Ronnie's dressing room at the BBC. He quickly came to the conclusion that the paper must have got it wrong, and that she couldn't possibly be 15. He'd seen her for himself, with his own eyes: those legs, her clothes, that slim figure; she was a woman alright! But then again, having thought about it at greater length, he reminded himself that many of his female school friends, even the ones who were in the same year as him at the Archbishop's School, had also developed a woman's shape. It was something he couldn't help but notice during school PE lessons, and the odd furtive glance at a tightly tee-shirted breast, or briefly exposed thigh were the only things that made this particular brand of enforced torture tolerable. If it turned out that she *was* only 15, then Ronnie couldn't possibly have known, he reasoned; after all, how old was he: 25, 26? Ideally, wouldn't he want to go out with a girl who was closer to his own age? It was not like he had no choice! They all seemed to like his uncle up at the BBC, and that girl who had shown David to his seat before *The Lulu Show*: she and Ronnie had seemed *very* friendly together! No, he concluded, if it *is* true, then Ronnie couldn't *possibly* have known. So, if that *was* the case, he wondered, what was Katie playing at? *Surely* she would have realised that if they found out how old she really was, then Ronnie would be the one in trouble, wouldn't she? He just couldn't understand it.

At 10:30, David was just about to read the 'Grimly Fiendish' page for the third time, when he noticed a taxi climbing the hill towards the house and then pulling up in front of it. He eagerly peered through one of the larger holes in the net curtain's floral pattern design, and then smiled. Sure enough, it was Ronnie who got out of the cab, clasping a holdall and what appeared to be a couple of suits, wrapped in plastic, draped over the same arm. He was wearing a long, figure-hugging Afghan coat, straight-legged jeans and a pair of circular shaped sunglasses. David waited until his uncle was almost at the front door before finally abandoning his post and rushing towards the hallway. Unfortunately, his father reacted with lightening speed, in response to the front door bell's harsh shrill, and managed to beat him to it. Len let his younger brother into the house without a word and a similarly silent Ronnie immediately dropped his holdall, suits and Afghan, in a pile at the foot of the stairs. David stood in the doorway leading from the lounge to the hall, waiting for the enthusiastic and demonstrative greeting the two brothers usually shared, but neither of them appeared to be about to embrace the other.

Ronnie removed his sunglasses, and then tucked them into the top pocket of his collarless shirt, before staring impassively at his older brother.

'Have you managed to sort it all out Len?' he asked, in an uncharacteristically grim tone.

'Yes I *have*!' came the stern-faced response. 'In fact, I'd better go over there *now* and wait, but when I get back, you and I need to *talk*!' he added, with an index finger extended in his brother's direction.

Ronnie nodded in resigned fashion and then threw a bunch of keys in Len's direction, which he pocketed prior to putting his jacket on. Looking grim he grabbed his holdall, scooped up his suits and then turned to go upstairs. He didn't seem to notice David at all, or if he had, he didn't acknowledge the fact.

Len paused at the threshold of the front door and looked back at his younger brother, who was already half way up the stairs.

'*Oh*, by the way Ronnie, you're staying in the caravan. *Sorry* mate, but there's no room at the inn!' he remarked, with a half-smile that gave away an underlying sympathy for his errant sibling.

Ronnie paused, sighed and stomped back down to the hall. David smiled as his uncle approached him; he was bound to greet him now, David thought optimistically. As his father had now disappeared outside, he held up his left hand for the secret 'scar brothers' ritual, but as his uncle was still not aware of him, it soon became a hollow, humiliating gesture. Staring fixedly ahead, Ronnie now crossed the threshold and, as he passed him quite unawares, David could see that his hair was greasy, his chin stubbly and, most shocking of all, those usually bright eyes were both dulled and puffy. What the hell had Katie done to him, pondered David, as the front door slammed; she seemed so nice!

*

Dave's solemn train of thought was suddenly disturbed by the sound and sight of a tourist punt slowly drifting past them on the river. And both the would-be gondolier and his passengers seemed more interested in studying them, sitting there against the trunk of the old beech tree, than they did the lovely Franciscan chapel whose gothic arches they were about to pass through. It saddened him to think that nowhere in Canterbury these days, not even this remote and secret place, seemed to be safe from the gawping eyes of tourists. Amanda-Jayne, who seemed equally affronted by the intrusion, quickly covered up her legs with her skirt and promptly pulled her gypsy blouse back up over both shoulders.

Dave worried that the special moment between them had now been lost; that all those questions he had just asked himself would drift away down stream, forever unanswered. But Amanda-Jayne could not have been aware that he had been pondering the future of his life, and possibly one to be spent with her, while they sat together in the shade of that ancient tree. All those thoughts had been in Dave's head alone, which was probably just as well, he decided, for it could be that the time was not yet right. It may even have been the case that the fates had intervened, in the form of those hated floating tourists, to slow down the pace a little. After all, the two of them had only met up again a few hours before. It then occurred to him that perhaps, Amanda-Jayne *had* been thinking along those lines as well; it could be that she *had* been speculating as to what he was feeling for her, and also wondering how she should be regarding him: as father, friend or potential lover. But then again, did she really know him beyond what she had heard from Julian? All that endless thought, the fantasising and speculation, was all very well, Dave mused, but it wasn't going to help them form a relationship of any sort. To achieve his dream, he knew he had to become more evolved, and get to know the third version of Amanda-Jayne who had now emerged: the all-encompassing person, the woman and the equal. He had to forget his perception of her solely as the daughter he never had, and, for the moment at least, put to one side those improper and premature primal desires he so obviously had for her.

The intermittent breeze had now dropped and through the warm still air, they could hear the sound of the cathedral clock striking three. Dave wondered why they'd not heard it before, and concluded that both of them had been too tied up in their own thoughts to have registered the sound on a conscious level.

Nonetheless, that well-loved campanological reverberation suddenly fired him with inspiration, and Dave quickly adjusted his position so that he was now facing his young companion.

'Did you know that *I* had a secret place of my own?' he asked, with eyebrows raised in eager anticipation of her response.

Amanda-Jayne did not disappoint him.

'Oh, *do* take me there now *please* David,' she responded keenly, and then immediately stood up to brush the dried grass from her skirt.

Her companion also got to his feet and smiled appreciatively. He found her child-like enthusiasm, and interest for everything, to be most endearing. It was certainly a refreshing change from Sheila's blind acceptance of God and nature, or the way her eyes glazed over when he talked about anything with a passion himself. Dave bent to retrieve his camera case and then slowly walked with her back down the ash path on the west bank of the Stour. After a few steps, Amanda-Jayne reached out and took his hand; it had cooled since he last held it, but that only made him more aware of the renewed and welcome physical contact between them. En route, he pointed out to her the old Tudor brick wall that ran parallel to the path, with its crumbling red bricks, and how the ancient chalk mortar had become an excellent growing medium for the red valerian and the few late wallflowers that were sprouting from it. Fortunately, she failed to notice that his familiarity with the old wall gave away the fact that he already knew her secret place, so wrapped up was she with the sight of those tumbling cascades of red, green and yellow along its entire length.

Before long, they once more found themselves standing on the little bridge that led back over the river. Dave paused, and stared down into the lazy waters below. Try to be more evolved, he told himself; whilst attempting to banish the previous well-ingrained image of Amanda-Jayne on the little drover's bridge, with all its inherent sexual associations. Having successfully managed that, with some difficulty, he also decided to finally disassociate himself from the surrogate father role by asking the teenager about her real father – a man who, according to Julian, was called Roger Roper – as she stood alongside him with her elbows also resting on the bridge's, tube-metal parapet.

As it turned out, Amanda-Jayne had only vague memories of a tall man, the frayed hems of his bell-bottomed jeans, and the smell of musky aftershave. He had been working for the local newspaper when he ran off with a young girl from the editorial office. His daughter was just three years' old at the time, and as a result, now had a great deal of difficulty separating out her actual memories of him from those later imposed on her from an understandably bitter and biased mother.

The pair walked slowly back through the darkened passage, to re-emerge in Stour Street, just as a crocodile of small school children passed by, no doubt, on their way to either the castle ruins or the nearby Heritage Museum. Amanda-Jayne went on to explain how devastated her mum had been following the split and subsequently, how she had spent some time in 'hospital' to get over it. She did not elaborate, but Dave assumed that this must have been a mental facility of some sort, rather than the usual sort of medical institution. Maternal grandparents had looked after the young Amanda-Jayne during this uncertain period, but it must have been a happy time, for she had many positive memories of those formative years with her Nanny and Grandpa Reynolds. When her mother finally came home, she seemed different somehow; she had lost that vital spark, and it soon became obvious to all that she had also developed a profound dislike for anyone who happened to be male. From the age of puberty onwards, all of Amanda-Jayne's friends had been viewed with suspicion and her boyfriends, whilst not exactly discouraged, were nevertheless strictly vetted. In defence of her harsh, interventionist actions, Mrs Roper claimed that she would instinctively know when the right one for her daughter came along. Dave derived no small amount of pleasure from the revelation that Amanda-Jayne's mother never liked Julian, but had tolerated him as a sign that she was now becoming less over protective and was allowing her daughter more leeway, more individual choice, as she got older. Amanda-Jayne had always looked out for her father's name against newspaper articles, but in recent years she had been finally able to show these to her mother, without fear of an adverse reaction. Both of them were surprised that he had actually made it to a national tabloid, even if it was only *The Sun*. Amanda-Jayne was also actively considering some sort of contact with the now well-known Roger Roper, and her mother had even obtained the newspaper's address and telephone number for her, as encouragement. So far, the seventeen-year-old had not acted on the information, but derived much comfort from it, and the knowledge that she could reach out to him whenever she felt the need, or sensed that the time was right.

As Amanda-Jayne and Dave turned out of Stour Street and rejoined the throbbing throng along Canterbury's main thoroughfare, they continued to hold hands. He reasoned to himself that this was no-less innocent looking, or more indicative of guilt, than when they'd earlier walked along with their arms linked. Therefore, it really didn't matter if anyone did see them. To take his mind off the many discovery scenarios he was running in his mind – all of which involved a well-meaning work colleague running to tell Sheila what he or she had observed that afternoon – Dave asked Amanda-Jayne to continue with the potted history of her recent past. Straightaway, his teenage companion admitted that she loved her mother, but for the best part of her life, it had always been just the two of them. After a brief, hesitant pause, she confessed to him the desire to strike out on her own, or even set up home with somebody, if the right person ever came along.

Dave's mind began to reel; he could very well see himself in the role as that person. Almost immediately, he began thinking along the same lines as he'd earlier done back in the Greyfriars gardens. He couldn't help but wonder if she was actually hinting that he might be that somebody. On the other hand, he had to concede that Amanda-Jayne could equally have been making it clear that she was still waiting for that special person. However, if he were free and not with Sheila anymore, Dave wondered if that would make any difference to her, and her attitude towards him. It was then that alarm bells began to ring, as he reminded himself that he'd been caught out like this once before. All too clearly, he remembered quitting his first marriage, in order to leave the way clear for Chloe, and then being left on his own when she pulled out of the deal at the last minute. Dave's own past had now brought him up short, and he realised that if he didn't learn from these experiences, he would go on making the same mistakes throughout life. But on the other hand, surely the circumstances were different now, he tried to convince himself; surely Amanda-Jayne was aware that things had not been going too well for him and Sheila. After all, the teenager had been there at Christmas when things were at their worst, and it must also be the case that Julian would have taken great delight in detailing to her all the rows that had taken place at home, either before or, to a lesser extent, since.

Dave bit his bottom lip as he thought quickly, and then decided to put the theory to the test.

'You may have noticed, *or* heard, that things haven't been…well, things haven't been too good at home this year,' he said, in quiet, confidential tones; but using words that surprised even himself in view of their frankness.

Amanda-Jayne seemed slightly embarrassed at first but then smiled, as if she was pleased that he felt able to share this fact with her.

'I *had* heard…I mean, I knew that all three of you were not hitting it off,' she confessed, somewhat gingerly, 'but I don't want you to think that I believed *everything* that Julian ever said to me about you… I mean, about the situation.'

'No, no…of *course* not!' he quickly responded, before giving her hand a reassuring squeeze.

It was obvious to Dave that she was having difficulty finding the right words; being both embarrassed and yet pleased that he had felt confident enough to involve her. However, rather than interrupt, he decided to let her continue to speak on the subject, when she was ready, and express an honest opinion; to say what she felt in her heart. Besides which, he realised that if he got started on the subject of Sheila, his desire to 'lay it on a bit thick' might become overwhelming, even allowing for their so-called cease-fire; the current pause in hostilities between them. He might be tempted to paint the situation even blacker than it actually was, in order for Amanda-Jayne to rush into his arms in sympathy and then agree to give him all the things that he didn't currently possess in his marriage, and so much more. Dave smiled to himself at that last rather fanciful idea of his, although for a while he had to fight the temptation not to put it into practise.

Once they were clear of the crowded and noisy High Street and had turned into the more peaceful Guildhall Street, Amanda-Jayne felt able to continue with what she was saying.

'I was a rather naïve and unworldly fourteen-year-old when I first went out with Julian, and believed everything he told me! But as I gradually got to know Sheila and particularly *you* David, I realised that much of what Julian had said concerning you was either patently untrue or else grossly exaggerated,' she confessed, in both calm and measured terms.

Dave was overjoyed at what he had just heard.

'Oh Amanda-Jayne, I can't *tell* you what it means to me to have you *say* that; it really *hasn't* been easy for me over these last three and a bit years!' he exclaimed, finally feeling a long-overdue sense of vindication.

'I'm sure *that's* true,' she said, with a sweet smile in his direction. 'You see, as I got older, I realised there was a special tension between you and Julian, and that anything he said to me about his *mother's new husband*, had to be viewed in that context.'

'*Wow*; I…I have to admit, I'm very impressed by your maturity *and* your insight, concerning our…umm, our somewhat difficult family,' commented a very pleased Dave, and with the merest hint of smugness, especially as he had come out of it rather well in her estimation.

'Mind you, that cuts *both* ways, you know!' she was quick to add; her words accompanied by a knowing smile. 'If *you* had said anything unkind about Julian to me, I would have treated it the same way!'

Dave was slightly taken aback by her comment, but he couldn't help but admire her even-handedness.

Amanda-Jayne must have seen or sensed his reaction, and couldn't help but giggle.

'I *know* it's hard for you to see, especially given the circumstances,' she remarked, with a maturity that belied her tender age, ' ... but Julian really *isn't* a bad bloke, and when he grows up a bit, *and* gets away from Sheila, he'll pretty soon realise that *you* are a very nice bloke too!' She concluded her statement by giving him a peck on the cheek.

As they resumed walking, Dave discreetly looked both to his left and right in order to see if there was anyone in their immediately vicinity whom he recognised, and who might have witnessed the kiss. Fortunately, he could see no faces he knew; nor did there appear to be any gawping tourists or staring shoppers who considered Amanda-Jayne's public gesture of affection to be the least bit noteworthy. Perhaps they had judged them as father and daughter, and thought no more about it, pondered Dave. However, in spite of his appreciation for the wonderful person this third version of Amanda-Jayne was turning out to be, it was still quite an effort for him to put to one side his sexual feelings for her; feelings that he knew could reassert themselves with a vengeance, given the right prompting, or stimulus. From now on though, he recognised that he had to be careful; he had to strive to be more evolved, and more mature, just like Amanda-Jayne herself. With that in mind, Dave refocused his thoughts and pondered on what she had last said to him. The notion of Julian *ever* realising he was a nice bloke was a hard one to believe, but then his lovely companion had also said that Julian himself was really a good person and, despite his reservations, Dave knew that he now really valued her judgement. She seemed to be one of those genuinely good, decent people, just like his Grandad Darwin in fact, who were a living reaffirmation of the basic goodness of man; if not an actual confirmation of the existence of God. So, if she thought that one day, he and Julian would bury the hatchet, then it might just happen.

The thought of God, reminded Dave of where he was taking her, and as they meandered up the narrow Sun Street, with its overhanging buildings on either side, he wondered if she had yet guessed their destination. They would soon be there too, but he didn't want to give her any indication that this might be the case. Therefore, in order to draw out the suspense, he once more engaged her in some diverting conversation.

'So why *did* you and Julian split up?' he asked, finally feeling bold enough to pose the question.

Amanda-Jayne didn't need to think before replying.

'To be honest with you, it had a *lot* to do with what I was saying earlier,' came the quick, if not somewhat cryptic response.

'Do you mean: our not getting *on* together?' Dave asked, eager for clarification.

His straight-faced companion nodded her head.

'Yes; Julian kept running you down, and I kept saying that you were a decent bloke…and in the end, he got fed up with hearing it,' she admitted, with a stoical chuckle at the end.

Dave's mind began to race again as he analysed what she had just revealed. Now he knew what his young companion had meant when she'd said that Julian needed to grow up a bit. Strangely enough though, he derived no sense of satisfaction from the knowledge that it was Julian who had ended the relationship, because the lad's ex-girlfriend was continuing to defend him. Given Amanda-Jayne's benevolent influence, Dave was even beginning to wonder if he could have handled things a bit better with Julian himself.

At the top of Sun Street, the vista opened out into the Buttermarket, with its collage of buskers, tourists, drinkers, beggars and hapless locals, trying in vain to get through the throng. Without saying a word, Dave steered Amanda-Jayne towards Christchurch Gate and then through its vaulted arch, complete with loftily placed stone boss depicting a Tudor rose. He was pleased to see that the crowds were thinner in the south precinct of the Cathedral, and was even more delighted to discover that there were fewer still people inside the tall perpendicular nave.

Dave pondered on the curious fact that almost without exception, anyone who came into the nave for the first time, invariably looked up and then walked around with their heads thus tilted. For most visitors though, this was more likely to be an appreciation of the fourteenth century gothic architecture, than it was a glance towards heaven. It was odd though, for whatever their motivation, very few people ever bumped into each other, or worse still, collided with one of the substantial perpendicular pillars that supported the high fan vaulting.

Amanda-Jayne let his hand go and, true to form, slowly walked around as she continued to look up in wonder. However, the seventeen-year-old soon reminded him that she was no stranger to Canterbury cathedral.

'I sang here in a performance of the Mozart C-minor Mass last month,' she said, averting her vault-ward gaze to look over at Dave.

'Of *course*!' he responded, as they exchanged smiles. 'I wish *I'd* been here to see it; especially with you singing one of the solo parts!'

Once more, the couple linked hands, and then proceeded along the nave's north aisle in the direction of the main crossing: the place where the principle transepts diverged, and the cathedral choir began. En route, they both regularly looked upwards, and neither of them bumped into anyone, or anything. Having reached that massive internal space beneath the central Bell Harry tower, Dave led the way up the main flight of stone steps, before turning left and then descending another flight into the north-west transept. In this venerated corner of the cathedral, Protestants and Catholics alike still congregated – some out of reverence, others from morbid curiosity – to see the place where Archbishop Thomas Becket had been so famously murdered by the four knights of Henry II. That was why this particular area had been known as the Martyrdom transept for many centuries.

With only a casual glance towards the stunning and recently restored Altar of the Sword's Point, Dave led his mystified, yet captivated young companion down a further flight of steps and into the darkness of the western crypt. Its coolness was in marked contrast to the balmy heat outside, and the familiar smell of aged stone was as welcoming to Dave as the aroma of frying bacon on a cold winter's morning, or perhaps, that of Rayburn-baked potatoes on fondly remembered Friday evenings. Luckily, few other people were with them in that semi-subterranean sanctuary.

With eyes that were wide with wonder, Amanda-Jayne approached an old tomb that was situated in one of the crypt's many dark recesses. As the teenager passed slowly by it, Dave watched in fascination as she ran her index finger along the carved stone facial features of the long dead archbishop. The ravages of time were all too evident in that effigy, exemplified by the man's missing nose; no doubt a victim of parliamentary troops, who had used the crypt as a stable for their horses, and the aged tombs therein, for target practise. This, together with the stone carving's sunken cheeks – in all likelihood, worn away by the countless other probing fingers of many pilgrims and tourists over the centuries – had resulted in a cadaverous appearance: dry skin stretched over brittle bone, which probably more closely resembled the remains of the holy man, secured in the sarcophagus beneath, than it did the benevolent features of the kindly priest it had originally attempted to depict in life.

The brief cry of a young child, echoed round the cavernous expanse of the crypt, as a family left by the southern steps. Amanda-Jayne and Dave were now completely alone. Having held hands yet again, they walked on a few more steps, before proceeding past the supposed secret burial place of the blessed Saint Thomas' bones. That unmarked slab in the floor was guarded by a red-hued sanctuary lamp that shone nearby. This was a subtle clue for those who recognised its significance, red being the symbolic colour of martyrdom.

Now acutely aware of every breath he took, Dave went on a few more steps and then opened the wooden half door of the Chapel of the Holy Innocents on the left. Standing slightly to one side, he allowed Amanda-Jayne to walk past him and be the first one to enter into his inner sanctuary. Awestruck, she cast her eyes about and, as they gradually became accustomed to the low light level available, Dave began to point out the chapel's special features: the elaborately carved twelfth century capitals, the tiny altar, with its unlit candle and, in between the massive round columns, the short row of rudimentary wooden chairs facing it. Without a word, the teenager sat down next to him, silent and elegantly upright, and then slowly looked about her as she absorbed her surroundings in more detail.

Dave reached out and encircled his fingers around the small, cool hand that was placed flat against her skirt-draped upper thigh.

'This is *my* secret place,' he announced in a hushed voice, appropriate to the tangible numinousness that seemed to be exuding from both Amanda-Jayne and the chapel in equal measures. Dave could clearly see that her face was transfixed with child-like awe and, at the same time, he could sense that the special indefinable vibe he always felt from this place, was now being fully experienced by her as well.

It seemed like an age before she finally looked in his direction again.

'Do you usually come here on your own?' she, at last, asked, in a low-pitched half-whisper.

'Yes…*sometimes* I do,' responded Dave, nodding gently, 'but I usually prefer the company of a like-minded friend.'

'*Oh?*' Amanda-Jayne said, with a mixture of curiosity and fascination.

In reply, he felt it appropriate to tell her about Tim: their friendship, the day trips out together and his friend's personal problems. Amanda-Jayne listened to him in attentive silence, until his hushed monologue was interrupted by the verger who, dressed as he was in dark robes, almost seemed to seep out from the aged stonework. As was his usual routine for God knows how many years – and Dave understood and respected routine – the verger had come into the Chapel of the Holy Innocents, to light the candle every day at four o'clock. Quite regularly, he came in to find Dave and Tim sitting there in quiet debate. Today, the man's double take at one of them in the company of a young woman for a change, made Dave smile.

Having lit the amber candle, the verger left them and once more, melted away into the ancient fabric, leaving only echoing footfalls that diminished with each step. Dave watched the candle flame strengthen in both height and intensity, as it bit into the wax-encrusted wick. He then looked back at Amanda-Jayne who, he was surprised to discover, now had tears rolling down her cheeks. In immediate response, Dave slid off his chair and dropped to his knees, in order to face her with his entire body. He then reached out to hold both of her hands in his, as her body gently shook with intermittent sobs. Acting on instinctive impulse, as opposed to some pre-ordained game plan, Dave moved his face closer to hers, so much so that he could see the candle flame reflected in the watery surfaces of her eyes.

In spite of her appearing to be upset, a broad smile soon broke across the young woman's face.

'Oh *David*, this is a wonderful place, I can feel…*everything*!' she said, gripping tightly on to both his hands.

Dave took in a deep but tremulous lung full of the numinescent air.

'I love you Amanda-Jayne,' he gulped, before a surge of emotion got the better of him.

'Oh I love you *too* David,' she responded; her brow furrowed with the intensity of her words.

Leaning forward still further, he kissed her gently, but warmly, on the lips in the English manner. It felt like he had been kissing those soft, pliant lips all his life. Just as the kiss ended, a warm, moist tear transferred itself from her cheek to his, but he made no attempt the brush the precious salty droplet away. Bewildered, Dave slowly returned to his seat, but still held on to one of her, by now, very warm hands. After he had settled, she leant over and put her head on his shoulder, and a small wet patch of tears quickly formed on his shirt as a result. As they sat there together, embraced by the rarefied religious ambience, neither of them felt the need to say anything to the other; in any case, there was nothing left that could either be said, or that needed to be said.

As they finally left the tiny chapel in silence, the notes from the base pipes of the organ in the choir above, vibrated rather than sounded in the air around them. Dave suddenly seemed to be feeling a heightened awareness in all his senses; it was as if everything he currently experienced was on an enhanced level. Looking over at Amanda-Jayne, he wondered if she was also feeling that same sense of spiritual awareness, but did not want to break the spell by asking her lest she confess to not having the same sensation.

In spite of his heightened senses, Dave had little memory of leaving the Cathedral, and then proceeding back along the main street in silence with his young partner. Nor could he recall walking round the Westgate Towers and passing into the city suburb of St. Dunstan's where she lived. However, instinct had compelled him to cease holding her hand as they approached this end of town.

Without making any physical gesture of either fondness or farewell, Dave left Amanda-Jayne at the junction of her road.

'See you soon', he said, half exclaiming, half questioning, as he struggled with another breaking wave of emotion.

Having swallowed hard, she nodded in reply, smiled and then walked away; turning briefly just the once to wave.

It was a very different Dave who made his way to Telecom House car park, sometimes running, sometimes walking. He felt thrilled; even exhilarated, and full of a power and confidence that he'd not experienced since the relationship with Chloe. It soon became clear to him that the ease with which he was able to cope with that chance meeting with his ex-lover, may have been due to the nascent feelings that were already beginning to form for Amanda-Jayne. Having reached Castle Street, he continued to run, quite un-puffed. Today though, his running was a physical manifestation of his joy, and not the fear that he might be late, or

Sheila, on time for once. This new Dave was suddenly aware that he no longer had anything to fear at home. From now on, he vowed that he would confront Julian himself, whenever appropriate. Not only that, but he would also demand loyalty from his wife, should she ever dare to put her work or son before him and his needs again. If they didn't like the new Dave, this confident and happy Dave, then that was too bad, he decided! Sheila and Julian could jolly well go off and resume the close conspiratorial family life they'd enjoyed before he came along and, as it turned out, had never lost! Nor would he have any worry about being left on his own for too long if they did, for Amanda-Jayne loved him; she actually loved him. That third version of this blessed creature with whom he had been reunited today: the woman, the person, whose love he returned with all his essence; she was all that mattered now. The daughter he once knew had now grown up; she had left home and gone. The young seductress; that now remote figure in those clandestine photographs: she had been utterly exorcised. However, before his teenage temptress fantasy was totally banished, he cut out his sexual desires from that soon to be redundant version of Amanda-Jayne and pasted them onto his feelings for that newly-formed third version: the real Amanda-Jayne, who loved him, warts and all. And now that his love was reciprocated, there could be no more doubts or fears about the future and, with any luck, he could avoid all that pain, humiliation and condemnation that poor old Ronnie had suffered. He reasoned that people would see how much in love they both were, to overcome any reservations about their age difference.

Dave arrived in the car park, at the same time as his wife. They were both exactly ten minutes late. With uncharacteristic cheeriness, he waved at her as they both approached the car from opposite ends of the tarmac expanse.

Sheila was mystified, rather than pleased at his up-tempo mood.

'*You* obviously had a very enjoyable time with Tim this afternoon!' she commented, feeling slightly irritated by his happy demeanour, as she yanked the seatbelt round her stout little body.

'Yep ... good old Tim!' beamed Dave in response, as he pushed his head back on the seat rest.

His wife frowned as she inserted and then turned the ignition key. She then thought for a moment, smiled and then turned to him with a wicked-looking squint.

'*Julian's* coming home at the weekend!' announced Sheila haughtily, in an obvious attempt to dampen his spirits; to 'piss on his fire' as it were.

'Oh *good*; it'll be nice to see the old chap again!' was Dave's unexpected and positive Grandad Darwin-like response, as he effectively pissed on the pisser.

As a result of his unexpected positive reaction to the news, Sheila nearly steered the car into one of the sturdy brick gateposts that flanked the entrance to Telecom House car park.

Throughout the stony silent journey home, Dave recalled that his beloved Amanda-Jayne had earlier asserted that Julian was really a good bloke, and he quickly decided that the coming weekend would be an ideal opportunity to test the theory. For his own peace of mind, he was determined to make a special effort to get on with his wife's son from the moment he arrived back from Dover and deposited his laundry bag in the hall.

As soon as they got back home, Dave hurried inside and, straightaway, strode up to the spare room. Once there, he pushed the door to, and then fumbled on the shelf for his childhood copy of *What To Look For In Summer*: the one with the intact dust jacket. Inside he found those two once deeply cherished photographs of a now exorcised version of his precious Amanda-Jayne. Without a second thought, he tore each picture into four, and then, after two unsuccessful attempts, succeeded in flushing all the pieces down the loo.

Helping Hands

From the very moment he arrived, Dave took up position beneath the shady canopy of the beech tree, just in front of the little medieval chapel. From this vantage point, he could see back down the ash path, along which he had just walked, all the way to the little access bridge that spanned the River Stour. Excited, he looked down at his watch: it was 12:50. He was ten minutes early, but then he'd planned it that way. Although he always liked to be early for appointments, the reason for this particular policy went beyond the usual margin of error he always allowed himself. Put simply, Amanda-Jayne always got there on time, and he loved to watch her arrive. It just wouldn't have been the same if they both arrived at their secret meeting place together, or if she ever managed to get there first.

Dave was so grateful to his best friend Tim for making these clandestine meetings possible. Not that the poor chap actually took an active role in the proceedings. No, Tim merely provided the excuse, to both Sheila and Telecom, for these lovely long summer afternoons that Dave was regularly taking off work. Saying that you were meeting an old friend for a drink was far less controversial than admitting you were meeting your seventeen-year-old girlfriend for an intimate afternoon together. In fact, as far as the real Tim was concerned, Dave was actually seeing far less of him these days. His friend's period of long-term sick leave had continued well into the summer, and it was becoming increasingly harder to get hold of him on the telephone. The really sad thing was that Dave was also making less of an effort to reach Tim, both physically and intellectually, because he was so diverted by this new relationship with the beautiful Amanda-Jayne. As the school summer holidays were still in full swing, he was currently meeting her two, and sometimes three times a week. Dave had always loved the Greyfriars gardens and now they had taken on an extra special meaning. This lovely oasis of solitude had long since been her secret place, but now it belonged to both of them. Even on the odd occasion when it was raining, there was always the broad leafy canopy of the old beech tree to shelter under.

His watch now showed five minutes to the hour, and a thrill of excitement coursed through his entire body. It wouldn't be long now, he told himself, as he imagined her hurrying along the main street towards the narrow Stour Street turning.

Right from the very beginning of their relationship, they had both agreed it was important that they should meet well away from the prying eyes of others. Early on, Amanda-Jayne had voiced her opinion that nobody else would understand their unique relationship; no one else could appreciate their *special* love. Other people would be only too keen to jump to the conclusion that a love between an older man and a young girl was somehow exploitative, or even sordid. As far as she was concerned, it was nothing of the sort, but she had to concede that they lived in a world where other folk always liked to see things at their very worst. Certainly, they were intimate, even passionate together, but there was no actual penetrative sex; their relationship was far too cerebral for that. From Dave's point of view, he was in full agreement that neither Sheila nor his work colleagues would 'understand' their relationship; it went without saying. Indeed, sometimes he couldn't understand it himself, or rather; he couldn't fathom his own role in the intimate arrangement. However, as time went on, Dave became aware that it was an ever-increasing struggle for him to stay 'evolved' and, in Amanda-Jayne's words, to keep things 'cerebral'.

He glanced at his watch again: the time was exactly one o'clock. It was as he lifted up his head, and then looked back along the ash path, that he saw her. There she was, his beloved Amanda-Jayne, crossing the little river bridge, fifty or so yards away downstream. The very instant she turned on to the path, she could see him waiting there by the tree, and proceeded to wave with wild enthusiasm. Following the usual routine, he waved back and as soon as he'd done so, Amanda-Jayne began to run towards him. This was the moment he looked forward to the most; this was why he always made sure he arrived at Greyfriars gardens before her. Dave could not express in words the sheer joy he felt, in knowing that this beautiful young girl wanted to be with him so much, that she ran so as not to waste the precious seconds better spent in his company. But he also delighted in actually seeing her run towards him: her brightly smiling face, the way her hair swished to and fro and that special feminine way she ran, with arms out to the side.

When Amanda-Jayne was only a few feet away, she called out his name as usual: '*David*, oh my *David*!'

The first time this had happened, it put him in mind of the finale to the film, *The Railway Children*, with Jenny Agutter running towards her father, in slow motion, on that smoke choked platform. It was a Freudian image he did not care to analyse too deeply and, on each occasion, he tried to put it out of his mind.

There next came another longed for moment: that first physical contact between the two of them as she literally flung herself at him. As always, Amanda-Jayne put her arms around his neck, whilst he held her round the waist. They would normally hold this tight embrace for about five minutes, with Amanda-Jayne on tiptoe and, on this particular occasion, they saw no reason to change the routine. Thus entwined, Dave could feel not only her pounding heartbeat, but also the exquisite pressure of her chest gently rising and falling. Both were physical consequences of her fifty yard dash, and became yet another reason why he wanted to arrive there first.

'Oh David, it's so lovely to *see* you again; to *hold* you again!' she panted; her lips brushing the skin of his neck as she spoke, her warm breath stimulating the hair follicles.

'I've missed you *too* my darling sweetheart,' Dave responded, slowly and gently stroking the sides of her body as she clung to him. He loved to carefully chart the curve of her waist inwards, and then outwards again, as he gradually moved his hand downwards, and then reversed the process.

Amanda-Jayne responded as ever by quietly and contentedly purring like a cat in his ear; her lips once more making intermittent and exciting contact with his sensitive skin.

Despite the obvious pleasure that Dave was experiencing, and evidently giving, in the arms of his young partner, he was also aware of the fact that this was a prime example of the problem he was having with the understanding of their relationship. Her reaction to his caresses: was it a sexual response or merely a platonic appreciation of his gentle touch? He certainly never did anything overtly sexual and always carefully avoided the more blatantly obvious erogenous zones. Unfortunately though, for him, his physical response to her close and intimate presence was all too predictable. Every time it happened, Dave wondered to himself, if Amanda-Jayne noticed that he had an erection. If so, then she made no indication of the fact and continued to press her body into his as they embraced. Then again, he was forced to speculate that, perhaps, she was actually flattered at the reaction she had so obviously caused in him. There were some occasions when it was almost like she was encouraging a sexual response from him. The previous Monday afternoon was a rather good example of this ambiguity.

It had been a hot day and they had arranged to meet at the Greyfriars gardens as normal. Amanda-Jayne, who was wearing a figure-hugging three quarter length dress, held him in the usual tight embrace as they greeted each other. Dave, who was in shorts and tee shirt, had remarked at the strength of the sun and how welcome the cool of the shade was under that familiar copper beech. Amanda-Jayne had agreed, and whispered that she'd decided it was too hot even for any underwear. As Dave gently stroked the contours of her sides: her ribs, her waist and then her hips, the warm smoothness of the teenager's skin, beneath that thin dress, was broken by neither strap nor elastic. He couldn't help but wonder whether she was deliberately trying to be provocative, or was simply confiding in someone she trusted and felt close to. And assuming that the sexual provocation was real, was it just a tease, or did she hope that he would act on the information? Dave had considered if he should, perhaps, test the water. However, he was all too aware that these were dangerously deep waters; just like those rivers or streams that were deceptively silent, still and dark green in hue.

Just as Dave's mind came back to the present, Amanda-Jayne kissed him briefly on the lips, and then as she finally pulled away from him, they went to sit against the trunk of that faithful beech. Almost straightaway, she reached for his hand and held it tightly.

'How's your grandad?' she asked with a genuine concern, implicit in both the tone and pitch of her voice.

As Dave struggled to formulate an appropriate response, his head fell forward, as if the weight of all those sad thoughts that were now rushing into his brain were too heavy to support.

Seeing his distress, Amanda-Jayne quickly adjusted her position to kneel on the ground in front of him. She then gently placed her now freed hand under her companion's chin and slowly lifted his head until their eyes met.

'*Tell* me David,' she whispered at close quarters, her eyes seemingly bigger and brighter than ever.

With his head thus supported, Dave met her plaintive stare.

'I...I have to confess ... I haven't been over there to *see* them for about a month!' he admitted shamefully, before briefly raising his eyebrows in resigned fashion. 'But I have been keeping in touch with my grandparents by telephone; almost every *day* I ring them! ... It's just that I've been so *busy* recently, what with...'

'Shush, it's *alright* David,' she said quickly, with soft, soothing reassurance. 'Just tell me how your Grandad Darwin's doing, okay?'

Dave grinned broadly and nodded in acquiescence, allowing Amanda-Jayne to settle back against the tree trunk next to him, and hear the latest report concerning the health of a man she'd never met, but through her intimate companion, had grown to care for very much. For his part, Dave had every intention of telling her everything, except that is, for the main reason why he'd not been over to Beltinge recently. The truth of the matter was that any free time he had, was now spent in the company of his teenage lover-of-sorts, and he didn't want her to feel guilty by confessing to the fact. Fortunately though, he now had an opportunity to put that right; to make it up to his grandparents, and this was something he could now happily report to her.

Only the previous evening, Dave had received a flustered call from Nanna Darwin, to say that Grandad was fretting about the state of his beloved garden.

She reported that, in the last three weeks or so, the old boy had begun to feel very tired and weak; preferring to while away the hours in the art room, working on his Kentish churches project. However, a few days ago, he had wandered outside for a breath of fresh air, and was soon registering distress at how quickly everything had become overgrown. Apparently, it was all Nanna could do to stop him from attempting to tackle the backlog himself, right there and then. Nanna Darwin's telephone call was effectively a cry for help. She had wondered if he, Len and perhaps Ed, could come over sometime at the weekend and tidy up the garden, or else she feared that Grandad – being the stubborn old devil he was would have a go at it on his own, and push himself too hard. Dave had then called his parents and, following lengthy negotiations, had managed finally to co-opt his father's help. He had secured the deal by agreeing to pick his dad up at 09:30 on the Saturday morning. Unfortunately, Ed could not be reached; he was away with some university mates dry-stone walling in Yorkshire, now that his exams were finally over.

Dave and Amanda-Jayne spent the rest of the afternoon together in the cool shade of the tree's canopy and mostly watching the water of the River Stour slowly slipping by them. This time, no tourist punts sullied the peaceful scene, and neither of them objected to the mallards that drifted by, singly or in pairs; all completely unaware of the human presence on the riverbank above them.

At some point during the contented calm of the afternoon, Amanda-Jayne asked Dave about when he was a boy, explaining that she was keen to find out his childhood likes and dislikes; his hobbies and influences, or anything that made him the person he was today. Inevitably, it wasn't long before the conversation got round to Rothermead Farm and, of course, back to Grandad Darwin. Dave also desperately wanted to talk about Uncle Ronnie, another major figure of his formative years, but something held him back. In all probability, this was owing to their mutual taste for teenage girlfriends. The story of poor Ronnie's downfall and the involvement of young Katie would surely be enough to send Amanda-Jayne running back down the ash path, and out of his life forever. As it happened, she seemed to be particularly interested in Grandad Darwin and asked many questions about him; questions that showed a remarkable perceptiveness and awareness of his importance in Dave's life, both past and present. He was both gratified and extremely flattered when she remarked on how much his grandad sounded like him. In fact, he told her that he did not deserve such high praise, and genuinely meant it, as had she.

The conversation having died down once more, they were perfectly happy just to be in each other's company and resume watching the languid river slip by, and listening to the ethereal strains of the cathedral clock as it chimed out each quarter-hour. It was Amanda-Jayne who first noticed the large clumps of vegetation that had begun to drift past them on the surface of the water. Dave thought that someone further up-stream must be scything the banks of their excess summer growth, and this possibility led Amanda-Jayne to wonder who that person may be, and what he might look like. They then both speculated how far back upstream the riverbank management was being carried out and also how long it had taken the severed clumps of weed to reach them in the Greyfriars gardens.

Later on, whilst Amanda-Jayne lazily leant against his chest, Dave mused on the notion that by the time it got dark, those green clumps of vegetation would be lapping around on the tides of the English Channel. He stared at the Stour with unfocused eyes and, remembering those earlier thoughts about his past and his grandfather, dared to vocalise a notion that had just occurred to him.

'D'you know my love: the course of a river, from its source to the sea, *well*... it's rather like a man's life, isn't it!' he said; his words being picked up by her as vibrations through his chest.

Straightaway, Amanda-Jayne lifted her head and smiled up at him.

'*That's* an interesting thought, David ... I'm very impressed!' she responded, with a slow, positive nod, whilst teasing out her flattened hair.

However, Dave soon seemed a little embarrassed by his statement.

'Come to think of it, *surely* much wiser men than me would have already come up with *that* one before; probably *years* ago!' he dismissed, with a resigned chuckle.

'Maybe, but it's a nice analogy in *any* case ... and it *sounded* nice coming from you!' she countered, before settling her head down on his chest once more.

What Amanda-Jayne hadn't picked up on was that it had been his Grandad Darwin's precious life he'd had in mind. For Dave, it was hard to accept that, just like those clumps of vegetation, the old boy would soon be coming to the end of his journey. But was there anything else beyond that seemingly final stage? For the weed, once it had reached the river's estuary, there was the vast expanse of the Channel. But what was there waiting for us, if anything? That was the fundamental question, he wondered, with an uncomfortable feeling of deja vu. Yet again, he had arrived at that same old unresolved struggle about religion: the logic of man's mere mortality, versus the more fanciful yet comforting notion of our immortality. Grandad Darwin's impending death had now made the resolution of that question more important than ever, and yet he was truly frightened about what the answer might be, especially if Tim's logical theory of nothingness turned out to be true. It then occurred to him that he had an opportunity to elicit a fresh new opinion on the subject in the form of his beloved Amanda-Jayne. There and then, he decided to confide in her about his religious fears, concerns and doubts. He did so, and she listened with patience as he poured out his heart to her, covering all the aspects that had comprised his many previous conversations with Tim on the subject.

As Dave paused to gather his thoughts, his caring confidante became aware of the cathedral clock chiming the three-quarter hour.

'Would you prefer it if we went to *your* old secret place to talk about this further?' she suggested thoughtfully, once again lifting her head up from his chest.

'No, here's *fine* thanks my love,' he replied, giving her a grateful smile, 'here with *you*!' Dave was happy that the Greyfriars gardens had the right atmosphere for such an intense religious conversation. True, the cathedral was inspiring, glorious, thought provoking and serene; it had all those elements that contributed to the special vibe he had always felt there, especially in the tiny Chapel of the Holy Innocents. But was that the essence of God or merely a sense of history? Perhaps a new venue for discussing religion was indeed necessary; a place where his love for the building wouldn't get in the way of his search for God.

Amanda-Jayne altered her position so that she was now sitting cross-legged on the grass directly in front of him, her legs exposed to the sun, and the material of her long skirt gathered up in front of her crotch.

'*So*, what is the single biggest concern you have regarding religion?' she asked, leaning forward

Dave didn't know whether to be more taken aback at the perceptiveness of her question, or at the sight of her lovely young, smooth legs. He couldn't help but remember her confession from last Monday concerning the lack of underwear, and wondered to himself if it might also be the case today.

Amanda-Jayne interpreted his hesitation as a sudden attack of reticence, and quickly sought to justify her question.

'I only ask because… well, you were earlier expressing so *much*, all at once; I just thought it might help if you slowed down and took one thing at a time!' She paused to giggle. 'After *all*, I wouldn't want you to short-circuit yourself!'

Quickly putting to one side all thoughts of his girlfriend's panties, or lack of them, Dave smiled reassuringly.

'*No*, no, that's alright, I…err, I just needed to think about the question for a bit, *that's* all,' he declared, knowing full well that if he hadn't been so distracted, there would have been no problem answering her question without hesitation.

'I suppose my biggest concern, or rather, I should say *fear*, is that a good, kind and selfless man like Grandad Darwin, who's the very embodiment of a good Christian as far as *I'm* concerned, might…might just *cease to exist* at the end of his life; be snuffed out with nothing left other than an urn full of ashes.'

Amanda-Jayne smiled benevolently and extended out her right hand for him to take, which he did.

'But we have a *soul,* David ... a spirit that lives on ...a part of us that *never* dies,' she said, with an air of absolute certainty. 'Leaving Christianity to one side for the moment, there are *billions* of people all over the world, from all the different religions, who believe in a human soul. As far as I'm concerned, they can't *all* be wrong!' She shuffled forward and then kissed him tenderly on the lips. 'Take it one stage at a time, my love. Once you accept the existence of our eternal spirit, once you believe in *that*, then the rest might just slot into place for you; it did for *me*!'

Almost immediately, he felt as if her sweet breath had blown away the fog that had been obscuring his path to the truth in this matter. Suddenly, agnosticism was yesterday's word. Dave pushed himself away from the tree trunk and hugged his youthful saviour tightly. As they embraced, he wondered how could someone so young, be so wise. Or rather, was it that he had been so bogged down with logic, information, cynicism and all the other baggage he'd picked up over the years, that he could not see the simple truth? Perhaps then, she was right: he *had* short-circuited himself; perhaps he had bypassed the basics every time he tried to over-analyse the problem. Was it Amanda-Jayne's youthful idealism that made her see it all so clearly? At the end of the day though, it didn't matter; she had really helped him, and he wanted to tell her as much.

'Oh, *thank* you my darling,' he whispered, quietly but fervently in her ear, at very close quarters.

In response, Amanda-Jayne gently pulled away from him and stared into his face.

'Did I *really* help?' she asked, with a facial expression that indicated she truly had no idea whether or not her words had made a difference.

Dave exhaled loudly as his brows furrowed.

'Oh my darling, I can't *tell* you how much!' he said before reaching up to stroke her left cheek. 'I love you *so* much; *promise* me that you'll always be there.'

She seized his caressing hand and encircled hers around it. 'David ... I promise that the *special* love I have for you will *always* be part of me!' she responded, with an accompanying smile.

Having let go his hand, she slowly got to her feet, and then smoothed down her crumpled skirt. A disappointed Dave rightly assumed that this was the signal that she must go, and he suddenly experienced a massive feeling of anti-climax. He discreetly glanced at his watch as she picked pieces of grass from her clothing, and was amazed to see that it was bang on half past three: the time she always departed. But then he began to wonder: how did she know that? The cathedral clock hadn't yet struck the half-hour as far as he was aware. Had she been sneakily studying her own watch all the while? Was it that she possessed some sort of amazingly accurate internal body clock? Whatever the reason, Dave knew that she could always be trusted to do the right thing, whereas he could have quite easily stayed there with her, arm-in-arm, until it got dark, irrespective of the consequences; that is, until they had to be faced.

As Dave stood up to join her, Amanda-Jayne kissed him one last time, and then walked back down the ash path to the little bridge over the river. Before crossing it completely, she paused to wave, and also to blow him a kiss. And then, as soon as he had responded in kind, she turned to go and within seconds, was completely out of sight. Dave waited for a few more lonely minutes, as was the arrangement, and then he too walked back down the path to the bridge. Gripping on to its tubular steel handrail, he paused to watch the water flow beneath him and pondered on what he and Amanda-Jayne had talked about that afternoon. If a river really was like a man's life, then he now recognised that it didn't end at the estuary that was corporeal death, but flowed into some sort of spiritual sea. Other rivers and streams also fed into that special sea. The sea then joined with others to form vast oceans that stretched round the world and continued to flow on a seemingly endless journey forward. That was a definition of eternity that Dave could understand and accept for the first time in his life. Although he himself had come up with that analogy, it was Amanda-Jayne who had provided him with that last vital missing element: that of man's certain soul. She had given him a rare gift that afternoon; she had opened the door for him on to a new level of spiritual understanding. This was something he knew he must share with Tim, if only he could reach him, in both senses of the word. If anyone needed some peace of mind, then it was his poor friend whose life was currently falling apart.

From the Greyfriars gardens, Dave walked the two and a half mile journey home, but not before stopping off at the Telecom House car park to leave a hastily scribbled note under the windscreen wiper of their car. Today, he did not want to wait for a lift from Sheila. After all, he told himself it was a wonderful day for walking; in fact, it was a wonderful day to be alive.

As Dave would be in Beltinge all day with his grandparents, and Julian not home at all that weekend, Sheila had duly organised a whole Saturday's worth of overtime for herself. Consequently, Dave made sure he was up in plenty of time to drop her off at Telecom House for 09:00, before going on to pick up his father. As it turned out, the traffic had been light that morning, and Sheila was dropped off a little earlier than planned. Dave also knew that the journey on to Westgate Court Avenue would only take five minutes, so he had plenty of time to spare. As a result, he soon found himself driving along Amanda-Jayne's street and then cruising slowly past her house, in the vague hope of catching a glimpse of his beloved, as she went down the town with friends, or out with her mother. Even better still, he dearly hoped that she would be gazing out of the bedroom window, still nightie clad, as a result of her somehow sensing that he was in the vicinity. Having achieved one completely unsuccessful drive-past, he turned the car at the end of the road in preparation for a second attempt. Sadly though, there was absolutely no sign of her, and all the curtains in the house were still firmly closed. As he pulled back onto the main street of the St. Dunstan's suburb, Dave consoled himself with the thought that it would only be a few more days until he could both see and hold her again.

Within ten minutes, having taken a rather time-wasting circuitous route, Dave was pulling up outside his parents' semi-detached house. Even so, in spite of his best efforts, he was still 15 minutes early. Having turned off the engine, he peered at the familiar house and, as he was often wont to, marvelled that it looked pretty much the same as it had when Len and Meg moved there from Tankerton nearly 30 years before. As he got out of the car, Dave recalled that he'd had his fifth birthday in this house, barely three months after the family had settled here.

Having locked the car, Dave studied his parents' front garden, with its regimented striped lawn and neatly clipped lonicera hedge. He reminded himself that Grandad Darwin had grown the hedge from cuttings, in the lean-to greenhouse at Rothermead, just after his parents had moved in, and also planted them for Len too. Dave's father was no gardener, but he did like his lawn tidy and a neatly clipped hedge also satisfied his sense of order. It was a shame that the gardening gene had skipped a generation, thought Dave, as he plucked a small, severed clipping from the hedge's squared-off top. He also regretted that neither Lucy nor Ed shared his own green-fingered passion; a love very much learnt in the company of Grandad Darwin during those fondly remembered formative days at both Oakenden Nursery and Rothermead Farm. Sadder still, it struck him that had Ronnie lived, and then accumulated the wealth that fame usually brings, perhaps he might have bought a large house with a huge plot, and subsequently created a wonderful wild garden after the well-established Darwin model. His uncle had certainly loved all the trees and plants that grew in the countryside; that much was obvious from those early walks. Sadly, he knew, all- too well, that this particular thought would forever remain a speculative one.

Dave went through the black-painted front gate but ignored the front door, and instead, took the path round to the rear of the house. This led him past the new caravan that was proudly parked on the drive: the latest in a long line of similar 'luxury' boxes, which his parents had owned since the late 60s. He let himself in at the back door, giving the family rhythmic knock, so as not to alarm his mother who, according to the routine, would usually be washing up the breakfast things at this time of day. However, the kitchen was empty and the breakfast dishes and plates already neatly stacked up on the draining board. Peering into the dining room and finding that similarly empty, he completed his journey along the hallway, and entered the front room, where he finally found Len.

Dave smiled to see that his father was sitting in his usual place, in front of the television.

'Only *me* Dad; I came in the back door to save you from having to get up!' he declared, with a grin, before dropping onto the end of the settee.

'*You're* early old chap,' his father said, before reaching for the remote control in order to reduce the sound level. 'Just watching the snooker highlights!' he added, with only the briefest of glances in his son's direction.

Dave looked over at his father, who seemed utterly transfixed by the coloured balls that currently coruscated and collided across the TV screen. Straightaway, it was quite obvious that Len was in one of his 'minimal' moods: one of those phases when he said and did as little as possible. This was in marked contrast with his 'manic' moods, when it was almost like being in the company of Groucho Marx on speed. During one of those more upbeat phases, the humour flowed freely and his father was as easily as funny and creative as Ronnie had ever been. Sometimes in the past though, those manic moods could also manifest themselves more darkly, in the form of violent tempers, shouting and the occasional punitive sanction; it was something that all three Darwin children could readily attest to. However, these days, Len's medication had curtailed much of the manic element to his personality, and the darker side rarely surfaced, and then only when he was behind the wheel. But, there were now more minimal moods than there were comic interludes: another inevitable, and less fortunate consequence of the beta-blockers and anti-depressants.

Len Darwin's medical problems had only really become debilitating for him in the aftermath of his brother's untimely death, when all the awful consequences of that terrible episode became apparent. He was finally forced to retire from Telecom at only 50 years' old, through chronic anxiety and high blood pressure. Had Len not done so, then his doctor had made it clear that there was a strong possibility of him suffering a stroke.

Dave's mother emerged from the hall and her cheery smile, upon seeing him, quickly banished much of his brooding.

'*Hi* Mum!' he greeted before standing up to embrace her.

'*Hello darling,*' she enthused warmly, before kissing him. 'I've just been on the phone to your poor old Grandad Maybury; I had to explain to him that we wouldn't be *over* today as per normal.'

'I think you spend far too much time over there as it *is*,' Dave retorted, reaching out to squeeze his mother's hand as she sat down alongside him. 'It's not like he would be on his own for *long* if you went less often. He *does* have his daily home help *and* twice daily nurses!'

Hearing the remark, Len glanced briefly at his son, and then nodded in grim agreement, but said nothing.

Ignoring her husband's silent acquiescence, Meg chose instead to respond directly to Dave.

'I *know* love, but since that last stroke, he says he only *lives* for our visits, even if he *does* spend the whole time moaning and complaining.' She paused and quickly looked at Len, who was once again nodding, and also biting his bottom lip, both literally and figuratively. 'But at the end of the day Dave, he's *still* my Dad… and I can do little else! But…it *is* hard…*especially* on your father!'

Having had his own difficult role in the proceedings acknowledged, a slightly guilty-looking Len smiled over at his wife.

'It's hard for *both* of us, my love,' he acknowledged, before winking at his son. 'But I'll always support you in this; you *know* that!'

Meg got up from the settee and kissed the top of her husband's head, just as his attention drifted back to the televised snooker championship highlights.

'As I will always support *you*!' she confirmed, before returning to her seat. She then proceeded to stare at the screen herself, as always, in an attempt to feign interest in the colourful table sport that, judging by their dress, only restaurant waiters seemed to play.

Since Ed had left home, Dave's parents had spent every hour of every day in each other's company. If one of them had to go to the doctor, dentist or even the gynaecologist, the other would go along too. Len had also accompanied his wife on those almost daily trips to her ailing father who, as a very emotionally demanding patient, was a drain on the health of his long-suffering son-in-law. It meant that on most days, Meg had to pick up the pieces when they finally got back home. But that was how they operated, and neither of them seemed to want it any other way. Therefore, it should have come as no surprise to Dave that his mother soon announced that she would also be coming to Beltinge with them as well, 'to keep Nanna Darwin company'. He was pleased in a way, because apart from his parents' daily one-mile journey to Grandad Maybury's and a weekly shopping trip to Keymarkets, they rarely ventured out any more, least of all to go over to Beltinge. The television had become their exclusive window onto the world; an existence of game shows, soap operas and snooker.

Dave waited patiently while both of them individually checked that the back door was firmly locked, and then that all the windows were closed before they were happy to leave the house. He was also glad that it was he who would be driving that day, thus avoiding the white-knuckle ride – with accompanying abuse and obscene gesticulations to other motorists – that would have resulted had his father been behind the wheel.

Len was the last to scramble into the car; both expecting and getting the front passenger seat.

'Did you remember to check the back door dear?' he asked of his wife, as the vehicle pulled away.

'*Yes* love!' replied Meg, with a tolerant smile. 'Did you check that the fanlights were closed?'

'*Yes* love!' responded her husband, before giving Dave a gesture with his eyebrows, as if to say: what *is* she like!

The family threesome made good progress on their journey to Herne Bay until, that is, they reached the village of Sturry, where a parked delivery lorry caused them, and everyone else on the road, a considerable holdup.

Len, who had been sitting there in frowning silence, finally couldn't help but comment.

'We always go via Broad Oak to *avoid* such delays!' he remarked, looking smugly vindicated.

Having eventually passed the stationary lorry, and eased round the bend towards the level crossing, Dave saw the twin lights flashing, and then the barriers dropping, about five or six cars in front of him. For once, that familiar sight brought Dave little pleasure, or reminiscent repose.

As the car ground to a halt, Meg tapped her son on the shoulder from the back seat.

'*We* always go via Broad Oak', she remarked, in a slightly piteous air.

'How's Lucy mum?' a slightly exasperated Dave asked, not only desperately trying to control his temper, but also attempting to stimulate some meaningful in-car conversation.

Fortunately, his mother immediately took the bait.

'Oh, your sister is *glowing*; she's nearly four months now. It looks like it's going to be a Christmas baby!' she enthused, in rapturous tones.

Poor little sod, thought a saddened Dave, only one set of presents then. He also began to feel sorry for his little nephew Jimmy who would, no doubt, soon be feeling supplanted by the arrival of a new sibling, very much as he himself had done.

Dave dismally watched as an eight-coach train pulled into Sturry Station, which he knew could only accommodate six. This meant the remaining two carriages would foul the crossing, resulting in a long wait, and a further delay. Having accepted that there was nothing he could do to hurry proceedings along, Dave decided to while away the time by thinking about the day's planned gardening duties at Beltinge. His only real concern was not regarding the amount of work they were likely to face, but about the possibility of a tense atmosphere between his parents and grandparents.

'How *are* you getting on with Nanna and Grandad Darwin these days, Dad?' Dave asked, in an effort to gauge the likely mood, once they'd arrived.

'The same as *always*,' Len replied, with a dismissive shrug. 'The cease-fire is holding, but since Grandad's ... err...illness, I *have* tried to keep in touch by phone.'

'*Yes*, but when did you last *visit* them?' Dave retorted, as the railway carriages began to ease out of the station unnoticed.

Len took this question as a personal criticism and quickly snapped back.

'We *do* have very busy *lives* you know ... Grandad Maybury takes up *all* our time. Come to think of it, when did *you* last visit *him*!' he countered, before grimly averting his gaze.

Touché, thought Dave; blowing out through pursed lips. He'd certainly hit a raw nerve that time.

Sadly, by now, Len was both brooding and fuming.

'My parents could have visited *us* at anytime,' he added irritably, and quite unable to let the matter rest.

Huh, only if Grandad Darwin was *well* enough, thought Dave crossly, but dared not say as much, lest he be seen as taking sides in this unhappy family situation.

Once more, Meg prodded her son's shoulder.

'*Look* darling, the barriers are up,' she said from behind, desperate to return to the safety of banal conversation.

'*Thanks* Mum!' Dave responded with a resigned nod; knowing that he'd better say nothing more on the subject.

'They could have visited *us*!' Len mumbled to himself, as the car began to roll forward; a remark that wisely went unchallenged.

As Dave bumped over the railway lines and then accelerated up Sturry Hill, he tried to trace the source of the animosity between his father and grandparents; a long-lasting bitterness that had much to do with Ronnie. Even as a child, Dave was aware that his father and uncle both competed for their parents' love and approval, but only with the benefit of hindsight, could he understand why Len might have felt some resentment. He was the older son after all, the responsible one; the one who had worked hard to secure a good engineering job with Telecom. He was also the son who'd provided his parents with grandchildren and yet, nothing had meant more to Nanna and Grandad Darwin than Ronnie's burgeoning career and eventual success, although short lived. In their effort to help Ronnie achieve his dream, they could have been accused of favouring their youngest son over the older, for example, by buying him a car and flat, whilst Len struggled on to bring up his family single-handed, and financially unassisted. Dave realised that none of this favouritism was deliberate on his grandparents' part, but at the same time, he could appreciate why his father might have felt shabbily treated as a result. To his considerable credit, the younger Len never challenged his family over this perceived grievance, but let it go and carried on as if nothing was wrong. Dave conceded that the strain on him must have been enormous.

The situation between Len and his parents only really became completely untenable after Ronnie's untimely death. Immediately prior to that, he'd been the one who had helped his brother all the way through that difficult period immediately prior to the end, and, at the time, Nanna and Grandad Darwin had fully supported him in this endeavour. Unfortunately, after Ronnie had died, rather than be grateful that their oldest son had attempted to help his little brother, Len very much got the impression that his parents actually blamed him for Ronnie's death. After the dust had settled, Len hoped that, being their only surviving son, his parents would have wanted to form the sort of special relationship with him, that they'd previously enjoyed with Ronnie. Sadly though, this did not happen. Instead, Nanna and Grandad Darwin began to forge stronger links with the teenage David. A lot more water would flow under that particular bridge in the years that followed, but Dave did not want to think about that painful period right now.

There was no one to greet them as they arrived, and then parked outside the Darwin residence at the end of Gainsborough Drive. Dave couldn't remember a time when Grandad Darwin wasn't working at the front of the bungalow in eager anticipation of the family's arrival, or else hadn't rushed out of the front door, immediately on hearing the car approach; newly washed, changed in to his best, and smelling of carbolic soap. His absence was most disquieting, and the disappointment Dave felt went far beyond that for the loss of a much-cherished routine greeting. As soon as Dave got out of the car, he cast his eyes over his grandparents front garden, and quickly realised that their work was really cut out. The front hedge and lawns were very overgrown and the borders, although still colourful and magnificent as ever, were choked with both annual and perennial weeds. Still no one appeared from the house, despite the slamming of the car doors, so rather than ring the doorbell, Dave led his parents round to the back. He was therefore the first of them to witness the much more extensive wilderness that now stretched out before them.

Unlike his son, Len couldn't help but express the horror he felt upon seeing the state of the back garden.

'Oh my *goodness*,' he said, placing a flattened hand on his brow, 'this is going to take *much* more than just one session.'

Dave nodded in agreement, but could not share his father's all too apparent hand-wringing dismay. Where Len could see only chaos, he could see a colourful romantic wild garden that was almost too wonderful to attempt to control. Meg meanwhile, passed no comment and seemed more concerned by her husband's disturbed reaction upon seeing the garden, than the state of the garden itself.

However, Len's mood quickly changed from the reactions of a victim, to those of a martyr.

'Better get *on* with it I suppose. *I'll* do the hedges and the lawns; I *know* about hedges and lawns,' he muttered, before beginning to push his way across the overgrown lawn, and then through the waist high plants, which crowded the path leading to the shed where the mower was kept.

An alarmed Meg made a futile grab for the sleeve of her rapidly retreating husband.

'Darling, *wait*!' she called out, before looking anxiously at her son.

'But *Dad*, aren't you going into the house with us to say *hello*?' Dave called to a figure fast becoming swallowed up by the undergrowth.

'*We're here to work aren't we?*' was the shouted response from somewhere further down the path, Len now having completely disappeared from view.

The raised voices finally attracted the attention of someone, and it was Nanna Darwin, who came out of the conservatory to greet her visitors with the customary peck on the cheek. In this respect, she was always far less demonstrative than her husband, bear hugs not really being her style. Sometimes even her pecks on the cheek were near misses; effectively becoming mere representations of affection.

Having greeted Dave and Meg thus, Nanna now glanced past them.

'Has *Len* not come with you?' she asked, with an anxious look on her face.

Meg smiled feebly and then looked to her son to be their immediate family spokesman.

'Err ... *yes*, he's gone to start the mower ... *ha*, you know him ... keen to get started and all that,' Dave responded in the most diplomatic way he could think of.

Rather than appear pleased on hearing the news of Len's declared dedication to the task in hand, Nanna Darwin frowned disapprovingly.

'Well, I wish he'd have *waited* ... I've drawn up a *schedule* of things that should be done!' she protested, before retrieving a neat, handwritten list from the right-hand pocket of her homemade tailored jacket.

The sound of the mower firing up could now be heard coming from further down the garden. As Dave and Nanna Darwin exchanged resigned glances, Meg looked anxiously in the direction of the noise. Even though barely three minutes had elapsed since she last saw him, Meg was already feeling discomfort at being separated from her husband.

Her painstakingly prepared list of tasks now seemingly superseded, Nanna sighed deeply.

'*Ah* well, I'll go and get my outdoor shoes,' she declared, before turning back in the direction of the conservatory.

Leaving his mother still staring towards the spluttering two-stroke sound of the unseen mower, Dave set off in pursuit of his grandmother.

'I'm just going in to say a quick hello to Grandad before we get started,' he announced, rapidly drawing level with her.

Nanna soon stopped, and then physically barred his way, just inside the conservatory door.

'He was *asleep* a few moments ago when I looked in on him,' she said in a half-whisper, and sounding more affectionate than when they were all outside. 'I *know* he wants to see you Dave, to see you *all*, but…do you mind waiting until later; until he's woken up?'

For a split second, her grandson looked crestfallen, but then smiled stoically as he nodded in agreement.

'Of *course* not ... but how *is* the old boy today?' he asked softly, furrowing his brow slightly.

Tears began to well up in her eyes, but she fought against them. Nanna was hardly ever known for any sort of emotional display, at least not in public.

'I'll just get my outdoor shoes,' she evaded before quickly turning away from him and disappearing into the house proper. The question was left hanging in the air, but there was clearly an unhappy reply implicit in her reaction.

Saddened, Dave went back outside to join Meg, who was still looking anxiously in the direction of the sound of the laboriously chugging motor, clearly hoping to catch a glimpse of Len as he finally set the contraption against the encroaching herbage. Their son realised that the day was not going to go well if Nanna constantly stood over them with her list, whilst his mother endlessly fussed round his father. Given that likely scenario, Dave concluded that absolutely nothing would get done except the shortening of tempers and the shredding of nerves.

Dave dwelt briefly on the problem, and suddenly inspired turned to his mother with a potentially ideal solution.

'Mum, what'd *really* help Dad and I today, would be if you could keep Nanna Darwin out of our *hair* for as much as possible!' he proposed conspiratorially; nodding and wrinkling his nose at the same time.

Meg examined him through narrowed eyes, and then smiled with a mild air of condescension.

'No love, I *don't* think that's a good idea,' she said, as a mother might if her toddler son had proposed eating earthworms for tea. 'I'd sooner help your father by *being* there for him ... you know, getting him drinks, making him rest ... *that* sort of thing!'

In response, Dave had to think fast, and soon realised that he would have to play an unkind if necessary card.

'*Yes*, but *you* know Nanna Darwin, and that list of hers; she'll have him doing *God* knows what,' he reasoned, with generous helping of exaggeration thrown in. 'Keep her out of the way, and then *I* could look after Dad *just* as well!'

'But...but, what can I say or *do* all day? Nanna and I have so little in *common* these days!' Meg responded, with the beginnings of panic, as the parent/child roles flipped once more.

'Why don't you offer to help clean up the ornamental pond?' he suggested in immediate response; both of them shocked and surprised by the spontaneous inspiration he'd again been granted. 'She's *bound* to want to do that with you, *and* you'll have the benefit of Dad never being too far away!'

His mother reluctantly agreed, much to Dave's considerable relief, and she went to find the formidable Nanna Darwin, armed with her pacifying proposal. Meanwhile, Dave himself set off to retrace his father's steps across the lengthy lawn, and then along the outer path, in the direction of the tool shed. He passed his father halfway along the path.

'Got her sounding as sweet as a nut,' Len beamed above the motor mower's very un-sweet sounding cacophony of coughing.

Dave gave his father the thumbs-up sign, before approaching the old shed, lifting the latch, and then entering into his grandfather's garden sanctuary. Once inside, he quickly located some gardening gloves, a trowel, a large fork and a pair of secateurs. Upon turning to go, he also noticed one of Grandad Darwin's old battered trilbies on the hook behind the door. Reverentially, Dave removed it and then studied its familiar contours. He held it to his nose and breathed in both slowly and deeply; the hat smelt of a fondly familiar blend of soil and carbolic. A small sprig of dried cherry blossom had got caught under the sweatband. Dave carefully removed it, but the tiny proto-posy crumbled in his hand. With a deep and symbolic sadness, he concluded that those particular blossoms were never destined to form themselves into cherries. It was an apt but sad thought, and one that completely occupied his mind as he replaced the beloved hat.

By the time Dave had returned with his tools loaded in Grandad's squeaky-axled wheelbarrow, Len was already charging up and down the vast back lawn at a furious pace, amidst huge clumps of long grass that were flying up in every direction. At the same time, he saw Nanna Darwin and his mother disappear between the cherry trees on the middle path that led to the pond, and breathed a huge sigh of relief.

For several hours, most of it spent either bent over or on his hands and knees, Dave worked along the huge curved border that flanked the vast back lawn, yanking out countless handfuls of both perennial and annual weeds. He figured that if they concentrated on the parts of the garden that could be seen from the bungalow, then Grandad Darwin would be suitably reassured by the return of some semblance of order, and then the remaining garden areas could be tackled later. Len had already located the other wheelbarrow and pressed it into service for the mountains of mown grass cuttings he'd created. Between them, they made dozens of trips to the compost heap in the furthest corner of the garden, behind the old shed, regularly passing each other halfway, to exchange weary smiles and exhausted exhalations.

On returning from yet another trip to the dump, Dave found his father sitting on the bench at the edge of the tidied lawn, his face both red and sweating.

'Are you *alright* Dad?' he asked with concern, quickly abandoning his emptied barrow.

'*Phew* ... just taking a breather old chap,' Len panted, before shifting his position towards the bench's left-hand armrest.

'Good idea, I think I'll join you!' replied his sweltering son, accepting the implied invitation.

Having mostly recovered, Len looked over in the direction of the bungalow, and then turned to Dave.

'I wish I could get on better with Grandad Darwin, now more than *ever*!' He paused, sighed, and then patted his son's knee. 'What went *wrong* then Dave, eh?' he asked, looking at him sadly.

This was the first time his father had really opened up to him on the subject, and he had no pre-prepared reply. However, Dave was grateful that he'd spent much of the journey over pondering on the family rift, and knew that it would certainly help him in this regard.

'I don't think anything actually *did* go wrong…well, *obviously* apart from losing Ronnie that is,' he replied, trying to find the right words; words that couldn't possibly be interpreted as apportioning blame on either side.

'But I couldn't match up to him in their eyes, even *after* he had died,' Len retorted in frustration, glancing back in the direction of the bungalow, and slowly shaking his head. 'I became second best to a ghost!'

In fact, Dave had been thinking a lot about the Darwin family tensions, not only on the journey over, but also while working his way along the herbaceous borders. He soon realised that in order to answer his father's question, he would have to draw on the experience of his own sometimes-troubled upbringing. It would be a difficult verbal journey to navigate, especially if one wanted to avoid the many potholes en route.

'The way I see it is *this*,' Dave began, pausing briefly to gather his thoughts.

His father paid close attention, all too evidently desperate to hear something that he'd not considered before, something that would allow him some much needed peace of mind.

'You see Dad, I don't need to tell you that when younger siblings come along, in your case Ronnie, they naturally need, and usually get, more attention from their parents. Sometimes, the older child might resent this, and I have to say: *I* certainly did when both Lucy and Ed were born!'

The comparison between the respective Darwin generations, and their reaction to a younger brother or sister coming along, was quite valid. However, for the young Leonard and Ronald, there were other factors to take into account. Len had been a sensible, placid youth, who always did as he was told, required little discipline and could always be relied upon in every respect. He had worked hard at school and each and every night, unfailingly did his homework without complaint. Young Len wasn't academically brilliant; he wasn't grammar school material for example, but his logical and methodical approach to life got him through technical school with distinction. In his spare time, he was happy to take himself off on his bicycle, or else cheerfully carry out any task at Oakenden Nursery that his father had set for him. There was never any doubt in either parent's mind that Len was going to grow up straight and achieve things. Ronnie, on the other hand, was the very antithesis of his steady older brother; it was a fact that became obvious almost right from the beginning of his life. He was hyperactive as a small boy and, more disturbingly, had displayed distinct behavioural problems. His young life seemed to be controlled by emotional peaks and troughs, best described as something approaching a manic-depressive pattern, though with much shorter episodes. When Ronnie was high, he talked non-stop and punned or spoonerised his words all the time. He described people he met in a fantastic and often, hilarious way, and then impersonated them, much to the delight of Len and his parents. He also exuded a sort of wild charisma that seemed to draw people to him. Later on, Dave would know this only too well, and would be bewitched by his uncle's indefinable charm right from as early as he was aware. However, when the younger Ronnie was low, he was very low and had a tendency to hide away. He would then either shut down completely and just cry, or binge eat in secret until he was sick. Consequently, most people only witnessed the 'up' side of his nature and had no idea as to the duality of his true character. Nanna and Grandad Darwin had taken Ronnie to specialists who ran many tests and then suggested drastic steps such as psychiatric 'treatment' or suppressive medication. At the end of the day though, his parents would have none of it and decided that the best way forward was to continue to help him themselves. In this unenviable endeavour, they achieved no small amount of success. Over much time, and with great patience, they managed to control the very extremes of his temperament, but also established much longer periods of 'normal' behaviour in between. Their major mistake, as Dave saw it, was to take their older son, Len, for granted and to assume that as he was so steady and reliable, he could be left to his own devices, while they concentrated on their younger 'problem' son.

Later on, when Ronnie decided that he could actually exploit his 'problems': that manic sense of humour, his talent for mimicry and wordplay, as well as his charisma, and become some sort of entertainer, his parents did all they could to encourage this ambition. At the same time, they tried to give him the same sort of stability and contentment that Len already seemed to possess, either naturally or through his own efforts, and which was apparent right from a very young age, right up until his mid-teens. The irony was, that in over-compensating for Ronnie's special needs, their neglected 'steady' son eventually began to display, although in a lesser form, some of the behavioural problems that were all too apparent in Ronnie. Everything Len had ever done: the unquestioning obedience, the many chores stoically carried out, and all the hard work at school, had been to please his parents, but in the eyes of their older teenage son, they did not seem to appreciate this. Was Len's change in behaviour, a subconscious desire to imitate Ronnie and thus attract the attention of his parents, or was it a genetic predisposition that only surfaced as a result of his being constantly sidelined? Whatever the answer was, his parents were too distracted to notice and when Len went off, got married and had children, they continued to concentrate on giving Ronnie some sort of viable future. Dave now tried to make his father see that all Nanna and Grandad Darwin were trying to do was redress the balance that had been thrown awry by nature, and bring Ronnie up to something approaching the same level of accomplishment in life as him. However, he had to concede that they failed to acknowledge Len's achievements and say in words, how proud they were of him for all he had managed through his own efforts. Effectively, they had thought of the young Len as already being an adult, so responsible and mature was he, but they completely forgot the needs of the child that were still very much within him.

As for Len's own part in all this, his quite understandable mistake was to resent what he perceived as his parents' favouritism towards Ronnie, and their rewarding of him for what seemed like bad behaviour. Sadly, the more jealous and resentful Len got, the more Nanna and Grandad Darwin thought he was trying to undermine their efforts to help Ronnie, and tried even harder. It was a vicious circle, down which their older son eventually spiralled.

The strange thing was that in all of this, there were never any problems between the two Darwin siblings themselves. On the contrary, as a small boy, Ronnie worshipped his big brother and often spent all day following him around the nursery. In turn, Len would often be there for his little brother when he hit one of his low spots. Many times on such occasions, Len would be the only one that Ronnie would allow anywhere near him. And then, when the worst moments had passed, and a tearful Ronnie ran into the arms of his concerned parents, there were no arms of appreciation left for a tired and exhausted Len. In all of this though, he never resented Ronnie; after all, his little brother couldn't help being ill. Nor did Len really mind his parents trying to help his troubled sibling. What he did mind though, was being shut out by them while they did so.

Dave did not even attempt to touch on the problems that had arisen after Ronnie's death; he had been too close to all of that himself, to form an objective opinion, let alone help his father with it.

As his son's overview of the sorry situation concluded, Len looked at him proudly. He marvelled at the remarkable insight Dave had in these matters, and was grateful to him for providing so much food for thought. Sadly though, Len never did realise that Dave was partly drawing on his own childhood experiences, to explain those of his father. It hadn't occurred to him that he and Meg had actually repeated some of the same mistakes with Dave that Nanna and Grandad Darwin had made with his own upbringing.

With both men now contemplative and quiet, Len once more glanced over at the bungalow. It was silent and there appeared to be no movement within. Grandad must still be asleep, he speculated. In fact, the only noise that could be heard at all was the distant voices of Meg and Nanna Darwin on pond duty.

'I've always been *there* for my parents,' Len commented, turning back to Dave, 'in *spite* of everything that's happened!'

'I *know* Dad,' Dave replied, with a warm smile and a reassuring hand on his shoulder. '*Hey*, do you remember the last occasion we all had to rally round and help in the garden; the last time when Grandad Darwin was ill?'

'How could I *forget*,' Len replied, with a weary chuckle, and a flicker of his eyebrows. 'What a taxing weekend *that* was!'

'*And* it was the last time that Nanna and Grandad saw Ronnie alive!' Dave reflected sadly, as both the circumstances and consequences of that occasion came into sharp focus in his mind.

*

'*Come* on Meg, you can do it,' Len pleaded, as he placed the tin tea caddy in the centre of the table. 'Just think of it as an ordinary weekend at Rothermead Farm, one that's no different from all the *others*'.

'*I can't*, I can't leave the house,' Meg sobbed, as she slowly backed into a corner of the kitchen. 'The press are out there somewhere ... they're *bound* to get us sooner or later!'

'Not if we're *careful*, and Ronnie keeps his head down!' her husband responded calmly, as he approached her, and then gently gripped her upper arms. 'This whole thing might just blow over. After all, it's only the papers making a fuss as usual. No charges have been filed, no formal accusations have been made.'

Sitting silently at the kitchen table, David looked from one parent to the other. He could tell that his father's slow reassuring voice was having the desired affect. Consequently, his mum gradually calmed down. The twelve-year-old vaguely remembered seeing her like this when he was very young; it must have been shortly after they had moved from Damascena to Westgate Court Avenue. That was the time when she had that weight problem, he recalled; that was the period when she never left the house at all, sometimes literally for weeks on end.

Len released one of his hands to reach behind his wife and then flick the wall switch in order to calm the frantically boiling kettle, which she'd been ignoring.

'You *know* I have to go, love ... Nanna sounded *desperate*. The Dutnells are away, so are the Carters apparently, and things are falling seriously behind,' he remarked, before moving to one side and pouring hot water into the teapot. 'You'll be great company for her if you come up too,' he added, glancing back at her as he stirred.

'But I need to stay and look after the children,' Meg said, crouching to take the milk out of the fridge.

'David is coming up *with* us, we can *all* go,' Len reasoned, as he pressed home the knitted tea cosy.

'But there won't be *room* in the car with Ronnie as well,' Meg countered, banging the bottle on the kitchen table with every other word she said.

David quickly looked up from his comic, and then smiled.

'Why don't we take the caravan,' he suggested in bright, cheery tones. 'Ronnie can travel up in that; *I* could too!'

His mother glared at him with an uncomfortable intensity, her face distorted crossly.

'*Please* keep out of this David; you're *not* helping matters!' she barked, with little obvious regard for his well-intentioned suggestion.

As the crestfallen lad looked forlornly at his father, his plaintive stare was met by a reassuring wink.

'People aren't allowed to travel in caravans whilst they're on the move I'm afraid!' he explained, before pulling out a chair at the table, and then sitting down. Furrowing his eyebrows, Len held a clenched fist against his mouth as he thought about the problems of the travel arrangements; all the while, stirring the teapot as he pondered. After a minute, he slowly looked back up at his worried wife.

'Yes it *would* be a bit of a squeeze in the car, and we *certainly* can't leave Ronnie behind,' he conceded, before another idea suddenly occurred to him. 'What if Nanna and Grandad Maybury were to have Lucy and Eddie for the weekend?'

'No, please, I just *can't face it Len*, I really can't!' Meg implored, once more backing herself into the comfort of the corner.

'Not even for *me*?' he pleaded, trying his best to effect a little-boy-lost face.

Seemingly softened by her husband's entreaty, Meg came back over to the kitchen table.

'Not even for *you* my darling, I'm *so* sorry!' she confessed, somewhat shamefaced, and at the same time, reaching to stroke his hair.

With resigned acceptance of the situation and memories of similar agoraphobic phases in the past, Len simply shrugged, poured the tea and then handed Meg a cup.

'Yes, Ronnie *has* to come with us and I suppose it *would* be unfair to spring the children on your parents at a moment's notice,' he said, before pushing a full cup towards David's seated position.

Meg smiled for the first time in the entire conversation.

'And didn't you say last night, that he wanted to explain to Nanna and Grandad Darwin, face to face, what had *really* happened up in London?' she added, in more optimistic tones, happy at the thought of finally being allowed to remain within the walls of her sanctuary.

'Yes, he *did*,' Len replied, with a nod of the head, 'and besides which, he'll be useful. We can put him to work in the garden of the big house, and keep him out of mischief!'

Now grinning from ear to ear with relief, Meg joined the two males at the table.

'Yes, and you three boys will be able to go on one of those farm walks that David so loves!' she enthused, giving her son a facial exclamation of glee.

Len nodded, sipped his tea and for a moment, seemed lost in thought.

'We'll *go* then, as soon as I've finished this,' he finally decided, in a calm but authoritarian manner.

David took a sip of his own rather hot tea, and then glanced across the table towards his father.

'What's actually the *matter* with Grandad Darwin?' he asked, not having heard any mention of the actual details.

His father looked at him from the top of his eyes, replaced his tea cup on the saucer, and then took a deep breath before replying. He then proceeded to explain that on the Monday just gone, Grandad had been cutting the sweeping front lawns of the 'big house' at Rothermead, using the sit-on motor mower. He had been turning a circle round one of the large ornamental trees, when a lower branch struck him on the shoulder and had thrown him from the mower. As well as a badly bruised shoulder, the doctor confirmed that he also had a mild concussion and prescribed bed rest for the next couple of days, at least. The problem was that as Lord and Lady Rothermead were abroad, not only were

Grandad Darwin's gardening duties not being performed, but also those other important tasks as caretaker of the 'big house'.

Having heard the tale retold, a possible reason for the old boy's fall suddenly occurred to Meg.

'You don't think the accident was caused by Grandad being distracted ... you know, having read the Ronnie stuff in the newspaper, do you?' she proposed, cupping her brew with both hands.

'Umm, I hadn't *thought* of that ... they do *have* a paper delivered!' Len responded, contemplating his cup.

Earlier, that afternoon, as soon as David had been told they'd be going to Rothermead Farm unexpectedly for the weekend, he had got his bags packed and ready within five minutes. Lucy was also told, but had soon confided in her mother that she was currently rather scared of Uncle Ronnie and did not want to go if he was coming along too. No one could get out of her exactly *why* she was scared of him now. Before all this Katie Townsend trouble had begun, she'd been almost as devoted to him as David. It was just like the Father Christmas episode, when she was six years' old. On the Christmas Eve of that particular year, rather than be excited, as all children of that age inevitably were, she was utterly petrified. Meg had finally managed to get her to confess that she didn't want an old man with a white beard, coming into her room at night, presents or no presents! It must have been the first occasion that a child had been positively relieved to be told that Father Christmas *didn't* exist. Now, as far as Ronnie was concerned, her parents' best guess was that Lucy saw her uncle as the reason why everyone in the family suddenly seemed so upset. Ronnie hadn't helped matters either by sometimes being snappy, or on other occasions, completely sullen and silent in the children's presence.

So it was eventually decided, to almost universal approval, that Lucy and Eddie would stay at home with their mother, while Len, Ronnie and David went up to Rothermead to help sort things out for Nanna and Grandad Darwin. Of course, David did not share Lucy's anxieties over Ronnie. On the contrary, he understood why his uncle was so upset, and why he was so unlike his normal self, or at least, he understood it in part. Ultimately though, David was looking forward to a chance to be with Ronnie at the weekend; to spend more time with his 'scar brother' up at the cherished Rothermead Farm, and hopefully, to cheer him up a bit as well.

Meg got up from the kitchen table, and began gathering together the empty tea cups.

'Where *is* Ronnie at the moment?' she asked, almost as if she'd picked up on her son's thoughts.

'As far as I'm aware, he's still in the caravan,' Len said, slowly pushing back his own chair. 'But he *does* realise we're leaving soon and I *know* he's looking forward to seeing our parents again, *and* of course, having that chance to explain *his* side of things. *Huh*, no doubt he'll be telling them that the papers have got it all *wrong*!'

'Yes, what *must* they be thinking!' Meg mused mischievously, as she ran hot water on the crockery in the sink bowl. 'Nanna Darwin has been boasting to everyone at the farm, from Smiler to his lordship, about Ronnie's recent fame and success!'

Her husband's brow furrowed on hearing the comment.

'Yes, and it's all *we've* heard since that blessed *Lulu* show screening!' he reinforced, with a tut and ceiling-ward glance. '*Still*, our new purchase should ease *that* problem somewhat!'

Meg looked at him, smiled piteously with her head on one side, and then nodded in general agreement, but said nothing in response to either exclamation.

'He *is* still Ronnie though,' Len added with a slightly cynical tinge to his voice. 'They'd forgive him *anything*, and besides which, I'm sure they will have *already* come up with a perfectly logical reason to neatly explain away what was reported in the papers!'

David peered at his father and wondered if he was being sarcastic. So far, it was a verbal art form that he himself had yet to master.

Len went upstairs to say goodbye to Lucy, who was holed up in her room, and also to Eddie, who appeared to be completely unaware of and, therefore, unconcerned about any of the current family problems. He then came back down to the hallway, with his already-packed holdall, and hugged a tearful Meg, who clearly did not really want him to go; even though she wasn't prepared to go with him either.

As his parents said their goodbyes, David went round to the side of the house and under the recently erected carport, where his father's pride and joy, the new caravan was proudly parked. The twelve-year-old was aware that had Uncle Ronnie's problems not flared up earlier in the week, then they might have been going away in it this very weekend. They might go next weekend instead, but it all depended on whether or not his unhappy uncle was still with them, and if all this Katie business had been resolved, or had blown over. Intrigued as he was by the thought of them all taking off together and camping somewhere for a weekend in the wilderness, he was also puzzled by the recent waning of his father's enthusiasm for going up to Rothermead as regularly as they used to. Perhaps it had something to do with what his father had just said inside; perhaps it had a lot to do with Nanna Darwin's endless diatribe about her youngest son's television-based fame and success, he thought with some unease.

David banged on the chrome-trimmed caravan door.

'*Uncle Ronnie*, only me; it's time to set off for Rothermead!' he announced cheerfully, trying to peer through the door's perspex window.

After a while, Ronnie appeared at the entrance, shaved and spruced up.

'All *right* then Dave ... looking forward to picking mushrooms again *eh*?' he said, ruffling his nephew's hair.

David nodded keenly in response. At the same time, he was feeling absolutely delighted; it was like suddenly having the old Uncle Ronnie back again, after the preceding three or four days of temper or silent brooding. Perhaps everything will be all right after all, he happily speculated. In fact, David was even tempted to offer Ronnie his 'Scar Brothers' hand, but held back at the last minute. Instead, he hoped that his uncle would be the one to make the first move, in their cherished secret rite, whenever he felt ready to.

The mushroom-coloured Ford Escort – with its newly fitted towing hook – pulled up outside the kitchen door of the farm cottage at the usual Friday evening time. David eagerly anticipated Grandad Darwin's familiar demonstrative greeting, as he scrambled out of the passenger door. This was the first thing he always looked forward to in that beloved sequence of routine rituals, spread out over the typical Rothermead Farm weekend; all of which meant so much to him. But then he remembered that Grandad was actually ill in bed, and that there would be no such bear hug greeting on this particular trip. By the time all three of them had disembarked, it was Nanna, and not Grandad Darwin, who had appeared at the kitchen door. Her anxious-looking eyes were fixed on Ronnie alone. And then, as she held out her arms, he ran into them, dropping his overnight bag on the way.

Len's head dropped, and he turned away unnoticed from the mother and son reunion.

'*Come* on David, let's go and get some logs,' he proposed, leading his son away and in the direction of the 'big house'.

Disappointed, David wanted to protest; he hadn't yet seen or heard the cuckoo clock strike six, and so sadly concluded that this was another much anticipated routine event that would be denied him. However, as the pair passed Grandad Darwin's tool shed, they both clearly heard the sound of Ronnie sobbing loudly from within the cottage kitchen behind them. David now understood: his father was being discreet; he was allowing Ronnie and Nanna Darwin some much-needed time alone together. Having reached the three-sided inner courtyard, the twelve-year-old showed his father where the door into the old north wing was situated, and they spent a good 20 minutes filling the two available baskets with logs and then re-stacking the remaining pile.

By the time they got back to the cottage, Nanna was in the kitchen preparing the evening meal, and she had some more bad news for David.

'Sorry boys, it will have to be baked potatoes in the electric oven tonight, I haven't had time to light the Rayburn,' she stated in resigned fashion, before giving them both a quick peck on the cheek by way of retrospective greeting. 'Oh and *thanks* for getting the logs, Len ... put them by the range, will you dear?'

As he watched his father take the basket through to the dining room, David could not believe what his grandmother had just announced. His beloved routines were falling like ninepins, and for a moment, he wished he were back at home again in Canterbury. It was like your favourite group releasing a bad record; it would be far better to have no record at all than one that disappointed.

Len, however, had other concerns; bear hugs, cuckoo clocks and Rayburn baked potatoes not being foremost in his mind at that moment. 'Is Ronnie alright?' he asked in hushed tones, having returned to the kitchen.

Nanna nodded, with a brief squeezing of her eyes.

'Yes, he is *now*. In fact, he's upstairs talking to Grandad,' she responded, giving him a weak smile.

'Oh, in *that* case, I'll leave them to it for now,' he said, before walking briskly back into the diningroom, where he knelt down and then peered quizzically into the cold black void of the Rayburn's firebox.

Although David agreed with what seemed to him as a further example of his father's discretion towards Ronnie, he still longed to rush upstairs and see his beloved grandfather himself, especially as he'd not been well. In the meantime, he followed Nanna Darwin into the diningroom and watched with interest as she rifled through a small pile of papers and envelopes on the sideboard beneath the cuckoo clock.

Having found a particular piece of paper, she waved it in the air with Chamberlain-like pride.

'I took the opportunity of making a list of jobs that need doing over the forthcoming weekend,' she announced proudly, handing it to Len, as he slowly straightened himself up.

David looked over his father's shoulder as he scanned through the many tasks detailed on it. His eyes quickly homed in on the third item of that neatly written list.

'*Greenhouse*,' David shouted enthusiastically, glancing from one relative to the other. 'I know what to *do*.'

'Off you *go* then,' Len responded approvingly. 'In the meantime, I'll try and get the Rayburn going.'

Without further prompting, David dashed outside and then nipped round the west end of the thirty-yard wall, to access the long lean-to greenhouse on the other side. The first section housed all the tender plants and he knew that each fanlight needed to be shut completely and then opened again first thing in the morning. The interior of the greenhouse was still warm, and the familiar smell of lemon-scented geranium leaves filled the air. The intermediate door led through to the grapevine house, where he remembered that the fanlights should be closed to the first notch in the summer months. He re-emerged at the east end and quickly glanced around Grandad Darwin's well-stocked, if somewhat weed-choked, walled vegetable garden, before walking through the arch in the thirty-yard wall nearest the 'big house' end. He then turned left, and walked passed Grandad Darwin's tool shed on his way back to the tied cottage.

The downstairs rooms were filled with the smell of baking potatoes by the time David had got back, but it wasn't quite the same eagerly anticipated aroma as usual. However, his father had managed to get the Rayburn going and the cuckoo clock reassuringly 'oo-donged' the three-quarter hour as usual, although on this occasion, no one laughed.

David watched in fascination as his dad laid the dining room table with the same fastidiousness and precision that he carried out many of his other domestic tasks.

'Is Uncle Ronnie still upstairs?' David asked keenly, before peering through the open door down into the sitting room.

'No, he's just gone to the farm cold store to get some more milk. He should be back soon,' Len replied, glancing at his son briefly in between careful placings of the cutlery.

Before he could question his father any further on the subject, Nanna Darwin bustled in from the kitchen.

'David, would you mind taking Grandad's tea up to him?' she asked, handing her grandson the well-loaded tray; thus making it an instruction, rather than a request.

'Oh *yes* I'd *love* to!' he responded, trotting towards her.

Gripping tightly onto the handles of the tray, David stepped down into the sitting room where, directly in front of him, he saw that the door to the stairs was already open. However, the stairwell light was not on. Feeling a sudden chill, a disquieted David slowly walked across the room and towards the opening, where that wall of darkness seemed to be both drawing him in and repelling him in equal measure. He stopped a few paces from the first step and thought he could hear the sound of floorboards creaking, but wasn't able to tell exactly where it was coming from. It was then that he felt a presence immediately behind him and, as adrenalin surged through his stomach, the petrified lad began to slowly turn his head.

'*BOO*,' was shouted at him at close quarters.

David cried out in fright and Grandad Darwin's baked potato nearly rolled on to the floor. He turned round completely to find Ronnie standing behind him, grinning away in delight.

'Scary old stairs *aren't* they, Dave?' his uncle remarked, in a low Vincent Price-type voice.

'Yes…a *little*,' David said, with a somewhat sheepish grin.

'Well *I've* always thought so,' Ronnie agreed, as he reached past his tray-wielding nephew. '*Here*, let me turn the light on for you.'

Leaving his chuckling uncle below, David gratefully hurried up the dimly lit flight of stairs, as fast as his load would allow. He passed through the bunk bedroom without a pause – where he was surprised to find the curtains shut – and then climbed the step into his grandparents' bedroom. Grandad Darwin was sitting up in bed, reading one of the *Look and Learn* magazines that David knew by heart; each one from cover to cover.

The old boy's face lit up immediately upon seeing his eldest grandson.

'Ah the *David*; good old boy,' he greeted with enthusiasm, whilst tossing the well-thumbed magazine to one side.

'*Hello* Grandad, I've brought you your dinner ... err ... your tea!' he beamed, before sliding the tray on to his grandfather's sheet and blanket-covered lap.

'Oo *lovely*!' came the familiar response, before he thrust out his uninjured arm in the lad's direction.

David allowed that rough gardener's hand to pat both his face and shoulder, whilst he gripped on to the beloved limb in question. Although pleasant, the greeting was an inadequate substitute for the bear hug that he knew was out of the question because of the old boy's bad shoulder.

Their greeting over, David sat on the edge of the bed and demanded to hear Grandad's version of his accident, which he knew would be made into a funny story.

'What a silly old Grandad I am!' he exclaimed, with self-deprecating good humour, once the tale had been concluded.

'No you're *not*!' David said loyally, smiling up into that beloved face. 'And you won't have to worry about the garden, *or* the big house ... me and Dad and Uncle Ronnie will have *everything* sorted out by the end of the weekend!'

'I can't tell you what it means to me to have this sort of back-up,' Grandad Darwin choked, with heartfelt sincerity, as his eyes moistened.

'Oh I'm looking *forward* to it ... we *all* are!' David said, as he slid back on to his feet. 'Anyway, I'd better let you get on with your dinner ... I mean tea ... *sorry*, mum calls it *dinner* in the evening, but I know *you* call it tea. In *any* case, I'll go down now and have mine, and I'll see you later!'

'Absolutely old boy; you go and have a good fill-up,' his grandfather said, with a cheery wink, as he studied his own meal.

'See you *later* then,' David reiterated, making for the door that led back down into the bunk bedroom.

'Oh, by the *way*,' Grandad spoke suddenly, turning his head awkwardly in the lad's direction, 'did you pat the lump in the wall for luck when you came up, my old David?'

'No, I was carrying the tray,' David replied, quickly realising that the old boy's current incapacity must have prevented him from carrying out this regular ritual. 'I'll do it on the way down,' he reassured with a smile, before finally leaving him to get on with his meal.

On his way through the bunk bedroom, the boy drew back the curtains to let in the evening light; some of which he hoped would allow him to better see the lump, and so perform the patting routine. Slowly descending the gloomy stairwell, David approached the lump in the wall halfway down, and felt honoured to be patting it for Grandad Darwin. However, as his hand hovered over the protruding mass, he thought he could feel an energy exuding from it, almost like static on a plastic surface. At the same time, he could have sworn he heard a peal of manic laughter, or rather, the residual echo of such a sound.

'Is that *you* Uncle Ronnie? I'm not *scared* you know!' he croaked, rapidly glancing both up and down the stairwell. There was no reply; there was only an eerie silence that almost seemed to be mocking him. As a result, David did not complete the lump patting ritual and, instead, ran back down the remaining steps and then through the sitting room, to the safety of the dining room and the familiarity of other family members.

The baked potatoes *did* taste different, thought David as he chewed his first mouthful, but he was almost determined that they would. The mealtime conversation also had a different flavour, and was not as lively as the usual Friday evenings. No one mentioned anything to do with Uncle Ronnie's alleged recent disgrace with that so-called schoolgirl. David speculated that, perhaps, they would have if he, a mere twelve-year-old, had not been present at the table.

It was his uncle who finally broke the long and awkward silence.

'Hey *Dave*, do you fancy getting up early tomorrow and then going to pick some mushrooms?' he asked, through a gob-full of home-cured ham.

David beamed at the prospect, but before he could respond, Nanna Darwin quickly intervened.

'But we always have *toast* on a Saturday morning,' she said, in a rather agitated manner. 'Umm, why don't you pick some on *Sunday* morning instead, eh?' The revised suggestion was aimed principally at Ronnie, and accompanied by a batch of indiscreet winks, each one seemingly more urgent than the previous.

Whatever she was desperately trying to communicate was completely lost on her youngest son.

'But I really want to go *tomorrow*,'Ronnie retorted, with a slight hint of petulance, almost as if *he* were the schoolboy at the table.

In response, David suddenly felt inspired to suggest the perfect compromise: 'then why don't we have fried mushrooms on toast?' David looked round at the adults present, none of whom could see the obvious solution to the problem.

Almost as one, everyone soon laughed and the ice was quickly broken.

A smiling Len looked at David proudly.

'My son, the diplomat,' he remarked cheerily, before leaning over to put his arm around the lad's shoulders.

With a far less tense atmosphere now established, Nanna Darwin went on to tell them – in a slightly edited version due to David's presence – of the terrible trouble that two of Lord and Lady Rothermead's children had recently got themselves into. One of the twin boys, Benedict, had been caught smuggling wine bottles out of his father's precious cellar. Apparently, he had been taking them up into the art studio he'd recently created from one of the deserted bedrooms in the old north wing, above the log store. Moreover, the cook and housekeeper to the 'big house', Mrs Cohen, had scandalised Nanna Darwin with talk of drunken teenage parties amongst the canvasses and of naked life models being the accepted norm. It was bad enough his having been expelled from school at Easter, for smoking cannabis of all things; now it seemed he was indulging in alcohol as well.

Ronnie raised his eyebrows at this 'terrible' story and looked at Len, who was trying to suppress a grin.

'Perhaps *I'll* help you get some more logs tonight, eh Len?' he proposed, with a sideways smirk.

'Yes, *lots* of logs!' Len responded, with a huge exaggerated wink. 'It'll probably take us quite a while!'

They both sniggered, and it was as if the clock had suddenly been turned back 20 years. David giggled too, his head rapidly vacillating between the two brothers.

Nanna Darwin was the only one not amused at the turn with which the teatime talk had suddenly taken.

'Now, now boys,' she scolded, looking over the top of her bifocals, 'think of David.'

'He's not *invited*!' chortled Len, a comment that made Ronnie nearly choke.

Now even the corners of Nanna's mouth were beginning to turn up.

'It won't do you naughty boys *any* good,' she smirked, behind a conveniently raised hand. 'That scallywag Benedict, and his *much* more sensible brother, Nigel, are currently abroad with the rest of the Dutnell family, so there won't be any of those scandalous parties *this* weekend!'

In immediate response to their mother's dismissive comment, both Len and Ronnie simultaneously distended their bottom lips in a collective mock sulk.

However, before they could have any more fun at Nanna Darwin's expense, she suddenly remembered the second part of her tale: an account of the other one of her employee's children to have disgraced themselves.

'When I said that the Dutnell family had gone abroad, what I *should* have said was that they'd all gone except Miss Victoria and, believe it or not, she's gone away for a week with the Carter family!' she announced with wide-eyed delight.

Whilst David and Ronnie both homed in on her words with great interest, Len stared back at his mother somewhat aghast.

'We are talking about the *same* Victoria, aren't we? ... that shy pear-shaped girl, with the long russet hair, who colours up whenever anyone says *hello* to her?' he asked, with brows furrowed.

'Yes of *course* I mean her ... shy or not, she's gone away with them alright; she's even taken that springer spaniel of hers as well; that's why Grandad and I aren't dog sitting for as long this year!'

'Well, *that's* a bit of comedown for her isn't it?' Len retorted, still unable to come to terms with the prospect.

'Apparently, Miss Victoria's got no choice in the matter,' Nanna responded, raising her eyebrows while giving a little shrug. 'You see, she's been sent down from school in disgrace, and her ladyship's placed her in the care of young Samantha Carter, as an older and more steadying influence!'

Len's facial expression now turned to one of shock, while Ronnie began to look decidedly uncomfortable, and wanted to know more.

'Err, being sent down…umm ... that means *expelled*, doesn't it?' he asked, by means of concerned clarification.

'Indeed it *does*!' Nanna Darwin gleefully confirmed; her mood governed more by the fact she had scandalous news to impart than it was the news' actual content.

'Doreen's keeping quiet, but Mrs Cohen reckons she'd been caught in the dorm getting up to goodness knows *what*, with another girl. We guessed probably alcohol or drugs,' she added in hushed tones; addressing her last comment principally to an open-mouthed Len, and completely failing to notice that Ronnie was now looking even more unsettled. Nanna leaned across the table, in conspiratorial pose, to deliver the denouement. 'And guess what: last weekend, we got a telephone call from her ladyship, all the way from France, asking, or rather instructing, Grandad and I to go down to Binningdene School and fetch her home!'

As soon as she had said the word 'Binningdene', Nanna Darwin realised that she had put her foot straight in it, and strayed on to the subject of Ronnie's recent indiscretion. She'd inadvertently touched on the taboo topic of fifteen-year-old schoolgirls and newspaper exposés, all of which was not to be mentioned in front of David. As a result, Ronnie hung his head and said nothing; in fact, no one said anything and the meal was finished in silence. David wondered to himself if Victoria Dutnell and Katie Townsend knew each other, and had been schoolfriends at Binningdene. He further speculated if the name 'Darwin' had ever come up when the two girls discussed either their boyfriends or their parents' employees.

A poker-faced Nanna finally collected the empty plates and shuffled off into the kitchen. At the same time, being desperate to escape the morose mood in the diningroom, David got up and grabbed the list on the sideboard, with a view to carrying out one of the many tasks written on it. The word 'boiler' was the first item on the list.

' 'Boiler'', he read with authority, whilst his father and uncle looked on, 'I know what to do there *too* ... I've watched Grandad *hundreds* of times.'

Both Ronnie and Len quickly stood up. 'I'll come with you,' they proposed simultaneously, and with equal keenness.

However, before David could dwell too long on the fact that there would be three of them going across to the 'big house', Nanna Darwin came back into the room, and was quick to decide just who would be accompanying David.

'*No* Len, I think you'd better go up and say hello to your poor father,' she strongly suggested, brandishing an extended index finger. 'And be a love and bring his tray when you come back down.'

Len nodded his reluctant acquiescence and slunk off, while David went

161

through to retrieve the bunch of keys to the 'big house' from the hook by the outside kitchen door. He and Ronnie quickly agreed to take the longer garden route to the cellar, as the Dutnells were away. Although somewhat circuitous, it gave them a rare chance to see much more of Grandad Darwin's horticultural handiwork. So they walked round the cottage end of the thirty-yard wall, past the door of the greenhouse, and then along the centre path of the vegetable garden. This led to a narrow brick arch. Walking through it they reached the second walled garden. This square-shaped area – which was not so well known to David, and even less so to Ronnie – was a riot of colour, largely from the neat rows of staked and supported perennials that seemed to occupy most of this garden. These were grown solely to be cut for Lady Rothermead's famous flower arrangements, which were usually displayed all around the 'big house'. Trained round the red-bricked walls were varieties of espaliered apples and pears, and in the four corners, sprouted spiky thickets of gooseberries and raspberries.

Another brick arch, set in the far wall, soon drew them into a long narrow garden area, set in an east-west configuration. This elongated space had an herbaceous border that extended along the outer face of the wall that in part enclosed the previous garden. On the opposite side of the central grass path, onto which they now turned left, was a thicket of shrubs that mostly hid the tall boundary wall of the grounds. David knew that beyond this was the lane to Rothermead Green: a continuation of the road they always took to get here from Beckensfield, and an alternative route to 'The Green', with its old windmill and cottages, if the more direct walk across the orchards wasn't chosen. The far end of this narrow linear garden soon opened out onto the sweeping, slightly sloping lawns in front of the imposing south wing to the 'big house'. This seemingly continuous green expanse was occasionally punctuated by mature trees, and bisected only by a long gravelled drive that led from the front gates, and ran in a southeast to northwest direction, right up to the property's imposing porticoed front entrance.

Halfway across the lawn, David and Ronnie noticed that the long swathe suddenly gave way to a strip of much shorter grass, just by an evergreen tree with low sweeping branches. However, it was David who first deduced the reason for this anomaly.

'*Look* Uncle Ronnie, this must be where Grandad Darwin was knocked off his mower,' he guessed, with the authority and deductive skill of a young Sherlock Holmes.

His uncle crouched down and then ran his hand over the uncut blades of grass and plantain heads.

'Looks like the old boy took his tumble just after he'd begun,' he said with a slow nod, scanning the entire lawn expanse. 'Most of it is still untouched!'

Moving on, the explorers crossed the gravel drive and onto more uncut grass before eventually coming to the large conservatory against the Regency half of the east wing. They now walked along the second less well used, metalled drive that led in from the outer courtyard, and then ran parallel to the east wing. David looked over at the 'big house' and noted the transition from the stuccoed early nineteenth century design to an earlier building phase. Having reached the timber framed part of the building's side elevation, David quickly located the crumbling brick path that led over towards the cellar steps. Never having ventured onto this part of the complex before, Ronnie looked about him with keen interest, as he followed David down the steep stone steps and into the darkened stairwell. Having reached that heavy old wooden door, David began sorting through the bunch of keys he'd been clutching.

'Which one *is* it then Dave?' Ronnie asked excitedly, as he stared down at the heavy bunch.

'It's this big black chunky one,' David replied authoritatively; holding the chosen item aloft, whilst the discarded keys hung off the ring below.

Taking the bunch, Ronnie inserted the key, turned it in the lock with a grating clonk, and then smiled triumphantly. Once the ancient studded door had been pushed open, David fumbled just inside to the right for the light switch, which soon pinked on before them. They then both descended the few further internal steps into the cavernous gloom of the boiler room.

'*Wow*,' a fascinated Ronnie exclaimed, as his eyes adjusted to the much-reduced light level, 'I don't think I've *ever* been down *here*!'

'*Fab*, isn't it!' David said as, like his uncle, he began to survey their surroundings.

After a minute or so of examining that rarely seen subterranean space, they approached the huge boiler in the recess to the left. A bewildered-looking Ronnie stared at the unfamiliar metal monster, with his hands on his hips.

'*So* then, what do we do with *this*?' he asked, before tapping on the glass-covered gauges with the nail of his right index finger.

With an air of confidence, David gently eased his uncle aside, and seized the blackened handle of the firebox door.

'As it's summer, and the Dutnell family are away, we only have to keep it ticking over!' he proudly exclaimed, before creaking the hatch open, and allowing a hot blast from the furnace to escape into the room.

Impressed, Ronnie turned the corners of his mouth down and nodded slowly.

'Yeah, I suppose the only person using the hot water at the moment would be Mrs Cohen,' he reasoned, before suddenly screwing his face up, but grinning at the same time. 'Hey *Dave*, imagine seeing old Ma Cohen in her bathtub, eh?'

'No *thanks*!' David giggled, trying to replicate Ronnie's grimace.

Still chuckling, David put a couple of shovels full of coke on the fire and then checked the temperature and water gauges, as if he'd carried out this task every day of his life. In reality, having seen Grandad Darwin do it only a handful of times, his performance was more bluff than anything else, but at least Edwina

Cohen would now be able to enjoy her regular Saturday-night soak tomorrow.

Having completed his task, David turned round to talk to Ronnie, but his uncle was nowhere to be seen.

'Are…are you *hiding* Uncle Ronnie?' David called timidly, 'I'm not frightened you know!'

'In *here* Dave,' came Ronnie's resounding voice from beyond the low arch in the opposite wall, which led through into his Lordship's wine cellar.

An anxious-looking David slowly walked over to the curved archway through which he had never ventured.

'Grandad always says that it's out-of-bounds in there,' he called out nervously, and surprising himself at the echo that resulted.

'Never mind that; just get *in* here mate,' said the unseen Ronnie, in an impatient manner.

Crouching down, David stepped forward into the forbidden territory and found himself in a low narrow passage which, after three or four yards, opened out into another barrel-vaulted cellar, similar to, but lower and much older-looking than the boiler house. In fact, the entire cavern seemed to be constructed from irregular pieces of cream-coloured stone, with regular patches of red Tudor brickwork visible here and there across the surface.

Unfortunately, it quickly became apparent that the cavern's undoubted antiquity was not his uncle's main concern.

'Look at *this* lot,' a beaming Ronnie enthused, motioning towards the high racks of dusty cobwebbed bottles. He then went in closer and, with almost reverential care, pulled one out of its slot.

David looked on extremely concerned, and was about to say something to his companion, but soon found that panic had rendered him temporarily mute.

'Don't *worry* Dave, I'm just looking,' a slightly amused Ronnie reassured him; glancing up briefly at his nephew before wiping dust from the aged label. 'Cor, these must be worth a *fortune*, and I bet they *taste* good too!'

However, David wasn't able to relax until Ronnie had safely put the bottle back into its allotted place. Breathing a sigh of relief, David quickly decided that coming into the wine cellar would definitely be another one of their shared secrets.

With the ancient cellar door locked behind them, the pair re-emerged into the subdued sunlight of a fine summer's evening. Straightaway, Ronnie squinted across at the vast expanse of largely uncut lawn.

'Where does Grandad Darwin keep the ride-on mower?' he wondered, looking back at his nephew with a quizzical expression.

'Over there,' Dave replied, pointing leftwards to a small lean-to shed, situated just to the right of the wrought-iron gates that led out into the outer courtyard. 'He must have somehow managed to put it away after the fall!'

'*No*, he told me that Smiler helped him in with it, and then walked with him back to the cottage,' his uncle explained, in matter of fact tones. Ronnie's eyes then narrowed, and a broad grin spread across his face.

'Do you happen to know which of the keys would unlock that shed?' he asked, his eyebrows now raised in hopeful expectation.

'I sure *do*!' David smiled, quickly realising what was being suggested.

Ronnie beamed and then held up his left hand.

'*Scar Brothers*,' he shouted with gusto.

'*Scar Brothers*', a delighted Dave responded, as their left hands banged together and gripped for the first time in months.

Laughing heartily, they both raced across the grass to see who'd be the first to reach the shed doors. It turned out to be a dead heat. The padlock yielded easily, thanks to Grandad Darwin's regular oiling, and the doors were rapidly swung open to reveal the monster mower within. It wasn't long before they'd managed to push it out into the evening's crepuscular light.

Wasting no time at all, Ronnie began to scramble onto the unfamiliar device.

'Do you know how it works?' he asked, lowering himself onto the driver's bucket seat.

'Only a bit,' David confessed, as he climbed up to a standing position immediately behind his uncle. 'That switch opens the fuel line and that first lever lowers the outer blades,' he indicated each in turn, with his left arm extended over Ronnie's shoulder.

Ronnie flicked the switch, and then yanked the designated lever into the 'down' position. As predicted, the huge rotary blades gently sunk to the ground either side of them. With that done, Ronnie pressed the starter button and she fired up at the first attempt. Straightaway, both of them laughed in triumphant unison.

Then Ronnie noticed a potential problem.

'The blades aren't rotating,' he shouted to David, above the noise of the chattering engine.

'It's that second lever ... the one on your right!' bellowed David from behind, and pointing at the same time for good measure.

Sure enough, as soon as the lever in question had been deployed, the mower blades began to rotate furiously.

'Here goes then, *hang on*,' Ronnie instructed, as he reached down to let out the handbrake.

Expectant with excitement, David grabbed onto his uncle's shoulders and, as the accelerator pedal was depressed, they were off with a violent lurch. Gradually, Ronnie went faster as his confidence grew, and as a result, grass cuttings flew into the air with ever increasing height. It wasn't long before David had to duck as the branches of a rowan tree – which they'd evidently passed by rather closely – brushed his head and shoulders, dislodging many clusters of its unripened green berries. If that avoiding action hadn't been taken, the alarmed boy realised that it could very well have been another Grandad Darwin-type situation. Ronnie hadn't noticed though; he was too busy having fun.

Having recovered from the near miss, David realised that there was another hazard rapidly approaching ahead.

'*The drive*,' he shouted, daring to loosen his grip enough to tap his uncle briefly on the right shoulder.

'*Yeah*, not bad for my first attempt is it!' Ronnie bellowed proudly, as he maintained his course.

'No, *the drive*, the *gravel drive*!' David was now panicking but too anxious to do anything but keep holding on tightly.

Unfortunately, David's dire warning came too late. The mower left the lawn and skimmed across the driveway amidst a shower of stinging gravel and a deafening clatter, before rejoining the turf on the other side with a jolting bump. Not the least bit discouraged, Ronnie hooted with manic laughter and even increased speed as he approached the top of the lawn, which terminated in a gentle semi-circular curve.

Relishing the challenge he saw coming up ahead, Ronnie narrowed his eyes, and gripped the steering wheel even tighter .

'*Lean to the right Dave*,' he shouted, as the speeding mower began to negotiate the curve.

'*Al...alright then*!' David bellowed, barely making himself heard above the roaring engine, as his uncle yanked the wheel to the right.

With the mower now lurching dangerously to the left, in spite of both passengers attempting to counteract the sideways thrust, pot marigold heads and lady's mantle leaves began to fly up as one of the outer blades sliced through the border's edge. As the mower finally came out of the curve at speed, on two of the four wheels, both Ronnie and David screamed out; the former in uncontrollable excitement, the latter in complete and utter terror. David barely had time to recover when he noticed that they were now flying down the straight edge of the lawn, next to the walled garden, and heading directly for the 'big house'. Worst still, with the added gravitational advantage of the gentle downward slope, the lawn mower seemed to be picking up speed all the while. Completely oblivious to any potential danger, his uncle let out a frenzied scream and, as his lordship's house got ever closer, a panic-gripped David seriously considered bailing out. Only the sight and sound of the mower blades, spinning wildly all around them, deterred him from taking that drastic step, but it was a very close call.

Now out of control, Ronnie whooped loudly like some demented cowboy.

'Another right turn, *Davey me old mate; you know what to do*,' he yelled, before yanking the steering wheel hard round in his intended direction.

David saw little point in replying, and considered it equally useless to mention the fact that the mower was once again about to join the main driveway, immediately in front of the 'big house'. In any case, his dry-throated bellows would probably never be heard above the jangling of the gravel that was about to erupt from all four spinning blades. The motor-mower barely made the turn in time; in fact, they came so close to the house that David could clearly see the reflection of his own fear-gripped face in the glass of the elegant Regency windows as they flashed past the frontage.

Ronnie was now ready for his second circuit and briefly glanced round with glee at his un-amused nephew.

'*And the vehicle slows round the chicane in front of the conservatory, before making another attempt at the speed record,*' he shouted, in a parody of the mannered style usually adopted by formula-one commentators.

Never had David been more glad to see his father who, at that very moment, could be seen coming through the open gateway from the outer courtyard. Ronnie saw him too and, sensing he was in trouble, steered the mower towards his brother, rather than back up the garden, and then slowed to a stop.

'I might have *known* it was you two!' remarked a grinning Len, with hands on hips. 'Mrs Cohen has just come running up to the cottage in a panic. She wanted to telephone the police as, in her owns words, there were two hooligans riding round his lordship's lawn on a motorbike and side-car!'

Ronnie screamed out with laughter; not only because of what had happened, but also as his older brother had attempted to impersonate the Dutnell's cook.

'The blind old bag,' he hooted, revving the mower up. 'This is hardly a fucking Harley-Davidson!'

Quickly recognising the warning signs, Len carefully studied his brother's features and the smile slowly faded from his face, to be replaced with a look of concern. He then discreetly motioned for David to dismount and the boy gladly stepped down on to the relative safety of the lawn. Len knew not to challenge or scold Ronnie directly, when he was so clearly in the midst of one of his manic highs. Experience taught him to play along, and then his little brother would come down on his own and, hopefully, avoid plummeting too far into a depressive episode.

'Well I *mean* ... does this thing *look* like a sodding motorbike to you then Len?' a still-laughing Ronnie said, as he bounced up and down on the mower's seat.

'*Quite*, and with eyesight like that, it makes you wonder what poor Edwina Cohen puts in her cooking,' Len commented, carefully keeping to the theme.

'*Yeah*, no wonder the Dutnells go abroad a lot ... it's the only way to get away from her 'orrible *dinners*!' retorted a chuckling Ronnie, unintentionally paraphrasing Grandad Darwin. He then stared up into the twilight sky and turned the mower's engine off. 'Umm, getting a bit dusky to finish this off now,' he added, before jumping down and then brushing the dried grass off his trousers.

'Yes, I think you're *right* mate,' Len said much-relieved, as he nodded in fervent agreement, 'besides which, we'd better go and reassure poor old Edwina, or she'll *never* get to sleep tonight!'

Ronnie sighed and shrugged his shoulders, but then, quite unexpectedly, struck a bizarre superhero-like pose.

'But tomorrow is another day and *Mower Man* will ride again!' he declared, in a mock American accent, before adopting another exaggerated attitude.

That harmless bit of horseplay finally coaxed David out of his shock, and he began to giggle. In fact, all three of the Darwin males laughed, as they first put the mower away and then made their way back to the cottage.

Len had never been included on one of the family's early morning mushroom gathering walks before; he'd never been up in time. So, this would be his first one and he made sure not to miss out by getting David to bang on his door, on the grounds that his son was usually the first one awake. However, on that particular Saturday morning, there was a problem. Ronnie, who was sleeping in the lower bunk that Lucy usually occupied, had evidently experienced a very disturbed night. David had been kept awake for long periods at a time. On each occasion that Ronnie moaned in his sleep, the wary twelve-year-old thought it was coming from the stairwell, and this had done little to help him drift off. Ronnie had also been rolling about violently in his sleep, and each time, this shuddered the upper bunk, where David was billeted as usual. Worst of all though, the unconscious Ronnie had talked almost continuously in a disturbed manner, as if having bad nightmares, and even called out Katie's name several times. As a result of all this disturbance, David was still fast asleep at 07:00, which was the agreed time for him to have been knocking on the door of the yellow bedroom. Luckily, Ronnie who, quite understandably, had preferred to be awake than have night terrors, was already up and so made sure that both his brother and nephew were awake in time.

Once Len was safely in the bathroom, an already dressed Ronnie came back into the bunk bedroom and shinned up the wooden steps to join David on the top bunk. He ruffled his nephew's hair as he often did in greeting.

'*Sorry* if I kept you awake last night Dave. I had *such* terrible dreams, well…*nightmares* really I suppose!' he confessed, with a sheepish shrug.

'Were they about Katie?' Dave asked quietly, and somewhat cautiously, realising that he was straying into a taboo subject that, thus far, everyone had skirted around.

Fortunately, rather than shrink from any reference to his recent trouble, as he'd done the previous evening, Ronnie merely looked at his nephew with an expression of astonishment.

'How did *you* know that I'd dreamt of her?' he asked, in a half-whisper, whilst leaning in towards the boy.

Relieved that his Scar Brother's privileges still held, David chuckled warmly.

'You were talking in your sleep, that's all!' he said with a knowing smile.

Ronnie puckered his mouth and then nodded slowly in acquiescence. 'Yes, they *were* about Katie…. you see Dave … I love her, and I miss her so much!' he sighed, with a pained grimace and fatalistic flick of the eyebrows.

In response, David quickly looked downwards, and instantly felt the hot embers of embarrassment on his neck and face. Not only was he taken aback at his uncle's frankness, but also he felt completely at a loss as to what to say in reply.

At once, his uncle picked up on his nephew's discomfort, and desperately sought to set the record straight.

'Dave, look...*please*,' Ronnie stuttered, with heartfelt passion, 'there's something you *must* understand and I'm telling you the absolute truth here. I did *not* know she was only 15. Do you believe me?' The answer was phrased as if so much depended on the answer it would receive.

Fortunately, David wasn't about to let him down.

'Yes, Uncle Ronnie, of *course* I do!' he responded, without a moment's hesitation.

Ronnie smiled and looked relieved as he patted the boy's pyjama-clad knee.

'*Thanks* mate, it means a lot to have you on my side,' he stated gratefully, knowing that David had spoken from the heart, and had not been influenced by any desire to say the right thing; to utter the appropriate words so as not to upset poor, fragile Ronnie.

David was pleased too, and yet, at the same time, somewhat puzzled by the comment.

'But we're *all* on your side ... Nanna and Grandad Darwin, my dad...'

'*No*, not Len I'm afraid,' Ronnie said. 'No...that's not quite fair, he *has* been very good to me over the last week, except that...'

'Except *what*?' his confused nephew queried, reaching to grab his uncle's arm.

Ronnie glanced briefly over at the doorway into the narrow passage, and then edged closer to the intensely attentive David.

'*Except* that he made me promise never to see Katie again!' he said forlornly. 'Your dad *means* well, I know *that* Dave; he's trying to protect me from more press intrusion and... err... prosecution, but we're *in love* Dave.'

Ronnie hung his head slightly and gave a half-hearted shrug of his shoulders.

'I just hope she still feels the same way, and is missing me too!' He paused once again to sigh deeply. 'And frankly, I don't care if she *is* only 15, I *love* her and one day, you'll know what that feels like, and it won't matter to you *how* old or young that person is.'

As Ronnie stared at him plaintively, the boy's head dropped again.

'Katie *is* very beautiful,' David said rather bashfully, as he stared into his lap.

Ronnie smiled and ruffled his nephew's hair once more.

'*Ah*, the surge of the old hormones ... I remember it well...and yes, she *is* very beautiful,' he happily confirmed, before his face returned to a more serious expression. 'And that's why I've decided that I must...I *have* to go and see her!'

David's head instantly shot up, and it was he who now looked very worried.

'But your promise to Dad, how will you...I mean, do you know *where* she...'

'I don't feel *good* about lying to Len,' Ronnie said quickly, 'but then I'd feel *worse* if I couldn't hold her again; if I couldn't tell her that everything is alright. You see Dave; things were…rather *complicated* when she and I last parted. So, when we get back to Canterbury, I'm going to jump ship at the first opportunity.'

He then fixed David with the most intense of stares, before extending out his left index finger to emphasize what he was about to say.

'This is just between you and me Dave; this is another one of our confidences. Do you understand mate?'

David swallowed hard and then nodded vigorously. 'Yes, Uncle Ronnie, you don't have to worry about me!' he vowed smiling broadly.

In response, his uncle's pointing gesture transformed into an upright flattened hand, and the 'Scar Brothers' ritual was performed to reinforce the understanding just reached between them.

Ronnie took himself off downstairs and David quickly slipped into the bathroom after his father. Within ten minutes, all three had assembled in the dining room. Len put some more logs on the Rayburn, while David quickly did his greenhouse duty, effectively reversing what he'd done during the previous evening.

That job done, David met his father and Uncle Ronnie at the top of the outer courtyard.

'Got the trugs?' he asked his grinning uncle.

'No, I always walk this way,' Ronnie quipped as he proceeded to swagger along like John Wayne.

'*I've* got them!' tutted Len, trying to conceal a smile as he held up a stack of three cardboard containers.

The trio set off, but it wasn't long before David wanted to establish just where they would be heading for that morning.

'Shall we go to the windmill and back?' he suggested, glancing keenly from one adult to the other. 'Assuming of course, that it's still *there*!'

'Oh my God, *yes*,' Ronnie frowned, coming to a sudden halt. 'I'd *forgotten* all about that. But wasn't there a local protest being organised to save it?'

In response to the enquiry, Len shrugged his shoulders, and then looked to his son for the answer.

'Nanna and Grandad Darwin *did* sign a petition I think,' David said, as they resumed their progress past the stable block. 'I should have looked out of the back bedroom window this morning, but then again, you never *can* see clearly up to the green when the cherry trees are in leaf'.

Having left the farm buildings behind, they soon found themselves in the first of the cherry orchards, where each of the trees were hanging heavy with ripening fruit. A stack of ladders and baskets, which had been placed at the orchard's edge, was a sure sign that the fruit picking was destined to begin the following week. From past experience, David knew that it would be alright to eat a few cherries as they walked through, just as long as it didn't spoil his breakfast. He located a particularly heavy-laden tree, and eagerly reached for a large juicy looking specimen that was hanging from a low branch. And then, just as his fingers made contact with the cherry's shiny black surface, there came a loud deafening bang that made David jump out of his skin. Both Ronnie and Len also looked rather alarmed, until it dawned on them all that the noise they'd heard must have been the automatic cherry gun; the one that old Bill Blackett set up every year to keep the birds away from the ripening crop. Having recovered from the shock, they began to pluck and eat the ripe and ready cherries, but only Ronnie and David spat the stones at each other.

Scrumping was soon forgotten when the first of the mushrooms was found. Unlike the cherries though, they were neither large nor plentiful. It didn't take Ronnie long to realise that his insisting the usual Sunday-morning mushroom hunt be brought forward a day, had probably scuppered Nanna Darwin's chance to obtain and then scatter some shop-bought mushrooms for David's benefit. But then again, he consoled himself with the thought that, given her preoccupation with Grandad's illness, she may never have been able to organise the deception in any case. As it turned out, the few mushrooms they were managing to locate were the first of the real batch; a crop that would become a lot more plentiful as late summer gave way to autumn. Nevertheless, by the time the hunter-gatherers were halfway through the second and older cherry orchard, they had amassed just enough between them, to fill one of the trugs.

As they neared Rothermead Green, both Ronnie and David began to scan for the first sight of the old tower mill above the treetops. The latter was soon anxiously peering upwards and wondering if it would still be there. Grandad Darwin would know, but sadly, the old boy wasn't there to ask that morning.

'*There* it is, thank *goodness*!' Ronnie shouted suddenly, his superior height having given him the advantage. 'But what's that draped around it?'

David began to run forward, his head still tilted upwards. 'I *still* can't see it yet…oh yes, *there* it is', he declared triumphantly, glancing back briefly at his companions. 'And I think there's some sort of banner tied to it!'

Even Len began to look interested now, and all three of them quickened their pace.

By the time they reached the edge of the orchard, they could see that it was indeed a banner, and one reading: '*Save our heritage, save Rothermead Mill*'. Ronnie breathed another sigh of relief: it seemed that the local people had done something about it after all. However, his initial feeling of optimism was soon dashed, when he reached the five-bar gate that accessed the green. From here, it became obvious that the demolition gang had already paid a visit, for nothing now remained of the pair of ruined eighteenth century cottages they'd admired back in the spring; nothing that is, save a spread of brick rubble.

Ronnie hurriedly led the party over the gate, across the circuitous gravel track and then onto the green itself, from where they were all better able to take in their immediate surroundings. It was still early, and as yet, there was no one else about. Rothermead Green was eerily silent, except for the distant and almost imperceptible barking of a dog. Even the birds were hushed, having now completed their nesting season and temporarily forgotten their territorial tunes.

It was Ronnie who finally broke the silence.

'If only I'd thought to bring my camera,' he said, throwing his arms out to the side. 'What a *damned* shame; this moment, this…this brief *interim* phase needs to be recorded!'

David very much empathised with his uncle's regret, but quickly sought to reassure him.

'At least you have all those pictures you took in the spring,' he pointed out, as they gradually approached the much-changed demolition site.

Now that closer inspection was possible, it became clear that one of the pair of semi-detached nineteenth century cottages, sited to the left of the mill tower, had also been pulled down, but the resultant untidy pile of collapsed bricks and structural timber had not yet been cleared away. The cottage on the far left, in other words: the one adjacent to the next occupied dwelling, was battered but still intact. However, the presence of a mechanical digger, parked adjacent to it on the green, no doubt heralded its imminent destruction within days, if not hours. With hands firmly placed on his hips, Ronnie studied the surviving cottage closely. A magnificent deep pink double rose in full flower hung in thorny tendrils from the dark red-bricked walls. In contrast, the whole floriferous mass seemed bound together by a dense tangle of yellow honeysuckle; the scent from which mingled with that of the roses and filled the warming early morning air.

Having paid homage to the one surviving home, Ronnie and David walked back over to where the older pair of cottages had, until recently, stood in glorious ruin. A still-smouldering heap of grey ash marked the spot where the cottage's few remaining beams and joists had been burnt, along with the smashed and severed branches of the elder and buddleia, with whom they had shared the roofless shell. Those shrubs had sought and been given refuge within the abandoned walls where they'd thrived for many years. Sadly though, they had now been put to the fire, along with the remains of their former sanctuary: a kind of pogrom for wild plants.

Ronnie picked up a charred buddleia branch from the edge of the bonfire. Its scorched leaves and unrealised flower buds clearly saddened him.

'What a superb flowering spectacle this would have made,' he said, before tossing the singed branch away.

Unaffected by such romantic concerns, or ruminous regrets, Len surveyed the scene from a different perspective.

'What are they planning to build here, d'you know?' he asked, glancing at his younger family members, and wondering why they both seemed so upset.

'I don't know…I don't really *care* either!' Ronnie said, before kicking at a fallen brick, and sending up clouds of demolition dust.

'At least the mill's still here,' David observed cheerily, once again eager to emphasize the more positive aspects for his uncle's benefit.

'Yes, you're *right* Dave!' Ronnie smiled, with an accompanying nod, before he looked up at the banner defiantly draped round the black brick conical tower of the old windmill.

The one consolation for the destruction of the old cottages, and the clearance of their excessively overgrown gardens, was that an unobstructed view of the old mill could now be appreciated. It was no longer cowering behind the Dutnell-owned dwellings with which it had been associated all its life, but standing proud and erect on its own.

Ronnie, once more took the lead as the party proceeded to pick their way across the rubble-strewn ground to the base of the tower.

'At least they won't be pulling *this* down,' he remarked, before reaching out his hand to touch the pitch-coated brickwork. 'And if they ever dare to *think* of it, the locals will stop 'em!'

'What makes you so sure about *that*?' Len asked, with furrow-browed seriousness. 'Do you think that a determined developer is going to take any notice of a few well-meaning, middle-class, middle-aged local protestors?'

'But…but the mill's still *here*, isn't it?' Ronnie reasoned, gesturing towards the structure with both arms. 'Perhaps they'll build *round* it instead!'

David, who had been following the exchange intently, nodded in optimistic agreement at his uncle's comment.

His father saw this and didn't want to raise his son's hopes, only for him to be disappointed, as happens so often in life.

'Well, the mill looks *very* vulnerable to me!' he stated calmly and coldly, whilst giving a dismissive shrug. He then placed his hands in his trouser pockets, turned away, and looked out across the empty green.

Len had seen many beloved and familiar historic buildings torn down in 1950s Canterbury, and that was in spite of much vigorous local opposition. As a result, he was somewhat cynical about the effect that any protest might have once a developer had it in mind to clear a particular site. Ronnie, on the other hand, had acquired no such experience, and did not know what to say in response to Len's pessimistic prognosis. His assuredness that no harm would come to the windmill, was based as much on a child-like belief that no one could possibly want to destroy something so beautiful, as it was in his faith that the residents of Rothermead Green would not let anyone demolish their precious mill: the very symbol of the local primary school. For his part, David understood the idealistic concepts of his uncle, far more than he did his father's experience-based cynicism.

Having ruminated on the remains, Ronnie and David walked round the base of the tower, while Len peered inside its small, low front entrance, where the door had been forced open, presumably by local children. Apart from this way in, they quickly established that there was another, much wider, access point further round to the right, but secured by a pair of stout wooden doors and a well-rusted padlock.

Ronnie paused by this and then took a step back in order to better study it.

'Look Dave, I wonder if these doors have been inserted more recently ... you know, after it ceased to be working mill?' he suggested, before running his fingers over some of the slightly newer-looking brickwork that surrounded this larger entrance.

'Well, Grandad Darwin once told me that one of the last cottagers had converted the base of the redundant mill tower into a garage,' David declared, with a proud, authoritative-looking expression.

Satisfied that David had given a reasonable enough explanation to confirm his hypothesis, Ronnie joined Len at the front of the mill. He too leaned in at the small original entrance, and straightaway noticed an intact flight of wooden steps, on the left, which he assumed led up to the next level.

'Fancy trying to get to the top?' he asked, looking back at Len and David.

'Oh *yes*, uncle, *let's*!' David exclaimed, clearly excited by the idea.

Len, on the other hand, seemed hesitant, if not a little worried.

'I dunno, I wonder if it's safe?' he speculated, once more studying the mill's dingy interior. However, his curiosity and long suppressed sense of adventure, finally won the fight over his fatherly sense of responsibility, and he became the first of the three to step inside the old tower.

'Just don't tell your *mother*,' warned father to son, as the others quickly joined him. 'Come to think of it: don't tell *my* mother *either*!' he added for good measure, much to the amusement of Ronnie who was not far behind.

Len was pleased to discover that the series of wooden steps, and the various floor levels between, seemed to be in a remarkably good state of preservation and easily took their combined weight. However, all of them noticed that every trace of the old mill mechanism, except for a huge pair of millstones dumped at ground level, appeared to have been removed long ago. The final flight of wooden steps, a much narrower and steeper one, terminated at a trap door that was secured by a simple slide bolt. Ronnie, who led the final assault, soon had it shifted and then threw open the hatch to reveal, not the interior of the mill's cap, which was long gone, but instead, a vast area of clear blue sky above them.

Ronnie pulled David up after him and then offered Len a helping arm. Soon, all three of them were standing in transfixed awe on the flat roof, at the very top of the mill tower. There was neither cloud nor mist, nor even a heat haze to compromise the magnificent view that could be enjoyed for miles in every direction. Len was quick to point out the series of smoke-belching paper mills that stretched along the Milton Creek from Sittingbourne, right up to the Swale Estuary and the Isle of Sheppey.

David listened to his father, but was more interested in the much closer Rothermead Farm that stood out well in the landscape, surrounded as it was by the dark green mass of foliage from the many trees that crowded the acres of cherry orchards.

'I think I can see the smoke from the cottage chimney,' David said, as he squinted hard against the sun and pointed in the appropriate direction.

'Good ho!' Ronnie replied, rubbing his stomach in an exaggerated fashion. 'That means the Rayburn will be nice and hot for our breakfast.'

Having got over the initial impact of that magnificent 360 degree view, Len became more aware of exactly where they were, and began to become concerned for his son's safety.

'Don't get too close to the edge, David ... there's absolutely nothing to prevent you from a nasty fall!' he warned, holding out a restraining arm that David was only too keen to take heed of.

Ronnie however, took absolutely no notice and almost as a gesture of defiance, proceeded to stand right on the edge in order to look down at the demolition site below. Having done so, he once again surveyed the surrounding countryside.

'When I've got my own television series and a bit of money, I shall buy this mill and convert it into a house,' he vowed, glancing briefly back at his two relatives, before throwing his arms out to the side in a Christ-like pose. 'Imagine looking at this view *every day*!'

'Oh uncle, that's a *brilliant* idea!' David enthused, daring to take one more step closer to his edge-perching relative.

Len smiled, but said nothing in response. In fact, he was dubious about the proposition for a number of reasons. Firstly, he wasn't convinced the mill would survive the coming week, let alone the undefined period ahead, during which Ronnie might achieve the success he had just envisioned. Secondly, and more crucially, Len knew that his brother would need to first ride out this current Katie controversy with no ill effect, or lasting consequences, before there could ever be any talk of a television series.

At that moment, Ronnie's attention was diverted by a person below, who was hurrying across the green in their direction, and waving his arms about in an agitated manner.

'Who's *this* joker?' he asked, before beckoning his brother towards him, and then waving back to the anonymous, yet animated figure at ground level.

'*Excuse me, excuse me,*' could now faintly be heard from this person, who had broken into a trot as he approached the demolition site.

In alarmed response, Len leant forward as far as he dared in order to monitor the man's progress.

'He's not coming up *here*, is he?' he asked anxiously, his newfound sense of adventure rapidly deserting him.

The question was soon answered by the clatter of urgent footfalls that could be heard coming from within the mill tower, and which were getting progressively louder.

Ronnie soon noticed that David was beginning to look even more nervous than Len.

'Don't worry Dave, I'll shut the trapdoor and then stand on it ... whoever it is, he'll not get up *here*!' Ronnie said unfazed, as he gave the lad a reassuring wink.

Len looked at Ronnie with even more concern, and couldn't decide if he was joking or not, but didn't want to take the risk.

'No, leave this to me,' Len ordered, as he glanced briefly at the still-open hatch. 'And remember Ronnie: keep a low profile, do nothing, *say* nothing, okay?'

Ronnie met Len's intense stare and grimaced crossly.

'What do you think I'm going to *do*, offer to shag his fifteen-year-old daughter?' he retorted, in an angry manner. 'Of *course* I'll say nothing!'

As the echoing footfalls became louder still, Len began to imagine a mill-top altercation and the resultant newspaper headlines the next day, reading: '*Trespass trio topple teacher from top of tower*'. He assumed that the man currently climbing the tower was a teacher; only because it scanned better than if he had been a quantity surveyor, or chiropodist

Finally, the head of the unknown man, of indeterminate employment, appeared through the open trap. Anxiously, he looked round at all three of them, who were staring just as anxiously back down at him.

'Oh, thank goodness for *that*,' the villager said, scrambling to his feet, 'you don't *look* like demolition contractors to me.'

The Rothermead Green resident was quite short, and had dark curly hair that was receding at the front. His dark-rimmed glasses were round and made him look studious. His facial features were small by comparison. Age-wise, he could have been anything from 25 to 40. As with the man's chosen career, Len could not pin this down.

Len now stepped forward and quietly cleared his throat.

'Err *no*, we're not contractors; my name is Leonard Darwin and ... umm ... we've walked up from Rothermead Farm,' he explained, in an overly authoritative manner.

'Ah *yes*, you must be George and Elizabeth Darwin's son,' the now-smiling man responded, tucking his stripy shirt into his trousers; a legacy from having dressed rather rapidly. 'I know your parents quite *well*; they live next door to the Carters, *don't* they!'

Straightaway, Len seemed to relax, having established friendly contact, and even offered his hand to shake in proper greeting, although he didn't yet know the man's name. David, on the other hand, had only just finished wondering to whom the man could be referring, having only ever heard his grandparents called 'Nanna and Grandad' by each and every family member, including themselves to each other.

Having established they were no immediate threat, the villager introduced himself.

'Anyway, my name is James Garrison ... I'm a teacher at the local primary school,' he announced, once more shaking hands with Len, for good measure.

Well I'll be buggered, Len thought to himself; he *is* a teacher!

Garrison stared briefly, but quizzically, into Ronnie's face as he shook hands with him, and then quickly looked away.

'Umm, for my sins, I'm organising and…I suppose, *leading* the protests against the proposal to demolish the mill. You see, when I saw the three of you on top of the tower, I naturally feared the worse.'

Ronnie beamed, and couldn't help but break his enforced silence.

'So how *did* you manage to save the mill in the end?' he asked, with a look of delighted relief on his face.

In immediate response to the question, the teacher puckered his mouth, and screwed up his eyes.

'Unfortunately, we *haven't* as yet,'he responded, with a regretful air before, once again, studying Ronnie's face and seemingly registering a faint glimmer of recognition.

'You…you mean they really *are* going to pull it down?' gasped a distressed Ronnie in open-mouthed disbelief.

'Sadly, it seems that way, yes,'Garrison sighed, with a fatalistic shrug of the shoulders. 'The contractors could return and finish the job at *any* time, and at the end of the day, there's *nothing* we can do about it, except, perhaps, hope and pray for some eleventh-hour *miracle* to occur!'

He walked slowly over to the edge and then looked down at his own cottage, nestling within its lush, leafy garden, on the other side of the green.

'Every morning of my life, after I've woken up, the first thing I see, opening the curtains, is this old windmill.' He then turned to face the three Darwins, and Ronnie in particular. 'If *only* we could have made the protest more high-profile, engaged the support of a famous person, or something like that, it might very well have made *all* the difference!'

A suddenly alarmed-looking Len held his breath, as Ronnie opened his mouth to respond. Fortunately he managed to catch his younger brother's eye and tried to appear as facially threatening as he could.

Ronnie returned his stern gaze, and held it for a few seconds, before appearing to finally relent.

'What a shame!' was his only comment in response to the sad news.

The mushroom trugs were exactly where they had left them, against the post of the five-bar gate that led back into the cherry orchard. Having climbed over the gate, a crestfallen Ronnie continued to glance back at the old mill tower with every other step he took, until it could no longer be seen, beyond the dense foliage of the cherry trees.

'I wonder if I'll ever see the old mill again', he mused miserably, and quietly to himself. After that, Ronnie hung his head and said nothing more, as they all trudged homewards.

Len immediately recognised the signs and was very concerned for his younger brother. The 'high' that Ronnie had been on since Friday evening was now all too evidently at an end. However, he reassured himself that it hadn't been an extreme high, not one of the more manic episodes, so he hoped that the corresponding fall would also be a moderate one. All Len knew for certain, was that as sure as the old windmill on Rothermead Green was coming down, so was Ronnie, and that, as always, he would be there for him throughout.

Arriving back at the cottage, David and Len were surprised to see Grandad Darwin up, dressed and cutting slices of bread at the dining room table.

'But, didn't the doctor say you couldn't get out of bed until Sunday *afternoon* at the earliest?' Len protested , his words and manner not giving away whether he was pleased, or not, to see his father up.

Grandad merely smiled and winked at his eldest son, before greeting David with his usual enthusiasm.

In fact it was Nanna who responded to Len's concern.

'Yes the doctor *did* say that,'she muttered with a wry smile on her face, carrying a pile of plates through from the kitchen, ' ... but once that stubborn old devil's made up his mind, you all *know* what he's like!'

What she neglected to say was that her husband wanted to get up and about as soon as possible, so that he wouldn't be treated in the same shabby manner as poor old Bill Blackett had been. The Rothermead Farm foreman, who'd been rather ill since Easter, had recently learnt that he was to be dismissed by the Dutnells, and replaced by a younger man, who was due to arrive sometime that very weekend.

'Yes, he's a stubborn old Grandad,' the man in question mimicked, grinning broadly in his tension-defusing way, before winking at his grandson, who now sat at the table next to him.

David busied himself slicing the gathered mushrooms for the pan, while a quiet and forlorn-looking Ronnie tried to slip off unnoticed in the direction of the sittingroom. Straightaway, both Nanna and Grandad Darwin looked at Len with concern, for they also recognised those telltale signs in their youngest son's behaviour. Len quickly confirmed their suspicions with a discreet nod of his head and then, raising his eyebrows, pointed in the direction of the sittingroom to indicate his next course of action. Nanna nodded in response, as if confirming her approval, and Len slipped off quietly to seek out his brother. David observed this silent communication with fascination, for he had seen it in operation on previous occasions. In fact, his family had found themselves in this very position many times before and, as a result, words were no longer necessary.

Within five minutes, Len returned to the diningroom, his arm around the shoulders of his unhappy, head-hanging brother.

'Now, if you could make the toast, Ronnie ... that would be very helpful,' he gently cajoled, giving his brother's back a friendly and fraternal series of pats.

A blank-faced Ronnie gave a resigned nod, reached for the faithful old brass toasting fork and obediently pushed a piece of the cut bread on to its blackened prongs. He then turned one of the diningroom chairs round to face the Rayburn, dropped on to it heavily, and positioned the slice in front of the opened fire door. During this process, the unhappy man neither looked at nor said anything to anyone in the room. However, in spite of this, Nanna Darwin seemed relieved, even unconcerned, as Ronnie appeared to be compliant, and that was always a good sign at critical times like this. He would soon get himself out of it, she reassured herself; this would be a short episode, thank God. As his mother happily busied herself with the breakfast preparations, and Len pretended to read the Saturday morning paper, Ronnie gazed hypnotically at the glowing orange embers in the firebox, but it was one of those deeply introspective stares that went far beyond the mere subject of the visual study. He therefore, did not notice when the toast went black, nor did he move an inch when it burst into flames.

However, his ailing father had noticed the potential hazard.

'*Look out the Ronnie, look out*' Grandad Darwin warned loudly, whilst painfully raising himself out of his seat.

Having been shaken back into the real world, Ronnie suddenly felt the heat travelling up the shaft of the toasting fork and dropped it with a cry of pain and a clatter upon the brick hearth. He got up quickly and, still without a single word or the merest glance at anyone, rushed out of the diningroom and into the kitchen. It was with the greatest consternation that they all soon heard the sound of the back door slamming shut. It had not gone as well as any of them had hoped. Nanna's overly optimistic prognosis now appeared to have been wrong. Standing swiftly, Len pointed in the direction of the kitchen with eyebrows raised, but Nanna sighed and then shook her head in reply. Her son's wordless gesture was clear in its meaning, but had been rejected. Ronnie was going to ground and clearly wanted to be alone. The time for his older brother to seek him out could wait until a little later. There was no choice therefore, but for Len to take over the toast making duties, but he had to struggle to resist the urge to chase after Ronnie right there and then. As he reluctantly sat on the chair so recently vacated by his brother, Len felt at his right leg and sighed with relief to confirm that his car keys were safely in his trouser pocket. Ronnie wouldn't be able to get far, and hunger would soon compel him to return. At that moment, the cuckoo clock struck nine 'oo-dongs'. No one seemed to notice it, let alone laugh.

David and Len spent the rest of the morning in the walled vegetable garden, uprooting the troublesome annual weeds that had so quickly seized occupation without having received any recent opposition. In fact, no less than twelve barrow loads of groundsel, fat hen and pineapple weed were taken to the compost heap in the corner. Watering was the next task, and father and son had a great amount of trouble connecting the various seemingly un-connectible short sections of hosepipe together, so that they would reach from the tap by the east end of the greenhouse, and then extend round the entire vegetable garden. There was obviously a knack in the connecting together of those seemingly arbitrary lengths of hissing and leaking pipe, and it appeared to be one that only Grandad Darwin had knowledge of. But both Len and David knew that to ask him, would be to have him take over and do the job himself and thus, risk his recovery. He was a stubborn old Grandad indeed. They both agreed that it was bad enough that the old boy had defied Nanna by coming into the garden, but now they could see that he'd even managed to sneak into the greenhouse and was currently thinning bunches of grapes with his one good arm.

All these various tasks were accomplished by each of the Darwin males, with half a mind on where Ronnie might have fled to that morning. Experience told them that he would have gone to ground somewhere quiet, but that he never usually went too far from his home base, and this was of some comfort to his family. However, of all of them, David was the most concerned, as he was the only one to be aware of the fact that Ronnie had planned to defy Len's ban and to go to find Katie. As he yanked up yet another handful of cleavers, David wondered if his errant uncle knew exactly where she currently was. He hadn't liked to ask Ronnie when he'd mentioned it earlier, and there was no way he could consult anyone else about it. David certainly couldn't betray his fellow Scar Brother's confidence by sharing this concern with his family, and especially his father.

Sometime around mid-morning, David used a trip to the loo as an excuse to check quickly that Grandad Darwin's red Ford Escort was still where it should be, and had not been requisitioned by Ronnie for his heartfelt quest. The boy was greatly relieved to find the vehicle positioned in its allotted space within the long outbuilding that served as a garage, and parked next to Lord Rothermead's vintage yellow and black Rolls Royce. The Dutnells' more modern Rolls, and the Carters' Vauxhall Victor estate were not there, but he reminded himself they were both on holiday, so that was alright, and nothing to worry about. It was an interesting fact that both David and Len had nurtured a concern that Ronnie might use a family car to flee the scene, but each for their own reasons, had checked on this fact independently, and neither had voiced that worry to the other.

Missing Ronnie or not, lunch – or rather dinner in the Darwin grandparents' household – had been set for 01:00 that day as usual. However, when the three gardeners assembled for ritual hand washing in the kitchen, they were all concerned to discover that Ronnie had still not returned. Len decided that he would now go and look for his brother, despite any nodding or shaking of the head that Nanna Darwin might want to indulge in. He knew that he was the best person to seek Ronnie out and do it alone too, because he was the only one whom Ronnie would allow near him during these dark despairing moods. If pressed, both Nanna and Grandad would have to concede this point. However, there was another reason for his decision and, this time, it was one known only to Len. The sad fact was that he knew exactly where to look for Ronnie, for they would be the same places he himself would go too if he ever felt the same way. Sometimes, he did indeed feel the same way, but no one else knew this; it was closely guarded, slightly shaming secret.

After a good half-hour's worth of searching, a glum-looking Len returned empty handed.

'I've looked all over the grounds and I can't find him *anywhere* and most of the outbuildings are locked up for the weekend,' he sighed dejectedly, slumping down on one of the dining room chairs. 'That strange grinning stable hand says *he* hasn't seen anyone, except his mother, old Bill Blackett and Mrs Cohen all weekend ... what with everyone else being on holiday!'

Nanna, who had been listening to this somewhat glumly, now became much more animated.

'*Yes*, and as I told you yesterday evening, Edwina Cohen says that young Miss Victoria has gone away with the Carters, rather than returning to France with the Dutnells,' she gossiped, temporarily forgetting her absent son. '*Apparently*, her ladyship thinks very highly of Samantha, who is such a sensible and straight young woman. *She'll* get her out of any bad habits their daughter might have picked up at that school!'

She had barely finished her last sentence, when Len pushed back his chair noisily, and stood up in frustration.

'This is *all* very interesting' he said, somewhat irritably, 'but it doesn't help us to find Ronnie, *does* it? Unless *he's* decided to go away with the Carters too!' He was tempted to add: if you had let me go after him when I wanted to, none of this would be happening now; but bit his tongue, as he so often had in the past during similar situations.

His mother looked a little cross at being cut-off in mid flow, but had the good grace to concede the point.

'Fair enough, but where can he have *gone*?' she asked, with an open-hand gesture, looking principally at her husband.

Grandad Darwin had just begun to play chess with David on the diningroom table; the abandoned lunch setting now pushed to one side. However, having heard the frustration in his wife's voice, he looked up from the game and joined in with the conversation.

'When the Ronnie was a little boy, and did one of his disappearing acts, we *always* knew just where to find him, *didn't* we Nanna!' he recalled, with a wistful smile, and a faraway look in his eyes.

'Oh *yes*,' Nanna Darwin confirmed, nodding vigorously. 'More often than not, I would find him at the back of that walk-in larder at Oakenden, bingeing on something sweet. Do you *remember* Len ... we had to limit the amount of chocolate or cake that we kept in the house? '

'Only too *well*,' Len replied, clearly deriving no pleasure from that recollection of restrictions. 'But it's not sweet things that he turns to now, *is* it?'

Everyone knew what Len was referring to, but no one dared say it; no one dared utter the word 'alcohol'. Of all of them, this was a particularly hard concept for Grandad Darwin to either understand or accept. He himself had been given a strict, yet loving nonconformist upbringing, where the demon drink was just that: something with which to frighten children at night. Grandad had even spent over 25 years in the navy, from sea scout to chief petty officer, without having voluntarily taken a drop. How hard it was for him therefore, to understand why a son of his would embrace such an evil indulgence; why he would want to drink something that only made him feel even lower and magnified his apparent lack of self worth.

Whilst his father had been brooding, Len had been thinking, and was suddenly hit with a flash of inspiration.

'What about 'The Fruit Picker's Arms' ... *you* know, the pub at Rothermead Green?' he suggested, glancing hopefully from one parent to the other. 'It's possible he would have made for *there*!'

As much as Grandad Darwin felt the concept of Ronnie being in a pub rather repugnant, he was nonetheless cheered by the notion of finding him, and then bringing him home safely. 'It's worth a try; let's go,' he replied with a slow thoughtful nod, before struggling to get to his feet.

With a course of action now agreed, Len also stood up and plunged his right hand into his trouser pocket, in order to retrieve his keys. '*Right* then, I'll take my car. *Nanna*, you wait here in case Ronnie comes home in the meantime. *Grandad*, you sit back down again and rest that shoulder. *David*, you come with me,' he instructed each of them in turn, calmly but firmly.

Len had now taken complete control and both parents knew that his proven organisational skills would serve them all well at this time of crisis. However, that stubborn old devil would have no truck with being left behind, so it was all three Darwin males who drove up to Rothermead Green. From the back seat, David thought how strange it was, not to be walking there through the cherry orchards. In fact, he could count on the fingers of one hand, the number of times he had been taken up to the green by car. On the other hand, he perfectly understood the need to get there quickly, and knew he would happily sacrifice any of his cherished routines to help his Uncle Ronnie.

The lane reached Rothermead Green by the small primary school, with the pub, village shop, and telephone box immediately opposite. The old windmill was now at the far end of the wedge-shaped green, and David gazed back at the familiar black conical tower in the distance, as the family car slowed and then pulled off the road. As the boy stared, he recalled that Ronnie had been so very happy that day, until of course, he'd heard that the old mill could probably not be saved. In his uncle's own words: what a shame, he thought sadly.

Grandad stayed in the car with David, while Len crossed the road and then disappeared inside 'The Fruit Picker's Arms'. The pub was an alien environment for the oldest and youngest of the Darwin males, one by upbringing and the other by age. Len could not really be considered a frequent pub goer himself, although he occasionally enjoyed a glass of 'Mackeson' with other Telecom colleagues at Christmas, or on other significant dates.

Having entered by the saloon door, Len eventually emerged by the public bar entrance and, with a grimace, shrugged his shoulders. The gesture was absolutely clear in its meaning: no Ronnie.

'Well, I can't think of where *else* he could have gone,' a very fed-up sounding Len said, as he got into the car and slammed the door behind him.

As his father started the engine, David peered out of the offside rear window to see if it was clear for them to pull out onto the lane. Whilst doing so, he once more caught sight of the far end of Rothermead Green.

'What about the old mill?' he suggested, with an excited sense of urgency. 'Remember; Ronnie *was* very upset at the thought of it being pulled down.'

'Good *idea*, my old boy,' Grandad Darwin said passionately, turning his head round as far as the pain would allow.

In response, Len shook his head wearily.

'Oh *well*, we might as well check it out whilst we're here!' he agreed, seemingly unconvinced by the suggestion, but clearly still willing to explore any avenue in their quest.

With the lane clear of traffic, David's father pulled forward, and then, almost immediately, turned right in front of the post office-cum-shop. This manoeuvre allowed him to join the gravelled track that circumnavigated the actual village green. After 300 yards or so of crawling round potholes and puddles, Len pulled up just in front of the demolition contractor's machine that he and David had seen earlier on their mushroom-hunting walk with Ronnie.

For Grandad Darwin, this was his first glimpse of the recently devastated site.

'Good *grief*, look at all *this*,' he remarked, with a mixture of shock and sadness.

Unseen on the back seat, David silently nodded his agreement.

However, being more concerned with the task at hand, Len ignored the comment and quickly turned round to address his son.

'Do you want to do the honours then, David?' he suggested, with an encouraging smile. 'I don't think I could manage *two* climbs in one day!' The proposal gave away the fact that he did not think Ronnie was here. If Len had, then he'd surely have searched the mill's interior himself; after all, at times like these, Ronnie responded to no one else other than his big brother.

Without any further prompting, David hurried out of the car, carefully picked his way over the rubble, just as they'd done earlier that day, and then entered the old mill tower. He was very puffed by the time he poked his head through the trapdoor in the roof, but sadly, there was no sign of Ronnie on any level. Lacking the sense of urgency that had accompanied his ascent, David came back down at a much slower rate, that is, until a rat ran over his feet on one of the upper levels. After that, David moved very quickly indeed.

On re-emerging through the low doorway at the base of the mill, David shrugged his shoulders, just as his father had done outside the pub.

'Never mind David, it *was* a good idea though ,'his father consoled him, as he stood by the open driver's door. Len waited until the boy had got back into the car before climbing in himself. He then indulged in a moment's contemplation; in other words, a quick verbal recap of the problem at hand.

'D'you know I...I *still* think Ronnie would try and get a drink from somewhere…but *where*!'

Mention of the word 'drink' sent Grandad Darwin into a sudden spiral of despair.

'Oh dear, the *pity* of it,'he bemoaned, bitterly shaking his hanging head.

'Yes it *is* a pity,'Len retorted with a slight air of impatience, 'but we can't stop him; we can only *help* him, and to do that, we need to *find* him ... but I *can't* think of anywhere else he could *get* a drink. There *is* no other source of alcohol around here!' he added, before thumping the steering wheel with both hands in frustration. Feeling despondent, and unsure of his next move, Len nevertheless started the car up again.

It was then, having reflected on his father's words, that David suddenly realised with horror, *exactly* where Uncle Ronnie was, a place where he could get as much alcohol as he wanted. A stomach-churning panic now gripped him, and as much as he didn't want to blab on his 'Scar Brother', he realised that Ronnie needed to be found as soon as possible and then helped. But on the other hand, did his uncle want to be found, he pondered; it was a terrible decision to have to make: betrayal or benevolence? He just didn't know what to do.

As Len, went to pull back onto the gravel track, he glanced in his rearview mirror and caught sight of his troubled-looking son. He knew that introspective look only too well, as any father would. And there was no doubt in his mind as to what it meant: David was hiding something. Leaving the engine running, Len returned the gear stick to neutral and then turned round to face his son.

'Now David, this is very important. Do *you* know where Uncle Ronnie is?' he asked in a firm, but friendly manner, and maintaining constant eye contact.

David looked back at his father anxiously. He had no problem withholding information, but if asked directly, he knew full well that he found it very hard to lie. However, if he *did* ever lie, and there had been such occasions in the past, then he conceded that it was even harder for him to make it sound convincing. Like sarcasm, it was a verbal art he had yet to master. Therefore, he quickly came to the unhappy conclusion that he had no other choice but to tell the truth.

'I...I've only just *thought* of it... just now, when you said about where he could get a drink... *honest* dad!' David stammered, in an attempt to preface his confession with qualifying reasons.

'That's alright David, I *believe* you,' his father reassured him, with carefully controlled cajoling. 'Now tell us where you think Ronnie might be.'

With a tremulous intake of breath, David stared at Grandad Darwin and then his father, who were both now peering back at him expectantly. 'The wine cellar,' he began, in hesitant tones, 'I think he must have gone down into Lord Rothermead's wine cellar!'

Grandad Darwin's reaction was both instantaneous and passionate.

'Oh *no*,' he bewailed, screwing up his eyes and imagining a probable sacking scenario. 'How would he know how to get in *there*?'

'The *boiler*!' David confessed, as his jaw began to tremble. 'He came with me to look after the boiler and he...he just wandered into the wine cellar for a look around ... I...I couldn't *stop* him'. At that moment, David burst out of the car and then ran towards the demolition site. He was completely beside himself with grief at the thought of managing to let down both Uncle Ronnie and Grandad Darwin, at the same time. What a horrible person he must be, came his confused conclusion. With tears now blinding his eyes, he continued to stagger forward, but it wasn't long before he tripped on a chunk of brickwork and went crashing to the ground.

His son seemed so very still, lying there on the rubble-strewn ground, as Len came rushing over towards him. Fortunately, David had already begun to stir as he reached him, and having helped his dazed son to slowly sit up, Len then enveloped the lad in a tight embrace.

Grandad Darwin wasn't far behind, and quickly dropped to his knees beside the father and son huddle. With his one good arm, he encircled the both of them.

'Oh my old David, *forgive* me. I didn't mean to speak harshly,' the old boy pleaded, now very close to tears himself. 'It was the bloomin' *situation* I was cross with, *not* you!'

Len nodded in agreement with his father, and then smiled down at the tear-stained, brick-scuffed face of his oldest son.

'It's alright old chap ... you've been *very* brave,' he reassured in calming tones. 'And you've helped your Uncle Ronnie by helping us to help him. '

'That's absolutely right!' Grandad Darwin reinforced, in a firm and quite unambiguous manner.

Now feeling forgiven, David happily nestled into the loving embrace that was willingly being given by the leading representatives of the two Darwin generations senior to him.

Having established that David wasn't too hurt, Len's thoughts once more returned to concerns for Ronnie. Consequently, it wasn't long before he loosened his grip, and helped David to his feet.

'Now let's go and get your uncle,' he said, with a reassuring wink, and a supportive arm. At the same time though, he subtly studied the graze on David's forehead with some concern, a wound that had begun to slowly seep blood.

All three of them walked back to the car in close formation, making sure that no one else tripped on the rubble en route. There followed a rather fraught car trip back to the farm, which was undertaken as quickly and as safely as the narrow country lanes would allow.

Throughout the brief journey, Len was trying to plan ahead. More specifically, he was wondering how they would be able to remove Ronnie from his lordship's wine cellar with a minimum of fuss, and then try and cover his tracks.

'God *knows* how many vintage bottles of wine that brother of mine will have drunk,' he remarked, turning towards Grandad Darwin with a worried expression on his face. 'And it's not as if one could pop down to the off-licence in Sittingbourne and buy replacements, *is* it!'

His father merely peered back at him, beetle-browed, and then shook his head in fatalistic fashion. This proved to Len, beyond all doubt, that any logistics behind the rescue operation would be entirely down to him. Firstly though, he had to establish that Ronnie had indeed secreted himself away in the wine cellar. In fact, Len prayed that they would find him down there, despite all the problems it would cause, because the unthinkable alternative was to have to call the police if he didn't show up by nightfall, and everyone knew that this would be the last thing Ronnie needed at the moment.

Having crossed the outer courtyard at twice the normal speed, the car came to an abrupt halt right outside the kitchen door of the farm cottage, and an anxious Len immediately rushed inside. Part of him still dared to hope that he would find Ronnie sitting there at the diningroom table, and grinning back at him sheepishly, having fully recovered from his depressive episode. Sadly though, seeing Nanna Darwin's concerned countenance, as she intercepted him in the kitchen, he realised that there would be no best case scenario that day.

'Did you find him?' his mother asked with anxious concern whilst, at the same time, trying to glance past him.

'No, but we think we may know where he might have gone,' Len replied, briefly giving his mother's shoulders a reassuring rub.

'Where…*where*?' came the urgent response, accompanied by a wide-eyed stare of expectancy.

Rather then reply verbally, Len instead turned to the wall-mounted hook, by the back door, where the bunch of keys to the 'big house' was usually kept. They were gone, and neither Nanna nor anyone else had noticed until now. She followed his gaze, quickly noticed the empty hook, and then stared back at him, with open-mouthed incredulity.

Len merely shrugged, and smiled back at her stoically.

'That *clinches* it: Ronnie *must* have gone to the wine cellar, and we have to get him out of there whilst Lord Rothermead still has a wine collection!' he said, before rubbing his chin and frowning, as he tried to work out the means of achieving that objective.

Having listened to his assertion, Nanna Darwin neither flinched in horror, nor questioned the logic behind her son's reasoning. It all made perfect sense to her, and she simply nodded in calm agreement as a result.

Len though, began to pace a small circle on the kitchen lino.

'But we can't just go rushing over there…I mean, what about Mrs Cohen? If she hadn't noticed Ronnie wandering past her cottage this morning, then she's *bound* to see *or* hear our efforts in trying to retrieve him!' he pondered aloud, whilst staring down at his shuffling feet.

Nanna Darwin thought for a moment, and then became very animated as inspiration hit her.

'No, no; I don't think we need worry about her!' she said brightly. 'I'm almost *sure* that she told me that on Saturday afternoon, she'd be helping poor old Bill Blackett move in with Queenie and Smiler, now that he's lost his job, and his tied cottage. I *know* it's only next door, but…'

'*Great*, so we should have a clear run!' Len interrupted, pointing excitedly back at her. 'Right then, let's *go*!' he added, spinning towards the back door, secure in the knowledge that there would be no witnesses, as far as the sharp-eyed and keen-eared cook was concerned. In fact, the only thing that might need further explaining away was the mower incident from Friday evening.

Once again outside, Nanna Darwin and Len rejoined David, who had just helped a very tired-looking Grandad out of the car. It was clear to all that the busy day's activities were beginning to take their toll, as far as his poorly shoulder was concerned, but he still insisted on coming with them to find Ronnie. In her concern for the task in hand, Nanna Darwin failed to notice the rapidly scabbing graze on David's forehead, and the boy himself did not want to draw attention to it by mentioning the headache he now had, for fear of being sent to bed to rest, or worse still, taken to the doctor.

The rescue and retrieval party found the cellar door shut but unlocked, and once inside, they discovered that light to the boiler room was on.

Leading the way, Len glanced through the gloom, to both left and right, as his eyes gradually became accustomed to the light level.

'Ronnie, are you *in* here mate?' he cajoled gently, in a hoarse half-whisper. As no answer was forthcoming, he turned round and shrugged at his mother, who was immediately behind him.

'He must be through *there* then!' Nanna Darwin said, pointing to the entrance into the wine cellar, and proving that she had at least some rudimentary knowledge of the place's layout.

Their worst fears seemingly confirmed once and for all, Grandad hung his head in despair.

'I'll be joining old Bill on the scrap-heap at this rate; you just *see* if I don't!' he lamented, in a very rare moment of self-indulgent pity. It was an emotion he allowed himself, only now that Ronnie had been more or less located.

David couldn't bear to see his grandfather so upset, and desperately thought of something positive to say.

'D'you know, Uncle Ronnie might be alright *after* all,' he said, glancing round at the huddle of adults. 'If he hasn't been able to find a corkscrew, then he couldn't have got any of the bottles open!'

That thought cheered the party considerably, and Grandad Darwin in particular, who now beamed broadly at the prospect.

'Yes, he might have just come in here for somewhere to be alone,' he said hopefully, before extending an appreciative arm round his grandson's shoulders.

Len though, began to feel a sense of unease, as he quietly walked towards the archway set in the right-hand wall, and then disappeared into the low connecting passage that led to the wine cellar. Seconds later, the head of the posse re-emerged alone, and looking somewhat confused.

'Ronnie's *not in* there', he said with much incredulity, whilst distorting his face appropriately. 'He must have come and *gone*, but the question remains: where *to?*'

'Were there any bottles missing?' asked Grandad with concern, as he shuffled towards Len.

'There's no way of *telling*,' Len replied, thrusting his arms out to the side, '*you* know what it's *like* in there!'

'Well, not *really,* the Len ... you see, I've never actually set foot in the wine cellar,' confessed a rather sheepish-looking Grandad Darwin.

For a moment, having once more reached stalemate, the three adults stood in silence, gazing at each other, all unsure of their next move.

David, however, continued to peer into the darkened recesses of the boiler room. His eyes then slowly scanned up the internal flight of stairs against the opposite wall: the one he knew gave access to the inside of the Dutnell's residence. '*Look, the door,*' he shouted suddenly, pointing at the very top of the steps, to where the entrance into the 'big house' was situated.

They all focused their eyes to where David was pointing, and it soon became apparent that the door in question was slightly ajar.

Nanna Darwin immediately covered her nose and mouth with her hands.

'Correct me if I'm wrong, *please*, but doesn't that lead into the big house?' she asked, glancing anxiously at each of her companions in turn.

With Len a little unsure of the place's layout, and Grandad too stunned to speak, it was left to David to reply.

'Yes it does!' he said, with an accompanying nod. 'And if you look closer, there seems to be a bunch of keys hanging from the door lock up there!'

David was right again: the missing keys were indeed dangling from the lock of the internal door, when they should rightly have been hanging on their designated hook in the cottage's kitchen. There was only one inescapable conclusion: Ronnie was somewhere inside the 'big house'. Len began to mount the flight of steps with a terrible feeling of dread, as it gradually dawned on him that this scenario could turn out to be far worse than he ever imagined. He also realised that David must have been absolutely right about the corkscrew, but that none of them had credited Ronnie with any intelligence or ingenuity. It was now perfectly obvious to Len that Ronnie had gone into the 'big house' to look for one to open the wine bottles that he'd undoubtedly acquired from Lord Rothermead's cellar.

At the top of the stairs, Len removed the bunch of keys from the lock and then passed them back to Nanna Darwin, who had followed him up the steps, with both Grandad and David in close formation behind her. With a sense of ever-increasing trepidation, he then pushed open the connecting door and stepped into the private interior of the 'big house'. Len found himself in a short but broad passage, with oil paintings hanging at uniform intervals along the panelled walls on both sides.

Nanna was the next to take a very hesitant step in to the passageway, as if she was undeservedly crossing onto hallowed ground.

'Perhaps he didn't go into the wine cellar at *all*, but just came up here to wander about,'she whispered to Len; a proposal clearly made more in hope than belief, and one he chose not to respond to.

Unsure of the direction in which to head, Len quickly studied his strange and unfamiliar surroundings. To the right, the passage ended in a door that was firmly shut, and to the left, it appeared to open out into a large well-lit room. Len instinctively knew that Ronnie would have been more attracted by the light, than the obstacle of a further shut door. Having chosen to go to the left and then walked along the low-beamed gloomy passage for about 20 yards, Len and Nanna Darwin emerged into the light, and found themselves in a high-ceilinged Regency-style room. From the left, ample quantities of sunlight were streaming in from two pairs of double French windows that led through into the adjacent leafy conservatory.

With the room thus lit, it didn't take Len long to locate Ronnie. He was sprawled out on a chaise-longue, towards the centre of the spacious room, and appeared to be asleep. There were three empty bottles and a fourth half-full one, standing on the circular table positioned by his slumbering head. Several framed photographs had been pushed on to the floor, to make way for the impromptu wine collection. The last thing he noticed was an empty sediment-stained glass that was still being firmly clutched in the right hand of the comatose figure.

By this time both David and Grandad Darwin had caught up with Nanna, who had been hovering anxiously at the end of the passage. Len looked back and silently motioned for them all to stay well back, and not enter the room, before he himself began to creep closer to the still-sleeping Ronnie. He had almost completed the journey over to the chaise-longue, when his brother's eyes gradually flickered open.

As soon as Ronnie realised he was no longer alone, he slowly propped up the top half of his body, using a precariously wobbling elbow as support.

'*Hello* there Len,' Ronnie said; his head gently swaying from side to side, 'fancy a drink?'

'Only if you've got a bottle of Mackeson,' Len replied, as he slowly leant forward and gently took the glass from his brother's sweaty hand.

'*Hey*, don't snatch,' Ronnie spluttered jokingly, with an exaggerated wag of his finger.

'Good stuff was it?' Len asked, smiling so as not to appear too adversarial, while at the same time discreetly placing the glass on the rug by the foot of the chaise-longue, and well out of his brother's reach.

In response, Ronnie screwed up his eyes to think, and then with a sudden movement of his head, remarked: ' ... highly over-rated old boy,' in an imitation of Len, complete with characteristic lip-smacking noises.

'Umm, was that meant to be me?' Len asked, with a sideways grin, knowing full well that it was.

'*Yeah* ... I'm thinking of introducing a few impressions into my act!' Ronnie chuckled, as he slowly sat up.

'Okay, but just don't think of doing Mrs Cohen!' retorted Len, maintaining the carefully calculated air on bonhomie.

Still chuckling, Ronnie gradually got to his feet with some difficulty, at the same time reinforcing his desire not to be helped up with wild arm-waving gestures. It was then that he noticed his parents and nephew, who had slowly crept into the room, despite Len's earlier warning.

'*Leave me alone*!' he suddenly shouted, in a rapid reversion to a much more agitated state.

Undaunted, Grandad Darwin stepped forward still further from the alarmed-looking trio of relatives.

'But *Ronnie*, we only want to…'

The sentence remained incomplete as a result of Len, whose urgent arm gesticulations now clearly urged them all to both shut up and withdraw.

Unfortunately, before Len could intervene – or the others comply with his wishes – Ronnie made a lunge for one of the empty bottles, toppling the others in the process, and then held it up in front of him.

'Worried that his lordship will miss his precious wine, *are* we?' he blubbed at high volume, waving the vintage bottle around in front of him.

'More worried about *that* than *me*, *aren't* you…*all* of you,' he added , distressed and still brandishing the bottle about, as if it were a dagger.

In a desperate attempt to halt the slide into chaos, Len reached out to gently hold the upper arm of his brother that was wielding the potential glass weapon.

'Hey...*hey*; my only concern is for *you* at the moment mate!' he urged, with an intense but sympathetic stare.

The intervention had the desired affect and the bottle was lowered, along with its brandisher's head, and also his mood.

'You don't know...you *can't* know what I've been through,' Ronnie pleaded, before looking up again and glaring, not at Len with whom he was in physical contact, but at his parents, who had still not left the room as repeatedly urged so to do. 'So I went to the ...wine cellar ... that dungeon of drink ... that cellar of Chablis ...that...that catacomb of Claret...so fucking *what*!'

'Steady on Ronnie,' Grandad Darwin intervened, once more defying Len's tactfully signalled urges for him not to interfere.

Sadly, Ronnie was not about to be steadied.

'*Go*...go, *all* of you,' he pleaded painfully, shaking loose his brother's grip, and once again waving the bottle about. '*Get out*...only Len stay...the rest, *go away*.'

Desperate and drunk, Ronnie slumped back down on the chaise-longue and covered his head with both hands, the empty bottle dropping unbroken to the rug-covered floor. Len took this as a cue to motion, with even more vigour, towards Nanna and Grandad Darwin, as well as a clearly upset-looking David, for them to leave him alone with his brother. He had to repeat the unspoken gesture, accompanied by a more threatening facial expression, before they reluctantly turned and retraced their steps; Grandad putting his good arm around David's slumped shoulders as they did so. Len watched impassively as his loved ones gradually disappeared into the relative darkness of the picture-hung passageway.

'Have they gone?' Ronnie asked, anxiously peering through his fingers, once no more sounds from his retreating relatives could be discerned.

'Yes, they've gone,' Len confirmed, with a gentle nod of his head.

'*That's* a relief!' Ronnie said, now much calmer, as his hands slowly fell from his face.

Now that the situation had quietened again, the older of the two brothers proceeded to stand all the wine bottles back up on the adjacent circular display table, including the one that Ronnie had been brandishing. He then spread his handkerchief out onto a small pool of red wine that had formed on the table's surface, thus preventing it from dribbling on to the carpet.

With the preventative task complete, Len sat down next to his bleary-eyed brother, and adopted the tried and tested Darwin gesture of support, by extending an arm around his shoulders.

'Is it Katie that's getting to you?' he asked gently, with fraternal empathy.

Ronnie nodded and then blinked rapidly, as silent tears rolled down his face.

'Katie *and* the windmill,' he mumbled in reply, before giving a brief resigned grin.

Len sighed deeply before smiling sympathetically at his unhappy brother.

'Well, I can do *nothing* about Rothermead Mill I'm afraid!' he explained, with a slow shake of the head. 'But, as far as Katie is concerned, I haven't *enjoyed* keeping you and her apart ... you *must* believe me!'

'Yeah…yeah I *do* mate!' Ronnie said, with a circular motion of his head, and a pat of his adjacent brother's thigh.

'*Look*, I know how important your career is ... *that* has been my priority!' Len continued; gently justifying the recent restrictive measures he'd placed on his errant brother. 'And, if we're careful, this whole under-age business might just blow over. Vanessa Townsend, Katie's mother, *already* considers the matter closed ... she told me so *herself*!'

Ronnie looked across at his brother, but then hung his head, and studied the well-worn rug beneath their feet.

'Right now though, I couldn't care *less* about my so-called career,' he said, with a violent head-shaking gesture. 'I don't think I could cope with the stress, the rehearsals, or having to have people like the bloody Black Theatre of sodding Prague, as guests on my pilot show.' His older brother smiled in response, so did Ronnie himself, but that sad-cum-serious countenance soon returned. 'You see Len, I don't think the press *will* let it drop!' he added, as a despairing coda.

Anxious to express a more optimistic prognosis, Len adjusted his position to face Ronnie, and then grabbed both his hands.

'I think they *might*, but not if they found that you'd carried on *seeing* her,' he emphasised in ominous tones. 'But that *won't* happen, *will* it ... I've seen to that!'

With the expression of a scolded child, Ronnie looked back at Len from the top of his watery eyes, but said nothing in response.

The matter now seemingly resolved, the brothers sat there in silence, but for the distant thudding tick of a long-case clock in the corner of the room; a sound that neither of them had hitherto noticed.

Finally, Len decided it was time to take the rescue operation onto the next stage.

'*Come* on then mate, let's get you home,' he said cheerily, before slapping his brother's upper leg playfully, and then standing up.

This time, Ronnie willingly allowed Len to help him to his feet, but was not too drunk to notice when his brother discreetly checked the fabric of the chaise-longue.

'Don't *worry*,' Ronnie slurred, thumping Len rather hard between the shoulder blades, 'I *didn't* piss myself. Do you think me uncivilised?' he added, pressing the spread fingers of his left hand into his own chest.

'Not at *all*, old chap, but you're only human,' observed a smiling Len, with a shrug of the slightly sore-feeling shoulders.

In response, Ronnie tapped his left-side temple with one hand, and then pointed towards the conservatory with the other.

'When I wanted a wee, I merely watered her ladyship's plants!' Ronnie swayed with loud laughter at his own comments.

Len couldn't help but join in.

'I don't think *that* was on Nanna's list of chores!' he commented, before encircling Ronnie's torso with a supporting arm, and then guiding him towards the passageway.

The brothers had no choice but to leave via the cellar steps and boiler house, as the bunch of keys had gone back with Nanna Darwin. Moreover, Len wasn't so familiar with the 'big house' that he could have negotiated an alternative route in any case. As it turned out, reversing course proved hard enough, especially when one had charge of a giggling drunken idiot, who took great delight in making it as difficult as possible. Once they'd reached the boiler house, Ronnie suddenly became Frankie Howerd, and then segued into Hilda Baker, when they finally re-emerged into the sunlight. However, by the time they had got back to the cottage, he was nearly asleep, so Len was able to hand him over to Nanna Darwin, who gratefully guided him up to bed.

Freed of his charge, Len was able to grab a moment's breather, and receive a gesture of appreciation from Grandad Darwin, but he knew that his task was still far from over; he had to return and cover Ronnie's tracks. Having recruited a willing David, Len retrieved the bunch of keys and began to make his way back to the 'big house' in order to tidy up after his brother's little adventure.

As the pair were about to cross the outer courtyard, Len noticed Mrs Cohen returning to the cook's cottage in the old north wing, having completed her Saturday afternoon task over at Pond Cottages.

'*Bloody hell*; that nosey old moo is *bound* to see us bringing the bottles back!' he grumbled, before dragging his son over to the careworn wall at the corner of the wing.

They both waited and watched, quite unseen, until Edwina's front door slammed shut, but each of them knew that her curtains would be twitching if she heard the faintest noise, or detected the slightest movement outside.

Pondering on the problem, David stared along the wall against which they were leaning, and noticed the old window, with its rusty corrugated iron shuttering, near to their huddled position. It was then that a possible solution to the problem occurred to him.

'I've got an *idea*,' he announced excitedly, 'let's go and take one of the log baskets, and put a few logs in it. And then, if she sees us going past, she'll think they're for the boiler…'

'…And we can bring the wine bottles back in the basket as well!' Len said, quickly picking up on the proposal. 'Well *done*, David. My son, the thinker,' he added with a delighted smile, before ruffling the lad's hair, in Uncle Ronnie fashion.

They wasted no time in hurrying round the east end of the old north wing, and then entering the exclusive inner courtyard. A basket was then quickly requisitioned from the old log store, and the two of them confidently marched past Mrs Cohen's cottage, both whistling the theme to *The Great Escape*. As they passed through the garden's rear gates, David reminded his father of the fact that the Dutnell's cook and housekeeper had an adjoining door from her cottage in the old north wing, through to the kitchen rooms of the 'big house'. As a result, they would have to work quickly and, above all, quietly. Firstly though, they needed to get rid of the logs, in order to make room in the basket.

As David searched through the bunch to find the cellar-door key, his father peered into the basket he was holding, and the obvious solution to the problem dawned on him.

'Hey, we could *really* put the logs on the boiler fire, couldn't we?' he suggested, watching his son push open the old studded door.

'No, not really .... it only takes coke,' David said authoritatively, fumbling for the light switch.

'Ah, I'm *sure* it won't matter just this once, although it might make old Ma Cohen's bath water a little hotter than usual,'Len grinned wickedly, as they quickly made for the boiler.

The logs disposed of, the intrepid pair crept back into the 'big house' and made their way along the passage to Ronnie's chosen room. Once there, Len carefully placed the four wine bottles in the bottom of the basket, while David traced all four corks and threw them in as well. The corkscrew was then retrieved and replaced in a drawer of the vast dark oak dresser that stood against the wall between the pairs of French windows. Following that, the remaining wine spills were mopped up with the already red-stained hanky, and the tumbled pictures carefully replaced. Len was both relieved and delighted that none of them had been broken during the incident. Then, having also consigned his wine-soaked handkerchief to the log basket, Len gave the scene-of-the-crime one final check over, and then nodded slowly with satisfaction. As far as he was aware, the room had now been returned to the same state it was in before Ronnie's intervention. The corkscrew may very well have been put back in the wrong place, but without an intimate knowledge of the contents of the Dutnell's drawers, he realised there was nothing that could be done about that. Len gave David a thumbs-up sign before picking up the basket and then beating a hasty but silent retreat. They had done it!

The dynamic duo had just reached the passage with the oil paintings, when Len suddenly remembered that they'd not retrieved the wine glass; in fact, he couldn't even recall seeing it during his final check round. Leaving David standing just inside the passageway, in charge of the full basket, he hurried back into the room and, straightaway, noticed the glass just under the foot of the chaise-longue. It was on its side; either he or Ronnie must have kicked it there unawares. Dropping onto his hands and knees, Len reached under to retrieve the missing wine glass. It was then that, with utter horror, he heard the unmistakable sound of footsteps coming from the slightly-open doorway in the wall directly opposite the French windows.

Still on all fours, Len froze with fear, as the footfalls grew ever louder. If that wasn't bad enough, they suddenly stopped, and then a familiar voice rang out: ' ... hello...*hello*...is anyone there?' asked an anxious-sounding Mrs Cohen. 'Hello, hello George...George Darwin, is that *you*?'

As the footsteps resumed, Len sank completely to the floor, so that he was now lying face-down on the rug parallel to the front of the chaise-longue and, as he hoped, hidden from view if the Dutnell's cook merely glanced into the room. Holding his breath, and with both eyes screwed-up tightly, he soon noticed a change in the acoustic resonance of the footfalls as they resounded against the parquet flooring: Mrs Cohen had entered the room. Also rigid with fear, David pinned himself hard against the wall at the end of the passageway. From here, he could see right across the room, and into a large mirror that hung on the opposite wall. It was positioned between two firmly draped windows, which would otherwise have offered views of the sweeping front lawn and driveway. Daring to lean forward slightly, David quickly discovered that this new position allowed him to see the reflection of Mrs Cohen, in the mirror, as she stood inside the doorway through which she had just walked.

'Hello...*hello*,' she repeated, in nervous tones, before taking three more steps forward.

As a result of this latest development, a nervous David quickly dropped to his knees. It soon dawned on him, with much alarm, that if he could see her reflection in that massive mirror, then she might also be able to see his. From this much lower vantage point, he could now see his hapless father, pinned to the floor by the chaise-longue. Len noticed his crouching son at the same time and, with a heavy frown, put an index finger to his lips in the shush gesture. It was clear to David that his father was extremely worried. Indeed, Len had much to look worried about, and he knew full well that it would not look good if they were caught in the possession of four of his lordship's beloved and highly prized wine bottles, especially ones it would appear for all the world that they had consumed. He concluded that there were now only two choices should they be discovered: either murder Mrs Cohen and put her in the boiler too, or risk tomorrow's newspaper headlines reading: '*Drunken Darwin Duo Diddle Distinguished Dutnell Dipsomaniac*'. The idea of doing away with the inquisitive cook lasted only two seconds, but for Len, it was a very tempting two seconds.

The father and son team once more held their breath, as the sound of footsteps on the parquet flooring resumed. Luckily though, they were soon both able to exhale with relief, when it became apparent that their would-be discoverer was actually leaving the room. Len remained utterly still until the sound of the retreating Mrs Cohen died away to nothing, followed by the distant echoing thud of a door being shut. Even then though, he stayed in position for a good minute afterwards, to make sure that only the ticking of the long-case clock, which had been keeping pace with his own heart beat, could be discerned from anywhere in the 'big house'. And then, completely satisfied that there was no further chance of discovery, Len quickly crawled on his hands and knees back to David's position, gripping the stem of the wine glass between his teeth. Having deposited it in the log basket, Len got to his feet, somewhat awkwardly, and then stared at his son in utter disbelief. It was with the stealth of a couple of bird-stalking cats that they finally tiptoed back along the passage, and then locked the door into the 'big house', before creeping back down the cellar steps.

It was only when Len felt the boiler room floor beneath his feet that he was finally able to fully relax, for it was Dutnell territory they could justify being on. Temporarily putting his load down, the head of the rescue party gave his son's shoulder a playful prod.

'The things we do for that Uncle Ronnie of yours!' he commented wryly, trying to steady his still-shaking legs.

With a serious countenance, David nodded in grim agreement, but within seconds they both broke out into nervous giggles.

Having exorcised themselves of that much-needed outpouring of mild hysteria, they left the boiler room, clicked off the light, and firmly locked the outer door. And then, having withdrawn from the garden of the 'big house', the pair walked un-whistling back to the log store. En route, neither of them dared look to see if Mrs Cohen's curtains were twitching.

David was glad to reach the spidery sanctuary of the old log store, but he soon realised that their task wasn't yet quite finished.

'How are we going to get rid of those wine bottles?' he puzzled, once more staring into the basket that this father was holding.

Len looked round the log store, and thought the problem through. It was then that he noticed the steps in the far left-hand corner of the room; the ones that allowed access to the upper floor.

'*Ah*, now it's your old *dad's* turn to have a good idea,' he smiled, with a wicked glint in his eye. '*Come* on, follow me!'

With an intrigued David in tow, Len went up the banister-less stairs, and then slowly but quietly lifted the latch of the door at the top to reveal Benedict Dutnell's art studio. Neither of them had ever seen anything like it outside of magazines or films. The old panelling around the room had been painted with colourful geometric patterns and swirls, and above them, the ancient oak beams, and plastered ceiling in between, were daubed in various shades of blue and white, presumably to imitate the sky. The furniture they found consisted of a number of old settees, adorned with a miscellany of throw covers, and positioned against the walls on either side. There were also several old Georgian-style tables and bureaus, all thickly coated in bright gloss paint of various hues. On top of every available flat surface were placed an array of ashtrays, drinks coasters and miscellaneous objets d'art that appeared to have been purloined from a bric-a-brac shop, presumably, as items of artistic inspiration. There was even a blackened human skull, on top of which had been welded a large, red, dripping candle.

In the centre of the long oblong room was a raised platform, seemingly constructed from wooden pallets, and with an elaborate but well-worn carpet nailed over them. On top of it all had been placed a moth-eaten chaise-longue, which appeared to be very similar, if not identical, to the one on which Ronnie had recently reclined, apart from its careworn condition. Positioned in front of this central platform was an easel supporting a large canvas, with a paint-splattered sheet draped over it. Resting the log basket on the dry-dripped floor, Len stood in front of the painter's easel and, as curiosity got the better of him, threw back the dustsheet to reveal the canvas beneath. Straightaway, it was an action he deeply regretted, solely on account of David, who was standing right next to him. The largely completed painting featured a young, thin, dark-haired woman reclining on the studio chaise-longue. Not only was she was naked, but also her legs were splayed open. Moreover, the dark pubic hair and genitalia had been rather graphically depicted.

Len quickly glanced down at David, whose eyes were out on stalks, and realised there was no point in pretending that the pornographic picture wasn't right there in front of them.

'Umm, err, rather clever use of colour, don't you think?' he remarked, as if it had been a prissy painting of a sunset, or one of Grandad Darwin's pastoral watercolours.

David nodded in silent agreement, as his cheeks flushed as red as the skin tones used in the painting. It was embarrassing to view such things in the presence of your father; much better to study them alone. Nevertheless, he looked from the canvas to the empty chaise-longue beyond, and tried to imagine that the alluring young model, whoever she might be, was still displayed on it.

The art appreciation lesson now over, Len hastily covered up the 'study' again and then turned his mind back to the task in hand. Returning to the log basket, he lifted out the three empty wine bottles and placed them on the floor by one of the old sofas. The half-full bottle and dirty wine glass were then positioned on the table with the brushes and paints, next to the easel. The corks, he just threw round the room in haphazard fashion, and replaced the partially dried wine-stained handkerchief in his trouser pocket.

David looked on with a mixture of fascination and concern. He knew why his father was doing this: he was making it appear as if Benedict had taken the bottles, and it was a crime for which the would-be artist had previous form. However, he couldn't help but wonder if his father had thought it through properly.

'*Dad*, won't this be getting Benedict into terrible trouble?' he asked, recalling the more flamboyant of the two Dutnell twins, and the one who always said 'hello' to him.

'*Huh*, it'll teach him not to be such a smug little smart arse,' Len replied, with a dismissive shrug, 'you see, I remember an incident many years ago, when a young Benedict Dutnell thought it jolly *funny* to lock Grandad Darwin in his own tool shed for a prank. In *any* case, my concerns are for Ronnie at the moment!'

'Yes, or *course!*' David said, feeling rather ashamed of himself for ever having raised the issue.

Silently accepting both his father's judgement, and sentence, in the matter, David wandered to the opposite end of the oblong studio, and soon noticed an old internal door set in the centre of the far wall. It had no handle and appeared not to have been opened for many years. Stacked against the wall to the right was a large collection of variously sized and completed canvases; the front one of which was a still life study, prominently featuring the black skull. However, what was of infinitely more interest to David could be found on the left of the blocked-up doorway. Here was the base of an old dresser, on which was placed a very impressive-looking record playing deck and amplifier. Two large teak-veneered stereo speaker cabinets, which were positioned on the floor on either side, completed the hifi unit. Next to the perspex-lidded deck was a stack of LPs that David began to flick through: *Disraeli Gears, Electric Ladyland, Children of Oakwood*; these were all albums he'd heard of, thanks to Uncle Ronnie, but had never seen before.

By this time, David had been joined at this end of the room by his father, who was soon flicking through the stack of finished and partly-finished paintings; no doubt, in search of further salacious nudes to frown over.

David straightened the pile of records before returning his attention to the handle-less internal door.

'Where do you think *this* leads to Dad?' he asked, rubbing his hand across the paint-peeling surface of the door in question.

Pushing the canvases back into position, Len came over to join him, rubbing his chin while pondering the question. It wasn't long before his face broke into a broad grin.

'Blimey, it must be Mrs Cohen's cottage on the other side of that wall, perhaps even her bedroom!' he deduced before beginning to chuckle. 'No *wonder* the poor dear has nightmares about drunken orgies; they're going on only a few *feet* away from her!'

Their task of concealment completed, and their curiosity satisfied, the father and son team turned to leave the studio. As they approached the doorway to the rickety staircase, David noticed a tall pot plant by the cobweb-covered window in the corner. He was unfamiliar with its long serrated fingerlike leaves, it being quite unlike anything to be found in Grandad Darwin's greenhouse.

'What *is* this?' he asked, with child-like curiosity, as he began to head towards the strange botanical specimen.

'Err...*just* some sort of herb,' Len replied, quickly and curtly, before ushering his son away from the 'exotic' plant.

Having replaced the empty basket in the log store below, Len and David walked in triumph back to the tied cottage. En route, Len marvelled at what an adventure the day had been and what a rite of passage it had turned out to be for David: detective work and drunken uncles, deceit and derring-do, naked girls and marijuana plants. There was no doubt that both of them would certainly have earned extra-large portions of Nanna's curry that Saturday evening.

*

'Look!' Len suddenly said, pointing over at his parents' bungalow.

Dave turned round and there, in the conservatory, was Grandad Darwin, standing close to the glass and waving away in their direction. Straightaway, they both waved back, far more vigorously than the old boy could evidently now manage, and then got up to walk over to the bungalow. By the time they had crossed the vast freshly cut lawn to the side entrance of the conservatory, Grandad had managed to take the few feeble steps over to the door to meet them. As soon as he saw him, Dave was shocked at Grandad Darwin's appearance, although he did his best to conceal the fact. For Len though, the impact of his father's physical deterioration was far greater, as it had been longer since he last saw him. Grandad was skeletal, hollow-cheeked and no longer able to hold himself erect, but was no less enthusiastic as he'd always been in his greeting of them.

Dave was the first to embrace him.

'Hello me old mate ... good sleep?' he asked, briefly screwing up his eyes to resist the surge of emotion he now felt.

'Ah, the *Dave*,' the old boy responded emphatically, and just able to put his arms around his grandson. 'Good to *see* you again!'

Len felt a lump in his throat as he followed Dave's example.

'Hello Dad!' he greeted warmly; this time, preferring to address him more personally, rather than use the old family familiar.

'Ah the *Len*…the Len,' Grandad Darwin choked, his voice trailing away. He even managed to summon enough strength to give his son, something approaching one of his old bear hugs.

As his father and grandfather held the reconciliatory embrace, which was both loving and long overdue, Dave turned discreetly away and stepped quietly outside. He felt pleased to have played a small part in this patching-up of sorts, and knew how hard it had been for his father to lay aside all those years of resentment. Dave was extremely proud of him for that.

After a few minutes, Len joined his son in the fresh air, and immediately extended an appreciative arm around his shoulders. Grandad Darwin followed slowly behind; his gait being both weak and hesitant, but his determination to walk unaided as strong as ever.

Once they were all outside, Grandad lifted his head in order to scan the garden.

'Oh, you boys have done a *grand* job,' he said appreciatively, before following up his verbal pat on the back with the actual physical gesture. 'That's a *huge* weight off my mind.'

At that moment, the two women reappeared from beneath the foliage of the two cherry trees that flanked the path to the pond.

Nanna Darwin was the first to notice Dave and Len's handiwork.

'You boys *have* been busy,' she remarked, with an approving nod, as she scanned the garden in her immediate vicinity. 'It's a jolly good start!'

'It's *fine*; it couldn't be better,' Grandad said, before he noticed Dave's mother. 'Ah, the *Meg* ... you're here as *well*. How marvellous to *see* you all!' he added, with his usual enthusiasm. The old boy then motioned to embrace her and she rather bashfully reciprocated. 'Just look what these boys of yours have *done* for me,' he mumbled chokingly, close to her ear.

Either unable or unwilling to witness her husband's demonstrative display of emotional appreciation, Nanna hurried towards the conservatory door.

'*Lunch* then anybody?' she asked, with almost mock-jollity, whilst pulling off her Marigold gloves. 'I've got chicken soup on the boil. It's *homemade* you know!'

Her grandson noted with interest that she now referred to the midday meal as lunch. Would she be providing napkins and serving wine as well, he wondered none too seriously, as the family followed her indoors.

In the diningroom, the same old familiar table had been laid for the meal and Dave was pleased to see that, as ever, much of the crockery had survived from the old Oakenden and Rothermead days. Much of the room's furniture was also the same as he remembered from many different stages throughout his youth. There was a familiar smell too; it wasn't quite like Oakenden, or that of the Rothermead cottage, for the dwellings themselves surely must have contributed to the overall olfactory sensation. And yet it was familiar enough to trigger cascades of memory fragments that began to happily whirl around in Dave's mind like an ingested narcotic. He couldn't help but wonder: did this make him a nostalgia junky? Perhaps, but then again, it did him no harm, and there were no discernable side effects, except, possibly, a feeling that the future had a lot to measure up to by comparison.

Dave was the first to sit at the table; in fact, for as long as he could remember, this had always had been the case. Indeed, it had become a rather wellworn family joke. Everyone assumed this habit was indicative of Dave's keenness to get stuck into the grub, although as a child, his sister Lucy had been less discreet and regularly called him a greedy fat pig. Certainly, his family were partly right; he *did* love his food, and that constant lifelong struggle with being overweight was testament to the vice. However, there was more to it than that, much more. It was true to say that Dave derived more pleasure from the anticipation of something than he did in its actual realisation, and this applied to many things in his life. The thought of the summer garden-to-come meant more to him in winter, than it did when the borders were full of June colour. That is not to say he didn't appreciate the flowers when they were there; he did. But then again, the idealised midsummer garden of the dark January evenings had no persistent tap-rooted weeds, or disappointing ungerminated seeds, and the clumps of perennials never flopped into a tangled mess at the first puff of wind.

Dave had a similar attitude towards the changing of the seasons in the wider sphere of nature. Along with most people, he always longed for spring to appear and then marvelled at the gradual greening of the hedgerows and the emergence of those early hesitant flowers. Then, once it was in full swing, he looked forward to the early summer and the thought of all those old roses, rather than immerse himself in the moment and enjoy what was to hand right there and then.

So it was with Dave's food and also his meal times. The ritual of the meal being brought to the table, be it breakfast, lunch, dinner or tea, utterly fascinated him and excited that same sense of anticipation. Quite often in his experience, food and drink looked or smelt much better than it actually tasted; fresh ground coffee being a good case in point. Dave also remembered a baker's shop in Tankerton High Street, which they would often walk past back in the Damascena days. It was another good illustration of this tendency within him, and could very well have been its root cause. The window would always display a mouth-watering array of gorgeous-looking cakes: coconut pyramids, iced buns, custard tarts and those puff pastry ones with the white icing and shredded coconut on top – which the Darwin children called tobacco cakes – to name but a few. On the odd occasion when his mother had been cajoled into buying a selection of these, each and every time, they tasted of nothing much in particular, which was a huge disappointment to both him and Lucy, especially given their visual promise. There were also those wonderful Christmas fizzy drinks; a delight not enjoyed at any other time of year, which only served to enhance their special nature. Six bottles of Corona would be delivered by the milkman, a few days before the twenty-fifth, and then lined up on the sideboard for David and Lucy to worship beneath. Oh, how exciting those different coloured liquids looked, and those names: cherryade, limeade, cream soda; they promised exquisite taste sensations that both children, and David in particular, very much looked forward to. And yet, when the first metal cap was fizzed off on Christmas morning, the magic spell seemed to disappear; it escaped into the atmosphere along with those many carbonated bubbles. True, the Corona was nice, but it was never as good as the eager anticipation of it had been during those preceding days of denial.

Dave began to wonder if this whole concept could be extended towards his relationships with women, both past and present. Certainly, as far as his two wives were concerned, it was hard to say as in each case, the pre-marital period had been more about hoping for the best, than it was eager anticipation of a happy future. And, with Chloe, the precious few times they had actually gone to bed together, were easily as good as the anticipation of the experience, if not better. With regards to Amanda-Jayne though, there was insufficient information on which to form an opinion as so far Dave had experienced little else other than anticipation. Like those cakes in the baker's shop, she had much visual appeal, but the small piece of icing he'd thus far been allowed to break off, certainly tasted sweet, and left him hungering for more. Only time would tell if he was ever allowed to consume the soft, moist, fruit-laden cake beneath.

The much-anticipated lunch, which Nanna Darwin and Dave's mother were now bringing to the table, consisted of homemade chicken soup, wholemeal bread and butter, and a cheese or ham salad to follow. The choice of soup was so that Grandad Darwin would feel comfortable having the same as everyone else, as the old boy rarely managed solid food these days. Dave always associated the smell of homemade chicken soup with his grandparents during their retirement years at Beltinge, rather than the earlier Rothermead Farm or Oakenden Nursery periods. No doubt, Nanna Darwin regularly made the soup up at the farm, but for him, the fond memory of other meals clearly predominated at the time. Funnily enough, the aroma of ham salad with bread and butter, reminded Dave much more of those Sunday afternoon teas at Nanna and Grandad Maybury's house in the 1960s, when the rarely used front parlour was pressed into service, and Nanna Maybury would switch on the light to illuminate her alpine valley mural, of which she was so proud.

Grandad Darwin and Len were the last to sit down at table, and the latter had a smile on his face.

'I've just been looking at Grandad's Kent churches pictures,' he said, with much enthusiasm. 'It's absolutely *marvellous* work!'

Having regularly inspected the artwork on previous visits, Dave nodded vigorously in both agreement and empathy. 'How many have you done now, Grandad?' he asked, reaching over for a slice of bread.

'I finished the forty-eighth one yesterday,' Grandad responded proudly, after which, he gave Nanna Darwin a loving smile and a wink.

Not yet having seen the pictures herself, Meg was nonetheless impressed with the statistics.

'Good *grief*,' she remarked, brandishing her unused soupspoon. 'Well *done* Grandad!'

'*Thank* you, the Meg, but there are just over 150 names on my list of churches for which I have sketches and photographs ... *ha*, so I'm only a third of the way *there* yet,' he responded, with a slow resigned nod, as the smile gradually faded from his face.

Len and Dave exchanged ominous downcast glances. It was clear to each of them that they were both wondering how many of those pictures Grandad Darwin would actually complete in the time he had left.

'That *reminds* me,' Grandad said suddenly, after taking a single mouthful of soup. 'Would one of you boys quickly run me over to All Saints at Whitstable this afternoon? I need to take a few pictures, or maybe do a sketch of the top of the church tower. All the ones I took a few years back have the top cut off. What a silly old Grandad!' he added, with the same exaggerated self-deprecating grin that Dave had known and loved all his life.

Len responded straightaway, beating his son to the mark.

'We'll *both* take you,' he responded, in positive, unhesitant tones.

As a result, Grandad nodded gratefully and then smiled very contentedly as he took another small sip of his soup.

Nanna Darwin, who had anxiously monitored the exchange, clearly didn't want him to go, but could see how happy he now was at the prospect of a trip out with his son and grandson, however brief, so decided to raise no objection. Instead, she chose to change the subject, mainly in order to stop herself from worrying.

'They haven't noticed the addition to the room yet Grandad,' she observed teasingly, leaning towards her husband.

Dave quickly looked around him and soon noticed the old cuckoo clock from the Rothermead cottage, perched high up on the far wall. As if on cue, it struck two o'clock: '*dong, dong*'. The cuckoo appeared from its little trap door, but no longer made any sound at all.

'It's lost the '*oo*' now as well,' he said, with almost child-like disappointment.

'Yes, the bellows don't work anymore,' his grandmother commented, in between mouthfuls of chicken soup, 'the '*oo*' has gone the same way as the '*cuck*' I'm afraid.'

Grandad Darwin briefly looked up at the old familiar clock, before smiling in stoic fashion at his assembled family.

'I'm sorry to say that poor old Grandad has lost his '*oo*' as well,' he joked, concluding with the same silly grin as before.

Everyone quickly realised that he'd just made his first-ever open reference to his illness and weakened state as a result. Nonetheless, all of the family responded with polite laughter, as was clearly hoped for, although that was the last thing that any of them felt like doing.

Nanna joined in too, but was the first to stop, preferring to alter the emphasis of the conversation back to the cuckoo clock.

'*Yes*, I found it in one of those boxes at the back of the garage,' she explained with forced cheerfulness. '*You* remember ... the ones we never got round to unpacking after the move down from Rothermead. And there's *still* a few pieces of furniture in there *too* from the old farm cottage ... we just didn't have room for it *all* in here!'

Grandad listened to the explanation, and then smiled across at his grandson.

'Remind you of the old Rothermead days does it, the Dave?' he asked, with fond remembrance of a happier, healthier time.

'Oh it certainly *does*,' Dave smiled, as he wiped his last piece of bread around the inside of his soup bowl. 'Those days were the *best*!'

Over the next ten minutes or so, everyone drifted off into their own reminiscences about the old cottage and Rothermead Farm, as Nanna cleared away the things from the first course.

Having listened with great pleasure to the many stories from the late '60s, Dave was prompted to recall his own recent pilgrimage up to the fondly remembered farm.

'That *reminds* me,' he spoke up, pushing his chair back, 'I have *another* memory of the old days at Rothermead for you ... a tangible reminder if you will. Excuse me a moment.'

Accompanied by many puzzled looks of intrigue, Dave quickly left the table and went out to his car via the shorter frontdoor route. Within a minute, he was back, and proudly wielding the brass toasting fork that he'd discovered in the old rusting Rothermead Rayburn back in the spring. Straightaway, he handed it to an utterly speechless Grandad Darwin, whose eyes quickly filled with tears.

Nanna looked on with open-mouthed incredulity, and a sort of half-smile, as she returned to the table.

'Where…how did you get *that*?' she asked, staring intensely up at Dave. 'The very *reason* I went through all those boxes in the garage, the other week, was to look for that *toasting fork*!'

A delighted Dave slipped back onto his seat and then recounted the story of his pilgrimage up to the farm earlier in the year, and that fortuitous discovery in the far corner of the overgrown and abandoned vegetable garden.

Still battling to control his feelings, Grandad Darwin finally broke his silence.

'It was usually the Ronnie's job to make the toast,' he remarked poignantly, whilst fondly stroking the precious object. 'The number of times he must have held this!'

Dave and Len once more exchanged emotionally charged glances. Neither of them had heard either Nanna or Grandad mention Ronnie's name since just after his funeral all those years ago; it had been their way of coping with the grief. Dave also speculated to himself that, perhaps, Grandad Darwin was looking forward to seeing Uncle Ronnie again, in a spiritual sense. With such profound thoughts, Dave was drawing on his formative-faith and recalling the recent, almost Damascene conversion he'd had, with the help of Amanda-Jayne, concerning the human soul and man's immortality. Now more than ever, he wanted to believe fully that what they had discussed together in the Greyfriars gardens was absolutely true. However, part of him already did; indeed, those doubts *were* already beginning to resolve themselves gradually in his mind.

Everyone spent the salad course continuing to talk about their favourite individual Rothermead memories, and these now openly included many mentions of Ronnie. For Dave, as much as anyone, it felt so refreshing to be able to recall him at last, without fear of upsetting someone. Even so, he couldn't have failed to notice that Nanna still seemed a little uncomfortable at the mention of her deceased son's name. Nonetheless, many of the happiest and most animated recollections actually came from Grandad Darwin, who did not have any salad and was able to talk without pause. He even touched on the funny story concerning Ronnie's attempt to mow the lawn of the 'big house', and Mrs Cohen's panicked reaction to it, but did not go on to recount those other much darker memories of that last weekend, especially the momentous events of the Sunday.

The family were just finishing their after-lunch cups of tea, as the cuckoo clock 'donged' the three o'clock. Having been reminded of the time, Grandad Darwin pushed his half-drunk cup away from him, and then very slowly got to his feet.

'D'you think we could get going to All Saints now, the Dave?' he asked, hesitantly shuffling round his dining room chair. 'I want to take those pictures whilst the light is still good.'

'Yeah, *no* problem!' David responded positively, before standing up and then feeling for his car keys in the pocket of his trousers. At the same time, Dave wondered if Grandad had another unspoken reason for wanting to make the trip sooner rather than later. Perhaps he wanted to go while he still had the strength to do so; after all, at this time of year, it remained light enough for photography well into the evening.

Len got to his feet barely a few seconds after his son.

'And ... umm ... thanks for a lovely lunch Nanna!' he said, smiling across the table at his mother.

'That's my pleasure!' she replied, happily returning Len's positive facial gesture. 'And while you boys are off photographing churches, it'll give Meg and me the *ideal* opportunity to finish off the pond, *and* inspect the work you did this morning.' Her face then dropped a little. 'But don't be *too* long!' she added, with a brief but concerned glance towards Grandad.

'Yes ... don't be *too* long!' Meg repeated, with an ominous tensing of her mouth.

Although it sounded as if his wife were agreeing with Nanna Darwin, Len realised that her statement wasn't so much out of concern for her father-in-law, as it was the dread of having to spend yet more time in the exclusive company of her mother-in-law.

Just after retrieving his grandfather's camera from the artroom for him, Dave went on ahead to open any doors that barred their way. Grandad followed slowly behind, with Len alongside; not offering him any assistance, but being there should it be required. Having reached the car, Len allowed Grandad Darwin to occupy the front passenger seat and then made sure that the seat belt was safely round him before climbing in the back himself.

Satisfied that everyone was in and secure, Dave started up the engine.

'Any particular route you want to take then, Grandad?' he called out, with a brief glance over his shoulder, as they pulled away up Gainsborough Drive.

'Oh, the *back* way please,' his grandfather responded, in no uncertain terms.

Dave happily nodded in agreement, but knew the request was a subtle way of Grandad saying: please avoid the Thanet Way. This was an arterial road that had unhappy associations for the Darwin Family, and solely because of Ronnie. It was something Dave hadn't thought about for a long time now, and quickly blocked it from his mind, at least for the moment.

The so-called 'back way', was a slow tortuous route that had been replaced by the Thanet Way, at least for longer journeys, as far back as the 1930s. But that was the way they went; bumping through Beltinge, before crawling along Herne Bay high street, and then negotiating 'the bends' to Swalecliffe. Every yard of the journey seemed to be taken behind a succession of slow-moving vehicles. There followed the short distance to Tankerton, through a 1920s urban landscape of bay windows, bungalows, and birdbaths, after which, Dave took the left-hand turn into Pier Avenue. They soon found themselves crossing the humped-back railway bridge of Ham Shades Lane: the gateway into familiar territory for them all. Soon after, they passed the bungalow named 'Damascena', on the right, which had been one of Dave's childhood homes. It still looked very much as it always had. However, the same could not be said for the former Oakenden Nursery next door, which had long-since been replaced by a small housing development. The final stretch took them on to Church Street and, after a couple of hundred yards or so; All Saints Church soon loomed up on the left.

With the exception of an elderly Morris Minor saloon, the small church car park appeared to be completely deserted as they pulled up, so Dave was able to have his pick of the spaces. Soon, both Dave and Len were gently easing Grandad Darwin out of the car; there was no point in him pretending he could manage this on his own, and he knew it. Indeed, despite his uncomplaining nature, his helpers realised from the strained look on his face that this simple manoeuvre was causing him at least some small amount of pain.

With the old boy disembarked, and already looking exhausted, Dave pulled the compact camera out of the glove compartment before locking the car.

'*Right* then Grandad, where do you want to stand to take your pictures?' he asked, from one side of his grandfather, with Len in support on the other.

Grandad Darwin took the camera, but hesitated for a moment, and then glanced up at each of his companions in a rather sheepish fashion.

'I'm afraid I've been misleading you boys ... it was *only* to spare the Nanna any extra grief, but...but the *real* reason I wanted to come here was to visit Ronnie's grave,' he confessed, in a slightly hesitant manner; deception not being one of his strong suits. The old boy then looked up specifically at his son. 'Is...is that alright with *you* the Len?' he entreated, in somewhat nervous tones, anxious to seek his oldest son's approval.

'Of *course* it is,' replied a shocked but no less positive Len, before glancing open-mouthed over at Dave.

To the casual observer, this wasn't such an unusual request: why shouldn't a dying man want to visit the grave of his long lost son. It was just that Ronnie, and in particular Ronnie's death, had been such a family taboo, that it was strange for Dave and Len to hear the old boy voice such a request. They both knew, or rather suspected, that Nanna and Grandad Darwin had visited the grave over the years, infrequently, as had both of them, but it was something that had never been broadcast, or even mentioned to the adjacent Darwin generation.

Dave was quicker than his father to act on the surprise request.

'Umm ... from what I can remember, the grave is along *there* somewhere ... straight ahead a couple of hundred yards, then a bit to the left,' he said, in as-matter-of-fact a manner as he could muster.

'Yes, I think that's right,' Len confirmed, gradually coming to terms with the situation. 'It's…err, it's been a while, but I'm *sure* that's where he is!'

Grandad grinned gratefully up at his son, but then looked down at the camera he'd pushed into his right-hand jacket pocket, and turned to face Dave.

'Here, tell you what my old Dave, take a few pictures here *anyway*, then I've got something to show the Nanna if she asks,' he said, with a subtle sideways smirk.

As requested, Dave retrieved the small camera and ran off a few shots of the top of the tower, while Len supported his father from the left. That done, and the camera replaced, Dave took hold of Grandad Darwin's right arm and they all began the gradual, and yet determined, pilgrimage to Ronnie's grave.

They slowly walked from asphalt path to neatly mown grass, and back to asphalt path again; carefully avoiding any partially camouflaged tombs en route. It wasn't long before Len could feel his father both slow and tire, as he relied more and more on their joint support.

'Are you *alright* there Grandad?' he asked, after about one hundred yards into the graveyard.

'Yes thanks, the Len, but I *will* take a bit of a breather, if you don't mind,' he conceded, in between hard-won puffs of breath.

As they stood amongst the monumental reminders of man's mortality, neither of the younger men really knew how much, or little, discomfort he was in, for Grandad never made a fuss about anything; especially his health. He was indeed a stubborn old devil and neither Len nor Dave doubted that he would complete his mission today, no matter what.

'*Hey*, do either of you remember Mrs Cohen?' Dave asked, after a moment's contemplative silence, in order that they might pass the time more cheerily.

Straightaway, Grandad chuckled in response.

'Yes I do ... bloomin' woman was a pest. Always asking me into the big house kitchen, or bringing me out tea and buns ... her bloomin' '*orrible* buns!'

'She must have taken a shine to you!' Len commented, with a wry grin.

'That's what the *Nanna* used to say,' Grandad smiled, with a concurring nod, as they slowly resumed their progress forward. 'But I must admit that on *more* than one occasion, I hid in the tool shed, as she went round with her plate, calling out: *George, George, oh Mr Darwin*!'

They both laughed at Grandad's impersonation of Mrs Cohen's whiney little voice and the thought of him cowering amongst the cobwebs as she tried to track him down with her disgusting homemade love tokens.

Finally, the family threesome reached Ronnie's stone, and found the grave in good condition, despite the several years of neglect, during which time none of them had visited. In fact, the gallica rose, 'Tuscany Superb', which was planted by Grandad in 1976, had suckered, true to type, all over the grave area. As a result, the long grass was now liberally punctuated with tight blooms of many deep purple petals surrounding a bright yellow centre.

Grandad suddenly took one step forward, breaking contact with his supporters on either side.

'Can you boys leave me alone with the Ronnie for a few minutes?' he asked, in a somewhat choked and broken voice.

Len was the first to voice his concern at the proposal.

'But will you be able to *stand* alright without us supporting you?' he fretted, seeing how exhausted his father already seemed.

Dave was concerned too, and desperately tried to think of a solution to the problem.

'*I* know Grandad ... why don't you hold on to the gravestone immediately in front of *Ronnie's*,' he suggested, leaning over to read the inscription on the monument in question. 'I'm *sure* that...err ...'Josephine Pilcher' wouldn't mind.'

With the matter resolved, Len and Dave reluctantly walked away and put about twenty yards between them and Grandad. En route, Dave realised that there were so many things he didn't know about events in the immediate aftermath of his uncle's death.

'Why *was* Ronnie buried here, and why not a cremation?' he asked, in a cautious half-whisper.

Having listened to the question, Len hung his head and then shrugged.

'Well, you know what they've always *been* like concerning Ronnie, and this is only guess work, but I suppose they wanted somewhere to come and visit, should they feel the need ... And why *here* at All Saints? ... umm ... I suppose because it was near to Oakenden ... *you* know, a place where they thought Ronnie had been at his happiest. And there was also the fact that old Canon Wainwright was a family friend, who had christened Ronnie here, and much later, as it turned out, Lucy as *well*.'

Dave nodded in acceptance of the explanation, which all seemed perfectly logical, and could therefore think of nothing more to say for the moment.

After a while, Len stole a glance back at Grandad, who was still clinging to the gravestone adjacent to Ronnie's.

'He's probably saying *goodbye* to him,' he stated sadly, before turning away again.

'I'd like to think he was saying: *see you soon me old mate*,' Dave commented, with a hopeful smile that belied his underlying feeling of sadness.

Len nodded in willing agreement, although the tears were hard to hold back at the thought of this day being a sentence printed towards the end of the final chapter in his father's life.

After about fifteen minutes of keeping a respectful distance, the pair slowly wandered back to Ronnie's grave, and to Grandad. It was all too obvious that he had been through an extremely emotional experience, but neither of them embarrassed him by making any reference to it.

The church clock struck five as they began to make their way back towards the car park. At one point in the slow and hesitant journey, two squirrels delighted Grandad Darwin by watching impassively from the top of a chest tomb, as the three of them gradually wandered by.

It soon became apparent that the lunchtime conversation was still very much on Grandad's mind; he was still clearly in a reminiscent mood, and continued the dining table's theme as they slowly walked on.

'I *wish* we could all go picking mushrooms in the old cherry orchards right now,' he remarked wistfully, as they approached the car park. 'Oh I used to *love* those early morning walks!'

Len smiled at the happy nostalgic thought, even though he'd only ever participated in one such walk, but it took only a few seconds for his logic gene to reassert itself.

'But it's not the right season for wild mushrooms, *is* it?' he asked, looking across to his son for clarification.

'Ah, that was the odd *thing* about Rothermead, they seemed to grow *all year* round, to a greater or lesser extent!' Dave said, with a slow, thoughtful nod. 'But…it would only take us twenty minutes or so to get there, if you *really* wanted to go and pick some Grandad?'

'No, that's okay thanks, my old Dave! I've had my fair share of them in the past. I can't complain ... in fact, I can't complain about *anything*! I feel *very much* at peace!' he said, with a slow, satisfied smile. 'D'you know ... I'm not *worried* about anything *either*, not now anyway ... thanks to *you* two boys!' In support of his words, Grandad tightened both his arms, in order to bring Dave and Len in closer contact with himself.

It was an emotionally charged last few yards back to the car, and neither of the younger men could talk for the overwhelming feelings that were currently flooding their senses.

As Len gently lowered his father into the passenger seat, Grandad held out a thin shaky arm and then placed it on his son's shoulder.

'You've brought up your children to be *wonderfully* caring people, especially the Dave,' he said, in a firm but faltering voice. 'I'm so *proud* of you, my old Len!'

In response, Len smiled but said nothing; he couldn't. So instead, he kissed the top of his father's beloved bald head and then gently secured the seat belt around his emaciated form once more. With that comment, and its reciprocating gesture, the father-son reconciliation was complete, and all those years of animosity instantly evaporated as if they had never existed.

The journey home retraced the same protracted route as the outgoing trip, and Grandad Darwin dozed in the front seat for most of the way. And then, while Dave was helping him out of the car at journey's end, the old boy accidentally referred to him as 'Ronnie'. He didn't seem to notice that he'd made the mistake, and neither of his travelling companions felt comfortable in pointing it out. Funnily enough though, Dave found it rather reassuring to know that Ronnie was still very much to the fore in his grandfather's mind. Perhaps there *was* a familiar benevolent spirit hovering nearby, he speculated as they all slowly walked back into the bungalow: a friendly soul who was waiting to take Grandad Darwin mushroom picking through those elysian orchards, where the beautiful cherry blossom never faded.

Shouting From The Rooftops

For the most part, Dave did not enjoy being completely on his own, but the odd day here and there could be tolerated, even welcomed. Such was the case on that particular summer Saturday morning. Sheila had gone in for another day's overtime at Telecom – he had dropped her off there first thing – and Julian was in France for the weekend, in connection with his summer job. Dave's conscience told him that he should be spending any free time he had by going over to Beltinge and working on Grandad Darwin's overgrown garden, just as he'd done last weekend. However, his mother hadn't been keen to go over there again so soon, and his father wouldn't go without her, so it had given Dave the perfect excuse to stay at home and catch up with his own garden chores. Nonetheless, to make sure his conscience was completely in the clear, he had telephoned his grandparents just after breakfast, and spoken at great length to the both of them. Fortunately, neither made any mention of the garden, and Grandad Darwin was still utterly absorbed in his churches project. Happy, therefore, that he'd nothing to reproach himself for, Dave had looked forward to a day's worth of mowing, pruning and weeding.

Well-intentioned plans are one thing, but if any physical effort is required, things often turn out very differently. As it happened, Dave spent much of the morning in the lounge with the stereo turned up, playing some of his favourite prog-rock LPs; it was music that always seemed to irritate Sheila, so he simply couldn't pass up the opportunity to enjoy it, unhindered by her grimaces and mocking comments.

By midday, Dave had already long-since decided that the afternoon would be perfectly fine for gardening, but not before he went to fry himself something really unhealthy for lunch. Some nice butcher's own sausages seemed like a good idea, and he was soon relishing the prospect of tucking into a couple of sandwiches, liberally enhanced with Daddies sauce and dripping with melted butter. But best of all, today, they could be enjoyed without any accompanying comments, alluding to salads and his expanding waistline. Frustratingly, just as the hungry man was getting the bangers out of the fridge, the phone rang.

He took the call on the kitchen's wallmounted extension phone. It was Sheila from Telecom House and she sounded worried.

'*Listen* Dave ... that Monica clotheshorse from your office has been doing some overtime with me today,' she began, in an urgent-sounding manner. 'She's just returned from an early lunch break in town, and has told us all a rather dramatic tale about seeing *Tim* down there!'

'*Oh* dear, what's that old reprobate been up to now?' Dave asked with a chuckle, and resigned flick of the eyebrows.

There was no reciprocating laugh, only a brief moment of stony silence before his wife spoke again.

'Apparently, he's trying to *kill* himself!' she finally responded, in a stark manner that left no room for ambiguity.

'*What*?' he gasped, in a dramatic change of attitude.

Having got him to take the matter seriously, Sheila now softened her own tone.

'She was pretty sure it *was* Tim ... he was sitting at the very top of the multistorey car park, with his legs dangling over the edge,' she continued, in a concerned-sounding half-whisper. 'Monica said he was clearly very drunk and shouting down at the small crowd that was gathering in Gravel Walk below. Now *listen* Dave, apparently, what he had been saying was largely incoherent, *you* know, drunken ranting, but she quite clearly heard the names *Alison* and *Dave* being shouted!'

'Oh my *God*,' Dave panicked, screwing up his eyes, and placing his right hand across his forehead.

'You okay?' Sheila asked quickly.

'Yes…yes, *sorry* ... please carry on!'

'*Anyway*, a police car arrived just as she left to come back to the office. Now I *know* Monica is a silly bitch, who's prone to exaggeration for effect, but you have to admit, it does *sound* like him…and those *names*!'

Dave sighed deeply, as he nodded slowly.

'Yes, I *agree*, but what's the bloody fool think he's *doing*? *Damn* it, I better get down there,' he replied, with a slight air of irritation.

'Okay then, but *please* be careful and don't get too involved ... see you at the usual time then, *bye*.'

'It *has* to be Tim,' Dave said aloud, after Sheila had rung off. However, in order to be sure, he tapped the receiver buttons and then rang his friend's home number. If Tim answered, he could tell himself that it was all a horrible coincidence, and go and make his sausage sandwich. Dave let it ring for a couple of minutes, but there was no reply, very much as expected. He now tried to reassure himself that this didn't necessarily mean anything, but as images of

Tim atop the multistorey car park began to assert themselves in his mind, he knew that he couldn't afford to take the chance. '*Blast* him ... there goes my gardening, *and* my sodding lunch,' he grumbled to himself, running upstairs in order to change into something fit to be seen in.

Dave drove into Canterbury as rapidly as the heavy traffic would allow, but it was still faster than he legally should have. All the time, his mind was reeling over Tim and what the hell he might be up to. He could understand his friend being drunk, and he could even accept him being on top of the multistorey car park; indeed, it had been a vantage point from which he and Tim had often taken cityscape photographs on their afternoon excursions. But Dave simply could not comprehend why his work colleague might be sitting on the ledge, and was just not prepared to accept Sheila's rather brutal diagnosis of the situation. There had to be another explanation. Instead, he wondered if it was possible that Tim was trying to make a point regarding the impending Whitefriars redevelopment? Straightaway, Dave considered this most unlikely as, contrary to himself, Tim had a very laissez-faire attitude towards town planning; he'd all too clearly explained as much earlier in the year. Was he then so drunk that he didn't know where he was, or what he was doing? That could also be ruled out as well, because Tim was so hardened to large quantities of alcohol that he hardly ever reached that stage. This left Dave with only the one inescapable question: was he actually trying to kill himself after all? It was well known that a number of people had jumped from the top of the multistorey car park before, but the structure wasn't as high as it seemed on first inspection, and some of the potential suicide victims had ended up being badly injured instead.

Having accepted the probability of the situation, as described by Monica, Dave began to rack his brains for possible motives if, indeed, suicide was his friend's intention. True, Tim's marriage had broken up and he was also having to find a new place to live, but that had happened to many people, including Dave himself, and they hadn't all queued up to dangle their feet over Gravel Walk. However, if the last six weeks had shown him anything, it was that Tim just wasn't a coper, especially when the realities of life came along and, all too often, slapped him in the face, as was currently very much the case.

Given the situation, the very last thing Dave wanted was to be caught in traffic on the city ring road, as so often happened these days, owing to inept town planning. So it was that his car soon slowed to a stop when he was within breaching distance of the city wall. Even so, as his vehicle slowly edged forward, he couldn't work out why the ring road was so very choked in the middle of the day; a time when the weekday traffic was usually not quite so bad. It was then he remembered that this was a Saturday, but that thought soon brought with it a chilling realisation. Was it not the case that on every other weekend, Tim had custody of Henry and Phillipa? A queasy feeling surged through his stomach as he imagined them both, Tim's children, being up there with him, or else shut in the car somewhere, wondering where on earth their father had got to.

Dave entered Canterbury via the Riding Gate, which was the nearest city access point to the multistorey, and drove straight to the Watling Street surface car park, which was only a hundred yards or so away from where Tim was meant to be making a public spectacle of himself. Luck finally turned in his favour, as he was able to quickly locate and then occupy a space that had just been vacated by a departing shopper. However, Dave did not purchase a ticket; such things seemed so petty, given the nature of his mercy dash. Besides which, such was the urgency of his mission that he'd left home without any money.

Gravel Walk was situated on the far side of the massive multistorey car park: a brutalist concrete structure considered by many to be the ultimate in 1960s eyesores. Dave and Tim liked it though, and had often photographed its dramatic shapes during their afternoon excursions. Now it would seem that Tim was bent on a solo visit, and photography did not appear to be uppermost in his mind.

As Dave approached the Gravel Walk junction, it became obvious that there was something very wrong. Traffic barriers had been hastily erected, not only to prevent vehicular access, but also to contain the crowd that had obviously built up since Monica's lunchtime report. He also observed that two police cars and an ambulance were parked outside the Ricemans department store, which was situated beyond the junction, and just out of sight from Gravel Walk itself.

Dave could hear Tim before he could see him, but was unable to make out what he was saying. At least it served to confirm, beyond all doubt, that the multistorey man was indeed his friend. It was then, as he looked down Gravel Walk, that the full horror of the situation hit home to him. On the right, were the contained onlookers: a hideous hoard of gawping vultures, all with their eyes cast upwards. To the left, and perched high up on the concrete retaining wall of the structure's fifth parking level was Tim, with his legs dangling over the edge, very much as reported. He appeared to be holding a large bottle of something, presumably alcohol of some description, and was occupying his time by ranting at the gleeful gathering below.

Unsure of what to do next, Dave approached a stocky, shaven-headed young policeman.

'Err ... *hello* ... I hope I can be of help. The man up there is a good friend of mine,' he explained, pointing up at Tim; not that there could be any doubt about whom he was referring.

Initially, the officer frowned at him, as if he was just another interfering onlooker, but then his stern countenance transformed itself into a grin.

'You're not *Dave*, are you sir?' he asked, with eyebrows raised in expectation.

'Yes, *that's* me ... Dave Darwin!' came the emphatic response.

'Ah, *good* ... he's been shouting out your name for some *time* ... his best mate, *he* says,' the policeman declared in a surprisingly cheery manner, before moving closer to Dave, as if he was about to share a confidence.

'Chummy up there was also mentioning his ex-wife, Alison, in less *flattering* terms sir!'

The young PC then pointed along the edge of the barriers on the right, to where the unmistakable form of Alison Cross was waiting in the company of another officer.

'She arrived about five minutes ago and is about to go up with Sergeant Marlowe and try to talk him down,' he concluded, in hushed conspiratorial tones.

Dave studied Tim's spouse intensely; so far, she had not noticed him. He had to concede that Alison was not an unattractive woman, but she had those sorts of eyes that never engaged you for long. More disturbingly, she seemed to give out a signal that Dave had long since interpreted as: *I don't much care for you.* It was rather disconcerting to be acquainted with someone who had so obviously prejudged you, and found you wanting. Initially, he had tried to over compensate in this respect, on the occasions when they met, by asking her questions, and trying to show an interest wherever she condescended to talk on a subject. However, Tim's wife had remained doggedly unresponsive and the whole exercise proved pointless. In the end, for no other reason than the fact that she, apparently, disliked him, Dave found himself not liking her much either, and that was still the case today.

He watched as Alison and the police sergeant walked forward through a small gap in the barrier and began to cross the empty tarmac void of no man's land. Their destination seemed to be one of the concrete staircase towers that would then give them access to the fifth floor, and also to Tim.

From his precarious vantage point, the drunken dangler noticed Alison approaching him down below and decided to *introduce* her to the crowd.

'*Ladies, gentlemen and tourists,*' Tim bellowed in a loud, yet courteous manner, as he balanced a two-litre bottle of cider on the ledge beside him. '*The woman you see before you is my estranged wife and the mother of my children…*' He then looked down directly to Alison and continued in a much more aggressive tone: '*…aren't you, you bitch, you bloody bitch*!'

Alarmed at the sudden turn of events, Alison and Sergeant Marlowe stopped in their tracks, halfway across the empty road, and stared upwards in anxious anticipation of Tim's next move.

Her ex-husband did not disappoint, and continued to address her directly.

'*Come any nearer, you…you fucking child stealer and I'll splatter myself on the tarmac beside you,*' he threatened in a very agitated state. Then, in another dramatic change of mood, almost as if he'd decided that having a domestic argument in mixed company was somehow unseemly, Tim once more addressed the vastly increasing gaggle of spectators, just as a fire engine arrived quietly and parked nearby.

'My apologies, good people of Canterbury! You'll understand my chagrin when I tell you that I only get to see my children every other Saturday. But this morning, when I went to pick them up as usual, *her* down there ... that...cause of all my woes, kept them from me ... she wouldn't even let me *see* them. Do you know, ladies and gentlemen, my dear wife prefers to keep them secreted away in that...that lesbian commune she's become part of.' Tim pointed down at Alison as he gave vent to his frustration once more. '*That's it...that's it, isn't it, eh? You prefer them to me ... you're a bloody lesbian too*,' he announced, almost as if the prospect had never occurred to him before. It was then that he began to cry. 'You can't *do* this to me Alison...Alison? Bring them...bring me my children...*please*, please... Henry... Phillipa...'

As his plaintive, pathetic words petered out to nothing, Tim took a large draught from his bottle, presumably to soothe his throat after all that shouting. At the same time, Sergeant Marlowe guided Alison back to the barriers, their mission all too evidently a failure. The pair then came over to where Dave and the young officer were standing. The best friend and the estranged wife merely nodded at each other in cold acknowledgement; the one thing they finally had in common being their names shouted out by the pathetic drunken figure above.

Her role now seemingly over, Alison began to walk away, but then after a few steps, paused and turned back to face Dave.

'It's not *true* you know,' Alison pleaded, in a rare display of vulnerability.

'*What* isn't?' he responded in a deliberately disinterested tone.

Alison sighed, stepped closer and made rare eye contact with Dave.

'What Tim's saying up there; it's not *true*!' she reiterated, in softer tones than before.

'But you've left him and taken the children, *haven't* you?' Dave challenged irritably, matching her stare, and expecting her to turn away at any moment.

However, to his surprise, Alison held her ground.

'Dave, I had no *choice*,' she reasoned, in absolute earnest. 'He was drunk *all* the time, abusive to me and neglectful of the children. Dave...his Uncle Stephen had to send me *money in the post*, to enable me to feed them!'

The shock he felt upon hearing her words immediately shook Dave out of his dismissive attitude towards her, and also forced him to re-evaluate his opinions. He began to wonder whether he had really misjudged the situation. Had his close friendship with Tim made him all too willing to accept everything that had been said about their deteriorating relationship? Was he too keen to think of Tim as the victim, because it served to justify his own stated position with Sheila? Dave looked up at Tim, who was still sitting there quietly, and then referred back to Alison again.

Tim's estranged wife must have sensed that she was getting through to him, and continued to plead her case.

'And I'm *not* a lesbian either, far from it! You see, it's not a women's commune I've gone to, it's a women's *refuge*! Dave, I'm *scared* of him!' she entreated, with an air of genuine sincerity, edged by real fear.

Dave was now more confused than ever: *just* a minute, this is not the strong willed Alison that *I* know, he told himself. Where was the assertive woman who had challenged them both at the dinner party the other month? Then again, it occurred to him that, perhaps, this was just an act to win him over after all.

'Alison, are you preventing Tim from seeing the children, or not?' he calmly asked, in order to obtain some much-needed clarity.

'I have to protect Henry and Phillipa *too* you know,' she responded in a brusque, defensive manner that was much more like the Alison Cross he knew of old.

'Do you think he'd really harm his own *children*?' Dave barked angrily, making a sideways grimace. He was also aware, from the corner of his eye, that the senior officer had just glanced impatiently at his watch, but tried to ignore it.

Alison maintained her intense eye contact with Dave, but did not reply to his question. Nevertheless, he interpreted her silence as confirmation that she did indeed have a concern for Henry and Phillipa's safety, should Tim be allowed to get anywhere near them. This left Dave wondering where he stood in all of this: was Tim right to be aggrieved at having his access to the children denied, or were Alison's concerns in doing so, somehow justifiable? A judgement had to be made, and a snap one too. In the end, Dave decided to go with loyalty to his friend, as that was the only thing he could think of to sway it for him: he was with Tim on this one.

Dave stared hard at Alison, and then narrowed his eyes with dismissive derision, before slowly and haughtily averting his gaze.

Having obviously been judged as a horrible person who had acted unreasonably, Alison exhaled audibly in frustration and quickly turned to go. However, as before, she stopped and once again turned back to face him.

'*Look*, I don't care what you think of *me*, but…but *try* and get him down from up there, will you Dave?' she entreated, her rapidly moistening eyes meeting his and holding the gaze.

'I'll do all I can, I promise!' Dave stated, with a slow nod and the merest flicker of a smile.

Alison repeated the gesture, took one last look up at Tim and then stormed off.

Sergeant Marlowe, who, like his younger colleague, had been silently observing the exchange, decided that now was the time for him to intervene.

'Go and get Mrs Cross back, will you lad? We might have to have another try with her later!' he said, with a slow, weary delivery.

'Right ho Sarge, but before I do ... this is Dave Derwent, chummie's mate!'

'*Yes*, I'd already worked *that* one out, now off you go constable.'

Having been given a friendly one-armed shove by his senior colleague, the young PC shot off in pursuit of the rapidly retreating Alison Cross.

Dave now had a chance to better study this Sergeant Marlowe with whom he'd been left. He was a short, rotund man, at least in police officer terms, with dark close-set eyes and an equally dark, ungraded moustache that seemed to completely cover his mouth. The flat-topped hat that he wore seemed incongruously bright and new, compared with the rest of his uniform; it was as if it rarely came out of its box.

Having monitored the progress of the younger policeman, until he disappeared into the crowd, Sergeant Marlowe turned to Dave and then shook hands with him.

'Very eloquent, your friend up there; an educated man I assume?' he asked, glancing briefly up at Tim, who was sitting there drinking silently and swaying gently from side to side.

'Yes, he *is* very well read,' Dave said, with a smile, as he shook hands.

'And *so* polite to everyone, except that poor ex-wife of his,' the sergeant commented, with a broad grin that couldn't actually be seen because of his moustache, but was assumed by the bulging of his cheeks and the narrowing of his eyes. 'I like him, Mr Derwent!' he added, with an approving nod.

'It's *Darwin* actually!' Dave corrected, now feeling comfortable enough to correct the earlier error.

'Sorry, Darwin! *Now* then, as his best friend, do you think you can get him to stop playing silly beggars and come down?' the middle-aged officer asked, with a more serious countenance.

'I'll do my *best* sergeant,' Dave responded, swallowing hard against his fear.

From the moment he had arrived, Dave knew in his heart of hearts that he'd probably have to go up there in an attempt to bring Tim down, but now the moment had actually arrived, he dearly wished that Alison had been more successful in her efforts. Dave took a deep breath and then slowly walked forward on his own. Straightaway, he sensed numerous pairs of inquisitive eyes focused on him.

If there were people in the crowd who had not seen Dave's intervention, then this was certainly no longer the case once Tim had noticed his friend.

'*Dave*, you old wanker ... you've *got* here at last!' came the cheery welcome from on high. 'Come up, have a drink, and tell me why all these people are *staring* at me!'

Having given Tim a quick thumbs-up sign, Dave approached the projecting staircase tower of the multistorey car park and stepped into its dank, odorous interior; grateful to have escaped the scrutiny of the crowd. He plodded up each successive flight of concrete steps with ever increasing trepidation, as it sunk in just what a huge responsibility he had taken on. His task: no lesser one than to save a man's life. Dave's advantage in this endeavour was that he knew Tim very well, perhaps as well as anyone could, with the probable exception of Alison. On the other hand, he had to acknowledge that a huge disadvantage to him was his friend's undoubtedly advanced drunken state. To anyone else, Tim wouldn't have seemed that inebriated; he certainly didn't sound it. He wasn't slurring his words and his unique command of the English language was utterly undiminished. And yet, Dave knew all too well that Tim must have had an absolute skin-full, otherwise he wouldn't be up there, facing public scrutiny and the summary judgement of far lesser men. His poor friend was clearly beyond caring and this is why he was acutely aware that Tim *was* capable of jumping.

Dave reached the fifth floor and once more re-emerged into the Saturday afternoon sunlight. There were still many cars parked on this, the uppermost level. No doubt, the disgruntled owners, who had been unable to retrieve their vehicles due to Tim's impromptu rooftop performance, were currently swelling the crowds in the street below. Dave had not yet seen those predatory packs of people from this high vantage point, but it soon dawned on him that there could very well be folk down there that he knew; Amanda-Jayne might even be watching, and would certainly have seen him approach the building if she was one of the many onlookers.

After a few steps forward, Dave saw his drunken friend's aged estate car parked half way along on the right, and just beyond that, sat on the retaining wall and facing outwards, the swaying figure of Tim himself. As he approached, Dave made sure that he made lots of noise, so as not to startle his precariously perched friend.

Sure enough, Tim heard the approaching footsteps, as well as the nervously whistled rendition of 'Yellow Submarine' and turned his head to greet Dave.

'*Dave* ... good view from up here, me old matey. Wish I'd brought my camera,' he declared, with a clarity that belied his drunken state.

'Hello there Tim,' Dave said, as he slowly squeezed between the front bumper of the old estate car, and the crash barrier. 'Mind if I ... umm...mind if I join you?'

In response, Tim merely made a flourishing arm gesture towards the broad concrete parapet top alongside his seated position.

With his limbs a tremble, Dave sat on the wall right next to him, but facing inwards, and with his feet tucked under the crash barrier for extra safety. During the manoeuvre, he deliberately avoided looking either outwards or downwards until his bottom was firmly in place, but even then, couldn't quite bring himself to do so. From this inward-facing vantage point, the first thing he noticed were three empty two-litre cider bottles discarded at his feet. Nonetheless, despite his massive intake of alcohol, Tim now seemed calm, even cheerful, and his potential saviour hoped that the rescue mission would be a straightforward one as a result.

Unfortunately, before Dave could utter any mollifying platitudes, there came another potentially disastrous intervention from street level, as an unknown voice suddenly boomed out.

'*Tell him to bloody well hurry up and jump!*' yelled a young male voice from the crowd below, followed by several other approving and disapproving mutterings from other on-lookers.

Fortunately, despite his dulled senses, Tim was quick to respond.

'*My dear fellow, God wasted a perfectly good arse-hole, when he put teeth in your mouth!*' he retorted loudly; a comment that prompted a huge roar of laughter from the Gravel Walk audience.

Relieved that Tim had got the better of the ghoulish heckler, and quickly abandoning any thoughts of saying anything meaningful, Dave turned his head so as to address his friend directly.

'*So* then, what are you doing up here you silly old sod?' he asked, after a short pause, and very much in the same casual manner he'd have adopted if they were sitting together in the pub.

Tim took another long, slow drink before replying.

'To paraphrase a certain bearded Victorian would-be ancestor of yours, I'm not fit to *survive* any longer…I'm not a fit husband, father *or* Telecom drone!' he responded in a chilling, matter-of-fact voice that displayed not the merest hint of emotion.

'But what about *friend?*' Dave interjected quickly. 'Don't forget, you *are* a good friend to me. Jump, and you'll selfishly rob me of that friendship!'

Tim stared impassively into the air and said nothing; he had obviously heard what his friend had to say, but gave no clue as to what his silence signified. Dave was now very worried indeed. Tim's calm air of fatalism was extremely frightening; it was almost as if he'd already made up his mind how the afternoon would pan out. For the first time, Dave very hesitantly turned his head round to look behind and below him. Because of the deep walled light well that surrounded the multistorey, the firemen had been unable to deploy their safety net. If Tim *did* jump, he quickly worked out, with much concern, that they would not be able to catch him.

A dizzy-headed Dave now restored his gaze inwards and forwards, and then gripped tightly on to the edges of the concrete wall upon which he sat. Gradually, his senses restored themselves to something approaching normality.

'Hey Tim, give me some of that cider will you?' he asked, daring to release his right arm in order to receive the bottle.

Tim willingly offered up his last remaining drink without a word. Dave put the bottle in his lap to steady it while he unscrewed the plastic cap; a cap that Tim had religiously replaced after taking each draught. Uppermost in his mind was how the hell he was going to get his best friend out of this sticky situation. As he slowly removed the bottle-top with his left hand, Dave noticed the small but prominent crescent-moon scar just below his thumb. This put him in mind of Ronnie, his Scar Brother, and a similar rooftop incident to this one back in the summer of 1969. All those years ago, he attempted to recall, how did they manage to get his uncle down?

*

David couldn't sleep, so he just lay there in the top bunk, watching the night slowly segue into day through the draped bedroom window. Once a sufficient quantity of daylight had penetrated the room, he carefully leaned over and gazed down at the sleeping occupant of the lower bunk. Yesterday evening, Ronnie had been put to bed in the yellow bedroom, in order to give him sufficient quiet and isolation to sleep off his vintage wine tasting experience. Therefore, David's bunk bed companion for that night had been his father, but it still came as quite a shock to see him lying there below.

As dawn gradually asserted itself on that Sunday morning, and a few birds made their presence known, David finally abandoned any idea of going back to sleep, and instead, continued to lay in bed awake, both thinking and casually flicking through one of the familiar *Look and Learn* magazines. Saturday's adventures had meant that they were falling behind with Nanna Darwin's schedule, but with Ronnie's famous powers of recovery, coupled with the fact that Grandad Darwin was now up and about, David felt confident that they could clear the gardening backlog by the time they went home on the Sunday afternoon.

As the minutes slowly slipped by, David tried to resist the urge to go to the loo, but the matter had now become rather urgent and he could no longer put it off. He concluded that there was no choice but to shrug off his sloth, and leave the safety and sanctuary of his well tucked-in bed, in order to go to the bathroom. Having finally accomplished this feat, he hurried back down the narrow passage and, quite unexpectedly, bowled straight into Uncle Ronnie, who was coming out of the yellow bedroom. Ronnie motioned to David to keep quiet and then quickly dragged him back into the small front bedroom.

It hadn't escaped his notice that Ronnie was already dressed, but that wasn't uppermost in his mind at the time.

'Are you feeling better now?' David asked in a half-whisper, as the bedroom door was quietly pushed to behind him.

'Yes, but I don't *deserve* to be,' his uncle responded, with a smile and a shrug. '*Huh*, not even a headache to shame me for my little episode yesterday.'

Now that Ronnie was well again, David desperately wanted to tell him all about the adventure they'd had in the 'big house' trying to cover his tracks, but his uncle seemed preoccupied. David was now eager to find out why.

'You're not going out to pick mushrooms on your own are you?' he asked, before glancing at the room's yellow curtains. 'It's barely light outside.'

'But it's early enough for the birds; can't you hear them stamping their feet and hollering?' Ronnie said, paraphrasing one of Grandad Darwin's favourite sayings. He smiled and then sat on the edge of the bed. 'No Dave, no mushrooms this morning ... what I have to do is *far* more important than that. You see ... I'm going to save the windmill!'

'*Wow*, do you really think you *can*?' David enthused wide-eyed, lowering himself onto the opposite corner of the yellow counterpaned mattress.

'I'm going to damn well try ... I can't just sit back and watch it happen!'

Ronnie paused briefly, during which time he chewed his bottom lip. 'You see Dave, there were two things that were said yesterday, which have helped me decide to take this course of action. That teacher, James Garrison, had wished for a more high profile campaign, with perhaps a celebrity being involved for better publicity .. d'you remember?'

David nodded keenly in response.

'The *second* influential comment actually came from your dad! It was Len who told me there was nothing that *he* could do to save the old mill. But don't you see Dave? *I can*', Ronnie declared, with passionate enthusiasm, before gripping both his nephew's hands. 'I'm going to go to the very top of Rothermead Mill, where, loudly and very publicly, I will do my act and I will keep on doing it until something positive happens!'

Straightaway, David thought what a brilliant idea this was, but it didn't take long before parentally inspired good sense and level headedness took over.

'Dad will go up the *wall*!' he stated with furrow-browed concern. 'Aren't you meant to be *avoiding* publicity?'

Ronnie did not respond to the question that had been asked of him, but instead leant forward and squeezed the lad's hands a little tighter.

'Answer me *this,* Dave ... if you had a chance to actually prevent the mill from being demolished, and you were the *only* one who could accomplish that, wouldn't you at least give it a *try*?'

With the question being posed like that, David could answer in only one way.

'Oh *yes* Uncle Ronnie, I *would*,' he said, with a vigorous nod.

Ronnie smiled again, winked and then ruffled his nephew's hair.

'Wish me luck then,' he whispered, getting to his feet. 'Oh, and by the way, having slept in the yellow bedroom last night, I'm even *more* determined to see Katie next week ... you wouldn't know why ... I'll *tell* you one day. But remember ... mum's still the word on that one, *okay* mate?'

David nodded again, and even more emphatically than before.

'In *fact*,' Ronnie added, as he crouched down in front of David, 'you're the *only* one I would tell this to, but everything I do today, no matter *what* the outcome, is also a gesture of love for Katie. Hopefully soon, I'll be able to tell her that *myself*. However…' Ronnie paused and took a deep tremulous breath, ' ... if I never get the chance, then *you* must tell her the reasons why I did what I did today.'

'*When* should I tell her?' David asked confused, as an unexpected wave of emotion surged through him.

Ronnie smiled benevolently, before straightening up again.

'*You'll* know when the time is right!' came the calm reassuring reply.

David nodded in compliance for the third and final time, before watching his uncle steal out of the room, over the passage, and then quickly creep across the bunk bedroom, where his brother Len slept on undisturbed and unaware. David followed and returned to his bed, but knew there was no way he'd be able to sleep now. This time, it wasn't because of the evil presence of the stairwell, or wanting the loo, or even his dogged headache, which had still not quite left him. On this occasion, his mind was too occupied with thoughts of Ronnie for sleep to claim him. It buzzed with the incredibly exciting, yet foolhardy adventure that his uncle was about to embark upon. In fact, David quickly decided that whether the idea was wise or not, he neither knew nor cared. What he could be absolutely sure of though, right there and then, was that he was incredibly proud of his uncle, and that Ronnie's love for Katie was absolutely genuine. And he didn't even mind that they'd forgotten to do the 'Scar Brothers' ritual before separating; it was not as if it would have been their last chance ever.

'Ronnie's sleeping in late,' Nanna Darwin remarked, as she teased the bacon around the large frying pan on the Rayburn hotplate.

'He's got a lot to sleep off, *hasn't* he!' Len tutted from behind the Sunday newspaper.

Grandad Darwin, who was also sitting up at the diningroom table, nodded in agreement.

'Although I expect that when the Ronnie *does* re-appear, he'll behave as if nothing has happened,' he asserted, through many years of experience. '*You'll* see ... he'll be down any minute, as bright as a button.'

Nanna huffed loudly in response. '*Well*, if that naughty boy doesn't hurry up, he'll miss breakfast!' she retorted, before transferring the cooked bacon to a plate in the warm oven.

David, who had been following the conversation with growing unease, could stand it no longer, and knew he would have to say something; after all, it wasn't as if Ronnie had told him in confidence. It wasn't like the Katie secrets, he reassured himself.

'He's, umm…he's not upstairs,' the boy confessed, in a nervous mumble, and almost too afraid to meet the eyes of anyone in the room.

Len quickly dropped the newspaper, and then motioned to both Nanna and Grandad Darwin for him to be allowed to question his son uninterrupted. He knew not to go in like a bull in a china shop, especially where those special confidences between David and Ronnie were concerned. However, every instinct he possessed urged him to pick his son up and shake the information from him.

'It's alright David, *look* at me,' he said soothingly, leaning forward in his seat. 'Do you know where your Uncle Ronnie has gone?'

David slowly raised his head, but hesitated before replying; he needed to find the right words.

'Has he returned to the wine cellar?' his father prompted, with a little more urgency, but no less gently. At the same time, Len once more raised his hand in order to remind his parents not to chime in and interfere in the interrogation.

'No, he's gone up to the windmill,' David replied quietly, but with his confidence restored.

'Well *that's* not so bad,' Len responded with a sigh of relief, as he relaxed back into his chair. 'He probably just wants a last look before they pull it down.'

'*No* Dad, he's going to *save it* from being pulled down!' David said in a much more assertive manner.

'How?' his frowning father queried, almost not wanting to hear the reply, as he resumed his previous forward-leaning stance.

David sat up straight and glanced briefly at both Nanna and Grandad Darwin before replying.

'Uncle Ronnie is going to do his comedy act on the flat roof of the old mill, to get some publicity for the campaigners,' he announced, as pride in his uncle's aspirations finally overcame his earlier reticence.

Almost immediately, Len's head dropped into his hands in sheer desperation and the room fell ominously silent. Sadly, as he glanced back up at David, it quickly became obvious that the interviewer could no longer keep his cool.

'Didn't it occur to you to *stop him*?' he asked, in a voice that got louder with each word.

'But he said he was going to *save the mill*,' David shouted in belligerent response, as he stood up in frustration.

'I'm more concerned with saving Ronnie!' Len retorted sharply, before rapidly getting to his feet himself. '*Come* on Grandad, let's go up there and fetch him home ... you'll have to keep breakfast warm for us Nanna!'

She nodded in silent but concerned compliance, as both Len and Grandad Darwin made for the back door.

David hurried to join them, but was quickly and unceremoniously dissuaded.

'Oh no you *don't*, young man,' bellowed his father, with a finger wagging furiously. 'Help Nanna, do something on the list ... but *stay here*'.

Before long, the crestfallen twelve-year-old heard his father's car start up and looked to Nanna Darwin for support, but there was none to be had, and as he slumped back into his diningroom chair, the sound of Len's Ford Escort accelerating away across the outer courtyard, could clearly be heard by the both.

Within seconds, Nanna had placed a loaded breakfast plate in front of him.

'Now eat that and *remember*, Ronnie's career is more important than any old windmill!' she exclaimed coldly, before turning briskly away.

David glared unhappily at Nanna Darwin's back as she busied herself at the Rayburn. He did not like the implication that he was unconcerned about his uncle's career; after all, he'd only been trying to support him with the best of intentions. He reluctantly picked up his knife and fork, but did not enjoy the eggs and bacon, and even the mushrooms they'd not got round to eating yesterday gave him no pleasure.

Just as David finished that miserable meal, the phone rang, and Nanna Darwin rushed over to the sideboard beneath the cuckoo clock in order to answer it. After a few seconds, her face dropped and David immediately began to pay attention to what she was saying:

'Demolition contractors…what, *today*? But it's a Sunday…my husband and two sons are up there already…yes…yes, *the* Ronnie Darwin…television as *well*… okay, thank you…yes…goodbye.'

Having replaced the receiver, she dropped onto one of the diningroom chairs at the table, with a bewildered look on her face.

David waited anxiously for an explanation, but could only contain himself for a few seconds.

'Who *was* that Nanna ... is everything alright?' he asked, with both interest and concern.

'That was Mr Garrison from Rothermead Green ... he's ringing everyone who signed the windmill petition,' she explained, with a slow, straight-faced delivery. 'He's heard that they're going to pull the old mill down *today*! Apparently, one of his contacts has informed him that the demolition crew are preparing to leave from their Sittingbourne premises right at this very *moment*, and he's going to try and organise a massive protest.'

It was then that the full implication of the surprising news struck her, and she suddenly shot out of the chair in a very agitated state. 'Oh my *God*, we have to warn the boys ... Ronnie simply *can't* get caught up in all this!'

As his grandmother fretfully paced the room, David thought quickly and realised that this was the ideal opportunity for him to finally be allowed to play a part in the day's events, and also redeem himself in everyone's eyes.

'I'll run across the cherry orchards and warn them ... I can *get* there in ten minutes,' he said, pushing his chair back noisily. '*Please* let me go Nanna!'

His grandmother paused from her pacing, fixed him with a long impassive stare and then slowly nodded her head.

'*Go* on then, but please *be careful*,' she said; clearly more concerned to protect Ronnie than she was in defying her oldest son's clearly stated wishes.

By the time David had reached the stile into the first orchard, he was already puffed out. He was certainly no athlete and had always hated school sports. To make matters worse, his stomach now griped with indigestion from his recently consumed breakfast. However, he knew that he was on an important mission, and soon surprised himself by summoning up additional energy from somewhere, which allowed him to press forward in defiance of his own discomfort.

David finally reached the five-bar gate that led onto Rothermead Green, and threw himself against it in a state of complete exhaustion. Straightaway, he could hear voices above the sound of his own laboured breathing, and when he had composed himself enough to look up for the first time, an extraordinary scene met his eyes. A large crowd had gathered round the base of the old mill tower; some with protest banners, others brandishing cameras. And then, as he clambered over the gate, he was excited to see that, positioned slightly further back on the green itself, there was a film crew from Southern Television. David soon noticed that the large shoulder-mounted TV camera, rather than being trained on the bespectacled and microphone-wielding front man, was angled up as if focusing on the top of Rothermead Green Mill. He looked back to the throng of local protestors and realised that the vast majority of them were also gazing upwards. It didn't take him long to scan his eyes up the fullest length of the mill tower to the very top, where Ronnie could be seen, very much fulfilling that earlier declaration of intent. However, rather than performing the act as expected, his uncle was striking another super-hero pose; standing proud and erect at the edge of the mill's flat top, with his hands defiantly on his hips.

David began to make his way towards the crowds at the base of the tower. He had only taken three or four steps when, as if prompted by some subconscious cue, the loftily-placed young comedian at last began to perform his regular routine. His impressed nephew looked up appreciatively, and before very long, Ronnie was being chased round the mill top's circular perimeter by an imaginary gorilla. Ripples of laughter and applause soon began to erupt from the crowd at regular intervals.

Suddenly remembering his rescue mission, David completed his journey over to the mill in more haste. Even though the crescent-shaped throng, gathered around its base, was about three or four people deep, it didn't take him long to locate his father and Grandad Darwin amongst them.

Before either of them could react to his unauthorised presence, the agitated lad delivered his urgent message:

'Nanna Darwin's had a telephone call from that teacher person ... they're gonna come and pull the mill down *this morning*!' he announced; looking rapidly from one to the other.

Straightaway, Len frowned with grave concern.

'Garrison hasn't mentioned this to us or anyone *else* here, as far as I know,' he remarked, above the noise of another wave of laughter. 'Mind you, most of these people were *already* here when we arrived!'

Whilst an anxious Grandad Darwin stared up at his performing youngest son, Len glanced back through the crowd and across the width of the green. It was then that he located James Garrison, who had just come out of his cottage, and was now standing on the perimeter track. He had his arms folded, and was looking extremely pleased with himself. Unlike the teacher, Len was far from happy with the developing situation, and began to push his way out of the protesting pack; his narrowed eyes fixed on the undoubted architect of all this. As he crossed this end of the green, Len became aware of the television crew for the first time. Luckily, they were too focused on the animated antics of Ronnie to notice him.

As the now seething Len homed in on him, James' smile weakened somewhat, and he was soon summarily challenged before being able to offer a word of explanation.

'Why didn't you *tell* us you'd heard that the mill was being pulled down today? That's my *brother* up there!' Len yelled angrily, before pointing up towards the top of the windmill.

'And I want to *keep* him up there too,' rejoiced the unrepentant protest organiser. 'Look *around* you ... the crowds, the press, the television; what better publicity could there *be*, and it's all thanks to your brother, *and*, of course, a few well-placed telephone calls from *me*!'

Gritting his teeth, Len grabbed the teacher by the lapel of his blazer, and then formed a threatening fist shape with his right hand.

'*If* you're going to hit me, make sure the television camera is focused on us first, there's a good fellow,' Garrison said, in a remarkably calm manner, given the predicament he was in.

Len huffed and quickly dropped his hold; in fact, he could think of nothing to say in response.

James, on the other hand, was all too keen to explain his actions, as he straightened his blazer.

'*Look*, I don't want to fall out with anyone. All I want to do is *save the mill*, just like *him* up there,' the teacher reasoned, pointing up at the rooftop performer. 'I *thought* I recognised him yesterday,' he added, with a wry smile. 'Ronnie Darwin eh? Well I *never*!'

Beaten, Len turned away in frustration and began to storm back across the green. As he watched him go, Garrison saw that the TV crew must have noticed their altercation, and that the camera was now focused on him. He soon decided to take advantage of the opportunity for more publicity.

'*The demolition crew may come, but they'll never pull the old mill down; not in these circumstances*,' he yelled, after the rapidly retreating Len. He then signalled a thumbs-up sign to Ronnie, who responded in like manner, whilst the television camera swiftly swung between teacher, protestor and an unsuspecting Len.

Having rejoined Grandad Darwin and David, Len extended an arm around each of them, and then looked up at his brother in confused contemplation. When they'd first arrived, he had tried to shout up at Ronnie, but without any apparent success. Now though, he felt that there was no choice but to try again.

'Ronnie, Ronnie,' he bellowed loudly through cupped hands, '*they're coming to pull the mill down today ... get back down here, you silly sod*!'

It was soon clear from the various shouts of '*stay up there*', which emanated from the crowd around him, that most people *did* know what was in the offing that morning, and if Ronnie *had* heard his brother's warning, then he wasn't responding. However, Len quickly worked out it was likely that he had, in fact, perceived what had been shouted up to him, for as the young comedian went through his act once again, it was performed in a much more manic fashion than before.

As the familiar routine progressed, David looked up and was laughing along with the rest of the crowd. Never before had he seen his uncle so focused, so professional and above all, so very, very funny. As far as the lad was concerned, it was a superb performance, and quite his best to date. But, when David caught a disapproving look from his father, he fell silent and became rather ashamed that he'd managed to get into trouble yet again.

At that moment, Len became aware of an additional clamour behind him, and turned round to discover that the TV camera was now trained on him. Worse still, a person he recognised from the local news, but couldn't name – a man with black, plastic-framed glasses, a five o'clock shadow and protruding chin – was pushing his way towards him with a microphone.

'Oh bloody *hell*; that's *all* we need,' Len muttered to a somewhat bewildered Grandad Darwin.

However, before the television reporter could get to him, everyone's attention was suddenly diverted towards the sound of an urgent two-tone siren, coming from the farmost end of Rothermead Green. Within a few seconds, a fire engine appeared, lights flashing, and bumping rapidly along the track to the north side of the long wedge-shaped green. Len immediately suspected that arch-publicity seeker, James Garrison, was responsible for this latest intervention and turned round in order to glare at him hatefully.

The troublesome teacher responded with another thumbs-up sign.

'*I thought the poor man was going to jump,*' he shouted back to Len with a sideways smile, and then a double-handed gesture of culpability.

With panic now beginning to set in, Len averted his eyes from the unrepentant organiser and once more stared up at his brother, whilst realising that they were running out of both time and options. Ronnie, on the other hand, seemed completely unperturbed, and cut a defiant figure as he stood at the roof's edge, watching the goings-on below.

David began to feel the sense of helplessness that Grandad Darwin, and his father were now experiencing.

'Can't we go up and fetch him down?' he asked Len, anxious to play a part in the resolution of the family crisis.

'That was the *first* thing I tried,' his father responded, with a sense of despair. 'Ronnie has somehow barricaded the door from the inside. Oh *God*, what a bloody *nightmare* this has become!' he added, briefly rubbing his brow.

The television crew were now filming the firemen who, having arrived close by, were unpacking what appeared to be a massive handheld safety net. Realising that the intention was for Ronnie to jump into this trampoline-like device, Len began to fear for his brother's life. Avoiding publicity now seemed a rather low priority objective.

'*Ronnie, Ronnie, Ronnie,*' he shouted, much louder and more desperately than before.

This time, Ronnie could not fail to have heard his brother's urgent cries, and clearly chose to ignore them. However, it soon became apparent to Len that his words had not gone unheard in other quarters, when many of the people who were packed round the base of the old mill in his immediate vicinity, began to ape him in a rhythmic chant: '*Ro-nnie, Ro-nnie, Ro-nnie.*'

Further vehicles could now be seen bearing down on the already lively scene. Much to the extreme consternation of all three ground-rooted Darwin males, it turned out to be the demolition convoy, consisting of several tipper lorries and a transit van; all being accompanied by no less than three police cars. The police, who were the first to pull up, immediately began to push the protestors away from the mill tower and then herded them onto the centre of the green.

Now trapped with his son and father within the mass of banner-waving locals and press photographers, Len tried to observe what was going to happen next. The first thing he saw was the fire chief approach the police sergeant, and then point up in the direction of Ronnie; presumably to make him aware of their biggest problem and potential danger. Shortly afterwards, as if responding to some unseen signal, numerous men spilled out from each of the contractors vehicles. One of them hurried over to the yellow mechanical digger that was already parked there, and quickly scrambled up into its cab.

As the machine roared into life, the corralled crowd began to jeer, and then the chanting resumed: '*Ro-nnie, Ro-nnie, Ro-nnie.*' Ronnie responded by crouching over the edge of the mill top; first to make beckoning motions and then to wave a clenched fist at the demolition workers below. It was almost as if he was defying them to try to get him. All the while, the anxious firemen hovered nearby with their safety net.

Undaunted by either Ronnie's threatening gestures or the jeering crowd, the mechanical digger swung round and then tore into the last remaining cottage. Bricks and roses fell to the ground together, as the crowd and emergency service personnel alike became engulfed in a choking wave of demolition dust. The whole thing was over in a matter of minutes, and it was then that the machine turned ominously towards the windmill. As the arm-linked police officers strained to hold back the agitated protestors, the gang foreman approached the tower and tried to manually move the firmly barricaded small entranceway at the front of the mill tower, but was as unsuccessful as Len had earlier been in this endeavour. Undaunted, he then went over to the hovering demolition machine and climbed up next to the driver, before gesturing towards the mill structure with a rotating motion of his right arm. With roaring engine and belching exhaust, the machine turned a slow semi-circle in front of the mill and then positioned its hydraulic pincer towards the old garage doors at the base of the conical tower. With one small movement, the doors splintered into so much kindling, and then in response to another sudden movement of the foreman's arm, four of the gang entered the mill structure by this new enforced opening.

A deeply distressed Grandad Darwin could remain silent no longer.

'*Look out, the Ronnie,*' he shouted up at his defiantly gesturing son.

The crowd quickly responded in like manner: '*The Ro-nnie', 'the Ro-nnie', 'the Ro-nnie'*; a chant that David joined in with, in his head.

At the same time, a couple of the more determined protestors broke through the uniformed cordon and ran forward; only to be unceremoniously rugby-tackled by two of the other police officers. As events now rapidly unfolded, James Garrison looked on from further back, having escaped being rounded up with the rest of the press and protestors by hiding behind Len Darwin's parked Ford Escort outside his cottage.

From his lofty vantage point, Ronnie could also clearly see what was happening below, and appeared undeterred by the jolt he no doubt felt from the mechanical digger. In fact, the rooftop protestor was now standing still and looking as if he was quickly working out what his next move would be.

By far the keenest observer of these dramatic proceedings was Len, and he was becoming ever more desperate as the chances of Ronnie escaping unscathed gradually ebbed away. And now there were muscle-bound, tattooed demolition workers making their way up the inside of the windmill towards his brother. It was then that despair suddenly gave way to hope as Ronnie suddenly moved away from the edge and thus disappeared from view. A hopeful Len quickly looked down at his son.

'Perhaps he's finally given up ... perhaps he's decided to make his way back down,' he said, with eyebrows raised in expectation.

David chuckled and then shook his head.

'I'll bet he's gone to stand on the trap door,' he countered, before looking back up at the seemingly empty mill top.

All signs of hope quickly fell from Len's face, as he reluctantly agreed that his son's hypothesis was far more likely then his own. Likewise, Grandad Darwin, who had been following the conversation and riding the same roller coaster of emotions as his oldest son, hung his slowly shaking head in despair, and tears began welling up in his eyes.

Despite the sheer number of people currently gathered there, an eerie silence now fell across Rothermead Green. Even the idling engine of the demolition machine had been switched off. Policemen and protestors alike eagerly awaited the next turn of events, but didn't know whether to look at the top or the bottom of the mill in order to observe it. A sudden loud crash emanating from the top of the tower, quickly followed by a man's hoarse bellow, soon settled the matter. As a result, cameramen and contractors alike either jumped or gasped in fright, and then all eyes turned heavenwards, eagerly awaiting the first sight of someone.

There was an audible collective gasp as Ronnie suddenly came back into view at the roof's edge, but now one of the demolition workers was clearly visible up there with him. However, it soon became apparent that the rooftop protestor was far from giving up the fight. He soon began to run round close to the edge of the mill top, as he had already done several times for the finale of his act. This forced the demolition contractor to chase him and therefore, unwittingly, play the part of the gorilla. As a result, loud peals of laughter echoed up from the crowd, and more than one police officer could be seen suppressing a smirk. The young comedian responded by behaving as if he were a silent movie actress, being pursued by that archetypal villain with the big moustache. The hapless demolition contractor soon tired of being made a fool of and decided to lunge at his nemesis. With an instinctive defensive reaction, Ronnie pushed him away, and then, with arms flailing wildly, the unfortunate workman toppled over the edge. As the falling figure emitted a deafening scream, the crowd cried out as one, and the firemen desperately raced with their net in order to catch him. Fortunately, they succeeded in their rescue attempt, but the fallen contractor was not a happy man. Neither were his three colleagues who, having finally reached the top of the mill, had all witnessed the fall. Now clearly outnumbered, Ronnie was quickly overpowered and forced to the bitumen-covered surface of the mill roof.

Now only able to observe the random thrashing of an arm here, or a leg there, Len shut his eyes and then winced sorrowfully. He was powerless to help his brother now, and as far as he was concerned, it was all over for him: his future, his career, everything. At the same time, Grandad Darwin and David embraced, both now in tears, and the television camera, which was now trained on them all, kept on filming, regardless of the personal intrusion.

However, they were soon shaken back to reality by the sound of vicious fighting coming from inside the mill. It got progressively louder, until finally, Ronnie literally came tumbling out of the splintered doorway to the right, closely followed by his three sparring partners. Suddenly seeing an opportunity present itself, Len quickly thrust his car keys into Grandad Darwin's hand.

'*Go, get the car started and wait for us,*' he instructed, both loudly and firmly, '*we're going to get Ronnie!*'

Len and David rushed forward, just as the crowd of village protestors broke through the police cordon, effectively to act as cover for them. Seeing the approaching grey-haired hoard, the three contractors quickly backed off and Len managed to get Ronnie to his feet, although straightaway, it was apparent that he was badly hurt; blood clearly pouring from at least two nasty wounds on his head. Then, under the cover of the surrounding mayhem, David helped his father to get the fallen hero of Rothermead Mill back across the green and over to the waiting Ford Escort. James Garrison redeemed himself by clearing a path through the jostling throng, and then distracting the television camera away from the fleeing Darwins, by suddenly leaping on to a startled young policeman's back.

Len was quick but careful in helping his injured brother into the back of the car, before getting in alongside him. David scrambled into the front seat, and then looked back with concern at his dazed uncle. However, from the corner of his eye, he couldn't help but notice the contractors removing rafters, doors and floorboards from the demolished cottage and then placing them inside the base of the old mill. It soon dawned on him, with absolute dismay, that they were making a bonfire; they intended to set fire to the windmill as a means of destroying it. As the car accelerated away, David could clearly see that the fire had not only been lit, but was already beginning to take hold. Finally, as the Ford Escort turned off the green's perimeter track at the far end, none of its occupants could fail to observe that the mill tower had become a flaming beacon, with orange fire and black smoke rising into the clear blue sky.

Grandad Darwin drove home as quickly as he could, all the while casting anxious glances at Ronnie through the rear view mirror. Len, who was supporting his swaying semi-conscious brother on one side, was all too aware that he was in a bad way, having clearly been ruthlessly roughed up by the three demolition workers. There was a nasty gash on his forehead and his right eye was puffed up and closed. His lower lip was split, and when he eventually tried to speak, it became clear that one of his front teeth was missing.

Once back at the cottage, Grandad Darwin held all the doors open as Len and David helped Ronnie inside. A shocked and distressed Nanna Darwin nearly fainted at the sight of her bloodied younger son, but Len could only afford to have concerns for one person.

'Can you get him cleaned up as soon as possible? I think we need to get Ronnie away from here before the police decide to come looking for him,' he instructed his mother, lowering Ronnie onto a diningroom chair. Having done that, Len quickly turned to his son.

'Now David, go upstairs and pack your stuff *and* Ronnie's things ... I need to make a quick telephone call home to Canterbury, and then I'll come up and join you!' he ordered firmly, before making his way over to the phone on the sideboard.

'I'll go and get the first-aid box,' Grandad Darwin said, as he retreated back into the kitchen.

With the call made, and a bewildered Meg brought up to speed, Len left his parents to patch Ronnie up, while he went upstairs to pack his own belongings. Father and son eventually met up again in the bunk bedroom and, straightaway, Len beckoned David over to him. Len held David by the shoulders, and then looked into his eyes with a serious countenance.

'You *obviously* realise that Ronnie is in a lot of trouble now. He's likely to be on the front page of *every* damned newspaper tomorrow, I shouldn't wonder, *and* on all local television bulletins tonight,' he said, clearly deriving no pleasure from the prospect.

Trembling, and beginning to snivel, David nodded in response.

Moved by his son's reaction, Len smiled warmly and allowed one of his hands to fall away before resuming.

'Now I *know* you didn't want to let your uncle down by telling us of his windmill fiasco, but if I'm going to be able to protect him from any *more* trouble, which might result in yet *further* press interest, I will need to know if he's got any more harebrained schemes up his sleeve ... do you understand?'

Rather than answer him, David merely nodded feebly and then looked down to his feet.

Immediately, Len could tell from his son's demeanour that he was hiding something, just as he was able to yesterday. However, on this occasion, he had neither the time nor patience for a gentle approach.

'*Out* with it David,' he bellowed, forcing the boy to look at him again, 'or you'll *feel my hand*!'

Straightaway, David realised that the game was up and, abandoning his Scar Brother's pledge, told his father all about Ronnie's plan to escape house arrest and go and find Katie. At the conclusion, he also sought to limit the damage he had done, especially to his own conscience.

'*Please* don't tell Uncle Ronnie that I've let him down by telling you all this,' he begged, in a shaky voice and through trembling lips.

Unmoved, his father stared back at him blankly, before bending to pick up his holdall, and then turning towards the stairwell door.

'I'll make no promises on *that* score, young man ... it's about time you learnt where your *true* family loyalties should lie!' he said coldly, before disappearing into the darkness.

With both hurt and disbelief now etched on his face, David scooped up the two remaining travel bags and followed on. The sense of betrayal he now felt was all encompassing. At great cost to his formative principals, he had betrayed Ronnie, only to be metaphorically slapped in the face for his troubles. Indeed, it would probably have hurt less had he been on the receiving end of a real blow. As he entered the top of the stairwell, David felt a small seed of resentment for his father begin to germinate in his mind.

Once downstairs with the bags, the pair went through to see how Ronnie was doing. He looked less bloodied now, and was certainly more alert, but his swollen eye was already beginning to blacken.

Seeing his brother and nephew enter the diningroom, Ronnie forced a weak smile.

'I didn't save the mill, *did* I?' he spluttered through sore, inflamed lips.

'No, you didn't, mate,' Len responded in frank, fatalistic tones, 'and I didn't manage to save *you*!'

Ronnie shrugged feebly, and then reached out for his brother's steadying arm as he slowly stood up.

'There's nothing to keep us here now, *is* there?' he said, sounding keen to escape the scene of his defeat.

Len helped him to his feet, and then noticed how hurt and confused both Nanna and Grandad were currently looking. The single-minded attitude he'd adopted for his brother's welfare alone, now softened a little as a result.

'When we're gone, please lock the door, and answer it to *nobody* ... it could be that the police will come here looking for Ronnie, regarding his part in this whole sorry saga!' He now did his best to force a reassuring smile. 'And *don't* worry you two ... *I'll* look after him ... *I'll* make sure that no further harm comes to him, okay?' he vowed, looking at each tired and bewildered face in turn. Unable to bear waiting for a reply, which might have only exacerbated the already emotionally charged atmosphere, a choked Len turned away and, supporting Ronnie's sagging body, they both made for the back door.

As the car slowly pulled away from the farm cottage, David looked back at Nanna and Grandad Darwin, who were standing motionless in front of their home. No one waved. Len's car left the outer courtyard and followed the track as it curved round the hornbeam hedge perimeter of the 'big house' garden to the right. As they trundled along, David studied the impassive heads of both his father and Uncle Ronnie. From the back, they looked as different as they did from the front, but he knew that, in their own way, each one was hurting just as much as the other.

As the car came out of the curve and approached the junction with the lane, a somewhat distracted Len had to suddenly swerve to avoid colliding with an incoming green Land Rover, driven by a rather startled-looking man whom he didn't recognise. Having avoided contact with both Land Rover and the farm track's left-hand metal perimeter fence, a now very much alert Len righted the car, whilst David looked behind and watched the green farm vehicle disappear round the bend. It was then that he recalled Nanna Darwin saying that the new farm manager was due to arrive this weekend, and he wondered if that was indeed him.

The Darwin's Ford Escort was soon leaving the metalled farm track and turning onto the lane to Beckensfield. Once more, David peered through the rear window and took a final look at Rothermead Farm as they pulled away. In the sky, a mile or so beyond the 'big house', a wide column of black smoke could clearly be seen, and was even beginning to block out the sun. Nothing will ever be the same again, concluded David sadly, as he looked away for the last time.

*

Dave looked over at Tim, gently swaying away next to him on the parapet, and for one brief moment, considered wrestling him to the ground, but then he could see them both going over the edge and quickly dismissed the notion. Indeed, he was too young to die and had plenty more to live for: bedding his beloved Amanda-Jayne being on top of the current 'must-do' list.

Strange as it might seem, the thought of death and the attractive teenager, in the same sentence, gave him another much more constructive idea.

'*Tim*, my old mucker,' he began, carefully calculating each of his spontaneous-sounding words, ' ... if you jump, splatter yourself and die, you might then go to *heaven*. Now that'll prove me *right*, with regards to the divine beyond, and you wouldn't be able to stand *that* now, *would* you!'

Tim glanced across at his friend and briefly cracked a smile.

Dave recognised that he was beginning to get through to him, and thus encouraged, knew he now had to try and deal a trump card.

'Tim, do you remember the day when we were both taking pictures up here, and also discussing the concept of fate?' he said, harking back to a cold Monday afternoon right at the beginning of the year.

His friend looked over more lingeringly, and then nodded.

'*Well* then,' Dave continued, daring to touch Tim's shoulder, 'do you *really* believe that it's your destiny to die today? Let's put it *this* way then ... if you can give me a sound philosophical reason why it has to be *right* here and *right* now, I'll push you off myself!'

Tim's face gradually broke into a more definitive smile, and then after an indeterminate pause, he slowly swung his legs round in order to face in the same direction as Dave. And then, almost imperceptively, he began to lean ever-so-slowly backwards. Alarmed, Dave quickly grabbed his friend and prevented him from toppling over the edge, albeit accidentally this time.

'Phew, *that* would have been ironic!' Dave chuckled, as he slowly got Tim righted.

'*Very*!' his friend agreed emphatically, with a vigorous shake of the head.

As Dave slowly got Tim to his feet, he was only vaguely aware of a ripple of applause that had risen from the crowd behind and below them both. It then began to dawn on him that he had actually succeeded in his mission; he had put on a successful rooftop performance, thank God. At that moment, he thought back to the Rothermead Mill incident, and how proud his Uncle Ronnie would have been of him today.

The gathered masses had thinned considerably by the time Dave and Tim had descended the staircase tower and reached ground level. The more sober of the two men instantly had a vision of hordes of disappointed old ladies, all with shopping trollies, shuffling away from the scene in every direction, eagerly in search of another parked ambulance and an excuse to gather round and resume gawping.

A delighted Sergeant Marlowe was in Gravel Walk to meet them.

'*Come* on then Peter Pan,' he said, gently taking hold of Tim's arm. 'You're *not* under arrest but I *would* ask you to go with the ambulance guys for a quick check up ... is that okay with you?'

Tim regarded the police officer with some suspicion, and then clung to Dave's arm like an alarmed child on the first day of primary school.

'Only if Dave comes too!' he insisted, with uncharacteristic timidity.

Marlowe looked to Dave with his eyebrows raised in an interrogative gesture, and was met with a stoical nod of agreement. With the bargain struck, the sergeant relaxed his grip of Tim's arm, and allowed the friends to make their way towards the nearby ambulance; a route that seemed mercifully devoid of any trolley-pushing pensioners.

'Well *done* sir!' called out Sergeant Marlowe after the departing Dave.

On approaching the waiting medics, who were standing by the ambulance's open rear doors, Dave noticed Paul Fisk, a tall, thin ginger-haired reporter he knew from the Gazette. Mercifully, the journalist seemed to be the only visible member of the press present; there being no evidence of a television crew having visited the scene.

Dave took Tim over to the friendlier-looking of the two waiting ambulance men and smiled broadly.

'Look, I know it's a bit of a cheek, but could you give me just two minutes to sort something out before we go?' he requested, in slightly obsequious tones.

'No problem at *all,* sir,' responded the grinning medic. 'We want to give your friend a few check-ups before we depart *anyway*!'

Paul spotted his friend from the moment he turned away from the ambulance, and then hurried over to greet him.

'Bloody hell Dave, I *thought* it was you up there! You *know* this guy then?' he asked, quickly flipping back the cover of his notepad.

'Yes, *very well* ... Tim and I work at Telecom together,' Dave responded, with a friendly grin. 'As it happens Paul, I was going to come over and talk to you about it *anyway*!'

'Ah, good *man*!' the journalist said as he began to scribble furiously. '*So* then, is it true what he was saying about his wife going *lezzie* and also stopping him from seeing his kids?'

'Essentially, *yes*!' Dave replied, in answer to the second part of the question only. 'She thinks he's going to *harm* them…which is nonsense!' he added in a close-to half-whisper.

'*Really*!' Fisk retorted, scribbling away.

'Oh *yes*, Tim Cross wouldn't harm a *fly* ... he's a very gentle guy,' Dave asserted, as he watched his friend's pen hurrying across the page. 'That wife of his has got it *all* wrong!'

'Umm, she *does* seem a little unhinged,' Fisk said, as he looked up from his scribbling. 'In fact, I tried to talk to her *earlier* and she used some *very* choice Anglo-Saxon! *Anyway* thanks Dave ... I won't hold you up any longer. *Yep*, this should make a good piece ... I *owe* you, mate!' he concluded before consigning his notebook and pen to his inside jacket pocket, and then rushing off.

Satisfied that he'd now set the record straight, Dave went back over to the ambulance and climbed in the back to rejoin Tim, who was actually asleep on the stretcher bed. However, as the vehicle pulled away, he started to have second thoughts, and was beginning to regret saying what he'd said to the reporter. Paul Fisk was bound to quote him he speculated, and the resultant article would certainly put Alison's nose firmly out of joint. Dave had to hope that his well-intentioned intervention wouldn't, in fact, make matters any worse for his poor friend.

It wasn't until 17:00 that the hospital finally finished with Tim, during which time he had reluctantly agreed to see a psychotherapist for a course of sessions. The doctor also arranged to take Tim home to Thanet by ambulance, which meant that Dave had to walk all the way back into town in order to pick up his car. Beforehand though, he telephoned Sheila from the hospital payphone to say that he would be approximately half an hour late picking her up, and gave her the choice of either waiting for him or getting a taxi home. She opted to wait for him, but didn't sound at all pleased. So, having told her half an hour, a daunted Dave concluded that he'd jolly better make sure it was no longer, or else be in even deeper trouble.

Having half-walked, and half-run all the way back to the car, Dave was hot, hungry and very, very thirsty. Leaning against the driver's door, he fumbled for his keys and then wearily retrieved the parking ticket that had been placed behind the windscreen wiper.

What a month it was turning out to be, Dave told himself, as he edged his way out of the car park. Not only had he engineered a reconciliation between his father and dying grandfather during the previous weekend, but also, in all probability, he'd saved the life of his best friend during this one. And what had been his reward for the more recent good deed: no more or less than a ten-pound parking fine. As far as he was concerned, it certainly seemed to be the case, in this life, that no good deed ever went unpunished.

By the time he was turning into the Telecom House car park, Dave knew that he'd just crept beyond his own time estimate and was now some thirty-five minutes late. Sheila was already waiting outside the foyer of the main building and her furrowed brow and stern countenance did not bode well for a row-free journey home. It only served to reinforce his faith in that recently learnt, rather cynical truism about good deeds.

However, when his wife got into the car, her first question was not about his inability to accurately estimate periods of time, but was concerning Tim.

'*Well*, was it him then?' she asked coldly, and without any eye contact, as she drew her seatbelt over her body and assertively clicked it in place

Dave gave out a single, weary chuckle as he accelerated away.

'Yes, it *was* him, the bloody idiot ... just as Monica reported,' he said, slowly negotiating the many twists and turns of their workplace car park. '*And* he was filthy drunk and ranting away about Alison not letting him see the children.'

'Were you able to *do* anything?' Sheila asked, glancing over at him for the first time, as they pulled on to the ring road.

'I talked him down ... well *sort* of,' he said, by way of a self-imposed understatement.

'Oh, *well done Dave*!' Sheila replied, with genuine delight, as she gripped his left arm. 'Tim is so lucky to have a friend like you!'

'Huh, *I* should say so...but I *suppose* he's going through a lot at the moment,' Dave countered, 'which is why I'm chuffed that Tim has agreed to have a course of counselling.'

They drove on in silence for a minute or two before Sheila responded.

'I can understand you wanting to defend your friend, especially as you don't like that Alison much,' she remarked; neither expecting nor getting any opposition from her husband on the topic. 'But I don't much care for *either* of them to be quite honest, so I can be dispassionate and offer a more objective viewpoint. I can see fault on *both* sides, but it's those two children I *really* feel sorry for!'

Dave nodded in firm agreement.

'It seems they're living in some sort of women's refuge with Alison now,' he said; his disapproving tone clearly giving away his feelings in the matter.

'*Yes*, but don't you think it ironic that Tim would choose to protest about his lack of access to the kids in such a public way?' Sheila challenged, with emphatic hand gestures. 'To *me*, it only serves to prove his unsuitability to have anything to do with them *at all*!'

Dave shrugged and then nodded in a fatalistic manner. He couldn't disagree with anything that Sheila had just said, however harsh it might have sounded. Her astute comments only served to demonstrate that he was too close to the subject to be objective, and too close to Tim to have clearly seen any other point of view; that is, until now.

As the Darwins' car slowed at the end of their close, Dave noticed that there was another vehicle already parked in their designated space.

'Bloody *cheek*; will you look at *that*,' he grumbled, as they slowed to a stop. 'Someone's put a grotty old Mark Two Escort in our parking bay!'

The couple left their car on the side of the road, a few yards away, and as they approached the house, Dave realised that there was a person sitting in the driving position of the parked vehicle. The driver looked round and on seeing the pair pass by, quickly got out of the car.

Dave was delighted to discover that the space-invading stranger was actually his brother Ed.

'*Hello*, you old sod,' Dave said, as he approached and then put his arms around him. 'What are *you* doing here?'

'Waiting for *you*, of course!' Ed replied, returning the Grandad Darwin-style bear hug.

Dave thumped his brother on the back before they separated.

'Well, come *in*, come *in*!' he enthused, looking into that familiar face. Ed was as tall as Dave, but was much stockier and broader in the upper body than he was, very much taking after their paternal grandfather in that respect. For brothers, their faces were very different as well, Ed favouring the Maybury side of the family with his close-set eyes and small mouth. Their voices however, were absolutely identical and not only confirmed their fraternal status to doubting strangers, but also confused their parents on the telephone. Ed had also grown a luxuriant beard whilst up in Yorkshire, to disguise the last stubborn traces of teenage acne.

All three of them walked slowly over to the house and, en route, Sheila and Ed exchanged happy but far less demonstrative pleasantries than the brothers just had.

Once inside the house however, Sheila became much more relaxed.

'Would you like to stay to dinner, Ed?' she asked, as she put her bags down in the hall. 'That is, as long as you're prepared to take the risk,' she added with a flirtatious giggle.

'Err...yes, *please*; if that's alright with you!' responded Ed happily.

Dave smiled to himself as he unlaced his shoes. His wife's ability to call on this alternative warm and friendly personality, whenever there were guests about, never ceased to amaze him. Of course, it all depended on whether or not she approved of the guest, Tim and Alison Cross never having seen this side of her personality. Ed, however, must have passed the test; after all, he *was* young and good-looking, Dave concluded, with more than a mild dose of cynicism.

Having quickly and discreetly checked her hair in the hall mirror, the sham Sheila turned to her husband and smiled sweetly.

'What are we having tonight, my dear?' she asked, in a manner Dave thought utterly incongruous, especially having come from her lips.

In response, her husband inverted his mouth and thought briefly.

'I *was* just going to throw some leftovers together, and have it with baked beans and pickled onions!' he admitted, with a shrug of the shoulders.

Straightaway, Ed nodded emphatically. 'That sounds *fine*,' he replied, with matter-of-fact politeness.

'*Oh* but I think we can do better than that, *in* the circumstances,' Dave countered as he reached for the phonebook. 'Anyone for an Indian takeaway?'

Both Ed and Sheila quickly nodded their approval, and after scribbling down everyone's requirements, Dave phoned the order through and also requested a home delivery. That done, Sheila went to throw a cloth on the table and warm up some plates, whilst Dave agreed to fix some drinks.

Ed followed his brother into the lounge, where the well-stocked drinks cabinet was kept.

'It's very *kind* of you to have me to stay to dinner. I only intended to pop in for a quick chat, but I was beginning to think you'd never get *home*!' he explained, re-familiarising himself with the room.

'Busy *day,* I'm afraid, but we're glad to have you. It's not every day that my university educated little brother deigns to pay us thickies a visit!' Dave joked smiling , as he motioned for Ed to sit down. '*Anyway*, how *was* the Yorkshire holiday?'

'Very *nice*, good *beer*, but I shan't mind if I never see another dry-stone wall *again*!' his bearded brother bantered.

Dave laughed and then turned back to rifle through the drinks cabinet.

'Small whisky to wet the whistle?' he proposed, brandishing the bottle in question.

'Not for *me* thanks,' Ed replied, with a vigorous shake of the head, and an extended hand giving a halt sign.

'You'll probably prefer a beer then; there are some cold ones in the fridge,' announced Dave, eager to make his little brother feel at home. 'I'll get one for you when we go through.' He poured two glasses of whisky and then passed a bottle of red wine to Ed for him to carry through.

The brothers found Sheila in the diningroom, arranging cutlery on the table.

'Here's your stress buster, love,' Dave smiled, as he passed her the short drink. 'And is red wine okay with your meal?'

'Lovely, *thanks* darling, and there should also be some cold beers in the fridge, if *either* of you lads would prefer one,' responded a beaming Sheila in an uncharacteristically vivacious manner.

It wasn't long before the threesome were all sitting round the dining room table with their respective drinks and a bowl of Bombay Mix to pick at until the meal came. As they talked, Dave looked across at his younger brother, who was ten years his junior, and reminded himself that the same gap had existed between their father and Uncle Ronnie. As he had earlier noted, of all the Darwin males of more recent generations, Ed most resembled Grandad Darwin in physical stature. This was very unlike the tall and lanky brothers, Len and Ronnie, or, as Dave was forced to concede, the equally tall, yet weight-conscious figure of himself.

Ed met his brother's gaze, and then smiled.

'So, what have *you* two been up to today then?' he asked, in between sips of his beer, and before casting his hostess a courteous glance, should she be first the one to respond.

As it turned out, his hostess motioned to Dave for him reply on their behalf.

'Well, let's *see* ... Sheila's been working overtime at the dreaded Telecom, and I've prevented someone from jumping off the multi-storey!' he declared, in a matter-of-fact manner.

The dinner guest laughed heartily in response, until he noticed that both Dave and Sheila were looking back at him with lowered eyebrows and quizzical expressions.

'You're *serious,* aren't you?' he asked timidly, returning his big brother's gaze.

Dave nodded and then proceeded to relate the entire story of Tim's drunken adventure, and his own vital role in it.

Ed listened impassively throughout the entire tale, and then silently stared down at his beer can for a short while before commenting.

'Your poor friend must have been in a pretty desperate state of mind to pull off a stunt like that, even if he *did* have a skin full!' he said quietly, and with surprising poignancy, before finally looking back up at Dave.

The remark sounded strange coming from Ed, who was usually intolerant of such bizarre behaviour and quick to both judge and condemn those who indulged in it. In fact, his brother's unexpected reaction made Dave feel rather ashamed at the lack of understanding for Tim's position that he and Sheila had displayed earlier on their way home. However, they had both been tired and hungry when the remarks were made he reasoned, so felt able to forgive himself.

Fortunately, the subdued atmosphere around the table was quickly dispelled when the doorbell rang out, to indicate that the curries had arrived. Sheila rushed into the hall, and soon returned in triumph with two brown paper carrier bags, both liberally sprouting the usual grease stains. The small, hot, oblong silver dishes were soon being passed to and fro, as their cardboard lids – complete with indistinct blue-penned scribble – were prised off and their contents quickly identified. Luckily, the order was complete and correct, and soon the room was filled with the mouth-watering aroma of biryanis, bhajis and Bombay aloo.

Dave quickly gathered up the containers that were empty, and then sat down gleefully behind his well-loaded plate.

'*So* then, what have *you* been up to today then Ed?' he asked, before tearing a huge chunk from his garlic naan.

'Well, this morning I was just relaxing at home ... you see, I'm back staying with Mum and Dad at the moment,' Ed explained, glancing between his older brother and his meal. '*Cor*, they don't get any better, *do* they?' he added quickly, with a wry sideways grimace.

Dave laughed heartily, behind his hand – an impromptu splatter-guard – and then shook his head in empathy with the observation.

'And *then*, after an early lunch, I went house hunting.'

Hearing the comment, Sheila's head quickly shot up from her meal.

'*Really*; what are you looking for?' she asked keenly, before spooning a portion of mushroom bhaji on to her plate.

'Just a *small* place really, something to get me on the property ladder!' he replied, with a spoonful of chana masala hovering in front of his face.

Sheila nodded in acknowledgement before returning to her meal, and thus allowing Dave to take up the interrogation.

'Any particular location in mind mate?' he asked through a large mouthful of meat madras.

'Obviously, I'd like Canterbury, because of where I hope to be working. But realistically, I suppose that Whitstable, Herne Bay or somewhere in between would be more affordable for me.'

'Where you hope to work? You're not gonna become another Telecom Darwin, *surely*,' Dave joked, before emitting a loud a roar of laughter.

'Actually, *yes*!' responded a straight-faced Ed, turning the tables on his older brother.

'Oh Ed, Ed, *Ed*; surely *not*!' despaired a suddenly shocked and disbelieving Dave, nearly choking on a chapatti.

Sheila immediately glared disapprovingly at her husband.

'Not everyone shares your dislike for *The Firm,* Dave,' she declared with haughty superiority. 'Some of us are *proud* to work for Telecom!'

'Well *said* Sheila!' Ed agreed, with a chivalrous nod in her direction. 'You wait until I'm Dave's boss. I won't stand for any crap *then*!'

Everyone laughed, as Dave proceeded to feign sycophantic gestures in his little brother's direction.

Once the mirth had died away, Ed resumed the conversation, on a darker note.

'And then, later in the afternoon, I went over to see Nanna and Grandad Darwin.' He paused and his face fell into a frown. 'Dave…I was…I was *shocked*; he's so…*thin*! It's only been six weeks since I last saw him, but…'

Ed stared down at his meal. He hadn't finished what he wanted to say, and was evidently having trouble finding the right words. Finally though, he slowly looked back up at his older brother.

'D'you know Dave; sometimes I wonder…the void he'll leave…you *know*? How incomplete…will I be able…oh, *I* dunno,' he despaired, with a dismissive hand gesture, having been unable to express what he felt.

'*Basically*, what you're saying is ... you can't imagine life without Grandad Darwin *being* there,' Dave said shrewdly, and in soft tones.

'Exactly ... that's *it*!' Ed confirmed, with an emphatic arm gesture. 'You *see*? I *knew* you'd understand!'

'That's because I feel the exactly same way, mate ... he *has* always been there,' Dave said, before passing his brother another can of beer. 'He's a *very* hard act to follow!'

'Indeed he *is*! And *another* thing ... he talked about Uncle Ronnie this afternoon.' Furrow-browed, Ed looked over, firstly at Sheila and then to Dave, 'I couldn't *believe* it!'

'*That* all began last weekend,' Dave explained, holding his fork motionless and prongs downward in the middle of his plate. 'I went over with Mum and Dad to tidy up the garden and, after *all* these years, Dad and Grandad Darwin actually managed to patch up their differences. And *then*, the old boy asked to see Ronnie's grave, so we took him over to All Saints. It was like ... you know, he was putting all his emotional affairs in order.'

'That must have been very moving for you both,' Ed remarked, with both sympathy and sincerity, as he smiled across the table at Sheila.

'I'm afraid I had to *work* that day!' his sister-in-law replied, in a curt yet chastened manner.

The conversation petered out at this point, and Sheila, feeling both awkward and embarrassed, took another couple of small mouthfuls before putting her fork and spoon together, and then pushing her plate away from her. Looking up, she was pleased to see that an equally silent Dave and Ed had also now finished their curries.

'Why don't you two take your drinks into the lounge while I clear up in here,' she said, beginning the task she'd assigned herself. 'I'll come and join you in a while.'

'Are you *sure*?' Dave asked, as he eased himself out of the seat.

'*Yes*, off you go!' she replied, without looking up, as she began gathering up the remaining foil trays.

'Thanks, and ... umm ... don't forget to save all the leftovers; they'll be nice to…'

'*Yes*, I always *do*, now off you *go* Dave!' Sheila said, with a vigorous shooing arm gesture.

As she watched the brothers leave the diningroom, Sheila felt wretched that she couldn't be more supportive of Dave in this troubled time. However, that dinner table conversation had made her feel uncomfortable, and she knew that it would inevitably carry on in the lounge. So, rather than have to listen to it, Sheila concluded that she'd much rather take her time in clearing the dinner things through, and let them get on with it. But that was how she had dealt with the whole Grandad Darwin business: by avoiding it as much as possible. It then occurred to her that she might have had another subconscious reason for doing all that overtime at Telecom recently. Were all those extra hours she'd put in really to advance her career? Or was it a good excuse to avoid having to cope with her husband's understandable distress at having to witness his grandfather's slow decline? It was a question Sheila left unanswered as she took a pile of dirty plates through to the kitchen.

Having plodded into the lounge, Ed flopped on the sofa, whilst Dave put on an *Emerson, Lake and Palmer* CD. As soon as he recognised the music, the younger Darwin brother chuckled to himself.

'It's thanks to sharing a bedroom with *you,* Dave, that I ended up having the untrendiest musical taste in university!' he smiled, before taking a swig from his beer can.

'I'm just glad to have been able to save you from *The Smiths* or *The Cure*!' laughed an unrepentant Dave in response, as he joined him on the settee.

Ed's smile, then gradually faded as he recalled their earlier conversation.

'You know we mentioned Uncle Ronnie earlier?' he asked, running his finger round the rim of the can.

243

Dave immediately sat forward in a more alert posture, and then nodded in acknowledgement.

'*Well*, it's funny that everyone in the family seems to have a different attitude about his memory, that is, when you can actually persuade them to *talk* about him!' Ed commented, with both accuracy and astuteness. 'But what was he *really* like Dave? You see, I wasn't even *three* when he died!'

'Do you have *any* memories of him *at all*?' Dave asked, with evident keen interest.

'Only *vague* ones really ... you know, fragments, Ed said, screwing his face up with the effort of thinking back so far. 'I remember a very tall man with dark hair…and being picked up by him,' he remarked, with a smile that quickly faded, as a further memory morsel bobbed to the surface. 'There's also *another* image, which may have been a dream, but I seem to remember his face being hurt ... like ... umm, like him having *injuries* of some sort!'

'No, that's *right* Ed ... that *was* him,' Dave agreed straightaway. 'He sustained those during the unsuccessful attempt to save Rothermead Mill. Do you *know* anything about that?'

Ed grinned warmly, and then nodded.

'*You* told me all about it just before you left home in the mid-70s. I thought it was a *wonderful* adventure story ... the bulldozer, the man falling off the top, and all those people chanting: *Ro-nnie, Ro-nnie, Ro-nnie*. And you told it to me so well *too*, complete with actions and all that ... I may not have *been* there, but you really helped me conjure up a mental image of that day,' he chuckled, once more looking over at his brother with much fondness. 'But I always use to wonder why Mum and Dad never talked about it, or much *else* about him, come to think of it.'

'*Huh*, you know what *they're* like,' Dave tutted, with a dismissive toss of the head. 'But I suppose it must have been especially hard for them in those early days, you know, when Ronnie's memory would have still been rather raw ... not to *mention* the problems that Dad was having with Nanna and Grandad Darwin at the time. At least Mum and Dad *did* talk about him sometimes, unlike Nanna and Grandad!'

Ed nodded reflectively.

'So what was he *really* like; Uncle Ronnie I mean?' he urged, repeating his initial question.

What was Uncle Ronnie like, Dave pondered to himself. Now there's a tough question. Where does one begin? He realised it would be much easier to say *nothing* about him, just like other members of the family, but Ed seemed so passionate about the subject, almost as if he needed to get to know Uncle Ronnie. For this reason, Dave decided he would try and do very his best to accommodate him.

'Like *most* of us Darwin males, except *Grandad* of course, Ronnie lived his life experiencing a rollercoaster of emotions, you know? There was nothing moderate or indifferent about the way our uncle *felt* things! For him, it had to be either the heights of joy or the depths of despair; the laughing and humour on one side and the tempers and intolerance on the other; the need to give and receive demonstrative affection, versus the desire for solitude and one's own space,' Dave explained, making parallel pendulum-swinging gestures with his arms as he spoke.

'That pretty much sums us *all* up,' Ed laughed, as he sank back in his chair.

'Allowing for personal differences and some variations, you're right, it *does*,' Dave affirmed, with a vigorous nod. 'But with Uncle Ronnie, *all* of that, including those polar extremes, seemed to be amplified *ten*-fold. I suppose *that's* how he managed to conjure up all that raw creative energy ... all that joyous humour for his fantastic performances!'

'But what about the *other* side of the coin, Dave?' asked Ed emphatically, leaning forward once again. 'What about when he was *down* ... how was it when he was *depressed*?'

Dave stared back at his brother, and then blew out loudly through pursed lips. These were *big* questions that were being asked of him, but he quickly concluded that Ed had every right to know, if not, an apparent need to know.

'Those dark episodes weren't pleasant for *anyone*, least of *all* Ronnie,' he began, trying to find the most appropriate, descriptive words. 'I suppose it's best summed up in Ronnie's own shorthand for those dark moments ... withdrawal, alcohol, tears, exhaustion, recovery, or '*water*', clever *eh*? And he could come down *very* quickly, usually after either a corresponding high or a particularly stressful moment. He'd then go to ground and nearly always indulge in a solitary binge-drinking session. *No one*, except Dad, could get through to him during those periods. Eventually, Uncle Ronnie would wear himself out with both crying and the drink. *Then*, after a long sleep, he'd always wake up as if nothing had happened!'

Ed, who had been studying Dave's words intently, got up and slowly paced round the lounge.

'Thank *goodness*; I thought I was going *mad*,' he commented quietly, almost to himself.

'*Why*, what's happened?' Dave asked immediately, and with much concern.

Ed sat back down next to his older brother, and looked at him at close quarters.

'Those extreme episodes of Ronnie's you described...I've started to experience something like that *myself*,' he confessed, in boldly frank terms. With his brother listening most intensely, Ed went on to explain that at University, especially during the last year, he had experienced exhilarating highs when psyching himself up for exams. They would carry him through the sitting with ease and then, usually continued into the following evening of frenetic celebrations with his friends. Ed, the unexpected life and soul of the party, would then accept and carry out the most amazing dares and stunts, winning himself both money and kudos from his peers. However, one morning, he'd woken up on the flat roof of the five-storey science block on campus, and felt the most intense despair, not to mention confusion. It wasn't until he was seen sitting on the edge of the roof, crying with uncontrollable grief, that several friends of his carefully dragged him off there and put him to bed.

Dave was both shocked and moved by his little brother's admission.

'It *must* be something that runs in the family ... after *all*, Dad's had his fair share of the old ups and downs too,' he asserted, with a contemplative expression. 'But it's funny how *I've* not been affected, *isn't* it!'

'*Ha*, you don't get away with it *that* easily, Dave ... you're *just* as bonkers as the rest of us,' Ed said, in a none too serious retort. 'Remember ... *you're* the one who saw ghosts, and also heard weird voices back at the old Rothermead cottage, when you were a boy, eh?'

'Very *true*, but I don't seem to *have* that perception, or is it *imagination*, any more', Dave responded, almost with a tinge of regret. 'But it's the other way round for you though Ed, *isn't* it? I mean, it's *strange* you never experienced those behavioural extremes at an earlier age,' he commented, placing a supportive hand on Ed's shoulder. 'From what I've been told, Ronnie went through those up-and-down episodes all his *life!*'

'Yes, I *thought* that was the case ... I've been *thinking* about this, and have come up with a theory as to why it's only been a recent thing for me,' Ed responded, in a slightly more upbeat mood. 'Do you remember those dizzy spells I used to get as a child, and Mum and Dad taking me up to London for all those tests?'

And all those treats you used to get as well, thought Dave darkly to himself.

'*Yes*, I remember,' he replied, desperately trying to put his childish bitterness to one side. 'It was some sort of mild pre-pubescent epilepsy wasn't it?'

'*Something* like that!' Ed agreed quickly. '*Anyway*, I was put on that phenobarbitone stuff until I was 16, and the doctors had decided that all dangers of the attacks had passed. So, it *could* be that the drugs also suppressed those manic-depressive tendencies as well!'

'Or could the childhood epilepsy have been something to *do* with it?' Dave posed, as a credible alternative to his brother's theory.

'Umm, I hadn't *thought* of that, but who *knows*! The main thing is that as soon as I was free from the medication, the new symptoms very gradually made themselves known. That fact, coupled with the stress of the exams, and bingo ... Uncle Ronnie Mark Two!' Ed slumped back in his chair and threw his hands in the air with a gesture of resignation. 'So, what do you think I should *do* about it?' he asked, with an air of despair. 'I *certainly* can't tell Mum and Dad about it!'

Dave was utterly floored by yet another difficult question, and had to think quickly, given the gravity of the topic. He asked himself: what had Nanna and

Grandad Darwin done about Ronnie's mood swings? The answer: nothing major! The low periods had certainly required careful handling, but apart from that, they'd let each episode run its course. Crucially though, all the way through their troubled younger son's life, they'd rejected all suggestions of using controlling medication.

'I suppose any sort of tranquillising drug could even out your temperament, but they would also flatten both the highs *and* the lows, and I *know* that Ronnie didn't want that for himself,' Dave commented, with absolute assuredness.

'I'm not keen on that idea *myself*!' Ed confirmed, passing his beer can from one hand to the other. 'I've been on that suppressive stuff most of my life, and you know how changed *Dad* is as a result of *his* tablets! But the thing *is* Dave, I don't really know which is the real *me* ... the person *on* or *off* the phenobarbitone! Besides which, I know it sounds weird, but I'd really miss the exhilaration of the highs if I took more suppressive medication.' He paused to drain the last of his beer. 'So I guess I'll just have to learn to *live* with it and keep off high roofs,' Ed chuckled, in fatalistic conclusion.

'*Yes*, and find yourself a really placid, tolerant partner ... one who can put up with the variable temperament of a Darwin male,' Dave added, with a sideways smile, 'in *other* words, find yerself a bloomin' *saint*!'

They both laughed, as much at Dave's words as his unintended Grandad Darwinism.

'Is that what *you've* got in Sheila then, Dave ... a saint?' asked a smiling Ed.

Dave grinned, but just did not know what to say. He certainly couldn't bring himself to lie, or claim that his marriage was perfect. Nor could he state that his wife was a model of patience and understanding; in fact, he couldn't think of anything to say in reply to Ed's question. However, Dave realised that his hesitant silence must have spoken volumes, and the pathetic grin still forced across his face must have only made matters worse.

Ed was about to press his brother on the subject, when Sheila joined them from the other room.

'So what have *you* two been discussing then?' she asked, placing her wine glass on the coffee table, and then sitting on the adjacent armchair, but with her knees positioned closely to those of her brother-in-law.

Dave stared impassively at his wife, as she gave Ed one of her well-practised social smiles. No after dinner cigarette, eh? She really *is* on her best behaviour, he observed, with great interest.

Their dinner guest noticed that Dave hadn't leapt in to answer his wife's question, so thought he'd better do so instead.

'*Oh*, we've been discussing how you women need to be absolute *saints* to live with a Darwin male,' he replied, in a jovial, light-hearted manner.

'You can certainly say *that* again!' Sheila responded, with a skywards huff, misunderstanding Ed's words as a serious admission of the Darwin males' shortcomings. '*Still*, I'm sure I'll get my reward in heaven,'she smiled, before crossing her legs and then demurely smoothing down her skirt.

Feeling somewhat bewildered at Sheila's response, Ed glanced over at Dave to gauge his reaction to what had just been said. As it turned out, his older brother laughed, but it was clearly a forced response, and Ed could sense how uncomfortable he was now feeling. A long awkward silence then followed; the CD had finished, and no one seemed to want to put on another.

It wasn't long before Ed stared down at his watch.

'*Well*, I'd better be getting along,' he declared, springing up from the sofa; all too keen to escape the strained atmosphere. 'We've *all* had long days ... especially you with your Superman act, Dave!' Ed paused to emit an awkward-sounding chuckle. 'And ... umm, *thanks* for the meal ... when I get my own place, I'll return the compliment,' he concluded, whilst already beginning to make for the hallway door.

Dave also hurried to his feet.

'I'll ... err, I'll show you *out,* mate,' he said with a forced joviality that barely disguised his embarrassment.

'*Good luck with the house hunting*,' Sheila called out, in a musical manner, before reaching for her cigarettes on the coffee table, and casting the briefest of glances up at the disappearing brothers.

Ed was not stupid; he realised that both Dave and Sheila had let their guard down for a moment just then, and made him aware that something between them was not quite right.

'Listen, *thanks* for the chat, Dave ... I really appreciate the support. And you *know* where I am if ... umm, if *you* ever need to talk,' he offered rather revealingly, as the pair crossed the hall.

Dave opened the front door for his brother and then stepped outside with him.

'Yes, *thanks* mate! I might just take you *up* on that,' he responded, before staring up at the few stars that had already appeared in the sky.

For Ed, his brother's response pretty much confirmed his suspicion: all was indeed not well in this particular Darwin household.

'Take care!' he said, with a friendly wink, before strolling over to his car.

Dave waved goodbye, Grandad Darwin style, as Ed drove off into the rapidly descending night. He was still standing there some minutes later, when the old Escort Mark Two, was long-since out of sight. Not yet ready to rejoin Sheila in the smoky fug of the lounge, Dave walked slowly onto their small green with his hands in his pocket. Turning a broad circle around the small sycamore tree growing on it, he thought about what his brother had just said. With Tim now hardly suitable as his confidante, it could be that Ed might fulfil that role sometime in the future, he suggested to himself. In any case, if things worked out well with Amanda-Jayne, and he did decide to leave Sheila, Dave vowed, right there and then, that Ed would be the very first person he'd tell.

A Bitter Aftertaste

Pushing aside the net curtain, Dave opened the front bedroom window, and then stuck his head out into the cool late afternoon air. From here, he looked down onto the small green around which their houses were gathered, and his eyes immediately focused on the sycamore tree, which was closest to the Darwin residence. Straightaway, he marvelled at the various hues of brown and orange, displayed in its autumnal leaves; in fact, death never looked so beautiful. This tree had seeded itself there, as sycamores were wont to do with promiscuous regularity, and now he was being visually rewarded for persuading the village green committee to retain it. On the far side of the small green was a copper beech, looking very much the same as it had back in the summer. But soon, Dave knew that it too would soon feign death and shed its foliage, but not after many weeks of hanging on to those crisp, brown and dry leaves, like a grieving Victorian widow, unable to release the cold hand of her hours-long departed husband.

 A gentle breeze rustled the leaves of both trees and stirred those that had already fallen to the ground. That susurrant sound always reminded him of those hot summer's days in Greyfriars Gardens and of course, Amanda-Jayne. They had met on a regular basis for the rest of the school summer holidays; holding hands, talking incessantly and stealing the odd brief kiss. They told each other 'I love you', on a regular basis, but the relationship had not progressed beyond that stage. Dave was happy with what they had together, more than happy in fact; it was the first thing he thought about when waking up every morning. But he longed to be able to express that love in a physical way; he wanted to have sex with her, as all adults who loved each other wanted. Moreover, he desired her as the woman he loved, rather than as that long banished latter-day Lolita fantasy figure of earlier in the year, so there was nothing sordid about the way he felt, he told himself, in spite of her tender age. In fact, his physical need for her was now becoming a bit of a problem, which had a very unsatisfactory solution. Indeed, sexual relations were something he wanted to share with her, rather than continually having to sacrifice himself, secretly and alone, at the altar of Onan.

Sometimes there were occasions when Dave wondered if he was still misreading the situation and perhaps, misinterpreting the love, or type of love his teenage girlfriend claimed she had for him. On the other hand, he reasoned, it could be that the continued presence of Sheila in his life was causing Amanda-Jayne to hold back, out of some sense of decency or respect for her. He realised the matter could not now resolve itself naturally, and that things would continue indefinitely as they were at the moment, unless he took some decisive action to effect a change. Such actions, like leaving Sheila for example, took courage and he was selfish enough not to want to burn his bridges unless he was sure of being able to build a new life for himself and Amanda-Jayne on that far riverbank. However, he quickly concluded that now was not the time for either a lengthy inner debate or for making life-affecting decisions. There was a guest expected, and he would be there any minute now.

The breeze suddenly strengthened on that September Saturday afternoon, and the light faded slightly as a bank of clouds scurried over the sun. Even with his head leaning outwards, Dave could still hear Sheila clattering around downstairs as she laid out the cutlery on the diningroom table. The noise reminded him that it hadn't been easy to persuade her not only to let Tim come to dinner, but also stay over as well, so that they could all enjoy a drink together. But agree she had, and he was both surprised and grateful as a result.

Sheila had long made it clear that she didn't really like Tim, and it wasn't just a case of not being able to get along with him. She disliked his crudeness, that continual wordplay and those 'dirty jokes', which were really more like smutty observations, puns and metaphors, as opposed to the 'a man goes to the doctors' variety. For Dave however, these characteristics reminded him of his Uncle Ronnie and, as a result, only served to make his friend more endearing. In his own defence, Tim always maintained that words were merely words and caused far less offence than what could usually be seen on the news every night, or that they hurt far less than a swift kick in the bollocks might.

It was also the case that Sheila harboured concerns about the influence Tim Cross was having on her husband, and often wondered what they got up to on those long afternoons off. She was especially worried about their excursions of more recent months, which had escalated in number to two, and sometimes three times a week. It was also rather irritating for her when Dave came home each time with that silly grin on his face. Sheila didn't really like him to be too happy, unless she had been the cause of it; after all, she reasoned, it was her Christian duty, and if she could feel that she'd done some good, this in turn made *her* feel good. That was the reason why she had finally agreed to Tim coming over and, of course, Dave was so grateful to her for it. In spite of that, even *she* had to concede that it couldn't be easy for a man living on his own, especially one who had absolutely no domestic skills, with the exception of being able to open a bottle of wine.

There was also another reason why Sheila had relented in respect of Tim's visit. In the last few months, she had noticed that Dave was becoming more and more assertive in his requests, sometimes even forceful, and she did not want to fight back and risk ending the understanding they'd reached at the beginning of the summer; the one that had kept the peace so well. However, Sheila cannily felt that she had to name one condition before agreeing to the visit – if only to keep one hand firmly on the tiller – and it was that Dave must cook the dinner. Unsurprisingly, he had been happy to oblige and even wickedly suggested he do lasagne again as, on the last occasion, Tim hadn't so much eaten it as worn it. Sheila thought it an amusing idea, which only went to show that there were still occasions when they could both laugh together. Consequently, earlier that very afternoon, he had made the Bolognese sauce and cheese roux for the lasagne, so that it could simply be assembled and then cooked as soon as Tim arrived.

So it was that Dave was looking out of the front bedroom window for any sign of his dinner guest's arrival. The breeze had dropped again, and the leaves no longer rustled, but the sun remained obscured by a bank of greyish cloud. At that moment, an old Dormobile camper van turned into the close and, with much spluttering of engine, positioned itself in the last vacant space along the edge of the green. Bloody hell, thought Dave crossly, where will Tim park *now* when he arrives! However, to his amazement, it was his friend who got out of the aged camper van, retrieved something from the passenger seat and then made his way towards the house.

Before he could be spotted, Dave withdrew into the bedroom, quietly closed the window, and then ran towards the landing.

'*He's here*!' he shouted, rapidly making his way downstairs to let his friend in.

'Okay, okay,' came the slightly weary response from below. Determined to make an effort, Sheila was already waiting in the hall.

Tim rang the doorbell, and allowed his finger to remain on the button for an annoying ten seconds. Dave opened the front door and Tim immediately pushed past him, holding a couple of two-litre bottles of strong cider. The host quickly deduced that they were the very same type his friend had been consuming on top of the multistorey, during that dreadful day back in the summer. It was a rather ominous start to the visit.

Seeing Sheila, Tim beamed broadly and then thrust both bottles in her direction.

'Hello Chloe; long time no see!' he shouted, almost knocking her backwards with both the bulky alcoholic gifts, and his cider infused breath.

As the hostess steadied herself, an undaunted Tim turned to Dave, who had just closed the front door.

'*Hello*, you *shitty* old bastard,' he said at high volume, before giving his friend a playful punch in the stomach, which was woefully misjudged and therefore a little too hard.

Dave slowly straightened himself and laughed, all the while pretending that the blow had not bloody well hurt. Sheila winced too, but it was more at Tim's language than as a result of her husband's all too obvious discomfort. Barely one minute into the visit and it was already obvious to them both that Tim had already imbibed that day.

Aware of the discomfort of Sheila's eyes boring into him, Dave tried to progress things as normally as he could, and ignore his guest's intemperate state.

'Did you leave your overnight things in the camper van?' he asked, with a forced grin, as he tried to get back both his wind and his confidence.

'*What* overnight things?' Tim asked, with a puzzled look that was quickly replaced by a broad smile.

Seeing his friend at close quarters for the first time, Dave was shocked to observe that one of his capped front teeth was missing and only the supporting pin now remained.

'*Tim*, your *tooth* ... how did *that* happen?' he asked, with beetle-browed concern, imagining a painful fall, or a drunken bar brawl.

His guest grimaced whilst flicking his tongue around the vacant space at the front of his mouth.

'Oh *this*...ha ... I was trying to get the top off a beer bottle!' Tim paused to laugh heartily whilst clutching his stomach and swinging his head between Dave and Sheila's position. 'Bloody well *swallowed* it, *didn't* I!' He then calmed down and turned to Sheila alone. 'Couldn't *bear* to sift through my poo, so I *lost* it!' He then snatched one of the bottles back from her and wandered into the lounge.

As soon as Tim had left the hallway, Sheila rushed over to Dave; her teeth gritted menacingly.

'I think he's had at *least* one of those *already*,' she remarked in a scornful half-whisper, and at close quarters, before pushing her husband towards the lounge door. '*Go* on, and make sure he uses a coaster!' Dave had only advanced a few steps, before Sheila grabbed her husband's waistcoat and pulled him back. '*Camper* van?' she queried, with her face screwed up, as she recalled a fragment of the earlier conversation.

'I'll tell you *later*,' responded Dave, with a heavy sigh. 'I'd better go in and see what he's up to!'

'Remind him of my *name* will you,' Sheila called out, as he disappeared through the doorway.

By the time his host had joined him, Tim had already ejected Sheila's *Clannad* CD, which had been playing away inoffensively in the background, and inserted one of his host's *Miles Davis* albums. Dave shrugged his shoulders and then retrieved two pint glasses from the sideboard, but not before he'd discreetly lowered the volume setting on the stereo.

Tim sat there playing air drums to *Freddie Freeloader* while he watched Dave pour the drinks.

'That cider has got quite a *kick* to it,' Tim enthused, as he stretched out his hand to eagerly grab the pint glass that was being handed to him.

'Yes I *remember*!' Dave retorted ruefully; with a head full of images from the day when they were both perched on that concrete wall five storeys up.

'In a *glass* eh? *Very* middle class!' was Tim's only gesture of thanks as he drained the contents in two lengthy open throated draughts.

Dave took two mouthfuls of his own pint, before remembering that he should be getting the dinner preparations underway.

'*Here* Tim, help yourself to another drink, mate,' he advised, before rising out of his armchair and then pushing the opened two-litre bottle in his friend's direction. 'I just need to get the main course sorted out, and I'll be back in a jiffy.'

Tim made a vague gesture of understanding and acceptance, before Dave quickly exited the room with pint in hand, and made for the kitchen. He got there, only to find Sheila already assembling the components of the lasagne.

She gave her husband the briefest and coldest of glances.

'*I'll* do this,' she declared, making her displeasure quite plain, 'you go back and keep an eye on Oliver Reed in there.'

'Are you *sure*?' Dave asked, hovering by the doorway with one hand on the wooden jamb.

Sheila cast him another icy glance, but said nothing in response.

'Would you like me to get you a drink?' he further probed; keen to get back into his wife's favour.

'Just *bloody well* get back *in* there!' she barked; pausing from her preparations only long enough to screw up her eyes tightly, and tense her whole body in frustration.

A crestfallen Dave returned as ordered, to find that Tim had not only poured himself another pint of cider, but also spilt some of it on the CD booklet that he'd carelessly extracted from the casing. Dave felt rather irritated, not to mention embarrassed that Tim was behaving so badly, especially after he had worked so hard to persuade Sheila to let him come and stay over. Nevertheless, he bit his tongue, and lowered himself back down on the armchair diagonally opposite his friend's settee-sprawling position. Unfortunately, despite his attempts at a conciliatory frame of mind, he couldn't help but recall Alison's words, spoken to him in Gravel Walk during the multistorey car park incident. He was forced to wonder: could she have been right about him? If Tim was behaving so badly as a guest in someone else's house, even if it was that of a close friend, how much worse would it have been in his own home? Did Alison have cause to be scared of him after all? Dave had no choice but to concede that she might. Then was she justified in preventing Tim from seeing his children? No, not at all; he still couldn't bring himself to believe that.

By the time the delicious aroma of cooking lasagne had reached the lounge, Tim had finished the cider and was starting on the cans of Favershams that Dave had supplied. However, whereas his host carefully poured the locally brewed bitter into a clean glass – his second drink of the day – Tim no longer had any time for such niceties and was now quite content to suck it straight from the tin.

In spite of the fact that his houseguest was speaking sparingly, whilst imbibing extensively, Dave had to remind himself that this was more than just a social visit. He had invited Tim over to encourage him to talk about his marriage, his job and his future, not to mention the alarming deterioration in both his physical and mental health. Indeed, there had been some rumours circulating at work that Tim had been seeing a counsellor, but Dave had always refused to be drawn on the subject. Sadly, it seemed that today, his dinner guest was being equally tight-lipped. Despite a number of attempts by his host, he could not be persuaded to talk about any of the important issues. On the contrary; it seemed that anything that caused him pain had to be blanked out or heavily sedated with alcohol; as opposed to being drawn out, put on display and scrutinised. As a result, all Tim wanted to do was drink, have a bit of a laugh and talk in a loud voice about trivialities. Therefore, Dave let him ramble on in the hope that one of the minor, seemingly insignificant, topics would lead him into something more serious, as had happened on such occasions in the past. And then, with any luck, Tim could resist the need for all that anaesthetic and face up to some of the pain he was currently feeling.

As the minutes ticked by, and the Miles Davis sextet played on, Tim continued to resist being pushed down onto the metaphorical analyst's couch. And although Dave felt very sorry for his friend, he was also fighting the annoyance that was beginning to build up within him. Why wouldn't Tim let him help by talking about his many troubles, Dave asked himself; why was his troubled friend bottling up his feelings, whilst at the same time, hiding behind a different kind of bottle? They always used to be able to confide in each other, be it in the crypt of the Canterbury Cathedral or the private bar of the Canterbury Arms, and this had remained the case until recently; until the summer in fact. Sadly though, all that now seemed to have been lost. It then suddenly occurred to Dave that he was just as guilty as Tim, for he had not told him about Amanda-Jayne; he had chosen not to confide in his former soulmate about the most momentous adventure in his life so far. Then again, Dave recognised that, given Tim's current state of mind, he would probably have forgotten all about the confidentiality of such a delicate matter, and ask him, across the dinner table, if he'd shagged her yet. The stark reality of the situation was that neither man confided in the other any more, and for this reason alone, Dave sadly concluded that he was absolutely powerless to help his friend. All he could do was to watch this inebriated lemming weave his way along a circuitous route that would ultimately and inevitably lead towards the cliff edge.

Dave was positively relieved when Sheila called them through for dinner, and he had completed the short distance through to the diningroom before she'd finished her announcement. To her credit, the table was laid immaculately and she had even used one of her grandmother's old cotton tablecloths to make the entire ensemble look more homely. Tim did not follow his host in straightaway, but stopped off to pay a call at the downstairs cloakroom en route. This fact soon became obvious to the occupants of the dining room, as he'd neglected to close the door, and the sound of his tinkling cascade came through both loud and clear.

By the time Tim had rejoined his hosts, Dave had opened and poured a bottle of red wine, and Sheila had served up three steaming, savoury portions of lasagne. Without making the merest mention of either the meal or its elaborate setting, their guest proceeded to take alternate gulps from his wine glass, and then his beer can, which had accompanied him on the trip to the loo.

Still somewhat shocked at both his friend's continued bad behaviour, and his own inability to help him, Dave said nothing, and sullenly sipped at his wine in between miserable mouthfuls of lasagne. It therefore fell to a rather bemused Sheila to instigate any dining table conversation; a task she now undertook with Job-like stoicism.

'I see that you've bought a camper van then, Tim,' she observed, making a good fist of feigning interest.

Tim nodded vigorously without taking his eyes off his meal, which he was now despatching with rapid rapacity.

'Yep, my rich Uncle Stephen gave me a loan to use as a deposit for a flat, *you* know, somewhere for me to go when the house was sold. So, I got the van,' he stated, before swallowing his mouthful, and then draining his wine glass.

Sheila dutifully emptied the remains of the bottle into his glass while, at the same time, staring across the table with a quizzical expression on her face.

'You're going to *live* in it?' she asked in incredulous tones, whilst also casting a brief angry glance at her stony silent spouse.

'Yeah, why *not*!' Tim reasoned, through another mouthful of lasagne, and in so doing, spraying little droplets of tomato sauce that speckled the heirloom tablecloth. 'Besides which, I can also get my drum kit in there and travel to paying gigs; make myself a bit of extra money on the side!'

This assertion finally made Dave look up from his plate and stare at his erstwhile colleague, but only because he considered his claim to be able to get paid work as a drummer rather overly optimistic.

So it was that both host and hostess were looking at Tim as he proceeded to remind them of how accomplished he was on his chosen instrument. With his knife and fork, he began to use the items on the table around him as an impromptu drum kit and played a loud clattering solo. The dinner plate became his snare drum, whilst the side plate and salad bowl stood-in for his tom-toms. Unfortunately, he chose his re-charged wine glass as the cymbal. Dave could foresee an unhappy ending to the self-indulgent display, but was unable to utter his words of warning in time. Sadly, the cacophonous drum solo concluded with a cymbal crash and the spilling of the wine glass all over the table.

Straight away, Sheila shot up out of her chair.

'*For God's sake, Tim*,' she screamed and then stormed out of the room in a petulant frenzy.

Tim picked up the toppled glass, looked sheepish for a few seconds then held it out in Dave's direction for a refill. His host merely stared back at him impassively, and then slowly got up from the table and proceeded to uncork a second bottle that was waiting on a side table, with the coffee crockery. In fact, Dave was now feeling pity for Tim, but it was a detached emotion, as one might feel for a condemned prisoner, or any other remote pathetic figure from the television news that one was powerless to help.

Sheila soon rushed back into the room with a cloth and some salt to try and absorb the wine stain. As she sprinkled and dabbed, Dave retrieved their three wine glasses, and re-filled them from the safety of the side table.

Tim watched Sheila's damage limitation exercise, with a hint of mild amusement.

'Tim is *ever* so sorry, Chloe my dear,' he fawned, in a hand-wringing Uriah Heep impersonation that was meant to break the tension, but which utterly failed to do so. Undaunted, Tim tried a different tack. 'Fucking terrible waste of good *wine* if you ask me!' he exclaimed, in the manner of a punch line to a joke. He then hooted with laughter and looked over in Dave's direction for endorsement.

Unfortunately, as his anxious-looking host brought the full wine glasses back to the dining table, he was staring only in the direction of a seething Sheila, whom he sensed, was about to respond to their guest's last verbal obscenity.

His wife wasn't about to disappoint him, and regarded their guest through tightly narrowed eyes.

'Tim, I would appreciate it if you would moderate your language,' she uttered in crisp distain, before slowly averting her eyes in a downwards direction, and then picking up her fork.

Dave also looked down, but it was more out of a sense of embarrassment than it was a desire to return to his rapidly cooling meal.

In response to the telling off, Tim held up both his hands in a sarcastic '*who me?*' sort of American style gesture of culpability.

'Sorry ma'am, fair do's ... I'll be a good boy!' he retorted, with the corners of his mouth turned down. And then, having taken another mouthful of his dinner, he once more looked across the table to his sour-faced hostess, and quickly decided that he needed to win back her favour. 'But this is a *great* lasagne, Chloe ... it's been *ages* since I had home cooking!' he praised, accompanied by what he considered to be his best conciliatory smile. It was a facial expression that gradually fell away as it became clear to him that neither of his dinner table companions was going to respond, or even look up at him. 'What... what... *what*?' challenged a rather bewildered-looking Tim, as he glanced from one to the other and then back again.

Sheila gradually straightened herself in the chair and even more slowly lifted her head in order to fix Tim with a rigid stare. And then, after what seemed like an eternity, she smiled at him, but it was an expression in which her eyes played no part.

'*Dave* made the lasagne…and my name is Sheila, S, H, E, I, L, A, *Sheila*!' she declared both quietly and calmly; an approach which had more impact than if she'd bellowed out the words.

Initially, Tim looked crestfallen, but after draining his glass, a grin gradually broke across his face and this, in turn, developed into a series of half-heartedly suppressed schoolboy sniggers.

'Sheila, Schmeila ... I *know* who you are for goodness sake ... you're my old mate *Dave's* wife!' he said, before swivelling round to face his forlorn-looking friend. 'And the love of his life, *eh* Dave, *eh*?' he added, accompanied by vigorous prods of the man's left shoulder.

Dave responded to neither jab nor jibe, preferring to cup his wine glass with both hands, and stare at the blood red liquid. At that moment, sympathy for Sheila had taken over from pity for Tim as the predominant emotion he was currently feeling. She had overcome her personal prejudice, and allowed his troubled friend to come over, only to be personally insulted and have a valued keepsake damaged through sheer carelessness.

For her part, Sheila was feeling more angry than sorry for herself, and currently looked like an unexploded bomb. She had taken just about as much as she could from this man, whom she'd allowed into her house; this drunkard who had already alienated his own family; this ultimate in life's losers who was no friend of hers, and who couldn't even get her name right. It was then that an overwhelming desire to strike a retaliatory blow, to hurt him back, completely engulfed her.

'*Tell* me Tim, when did you last see your children?' she asked, leaning forward and resting her chin on an A-frame of her linked arms. Having delivered the deadly dose, she then waited for the poison to take effect.

Almost straightaway, Tim put the empty glass down and stared impassively at his plate. The man's mood also palpably darkened and his breathing became more laboured, as the verbal venom coursed through his body. He then proceeded to mumble short snippets of muddled information, the upshot of which, as far as either Sheila or Dave could gather, was that he'd made several attempts to gain forced entry into the women's refuge, where Alison and the children were currently staying. But this was only after half-arranged, half-implied promises to be allowed to see his kids more regularly had failed to materialise. There was now a court injunction against him, barring any access to either of them. However, his Uncle Stephen, a solicitor, was trying to sort something out for him. Conversely, and on a slightly brighter note, his estranged wife had sent him some Polaroid shots of the children in the last week. Unfortunately however, he had since mislaid them.

During the subsequent lull in the conversation, Tim unhappily stirred the remains of his uneaten food, while Dave glared at an utterly unmoved Sheila. As a result of her cruel intervention, he felt all his sympathies and loyalties rapidly swinging back in Tim's direction. It wasn't what she had said, but the reason behind why she'd said it, that he now felt so completely betrayed by her. It had been the very subject of Tim not being able to see his children, which had, both literally and figuratively, nearly sent him over the edge. Sheila was all too aware of the fact, and yet she'd still asked that loaded question. As Dave continued to stare at her cruelly-etched, concave-shaped face, he felt the last grains of his love for her slipping away.

In spite of her external appearances to the contrary, Sheila was actually beginning to regret the very un-Christian motive that had been behind her question to Tim. The blow was perhaps a little too low, she judged. However, the nascent remorse she was currently experiencing for their dinner guest would be short lived.

The pain that Tim now felt was overwhelming him and, in his estimation, needed to be anaesthetised again. Consequently, he reached across for the wine bottle that Dave had not long since uncorked and then set by his place at the end of the table. Unfortunately, as he leaned over, Tim over-balanced, and in an effort to save himself, grabbed the tablecloth, much of which slid off the table's shiny surface as he crashed to the floor. Dave's dinner, his own dinner, the half-full wine bottle and sundry bowls and items of clattering cutlery, fast followed him to the ground. Sheila, whose dinner plate had ended up in the middle of the table, watched the now vacant space opposite her with utter incredulity. Gradually, she saw a groping hand appear, followed by an arm and finally an all too familiar head. Much to her chagrin, Tim was convulsed in helpless laughter, with both tears and tomato sauce running down his face.

Despite her recent regret, Sheila was now ready with more hemlock for his cup.

'Tim, for *pity's sake*; you're not the *first* man whose wife has ever left him,' she barked, whilst yanking the drifted table cloth back towards her. 'We've *all* been through marriage break-ups you know, but we don't *all* turn to the bottle and…and make *fools* of ourselves on top of tall buildings. You have to get a *grip* and get *on* with your life!'

As Tim slowly straightened himself in the chair, and listened to Sheila's brutal barrage, the laughter gradually petered out, and an expression of child-like distress appeared on his face. Dave could not bear to watch his friend in such a state, with pieces of lasagne, together with all traces of his dignity, dropping away from him. Consequently, he lowered himself on to the carpet and began to retrieve all the items that had not broken. Whilst on all fours, he sadly reflected on the fact that Tim *had* ended up wearing his dinner again, after all.

By the time Dave had climbed back onto his seat, Tim had begun to sob.

'Are…are you *alright* mate?' he asked, realising how redundant, even trite his question was, given his friend's current condition.

As it soon became clear, Tim hadn't even noticed his friend's concerned query; he was too focused at venting his spleen in another direction.

'You don't know what it's *like* Sheila', he said, unambiguously addressing her directly. 'You can't *possibly* know what it's like to have your wife leave you, and…and…and then for her to prefer being with other *women*… to not to be able to see your *children*…I'll soon have no *home*…there'll be *nothing*. Has any of *that* happened to you, eh? I …I just can't see any way forward! *Nothing*…no life…'. The rest of what he had to say was completely incoherent, the bitter sobbing having taken over almost entirely.

An unmoved Sheila said nothing in response and looked away dismissively.

Dave, on the other hand, could bear it no longer.

'*Come* on, old chap,' he proposed pityingly, before standing up and then holding out his left arm. 'Let's go for a few turns round the block and get some fresh air eh? You'll feel *better* after that!'

Tim threw him off with a flailing right arm.

'*No*…no…I think I'll go to bed!' he decided, before staggering to his feet, and knocking his chair back against the wall in the process. 'Goodnight…err Sheila; *sorry* about…' he added, whilst motioning in the general direction of the trashed table.

Dave gently guided a tottering Tim upstairs, found him a clean towel and left him in the spare room. He considered that to be the easy part, compared to the prospect of going back downstairs and facing Sheila's displeasure, but downstairs he went, albeit gingerly, whilst at the same time, reminding himself that she was hardly blameless as far as the evening's outcome was concerned.

He found his wife in the diningroom, picking up pieces of broken crockery and congealed lumps of lasagne from the carpet. She was saying nothing, but moving things about with extra brusqueness so as to clearly register her extreme exasperation. Dave kept out of Sheila's way by ferrying the breakages, empty cans and bottles out to the bin, while she stacked the surviving china on the kitchen work surface. Neither of them could face the washing up, and so both turned in for the night.

Sheila undressed both unhappily and wordlessly in the bedroom, her back towards him throughout the process. However, she quickly turned round upon hearing a sudden loud crashing noise, followed by a series of nearby thumps.

'It's coming from the spare room,' she exclaimed with alarm, before pressing her ear against the wall.

Her husband didn't need to get any closer to tell that they were hearing the sound of furniture being overturned, and this spurred him into action.

'*Stay* here; I'll sort this out!' he said, rapidly pulling his trousers back on.

'What a bloody *nightmare* this is!' was his wife's only response as she disappeared into the en suite.

Dave hurried onto the landing and then knocked on the spare room door.

'Tim…*Tim*, are you alright?' he whispered, as loudly as his throat would allow.

There was no verbal reply, and only the sound of something banging against the door from the other side could be heard. Dave quickly decided that he had no choice but to open the door, although only managed to move it a few inches before hitting a long, large metal object. It soon became apparent that the fold-down stepladder, which they used for accessing the loft, had been placed against the inside of the door. He could also see a bare, hairy leg tangled up in the lower rungs of the ladder.

'*Tim*, back away from the door; I need to get in,' Dave pleaded, trying once more to widen the gap. '*Tim*, for God's *sake*, will you *please* get away from that sodding door.'

There followed some muddled movement from the other side of the door, and Dave finally managed to push his way into the spare room. Once inside he also succeeded in getting Tim and the foldaway ladder separated. A frowning Dave then looked to his friend for some kind of explanation.

'I…I couldn't find the toilet,' was the only excuse that Tim could offer.

It soon became obvious that their guest did not know where he was, so Dave ushered him out of the room and then pointed towards the main bathroom at the other end of the landing. Tim shook his head feebly and then padded off in the advised direction, his long white shirttails flapping against his bare spindly legs. In any other circumstance, Dave would have been found that image quite comic, but now, it was merely pathetic. He then peered back into the spare room and saw, in the half-light, that it was in complete disarray. His precious Ladybird books and Dinky toys were scattered all round the room and the chest of drawers was completely overturned.

By the time Tim had finally finished in the bathroom, Sheila was out on the landing in her dressing gown, her arms rigidly folded and mouth set in a thin downward sweeping line, like a nagging mother-in-law from a Donald McGill seaside postcard. She stood in a position that barred Tim's way back into the spare room. Consequently, he slowed his pace and then stopped dead in front of her.

'Why *the hell* don't you pull yourself together? ... snap *out* of it, Tim,' she shouted directly into his face. 'And for pity's *sake,* go and see a doctor before you *drink* yourself to death!'

*

'Are you *sure* you don't want to go to the doctor with that?' Meg asked, as she leaned over a seated Ronnie and examined the gash on his forehead. 'It might need stitches!'

'No I'm *fine* thanks ... it's stopped bleeding now, I can see out of my black eye and…'

'But a few stitches might prevent a scar…'

'Don't *worry,* Meg,' Ronnie interrupted, reaching up to squeeze her hovering hand. 'So, I'll have a sexy scar ... it's not a problem! Like I said last night, *all* I needed was a good sleep and I'd be fine,' he added, smiling with cracked, swollen lips to reveal the gap left by his missing front tooth.

Len looked across from the opposite end of the kitchen, where he was cutting slices of brown bread for lunch. In his estimation, Ronnie looked anything other than fine, but so far, there hadn't really been an opportunity to get him proper medical attention, even if he'd wanted it. After Len had brought his brother home from Rothermead yesterday, all he had wanted to do was to go straight to bed, but Len didn't think it wise for him to continue sleeping in the caravan. The real reason for this, however, was that if Ronnie moved into the house, it would make it less easy for him to abscond and go off to find Katie, about which, he had earlier confided in David. Nonetheless, what Len actually told him was that, with his injuries, he would be much more comfortable in a proper bed. Firstly though, they needed a volunteer to move into the caravan in order to make room for him. Both David and Lucy had quickly raised their hands, but it was Lucy who was chosen, as she was the one with a room of her own. As it happened, she was relieved to be out of the way, having grown wary of Ronnie since the troubles began and he'd come to stay. Indeed, this fear had now worsened because of the frightening looking injuries on his face. Her uncle was grateful for a proper bed, but could not sleep for the pain in the root of his broken off front tooth. Len had suggested that a large measure of whisky might dull the pain and knock him out for the night. It did the trick, at least as far as his sleeping was concerned. At the time, Len hadn't been too concerned about giving Ronnie alcohol, because experienced proved that he only binge drank when he was in a very depressed state.

By midday on the Monday morning, Ronnie was up, dressed, and still sipping whisky to soothe the persistent pain in his head.

'You might *have* to go to the dentist for that tooth,' Len said, with a sympathetic wince, having turned away from his margarine-spreading duties.

'After all, you can't keep on *forever* with that scotch!'

'It was *your* idea, Len ... and it works ... *huh*, to a certain extent,' Ronnie stated, with a rather unreassuring closed-eyed grin, 'so don't *you* worry *either*. As I said, I'm *fine*. It's just this tooth and a little bit of a headache, which I'm sure will all sort itself out before very long!' He took another large mouthful of whisky and then closed his eyes tightly again. The man was clearly still in much pain, in spite of what he claimed.

Len was now very worried; he couldn't help it. On top of everything else, he had turned his little brother into a daytime drinker. And then there was that morning's newspaper, coming as it did exactly one week after the first bow-wave of Ronnie Darwin revelations. The man of the moment had not seen it yet, nor had he viewed himself on the local television news that Sunday evening, as he'd already gone to bed by then. However it had been the newspaper article that Len was especially worried about, as it would be seen all over the country. And although the front page appeared to portray Ronnie in a seemingly favourable light, it still repeated the claim of under-age sex and now added a new allegation.

With the headline stating: '*Randy Ronnie's Rothermead Rant*', what person could resist reading the accompanying article:

'*Popular new comic Ronnie Darwin, who went to ground last week following allegations that he was having a relationship with a minor, re-surfaced in dramatic fashion yesterday, on top of a windmill. The derelict tower (pictured below), at Rothermead Green, near Sittingbourne in Kent, was due to be demolished for a development of luxury bungalows. However, cheeky comic Ronnie, 25, was having none of it. Daring Darwin was cheered on by local villagers, who had so far unsuccessfully campaigned for the mill to be saved themselves. The funny man told jokes from his lofty stage set and ranted at demolition workers who had come to destroy the symbol of the local village school. At one point, eighteen-stone labourer, Mick Tyner, toppled over the edge of the windmill and into a fire brigade safety net, following a tussle with brave Ronnie Darwin. On the scene and after his dramatic fall, Tyner, 37, alleged that the protesting comic had tried to murder him. Sadly, Ronnie was cruelly set upon by a number of Tyner's cronies and sustained several bad injuries. The windmill itself crumbled before the bulldozer shortly afterwards, another victim of so-called progress! This paper says: well done Ronnie Darwin – the hero of Rothermead Green and defender of our English heritage. This country needs more men like him*'.

Len had no intention of letting Ronnie either see or read the article. He knew full well that his brother would only consider it justification for what he had done and might even be encouraged to perform more bizarre stunts like that in the near future.

Earlier that same morning, whilst Ronnie was still sleeping, David had read the article and thought it a splendid piece, that is until his father had sat him down and pointed out two problems with it. The first was the article's overall tone. Had he not noticed how so full of high praise it was for Ronnie, when exactly a week ago, the self same paper had damned him as the man most likely to corrupt the morals of Britain? It was a valuable lesson in how a newspaper could make or break a person, especially if their editorial policy was anxious only to appease the opinions of the most ignorant and reactionary amongst the British population. David could now fully appreciate why his father had been so keen to keep Ronnie away from any press interest. The second problem was something the newspaper article had reported, almost as an amusing aside.

'David, do you remember what happened on top of the mill, when that huge man tried to grab Uncle Ronnie?' asked Len of his son as, with the paper in front of them, they recalled the momentous events of the previous day.

'*Yes*, Ronnie pushed him away and he accidentally fell over the edge,' replied David, giggling from behind his hand, 'and then the silly man told a reporter that Uncle Ronnie tried to *murder* him!'

Len nodded in agreement, but did not laugh along with him.

'The point *is*, the paper *printed* the allegation, *didn't* they? So imagine, for one moment, that it had been the other way round,' Len proposed, making rotating movements with his arms. 'What if that demolition worker had pushed Ronnie, and *he* had then fallen? Having read in the paper that he tried to murder your uncle, wouldn't *you* want the police to look into it?'

'Yes, of course ...oh I *see*!' David replied, as the awful truth behind his father's point suddenly hit home.

'At the end of the day though, if anyone *did* make a fuss, there would be plenty of witnesses to say that Ronnie was merely fending off a physical assault, and that the man fell as the result of, as you say, an *accident*,' Len added, before closing and then folding up the newspaper.

'So that's *okay* then, isn't it?' David asked, looking up at his father with his forehead furrowed.

'*Eventually* perhaps, but not until after a long drawn out court case, where you, me *and* Grandad Darwin could be cross-examined as witnesses, not to *mention* what Ronnie might be put through by any prosecuting barrister,' he asserted in grim tones. 'And *then* there would be all the resultant press speculation and interest that would inevitably arise from a case that had featured the controversial comedian, Ronnie Darwin!'

David nodded in glum agreement; even he could see now how his uncle's career would be irreparably damaged by such attention, that is, if it wasn't already too late by then.

It was with a mild sense of personal triumph that Len now smiled.

'So, *now* do you appreciate why Ronnie can't go haring off after Katie Townsend at the moment?' he asked, finally satisfied that his harsh-sounding words would be heard in the proper context.

'Yes, I *suppose* so,' David agreed reluctantly. Although he both understood and accepted the logic of the situation, part of him still felt much of the emotional consequences of having previously betrayed his uncle's confidence on that very subject.

At that point, the conversation was interrupted by the telephone ringing. It was Grandad Darwin, wanting to speak to his oldest son. It was a call that Len had been both expecting and, therefore, preparing for.

'*Len*, how's the Ronnie this morning?' enquired the strained, stressed voice from Rothermead Farm.

'He's still asleep at the moment; I'll get him to ring you back as soon as he emerges,' Len promised; looking across at David and giving him a brief wink. 'So, how are things up at the farm?'

'Well, yesterday afternoon was a bit worrying ... there were several knocks on the back door. We didn't answer it, but the Nanna sneaked upstairs to peer out of the yellow bedroom window. *Len*, there were at least three police officers in the outer courtyard ... one of them was a woman!'

'But you didn't *speak* to any of them?'

'*No*, I *told* you ... we didn't answer the door!' came the emphatic response. 'You told us not to, and we *didn't*!'

Len took a deep breath before asking the next question.

'So what happened *this morning* then, Grandad?' he patiently asked, casting David a long-suffering look.

'Well, we got the newspaper earlier on, and were surprised by just how highly poor old Ronnie was being *thought of* now!' he exclaimed, with the same overly optimistic reaction that had also thrown David. 'So when the police called again, we didn't feel so worried about letting them in'.

'*And?*'

'And they wanted to speak to Ronnie about what happened yesterday. The sergeant took some convincing that he wasn't here, but then they wanted to know where he *was*!' explained Grandad, beginning to sound a little hesitant. 'And I didn't know what address to give them ... the Herne Bay flat to throw them off the scent a bit, or yours in Canterbury.'

'And err…which one *did* you give them in the end?' asked Len anxiously, gritting his teeth.

'*Well*, you know me ... I never *could* tell a fib convincingly, so gave them your address *there*! I'm sorry if I said the wrong thing the Len.'

'No, don't *worry* Grandad ... that's fine ... I'll take care of it from here,' he responded, with a broad smile of relief. 'And I'll get Ronnie to call you later ... bye!'

The conversations with David and Grandad Darwin, had taken place several hours ago and now Len was looking across the kitchen table and watching Ronnie sipping whisky, whilst the lunch simmered away on the stove. Meg had made a chunky chicken and vegetable soup with some leftovers from the Sunday lunch she'd had with Lucy and Eddie. It had been a meal that the Rothermead contingent never got round to eating.

However, unlike both Len and Ronnie, David had more than made up for it by despatching, not only a big Sunday evening tea, but also a hearty Monday morning breakfast. And now he was back in the house in plenty of time for lunch, having been playing with his sister and little brother out in the caravan for the last hour. He also had some rather awkward news to break.

'*Mum*, Lucy and Eddie want to have their lunch in the caravan ... is that alright?' he asked, watching her ladle out bowls full of the steaming soup.

Ronnie, who was sitting at the kitchen table with Len, looked up through half-closed eyes, as soon as he heard the request.

'Huh, I expect they're scared of the way I look!' he said wearily, and with remarkable perception, peering across at his unsettled-looking brother.

'No, not at *all* mate!' Len countered, with a slow, sympathetic shake of the head.

'*No*, that's not the case at *all* Ronnie!' Meg reinforced, with a wince and a smile, and an exaggerated manner that only served to confirm the lie she was telling. '*No*, they just want to play *houses*, that's all ... I'll ... umm ... I'll take their lunch out to them now!'

Whilst his mother quickly loaded up a tray, David sat up at the table with the two men, and then helped himself to a slice of the bread and spread. Ronnie gave his nephew a weak smile, but found that he couldn't properly focus his eyes on the lad's face. This worried him somewhat, but he soon gave up the effort, and merely took another sip of his Scottish painkiller. Meg was soon back, and with a nervous chuckle, brought the remaining bowls of chunky soup to the table.

It wasn't until lunch was well underway, that Len broached the subject of his earlier telephone call from Rothermead.

'I say, Ronnie ... I was speaking to Grandad this morning, and he told me that they'd had a visit from the police!' he said, in as cheery a matter of fact manner as he could muster.

Ronnie looked up from his barely-touched bowl, on hearing the news, but his facial expression of weary indifference did not change in the least.

'Yes, they wanted to talk to you about the ... umm ... the windmill incident,' Len further explained, trying not to attach a too glamorous-sounding epithet to what he considered to be his younger brother's foolhardy prank. 'They're going to be coming *here*, sooner or later Ronnie, and I wouldn't be surprised if it were this afternoon!'

Still appearing somewhat unconcerned by Len's assertion, Ronnie soon began to nod slowly. He seemed unfazed by the news; on the contrary, he welcomed it.

'*Good* ... I've been seriously thinking about bringing assault charges against those un-evolved *gorillas* who beat me up, and then tore down Rothermead Mill,' he declared, with the briefest flick of the eyebrows, before lowering his head once more.

As Ronnie looked down, Len's head was quickly raised in corresponding action.

'Oh, I don't think *that's* a very good idea,' he responded, with a frowning shake of the head.

Straightaway, his younger brother stared at him aghast.

'Why *not*?' he asked crossly. 'Those bastards really kicked the *crap* out of me!'

Len still looked rather worried, even though, as far as David was concerned, his uncle had more than justified any action he might want to take against those bullies. Ronnie sensed this support, and gave his nephew a pain-causing grin. It was then that Ronnie noticed that he was getting a steely glance from Meg, and soon realised that, as David was at the table, his language had been judged as inappropriate. Now feeling rather embarrassed, he quietly resumed eating his lunch, though with some difficulty. Sadly, the whisky had loosened his tongue, but was no longer sufficient to dull the pain of that broken tooth.

Seeing his brother's downcast state, Len now sought to pacify him.

'Anyway, let's just wait and see what the police have to say first, and then we can take it from there,' he suggested, in a calm, quiet manner, before reaching for a slice of bread.

'But why *are* they coming?' Ronnie asked, with a mixture of frustration and petulance. 'I haven't done anything *wrong*,' he added, letting go his spoon and allowing it to splash into the bowl; creating little soupy speckles on the tablecloth.

Len glared at him as if he couldn't believe what had just been said.

'You pushed a man off the top of the *windmill* ... he could have *died*!' he said, with an incredulous glance.

'It was an *accident*, and he *didn't*,' Ronnie countered; his sense of frustration increasing as he firmly pushed his bowl away and allowing its contents to slop over.

'Look, *I* know that,' Len agreed, with emphatic hand gestures, 'but let's just hope the police see it that way too!'

As if fate was organising the day's events, the doorbell rang through from the hall at that very moment. Straightaway, a surprised David looked across at his mother, a worried Meg stared over at Ronnie, and a concerned-looking Ronnie peered at his brother.

'That must be the police,' Len stated straight-faced, as he quickly rose from his seat.

'Unless, of course, you were expecting the Avon Lady?' smiled Ronnie, flashing the gap where his tooth had once been.

Len ignored his brother's attempt to make light of the situation, and instead, beckoned him up from his chair.

'Okay Ronnie, lets take this calmly,' he advised, already making for the door to the hall, 'after *all*, you haven't done anything wrong!'

'That's easy for *you* to say, you haven't pushed a man off the top of a windmill!' Ronnie remarked frowning, ironically echoing Len's earlier statement, just as his brother had unwittingly repeated his.

Len answered the door to a middle-aged moustached man, who introduced himself as Sergeant Reginald Workman, from the Swale Police. Straightaway, he recognised him as the senior uniformed officer who had attempted to oversee matters back at Rothermead Green during the previous day's disaster. His companion was a young fresh-faced policeman, who was not introduced but looked as equally familiar to Len. They were shown into the lounge where a nervous-looking Ronnie now sat waiting. He had brought his whisky glass through with him although, for the moment, he did not sip from it. Both policemen recognised Ronnie as soon as they saw him, in spite of, or perhaps because of his facial injuries. Either way, having made themselves comfortable, the uniformed pair proceeded to chat with him for some minutes about his career and television appearances. In fact, Len was rather surprised, if not a little relieved at their almost casual approach to the visit and expected one of them, at any time, to actually ask for his brother's autograph.

Inevitably, the celebrity gossip eventually died down, as both Ronnie and Len realised it surely must, and Sergeant Workman called the meeting to order by first addressing the latter.

'Before we begin this informal interview, would you mind sir, if your lad – *David*, isn't it – joined us, as he had been present on the day in question?' the sergeant requested, uncrossing his legs so as to adopt a more professional posture, and also retrieving his note book from the right breast pocket of his uniform.

'Umm ... *yes* ... err, I'll get him!' Len responded slightly taken aback, before disappearing into the hallway. Within a matter of seconds, he had returned in the company of a sheepish-looking David. Rather then sit on the vacant space on the settee, in the middle of the two police officers, David chose to perch on the armrest of the chair in which his father was sitting.

The sergeant both winked and grinned at David, before clearing his throat and then looking straight at Len.

'I have to inform you that yesterday evening, one Michael Tyner, an employee of Bring-it-Down Demolition Company, made some serious allegations against Mr Ronnie Darwin here,' he announced, raising and lowering his bushy eyebrows as he spoke. 'However, having discussed the matter with his work colleagues, it appears that he's subsequently withdrawn them ... this *morning* in fact!'

Len glanced at his brother with mouth open and eyebrows raised. At the same time, David's body posture became a lot less stiff, but he now looked with even more intensity at their potential saviour; almost as if he was expecting there to be a catch.

Having allowed time for the Darwin family to react to the news, Sergeant Workman now turned to Ronnie, with a rather serious-looking countenance.

'That notwithstanding, I am still obliged to look into the incident for the record, and of *course*, there is still the matter of the serious and all too evident assault against your good self,' he said, raising his eyebrows at the conclusion of his sentence.

Ronnie slowly leaned forward in the armchair, screwing his eyes up in pain throughout.

'Yeah, *I* should say!' he firmly agreed, reaching for the whisky glass that was on the end of the coffee table in front of him.

In response, the senior officer regarded him through narrowed eyes, and took a deep audible breath.

'Now, I'm a very busy man,' he continued, in a somewhat wearisome manner, 'and if *no one* was to make any allegations, or likewise file any complaints, then I would have no choice but to *close* the case ... say in my report that you fell down a steep flight of steps, or something like that…if you get my meaning?' he proposed; his eyebrows raised so as to resemble two hairy caterpillars crawling across his forehead.

Immediately, Len sat up straight in his chair, with a suddenly very excitable look on his face.

'*Yes*, we do indeed Sergeant!' he interjected knowingly, before casting a wide-eyed stare over in his brother's direction.

Ronnie glared back from the top of his eyes, and gave a little cough, but did not respond, or give any other indication that he understood what was being proposed. Len had to hope that he was just thinking about the implied suggestion, and would not insist on any legal retribution for his injuries.

By now, the sergeant was also staring at him, clearly keen to resolve the matter one way or the other.

'*So* then ... err, Ronnie, if I may be so bold as to address you thus. Do you intend to file charges, or not?' he reiterated, in more blatant terms than before.

A head-hanging Ronnie took a long sip of his drink, whilst all eyes in the room were anxiously fixed on him. He finally looked up, but focused on no one in particular.

'Why *should* I file charges, when I got these injuries falling down the windmill steps…*clumsy* old me!' he responded at last, in a very tired-sounding voice, and with exaggerated opening and closing movements of his eyes as he spoke.

Reg Workman smiled and immediately replaced his un-used notebook.

'Well in *that* case, I can shut the file, take off my metaphorical policeman's hat and tell you what a bloody good job you did for us yesterday!' he declared before springing his rotund body off from the settee, and then approaching the injured comedian with his right hand extended.

'But I didn't save the mill, sadly,' replied a more downcast Ronnie, as he reached up to respond to the gesture, albeit in a rather lacklustre manner.

His erstwhile interviewer sighed and then nodded in stoic fashion.

'Indeed *not*, but young Stanley and I reckon that you had a bloody good try!' Sergeant Workman then gestured towards the young officer with him, and then chuckled. 'As it happened, Constable Smithers here managed to get himself on the six o'clock news *as well*, after some idiot jumped on his back, and then rode him around like Nijinski for a few seconds!'

The young policeman merely grinned and then shrugged his shoulders.

'It was worth it to be in the same company as the Hero of Rothermead Mill' Stanley said, recalling the morning's newspaper article, before standing up from the settee.

Workman nodded in vigorous agreement, before leaning in towards the still-sitting Len.

'When I was young many, *many* years ago, a little bit younger than your son here, I used to go to Rothermead Green Primary School,' he explained, in slightly conspiratorial tones. 'I must have climbed to the top of the mill *many* a time in my youth! So, you'll now understand my interest.' The officer straightened himself up and took another deep breath. '*Anyway*, I won't keep you all any longer ... come along Stanley.'

A delighted Len stood up swiftly and then shook hands with their three-striped saviour.

'*Thanks* for everything you've done ... it'll make things a little easier to cope with over the coming weeks!' he admitted, with a supporting nod of the head.

'I understand sir!' the sergeant said emphatically, before stooping slightly to address David. 'Are you proud of your uncle, lad?' he asked, with a sideways grin that made his moustache protrude somewhat.

'Oh, *yes*!' David replied emphatically.

Sergeant Workman smiled, winked at him, and then hesitated before turning to face Ronnie, who had since staggered to his feet.

'This is *strictly* off the record sir, but we've had an approach from the Metropolitan Police. It seems they've become aware that you have ... umm ... *re-surfaced* as it were, and have expressed an interest in interviewing you on, err ... *other matters*!' He made ominous eye contact for a further few silent seconds before averting his gaze.

As the sergeant made for the hallway door, Len and Ronnie immediately exchanged concerned glances, but David merely looked puzzled as he'd been unable to decipher the cryptic message.

Len showed the two police officers out, but as he stepped onto the front path, Sergeant Workman turned back and then grabbed his arm.

'My advice to you, is to get your brother a solicitor as soon as possible.' He touched his nose with his left index finger, before resuming his journey out to the police car that was parked in the roadway, just on the other side of the lonicera hedge.

Back in the lounge, Ronnie found himself alone with David for the first time since early on the Sunday morning back up in the Rothermead cottage; a period of time no more than a day and a half, but one that seemed so much longer. It was then that he noticed for the first time that there was something on his nephew's forehead. Leaning forward slightly, the woozy-headed man struggled to focus his eyes in that direction, and as soon as he realised it was a large scab, he pointed a finger at the gash on his own forehead and smiled.

'Scar Brothers *again*, eh Dave?' Ronnie chuckled, followed by a wink of his good eye.

'Oh *yes*, so it *is*!' David beamed, as the significance of another shared injury dawned on him. 'I got this up at Rothermead Mill!'

'Yeah, me *too*!' his uncle grinned, as if there could be any possible doubt. '*Still*, it's a slight improvement on falling through a cold frame at Oakenden Nursery, *eh*, Dave?' he said, fingering the small crescent-shaped scar just below his left hand.

'I suppose *so*!' Dave agreed, as he touched the spookily similar scar on his own left hand.

'Do you remember much about that, *you* know, the fall, and me carrying you up to the local hospital?' asked Ronnie, as he himself tried to recall that early 1960s incident.

'A little ... I remember being in the hospital, and the nurse asking me to look up at the light as she checked the bump on my head, but not much else!' he admitted, straining to recall the distant pre-school memory. 'You cut your hand on the broken glass trying to lift me out of the frame, *didn't* you uncle?'

Ronnie nodded his head, and then winced in pain, before once more raising a hand to his forehead.

'You *alright,* uncle?' asked a suddenly very worried David, as he crossed the room and lowered himself onto the now vacant settee.

'I've been *better*!' he sighed, before draining the rest of his drink in one draught.

At that moment, the sound of the front door closing could be heard, and Len soon rejoined his brother and son in the lounge.

Ronnie looked up at him, and gradually re-focused his eyes.

'Well, *that* was a piece of cake,' he declared; beginning to sound a little upbeat, due to both the success of the visit, and the long awaited effect of the anaesthetic.

Len, on the other hand, remained poker-faced, as he sat back down in the same armchair he'd earlier occupied.

'But aren't you *at all* concerned about these *other matters*?' he asked; clearly a little irritated at the prospect of another police visit, as much as his brother's dismissive attitude towards it

'Of *course* I am!' Ronnie retorted, with more than a hint of belligerence. 'Do you think it's about Katie?' he added, in softer tones.

'It can't be about anything else, *can it*!' Len shouted, once more frustrated at his brother's inability to grasp the situation, or its potential importance. 'Unless, of course, you've been holding out on me with regards to some *other* idiotic thing you've been up to!'

'You mean the marijuana plants the police took away from my London flat?' Ronnie asked with straight-faced seriousness.

'*What*?' Len screamed, lifting himself half-out of the armchair.

'Joking, *joking*!' Ronnie giggled, waving his left hand in a lowering gesture, as he looked over at David, with a comic expression of 'he's no fun!' on his face.

An unsmiling Len sat back down, but perched on the edge of the seat and then leant forward to emphasize what he was about to say:

'*Listen*, if the police *do* pursue this Katie Townsend business, as it now seems they might, then it will be far from a *piece of cake*, as you put it. This will be a jolly *serious matter*!'

'I *am* very serious, as far as Katie is concerned,' Ronnie countered, leaning forward to match Len's body language. 'I *love* her, I *miss* her…'

'*And* you're planning to visit her, *aren't* you!' cut in Len starkly, pointing an accusing finger in his younger brother's direction.

'*Sorry*?' Ronnie stuttered, in staggered disbelief.

'It's no good … I *know* you're planning to visit Katie, *despite* your promise to me!' Len said, once more stabbing the air with his extended index finger.

Ronnie glared at his nephew with a pained and pathetic look of betrayal on his injured face.

'*Don't* look at David … I *forced* it out of him,' Len declared unmoved, before folding his arms defiantly.

David felt the panic gradually build up inside him. He first glanced at his uncle, whom he'd earlier betrayed, and who now looked as emotionally hurt as he did physically. He then stared over at his father, who had just betrayed him by directly revealing the source of his knowledge regarding Ronnie's plans to see Katie. The tears now began to burn in his eyes and he soon rushed from the room in order to seek the shameful solace of his bedroom.

Ronnie pushed himself up from his chair, and somewhat zombie-like, set off in pursuit of David. However, he'd only gone a few staggering steps before Len intervened.

'*Leave* him, *he'll* get over it,' he instructed firmly, before pointing at the chair his brother had just vacated. 'Now *sit* down … we need to get this other matter sorted out right now!' Len got up and then stood over his now-seated brother. 'I must have your absolute assurance that you won't try and see Katie!'

Ronnie looked up at the figure hovering over him and chortled defiantly.

'My *car* is still in London, I've got *no* money, I feel like shit, *and* I've got a pounding headache! I'm not going *anywhere* Len, okay?' he vociferated, with a supporting open-handed gesture.

'Okay!' his older brother replied, in a calm, trusting manner before slowly straightening up his stance. 'Now, I'm going to make an appointment to see the family solicitor. Fingers crossed, we can get in tomorrow morning,' he said, before walking into the hall, and then shutting the door firmly behind him.

The sudden sound of the front door slamming shut resounded up the staircase and immediately alerted a somewhat surprised David, who had been reading the Tuesday morning newspaper on his bed. It was far too early to be his mother and younger siblings returning from the shops, he quickly concluded; which could only mean that it had to be his father and Uncle Ronnie who were now back from the solicitors. With stealthy speed, he crept onto the landing, crouched by the banisters, and then peered between the wooden struts and down into the hall below. Eager to learn how the visit had gone, David listened hard and caught the tail-end of one of his father's diatribes:

'And I usually hate people who say this, but you really *will* have to pull yourself together when you're in this house Ronnie, if only for the sake of the children,' Len lectured, as he hung his jacket on one of the hooks at the foot of the stairs. 'And for Pete's *sake*, tidy yourself up a bit!'

'At least I wasn't recognised by anyone,' Ronnie retorted as the pair walked along the passage towards the kitchen door.

'I'm not *surprised* ... you look like you've been dragged through a hedge backwards,' Len said, as their voices faded into the next room.

David agreed that Ronnie wasn't his usual spruce self, even allowing for the facial injuries sustained at the Rothermead Mill protest. But then again, he reasoned to himself that the rapidly forming beard and matted unwashed hair, together with the ubiquitous celebrity dark glasses, were all probably deliberate, so that his uncle could move about outside without constantly being asked to sign autographs.

Hearing his relatives speak again, but unable to make out any words, David leaned forward as far as he dared, and the space between the landing struts allowed. The kitchen door was open and he could now just about make out his father's voice:

'And *that* won't help!' he said, above the sound of the hissing cold tap.

'It helps *me,* or rather it helps the toothache and headache,' Ronnie replied, in much more mumbling tones.

'At least have a cup of tea as well ... I *am* putting the kettle on,' Len insisted, sounding slightly more conciliatory than before.

'Yeah, alright,' came his brother's joyless response.

Back upstairs, David continued to strain to hear. He knew very well that it was rude to listen in to other people's conversations, but then again, he told himself, how else could he find out how his Uncle Ronnie was feeling and also what exactly had happened at the solicitors? Of course, David longed to go down and join them both, but after his father had blabbed about the Katie confidence yesterday, he didn't think that his uncle would want to see him; and after all, Ronnie was in enough pain without him making matters worse by having betrayed their sacred Scar Brother's code, and then pretending that nothing had happened.

David was also aware that Ronnie had a much more pressing matter on his mind. Indeed, if that morning's newspaper was true, then he knew that his poor uncle was in big trouble. David had sneaked the paper into his room when the men had popped out earlier to fix Ronnie up with the family solicitor. David felt that he needed to read every inch of the coverage himself, rather than just rely on his father's edited version, so that he could try and find some meaning behind it all. Even so, it just didn't seem fair, especially when his uncle's career was really beginning to take off. Perhaps, all of them were jealous of Ronnie and wanted to take him down a peg or two; or at least, that was the only conclusion he could reach.

The newspaper headline had been bad enough: '*Show's Over For Schoolgirl Seducer*'. And then as he'd read on, David realised that everything his father had said yesterday, concerning the fickle nature of the papers, was absolutely true:

'*The BBC announced yesterday, that plans for a pilot 'Ronnie Darwin Show' had been shelved indefinitely. The statement came following the recent revelation that Darwin was having a relationship with 15-year-old schoolgirl, Katie Townsend. Ronnie had made no comment as he left his London flat last week; believed to be headed for a destination somewhere in East Kent. Then, as revealed in yesterday's picture exclusive, publicity seeking Darwin dramatically re-surfaced at the weekend, leading a protest to save a doomed windmill. The disgraced comic's rise to fame was rapid. Following his success with talent show Opportunity Knocks, he appeared on several other variety bills, the most notable being the Lulu Show, which was said to have attracted viewing figures of 10.5 million. Filming for the pilot show was due to have begun in August, with screening planned for a primetime slot during the autumn season. Our sources report that the Metropolitan Police are anxious to speak to Mr Darwin, concerning the allegations of under-age sex, although it is understood that no formal complaints have yet been filed by Vanessa Townsend, mother of the teenage runaway. Yesterday, there was no answer from the Townsend's Tunbridge Wells home and a family solicitor confirmed that both mother and daughter were staying with friends on the coast. Katie's older twin sisters, Carol and Christine were also both unavailable for comment*'.

As his ears were now beginning to throb, David freed his head, crept round to the top end of the landing and then sat halfway down the stairs, so as to better monitor the conversation. This was only partially successful, as it soon became apparent that the kitchen door had now been pushed to. However, from this newer vantage point, he could also keep half an eye on the front door, in case his mother, Lucy and little Eddie came back from their shopping trip. David was quickly able to establish that Ronnie and Len were currently in hushed but intensive conversation. He was a little annoyed that his father had apparently replaced him as Ronnie's confidante, but realised that this was all his own fault. On the other hand, David was also a little relieved, as he would not have known what to advise his uncle; especially now things had become so very complicated. He strained harder to hear what was being said in specific terms, but only vague snatches of conversation from within the kitchen could be made out, and these were usually the ones when each respective voice was raised in either anger of frustration:

'…career *ruined*…'
'…thought she was *older*…'
'…*silly* young fool…'
'…we *love* each other…'
'…sooner or *later*, the press…'
'…I *promise* you it's true…'
'…no I *don't* want a drink…'
'…you don't know what it's *like*…'
'…*steady* with that…'
'…not being able to *see* her…'
'…the family *stick together*…'
'…no way *forward*…'.

Quite unexpectedly, the front door knocker rapped both loudly and rhythmically. Alarmed, David turned with a start and then shot back up to the landing. Perhaps Mum has forgotten her keys and was cross, David thought, as he peered round the topmost newel post. However, he could not equate that theory with the two bulky figures he could now make out beyond the frosted glass and lace curtain of the front door; and besides which, if it had been his mother, why hadn't she used the bell? He soon became aware of someone coming back along the passage from the kitchen, so withdrew out of sight and once more took up the ear-stinging position between the landing struts. From here, he heard the front door opening and then a deep voice ask his father if he was Leonard Robert Darwin. The two men were invited in and, without delay, followed his father through to the kitchen.

David now slowly stole back to his staircase listening position, where the odour of stale cigarette smoke slowly assailed his nostrils. Once more straining to listen, the lad soon realised that he had at least three voices to try and decipher:

'…Ronald George Darwin…'
'…didn't *happen* like that…'
'…you can see the *state* he's in…'
'…serious offence sir…'
'…thought she was *older*…'
'…cup of *tea* officer…'
'…whereabouts of the young woman…'
'…we *love* each other…'
'…*all* a misunderstanding…'
'…do this the hard way sir…'
'…thought she was *older*…'
'…just need to leave a note…'.

Within a minute, all four men came back into the hall and a surprised David was pretty sure that he'd been seen, as he quickly scrambled back upstairs. He then heard the sound of the front door being opened.

'*We're just popping out again David,*' his father shouted up to him. '*Your mum will be home soon!*'

'*Right-ho,*' David yelled in a deliberately nonchalant manner.

Having heard the front door slam shut, the worried lad hurried into his parents' bedroom in order to look out of the front window. A large black Rover was parked in front of the house. David soon surmised that it was a police car and, therefore by implication, that the visitors had to be police officers. As all four men approached the vehicle, he could see that one of the non-uniformed policemen was holding firmly on to Ronnie's upper arm. The car's nearside rear door was opened and, as if he could somehow sense his nephew's presence, Ronnie glanced up briefly at the bedroom window. Thinking himself safely concealed behind the net curtain, David did not move or react, but soon sensed his feelings of shame become compounded; for not only had he let his uncle down by betraying that confidence, but also he was now spying on his public humiliation. However, David could see that he was not alone in this very unpleasant practice. Curtains twitched in two of the houses opposite, and a woman passing by with her shopping trolley, stopped to talk to another with a pram. They both proceeded to gawp quite unashamedly at the scene.

As soon as the car ferrying Ronnie pulled away down the hill, closely followed by Len in his mushroom-coloured Escort, David ran downstairs and then rushed into the kitchen. On the table was a half-full bottle of whisky, an empty glass tumbler and an envelope propped up against it. David picked it up and found that it was sealed. He looked over at the kettle, which had not long since boiled, and remembered an article he'd once read in one of the *Look and Learn* magazines up at Rothermead. It had shown how envelopes could be steamed open, and then resealed again without anyone finding out. Having thought about it for a moment, he lost his nerve, and put it back where he'd found it.

David helped himself to a biscuit from the old metal barrel on the work surface, and then sat at the kitchen table in order to think. He soon began to worry about Katie Townsend, although not for her welfare, but rather his own involvement in the whole sorry affair. David reasoned that she was the one who had got Uncle Ronnie into trouble and now, it would seem, arrested by the police. She must have told Ronnie that she was much older than she actually was, he concluded; otherwise none of this made any sense. Katie certainly seemed older to David when he'd met her at the BBC back in the spring, but now it turned out she was only three years older than he was. It was also the case that no one in the family except him had any prior knowledge about Ronnie and Katie. For that very reason, he was now forced to ask himself: should he have told his parents about her back then, and broken yet another, albeit unstated, confidence between himself and Uncle Ronnie? On the other hand, if he had mentioned meeting Katie, could his parents have somehow prevented all this from happening? Then again, if they'd gone on to meet her too, wouldn't they have also assumed that she was older? And wouldn't Ronnie have gone on seeing her irrespective of what they thought? Sadly though, whatever might have happened in the recent past; however many different scenarios he ran through in his mind, it was now all too late, and as a result of that chilling realisation, David began to feel really frightened. And there was no point in saying anything now, he sadly concluded; there was absolutely nothing he could say or do to help his poor old Uncle Ronnie anymore.

Hearing a key turn in the front door lock, David soon shook himself out of his glum musings, and rushed to the hallway door. Looking along the passage, he watched his mother coming in, her shopping bags banging against the doorframe as she manoeuvred herself over the threshold. Lucy guided Eddie's pushchair in behind her, making equal clatter and contact with the paintwork.

Having dismounted, his little brother ran into the kitchen. '*Unca Ronnie, Unca Ronnie*,' he shouted with enthusiasm, but stopped dead, with a very disappointed look on his face, at finding only David there by the door.

Lucy held back, as she didn't particularly want to see her uncle, but was greatly relieved upon finding out that he was not at home.

However, it was his mother whom David was anxious to see, and he waited until she had dumped two of her bags on the work surface, before it all spilt out of him in an excited gabble.

'*Mum*, Mum, the police came and ... and they took Uncle Ronnie away ... Dad went *with* them,' he announced excitedly, before reaching for the envelope on the table. 'Dad left you this *note*!' he added before holding it out in front of him triumphantly.

Meg quickly snatched it from him and, with shaking hands, tore the note out from the envelope in a panic. She then read the contents, with both Lucy and David looking on anxiously. Gradually, a smile of relief spread across her face.

'It's *okay* ... the police merely wanted Uncle Ronnie to go down to the station and answer some questions,' she explained, in a much calmer manner, 'he's *not* been arrested!'

Now feeling a little better about the situation, David busied himself by helping his mum to put the shopping away. It was a welcome distraction, and took his mind off thinking about what was happening down at the police station.

As Meg ferried another bag through from the hall, she tutted disapprovingly upon noticing the whisky bottle, but left it where it was on the kitchen table and simply unloaded the shopping around it.

Not long after that task had been completed, the sound of a key in the front door once more echoed through from the hall. As expected, Len came in, presumably in the company of Uncle Ronnie, but they didn't see him at all; much to both Lucy's relief, and David's disappointment, Ronnie had bolted straight upstairs without a word.

Len exchanged anxious glances with his wife as they met in the kitchen.

'You got the *note* I assume,' he exclaimed in a weary, lacklustre manner, as he flopped down on the nearest kitchen table chair.

'Yes, so what's *happened*?' she asked, in anxious tones, joining him at the table.

Len sighed deeply and then screwed his eyes shut.

'It was the *Metropolitan* Police this time, just as we'd been warned. And of *course*, they wanted to talk about the whole Katie Townsend business!'

Hearing the name of the family nemesis, Meg held up her hand to signal for her husband to pause, before turning towards the children, who were standing in a worried-looking huddle around the biscuit barrel.

'Why don't you children go and play in the diningroom,' she suggested, with a sweet, maternal smile. 'Your dad and I need to have a private talk!'

Without the least bit opposition, Lucy and Eddie trotted off hand-in-hand, but David stood his ground, leaning his back against the work surface, and looking over at his parents somewhat nervously.

'*Come* on David ... play the game!' his mother urged, with an encouraging hand gesture.

'No that's alright ... let him stay,' intervened a tired-looking Len, with out making eye contact. 'For good or bad, he's *part* of this now!'

David tried not to meet his mother's slightly resentful stare as he joined his parents at the table.

The boy's father gazed at the whisky bottle and dirty glass, and then completely unexpectedly, poured out a small measure before continuing with his account.

'There have been no formal allegations made, *or* charges brought ... it's all press speculation *so* far. But that…that silly young fool actually *admitted* having ... umm ... relations with that girl, in *spite* of old Mr Howell's best legal advice. So now the police have a *confession*!' he concluded, throwing his arms up in despair.

'But didn't he *tell* them he thought she was older?' queried a furrow-browed Meg, as she threw herself back in the chair.

'*Repeatedly*, like a broken record,' Len insisted, wearily rubbing his right temple, 'and I suppose that's why they didn't formally charge him today, but they *are* thinking about it, and want him to go in again tomorrow. *God*, I'll have to have *another* day off work!'

Len lifted the glass to his lips, but before he could take a sip, a large crashing sound resounded from upstairs, followed by loud screams of frustration from Ronnie. Both Eddie and Lucy soon came running in from the diningroom and began sobbing with spontaneous fear at the bizarre happenings.

Looking towards the ceiling, the children's father quickly stood up.

'I was *afraid* of this,' he stated, before making his way to the hallway door. 'He's like a coiled spring today, or…or a caged lion!' He motioned for everyone to stay in the kitchen as he shut the door into the hall and then hurried upstairs.

Meanwhile downstairs, Meg did her best to comfort the younger children, whilst David pressed his ear against the closed hallway door, despite his mother's continued disapproving looks. He knew it was unlikely that he'd be able to hear what would be said upstairs, but tried in any case. However, on this occasion, the voices of both his uncle and father were sufficiently raised in mutual anger and frustration, to once more allow key phrases to be discerned:

'…have to *see* her…'
'…make matters *worse*…'
'…*kill* myself…'
'…bloody *stupid* remark…'
'…need to go *now*…'
'…both keep a *low profile*…'
'…it's *no good* Len…'
'…might *not* be charged…'
'…I can't *forget* her…'
'…*snap out* of it…'
'…can't *stop* me…'
'…Ronnie, *please* don't!'

Following that last remark, David could quite clearly hear someone come bounding down the stairs and then, after a brief pause, slamming the front door. A second set of steps could soon be discerned, in close pursuit, and the front door being opened once more.

'Ronnie, *Ronnie, come back*!' Len shouted, in a panic-stricken voice that could be heard by the whole family.

David quickly moved himself away from the kitchen door as a pair of running footsteps became ever louder.

Sure enough his father soon burst in with a look of horror on his face.

'My *God,* Meg … Ronnie's taken my wallet *and* the car,' he announced, holding both hands to his head in a Munch-style parody. ' I just couldn't *stop* him!'

*

A panicked Dave stood in the close, at the front of his house and watched the aged camper van roar off into the night. The thought briefly occurred to him that he should get into his own car and attempt pursuit, but then how would he be able to stop him? Indeed, Tim was definitely in no fit state to walk, let alone drive, and Dave feared that the night could very well end with him, or someone else getting killed. He looked back towards the house, and then up at the front bedroom window where light was streaming through the un-curtained glass. And there was Sheila, staring down at him impassively from behind the nets. If anything *did* happen to Tim tonight, then blood would be on her hands, he angrily concluded.

Looking away with barely disguised disdain, Dave paced slowly over to the sycamore tree on the green and tried to recall the shocking events of barely ten minutes before. He soon pondered: what exactly *had* been said on the landing?

Tim, who was very drunk, had been coming back from the bathroom, and just beginning to compose himself, when a stern-faced Sheila had confronted him. It is widely known that no one in distress likes to be told to pull themselves together, or worse, to snap out of it. Dave didn't and Tim *certainly* did not. Sheila was either unaware of this fact, or more likely didn't care, for her sanctimonious scolding had been intended as much to hurt Tim as it was to control him.

As it turned out, their guest responded in like fashion.

'I *can't* pull myself together,' he countered crossly; his face only inches from hers. 'I've *tried*...but I *can't*! Do you think I actually *enjoy* being like this, you *stupid fucking bitch*!'

Sheila actually raised her hand to slap him, but then stopped herself as she realised that, as ever, her tongue could do a lot more wounding.

'You pathetic excuse for a man,' she retorted, with one of her mouth-only smiles. 'No *wonder* Alison left you, and I bet the women she's with right now have more balls than *you*!'

Tim really saw red this time and, suddenly lurching forward, pinned a shocked-looking Sheila against the airing cupboard door. She quickly glared at Dave, expecting him to intervene on her behalf, but he did nothing; he knew that his friend would go no further, at least in a physical sense. His only regret was that it was Tim and not he who had finally dared to challenge her control.

Moreover, it was soon obvious that Tim could inflict just as much verbal damage as she could.

'How *dare* a sanctimonious little *cunt* like you, talk to me like that. You...you, who prefer the company of your ungrateful *lying* son to that of your long suffering husband!' he spat, with well-chosen words, before delivering his devastating coup de gras. 'No doubt you'd probably prefer to fuck Julian as well, *I'll* bet!'

Summoning up a huge wave of strength, a snarling Sheila pushed Tim away and sent him sprawling on his back.

'Get out of *my* house, get out, get out, *get out*,' she screamed, almost standing over him, as she stabbed the air with her extended index finger.

Tim desperately tried to straighten his loose shirt, which had ridden up to reveal a pair of soiled underpants, and then slowly stumbled back onto his feet.

'Don't worry, I *want* to get out,' he loudly retorted, and then headed back to the spare room in search of his missing trousers.

A concerned-looking Dave quickly followed him into the room.

'*No* Tim, you're staying here tonight ... you *can't* drive like this!' he reasoned, with an arm round his friend's shoulders.

Sheila glared at her husband through the doorway, with eyes narrowed angrily and both hands firmly placed on her wide hips. 'Dave, how *dare* you...'

'Just *shut up* a moment will you?' he bellowed, for the first time in their brief marriage, before walking out of the room and then standing in front of her.

For a moment, she stood there on the landing, staring back at him in complete shock, but then recovered enough to stomp back in their bedroom and then slam the door shut behind her.

Tim soon re-emerged from the spare room with trousers restored and, without a word, began to walk down the stairs.

Dave set off in pursuit and, once more, tried to intervene. 'Tim, you *can't*...'

'*No* mate, I'm going to go ... I may not believe in God, but I recognise *evil* when I see it!' he firmly attested; pausing just long enough to point back up at the master bedroom. 'Besides which, I've driven home a *lot* worse than this.' Tim soon halted his descent again and then stared fixedly into his erstwhile host's face. 'Dave, if you're my friend, you *won't* stop me!' he challenged, with straight-faced seriousness. The man spoke with a logic that only other drunkards could fathom; it was a language that could only be countered coherently if one was in the same state.

Tim lurched down the rest of the stairs, closely followed by Dave, who was still trying to think of ways to make his friend stay.

'Look, why don't you sleep in the camper van outside?' he suggested, keeping pace with him in the hall. 'That's what you *bought* it for, isn't it?'

'There's no bedding in it yet,' his friend retorted, without making eye contact with him. However, just short of the front door, Tim paused, and then fixed Dave with a determined stare. 'You could come *with* me', he suggested, swaying gently as he spoke. 'Throw a few things into a bag, and get *out* of here, mate!'

Dave stood there and actually found himself tempted by the proposal, and this shocked him a little.

Sensing his friend's indecisive-based hesitation, Tim pressed the point.

'*Listen*, you could drive and then crash at my place. Huh, otherwise, *I* might be the one to crash, eh?'

His friend's attempt at black humour made Dave wince, but he couldn't really go with him and Tim knew it. He had Sheila to sort out, and besides which, despite her earlier comment, it *was* still half his house and crammed full of his things as well. At the end of the day though, he had always told himself that he would only leave his wife if there was somewhere to go and someone to be with. Tim and his elderly camper van hardly fit the bill, but that didn't stop him from feeling terribly sorry for his erstwhile telecom colleague. Dave tried to draw some comfort from the fact that Tim seemed calmer now, less slurred and also steadier on his feet.

Although Dave didn't say in words that he wasn't going with him, it was clear to Tim, by his friend's body language and embarrassed-looking countenance that he would be driving home alone. Consequently, having given Dave the briefest of smiles, he walked over to the van, in as steady a manner as he could muster.

'Please go carefully!' was the last thing Dave said to Tim, as he climbed into the Dormobile and then fired up its ancient engine.

Rather than reverse out of the parking space and into the close, the drunken driver lurched forward, demolished the small retaining wall and then drove onto the green. Gathering speed, he did a tight circuit of the small sycamore tree, loudly tooting his horn in the process, and then drove off back though the gap in the wall he'd just created, before roaring up the close and away.

So that was what had happened, but had Dave said and done the right thing? He ruminated on this thought, as his foot traced the indented tyre marks around the sycamore sapling. Feeling utterly joyless, and unable to draw any peace of mind from anything he'd done or not done during Tim's calamitous visit, he wandered slowly back towards the house. There in the brightly illuminated window above, Sheila was still staring down at him, and he could have sworn that she was smiling.

Dave could not go upstairs, so he sat on the settee in the lounge, with the light of one small side lamp as his only comfort. Several sticky rings, from Tim's drinks glasses, bottles and cans could just be made out on the shiny surface of the coffee table, as could the damaged booklet from his *Miles Davis* CD. If Julian had done this to his property, then he might have lost his temper, or even sulked a little; for all the good it would have done him.

Swinging his legs round and lying down, Dave tried to banish all thoughts of Julian, Sheila or Tim, and concentrate on something that would turn his miserable mood around. It only took a few seconds for an alluring image of Amanda-Jayne to form itself in his mind, and he was soon able to smile again. Now he had a definite future in mind for himself, and it was one in which Sheila played no part. Tonight felt like it was the beginning of the end, he conceded, before reaching over to turn off the side lamp. There was not a sound coming from upstairs; it was quite obvious to him that his wife didn't care a damn where he bedded down for the night, and had clearly gone to sleep herself, no doubt to dream of her triumph against Tim. Had she come down and asked him to join her upstairs, then there may have been scope for forgiveness, but not now, he concluded; it was too late.

Dave emptied his mind as best he could and then shut his eyes. There was little traffic noise coming from the bypass several hundred yards away, but in the distance, a freight train horn sounded, so he lay there and listened as the noise of the diesel engine growled away into the night. His last conscious thought was for Tim, and whether he'd made it home safely by then.

Dave Darwin slowly opened his eyes and soon felt that initial confusion one experiences when waking up in strange surroundings. This was not his bedroom; it was the lounge, but why? It was then that Dave remembered. But what was it that had woken him up: the low autumnal sun streaming through the wide gap in the curtains, or the persistently ringing telephone. The telephone? Bleary eyed, and still a little disorientated, he groped his way out to the hall in order to answer it.

'Is that Mr Darwin?' enquired a strange authoritarian sounding male.

Dave tried to concentrate, and clear his head.

'Err, *yes*…speaking,' he muttered, sounding somewhat croaky.

'Ah *good*, this is Canterbury Police Station, Desk Sergeant Marlowe speaking. *Sorry* to have troubled you so early on a Sunday morning!' the caller exclaimed; now in a much more jovial manner.

It was a voice that Dave was beginning to recognise, but he couldn't quite place it for the moment. Nevertheless, an adrenalin surge of fear now coursed through his chest.

'Umm ... what can I do for you?' he asked, feeling more alert by the second, and expecting to hear Tim's name at any second.

'The thing *is* sir ... we have in custody here, one Timothy Malcolm Cross! I understand he's *still* a friend of yours?' the dour officer enquired, in an almost avuncular style.

The identity of the caller finally clicked into place.

'Yes Sergeant, he *is* still a friend of mine and he's *still* a lot a trouble!' Dave responded rather wearily, trying to stifle a yawn. His initial reaction was one of relief; he thought he was going to be told that Tim had been killed, or worse still, had killed someone else. But no, thank goodness, that was not the case. However, he soon found out that the call had an unexpected sting in the tale.

'Mr Darwin, when it's convenient, I'd like you to come down to the station,'

Sergeant Marlowe announced, in slightly more obsequious tones. 'We need someone to stand surety for him, and...umm, also take 'im *home*! You see; his vehicle has been impounded. *T*hat wife of his doesn't want to know, his parents don't live locally, and his uncle, who *does* live locally, is away on holiday. So it seems that you're all he's *got*!'

'Oh well, I'd better get *down* there then ... no doubt I'll see you in a short while sergeant!' Dave said, before replacing the receiver, and then heaving a long frustrated sigh.

Dave stood in the middle of the hall and stretched wearily. He felt dirty and unshaven; his trousers felt damp and clingy, as they always did if you slept in them, and his bladder was full to bursting. A quick trip to the downstairs cloakroom took care of the last-mentioned concern, but he also had to tidy up before leaving the house and that meant the daunting prospect of going upstairs. But then he told himself: why be afraid of Sheila anymore? This was meant to be the new Dave, for goodness sake; the one with the possible escape route in the form of a beautiful young admirer, whom he dearly loved. Buoyed up by that positive thought, he happily leapt up those stairs two at a time.

At that moment, his wife came out of the bedroom and confronted him on the landing: her tried and tested battlefield.

'*So*, you've got to go down to the police station and collect Tim then!' she declared coldly, drawing her dressing gown tightly round her stout torso.

'You were bloody well *listening in*!' he accused crossly, almost goading her into starting a row.

'The phone woke me up, and I happened to answer it at the same time as you; *that's* all!' Sheila countered, in a flat matter of fact manner. 'I suppose you'd better get cleaned *up* then!' she suggested haughtily, before standing aside to finally let him into their bedroom.

As Dave went through as instructed, he was surprised that his wife hadn't seemed to have wanted a row. Perhaps she was saving it until the crisis was over, he speculated; after all, Sheila did like to let things simmer, and him, suffer.

Not only were the Sunday morning roads very quiet, but also Dave easily found a visitor parking space at the police station. As he locked the car, he noticed Tim's camper van in the firmly gated enclosure behind; its offside door and adjacent panelling both badly damaged. He wandered into the building through the swing doors, and immediately encountered the station's enquiry desk and waiting area, which was a rather grim place. Every inch of the wall surface was covered in printed notices warning of pickpockets, car thieves and house burglars; it was enough to turn the average man into a paranoid wreck. There were also many colourful pictorial posters, and one in particular, which showed the photo of a pretty young girl who had been missing from home for two weeks, quite unexpectedly engendered an emotional reaction from him. A discarded burger carton, a screwed up paper cup on the floor and the unmistakable stench of vomit, were all compelling evidence to suggest that Saturday night in here, had been a lot busier than it was now.

A familiar-looking middle-aged uniformed policeman, with a rather large moustache, approached the desk from the other side. He was too engrossed in the document he was carrying to allow the merest hint of a glance in Dave's direction. Eventually though, the officer looked up and tried to focus his eyes on the human shape that was silhouetted against the bright sun streaming in through the plate glass frontage.

'Hello, I'm Dave Darwin,' Dave said . 'You rang me earlier about Tim Cross?'

The sergeant leaned over the counter and his demeanour changed immediately upon recognising him.

'We must stop *meeting* like this sir, tongues will wag!' the droll officer exclaimed, as he flicked through the book on the front desk. 'Ah *yes*, here he is ... *Campervan-Man*! Believe it or not, he was brought in here following a citizen's arrest!' the sergeant added, with his bushy eyebrows raised.

Dave learned that, having collided with a pedestrian traffic island just beyond the Sturry level crossing, Tim continued to drive in a very erratic manner, along the main road to Thanet. Two other motorists, who had been following him, actually managed to force the campervan off the road just beyond Hersden, for fear that he might kill someone or even himself. They then held him there until the police arrived.

'We need more decent people like that, don't you agree, sir?' the officer asked, almost rhetorically.

'Yes, *absolutely*!' Dave replied, regretting his own inability, or even lack of effort, in stopping Tim himself.

'What I *don't* understand, Mr Darwin, is that if he was driving a Dormobile and had obviously had a skin full, why he didn't just find a lay-by and go to sleep in the back? *That's* what those vehicles are for, is it *not*?'

In response, Dave shrugged his shoulders and grinned somewhat feebly. He didn't want to say that the same thought had occurred to him the previous evening, for it would mean admitting that he and Tim had been together, and that might in turn lead to accusations of allowing a drunk and incapable man of driving home alone. It may not be a criminal offence, but it was certainly morally irreprehensible.

Still glowing with guilt, Dave waited whilst Sergeant Marlowe unlocked a side door, so that he could be taken down to the cells, where Tim was being held.

'*This* way sir,' Sergeant Marlowe beckoned, as he studied a clipboard he had now acquired.

'Thank you,' Dave replied, as he watched the door being shut and firmly locked behind him. He was then led along a narrow, deserted corridor, from which a number of empty offices led off.

'I hope you don't mind me *asking* you this, Mr Darwin,' the officer said, after a few paces, 'but are you any relation?'

'*Yes*, Ronnie Darwin was my uncle!' Dave responded brightly, with his favourite mantra.

'And a very funny man he was *too* sir!' Marlowe beamed from behind his moustache. 'Although I seem to remember a bit of a fall from grace ... with a young *girl,* wasn't it?'

'Yes, that's *right* I'm afraid, sergeant,' Dave responded, with a tinge of regret. 'It's a shame he neglected to ask her how *old* she was!'

'Mind you sir, *I'm* always being asked that,' the sergeant commented, smoothing down the corners of his tache.

'What, your *age*?' Dave asked, puzzled, as they descended a concrete flight of steps.

'*No*, no, my *name*,' his companion chuckled. 'With *my* name, I'm always being asked if *I'm* any relation. The trouble is, I can't tell if they mean Phillip or Christopher Marlowe!'

Dave chuckled empathically. 'With *me*, I always have to ask myself: do they mean Ronnie or *Charles* Darwin!' he said, recognising a kindred spirit in the middle-aged policeman.

'Well it could be *worse* I suppose, sir,' his newfound friend remarked, with eyes both narrowed and twinkling. '*Imagine*, there's probably some poor sod out there called Colin Hitler, who's being asked all the *time* if he's any relation!'

'No doubt,' Dave responded; his laughter echoing round the plainly painted, yet brilliantly lit subterranean passage in which he now found himself.

The policeman soon stopped by the second of four ironclad doors, peered through the little swing-covered hatch, and then untangling his bunch of keys, unlocked it with a resounding clonk.

'*Here* he is, sir,' the sergeant announced, beckoning him to the cell door, 'Jackie Stewart with a bad headache and, judging by the atmosphere in here, incurable flatulence!'

Dave approached the opening somewhat gingerly and then peered into the room.

'*Blimey*, it's a bit *bright* in there isn't it?' he squinted, having only caught a brief glimpse of Tim. 'How can they *sleep* like that?'

'They probably *can't* ... unless of course, they've had a skin full like *him*!' the officer replied, as he approached a panel of switches on the corridor wall. 'But on the *other* hand, it means that *we* can see what they're up to, and not doing …umm, something silly!' He then flicked one of the switches. 'But *there* you go; that should return things to what that twit of an inspector calls: *daylight mode*!' He chuckled again before briefly placing a hand on Dave's shoulder. 'I'll be back in a minute, once I've found the release papers,' he added, before walking off in the same direction from which they'd come.

Dave once more peered into the cell, and was now able to see Tim quite clearly, even though the only available light seemed to be that which was seeping in from the corridor. He was sitting quietly in the middle of the fold-down bed, and blinking his eyes rapidly as they adjusted to the lower light level. The friends acknowledged each other with a raising of the eyebrows and a brief nod. Dave sat down next to the hung-over jailbird without a word, and then looked around the small cell. There wasn't much to see except a rudimentary table against the far wall, above which, the small emergency back-up light still shone red in the gloom.

Tim soon joined him in a visual scan of the small room.

'When I was *first* put in here last night, before the *torture* lights came on, I thought that I was in that chapel we used to go to in the cathedral crypt!' Tim said, finally breaking the silence.

'*Yes*, I can appreciate why this cell would remind you of the Chapel of the Holy Innocents,' Dave replied, before a wry smile broke across his face, 'but in your case, I don't think you are *wholly innocent* ... d'you get it?'

Tim winced and shook his head, but then couldn't help but respond in like manner.

'Well, if I'm not innocent, why did the policeman say: *halo, halo, halo*, when he arrested me?'

They both laughed loudly, but more by way of a release of tension than it was an appreciation of the terrible puns. The laughter having died down, there was a long silent pause before Tim explained exactly what had happened to him the night before. His tone was very matter of fact, almost as if he was describing going down to the newsagents to buy a paper. Surprisingly, he had felt quite relieved when the two concerned motorists had pulled him over, and then sat there with him on the grass verge, each holding one of his arms, as they all waiting for the police to come.

'D'you know, Dave, one of them even said to me that if I had such a death wish, why didn't I just stay at home, take some tablets and kill myself *that* way, rather than risk the lives of innocent motorists!'

'What did you say in reply to *that*?' Dave asked with a mixture of shock and interest.

'I had to *agree* with him,' his friend responded, with an expansive hand gesture, before turning the corners of his mouth down.

The sound of echoing footsteps in the corridor outside could now be heard, and then grew steadily louder.

'Look out, here comes the verger,' Tim smiled, followed by a series of chuckles from Dave.

Sergeant Marlowe soon appeared at the cell's open doorway.

'*Okay* then gentlemen, come this way please,' he requested, gesturing in the direction of the staircase with both arms.

The two friends followed him back upstairs, and soon found themselves on the police side of the station desk.

'*Right* then, Mr Cross, you are now being released into the custody of Mr Darwin here, but you must return back here to Canterbury Police Station on Monday morning at 10:00, to be formally charged. Failure to do so would result in your *immediate* arrest ... now did you *understand* all that?' Sergeant Marlowe said, peering across at Tim from the top of his eyes.

'Yes, I understand!' mumbled the accused, staring down at his feet like a chastened schoolboy in the headmaster's office. It was at this point that Tim finally and fully realised the likely consequences of his actions. He was to be charged with several offences; the details of which would be spelt out to him the following day. There would inevitably be a court appearance – date to be set – and he knew that the prognosis was not good. He would likely be fined; probably banned from driving and worst of all, lose the use of his Dormobile van. This was not only his sole source of transport, but also his planned future home, which he had not, as yet, got round to insuring. And he hadn't even begun to think about how Telecom would view this latest incident. They had been good to him so far; he was still on fully paid sick leave, which was just as well, as the maintenance payments to Alison were absolutely crippling, as was his bill at the wine merchants.

Tim said little on the journey home to Margate; he was too deeply immersed in his own thoughts. Dave desperately tried to search for positive things for Tim to home in on, but it was not easy. For example, he pointed out that once the dust had settled, Tim could quite easily get himself a new girlfriend. He further claimed that there was more than one woman at Telecom whose eye he'd caught, but he would obviously have to get his act together first, or at least get that front tooth fixed. To reinforce his point, Dave was right on the verge of telling him about Amanda-Jayne, but something held him back at the last minute.

No train hampered their progress at Sturry level crossing, and just beyond that, Dave couldn't help but notice the bent lamppost and shattered directional beacons of the pedestrian island that Tim had collided with the night before.

As they pulled up outside Tim's house, Dave immediately saw the 'sold' notice by the front gate. And then, as they both got out, he noticed that the front garden was a neglected jungle. Worst of all, lying by the front path, amongst the nettles, were the broken pieces of a wood-chipboard veneered bookcase. It prompted him to recall that heavy drinking session back in the summer, when Tim claimed to have sold some books to enable him to finance the binge.

The inside of the property was airless and squalid; it almost seemed like someone had died. Cardboard boxes full of empty bottles were evident in the hall, as was a pile of ignored free newspapers by the front door. In the two livingrooms, Dave noticed huge dusty voids where, no doubt, furniture had either been sold for more drinks money, or collected by Alison for her use elsewhere. Unwashed plates, cups and empty beer cans seemed to occupy every available surviving surface. And where were all of Tim's precious books, wondered Dave: had he really sold them all? The saddest sight of all was to be found on the small coffee table next to Tim's food-stained armchair. Dave noticed that a Polaroid photograph had been used as an impromptu drinks mat. He lifted up the empty glass, and the picture came with it; it was firmly stuck to the base. However, Dave could see enough of the picture's glossy surface to discern that it was an image of two children: it was one of Tim's missing pictures, the ones that Alison had recently sent him, only for them to be quickly mislaid. Each time Tim had drained that glass, had he noticed the image of Henry and Phillipa staring plaintively back at him through the slops and the froth, or had he assumed the sight to be merely a manifestation of his alcohol befuddled brain? As thirsty men in the desert see mirages of watery wadis or tree-lined oases, had he written off the image of his children as nothing more than a poignant representation of his heart's dearest wish?

'The new people will be in next weekend!' Tim announced suddenly, as he stood impassively amongst the ruins of his home and marriage.

'But where will you *go* ... what will you *do*?' Dave asked, in genuine distress; an emotion exacerbated by the sure and certain knowledge that any remaining chance that Sheila might have let Tim stay with them, however remote, had been utterly eradicated the previous evening. And of course, the Dormobile was no longer an option, what with all that damage; not to mention the impending driving ban.

'Don't worry,' Tim responded impassively, as he motioned to usher Dave out. 'Uncle Stephen is back from Tuscany next week, I think. *He'll* be able to sort out all the police business ... he's a *solicitor,* you know ... perhaps he'd even lend me some more money *as well*!'

Dave was more than happy to leave the house, a property that exactly matched its owner in both squalor and degradation. However, he was not happy to leave his friend in such a hopeless situation.

'Look Tim, why don't you come over for dinner next week?' he offered, before placing a supportive hand on his friend's slumped shoulder.

'Are you *serious*?' Tim looked at Dave as if he had gone mad and that Saturday night had not happened.

'No, it's *alright* mate,' Dave retorted, as soon as he understood the reason for his friend's reaction. 'Sheila will be away on a Telecom management course. Come on *Thursday* evening; we'll have the place to ourselves and I'm *sure* we'll be able to work something out, *you* know ... think of a way forward for you!'

'Okay,' Tim replied, with a faint smile, and the briefest shrug of the shoulders, as they wandered up the garden path together.

'*Good*; it's a date!' Dave enthused; pleased to have been able to help his friend, and thereby ease his own conscience. 'I'll telephone you on Wednesday to confirm, and then come over and pick you up after work, the following day ... okay?'

'Okay,' Tim responded, with the same level of enthusiasm with which he had given the previous answer.

Having walked back up the front path, and past the unhappy reminder of Tim's lost library, the two friends stood by the front gate and the moment seemed frozen in time.

'Okay then, mate ... see you soon,' Dave said, half questioning, half exclaiming, as an unexpected wave of emotion washed over him.

An unsmiling Tim nodded and then, without a word, wandered back along the path, without noticing the shattered remains of his bookcase.

Dave waved in the Darwin manner as he pulled away, but his friend just stood there, motionless and emotionless, in the open doorway. And then, as he proceeded down the road, he felt that lump forming in his throat again.

'We'll think of a way forward for you, my old mate,' he vowed out loud to himself.

Dave looked back, as the car slowly turned left at the junction, and watched as Tim disappeared from view.

Mounting Expectations

Monday morning misery once more engulfed him. Telecom customer relations were getting no better, and Dave knew that if he wanted to live to a ripe old age, he would have to find some way of getting out of there, and yet still have enough money to be able to buy his plants, books and CDs. That was a pretty tall order, he thought grimly, as the incoming calls continued without pause; but sooner or later, it would have to happen if he were to avoid the sort of stress that cut short his father's own Telecom career.

At just after 09:45, Dave took a much-needed toilet break and further dwelt on the problem of getting out of Telecom. Nothing short of a pools win, or a large inheritance, could help him achieve his objective, he decided reluctantly, staring at the speckled-paint wall décor of the gents. The trouble was, he had no rich elderly relatives; in fact, Dave had no rich relatives at all. Years ago, he recalled that there had been talk of a very obscure but moneyed relative of Nanna Darwin, who had once asked her and Grandad down to visit for the day. Apparently, this relative had married into the minor Kentish Wealden aristocracy and, by all accounts, was very well off indeed. His grandparents went, out of curiosity, and subsequently, further invitations had been forthcoming. However, Grandad Darwin, being a modest, uncomplicated man of simple pleasures and nonconformist beliefs, had not wished to hobnob, or be seen to be hobnobbing, so the connection was gradually lost.

Inheriting wealth was one possible route of escape barred to him, but what about the other? Sadly, as far as the pools were concerned, the lines of the office syndicate had been checked first thing that morning and nothing had come up; not even anything close. Therefore, Dave had to accept that there would be at least one more week to have to put up with at Telecom.

To make matters worse, that Monday morning had not got off to the best of starts. Sheila's threatened row, postponed from the weekend, had still not happened, but the prospect of it hung ominously pall-like in the air. However, as far as Dave was concerned, something else definitely *had* occurred, and that was the beginning of the end of their marriage. Quite clearly, the ceasefire between them, which had been in effect for much of the year, was now unequivocally over. Since that last incident with Tim, Sheila had maintained a frosty persona and the journey in to work that morning had been particularly tense. However, this treatment no longer hurt him as it was intended to do, and he made no attempts to appease her, as he once might have done. This, in turn, had chilled his wife's mood into glacial proportions.

Coming back from the loo, and then looking around the office, Dave thought of a thousand other things he'd rather be doing, or places he would rather be, than taking complaint calls from whingeing losers and dotty old ladies. Having sunk back into the chair at his desk, he began to fantasise about his life's ideal scenario:

There he was, somewhere within his lush two-acre garden, which would be bordered on all sides by high hawthorn hedges, and situated right in the middle of the Kentish countryside. No doubt, he would be in the throes of creating the most sumptuous cottage and wild flower garden possible. In the middle of this controlled wilderness, would be situated an ancient Rothermead style cottage, with a much older cellar and later extensions including a lean-to greenhouse, or even a conservatory on the south side. In the kitchen, contentedly baking homemade bread in the Rayburn, would be Amanda-Jayne in a long thin cotton dress, having just discovered that she was pregnant with their third child. Tim, a successful if somewhat eccentric writer, would then pay an unannounced visit, as he was wont to do. Amanda-Jayne would bring them out some chilled elderflower wine, which she had made herself, and the two friends would chat from the deck chairs in the middle of a daisy-covered lawn, whilst the children played around them. She would then stand behind him, occasionally smoothing down his long thick hair and kissing the top of his head, as Tim talked enthusiastically about his latest novel. Later on, as she drifted back into the cottage, to make their dinner: a gorgeous lamb casserole with caraway seed dumplings, Tim would watch her disappear and then state with envy what a fortunate man Dave was to have all this, and such a beautiful young wife to share it with.

'Excuse me Dave...*Mr Darwin*, there's a call waiting in the queue,' Darryl Giles declared, as he leaned out of the doorway of his office.

The untimely intervention brought him back to earth, reality and the bitter awareness of his dull, repetitive and utterly futile career. He then flicked the switch to take the call in question.

'Telecom, Customer Relations, Dave Darwin speaking.'

'Dave *Darwin*, any relation?' came a familiar female voice in response, followed by peals of high-pitched laughter. It was Amanda-Jayne and she was on a half-term break.

'Oh, I *do* love your telephone voice, David,' she purred, having altered her own voice to a much lower pitch, '*very* sexy!'

'Thank you…err, madam ... it's nice to be receiving a compliment for once,' he responded, attempting to maintain an air of normality, so as not to attract the attentions of either Monica or Tiffany.

'I've been thinking of the wonderful summer we had together Dave, and I *am* missing you today!' she said, in an alluring half-whisper. There seemed to be a new tone in her voice, a hint of sultriness somehow.

Dave had long wanted the relationship to develop further and to him, this was a very good portent. Maybe, just maybe, the time had finally come, he speculated excitedly. Perhaps now, Amanda-Jayne was actually indicating that she was ready for them to begin expressing their love for each other in a more physical way. If that was the case, then he *had* to see her as soon as possible; he had to be with her in order to exploit and enjoy this new development. However, by implication, the meeting had to be in a much more intimate setting than their usual arrangement, but where? It was then that he remembered Sheila's course, and the fact she would be away for three days and two nights towards the end of the week. Amanda-Jayne could come to the house for dinner; it would be just the two of them.

Dave had been bragging to Amanda-Jayne about his culinary expertise for months, which in reality was a well practised half-a-dozen or so dishes that he could do blindfolded. So which one would it be: chilli, lasagne, his new ginger and lamb curry, bean and pepper hotpot, chicken cacciatore, or a roast? He quickly ruled out the last one, as everything was ready at the same time; inevitably leading to blind panic at the serving up stage, and anyone who knew Dave would attest to the fact that he could pass an A-level in panicking.

The next problem he needed to think about was how to propose this evening of sustenance and seduction to Amanda-Jayne. Dave decided that an evolved man would be honest about the circumstances; he would tell Amanda-Jayne that Sheila would be away and they could be alone together, with some wine, soothing music, good food and a warm house, all completely safe from prying eyes. Surely the teenager would know what that meant if she accepted his invitation! But even if she was unsure as to what to expect, Dave recognised that now was the time for taking risks, otherwise their relationship would continue on the same platonic level, wonderful though that was. There was no doubt in his mind: they had to move on to the next stage and become a proper couple, and as far as he was concerned, there was no longer any moral impediment why either he or Amanda-Jayne should hold back. Effectively, he and Sheila were now finished as an item. The last spark had been extinguished less than 48 hours ago, when she metaphorically kicked the blind beggar; when she maliciously made Tim feel even more wretched than he already did. He would make all this clear to Amanda-Jayne on the planned evening alone together; he would be honest about it, and do things by the book, in order to let Amanda-Jayne make informed decisions about their future together.

'Hello, *hello*, David…are you still there?' came the same familiar, beloved voice from the telephone receiver.

'Oh *sorry*, I was thinking, umm…I was just thinking about asking you round to dinner; I mean a *proper* intimate dinner with wine, soft music and candles that is,' he proposed, thus setting the whole thing in motion.

'Yes, I'd *love* to,' the teenager enthused, with unambiguous delight. 'Our first *meal* together; gosh, how *thrilling*!'

Dave went on to give her all the details about his plan for an intimate meal together at his place and left nothing out, short of asking her if he needed to buy condoms. Whilst doing so, he pretended to be tapping away on his computer keyboard, like all the other Telecom automatons in his vicinity. Fortunately, her reaction continued to be positive; she was looking forward to it, and if it was just the two of them, then so much the better. Moreover, it would give her the chance to wear a dress he'd not seen before. Dave was absolutely intrigued; it was all going far better than he could have possibly hoped. All that remained was to decide which evening she could come

'Now Sheila's going away first thing on Wednesday morning, and she'll be back Friday evening, so when do you fancy coming?' he asked, pretending to look something up on the screen.

'*Now* then, I can't make it on Wednesday,' she said, thinking aloud. 'I have a rehearsal for Handel's Solomon; I've got one of the soprano leads and can't miss it, I'm afraid. So, it will have to be *Thursday* evening.'

'So Thursday it *is* then,' Dave said, thrilled, 'I wouldn't want you to miss your rehearsal!'

'And can we have your cacciatore?' she requested, with genuine excitement coming through in her voice.

'I don't see why not!'

'Oh *good*, it sounds delicious, as does the wine!'

'So, shall I come and pick you up then?'

'Best *not*, eh ... I'll get a taxi.'

'Okay then, but what will you tell your…'

'I'll simply tell Mum that I'm coming to dinner with *all* of you; she'll be none the wiser!'

'*Brilliant*…seven o'clock alright with you?'

'Perfect! *So* then…see you Thursday, bye-bye David.'

'Umm ... goodbye Miss Roper, and thank you for your enquiry.' He heard the sound of Amanda-Jayne giggling as she replaced the receiver.

The call having ended, Dave drifted off into myriad fantasies concerning their planned Thursday evening together. The best of these culminated in a naked Amanda-Jayne sitting astride him on the settee, with his hands outstretched to fondle her breasts, as she rode him all the way to heaven. In the meantime, the incoming calls stacked up in the queue quite disregarded.

There seemed to be more complaining customers than usual that Monday, but this was an illusion brought on by the higher than normal number of absentees in the office. Dave looked at the empty space opposite him and thought of Tim, who was one of them. He knew his friend would be formally charged, that very morning, with a number of motor-related offences, including that of driving under the influence of alcohol, alcohol that Dave had served him. And then, there would be a court date hanging over Tim; it was the very last thing he needed. Fortunately, no one in the office seemed to know what had happened at the weekend, but judging by the way these things usually got around Telecom, Dave realised it would not be long before all the office gossips were talking about their absent colleague. Sheila wouldn't be able to resist spreading the word herself, given half the chance, especially if it showed her in a good light. Nevertheless, whatever his friend was charged with, whatever gossip went round the office, Dave could at least draw comfort from the fact that he and Tim would be able to thrash it out together on Thursday evening.

Dave suddenly gasped audibly, and also screwed his eyes up tight when the awful realisation hit him – a blow felt in the pit of his stomach – that he had double-booked himself. The panic, however, was short-lived when, having thought through all the alternative options, he decided that Tim's visit could simply be moved to Wednesday. For Dave, it would be a busy social period, but no less welcome for that.

After work that evening, Sheila surprised Dave in no less than three ways. Firstly, she turned up at the car at precisely five o'clock, which was actually a whole minute before Dave could manage it – he could see her climbing into the car, as he descended the stairwell. Secondly, rather than row about Tim, she actually asked about him; she enquired about the police charges he was likely to face, and what the likely outcome would be. It suited Dave's current mindset to believe that her interest was merely morbid curiosity and that she would no doubt derive some sense of cruel satisfaction at the knowledge of his friend's inevitable undoing. He could hate her even more then, and further justify the extramarital ecstasy he had planned for later in the week. But in all honesty, he had to concede that his wife's interest, if not quite concern, was nonetheless genuine.

Sheila's third and final surprise, perhaps the most astonishing of all, was saved by her until after dinner, when Dave was relaxing with a glass of whisky, and she, her ubiquitous cigarette. To her husband's utter amazement, Sheila expressed her regret at not having handled the situation on Saturday night a little differently. As always, her pride would not allow her to actually apologise, but she did admit that her attitude probably contributed to the evening's eventual outcome. However, the coup de grace was her explanation of why she had said what she'd said, and in doing so, his wife cleverly justified her behaviour by turning things around. Sheila's reasoning went something like this: would Dave have reacted any differently, if the drunkard smashing up *his* home and insulting him to *his* face, had been Julian or one of his friends? Dave was forced to admit that, given the same set of circumstances, he would probably have behaved in much the same way as she had. And yes, perhaps she had been a little unkind, Sheila conceded, but at the end of the day, we were all human and no one could guarantee to react in the correct or appropriate manner every time, especially given sufficient provocation. Her husband could not disagree; she had made her case well, and he could find nothing to come back at her with, in any respect. However, Dave thought to himself that, given the same situation, he would probably not have been so premeditatively cruel.

Dave had found the whole discussion regarding Tim, profoundly irritating. At any other time before that summer, he would have considered such a conciliatory conversation with his wife as a good reason for a celebratory drink or meal. But now, Amanda-Jayne was in his life, and it was almost as if he wanted to find reasons to hate Sheila. Ceasing to love her, as he now had, was no longer enough. Indeed, for him and Amanda-Jayne to progress in their relationship, he had to be completely rid of this marriage. However, such a major change like that was a very scary prospect for Dave; he knew that only too well, having been there once before with Chloe. It was for this reason that learning to hate his wife had now become a priority. If it were crystal clear in his mind that Sheila was a complete and irredeemably hateful bitch, who had no concerns for himself, his family or his friends, then it would be far easier for him to justify leaving her. Indeed, it was already the case that she put Julian and her career before him and his needs. On the other hand though, they still laughed together, enjoyed the garden with each other, and regularly dined with friends together. In addition, she was being as supportive as her character would allow, where Grandad Darwin's rapidly failing health was concerned. But given the present set of circumstances, this was no longer enough for him. Dave now recognised that he could have all that *and* so much more with Amanda-Jayne. But for him and Sheila, everything that was really important in a marriage had gone, if it was ever there in the first place. The patient was breathing, but brain death had occurred, and yet, he still hadn't the courage to switch off the life support machine.

Later that evening, Sheila suggested that Dave phone Tim and find out how he had got on at the police station. He thought it was a good idea, especially as the busy Monday hadn't allowed him any scope to call before. Dave went through to the hall and rang as suggested, but there was no reply.

Whereas Monday had been full of surprises, Tuesday turned out to be a day for irony. Firstly, Sheila was on time for going home again; a fact that Dave found profoundly annoying. It simply wasn't good enough, he thought on the drive home . His wife putting her career before him, was one of the foundation blocks upon which he was building his justification for considering their marriage a spent force. If she wasn't going to stay late anymore and do extra work, then that was something he would have to cross off his list of reasons to hate her. However, on reflection, he thought it might be a little premature to get the pencil out; after all, it had only been two nights of getting home on time and as they say, one swallow doesn't make a summer, even in mid-autumn.

Then, there was the Tuesday evening meal. Sheila made a superb lamb casserole with caraway seed dumplings, which was rather ironic considering his utopian Amanda-Jayne fantasy from the previous day. Nevertheless, the dinner was delicious and the wine, plentiful. And what made matters worse was that throughout it all, they were getting on so very well. What was happening, Dave thought; why was Sheila being so nice to him? Although he was not giving her any reason to be angry with him, he wasn't making any particular effort to get along with her either. He was no longer walking on eggshells around her, or minding his p's and q's whenever they talked. But therein could lie the ultimate irony, Dave pondered as he sipped his after-dinner whisky, having been excused washing up duties. Was the very fact that he was no longer making an effort any more, actually causing Sheila to over-compensate, in order to maintain that period of mutual non-aggression they had enjoyed since June? Another explanation could be to do with the fact that, in the past, Dave's desperation to say the right thing during disagreements, difficult situations, or just plain normal conversations, had often made matters worse. Could it be that his current verbal indifference and, therefore, lack of foot-in-mouth disease, was making things seem better between them? Unwittingly, he was improving their marriage by caring less about it: the ultimate in ironies! As the old adage had it - if one picked at a scab, the wound took longer to get better. He began to wonder: was that the solution? Perhaps now was the time to forget indifference and start getting nasty; begin opening up those old wounds instead. If the patient died of its injuries, then there would be no need for him to turn off the life support machine.

Sheila brought through a tray of coffee and liqueur chocolates and, giving him a sweet smile, suggested that it might be a good idea if he tried to contact Tim again. Dave looked at the lounge clock: it was just after nine, and wasn't too late, so he agreed, for they both wanted to find out how he'd faired with the Canterbury police. Dave also had another reason for wanting to contact his friend: he needed to change their dinner date from Thursday to Wednesday; to tomorrow in fact, and he hadn't been able to get hold of him at all during the day. With his wife in the house, he realised that he'd have to speak in code, especially if she came out to the hall with him, but she now had her nose in a large Telecom document, so the problem wouldn't be insurmountable. Frustratingly though, there was still no reply. Was he out, or was he out cold,

Dave wondered; could it be that his friend was lying in a drunken stupor and either unable, or unwilling to answer the phone? As he replaced the receiver, and slowly wandered back to the lounge, he felt a small surge of panic; time was running out. However, he calmed down by telling himself that there was still one more chance to rectify the matter; he would try and contact him one more time at work tomorrow, when Darryl Giles went out to the loo, or a meeting. If he could get hold of Tim by lunchtime and tell him of the change in dinner date, then it would still be okay. Sheila would be leaving for her course first thing in the morning and he could get all the shopping for the two dinners during his Wednesday lunch-hour. However, no matter how things panned out with Tim, he had already decided that cancelling on Amanda-Jayne was just not an option.

On Wednesday morning, Dave stood on the leaf-strewn green and waved as Sheila drove off in the office pool car. As soon as the vehicle was out of sight, he felt a thrill of excitement, and the keen anticipation that the next couple of days would be changing his life forever. Walking back to the house, Dave thought about phoning Tim before he left for work, but figured that if his friend had nothing to get up for, then he probably wouldn't be up yet. Dave resolved to call him at work as originally planned, and when the opportunity presented itself.

Darryl Giles left for a manager's meeting at 10:30, which gave Dave his first real opportunity to ring Tim, but his line was engaged. He was a little encouraged by this development, for at least it meant that his absent colleague was at home, and either making or receiving a call. And then, just after 11:00, Amanda-Jayne rang him; it was a brief but thrilling call, with the youthful excitement in her voice, a sheer joy to hear. She confirmed that the taxi would be picking her up at 19:00, as they had discussed, and she'd be with him around five minutes later. Her mother was aware that she was dining at the Darwins, so no lies had needed to be told. They managed to finish the conversation by exchanging discreet 'I love you' declarations.

Dave managed to find another chance to ring Tim just before he went to lunch, but the line was still engaged. This was particularly frustrating, as he was about to go out and get the shopping for both the hopefully rescheduled meal with Tim that evening, and Thursday's intimate evening with Amanda-Jayne. But now, not knowing the situation with his friend, or rather, Tim's not knowing that he'd been moved to Wednesday, Dave had no choice but to postpone his trip to Sainsbury's until after work; fingers-crossed that he would have contacted him by then. It would be a rush, but he could just about manage it.

At 15:15, when his manager called Monica in for her annual appraisal interview, Dave tried to ring Tim one more time, but got the engaged tone yet again. It soon occurred to him that the silly sod must have got drunk and not put the receiver back properly. On the other hand, he also considered the possibility that Tim was in lengthy conference with his rich Uncle Stephen, concerning another financial loan, his up and coming court case, or the problem of his having nowhere to live after Saturday, when the new people were due to move into his house. They certainly had a lot to talk about, he reasoned, and could quite easily explain why the phone was persistently engaged. Even so, this assumption didn't exactly assist Dave in his efforts to alter his dinner arrangements. Now it really was too late, he was forced to accept; the only option now left to him being to cancel Tim outright and then try to arrange a lunchtime pub meeting for early next week. But how would he let his friend know? It was then he remembered that Tiffany lived in Ramsgate and might be prepared to drop a note in at Tim's house on her way home, as the small estate where he lived, just outside Margate, was on her regular route. Fortunately, she agreed to help out, but only as long as she didn't have to hand it to him personally. Gossiping about someone's troubles in the office was one thing, but having to face a person in distress was another matter entirely.

The letter was hastily written and so Dave gave little thought to discretion. But then again, he reasoned that only his friend would be reading it, so there would be no problem if he were entirely and blatantly frank. He had to be completely honest, if only to justify messing Tim about like this at such short notice:

Dear Tim
You may be interested to know that the ringing noise in your head is not a hangover, but me trying to telephone you, you sozzled old bugger. And now you've knocked the bloody receiver off the hook; there really is no hope for you matey!
Anyway, this is just a note to say that I'm going to have to cancel you for Thursday evening. Sorry about this, but I do have a good reason and, I have to emphasize, you must keep this to yourself. For the last few months, I have been seeing this gorgeous young girl called Amanda-Jayne, and with Oedipus' mother away at the moment, she is coming round for dinner on Thursday, which is the only day she could make. There is a very good chance that, by the end of the evening, I'll have her playing 'horsey', if you get my meaning! Given the circs, I'm sure you'd do the same.
In all seriousness though, I think she really is the one this time.
So how about this then; next week, we will meet one lunchtime at the 'Olde City' and I'll tell you all about her and you can let me know what you and Uncle Stephen have managed to sort out re money, police, house, your bitch of an ex-wife etc, etc.
Tim, can you PLEASE ring me on Saturday or Sunday and let me know where you have ended up. Then, we can also firm up a date for next week. In the meantime, take it easy with the old demon drink.

Your shameless pal,

Dave.

After work that evening, Dave got the shopping in for the special dinner on Thursday, as well as some other items Sheila had asked him to buy for the weekend. He also picked up some fish and chips on his way home; a treat he'd not enjoyed for some years, and one that he had every intention of eating, not only straight out of the newspaper, but also in the lounge, and with plenty of ketchup too.

Later on, at about 20:30, with the odour of his supper still lingering in the lounge, the phone rang in the hallway.

'Ah, that must be Tim,' Dave said aloud to himself, getting up from the settee. 'He's got the note!'

He knew that any mention of Amanda-Jayne would have Tim on the phone straightaway, quite unable to wait until next week for more of the lurid details. And with Sheila away, he wouldn't have to concoct one of those cryptic discussions, full of over-emphasised '*yes's*' and '*no's*'. However, rather than Tim as expected, it was his father who had rung.

'*Hello* there, Dad ... nice to *hear* from you mate!' Dave said warmly.

'Hello Dave, *sorry* to ring you in the evening, son ... but I thought I ought to let you know that an old schoolmate of yours is trying to get in touch with you.'

'*Really*? I haven't heard a squeak from of any those blokes for *years*!'

'It *wasn't* a bloke, old chap, and *she* seemed very nice!' his father declared approvingly. 'Called herself Mrs Holroyd ... she knew all about you ... your schooldays at the Archbishop's ... your brother and sister, even your Uncle Ronnie, so I'm *sure* she's on the level.'

'Umm ... so what was her *first* name Dad ... or her maiden name?' a rather puzzled Dave enquired.

'Err ... *sorry* old boy, she either didn't say or I don't remember, but I *had* just got off the phone to Nanna Darwin and was a little, *you* know…unsettled.'

'I *see* ... so how *is* Grandad?' Dave asked, in a hushed slow voice.

'Not good I'm afraid,' his father replied, in grave tones. 'He felt too weak to get out of bed on Monday, and hasn't wanted to move from there since ... it can't be long now Dave!'

'*Look*, I'm so sorry, I just haven't been able to *get over* there to see him this week so far,' he confessed, suddenly overwhelmed by guilt.

'*Don't* be!' came the rapid reassuring response. 'You've done *more* than enough to help over these last months, especially encouraging Grandad Darwin and me to reconcile .... I'll *always* be grateful to you for that. *Anyway*, about this old friend of yours, I gave her your address and telephone number. Is that alright?'

'Yes, of *course,* Dad, that's fine. But if she *does* turn out to be gorgeous, I don't know *what* Sheila will say!' he speculated, in a half-serious manner.

'If she's *that* good looking Dave, ask her to ring *me* back then!' his father joked, with a chuckle that he quickly stifled.

'So, have you heard any news from Ed recently then, Dad ... you know, about all this house hunting business?' he asked, in a sudden change of tack.

'*Oh*, that *reminds* me, your younger brother is going to be joining Telecom as a middle manager, now that he's got his degree.'

'Umm, that's…that's *great*,' Dave replied, not wishing to deflate his father by saying that he already knew about his brother's dubious choice of employer.

'We're becoming a *right* old Telecom family,' Len said proudly, 'what with your sister being a 999 operator, at *least* until she has the baby, and James being an engineer ... not to *mention* you and Sheila!'

Dave was not proud of the fact, and couldn't be sure if his sister or brother-in-law took pride in 'the old firm' either, but he had never said as much to his father. Len wouldn't have understood, and more especially now, when he had so much on his mind.

'*Anyway* Dad ... thanks for the news, and be sure to let me know if there are any more…developments at Beltinge. Love to Mum ... *bye!*'

After the conversation ended, Dave pondered on the identity of the mystery woman who was trying to get hold of him. He remembered there being several very attractive girls who went through secondary school with him; ones whom he never had the courage to ask out, but no one came immediately to mind. Typical, just like London buses, he reflected, before once again running through his Amanda-Jayne fantasy for tomorrow night.

From the moment Dave woke up on Thursday morning, he was nervous. This state manifested itself in trembling, butterflies and massive surges of adrenalin whenever the reason for his condition was remembered. The night before had been little better, with a mind too active to be shut down and loins too active to ignore. But ignore them he did; he was saving himself for her.

During breakfast, he nearly jumped out of his skin when the phone rang. He prayed it wasn't Amanda-Jayne, with a change of mind or heart, and he hoped that it might be Tim in response to his note. It actually turned out to be Sheila, with her usual mid-course call home, to check that everything was okay. Checking up on *me* rather, he theorized, but this time with good cause.

Once Dave had got to work, things were no better. He could not concentrate, gabbled through his calls and said 'no' if anyone asked him if he was any relation. On more than one occasion, his manager had to tell him that there was a call in the queue. In fact, Dave was so preoccupied with the forthcoming evening that Tim was entirely forgotten. He did not try his home number, because he didn't think to do so.

Five o'clock took forever to arrive. The passage of time seemed not only to have halted, but also to be going backwards as well. But come it eventually did, and a highly-strung Dave drove home on autopilot. Just under two hours to prepare dinner and have a really good bath; no problem, he concluded, turning into his parking space at home.

As Dave dressed, he briefly considered wearing no underpants beneath his trousers, but dismissed the idea as rather too blatantly obvious. The last thing he wanted to do was give the impression that this was a planned seduction, by making too many assumptions. However, he did make sure to have a three-pack of condoms handy: an item that had been bought at the supermarket, along with the rest of the shopping, to reduce the usual embarrassment factor.

Having gone downstairs, and with the dinner well underway, his next task was to choose the appropriate ambient background music for the evening's events. *Enja* seemed suitably unchallenging, he decided, at the same time, wondering if anyone had ever tried making love to *Bitches Brew*.

With everything in the kitchen doing nicely, he went back upstairs to watch for the taxi from the bedroom window. From this vantage point, he could see that the remaining leaves on the sycamore were now nearly all of one rich golden colour. He also noticed that the tyre tracks around the tree's base, which had been created by Tim's Dormobile, were still very much in evidence. Moreover, it would appear that they had become useful conduits for the collection of those leaves that had already fallen. Abandoning his post for a few seconds, Dave dashed downstairs to pour the uncooked rice into the water, which had now reached boiling point, and then raced back upstairs to once more keep watch. It was only a few minutes to seven; she would be here soon, he enthused. He then checked his breath, yes; that was okay thank goodness. Knowing that there was only seconds to spare, he once more shot downstairs, put the music on, lit the candles on the dining room table and then raced back to his lookout point. It wasn't long before a pair of headlights blinked into view through the autumnal twilight. As the vehicle got closer, he could also make out an illuminated yellow sign in the centre of its roof: it was a taxi; it was her.

Dave didn't wait to watch her get out of the car, but instead dashed downstairs to his pre-arranged position in the hall. The doorbell soon rang out and he started to count to ten, as he'd planned beforehand, but ran to open the front door before getting to six. As he reached up to turn the catch, the adrenalin surge in the pit of his stomach was almost painful.

Amanda-Jayne stepped inside timidly, but he didn't want to look at her properly until he'd shut the door behind her, and she was safe and secure inside his sanctuary.

'Here I *am*!' she announced nervously, standing in the middle of the hallway, and bashfully studying her feet.

There she was indeed and, in his estimation, looking beautiful too. She was wearing a simple black, full-length evening dress – which to him, seemed just a little bit big for her – and a matching black wrap, which covered her shoulders and upper arms. As well as gripping the ends of the wrap tightly in both hands, she was also clutching a small silver oblong handbag in her right. He hair was pinned up and her face made up; neither of which, he had ever seen before.

'You look *stunning* my love!' he extolled, before reaching up to take her wrap.

However, she continued to hold it tightly.

'*No*, I'm leaving it on ... I've got fat arms,' she admitted bashfully, making brief eye contact with him.

'*Nonsense*,' Dave said, before gripping the garment at the back, and then pulling it off her body. She gave little resistance.

For Dave, the results were instantly gratifying, and despite her allusions to chubbiness, he thought her arms were lovely. Better still, he could now see that the dress was sleeveless, with thin shoulder straps and a plunging neckline to both front and back.

'Oh you are *beautiful*,' he reiterated, unashamedly admiring the tentative teenager from tip to toe.

'*Thank* you David,' she murmured, with a quivering smile, as large red blotches almost instantaneously appeared on her youthful cheeks and slender neck. She also lowered her head once more.

Dave stepped forward, placed both hands on her bare upper arms and then tenderly kissed the top of her head. She did not look up. They then embraced for a brief awkward moment; her arms slung only loosely round his torso. In spite of her uncharacteristic reluctance to make physical contact with him, he could still tell that her whole body was trembling. Was she really more nervous than he was? Dave was forced to wonder if, perhaps, this evening alone with him in his house was more of a big deal for her than he had anticipated. With that very much in mind, he decided to back off for a while and give her some breathing space.

Slowly releasing his grip of the tense teenager, he went to throw her wrap over the newel post of the banister. As he turned back in Amanda-Jayne's direction, she accidentally dropped her handbag. Quickly bending forward to pick it up, the loose bodice of her dress gaped open at the front and, for a short time, Dave could see her breasts fully exposed; that is until she straightened up again. Her breasts were small, but firm-looking and beautifully shaped; they were quite unlike the sagging stretchy udders his wife possessed. The sexual tension he was now experiencing was almost overwhelming, but he knew that tearing off her dress and making love to her on the hall carpet, right there and then, was just not an option, at least for the moment.

It wasn't long before Amanda-Jayne noticed the increase in his breathing rate.

'Are you nervous?' she asked hesitantly, but hopefully.

'Yes, *lots*!' he replied with a breathy chuckle.

'Oh *good*, me too!' she smiled with relief, pressing a flattened hand against her bosom. She then ran forward and flung her arms around him with all the old enthusiasm restored. It was as if his admission had put them back on an even keel again; he was no longer the seducer, and she the innocent victim. It made them equals in edgy excitability, ahead of whatever the evening might throw at them.

As she buried her head ever deeper into his chest, Dave gently caressed both the curves of her waist, and the small of her back. He then dared to move his hands just a bit lower than he ever had before and slowly traced the gentle-valleyed recess at the top of her bottom with his finger. She did not resist, but purred appreciatively, as she always had at such moments in the Greyfriars gardens.

Although things were now going very much more in the direction he'd hoped, Dave realised that he would have to slow down a little; they were both still nervous wrecks. In any case, he had always envisaged an after-dinner seduction, both in the warm glow of the lounge and their own alcoholic consumption.

Having shared a brief kiss on the lips, Amanda-Jayne followed her host and boyfriend through to the lounge, and immediately looked about herself in wonder.

'Oh *David*, this is your *home* ... I *know* I've been here before, but it's…it's almost like I'm seeing it now for the first *time*!' she declared almost rapturously, before hurrying from one piece of furniture to another.

'I'm so glad you like it ... there's a lot of *me* in this room!' he responded with genuine affection, and hands on his hips, as he looked about him and tried to see things as she might.

'Yes…that's what *I* feel ... this is…this is your *sanctuary* from the rest of the world, *isn't* it David!' she remarked, with spookily accurate insight that he found wonderfully gratifying.

Dave would love to have stayed with her and explained the family links behind all his things, but knew that his presence was required in the kitchen.

'I say my love; why don't you pour us some wine, sit down and relax, whilst I go and see to the dinner, okay?' he proposed, whilst gesturing towards the open bottle and glasses waiting on the coffee table, before beaming broadly at her.

'Don't be *long* then!' she replied, with a seductive tinge in her voice, and a crooked smile, before bending to pick up the claret.

Dave lingered long enough to catch another glimpse of her beautiful bosom before withdrawing.

Once he'd come through to the kitchen, Dave pinched himself that he could be so lucky as to be in this position. There was a beautiful young girl waiting for him in the next room and she was all his. And seeing Amanda-Jayne's breasts was a pivotal experience for him, especially after all that anticipation.

Dave had long recognised that much of his sexual stimulation was voyeuristic in nature, and put it down to the encounter with Uncle Ronnie's girlie magazine back when he was five. In fact, given the choice, he would rather look at, and perhaps caress a naked woman, than make love to one who was fully dressed.

Amanda-Jayne was only the third woman in his life so far, to have had such an all-encompassing erotic and arousing affect on his imagination. He recalled that the second one had been the lovely Chloe. And then there was the first, ah that first girl; now she had been very special indeed. As he stirred the simmering cacciatore, Dave found himself thinking about the last time he had ever seen her.

*

David wasn't prepared for it to have been quite so cold, dark and misty that morning, as it was still the late summer. The overnight rain hadn't helped either, but at least it had stopped for now. But none of this presented a real problem; he had wanted to make an early start in any case, whatever the weather. As he cycled along North Lane and parallel to the River Stour, he noticed that the damp mist seemed to hang in pockets over the abandoned races of the long demolished Hooker's water mill, through which the Stour still rushed and foamed. And was it the dark, still morning or the saturated mist that was causing all sound to be amplified, he wondered to himself? Indeed, the noise of the water, as it gushed through the mill ruins, seemed to be all around him. It was then that the cathedral clock announced the three-quarter hour, and those separately struck chimes hung in the air, prolonged themselves and seemed to segue into one long shimmering chord. David speculated that, perhaps, if he shouted out his uncle's name, the words would carry into the air and be broadcast to wherever he was; to wherever he had gone so angrily, in his father's car, late yesterday afternoon.

David wasn't sure that this mission would be successful, but at least it was better than sitting at home, like his parents were, waiting for the phone or doorbell to ring. They hadn't seemed to know what to do yesterday when Ronnie stormed out so crossly and, as his father later confirmed, drunk on the whisky he'd been ingesting in large quantities, ostensibly to soothe his sore head and bad toothache. Both his father and mother had expressed their concerns in short sentences, alternating from one to the other, like people shouting out the possible answers in a game of charades:

'He'll damage the car.'

'He'll hurt himself or someone else'.

'What if he's breathalysed?'

'The press will have a field day!'

'What if he goes over to Herne Bay?'

That last piece of speculation had appeared to concern them the most, but David could not work out why. He also wondered if there was any connection with his father's earlier assertion that Ronnie's flat was strictly off limits. The only answer he could come up with was that the press were aware of the address for his uncle's seaside flat and were camping out there, waiting to spring out on Ronnie, if he should ever be foolish enough to turn up there. In any case, out of bounds or not, the press being there or not, David had decided that Herne Bay was where he would be heading today on his trusty bicycle.

The plastic lunchbox, full of hastily compiled cheese and Daddies Sauce sandwiches, and bottle of diluted orange squash, rattled away on the rack to the rear of him as he left the city suburbs behind and sped along the empty and level Broad Oak Road. He worked out that his parents would be getting up about now, and would soon find the rapidly scribbled note that he'd left on the kitchen table: -

Dear Mum and Dad,
Gone looking for Uncle Ronnie. Be back by teatime.
'D'.

At least having read the note, his mum and dad wouldn't be worrying about him, he reasoned, before turning on to the Sturry Road, opposite the bakery complex. Both of them fretting about Ronnie was bad enough; at least they would now know that their eldest son was okay.

As he cruised past the sewage works, a panda car hurried by in the opposite direction. Perhaps they're on the same mission as me, he speculated, as the village of Sturry loomed up ahead.

When Ronnie hadn't turned up for tea yesterday evening, his father had wanted to call the police, but then hesitated. Instead, he had made a call from the hall phone, with all the doors closed, just as he'd done at the very beginning of the Ronnie crisis. And then, when the runaway still wasn't home by the time *Panorama* had finished, the police were finally called. 'It's a rather delicate situation!' he had heard his father tell them. Apparently, the police had agreed to put out a general alert and also to keep a lookout for the family's missing mushroom-coloured Ford Escort.

When David reached the Sturry level crossing, the gates were already closed. His bike squealed to a halt right against them, and then as he eased himself off the saddle, the early-morning cyclist looked around his immediate vicinity. The road and rails were still very wet from the overnight showers, and the rapidly darkening sky threatened to resume the downpour at any moment. On the opposite side of the level crossing, some cones and a warning sign surrounded an area in the middle of the road, where a pedestrian island was being installed. The only other waiting vehicle was a familiar red and cream double-decker bus, which was now purring away behind him, with a service to either Herne Bay or Thanet; he couldn't quite see which.

A loud two-tone train horn, blaring out from the right, suddenly shook him from his reverie. Within seconds, a high-pitched whining sound could also be heard. And then, amidst a noisy shower of yellow sparks from the 750 volt DC rail, two blue-painted electric locomotives screamed past him in tandem, with a long and heavy trainload of Kentish coal. Another shower of sparks fizzed out as both engines reconnected with the current on the other side of the level crossing; an audio-visual experience that was enhanced by both the dampness of the electric rail and the blackness of the sky. A seemingly endless rake of coal hoppers then thumped past him, their axles squeaking and complaining, as the two locomotives at the front struggled to pick up speed.

When the gates finally opened, David made a run for the daunting Sturry Hill that began almost immediately after the railway crossing, whilst the bus veered off to the right so as to follow the Thanet Road. With a series of other hills before him, David's progress now slowed considerably. The misery was compounded, not only by the gradual increase in traffic on the road as the day got into full swing, but also by that long-threatened shower of icy cold rain, which now stung his face, as he struggled onwards.

By the time David was finally peddling along Herne Bay seafront, the rain had stopped at last, and there was some hazy sunshine trying to break through. However, the rays were as yet too tentative to help dry off his sodden clothes. He soon found himself nearing the area where Uncle Ronnie's flat was situated, and therefore, approached it rather gingerly. However, he could find no evidence of the threatened hordes of television and newspaper reporters; there were no sign of any cameras, notebooks or microphones. In fact, there only seemed to be a few local people about, who were either quietly opening up the shops and amusements, or else walking their dogs.

David dismounted, wheeled his bike over to the bandstand and then sat at the top of a series of stone steps on its landward side. From this vantage point, it seemed certain that he would have a clear view of Ronnie's second-floor flat on the opposite side of the road. The next thing was to locate his uncle's particular pair of bay windows amongst all the other similar ones in this stuccoed regency terrace. It was a task quickly completed, and straightaway he noticed that all the curtains were closed. However, the smile soon faded from David's face, as he suddenly realised that he did not know what to do next. This was the bit he hadn't planned, when lying in bed last night unable to sleep for the sound of his parents' voices drifting through from the adjacent bedroom, as they talked well into the small hours.

Having stared along the seafront road to both left and right, David once more looked up at the curtained bay windows, and asked himself: was Ronnie really up there in his flat? Had his uncle got so fed up with his own brother telling him to 'pull himself together', or 'stop being such a silly young fool', that he'd come over here to get away from it all for a while? If that was the case, where then was the familiar mushroom-coloured car that he'd ridden off in? David looked along the street again, much more carefully this time, but there was no sign of his father's Ford Escort parked anywhere within his considerable visual range. As an alternative explanation, he was forced to speculate that his Scar Brother must have actually done what he'd threatened to back at Rothermead: he'd gone off somewhere else to find Katie: 'that wicked schoolgirl', to once more quote his father, who had caused all this, and yet somehow still had him under her spell. Having thought about all of those heated conversations between his father and uncle, and also being aware of Ronnie's desire to see his young lover, David now considered his last option to be much more likely. So, had cycling over there been a wasted journey after all? Perhaps, but even now, the boy's fervent hope was that his father's Escort would soon come coasting down the seafront road, with Ronnie at the wheel, both safe and sound, and grinning from ear-to-ear as if nothing had happened; just like in the immediate aftermath of one of his famous dark episodes.

Feeling a lot drier now, David unpacked the sandwiches, and took them back up to his bandstand perch. They were not bad for a first attempt, he thought, chewing on his second mouthful; although he had to concede that he'd been a little heavy-handed with the Daddies sauce. He took a swig of orange squash, and then peered up at the flat again. Uncle Ronnie could be up there right now fast asleep, David further theorised; he might have left the car somewhere else; it could even have run out of petrol. Buoyed up by his new theory, and in the absence of any other ideas as to what to do, David decided to stay put and keep watch. If Ronnie got up, and then drew the curtains back, he knew he would be able to see from there.

Just as he had finished his sandwiches, a middle-aged woman appeared at the pillastered front entrance immediately below Ronnie's flat. She closed the door, descended the stone steps, walked up the front path and then turned right, glancing only briefly, and unsuspiciously, in his direction. Dave hypothesised that she could very well be the woman whose stairs you had to go up in order to get to the flat. He watched until she had disappeared round the next corner.

It was while securing the empty packed-lunch things on the back of his bicycle, that he decided he'd waited long enough, and that now was the time to take some action. Surely, Uncle Ronnie wouldn't mind if he went over there and woke him up by banging on the door, he reasoned; assuming he was up there in the first place. Hopefully, he would be pleased to see him, and also welcome the opportunity for a friendly chat; after all, they had only exchanged a few words in the last few days. His fondest wish however, was for his uncle's forgiveness, for breaking the confidence between them concerning Ronnie's intention to seek out Katie, wherever she happened to be. He longed to grip his 'Scar Brother's' left hand and make things right again between them. With his next course of action clear in his mind, David locked the bike, crossed the road and then mounted the flight of stone steps up to the huge front door. Finding that the recently departing lady had left it on the latch, he pushed it open, crossed the lofty lobby and then mounted those familiar stairs.

Having finally reached Ronnie's second-floor landing, he tapped nervously on the door. Having got no reply, he put his mouth close to the letterbox, and then pushed at its sprung flap with his left index finger.

'Uncle *Ronnie*…Uncle *Ronnie*…it's me…it's *David*,' he announced, in a hoarse half-whisper. He waited a while, and was about to knock for a second time, when the door opened a few inches, or as far as the safety chain would allow.

A shock of blonde hair appeared in the gap.

'Is that David Darwin?' enquired a young female voice from behind the door.

'*Yes*,' he replied, in a somewhat confused manner.

The door slammed shut, and he began to wonder what was going on, but then he heard the sound of the chain coming off. Ronnie's door opened again to reveal the head and shoulders of a young woman.

'*Hello* David, come in,' she said, before standing aside for him. 'I must *say* … it's nice to see a friendly familiar face again!'

He could not believe it. She was half asleep, her hair was partly obscuring her face, and she had no make-up on. Nonetheless, there was absolutely no doubt in his mind who she was: it was Katie Townsend.

As he stood in the open doorway, his first thought was to hurl a tirade of abuse at her for lying to Ronnie about her age; for seducing him with her long hair and long legs, for getting him into trouble with the police and worst of all, for ruining his career, just at the very moment he was about to achieve all that he'd ever dreamt of: a pilot show of his own. His mouth did indeed fall open, although not with words of condemnation, but rather in sheer awe at what he now beheld. As Katie turned away from him, he studied her tall slender form as she walked lazily across the room and headed towards the settee. She was wearing a short white silk dressing gown, very short in fact, and it was obvious from David's vantage point, that she had absolutely nothing on underneath it. Katie sat back on the settee, with one hand on top of her bare crossed legs, whilst the other tried to straighten the dishevelled tresses that still covered her eyes, with a small plastic hairbrush.

Almost straightaway, David could sense her power; he could feel her sexual allure. It compelled him to consider if he was coming down with the same disease that had laid his uncle so low? He shut the front door, and then walked over to the nearest of the two large bay windows, to check that his bicycle was still where he had left it. Everything outside seemed to be in order, and so he slowly turned to face his hostess, who anxiously stared back at him; her big eyes now visible between the parted tresses of her long hair.

'Oh David, you must think I'm a *terrible* person,' she said, in a quiet timid voice, before lowering her head.

'Yes I *do* ... you *lied* to Uncle Ronnie ... you told him you were *older*!' he responded, both loudly and bitterly, as he attempted to ignore her diverting visual appeal. 'You're only *fifteen* ... that's just three years older than *me*!'

Katie slowly looked up at him, with a face that seemed etched in pain.

'I'm *sixteen* actually,' she said, in a voice clearly seeped with emotion. 'You see, it's my *birthday* today!'

'Happy birthday,' was the only thing the stunned twelve-year-old could think of to say in reply.

Over the next five minutes, Katie went on the explain how she had first got to know Ronnie, when her older sister Carol had taken her to see an *Opportunity Knocks* show as a special treat. Later on, she and Ronnie had met back stage, and hit it off straightaway. He had thought Katie was 18 and, in the intense emotion of the moment, she did not deny it.

'And then we fell in love, David,' she said frankly, almost as if he had been her life-long confidante. 'It was…the real *thing* and that's why I miss him *so* much!'

She seemed very upset and so very genuine. David had precious little experience concerning women, far less the affairs of the heart, but he believed her. The fact that her candid confession uncannily echoed Ronnie's own words on the same subject – confided to him up at Rothermead only days before – helped to reinforce his faith in her authenticity. Katie had not lied after all; she had just not broadcast her real age, and it was Ronnie who had made the assumptions. He suddenly felt completely liberated; everything was alright, and he didn't have to hate this beautiful girl any more. As a result, he slowly walked towards the settee, made eye contact with her, and then smiled warmly.

At that moment, Katie realised that David had believed her, and that she'd gained an ally in him; the boy whom, she was surprised to notice, had the same kind eyes as his uncle. At that moment, she could see right through the spots and the awkwardness, and knew that he would grow up to be a man with all the compassion and sensitivity of her beloved Ronnie.

Sadly, David's new found peace of mind proved to be rather brief, and lasted only until he remembered that the primary mission, for which he'd set out that day, had not yet been completed. Everything was not alright, he told himself, trying to avert his gaze from her long beautiful bare legs.

'Katie, have you seen Ronnie recently?' he asked, in as sensitive a manner as he could muster. 'Has my uncle *been* here in the last twenty-four hours…is he here *now*?'

His scantily clad companion frowned heavily, and then slowly shook her head.

'No, I haven't see him for about ten days,' she responded, in a voice that was already breaking up. And so, her joy at winning David over had proved as short-lived as his.

Now seemingly lost in her own thoughts, Katie leaned forward and cupped her hands around the coffee mug, which had been sitting on the wobbly little table in front of her. In so doing, her dressing gown gaped open, completely unnoticed by her, and for the first time, David caught sight of a woman's naked breast. From that moment on, he had been entirely won over by the sixteen-year-old; first emotionally and now physically as well. Having exposed himself to her germs, he had caught the same disease as Ronnie, and now imagined himself in love.

Katie took a sip of her rapidly cooling coffee, and then leaned back into the settee, and beckoned for David to sit next to her. He did so, but approached the seat as gingerly as he earlier had Ronnie's flat. He also sat as close as he could to the sofa's opposite end. The blonde birthday girl took a deep breath and then began to explain to him how things had been for her over the last ten days.

When it became clear that the press, not only were camping outside Ronnie's London flat, but also had found the Townsend residence in Tunbridge Wells, Ronnie quickly co-opted the help of his older brother Len, who subsequently arranged for Katie and her mother to hide away in the Herne Bay flat. So far, neither the papers nor the television had managed to track them down.

'Is your Mum here *now*?' David asked a little anxiously, before swinging his head between the two internal doors that led off the room.

'No, you're alright ... she's just popped out for some provisions, but I'm *sure* she wouldn't mind you being here!' Katie reassured him, with a brief grin.

'*Actually*, I think I saw her go out as I, umm…as I arrived!' he explained with a half-truth; feeling reluctant to admit that he'd been waiting outside for a while.

The teenage girl nodded in acknowledgement of what he'd said, and then gradually adopted a rather introspective countenance, as she resumed her story.

'Mum and I *knew* that Ronnie was staying with you in Canterbury for all of last week,' she said, clearly having derived no pleasure from the knowledge. 'Imagine how that was for me ... he was only a few miles away, but I couldn't get to see him, or even speak to him on the phone. *Huh*, never mind Canterbury Kent, it may as well have been Canterbury *New Zealand* for all the contact we had!'

David stared across at his lovely companion and felt a profound sympathy for her. He also felt an uncanny sense of déjà vu, for the emotional resonance in Katie expressing her longing for Ronnie, was identical to that of his uncle confessing to how much he had missed her, and in words confided in him only a few days before. Having recalled that previous weekend, he was very much put in mind of the windmill incident.

'Umm ... Katie, did you, err…did you see Uncle Ronnie on the telly last Sunday?' he asked rather hesitantly, for fear of upsetting her too much.

Straightaway, she puckered up her mouth and nodded rapidly.

'Mum and I were watching the local news when all that Rothermead Green business suddenly came on, and *there* was Ronnie right in the thick of it ... in fact, we saw *all* of you Darwins in the coverage!' she said, with just the briefest of smiles. 'Imagine how much *more* worried I was for him after *that*!' She paused, and then leant forward to cradle the coffee cup once more; her long tousled hair hanging down vertically on either side of it.

David could not bring himself to look at her gaping robe, even if he was able to see anything from that angle. She seemed so upset; he just wouldn't have felt right ogling her bare bosom at that moment. It was then he recognised the fact that his feelings for her had already transcended mere attraction to her physical form.

Without either lifting the mug, or drinking from it, Katie straightened up from the coffee table, and adopted a stiff upright posture with her knees together, and each hand placed on top of the corresponding thigh. She then turned her head slowly in the direction of the twelve-year-old, and stared at him with eyes that were both aqueous and angst-ridden.

'I *know* that Ronnie stormed off from your house yesterday ... Len telephoned my mum about it late afternoon!' she explained, in a voice only barely held together.

'Oh, so *that's* who he was phoning, with all the doors to the hall shut!'

'Yes, your dad wanted to warn us in case Ronnie turned up *here*. Mum was alarmed at the prospect, but I…well…Oh *David* ... for the rest of that *day*, I was hoping to see him come through the door …but he didn't. And this morning, I prayed that he would turn up here…but he hasn't!' That last declared disappointment proved too much for her to bear, and she burst into tears; her head dropping into her upturned, raised hands.

A distressed David watched the sorry sight for a few seconds, feeling both awkward and acne-ridden, and quite unable to help her. But it wasn't long before his inbuilt family sense of compassion got the better of him, and he slid along the settee in order to place a comforting arm around her slumped shoulders. Immediately, she leant over and nestled into his chest, and then poured forth her considerable grief. Instinctively, he enveloped her with his other arm too, as she sobbed and shook; the looser strands of her fragrant hair tickling his nose in the process.

As David continued to hold the inconsolable Katie, it occurred to him that at another location somewhere, his Uncle Ronnie might very well be grieving for the very same reason, but that in all likelihood, he wouldn't have someone there to comfort him. It then struck him, with a sickly thud, that all this unnecessary upset had one single common cause, and he wasn't blaming the press, Katie's tender age, or Ronnie's passionate nature. Suddenly, David had a new hate figure in mind, for was it not his own father who had prised the young lovers apart? Was the fact that this beautiful woman was now sobbing her heart out, not a direct consequence of his brutal actions? Would his uncle have stormed out in the way he did, if he'd not been denied seeing the woman he loved? On top of all that though, David could not forget that his sacred Scar Brothers' pledge had been forced out of him, and in the end, it was all for nothing. Ronnie was still missing, and David was absolutely clear in his mind that it was all his father's fault.

*

Those alluring images of the sixteen-year-old Katie Townsend had stayed with him for over 20 years, but that was then, and now was very much now, Dave thought, as he ripped the cling film from the salad bowl. All those voyeuristic fantasies that had been the very core of his sexual identity could at last be banished; he was finally going to turn the dream into a reality. Dave turned down the heat under the cacciatore and quickly threw the garlic bread in the oven. Everything else was done, which meant that he could go through and rejoin Amanda-Jayne.

On entering the lounge, Dave was slightly surprised to discover that his young dinner guest had obviously readjusted the dimmer switch, so that his carefully pre-set ambient and seductive light level had now been replaced by the harsh glare of an interrogation chamber.

Amanda-Jayne was over by the sideboard, holding the framed picture of he and Sheila's wedding with her left hand, whilst sipping a glass of the Bordeaux in her right.

'I *hope* you don't mind,' she said with a smile, turning her head in his direction. 'It's just that I couldn't see the photographs properly.'

'Umm ... not at *all*!' Dave replied, as he subtly re-adjusted the dimmer switch to a compromise light level. 'Do you like the wine?

'Yes, yummy thanks,' she said, still carefully studying the picture. '*Oh*, I've poured you one too,' she added, motioning towards the waiting wine glass on the coffee table.

'Ah *great*!' he enthused, and then sat down on the settee adjacent to his drink.

'I never knew you once had a beard ... you look *nice* with one David,' Amanda-Jayne smiled, carefully replacing the frame. She then walked over and sat in the armchair opposite him, rather than on the settee next to him as he'd hoped. 'How long ago was the picture taken?'

'Four years, we've been married four years,' Dave replied with little enthusiasm. 'And the beard had to go because Sheila didn't *like* it!'

Amanda-Jayne gave him a pitying smile, before crossing her legs, and then, with wine glass in hand, settling back into the chair. Dave did likewise, as an awkward silence ensued, except that is for *Enja*'s synthesized gaelic noodlings.

But there was so much he wanted to talk to her about. Indeed, the mention of marriage just then had been rather appropriate, as it was something he wanted to discuss with her. And it was not a case of going down on one knee in front of her, at least not yet. Instead, he wanted to be completely honest with her about, not only where his and Sheila's marriage stood, but also that he very much considered her to be part of his future. This carefully thought out evening was not going to be a 'wham-bam, thank-you ma-am' affair. On the contrary, he wanted it to be the first of many in a long-term relationship with Amanda-Jayne, and she needed to know that the way would soon be clear for her.

Dave leaned forward slowly, reunited his wine glass with the cork coaster, and then looked over at his beloved with a rather serious countenance.

'*Listen* my love, I have something to tell you,' he announced, nervously running his finger over the cut-glass shapes on the stem of his wine glass.

Amanda-Jayne suddenly looked rather worried, and slowly uncrossed her legs.

Undaunted, he took a deep breath and then exhaled audibly.

'I think you need to know, that I'm seriously considering leaving Sheila ... our marriage *isn't* going anywhere, and I want to be free to .... umm ... to consider *other* options!' Dave said, in the manner of a newsreader detailing the latest disaster. Having finally got it out in the open, he took several gulps from his wine glass and then anxiously waited for her initial reaction.

With a neutral expression, Amanda-Jayne slowly shuffled to the edge of her seat, placed her glass on the coffee table, and then got to her feet. Much to Dave's surprise, she walked round, and then knelt down on the carpet by his feet.

'I *must* say, I'm not surprised,' she responded, with a supportive smile, before grabbing his left hand with both of hers. 'It won't be *easy* David, but I want you to know that I'll be *there* for you!'

He leaned forward, gently raised her chin with his right hand, and then kissed her on the lips, in the non-lingering, and yet soft way that they always did. She had reacted to his awkward announcement rather better than he'd hoped. In fact, Dave felt encouraged to say more.

'I *hoped* you would react like that, in fact…'

'*After all*, what are friends for?' Amanda-Jayne interjected, with a supportive if somewhat sisterly smile, as she got up and then returned to her seat.

'I appreciate that!' Dave said rather crestfallen, as the *Enja* CD finished.

Although the moment had been lost, he told himself that the night was yet young. There would be plenty more opportunities to tell her how he really felt, and what is more, demonstrate to her just how he wanted to express that love.

The aroma of garlic bread soon began drifting into the lounge, and reminded Dave that their meal must almost be ready.

'*Right* then, I'm going through to serve up,' he announced, before briskly getting to his feet. 'Are you hungry?'

Amanda-Jayne gave him a close-lipped smile, widened her eyes keenly and then nodded her head in short but rapid movements.

'Okay ... give me about two or three minutes, and then come through to the diningroom with the wine, will you?' he requested, making for the open door to the hall, only to pause by the threshold, and turn back. '*Oh*, and ... err ... would you choose some more music please ... something you deem suitable for our meal together!'

'I'd *love* to!' came the enthusiastic response, as she immediately got up and then headed for the hifi.

Dave smiled, and then made his way towards the kitchen; secure in the knowledge that she would choose his new *XTC* album, which he'd earlier placed strategically on top of the small pile by the player.

Within minutes, he'd not only lit the candles, but also had two bowls of steaming chicken cacciatore, a side salad and the garlic bread laid up ready on the diningroom table. As if on cue, at that very moment, Amanda-Jayne came through to join him. It was as she placed the half-empty wine bottle in the middle of the table, that the unmistakable sound of *The Smiths* began, and to his utter dismay, he realised that she'd chosen one of Julian's CDs. Dave hated *The Smiths*: that boring self-indulgent repetitive whingeing drivel. For the first time, he regretted having wired those extra speakers through into the diningroom. Now, he would have to listen to that row throughout their planned perfect dinner. Never mind, block it out, Dave determined, as he pulled out the chair for Amanda-Jayne.

'Oh David, it all looks so lovely ... you *are* clever!' she purred appreciatively, gently lowering herself into the seat.

As he politely pushed the chair in for her, he again found himself glaring down into her gaping bodice. He tenderly kissed the top of her head, and then furtively watched as her nipples hardened. It was all too much for him, and he soon hurried back to the seat opposite her, before his own blood-flow problem became too obvious. With trembling hands, Dave then poured her some more wine and also recharged his own glass.

Amanda-Jayne picked up her fork and spoon, and with the dexterity and elegance of a native Italian, took a mouthful of cacciatore.

'Mmm, it's *gorgeous*,' she praised, and then smiled over at him with eyes that sparkled in the candlelight, just as they had on that distant day in the cathedral chapel.

'*Thank* you ... you're *very* kind,' Dave responded appreciatively, and with barely suppressed pride, as he watched her tuck in. As he did so, the mesmerised man felt a coming together of all the emotions he'd experienced since really getting to know her. All those feelings suddenly coalesced, and everything in the universe finally seemed to have meaning. No longer able to hold back, he stretched out his left hand across the table, and she dutifully reached for it. 'Oh,

Amanda-Jayne, I'm so *very* much in love with you!' he declared with much fervent emotion coming through in his voice.

Suddenly, it seemed as if time itself had stood starkly still; it felt like that sort of moment when someone farts during silent prayers in church. Amanda-Jayne slowly withdrew her hand and then stared down into her bowl. At the same time, those red blotches quickly began to break out all over her pale skin as before.

It was hard for Dave to determine what had just happened. Was she just being shy, he wondered; could it be that she was taken aback by the intensity of the feelings he'd just expressed? Perhaps she was just thinking of something to say in response to his earnest declaration! As she still sat there unmoving, unspeaking, and unresponsive, all Dave could hear was Morrissey of *The Smiths* bleating away, and defying all his attempts to ignore that monotonous caterwauling.

Eventually, Amanda-Jayne appeared to recover from the shock, if indeed that was what it was, and then slowly raised her head.

'David...do you know the difference between *being* in love with someone, and *loving* someone?' she asked, in a calm, unemotional voice he'd not known before.

A bewildered Dave stared back at her and felt that he'd been bowled something of a googly. It was a simple enough question, and yet he didn't know what she meant by it. A sense of panic began to take him over; it was almost like being a finalist on *Mastermind* with only one point needed to win.

'Yes?' he hesitatingly replied, with more than a slight hint of the interrogative.

'*Well* then, David, as I've told you *before* ... I love you!' she replied and then smiled reassuringly, before averting her gaze.

He nodded slowly to acknowledge her statement, but did not feel reassured by what she had said; in fact, the strongest feeling he now had was one of confusion. It wasn't long before he began wondering if she was actually setting limits on their relationship, but could not equate that theory with the way she had been behaving towards him. As far as he was concerned, Amanda-Jayne had given him all the right signals so far that evening. Nevertheless, Dave soon began telling himself that he must stop over-analysing her every reaction and just go with the flow of the evening, however difficult that might be.

After 20 more minutes of eating and intermittent small talk, each of them decided that they'd had enough and were too full either for second helpings or for dessert. In truth, Dave was far from replete, but said he was full-up so as to be able to move back to the lounge with her almost straightaway.

By the time the couple had gone through to the lounge, 'Meat is Murder' had mercifully finished, and Dave was determined that the next choice of music would be a joint decision. Scanning through the rack, he was inspired to select the Mozart C-minor Mass, and Amanda-Jayne readily agreed as she had recently performed it at the cathedral. So, with the music on and some after-dinner drinks poured, they both sank down into the settee together: his arm around her, and her head on his shoulder. The light level had been subtly restored to his preferred setting and they were both sipping from small glasses of port, whilst in close contact with each other.

As far as Dave was concerned, 15 minutes into the piece, and they were back on track, and the slight misunderstanding at the dining table had been forgotten. Here and there, Amanda-Jayne sang along quietly to some of the soprano parts she knew. He was both entranced and delighted; for the first time that evening, his lovely young companion appeared completely relaxed; she seemed totally herself.

'Are you *happy* my love?' he softly asked, in an effort to accurately gauge her mood, and thus avoid any ambiguity as had happened earlier.

'Oh yes *thank* you David, I feel very content ... you've looked after me *so* well,' she extolled, touching his leg to reinforce the genuine feeling of appreciation behind her comments.

Given his mood of mellow optimism, this was all the encouragement he needed. Without either thinking or planning, Dave slowly slipped his arm from behind the young girl, edged forward a little, and then dropped to his knees on the carpet by her legs, before turning to face her – in a reversal of the positions they had adopted before dinner. And then, leaning forward, he gently kissed her on the lips, in their usual way, but lingered a little longer than normal. She appeared to offer no resistance; joining in with what became a series of little kisses, as opposed to anything open-mouthed or penetrative. Building up courage, he next kissed her cheek and then that long, rapidly blotching neck. In response, she slowly raised her left hand, and cupped the back of his neck; it was hardly a sign that his attentions were unwanted. Encouraged still further, he slowly moved down onto her body, tenderly kissing her skin as he went, until reaching the exposed area immediately above her breasts. His kisses became more passionate and, as a result, she began to breath more deeply, her chest rising and falling against his lips. He also thought he detected a slight moan of pleasure from her. Soon wanting more bare skin to kiss, he reached for the right-hand strap of her evening dress and slowly pulled if off her shoulder. Immediately, her hand fell away from his neck, and he felt her body tense a little. Undaunted, he continued tugging down on the strap until her right breast was fully exposed. And then, wasting no time, he began to lovingly kiss her nipple.

Suddenly, her right hand came up into his chest and she thrust him firmly away.

'*No*, David, please *don't*,' she said in distress, before quickly replacing the shoulderstrap, and then sitting bolt upright.

'Sorry...I'm *sorry*,' he stammered in confused horror, whilst shrinking away from her and backing himself into the coffee table. 'I thought... I mean... you were...oh God, I'm sorry...I'm *sorry*!' Dave quickly stood up and hurried from the room.

Disorientated by panic, Dave ran along the hallway and soon found himself in the kitchen. And then, whilst trying to get a grip, he started to make the coffee in a very flustered state, banging the cups and cafetiere about, all the time, mumbling his manic mantra: 'Oh *God*...oh *God*...oh *God*', repeatedly in an agitated half-whisper.

After about a minute, Amanda-Jayne appeared in the doorway.

'*Hey* you, calm *down* in here,' she urged, clearly trying to lighten the situation.

He turned to her, and took a few hesitant paces forward.

'I'm *so* sorry ... did I rush things too much?' he entreated, still feeling absolutely crushed by the experience.

Amanda-Jayne now tried to take control of the situation. It wasn't that she was unaffected by what had happened; it was just that she was a little calmer than him.

'*Look*, it's only that I've...*well*, err, it's just that I had never considered loving you in *that* way before,' she said, with an open hand gesture of submission.

Dave heard the words, but found them rather hard to either accept or believe.

'But...but it seemed to me that you were *responding* to...'

'I *was*...but *only*...oh, I don't *know,* David.' Amanda-Jayne grimaced and then held her hand against her left temple. 'I'm so *confused* ... I need time to think about this,' she said, evidently becoming somewhat agitated herself.

Now that they appeared to be on an equal emotional footing, Dave walked forward in order to hug her. The gesture of both comfort and conciliation was willing reciprocated. Inevitably though, the pent up frustrations, disappointments and distress he was feeling finally came pouring out of him in the form of tears.

'*Sorry* about this Amanda-Jayne,' he sobbed in uncontrollable despair.

'Nothing to *worry* about David,' she reassured soothingly and softly into his ear. 'As I *said*, I need time to *think* about this. You see, I never make love to anyone unless I'm absolutely *sure* it's for the right reason.' She slowly broke away from him, gently lifted his chin up, just as he had done with her earlier, and then smiled sweetly into his face. 'Now, why don't you go and ring for a taxi for me, *okay*?'

Slightly shamed by her seeming serenity, Dave tried to compose himself and nodded in silent acquiescence to her request to ring for a cab to take her home. Whilst out in the hall, he tried to think about what Amanda-Jayne had said, regarding the fact that she only made love to someone for the right reason, and surmised that it didn't sound like the virginal seventeen-year-old he had thus far idealised. It didn't take him long to realise the awful truth; a fact very strongly implied by her choice of words: she must have had a full sexual relationship with Julian. Suddenly he felt seethingly mad with jealousy and wanted to go back through and challenge her about it there and then. However, he had already overstepped the mark once that evening, so decided to say nothing on the subject, at least for now.

With the call made, they both sat silently at opposite ends of the settee, whilst waiting for the taxi to come. It seemed to take an eternity, but finally the doorbell rang and she promptly got up to go.

Dave opened the front door and she went to leave, but he held on to her arm before she could cross the threshold.

'See you soon,' he said, half exclaiming, half questioning.

Amanda-Jayne looked up at him impassively, but said nothing, and then quickly walked on. She climbed into the taxi and neither waved nor looked back as it growled off into the night.

Dave touched none of the tidying up in the lounge, the clearing through in the dining room, or the washing up in the kitchen; preferring instead to clamber up the stairs, and then throw himself down on the double bed: the one he had optimistically re-made earlier, with clean sheets. He felt completely and utterly miserable; he was the child who had looked forward to a bike for Christmas, only to have been given socks. And yet, in desperation, he tried to tell himself that all was not completely lost. Indeed, it could be that, having reflected on the evening, Amanda-Jayne might come to realise she *did* actually have those sorts of feelings for him. And then again, perhaps something good had come out of the evening after all, he speculated; for at least she was now all too aware of exactly how he felt, after having played his trump card so clumsily tonight.

Sleep eluded him as much as it had the previous night, but now more through anxiety than anticipation. Same person, different reasons! During one particularly long period of worried wakefulness, he remembered the handwritten note that he'd sent to Tim: the one with all those lurid and, sadly unrealised boasts. At that moment, he would have given anything not to have sent it.

A Triple Blow

Dave looked at the bedside clock through blinking, bleary eyes. Its stark green digital display shone through the gloom to inform him it was 05:10. Although it was still early, he realised that snoozing was not an option, as there was so much to do downstairs.

Having washed and dressed, he wearily made his way down to face the legacy of his failure: all those unhappy reminders of his disastrous evening with Amanda-Jayne. But was it really a disaster? Although his optimistic half was very much on the wane, he still clung on to the hope that yesterday evening's calamity might become a catalyst for a new stage in the relationship with her. Only time and Amanda-Jayne, would tell.

Heaving a deep sigh, Dave opened the lounge curtains, but there wasn't sufficient daylight to illuminate the room, so he was forced to turn the dimmer switch up to full. It was an untimely reminder of his inability to have created the appropriate mood for the previous evening. Looking round the lounge, he discovered that the CD player was still switched on and loaded with the Mozart disc. Abandoned on the coffee table were two empty wine glasses and two smaller ones, each still half-full with port. Dave wrinkled his nose up and grimaced before gathering them up. He hated the vinegar smell and stickiness of morning-after glasses, and on that particular morning, it seemed so much worse. The diningroom had to be cleared as well and this was the next task he tackled.

With everything finally gathered in the kitchen, Dave then had to face the most gruelling job of all: the washing up, but he realised there was no choice but to put his head down and get on with it. Sheila would be home by the time he'd finished work for the day, so the house must be straightened out and all evidence of the doomed seduction completely eliminated, before he left for the office. She had been aware that Tim was coming over in her absence, but none of those intimate dinner party things could possibly be explained away as being for him. Luckily, the dustbin men came that morning, as there was a whole sack-full of bottles, cooking ingredient packages and uneaten cacciatore outside, which otherwise, would have had to be disposed of discreetly at the city dump. At the last moment, he also remembered to get rid of the unused packet of condoms: the ultimate metaphor for a failed seduction session. The dessert, a fresh fruit salad, hadn't been touched at all either; in fact, rather like Dave himself. Nevertheless, the sliced bananas had now gone dark and slimy, so there was no pretending that he'd made it for Sheila's homecoming, and this had to go out as well.

By 07:45, it was all done; every scrap from last night had been washed up, cleared away or disposed of, and it came as an enormous relief to him. If only memories could be so easily banished, he mused, as he flopped down at the small kitchen table. He worked out that he had just enough time for a bowl of Shreddies and a cup of tea before work, so quickly made the necessary preparations. As he took his first mouthful of cereal, the kitchen's wall-mounted phone unexpectedly trilled into action. Typical of Sheila to interrupt my breakfast, he thought, whilst getting up; no doubt she wants to confirm her e.t.a.

'*Excuse* my mouthful,' mumbled Dave, into the receiver. 'Would you like me to spit or swallow?' He waited for his wife's amused reaction, but none came.

'Is that David Darwin?' came the unfamiliar and utterly un-amused female voice in response.

My God, it's not Sheila, panicked Dave, as his heart banged on his chest wall in complaint. Who is this woman I've just been rather suggestive to?

'*Speaking*!' he at last acknowledged aloud.

'*Ah*, Mr Darwin,' continued the serious sounding woman. 'This is Mrs Roper speaking…Amanda-Jayne's mother!'

Dave felt a terrible shockwave pass through him from top to bottom, and then he stood there in abject horror, his breakfast entirely forgotten, as Mrs Roper detailed exactly why she had called him at this hour:

'Amanda-Jayne arrived home last night in a *very* distressed state, and when I challenged her as to why, and then pressed her on the subject, she finally broke down completely and told me *everything*; do you hear? every … single … detail. The worst thing is, Mr Darwin, she says you are in love with her.'

'*Yes*, but you don't…'

'*Do you realise* she's only *seventeen* for pity's sake?' continued the forthright Mrs Roper, completely ignoring his attempt to intervene. 'You're *twice* her age, and as far as *I'm* concerned, Mr Darwin, there is only one reason that men like you pursue young girls like Amanda-Jayne…and you know *exactly* what I'm talking about.'

'But I can assure you, it's not *like that*,' Dave interrupted in an exasperated but pleading voice.

'I *don't* think that I'm making myself *clear*, Mr Darwin,' she responded, now much louder and with more vitriol. 'If you come *near* my daughter again, I shall *contact* the police, I shall *speak* to your wife, I shall *ring* Telecom and I shall *go* to the press. I have contacts you know ... *o-oh* yes ... and I'm *sure* they would be only too happy to run a story about the continued paedophilic predilection of the Darwin family. Now do you *understand* me?'

By now, Dave was shaking with panic. He desperately wanted to challenge the inappropriate use of the word 'paedophilic', but was too scared by the barrage of threats to offer any further resistance. Therefore, he could see no choice but to submit to her demands.

'I *will* abide by your wishes, Mrs Roper ... I will cut all ties with Amanda-Jayne ... you have my absolute assurance,' he vowed, trying to steady his quavering voice.

'Do you *hear* me Mr Darwin, I shall *go* to the police, I shall *speak* to your wife; I shall...'

'*Please*, I've just *said* that *I will* abide by your wishes ... I *will* do what you say,' Dave pleaded, now metaphorically on his knees.

'We will leave it at *that* then Mr Darwin, but *be warned*,' she responded in a calm, cold manner, and then hung up.

Dave replaced the receiver and began pacing from one side of the kitchen to the other, like an institutionalised polar bear. And then, as the nerves got the better of his digestive system, he had to rush to the downstairs cloakroom.

Within minutes, the telephone rang once more. Luckily he had finished in the loo, so flushed, and then crept anxiously out into the hall. It must be her again, he panicked; she wants me on my knees again. He stared at the receiver and let it ring, but the caller was very persistent, and with the possibility that it could be Nanna Darwin with news, he felt there was no choice but to pick it up.

'Hello?' he trembled, like the hesitant victim of a dirty caller.

'It's about *time*!' scolded Sheila, on the other end. '*And* you were engaged a while ago ... is everything alright?'

'Yes *fine*,' Dave replied, feeling greatly relieved, but also having to think fast, 'I was on the loo, that's all ... trust you to interrupt my poo! And ... umm ... the phone wasn't engaged; I was trying to ring Tim again ... *huh*, no reply as usual!'

'*Never* mind, try him again at the weekend,' his wife responded in friendly tones. '*Anyway*, this is to let you know that, with *any* luck, I should be home by the time you get back, *just* as expected!'

'Okay then, see you later.'

'And *Dave*?'

'Yes?'

'I'm looking forward to the weekend!' she confessed, in a somewhat ambiguous tone.

'Yeah, me too, *bye*!' he admitted, more out of politeness than anything else.

Dave only just got to work in time, and then had to endure a day as miserable as a thousand Mondays. At just after 10:30, he took a call from Amanda-Jayne. As soon as Dave heard her voice, he wondered if she was ringing to reinforce her mother's earlier implied threat to have him hung drawn, quartered and put on display along the city walls. At the same time, his optimistic alter-ego speculated that she might want to run away with him and was waiting in the phone box at Canterbury West station; her suitcase already packed. Either way, he was almost too afraid to speak to her, lest Mrs Roper somehow found out. He therefore said nothing, and waited for her to kick things off.

'You must think I'm a *horrible* person,' she said at last, at the start of the conversation. 'I *never* wanted Mum to call you, I begged and pleaded, but she just wouldn't listen…and now it's all *done* with!'

'Are you saying that *that's it?*' Dave asked, trying to suppress his distress. 'I *know* I promised your mother that I'd not *see* you again, but…but can't we just go on meeting in secret, as before?'

'Oh *David*, please don't make this anymore difficult than…'

'But I *love* you!'

Amanda-Jayne sighed deeply before responding.

'My feelings for you haven't changed *either*, and…and maybe there *could* have been, you know, *more* to our relationship, given time, and a different set of personal circumstances,' she conceded, with a tantalising tinge of regret. 'But *I've* had to make promises to my mum *too*, and until I'm eighteen, I've got no *choice* but to do what she wants…and I also have to consider her ... umm, her well-being too, if you understand what I mean!'

'I see!' Dave retorted somewhat coldly, knowing she was alluding to Mrs Roper's fragile mental state. Thus, it appeared that the woman had them both under her control, as well as on their knees.

'I still love you David, *remember* that,' she sobbed before saying her final farewell.

He couldn't say goodbye to her; it sounded so final, but in his heart of hearts, he knew that it was over. As she had said just now: it was all done with.

In the lunch hour, Dave walked quietly by himself around the cathedral grounds. He did not want to go inside the building, least of all the crypt; it was all too full of painful memories. As it happened, the grounds were secluded enough, and the tourist hordes thin enough, to allow him some peaceful thinking time. Dave would be the first to admit that he usually had a tendency to push things as far as he could; a tenacity that allowed him to keep nagging away, if there was something he really wanted badly enough. However, this only applied if there was a realistic chance of his actually achieving the objective. Indeed, he was pragmatic enough to recognise that there were some circumstances in life when you could never win, and the reality of the situation had to be accepted, however painful or undesirable the consequences. Sadly, such was the case now with Amanda-Jayne.

Dave was a survivor and, unlike his friend Tim, he would neither flog a dead horse, nor indulge in self-flagellation. The Amanda-Jayne campaign was now lost; he had to withdraw, take stock and regroup the forces he still had at his command. The alternatives to not accepting the situation were none too appealing. Yes, he could continue to pursue the fair maiden, who was now locked up in an even higher tower, and stand a good chance of being killed by the wicked witch. Otherwise, he could surrender to fate, wallow in self-indulgent misery within a lonely prisoner-of-war cell, and lose the loyalty and respect of his remaining troops. But at the end of the day, there really was only one way forward: to put it simply, he still had Sheila. Now more than ever, he had to make it work with her, or end up on his own again, which to him, was the worst of all possible options. In the absence of Amanda-Jayne, there was no one to leave his wife for anymore, so he had no choice. Ironically, things with Sheila seemed to have been improving in the last week: a time when he, almost certainly, cared for her the least. He just had to continue down that same road and improve things by actually *meaning* to this time.

That evening, Dave arrived home from work to find Sheila there, very much as expected, and greeted her with more affection than he'd done for a long time. She was pleasantly surprised and happily reciprocated, which came as no surprise to him, as she'd been somewhat conciliatory all week, including in that morning's telephone call. Of course, he didn't actually feel what he was displaying; it was as much a case of pragmatism as anything else. However, Dave speculated that, given time to get over Amanda-Jayne in his heart, then he could probably learn to actually mean it again, or mostly so. Getting rid of the teenager in his head had been much easier; he had reasoned her away that lunchtime.

Sheila was further surprised when her husband announced that he had booked them a table for 19:00, at the new Mexican restaurant in St Dunstan's. En route, she took the opportunity to return the pool car – in which she'd travelled to and from her course – back to the Telecom House car park, and then joined her husband for the last, brief leg of the journey.

The evening went very well; in fact, for both of them, it almost felt like their courtship time all over again. Moreover, for Dave, there was the added bonus of keeping Sheila out of the house in case Mrs Roper decided to call again. Later, over coffee and brandy, Dave made a pragmatic leap of faith and told her that in the future, he wanted to make a special effort to get along better with Julian more. Bewildered and softened by both chardonnay and brandy, she readily accepted his words with tears in her eyes.

323

That night, Sheila slipped into bed without her nightie on, and came on to him for the first time in months. Dave saw it as a reward for his good behaviour that evening, and willingly acquiesced, being desperate for the comfort, affection and body contact, not to mention the sheer physical relief. For her part, she was touched that he had thought to put clean sheets on the bed for her homecoming.

Later that night, as Sheila snuggled naked into his back, he thought once more about Amanda-Jayne. He was proud that he'd not fantasised it was the seventeen-year-old when making love to Sheila; that was a good start. Now, he began to bring up all the other Amanda-Jayne files in his head: the ones that he wanted to delete in this pragmatic purge of the database. In order to expunge those memory files, he had to systematically run through the whole Amanda-Jayne saga; in so doing, he was forced to recall exactly what had been thought, said, and done. How things might have been handled differently was not the issue; it had been done with, and now it would be deleted.

It was during this purging process that he was brought up short by a rather disturbing discovery. In re-running the story, he realised that, apart from some unfortunate contributions from other parties, there was really no one to blame for what happened, but himself; it *was* all his fault. He fully acknowledged a past tendency of his to want to, nay, to need to find someone to blame for any negative situation that he found himself in. The whole Julian debacle had not been helped by this propensity. But not now, not this time: the calamitous conclusion to the whole Amanda-Jayne affair – if it could even be called that – really was his fault. This shocking piece of self-discovery, far from being disturbing, actually began to feel somewhat liberating. He was to blame, and therefore, what was there stopping him from becoming his own father confessor, giving himself absolution and then moving on? At least, that was the theory.

The whole scenario with Amanda-Jayne, naturally led him onto thinking about the similar situation that had existed with his Uncle Ronnie and Katie Townsend. Dave had been all too keen to apportion blame there as well. Firstly, it had been Katie's fault, but then, after a memorably emotional moment with her back in Ronnie's flat, the blame was swiftly shifted to his father. That one had festered away for years, until coming to a head when he was 18. And then, following a brief period, during which time he had no contact with his father whatsoever, the blame sort of drifted around, unable to find a home, but finally got re-attached to Katie by default, as she was no longer around to defend the Darwin family's, and in particular Len's, constant condemnation of her role in the whole sorry saga.

Dave was not prepared for where this train of thought took him to next, but in so doing, it brought about his second disturbing discovery of the night. If he was truly to blame for the whole Amanda-Jayne business, and there was now little doubt about that, then surely his Uncle Ronnie was similarly culpable for the consequences of the entire Katie controversy. And was it not the case that his uncle hadn't been able to let go, even when it was no longer practical, sensible, or safe to keep hanging on? It *was* all Ronnie's fault, Dave decided disturbingly. This second discovery was not quite as liberating as the first one; on the contrary, it would inevitably lead to the rewriting of other long-stored memory files, but the conclusion was inescapable.

Sheila rolled over in her sleep, with a soft moan; allowing much of the duvet to slip off the foot of the bed. He reached down and gently stroked her bare bottom, whilst musing on the thought that a lot could happen in a 24 hour period. This time yesterday, it might have been Amanda-Jayne lying there naked in his bed, but now, she was out of his life completely. Twenty-four hours ago, Ronnie was still his childhood hero; he was a deified figure who had been cruelly wronged by the whole world. Now, he was just another flawed human being, who had been the architect of his own downfall; he'd become a victim of his own poor judgement, just like Dave himself. The wakeful man sadly concluded that his own deeply engrained hero-worship for his uncle had blinded him to the truth for years; a truth that shone through so clearly now. He would certainly have a lot to talk to Tim about next week!

Sheila woke him at about 09:00 with a gentle shake.

'Cup of tea for you, love,' she said in a soft, soothing voice. '*Oh*, and don't forget, Julian will be home sometime this morning, so don't lay in *too* long.'

'*Thanks,* love,' he responded croakily, and then cracked his eyes open in time to see his wife leave the room, the bath towel barely covering her short, but well-rounded form.

Dave slowly sat up and was soon sipping his tea. He was aware that any mention of Julian would once have been as a red rag to a bull, but now he had to go with it; he had to be pragmatic – the theme word for the weekend it would seem – and Sheila would certainly appreciate the effort.

Having finished his tea, Dave got up, put on his dressing gown, drew back the bedroom curtains and then headed for the bathroom. 'Saturday, thank goodness,' he rejoiced aloud, noting the smell of bacon that was wafting up the stairs.

The very moment he closed the bathroom door, the telephone rang. Anxiously, Dave came back out and then hovered nervously on the landing, in case it was Tim, or heaven help him, Mrs Roper. He assumed that Sheila must have answered it on the kitchen extension, as he couldn't hear her voice drifting up from the hallway below. However, after a few seconds, his wife appeared half way up the stairs.

'It's Lucy,' she declared, in ominous-sounding tones, and with a frowning expression, 'and she sounds upset!'

Dave took the call in the bedroom and Sheila, being genuinely concerned, came upstairs and then stood in the frame of the doorway. He sat on Sheila's side of the bed, for she had the extension on her bedside cabinet, and then picked up the extension receiver.

'Hello?' he began, with a hesitant interrogative, whilst also experiencing the echoing ambience from the kitchen phone being off the hook.

'Dave, it's *me*,' Lucy responded, clearly too much on edge to realise that he already knew who it was. 'I shouldn't really be *telling* you this, and I've *agonised* over calling you for a couple of days now, but James *says* that I should.'

'What *is* it?' Dave asked, both anxiously and expectantly.

'The thing is, early on Thursday morning, I was on duty, at the 999 switchboard ... it was the second to last day there before my maternity leave started. *Anyhow*, at about 07:00, I took an emergency call from a gentleman, who gave his name as Stephen Cross.'

Straightaway, Dave felt the blood drain from his head and the room beginning to tilt.

'Yes...*go* on,' he urged, as myriad possibilities flooded into his mind.

'*Look* Dave, it may be a coincidence, but...,' Lucy paused, clearly starting to struggle, ' ...*well*, he said he had found his nephew...*dead*, and...'

'Did they...did they say what this nephew's *name* was?' he interrupted, in a breathy, shaky voice.

'Yes...Timothy...his name was Timothy.'

'Was the call from the Garlinge area, just outside Margate?'

'Yes it was ... *oh Dave*, I'm so sorry, so it *was* your friend and I...'

'Do you know any *more* Luce?' he cut in, now beginning to hyperventilate.

'*No*, this Stephen Cross fellow was very upset, *obviously*. We talked for a few seconds, whilst he gave me the details and I connected him through to the police and ambulance. *Listen* Dave, if there's anything I can do...'

'*No*...no thanks, that's okay Lucy ... I really appreciate you letting me know, bye for now.' His sister rang off, and a blank-faced Dave sat there holding the phone.

A concerned-looking Sheila came up to her husband, took the receiver from him, replaced it, and then sat down right next to him.

'What's *happened* my love?' she asked, in the tenderest voice he had ever heard from her, extending a comforting arm round his body.

Her husband looked at her with eyes that were lifeless.

'Tim is dead!' he replied both quietly, and with an eerie calm.

*

David cycled along at great speed, driven on by his own high spirits, and a mind that was alive with exciting images. At this rate, the journey back to Canterbury won't take any time, he thought to himself, having already left Herne Bay far behind. Of course, he was still worried about his missing uncle, but it was Katie who now occupied every corner of his conscience: those long smooth legs, that dishevelled blonde hair, her pert breasts, her perfumed smell, the silky warmness of her touch and that indefinable essence that she seemed to radiate. He may have been only twelve, but he was acutely aware of being post-pubescent at that moment. Some of the rougher council house-type boys at school sometimes referred to him as a poof, because of his sensitive nature, but boy, did he feel heterosexual today.

David flew down Sturry Hill at just under the speed limit and, as he could see that the road from Thanet was clear, shot over the level crossing, just as the signalman was beginning to close the gates. Although he didn't look back, David imagined that the signalman was shaking his fist at him, just like in those Saturday-morning films about wayward children.

The outskirts of Canterbury were soon upon him and before very long, he found himself peddling up the hill towards the family home. Looking up between leg-aching thrusts, he noticed a police car ahead. As he gradually got closer, it seemed to be parked outside their house. And then, as he completed his journey home, he could see that it was, and this led him to speculate that perhaps they'd finally found Uncle Ronnie.

David was leaning the bike against his father's neatly clipped hedge, when his mother and a policeman appeared together at the front door. The latter pointed straight at him.

'*Well* Mrs Darwin, it seems that the younger of the two runaways has turned up,' remarked the shorthaired, uniformed officer.

'Oh David, thank *God*,' Meg emotionally exclaimed, as she rushed up the front path towards him.

The policeman followed her at a more sedately pace.

'Now remember, you give us a call at the first sign of trouble,' he added cryptically, handing Meg a piece of folded paper.

As soon as the police car had pulled away, the relieved mother grabbed her son's arm.

'Where in God's name have you *been*?' she shouted, in a rapid change of both tone and manner.

'Didn't you get my note?' David asked, as he was being manhandled along the path; still wondering what the fuss was all about.

'Never mind *didn't you get my note* ... just get in the house *this minute*!' she said, propelling him over the threshold.

As soon as they were inside, and the front door had been shut behind them, his mother's attitude softened considerably, and he followed her through to the kitchen feeling a lot less anxious. Straightaway, David noticed how awfully quiet the rest of the house seemed, deadly quiet in fact.

Suddenly, David had so many questions.

'Have they *found* Uncle Ronnie? Where *is* everyone? *Why* was the policeman here?' he asked his mother, in one long gabbled outpouring.

She stared at him impassively, and then pulled out one of the chairs at the small kitchen table.

'Sit *down* please,' she requested, in a low-pitched monotone, before taking a seat herself.

David soon realised that he was in the house alone with his mother, and couldn't remember the last time that this had happened. The relationship between them had always been unconventional; a comment underscored by the fact that David had no memories of his mother before the age of five. On the other hand, he could draw on some quite early recollections of his father: tinkering with their troublesome three-wheeled car in the drive at Damascena, or clearing the garden with the sleeves of his white shirt rolled up. And then later on, there would be those much-anticipated Saturday morning walks into Canterbury. These would take place on the alternate weekends when they didn't go up to Rothermead. David would be bought a Crunchie bar and the two of them would stand on the city wall and watch the red and cream buses coming into the city from all over East Kent.

It was during the frequent father and son outings that David would sometimes ask his dad about Mum and why she never came on the trips with them. The usual explanation was that his little sister Lucy was such a handful and therefore occupied all of her time. Later on, he gathered that his mother had suffered some sort of breakdown after Lucy's birth and, at the same time, had put on rather a lot of weight. The combination of these two problems resulted in her displaying some noticeable agoraphobic tendencies, as well as having the apparent inability to deal with two small children at one time. Consequently, both sets of grandparents played a significant role in David's formative years and he would regularly be sent off, albeit quite willingly, to spend weekends and sometimes, whole weeks with either one set or the other.

Nanna and Grandad Maybury lived just outside Canterbury, in a pebble-dashed 1920s council house. She was a brilliant cook and David preferred her dinners above anyone else's; although his mother's nose would always be put slightly out of joint whenever he expressed that preference. As nice as the meals were though, he had completely failed to notice that Nanna Maybury never strayed from a well established weekly menu; so much so, that if you were given sausage meat for breakfast, then it had to be Friday and no other day. Likewise, a rich, tasty stew could be enjoyed on a Wednesday, whatever the weather or time of year. The Maybury house and its garden were both neatly kept affairs, each one being looked after exclusively by the appropriate grandparent. Nanna would not so much as pull a weed in the garden, and Grandad was never to be seen with a duster. For David, those were happy times up there along the Littlebourne Road and his love for a regular routine was developed quite early on in the Maybury house; a legacy that had stayed with him ever since.

If David were forced to choose, then it would be those wonderful times with Nanna and Grandad Darwin up at Rothermead that would rank as the very best. One major contributing factor was that both of his parents would be there too for all of the weekend visits, even though he'd still be alone for the longer weekly stays. And of course, there would often be the additional benefit of seeing Uncle Ronnie at those Rothermead weekends, although now, he didn't show up as often as he used to.

There David was, alone with his mother at the kitchen table, alone with her in the whole house it would appear, and what is more, he couldn't fail to notice that she seemed rather distracted, even upset.

'What's going *on* Mum?' he asked, suddenly and inexplicably, feeling rather frightened.

'David, the reason the house is quiet, is because Lucy and Eddie have gone to spend the day with Nanna and Grandad Maybury. Your father however...oh *dear*...' Unable to finish her sentence, she hid her face behind a small handkerchief that had now appeared in her right hand.

'Mum, what *about* Dad? *Mum*, please tell me,' her alarmed son urged, quite unable to allow her the time to recover from whatever it was that had upset her.

Taking a deep breath and, with a dexterous dab of her floral hanky, his mother quickly regained much of her composure.

'Your father's gone up to the hospital,' she said, looking at him with damp, doleful eyes, before reaching out to grip his hand. 'You see David, Ronnie has been involved in a serious car accident.'

With a lump in his throat the size of a tennis ball, David listened in chilled silence, as his mother related to him the known facts: at about mid-morning, the police had spotted the family car in a lay-by on the Thanet Way, near Tankerton. As they pulled up behind it, Ronnie was observed coming out of an adjacent telephone box. On seeing the police car, he seemed to panic, so scrambled into the mushroom-coloured Escort and then accelerated away in the direction of Herne Bay. The police followed him, no doubt, with sirens blaring and blue lights flashing. His mother's voice soon caught with emotion as she explained that further down the Thanet Way, Ronnie had negotiated the Chestfield Roundabout too fast. As a result, the car had rolled several times and then ended up in a garage forecourt, only inches from the petrol pumps. Soon after, Ronnie had been taken to Kent and Canterbury Hospital, apparently with serious head injuries. Unfortunately, a young woman, who had been waiting in a parked car on the forecourt, had also been injured.

'Your father's up at the hospital with your uncle right now,' his mother said, whilst squeezing her son's hand even tighter. 'Ronnie has had to have an operation.'

Although David's own escapade now appeared to have been forgotten, this came as small comfort to him given Uncle Ronnie's condition.

'Is he going to be alright?' he asked, desperately anxious for reassurance.

His mother sighed deeply and then shrugged his shoulders.

'I *really* don't know,' she replied, in frank, fatalistic tones. 'But do you know a funny thing ... the call that Ronnie was making from the phone box, when the police found him ... it was to *here* ... it was to this house. Your father *tried* to speak to him, but Ronnie was largely incoherent and very tearful.' She paused, and then intensified her stare; now looking across at him from the top of her eyes. 'Your uncle asked to speak to you *as well*, David…but you weren't here, *were* you. And then, his money ran out.'

Before David could react to that last shocking revelation, the telephone rang out in the hall. As a result, his mother jumped in her chair, jogging the kitchen table in the process, but soon recovered enough to rush through and answer it. It was her husband, calling from a payphone in the hospital foyer. He was happy to report that Ronnie was now out of theatre and currently recovering in the male surgical ward. However, there was another problem: the press were outside the hospital, and they appeared to know that Ronnie was there inside. At Len's request, his wife then peered through the front room curtains and was able to reassure him that, luckily, it still seemed to be all clear at home.

After her husband had rung off, Meg went back to the kitchen and updated her son on the latest developments. Although delighted that Ronnie appeared to be over the worst, she was nonetheless unsettled that the baying hordes of the press were now just outside the city walls, both figuratively and literally. To calm herself, she began to make a cup of tea, deriving as much comfort from the ritual as she did the prospect of a nice cuppa. David didn't want one, and was surprised that she raised no objection when he wandered out of the room.

With no particular destination in mind, David soon found himself at his usual favourite perch by the front room window. Having settled down between the many folds of the net curtain, David tried to both run through and make sense of everything that had happened and was still happening. This was not easy, as his head was currently reeling with hopes, facts, assumptions and assertions. And it was bad enough that his uncle had been seriously hurt, but to miss that call! The troubled twelve-year-old speculated that had he been at home to take it, then this would have been his chance to really help; to tell his uncle he was sorry; to reassure him that everything would be okay, and most especially, ask him to please come home. When Ronnie got better, David vowed he would make it clear to him, that the only reason he'd not been at home to take the call was because he had gone out on his bicycle to look for him. He would also tell him, in confidence of course, that he had seen Katie and she was fine, but missing him terribly. But most important of all, he would tell Ronnie that he must not to blame himself for anything that had happened. They could then perform the 'Scar Brothers' ritual and everything would be alright again, and back to normal, except that is, for one thing. The lasting legacy of the whole affair would be

David's sure and certain knowledge that his father had been terribly wrong in keeping Ronnie and Katie apart when they loved each other so very much.

After much solitary musing, David glanced out of the window and noticed an unfamiliar car ascend the hill and then pull up on the opposite side of the road. He pulled the net curtains aside for a better look and was then almost blinded by the sudden flash of a bright light. It didn't take him long to determine that it was a camera, or to deduce the awful implications of what had just happened.

David quickly abandoned his post, and ran for the kitchen.

'*Mum, Mum*, the press are outside,' he shouted, as he found her, teacup in hand, at the small table.

Without Len to turn to for either help or advice, his mother began to panic. She quickly stood up, spilling her tea in the process, and quickly locked the back door. And then, with David's help, she made sure that all the downstairs curtains were closed. Meg then remembered the piece of paper with the police contact number on it, and hurried out to the hallstand to retrieve it. As she reached for the telephone, she heard the sound of a key turning in the lock of the front door. A fear-gripped Meg turned to see three large shapes through the glass and, with an instinctive reaction of self-preservation, she fled back to the kitchen. However, it quickly became apparent that the feared interlopers were, in fact, her husband and two policemen, one of whom waited outside.

Len was ashen faced, and his eyes were both puffy and red. He sat down heavily at the table and then stared up at his wife with a look she'd never known before.

'Ronnie is dead,' he quietly announced.

*

A key turned in the lock of the front door, but it was too quiet for anyone else in the house to have heard. Julian came in, dumped his holdall and bag of dirty laundry in the hall, and then went to look for his mother. Not finding her anywhere downstairs, he quickly ascended the stairs, calling out as he went. Sheila, who was still comforting Dave in their bedroom, looked round just as a smiling Julian appeared in the doorway.

'*Hi* mum...what's *wrong*?' he asked with sudden concern on seeing the slumped back and hanging head of his quasi-stepfather.

'We've just had some rather bad news, love,' she quietly explained from over her shoulder, whilst still keeping her arm in place around her husband. 'Can you give us a bit of time alone?'

Dave didn't look round, but sat there waiting for his latter-day nemesis to raise some objection. However, he was to be pleasantly surprised.

'*Sorry* to hear that ... *sure* I can,' Julian said, both considerately and co-operatively. 'I'll just go grab something to eat and then I'm heading off into

Canterbury. You see, I'm hoping to bump into Amanda-Jayne,' he added cheerily.

'Oh *really*?' his slightly taken-aback mother said, whilst an alarmed Dave swallowed hard and dryly.

'*Yes*, I've been thinking about her *a lot* recently and realise now, how stupid it was of me to have ever given her up. *Anyway*, see you later Mum, *bye* Dave.'

After Julian had gone, Sheila turned to her husband and smiled.

'I wouldn't mind betting he's too *afraid* to ring her instead ... fearing that he might get to speak to that old dragon of a *mother* of hers!' she conjectured, in an effort to lift his spirits, if only a little.

Dave smiled politely in response, whilst reflecting on the fact that he knew only too well about that old dragon. It was then that he gradually began to experience a sense of unreality and felt like he was floating outside his body, as terrifying random thoughts assailed him from all sides: Tim, Amanda-Jayne, guilt, discovery, death, blame, humiliation, blame, panic, panic, panic. He just couldn't unravel one shocking revelation from the other: Tim's untimely death or Julian meeting Amanda-Jayne.

Although Sheila was curious about her son possibly reuniting with his former girlfriend, to her credit, she chose instead to talk to her husband about Tim, whilst she dressed.

'When did you last see him?' she asked, manhandling her breasts into the considerable cups of her brassiere.

'It was on that last Sunday, when I took him home from the police station,' Dave replied, with a heavy sigh.

She then placed a comforting hand on his shoulder.

'Do you think it might have been suicide?' she asked in a sensitive manner, standing there rather incongruously in a bra but no knickers.

'I don't know ... it's *possible* I suppose!' Dave said, as he slowly shook his head, but without looking up. 'All Lucy knew for *sure* was that his Uncle Stephen found him on the Thursday morning.'

Sheila looked puzzled at his reply.

'Wasn't that the day you and he were due to get together for a drink?' she asked, before finally pulling on her sensible pants.

My God, what do I say now? Dave thought as he looked up at his wife, and then forced a weak smile.

'Yes, that's *right* ... he didn't turn up, so I phoned him,' he explained, quickly formulating a false back story in his mind. 'I got no reply and just assumed he was *drunk* again!'

His wife stared back at him, and still didn't seem happy with his explanation.

'But hadn't you agreed to go over to Garlinge and pick him up?' she asked, more by way of clarification than a challenge.

The same sense of panic quickly rose up in Dave again, as he felt himself gradually being backed into a corner.

'Yes ... umm, we spoke on the phone, on the day *before*, I think it was… *yes* the Wednesday, *after* you'd gone away, and he said he'd arranged to go over to his Uncle Stephen's house in Faversham *first*, and *then* come back here for dinner,' he expounded, with many accompanying hand gestures.

Sheila looked at him, and then puckered her mouth as she nodded.

'Oh, what a *shame* you never got to *see* him again!' she said, before opening the top drawer of her dresser. 'In actual *fact*, you could very well be the last person to have *spoken* to him; oh *Dave*, how *awful*!' she added, looking back at him piteously.

'I don't know!' he replied, in a mumbled monotone. Lies heaped upon lies, Dave thought, as he watched his wife stretch on a red mid-length skirt. Although she had appeared to have accepted what he had said, the unhappy man wondered how much lower could he get in this whole sorry saga!

Whilst Sheila went downstairs to resume cooking the breakfast she'd begun earlier, Dave remained in the bedroom to dress, having already decided that washing could wait for later. As he wearily pulled on his clothes, he despaired at what a terrible day it was turning out to be. And then there was this potentially new problem with Amanda-Jayne. What would she say if Julian *did* manage to run into her? Indeed, what would transpire if Mrs Roper decided she would phone again, and Sheila happened to take the call? It soon occurred to him that he needed to build himself some protection against either possibility, and could think of no other option but to carry out a limited pre-emptive strike. Unfortunately, to make it really effective, poor Amanda-Jayne would have to be the target. But he was then forced to ask himself what this might say about his own sense of morality with regards his former girlfriend; what about his love for her, and his loyalty towards her? Sadly, as far as love, emotional love, was concerned this was something he could no longer do anything about, and hopefully, the passage of time would take care of that. But what of loyalty? True, he had secretly supported the Amanda-Jayne faction for much of the year, but its cause was lost and he had now sworn allegiance to Sheila's banner.

Dave wandered into the bathroom for the second time, and then stared at his stubbly face in the mirror. His dishevelled appearance unsettlingly reminded him of poor old Tim: his so-called best friend, who had died alone, driven to misery, drink, penury and squalor by an uncaring wife and a seemingly unstoppable self-destruct mechanism. Apportioning blame usually made Dave feel better, or rather, more able to cope with the situation, but not this time. As he'd already concluded last night: finding someone to blame for any given situation was a wasted exercise, and no longer figured as part of his curriculum. However, unlike the sad conclusion of his affair with Amanda-Jayne, Dave had no intention of blaming himself for Tim's death. Nevertheless, for some reason, he was all consumed by a terrible feeling of guilt.

Having spruced himself up a little, Dave went down for breakfast and was rather surprised to find that Julian had left him half the bacon. Not only that, but Sheila had done her best to lay a nice table for him complete with teapot and toast rack. He sat down and began to eat his full English, whilst his wife poured the tea. Although he was rather guiltily enjoying the breakfast, his mind was solely on the pre-emptive strike he'd just planned upstairs, and it wasn't long before he got the sortie underway:

'D'you know love, it's *funny* Julian mentioning Amanda-Jayne upstairs, and *then* you talking about her mother as *well*,' Dave remarked, planning both his words and facial expressions carefully. 'I didn't want to worry you, or spoil your homecoming, but I have to tell you that I had a bit of a run-in with *both* of them a few days ago and, on reflection Sheila, I think you have a *right* to know.'

He went on to explain that shortly after arriving home from work on Thursday, Amanda-Jayne had turned up at the door quite unexpectedly. In fact, he thought it had been Tim arriving early. Out of common courtesy, he had invited her into the house, even though she was acting a little strangely, and also saying that she missed them all and him in particular for some reason. But then, she went on to declare that she loved him. Naturally, he was a little taken aback and tried to tell her that she was just experiencing a schoolgirl crush. She had then gone away clearly quite upset.

At first, Sheila listened impassively, but then her eyes narrowed as she began to recognise a certain familiar trait.

'She always *did* seem a little overly fond of you, come to think of it,' Sheila commented, with a sideways sneer and a slow nod.

'*Yes*, sometimes it was quite *embarrassing*,' Dave said quickly, distending his eyes in exaggerated fashion, 'but I tried to ignore it, *you* know, on the assumption that it was the best thing to do.' So far, so good, he calculated and then decided to push his luck a little further. 'The trouble is though, that silly young girl must have talked to her mother about it, and the *next* thing I know, Mrs Roper is on the phone to me regarding Amanda-Jayne, and accusing *me* of being in love with *her* for goodness sake!'

'*Bloody hell*!' his grimacing wife commented, as she slowly looked from left to right.

Dave could see that Sheila was thinking, as she methodically chewed her bacon, and quickly decided that he needed to give her one more nudge.

'I *know* poor old Julian had a few run-ins with that old dragon,' he vigorously testified; quoting Sheila's own words back at her, 'and *now* it seems that she's got it in for *all* of us!'

Sheila was soon nodding in complete agreement.

'Mrs Roper never *did* get over her husband leaving her ... it turned her mind funny,' she affirmed, effectively reinforcing his words. 'And she was *always* trying to split up Amanda-Jayne and Julian. *Now* it would seem, she wants to make trouble for us *as well*.'

'*Absolutely,*' Dave confirmed, as he quickly got up from his seat and then rushed round to embrace his wife. 'And we must not *let* her. Sadly though my darling, it appears that her daughter may have inherited at least some of that family instability!' Lies heaped upon more lies; he didn't feel good about any of it, but at least now, every eventuality had been covered, determined Dave, as he squeezed his wife tightly. Let Mrs Roper ring and be damned.

With the deed finally done, Dave returned to his side of the table, but his stomach now felt too sick to eat any more. He had just rubbished the person with whom, barely two days ago, he'd been prepared to spend the rest of his life. Pragmatism: that was all his words were, but they had really hurt him inside to say, and he knew that those unkind and unmeant phrases would be echoing through his head for many months to come.

After struggling through the rest of his breakfast, Dave walked round the back garden with Sheila, in order to clear his head. All the flowers had gone, except for a few stubborn, straggly asters, and much of what could be found along the borders consisted of seed heads and withering stems. Autumnal leaves showered down upon them with each new gust of wind, as the couple promenaded across the surviving bit of worm-cast lawn. And still that relentless guilt ate into him; not because of what he'd said about Amanda-Jayne – that was merely a vocal veneer with no depth or meaning – but for Tim's death, and yet he just couldn't work out why. As Dave rubbed a dried bergamot head between his thumb and forefinger, he began to speculate if this inexplicable remorse was because he had been prepared to put Tim off in favour of Amanda-Jayne, but at least he'd tried calling him about it on many occasions, both at work and at home. Even then, when the calls had failed to connect, he'd written to him, so as not to leave him in the dark. It was at this very moment that he realised he would no longer need to search for the source of that persistent guilty feeling: it was the note he'd sent to Tim; it must have been because of the note. The awful realisation struck him that Tim would have received his hastily written note on the Wednesday afternoon, and if he *had* been planning to kill himself, then that blatant missive might have been what pushed him over the edge. Tim would have read that his best friend, the man who was going to help sort out all his problems, had put him off in favour of a schoolgirl he wanted to fuck. That must have been the final deathblow, concluded Dave, as feelings of guilty grief overwhelmed him. He had killed Tim; he was to blame. Yet again, it was all his fault!

Sheila could feel Dave's distress and see his tears, but was completely unaware of the magnitude of the emotion he was currently experiencing. Of course, she felt terribly sorry for his loss and would be happy to allow him some more time to grieve. However, she firmly believed that there came a point when enough was enough; a time would be reached when you should snap out of it and get on with your life. Sheila concluded that she would surely be failing in her wifely duties if she didn't tell him when that time had come; after all, limits had to be set.

By mid morning, Dave was still in the depths of despair, so in order to shake him from his misery, Sheila suggested that a long walk might help with the mood he was in, and also give him an appetite for lunch. Her husband agreed with no particular enthusiasm. As they splodged along the muddy tracks of Church Wood, amidst acres of golden-leafed trees, Dave talked about Tim and also expressed his frustration at not knowing more about the circumstances. Exactly how had his friend died: was it suicide, heart failure or kidney failure? Did he leave some sort of a note or make a will? He wished there was some way he could find out those answers, and Sheila agreed that if this was possible, it might help him get over it that much quicker. The rest of the walk home was spent musing, worrying and repeating himself. And yet, there was no way he could confide in his wife regarding the relentless remorse that was eating away at him, and in all probability, with good cause.

The mixed grill for lunch did nothing to lift Dave's spirits either, and things were further darkened by a telephone call that he took from Sheila's mother, to say that her Aunt Theresa, who was her mother's oldest sister, had been taken ill, and rushed into hospital.

'I dread to think what the *third* call today will bring,' muttered Dave, as his wife came back from the hall; remembering the old adage that bad news always comes in threes.

'Oh I don't really believe in that superstition,' she remarked wearily, flopping down on the diningroom chair. '*Still*, touch wood; that'll be the last of the bad news today!'

The couple then resumed their lunch, with Sheila worrying about her aunt, and Dave fretting about what that third telephone call might herald. He had become convinced that Mrs Roper would call again, even though he'd complied with her demands. Of course, the earlier pre-emptive strike would mean that his wife should take anything 'the old dragon' said with a pinch of salt, but he realised that his own credibility factor was already stretched to the limit, as far as Sheila was concerned. If Amanda-Jayne's mother did deem to call again, then Dave concluded that no good could come of it.

It was at around 14:00 in the afternoon, when it happened. Sheila had insisted her husband go and relax in the lounge, whilst she cleared through. Dave had only just sat down on the settee when he heard the ominous resonance of the telephone ringing. The ring tone stopped abruptly, followed by complete silence. However, it wasn't long before the sound of Sheila's mumbled voice drifted through the half-open lounge door, which told him that she had taken the call on the hall phone, presumably whilst en route to the kitchen. Within seconds, there was silence again, and Dave stared fearfully at the doorway through to the hall, where he knew his wife would be appearing at any time now.

Sheila came into the room, very much as expected, and her countenance was forebodingly forlorn.

'Dave, I'm awfully sorry, it's Len on the phone ... he's calling concerning Grandad Darwin!' she revealed in grave tones.

He rushed into the hall, where the receiver had been left off the hook next to a couple of dirty dinner plates that hadn't quite made it through to the kitchen. As Dave reached for the phone, it almost felt as if it had been his destiny to get that third call, as Tim might have put it.

'Dad?' he said pensively, already guessing that the news would not be good.

'Dave…Nanna Darwin has just rung me. Grandad has been slipping in and out of consciousness since mid morning; she thinks he's drifting away,' his father announced in hushed, sombre tones.

'Oh Dad, I'm so *sorry*!' Dave responded, putting his father's feelings before his own for the moment. 'Do you think he *really* is?'

'Apparently *so*, the home care nurse from the hospice is with him and has just administered a large injection of morphine as a painkiller, so at least he's comfortable. *Look* Dave, your Mum, brother and I are about to leave for Beltinge. Why don't you meet us over there?'

'Okay, we'll be there as soon as we can!' Dave responded, desperately hoping that the 'we' would be appropriate and Sheila, prepared to accompany him.

His father sighed loudly down the line.

'Now I have to ring Lucy and give *her* the bad news. *Anyway*, see you at the bungalow; bye!'

Dave dropped the receiver and rushed to tell Sheila, only to find that she'd been monitoring the proceedings from the lounge door. She looked at him, and gave a small shrug.

'I better get my *coat* then!' she declared, in a manner that was more resigned then sympathetic.

He watched his wife pace across the hall, as he sat at the foot of the stairs in order to slip his shoes on. He did not have the luxury of time to react to yet more grave news; the priority now was to get over to Beltinge in time to be able to say a final goodbye to Grandad Darwin, or just be with him at the end. He especially wanted to say *thank you* for everything he had done for him over the years: the guidance, the benign influence and most important of all, the unqualified love. The fact that he had never been given the chance to say a proper goodbye to Ronnie only made him more determined not to fail in that respect on this occasion.

Sheila soon softened her attitude and reassured her husband that she not only wanted to go over there with him, but also would be driving, as he was quite clearly in no fit state to concentrate on it. However, throughout the journey to Beltinge, she thought, with mounting dread, of how she would have to deal with her husband's grief in the weeks following this double blow. Moreover, Sheila also wondered to herself if she was up to the task.

Jostling away in the passenger seat of the car, Dave couldn't help but think about Amanda-Jayne, and in spite all his pragmatic reasoning of her away, he would have given anything to be able to sink into her arms at that moment. Unknown to his wife, the loss of the precious teenager, and the positive, happy future she would have been the catalyst for, meant that it was, in fact, a triple blow that he was currently having to deal with. So preoccupied was Dave with his quite justifiable self-pity that, he did not even notice that they had passed through Sturry, or that there had been no hold up at the level crossing.

As they finally drove down Gainsborough Drive, Dave could see both his father's and sister's cars parked outside the bungalow at the far end of the road. There was also a third unknown vehicle hurriedly positioned alongside. As Sheila slowed the car, and then pulled into the kerb, he hoped with all his heart that they were not too late, and that his beloved grandfather was still clinging to life. As he got out of the car, Dave noticed that the curtains of the bungalow's master bedroom were ominously closed. Having found the front door ajar, the couple entered and then crept quietly down the passage towards the sound of subdued voices and muffled sobs, emanating from the dining room. En route, they went past Nanna and Grandad Darwin's bedroom door on the left, which was firmly shut. Dave began to feel rather anxious, as he wondered if he was too late.

In the diningroom, his father greeted him with a firm Darwinesque embrace.

'Nanna and the doctor are in there with him at the moment. He's *very* weak…it won't be long now,' he announced, as the two of them separated, and then stared into each other's mournful eyes.

And then, as Len greeted Sheila in the same, if slightly less demonstrative manner, Dave looked round the room at the rest of his funereal family. Sitting in the centre of the sofa, was a heavily pregnant and utterly distraught Lucy, being comforted on one side by her mother and on the other, by her four-year-old son, Jimmy. Dave's brother-in-law James and his younger brother Ed were in the conservatory together, in close conference. He assumed that discussing music and their own respective record collections, which they surely must have been, was their way of coping with the situation.

Having turned full circle, Dave's gaze returned to his father.

'Have you been in to see him yet?' he asked discreetly, and at close quarters.

'*Yes*, with your mother, but I don't think he knew we were there,' Len replied, with a heavy sigh, and solemn shake of the head.

At that moment, the doctor re-emerged from the passageway door, with a very solemn countenance, and immediately walked up to Dave's father.

'His will to live is *incredibly* powerful, but his body is rapidly giving up on him. He'll slip away soon, but I can assure you, he's in no pain.'

'Thank you Doctor Manning … at least it's comforting to know *that*!' Len responded with equal measures of remorse and relief, as he shook the medical man's hand. 'I'll show you out.'

'There's nothing more I can do for now, Mr Darwin,' the doctor added, as the pair slowly left the room, 'just give me a call…you know…after…' The sentence, although left unfinished, was nonetheless clear in its meaning.

Sheila watched as the doctor and her father-in-law disappeared, and then approached her husband.

'Dave, why don't you go through and see your Grandad *now* ... you may not get another chance!' she softly suggested, unwittingly paraphrasing one of Uncle Ronnie's often used expressions.

Dave desperately wanted to, but was suddenly overcome by a mixture of fear, and a desire not to be presumptuous.

Sensing her son's anxiety, Meg temporarily transferred her attentions away from her inconsolable daughter.

'*Go* on love ... *we've* all been in!' she urged, with a sweet encouraging smile.

He nodded grimly and then began to walk back into the passage, where he could see his father and the doctor outside through the open front door. It then occurred to him that Sheila had not offered to go and see his grandfather with him, but it was a thought he was too preoccupied to dwell on. Dave approached the shut bedroom door with a mixture of churning emotions, but all of them, determined to flip his stomach over and wrench tears from his eyes.

From the moment he opened the door to that dimly lit and stale aired room, Dave saw his grandad, lying in the centre of the double bed, and propped up by a stack of pillows. His eyes were closed, as was his mouth, and both of his arms were outstretched on top of the bedclothes, and angled away from his motionless body. To the left was Nanna Darwin, who was sitting on the edge of a small chair and leaning forward in order to hold his right hand.

She looked up at Dave, with wistful watery eyes, as he approached the bed on the opposite side.

'He hasn't said *anything* for over two hours now,' she whispered, as her grandson went to sit on the matching bedroom chair, which had been similarly pushed forward towards the bed.

He reached out and clasped his grandfather's left hand, and was taken aback by how cool it was; recalling that those massive, rough hands were always very warm.

Nanna noticed his surprise.

'Feel cold, don't they? The doctor said it was because the body's circulation gradually retreats from the extremities,' she explained, in calm, and yet strangely unemotional terms. 'That's why the rest of him is so ragingly hot; *here*, feel!' She then placed her free hand on her husband's forehead.

Dave followed suit, and gently stroked the familiar and beloved bald head that he'd never known hirsute. It was alarmingly hot.

Nanna briefly patted Dave's hand before withdrawing hers and then pushed her chair back in order to stand up.

'Will you stay with him while I go to the loo?' she requested, already making for the bedroom door.

'Of *course*,' her grandson replied, in a half whisper, and then watched as she quietly closed the door behind her.

Dave and Grandad Darwin were now in each other's exclusive company, just like those many long and happy days at both Oakenden and Rothermead, when he'd been the old boy's willing assistant and constant shadow. He once more squeezed the benevolent hand, and also looked at the kind old face that he'd known all his life. Thinner now, inevitably, but it was still very much him, and a powerful life force could still be perceived, even though he was dying. Dave now took the opportunity of the two of them being alone, to say all those things he had wanted to say, and hoped that some of it got through, but there was no way he could be sure. The old boy's breathing was very shallow now and there was such a long pause in between each laboured inhaling, that Dave thought every single breath might be his last.

Over the next few minutes, something amazing happened. Grandad Darwin's eyelids began to flicker and, after what seemed like an age, he opened his eyes completely. Straightaway, Dave stood up and then leaned close to his grandfather's head, so that he could be made aware of his presence. And he was delighted to see that, not only did Grandad's eyes tense in recognition, but also the corners of his mouth turned up in a valiant attempt at a smile. The old boy strained to speak, but his throat was dry. Dave quickly looked round the room, and seeing a glass of water on the opposite side of the bedhead, rushed round to retrieve it. Returning to his original position so as not to disorientate the old boy too much, he moistened his lips, and then held the cup, and also the back of Grandad Darwin's head, as he took a little water.

'*There* you go ... is that better me old mate?' Dave asked, as he gently lowered his grandfather's head back on to the pillow prop.

Thus refreshed, the old boy made another attempt to speak.

'Lovely... Good old... Dave,' he eventually responded, between hard-won shallow breaths. With frame-by-frame slowness, he then turned his head round to face where Nanna had previously been sitting.

'And... the Ronnie... too,' he croaked approvingly. Grandad gradually lifted his right hand in the direction of the empty chair as if to wave, before the effort became too much and his arm dropped back down heavily on the bedclothes. Grandad Darwin then turned back in Dave's direction and forced a smile. 'Everything's... going... to be... alright!' he whispered, before slowly returning his head to the forward position and also closing his eyes again.

'I love you Grandad!' uttered a choked Dave, in a broken wavering voice; not knowing if he had physically heard him, but certain that the message had got through on a spiritual level.

His grandfather's previous laboured breathing pattern now resumed, and it was almost as if none of the previous few minutes had ever occurred.

Within seconds, Nanna Darwin re-entered the room and once more took up her vigil.

'Any change?' she asked; the fact she was expecting none implicit in her tone of voice.

'No, I'm afraid not,' Dave responded, with a slow shake of the head; he didn't want to increase his grandmother's distress by letting her know that she'd probably missed her beloved partner's last words.

'He looks *very* peaceful, doesn't he!' she stated, with a brave grin, before slowly shuffling along the side of the bed, and back to her seat.

As Nanna resumed her hand holding vigil, Dave finally severed the physical link with his grandfather.

'I'll leave you with him now,' he whispered, and slowly got up to exit the room.

His grandmother nodded in reply, but did not avert her gaze from her husband's still but sedate features. Nor did she seem to notice that the glass of water had inexplicably changed from one side of the bed to the other, during her absence.

At the door, he took one last glance back at the beloved man who would soon be leaving them all for good.

Once Dave was back in the hall passage, he paused before rejoining the rest of his family, in order to try and make sense of what he had just witnessed in his grandparents' bedroom. Was it really the case that the spirit of Uncle Ronnie had been there in the room with them? Had he come to guide Grandad Darwin on his forthcoming journey? Or was it merely an hallucination brought on by the morphine? Whatever the truth was, Dave had definitely felt a surge of positive energy sweep through him, when Grandad told him that everything was going to be alright; he could not explain that, but wondered if there was indeed some spiritual element at work.

A strangely serene Dave finally wandered back into the diningroom, where all the other members of his family looked at him anxiously.

'He's still hanging on,' Dave reported, with a stoical smile. 'As he always used to say of himself: he's a stubborn old Grandad!'

As Len, Meg and Lucy all smiled in fond remembrance, Dave sat down next to Sheila, who gave him a supportive wink, and then reached out to hold his hand.

Within five minutes, Nanna Darwin appeared at the door, her face drawn and lifeless.

'He's gone,' she announced, before her usual powers of emotional control rapidly slipped away.

Len was the first of the family to comfort her.

Dave remembered nothing of either the journey back to Canterbury, or of Sheila pouring them both a large drink, once they'd got home. However, he did remember her genuinely well-intentioned words of comfort that Grandad Darwin had now gone to a better place. He happily accepted what she said, not only as the alternative, oblivion, was too painful to contemplate, but also because it supported what he'd witnessed back in the bedroom. Moreover, the emergent faith, which Amanda-Jayne had nurtured within him, had now been re-enforced by tangible evidence. There was no doubt that he owed the seventeen-year-old girl a great debt, but she was in the past now. In the months to come, it would be Sheila to whom he would turn for both comfort and support, for she was his pragmatic alternative to solitude and loneliness. However, he knew in his heart of hearts, that her ability, or willingness to either comfort or support him would run out long before his need of her succour had been satisfied. In truth, Sheila herself would be the first to acknowledge this assessment as completely correct.

That evening, Julian came home saying that he had failed to track down Amanda-Jayne. This helped to lift Dave's spirits just a little, by postponing the possibility of embarrassing revelations being made until sometime in the future. Of course, Julian hadn't gone to the Roper family house, preferring instead to hang about in her favourite haunts for much of the day. However, it seemed that none of her friends had seen her for a couple of days either; it was as if she had completely disappeared. Having heard the statement, Dave wondered to himself if Julian was aware that the Greyfriars gardens had been her most favourite haunt of all: her 'secret place'. It was certainly somewhere he could imagine she would withdraw to in order to recover, and also contemplate the future.

For the rest of the evening, Julian not only offered to make continuous cups of tea, but also allowed Dave to watch what he wanted on the television. Sheila too, was doing all she could to help ease his grief by offering a physical presence: the literal shoulder to cry on. However, although she was trying her very best to be supportive, by bedtime, it became obvious to him that she was beginning to show a little irritation at his continued unhappiness, which did not help the situation at all.

Laying awake that night, Dave pondered on another 24 hour period, where the leading players in his life had again adopted different masks. Poor Tim was no longer dead drunk, just dead. Amanda-Jayne had gone from his lost love, to a prick-teasing Lolita who had inherited the family nutter gene, at least in Sheila's eyes. And worst of all, his beloved Grandad Darwin had passed from being a relative he was very concerned about, to one he now deeply mourned. The last bitter blow had long been expected but was no less painful for that. And what of Uncle Ronnie: had his attitude towards him changed in the last day? No, he was still a loser; rather like Dave himself. But what of this new spiritual element, it was all very intriguing!

As for Dave's so-called, immediate family: Sheila was not naked and compliant that night, but securely protected by a full-length nightie and bed socks, her back towards him. He knew she was very worried about being able to cope with his grief and that he would have to either hide or suppress his feelings, in order to spare her the stress. By contrast, Julian had been surprisingly non-confrontational, even thoughtful. Moreover, he'd been genuinely upset by the news of Grandad Darwin's death and had shown a new maturity; he'd displayed a new level of understanding that went beyond his own selfish needs and feelings. Dave speculated that it might have been those months away from his mother, living effectively as an adult that was bringing out the real him. He couldn't help but recall that it had been Amanda-Jayne who predicted this; she had also been the one to recognise the 'good bloke' beneath all that teenage attitude.

As he finally drifted off, more out of exhaustion than anything else, Dave looked forward to a quiet, peaceful and reflective Sunday with his immediate family – and it helped to think of them as his family – and time to try and adjust to the new set of circumstances.

Revelations

When Dave awoke, he was completely on his own. There was no sign of Sheila and no comforting cup of tea. But at least it was Sunday, he told himself, so there was no work and no one to have to deal with whilst he was feeling so very low. Sunlight leaked through the gaps in the curtains; it was going to be a nice day and Dave imagined that families everywhere were happily planning to take advantage of what might be the last warm Sunday of the year, by organising picnics, or perhaps going on a long drive, or maybe even a walk. However, he wanted none of those things for himself today; he desired only peace and a little comfort, some tolerance and a lot of understanding, while he tried to accept everything that had happened yesterday. Unable to make any sense of it for the moment though, he got up, and slowly dressed, remembering to honour his Sunday no wash, no shave policy.

Dave came downstairs to find Sheila and Julian already at the breakfast table. Their conversation continued in spite of his presence, proving to him that things were looking up, at least on the home front. Moreover, they both smiled at him warmly.

'Morning all!' greeted a croaky, creased and crusty Dave, as he pulled out his usual kitchen seat.

'Morning Dave, how are you feeling this morning?' Julian asked, with an uncharacteristic cherubic smile.

'Oh *you* know ... so, so!' he responded, wobbling his flattened right hand.

'I thought you'd like me to let you sleep in,' Sheila said, as she poured and then passed him a cup of tea.

'Yes…yes, I appreciate that!' her husband smiled, reaching for a piece of tepid toast.

'*Oh*, and don't eat *too* much breakfast,' she said with a bright countenance, 'I've prepared a nice roast for lunch, and you can have it as early as you want!'

Julian was the first to respond to the announcement.

'Yeah that's *brilliant* Mum, thanks!' he said, before giving Dave an enthusiastic grin; a gesture which signalled that lunch would be a shared pleasure, and not something for them to compete over as of old.

As Dave spread margarine on his sagging slice, mother and son resumed their conversation. It was concerning Amanda-Jayne. Julian was continuing to declare his intention to re-establish a relationship with her, whereas Sheila was gently and discreetly discouraging him: 'you can never go back', being the main tenet of her argument. This line suited Dave, but he felt it inappropriate to contribute to the debate, which would mean siding with Sheila against her son, after he had been so conciliatory yesterday. The exchange finally ended in a stalemate, after which, Julian got up to make a fresh batch of toast, whilst Sheila shared out the various components of the Sunday paper.

Dave sat there trying not to focus too closely on the events of the weekend, and when a Grandad Darwin memory proved too persistent to ignore, he thought he'd turn it into something positive.

'I'd like to start using coal-tar soap, if that's alright with you,' he asked, from over the top of the colour supplement. 'It'll be a nice way to remember Grandad by. In *fact*, I've decided that the best way of *all* to honour his memory, is to try and be more *like* him ... huh, although I don't know if I'm up to the task!'

'He *will* be a hard act to follow,' Sheila agreed, with a supportive nod, ' but I doubt that *any* of us have it in them to be so...so *selfless*. I know *I* don't!'

Dave signalled his agreement, feeling quite touched that his wife had claimed his grandfather as being a better person than herself.

The next five or so minutes were spent in quiet contemplative reading, tea sipping, and almost imperceptible toast munching. This was why, when the doorbell rang unexpectedly, it caused both adults to jump in shock. However, it wasn't long before Sheila began to look irritated.

'Oh *no*, go and see who that is, will you Julian?' she asked, with a pained expression on her face.

Complying with his mother's request, Julian bounded into the hall, humming some cheery, although disjointed melody.

Dave looked across at his wife and then screwed his face up.

'I'm not really in the mood to see anyone today,' he remarked, briefly glancing behind him at the hallway door.

'I'm not *surprised*,' Sheila responded, her browed furrowed in sympathy.

Julian was gone quite a while, during which time, Dave continuously cast anxious glances at the internal door. Although Sheila didn't appear to have noticed, he could just make out the sound of a soft female voice joining Julian's, both of which were emanating from the far end of the hall.

Julian finally re-entered the room in a joyous burst.

'*Look* everyone, it's Amanda-Jayne!' he announced, with excited enthusiasm, as he gestured towards the door, through which he had just passed.

Sheila and Dave exchanged incredulous glances, just as the young woman in question appeared, and then stood bashfully in the doorway, like a shy guest on a chat show.

'*Hello* everyone, *hello* David,' she said coyly, in full Diana Spencer mode.

He nodded nervously in response; his mouth too dry to make any sort of verbal greeting, especially as she seemed to be wearing the same gypsy blouse and long skirt that had once so ensnared his passions.

Sheila, however, had no such verbal difficulties.

'*Well*, what brings *you* here again?' she asked suspiciously, her facial expression completely passive.

Dave drew in a shocked breath at her poor choice of words, while at the same time wishing to know the answer to that very question himself.

Julian looked puzzled, not only at his mother's cold greeting of the teenager, but also because of her choice of words.

'*Again*? It's been *ages* since Amanda-Jayne last came up here!' commented her confused-sounding son.

Dave could have kept quiet, but now saw a chance to shut down Sheila's line of potentially confrontational questioning.

'Err ... *yes*, you were here last...*in the spring*, wasn't it?' he asked, in the exaggerated manner of an amateur dramatic player. He then looked at Sheila with eyebrows raised, hoping she would follow his somewhat awkward lead.

Having briefly been very tempted to accuse Amanda-Jayne of sniffing round her husband whilst she was away, Sheila had now thought better of a confrontation, not wishing to involve Julian, at least for now.

'Yes, the *spring*,' she confirmed crisply, with a look of disdain in their visitor's direction, before picking up the paper's business section, and then disappearing behind it.

Seemingly impervious to Sheila's icy reaction to her presence, Amanda-Jayne smiled back at the wall of print.

'Although David and I *did* bump into each other in the town during the summer,' she said, before turning towards David. 'Don't you *remember*? You were photographing those shops being pulled down near the clock tower.'

Dave glared back at her, his wincing smile barely covering his gritted teeth. Shut up, shut up, you stupid little bitch, he thought angrily; haven't you heard of discretion?

'Oh yes *that's* right ... the shops, I'd forgotten!' came his carefully considered response. He then glanced over worriedly in his wife's direction.

As expected, Sheila slowly re-emerged from behind her paper partition, and then glanced between Dave and Amanda-Jayne in rapid succession.

'My, *my*, what a small world ... you two *do* seem to be bumping into each other a lot,' came the cold, contemptuous-sounding comment. Indeed, Sheila had not been privy to their summer's meeting: the one that had actually started the clandestine relationship.

A fearful Dave once more tried to dilute the vitriol currently pouring out of his suspicious-sounding wife.

'*So* then Julian, are you and Amanda-Jayne…umm, back together again?' he asked guardedly, as he stared at his wife's son, desperately trying to make him the focus of the conversation.

'*Well*, that's completely up to Amanda-Jayne,' Julian declared, before looking expectantly in the direction of his former girlfriend.

Amanda-Jayne soon smiled and then reached out to hold his hand.

'Angelica came round last night, saying that you were trying to get hold of me, for some sort of reconciliation. So I came round here this morning to hear it from your own lips!' she said coyly, swivelling her upper body from left to right.

Straightaway, Julian enveloped her waist with his right arm.

'Okay, let's go upstairs and ... um, *talk* about this,' he beamed, before swiftly leading her from the room.

Sheila and Dave stared at each other in horror, at this latest unexpected development. For him, it was especially disturbing; not only as Amanda-Jayne was the last person he expected to see that morning, but also at the thought of the two teenagers tearing each other's clothes off, and then tumbling on to Julian's bed to celebrate their reconciliation. It could be that his wife was thinking the same thing, but jealousy wouldn't exactly be figuring in her feelings.

Neither husband or wife said anything straightaway, but waited until the footsteps on the staircase had died down completely before either one of them spoke. It was Sheila who was first off the blocks.

'*Listen* Dave, I don't *want* Julian going out with that girl, but you seemed to be *encouraging* it!' she snarled, clearly in a mood for a verbal fight.

'No, not at all,' Dave said, with a defensive hand gesture. 'I just did'nt want to start a row in front of *Julian*, and…and I thought you wanted the *same*.'

His wife thought for a moment, and then softened her attitude a little.

'Yes I *do*, but he needs to know what he's *getting himself into*,' she responded, violently gesticulating with a conjoined thumb and forefinger.

'True!' he replied, with a brief nod, before looking back down at the colour supplement magazine.

Sheila stood up and then began pacing round the room in frustration, but she'd only managed to stride out two complete lengths of the kitchen before the front doorbell rang again. She froze, looked in the direction of the hallway door, but then turned away, and leant over the sink.

'Oh bloody *hell*, not *again* ... what's *happening* this morning?' she implored in frustration; clearly showing no desire to respond to the bell, which now rang out for a second time.

'We *do* seem to be very popular this morning,' Dave remarked, somewhat wearily before getting up to answer the front door.

After thirty seconds or so, curiosity had taken over from annoyance, and Sheila went into the hall to see whom Dave had discovered on the front door step. She was surprised to be confronted by a very striking white-haired man, who was easily the equal of Dave in height. He had on a tweed jacket, under which was a white shirt and burgundy cravat. The faded blue jeans he was also wearing did not seem to match the rest of the outfit, yet he wore it all with such an air of confidence, that the trendy trousers did not appear the least bit incongruous.

Dave soon noticed his wife's presence, and turned to her with a shallow smile.

'Sheila, this is Stephen Cross ... Tim's uncle,' he announced politely, gripping a large jiffy bag, which had just been handed to him by the visitor.

'Umm ... delighted to *meet* you,' she responded, in the charming manner that could instantly be drawn on if required. 'And I must say, how *shocked* we were to hear about your nephew ... Tim was very close to us *both*!' she added, whilst holding out an elegantly poised hand in greeting.

'Oh *absolutely*!' Dave reinforced, wanting to ally himself with the sentiment, even if it had been uttered through his wife's dissembling lips, as she was taken over by the alter-ego personality she'd last used on the visiting Ed.

'Thank you, err...you're both very kind!' responded their distinguished visitor, staring down at the hallway carpet.

'I'm just very relieved that you'd both already *heard*... I wasn't looking forward to having to *announce* it!'

Sheila soon ushered the two men into the lounge, staring back and smiling at Tim's uncle with each alternate step. It soon occurred to her that this person may very well have answers that would help her husband's grieving process, and therefore, indirectly help her too.

Stephen sat down, as invited to do so, and without pause, began to address Dave quietly.

'This is a *personal* visit that I, with Alison's full support, wanted to make to you ... the person whom Tim considered his best friend!' he announced; his calm voice and confident manner standing in stark contrast to the tiredness and grief that so clearly showed through on his face.

'No doubt, you are *both* burdened with questions, and if that *is* the case, then I may be able to help you with some answers!'

Dave listened carefully to the kind, selfless words, and then leant forward in his armchair to better respond to their compassionate caller.

'I *really* appreciate you taking the time to come here, and…and also saying what you've just said, *especially* as I know so little of the …you know, the circumstances behind…' Dave just could not find the right words to complete the sentence, but their visitor's slow, close-eyed nod made it clear that he didn't need to.

'*Well*, to be brutally *frank* ... err Mr Darwin ... the post-mortem has unequivocally concluded that Tim died from a massive ingestion of sleeping pills and alcohol... taken in the early hours of Wednesday morning. The time of death would have been around noon the same day.'

Stephen Cross paused for a moment to gather his thoughts and also reinforce his emotional control. Finally, having briefly massaged his forehead with the tips of the fingers from his right hand, he looked back up at Dave.

'I *would* ask if you could respect this confidence ... you see, an unofficial report was given to me by an insider '*friend*', with whom I've had *dealing*s before.'

'*Thank* you for sharing that with me,' Dave declared, in a hushed and emotionally charged baritone. 'And we *won't* let you down in this respect.'

Tim's uncle once again nodded slowly, this time in acknowledgement to the assertion.

'Alison is *naturally* very upset and...and carries a certain burden of guilt as far as this matter is concerned,' he conceded, clearly deriving little pleasure from the admission. 'However, she and the children have *always* been close to my wife and I, and, *of course*, will continue to be so. '

Sheila listened to the rhythm of the exchange, rather then the actual words, with a series of nods, shakes and supportive smiles inserted wherever she deemed the conversation required them, and then waited for a pause before trying to inject a little social etiquette.

'Would you like a cup of tea, Mr Cross?' she asked, with a polite smile, as she hovered half-in, and half-out of her chair.

'Err ... *no* thank you, Mrs Darwin,' Stephen said assertively, with an accompanying hand gesture. 'I *have* to say ... I'm rather awash with tea at the moment ... it's Muriel's, my wife's, way of trying to help me cope, *you* know, by keeping me topped up!' he admitted, letting let out a single chuckle at the end.

Dave smiled at the tiny crack in his guest's formal façade that, now and then, allowed a sliver of his all too human vulnerability to slip through.

Sheila also seemed to appreciate his carefully confessed candour, and also his emotional self-control in the face of adversity. It was the mark of good breeding, in her opinion; as well as being a quality that her husband lacked.

'This whole thing must have been *very* hard for you Mr Cross; *especially* as you'd already arranged to *see* Tim on the Thursday afternoon,' she remarked with genuine pity; staring at him with her head tilted to one side, and hands clasped together as if in prayer.

Stephen Cross looked back at her with a confused countenance.

'I think *not*, Mrs Darwin ... *no* such arrangement had been made to my knowledge. Muriel and I only returned from Tuscany on the Wednesday evening, and I'd had no contact with Tim for some *time* before then...regrettably!' he said, in words that left little room for doubt.

Sheila nodded politely in acknowledgement, but then glared over at Dave suspiciously, through tightly narrowed eyes.

Happy that he'd straightened out the facts, Tim's uncle continued: 'I rang him *repeatedly* on the Wednesday evening, as Muriel unpacked, and got that damned engaged-tone each and every time. *That's* why I visited the premises first thing on the Thursday morning and that was when I…err, that was when I found him.'

'*God*, what a *terrible* shock for you,' Dave said, with a shake of his lowered head. 'I last saw him the previous Sunday and he was down and dishevelled, but I *never* thought he'd, well, *actually* take his own life.'

Stephen also shook his head in fatalistic fashion.

'Alison told me he'd taken their separation very hard and that she'd been worried about his state of mind; as you *yourself* know, only too *well*, from the multistorey car park incident. And *yet*…her taking out of that injunction *against* him … it was…it was *very* unfortunate!'

Stephen Cross obviously had some mixed feelings concerning his niece-in-law, but family loyalty prevented him from being too explicit, and he quickly composed himself.

'I *have* to say … Alison has been *enormously* helpful to me over the last three days; going through … umm…what was left of Tim's possessions. In fact, the packet I gave you earlier contains some things that, she believes, belong to you … a CD or two, some photographs, as well as other personal items; documents, correspondence between yourself and Tim, etcetera. She assembled the items *herself*, bless her, and insisted I deliver it to you today.'

'That's … umm, very kind of her I'm sure!' Dave replied, with a politely forced smile, as he firmly gripped the A4 size jiffy bag in question.

Having now fulfilled his mission, Tim's uncle stood to leave, straightening the front of his jacket as he did so.

'*Anyway*, I've taken enough of your time and regrettably, I have a funeral to arrange. I'll be sure to let you know the date.'

'Thank you!' Dave responded, in a head-hanging half-whisper.

Stephen nodded politely in Sheila's direction and exited smartly from the room. He stayed long enough to shake hands and also exchange mutual condolences with Dave in the hall, before he departed as swiftly as he'd arrived.

Having watched the second of that morning's unexpected visitors leave, a rather nervous Dave closed the front door and then returned to the lounge, knowing full well that part of Stephen's story had not gelled with his own earlier explanation and, what is more, he realised his wife had noticed.

However, Sheila did not challenge him, as they met up again, but appeared to be in a supportive mood.

'Would you like to go through this now?' she asked, picking up the recently delivered jiffy bag from the coffee table in front of her.

'Oh, I don't think I can bring myself to look at it *right* now love,' Dave said, as he stared out of the window and across the drab, dying garden. 'Would you do me a favour and quickly go through the contents, to see if there's anything worth keeping; you know, a memento that hasn't been ruined by beer stains or fag ash,' he asked, remembering Tim's carelessness in the latter months. 'I think I need to go and grab some fresh air!'

'Of *course*,' she replied calmly, and with seeming sympathy. 'I expect you'd *welcome* some time on your own as well!'

'*Something* like that ... see you in a minute then,' he said before wandering back into the hallway.

Knowing that the back door in the kitchen was still double-locked and bolted from the night before, Dave grabbed his bunch of keys from the dish on the hall table, and left the house by the front door. He couldn't wait to get out into the garden for a welcome, solitary emotional release, although not because he was upset, but for the very opposite reason.

Sheila meanwhile, had stood up and was pacing the room in an agitated fashion, fiddling with the corners of the jiffy bag. She was still troubled by something that Stephen Cross had said, and now began to run through it slowly in her mind. If Tim had not arranged to see his uncle on the Thursday, as their visitor had unequivocally claimed, then either Tim had been lying to Dave, or Dave had been lying to her, she reasoned to herself. Sheila paused by the lounge window and looked out at her husband, as he wandered slowly round the autumnal garden. And then, as he receded into one of the far corners, she quickly sat down and ripped the flap of the packet open. Inverting the jiffy bag and then giving it a vigorous shake, she watched with interest as its many and various contents cascaded onto her lap.

Dave paced round the edge of the new herbaceous border and fingered the many drying seed heads within his reach. He had dared not show the relief he felt whilst Stephen Cross was with them, nor even in Sheila's company, but now he felt like screaming it out aloud. Tim's death was *not* his fault after all, thank God, he rejoiced. His friend would have been dead by the time his note had been delivered, and therefore he would never have seen it after all. Any sadness he had previously felt over Tim's death was now temporarily put on hold, whilst he willingly cast off that huge burden of guilt he'd been carrying around for the last 24 hours. Of course, his newfound relief from remorse was not something he'd ever be able to share with anyone else, especially not Tiffany at work, he quickly concluded. She would surely freak out if he told her that when she pushed his note through the letterbox on that Wednesday evening, Tim was lying dead inside the house. He also speculated that the note must have been the '*correspondence between yourself and Tim*' to which Stephen Cross had earlier referred.

It only took a few seconds for the penny to drop, and when it did, Dave suddenly experienced one of the worst heart-stopping shocks he'd ever had in his life so far. He realised that the very note he'd written to Tim was no doubt part of his padded-packet legacy; the one that Sheila was currently going through. Completely possessed by panic, he rushed back towards the house, telling himself that it may still not be too late; it could be that Sheila had stopped to look at a CD, or perhaps one of the photographs therein.

With shaking hands, he fumbled for his front door key, which refused to insert itself in the lock until he'd tried at least four times. Finally gaining entry to the house, Dave raced blindly across the hall, before nearly colliding with Amanda-Jayne and Julian, who had just come down the stairs hand in hand. Trying to maintain his cool, he apologised, made light of the incident, and then followed the pair into the lounge.

Straightaway, Dave could see that Sheila was sitting quite calmly on one of the two armchairs. She looked up briefly, and impassively, as the three of them entered the room. It didn't take very long for her horrified husband to realise that his worst fear was about to be confirmed. He could clearly see a small collection of miscellaneous papers on his wife's lap, together with some black and white pictures. On the coffee table, immediately in front of her, were two or three CDs, and a paperback book he'd once lent to Tim. The opened and empty jiffy bag was lying discarded at her feet, but worst of all, on top of the paper pile, was a torn envelope, addressed to 'Sheila' in an unfamiliar hand.

The happy teenage couple sat on the settee together, whilst a fearful Dave lowered himself into the other armchair. He could feel his heart trying to force itself from his chest and his mind was racing just as fast, trying to find inspiration for what might prove to be an impossible escapee act. Sheila sat there quietly with an alert but expressionless countenance; her eyes darting from one of the assembled gathering, to each of the others in turn, whilst all the time, slowly and repeatedly running what appeared to be a folded letter through her fingers.

Completely unable to sense the atmosphere of tension that pervaded the room, Julian leant forward in order to make an announcement.

'Mum, you will be delighted to know that Amanda-Jayne and I are together again,' he enthused, smiling broadly, as he gripped the hand of his regained love, and then glanced round the room.

Neither a sternly-staring Sheila, nor a head-hanging Dave responded to the proclamation with either words or a smile.

A little taken aback by the air of indifference that had greeted their happy news, Amanda-Jayne nevertheless, tried to press the point home.

'Yes, and *think* David' she added beaming, glancing with glee at the man in question, ' ... we'll all be able to go on those *lovely* long walks together again; you can teach me more names for the wild flowers, *and* the trees!'

Dave's eyes alternately tensed and relaxed, as his mouth twitched a kind of staccato smile in response to her unexpected assertion. What the hell was she up to, he wondered? Was this reconciliation with Julian genuine, or was it some ruse she had quickly concocted to allow them at least a little time together? Either way, he considered her sense of timing to be utterly deplorable; after all, over the last 48 hours, he had already tried, executed and buried her beneath a mountain of pragmatic lies, told both to himself and to Sheila.

It soon became obvious that Sheila had been thinking along the same lines as her husband, but unlike him, she was about to vocalise her misgivings.

'So *tell* me, Amanda-Jayne,' she began, in a low voice, with carefully placed gaps between each group of words, 'which one of them are you *really* re-establishing relations with: Julian or Dave?' She pointed to each male in turn as she spoke.

'I'm *sorry*?' Amanda-Jayne asked, with a brief but alarmed glance in Dave's direction, as her chest began to visibly rise and fall in panic.

He momentarily returned her glance, before staring anxiously over at his wife.

'*Look*, I think we'd better discuss this between ourselves *first* Sheila,' Dave said, as he hovered half-in, and half-out of his chair.

His wife glared back at him with wide-eyed insolence.

'Not at all, *I* think we should discuss it right *here* and *now*,' she retorted crisply and coldly, but with a sideways grin. Sheila now turned her head ever-so-slowly in the direction of their young female visitor. 'Don't you *agree* Amanda-Jayne?' she asked, her brows raised in an interrogative gaze at the teenage girl, whose skin was now beginning to blotch uncontrollably.

All those cryptic questions and anxious assertions finally became too much for Julian.

'*Mum*, what *is* the matter?' he asked, with a mixture of confusion and irritation. 'Aren't you *pleased* that Amanda-Jayne is my girlfriend again?'

'No darling, *Dave's* girlfriend,' she responded, smiling with calculated sweetness at her troubled son.

Straightaway, her accused husband leapt to his feet and then stood in front of Julian.

'Would *you* and Amanda-Jayne mind leaving your mother and me *alone* for a while?' he insisted, and more by way of a command, making sure he was blocking the lad's view of his mother. 'She's *obviously* upset at me, for some reason, and there's *no* reason for either of *you two* to get involved.'

'But Dave, Amanda-Jayne *is* involved,' Sheila countered with a calm smile, and gentle head-rocking movement. 'Now, will *everyone* please sit down ... I want to read something to you all.'

She slowly unfolded the letter that she'd been toying with throughout, and then cleared her throat.

Still on his feet, an angry Dave now rushed towards his wife.

'*Give* me that ... it belongs to *me*!' he demanded, before making an unsuccessful lunge for the document.

'*Ah*, so you don't deny *writing* it then!' Sheila said in a raised musical voice, as she teasingly waved the letter in the air from side to side, and just one move ahead of his grabbing hands.

Fight, having proved woefully unsuccessful, flight now took over and Dave turned in haste to leave the room.

'*Stay where you are,*' Sheila shrieked, with a snarling grimace, 'or I might be forced to have a telephone conversation with Mrs Roper.'

A disconsolate Dave froze to the spot, an anguished Amanda-Jayne began to sob, and a jumbled-up Julian looked at his mother through narrowed eyes, as if he instinctively knew that she was about to deliver the damning coup de grace to her whole accusatory monologue.

Sheila held up the unfolded letter and, with her practised icy calmness, began to read, skipping, of course, what she considered to be some irrelevant 'schoolboy' nonsense:

'*You must keep this to yourself. For the last few months, I have been seeing this gorgeous young girl called Amanda-Jayne and with Oedipus' mother away at the moment...*'

Sheila paused and glared briefly at Dave, from over the top of the letter, before resuming:

'*She's coming round for dinner on Thursday, which is the only day she could make. There is a good chance...*'

She left a long pause here, looking at Amanda-Jayne and Julian, who both stared back at her in goggle-eyed disbelief. ' ... *There is a good chance that by the end of the evening, I'll have her playing horsey, if you get my meaning...*'

Having just heard herself so publicly humiliated, the wretched girl could take no more, but it was not the reader of those devaluing words who now felt the full force of her anguish.

'But you said you *loved* me, David,' Amanda-Jayne screamed, in tearful hysteria, as she raised herself slowly and stealthily to her feet.

'I did… I *do* love you,' Dave pleaded loudly in response, accompanied by wild hand gestures.

Sheila now stood up and placed both hands on her hips in triumph, knowing that she had just forced a mutual confession from both guilty parties.

However, Dave was not about to get down on his knees and accept his wife's mocking judgement. Once again, he approached her at speed, but this time managed to grab the letter. He then pushed her hard in the chest; as a result of which, she fell back roughly into her chair. He then turned to face the woebegone girl.

'You'll *soon* see that I was sincere ... *here*, let me read the rest of the letter,' Dave entreated, as he feverishly straightened the crumpled document.

Unfortunately for him, Amanda-Jayne soon slapped the letter from his hand.

'*No*, you only wanted to have *sex* with me,' she retorted, through hysterical crying, as she slowly walked backwards and away from him.

'*No*, no, not *just* that,' Dave insisted, as he grovelled on the ground for the letter. 'Let me read the *last* bit of the letter, you'll see…'

'You *bastard* Dave,' Julian interrupted, as he stood up; now quite unable to stomach any more. 'Why did you come into our lives in the *first* place, eh? Mum and I were better off *without* you!'

Years of pent-up frustration within Dave suddenly boiled to the surface and, leaping to his feet, he took a swing at Julian. Unfortunately for him, his agile and much younger opponent easily managed to dodge the blow and, as a result, Dave went sprawling back on the carpet from where he'd only just risen.

From the slumped sitting position where her husband had pushed her, Sheila had been quietly observing the unfolding drama she had so maliciously initiated.

However, things were about to take an unexpected twist, and her son would be the architect.

'*That's* it, I'm *out* of here,' yelled Julian loudly in his mother's direction. 'And I will *never* return, all the while *that man* is in this house!'

Baring his teeth, Julian pointed a threatening finger at Dave, who was slowly straightening himself, and then stormed out of the room, without either a glance to the left or right, slamming the door as he went.

Amanda-Jayne was still standing with her back against the sideboard, her red face running with tears.

'My mother was…was *right* about you,' she accused, whilst pointing at Dave; her sobs now in rhythm with her agitated breathing.

'Yes she *was,* dear,' agreed a smiling Sheila, finally breaking her long silence. 'Now why don't you run along ... *there's* a good girl.'

As bidden, Amanda-Jayne slowly walked to the door and opened it, but paused on the threshold, and looked back into the room.

'I thought you *loved* me,'she sobbed and then ran for the front door.

A numbed Dave didn't have a chance to respond in any way whatsoever; not that anything he could have either said or done, right at that moment, would have made the least bit of difference to the outcome.

Sheila stood up, leant over and then calmly retrieved the crumpled note from Dave's hand without any resistance.

'I believe you were going to read on,' she said in a matter of fact tone. 'Allow *me* ... after all, this last bit does rather affect me too:

In all seriousness though, I think she really is the one this time!'

She calmly folded the letter back up, smiled and then shrugged her shoulders.

'If it was only the sex, if all you wanted to do was *fuck* the little tart ... make her play '*horsey*' as you phrased it, then I could have…I *might* have forgiven you, and put it down to the stress of losing your grandfather. But *no*, you were *in love* with her. Made plans to *leave* me for her…*had* you, eh Dave?'

Dave had maintained eye contact with his wife throughout the entire diatribe, but now he looked to the ground in shame.

'I…I don't know…*probably*…but…' the sentence petered out into silence; he had nothing more to say, and was heartily sick of lying; it seemed to be all that he'd done over the last 48 hours, at least as far as his home life was involved.

For the first time, Sheila's face began to show some emotion and her mouth had started to quiver, but she was not yet quite finished judging him.

'*God,* Dave; d'you know what? ... you're no *better* than that paedophile uncle of yours. At least Ronnie had the decency to *kill* himself!'

Just as Sheila reached her bile-soaked finale, Dave swung his right arm and slapped her across the face, very hard in fact, and he made sure not to miss this time. The resultant blow dislodged her glasses, which resulted in her resembling some sort of hideous parody of Captain Mainwaring from *Dad's Army*.

Sheila looked at him as if she hadn't felt a thing, her eyes tensing and relaxing at random, before calmly straightened her spectacles. It was then that her breathing gradually became more and more pronounced, as she maintained that intense stare.

'Get out, get out, *get out of this house,*' she screamed, having built herself up to a hyperventilated crescendo.

*

'Go on, get *out* of this *house* ... get out *right* now,' his furious father shouted, from the other side of the lounge. 'I don't think I can stand *another minute* of your confrontational attitude, you silly young fool!'

Things had become rather strained between Len and Dave in the six or more years since Ronnie's death, and the tension that had been building between them for some time finally boiled to the surface that very Thursday evening.

'*Please* Len, it's dark outside now *and* it's raining down hard; he *can't* go like this,' Meg pleaded, well used to her role as peacemaker between the two Darwin males; those two superpowers who had been building up arms and threatening each other's borders for seven years. 'Look, I'm sure if Dave apologises…'

'*He's* the one who should apologise,' her angry son interrupted, pointing accusingly at his father, ' ... he's the one who *started* all this!' Dave got up to storm out of the room, being one of his well-practised teenage acts of defiance, but was halted by what he initially perceived as a climb down.

'Your mother's absolutely right son,' Len said, with some reluctance, from over the top of the *TV Times*. 'Say sorry, and I'll let you go to your room. But I *still* want you out by the weekend!' he added, in order to imprint his authority as man of the house.

The conciliatory gesture was made purely for his wife's sake, to spare her the worry of having Dave tear off into the night on wet dangerous roads. But it was a hollow gesture and everyone in the room realised it. Firstly, Dave was due to move out into his own bedsit on Saturday anyway, and secondly, Len knew very well that his son was not going to apologise; they were very much alike, and *he* wouldn't have said sorry, if the roles were reversed.

'*Huh*, I'm not *going* to apologise!' Dave responded to his father, very much as predicted '*You* want me out of the house, so I'll go *now*.' He tore out of the room and then clumped noisily up the stairs.

Almost straightaway, his mother ran into the hallway a few seconds behind him.

'But *David*, where will you go?' she called out anxiously after him.

'As if *you* care!' her son shouted back down the stairs. 'And call me *Dave*; I *am* nineteen now you know!'

They were only words though; words without meaning. He knew his mum cared and realised that she would be worried about him, but upsetting her was an indirect way of getting back at his father. Later on, she would no doubt scold her husband for his intolerant attitude and perhaps, make him feel guilty by conjuring up images of park benches, strange predatory old men and discarded bodies found later in a ditch by the roadside. The problem was, those images were worrying the troubled teenager as well. Where *would* he go tonight?

Dave crept into his bedroom and then gazed at the stack of sellotaped-up boxes against the empty shelving unit. Luckily, a lot of his things had already been packed for his move at the weekend, so all he had to do was get some clothes together, retrieve his washing things from the bathroom and then he could finally be off and out of that house for good. His only regret was not being able to say goodbye to his brother and sister, with whom he had no gripes. Unfortunately though, Lucy was round at a girlfriend's house, and Eddie, who was sound asleep at the other end of the bedroom they were forced to share, would be upset if he woke him now, even if it did mean that he would be getting the bedroom to himself a whole two nights earlier.

As soon as his bluster had cooled a little, Dave thought about his mother's words once again. The problem remained: where *would* he go for the next two nights? He pondered this predicament whilst carrying the boxes out to his car. Crawling back to his father was definitely not an option; he'd done so a number of times in the recent past, especially following threats of being banished from the family home. Also ruled out was the alternative of going to stay with Grandad Maybury. He was in no fit state to put the nineteen-year-old up, what with Nanna Maybury being so ill in hospital and he himself getting over a minor stroke suffered earlier that year. Dave did think about going all the way to Rothermead, secure in the knowledge that Nanna and Grandad Darwin would be only too pleased to take him in. However, it was a long way to commute back to Canterbury for work each day, and besides which, it was rather late and they would have already gone to bed by the time he got there. No, he would have to think of another option.

An inspiring idea finally occurred to Dave, just as he went back into the house to fetch his very last box: the most precious one of all; the one that contained all his childhood Ladybird books and Dinky toys. As he passed the hallstand, he quickly and quietly opened the drawer and sure enough, there they were: the two 'special' keys with the thick buff card label attached, upon which, was some indistinct faded writing. Reaching inside, he stealthily slipped them into his trouser pocket, and then quietly closed the drawer.

As Dave came downstairs with that last box, his parents met him in the hall. Whilst his mother looked regretful and close to tears, his father stood there upright, with his arms folded, and a face like a rugby full-back's passport picture. The evicted teenager did his best to act bravely.

'*Right* then, I'm off!' he declared; any sympathy he felt for his mum easily cancelled out by his dad's defiance.

Looking straight ahead, Dave marched towards the front door, holding the heavy, bulky box in front of him. However, as he drew level with his parents, his father stepped forward and barred his way.

'*Keys…now*!' he barked, holding out an upturned, flattened hand.

Dave was shocked; he couldn't believe that his father had seen him take them out of the drawer. However, it soon dawned on him, with much relief, that he must be meaning the keys to *this* house. Even so, he realised that once they were handed over, his bridge back would be well and truly burned. Dave banged the box down and then retrieved the key ring from his trouser pocket, being careful not to let his newly acquired 'special' keys fall out at the same time. With some effort, he eventually managed to slip off both the front and back door keys to the house he'd lived in for the last 13 years, and then slammed them down on the hallstand, completely ignoring his father's outstretched hand.

Len didn't wait to see his oldest son walk out of the front door, but calmly ambled back into the lounge, with seeming emotional indifference.

Meg however, followed her first born out into the dark, rainy night. She watched as he loaded the last box in the back of his car, and then intercepted him by the driver's door.

'*Please* keep in touch David,' she begged, with tears in her eyes, before hugging him tightly.

As Dave willingly settled into the embrace, he felt something being slipped into his jacket pocket.

'Yes of *course* I will, Mum,' he replied warmly, and close to her ear. 'I'll call you from work in a few days' time ... I promise!' After a brief smile, he got in his car and drove off without either a backwards glance or a Darwin wave.

Dave waited until he had descended the hill and then rounded the corner before he pulled over and then felt in his pocket for what his mother had just secreted there. To his delight, he found not only a folded ten pound note, but also both his house keys. With a warm smile, he looked back towards the house, which of course was now out of view, and hypothesised that his mum would surely experience some trouble from his dad for that act of kindness.

As Dave pulled away to start his new solitary existence, he glanced briefly at all the many boxes, containing his life, which were packed tightly around him, and thanked the lord for Grandad Darwin's old Ford Escort. He had purchased the seven-year-old, red Mark One from his grandfather, shortly after passing his test. They had allowed him to pay by monthly instalments, and then cancelled the debt after only three payments. He was eternally grateful to his grandparents for that kind gesture, as his wages as a junior clerical officer at Telecom were not considerable, especially after his parents had taken the excessive £25 per week 'house-keeping' money they insisted on.

Well, at least that's another payment I won't have to make, he thought ruefully, as his car splashed along an otherwise deserted Broad Oak Road.

Sod's law dictated that, more often than not, Dave would get caught at the newly installed automatic barriers at Sturry level crossing, and on each and every occasion, he would think of that very first time with Uncle Ronnie, when the last steam train had sped through. The nineteen-year-old stared at the hypnotic alternate flashing red lights of the new automatic crossing and realised it was because of his uncle, that he now found himself in this position, in other words: homeless. But he knew that he wouldn't have changed a thing. Indeed, those words had long needed to be said to his father, and tonight he'd finally unburdened himself.

Dave's concentration at recalling that evening's row was soon broken by a snarling sound, as a diesel locomotive slowly passed in front of him with a railway engineering train. The barriers went up after it had cleared the crossing, and he took the Herne Bay road, commencing with that steep Sturry Hill.

Having been lost in thought for much of the journey, it seemed like no time at all before he found himself pulling up along Herne Bay seafront, just in front of the old bandstand. Looking over at the now somewhat shabby regency terrace, it struck him as extremely odd that his father had not sold Ronnie's old seaside home long ago. The London flat had been disposed of very quickly, as far as he could remember, but not the original one here in Herne Bay. Every few months or so, his father would take those keys from the hallstand drawer and then drive over to the coast to check that everything was still in order. Although the offer had always been there, especially in the early years, Dave never went with him; he hadn't wanted to. In fact, his last visit had been on the very day that Ronnie died, the day he'd found Katie there, looking so lovely and so vulnerable. He hadn't wanted to sully that special memory with subsequent visits to an empty, lifeless flat; not until tonight, when absolute necessity forced his hand.

Dave locked the car and then stooped to look at all the boxes in it. He briefly considered unloading them, but felt far too tired, so in the end, decided to risk leaving them there and took only his holdall that contained most of the essentials.

To his relief, the first of the recently acquired keys successfully opened the huge front door, at the top of those stone steps. A single dim light bulb illuminated the lobby and grand staircase; the sharpness of its splendid regency carving dulled by successive layers of white gloss paint. Having reached the second floor landing, Dave hesitated outside Ronnie's door. He knew there would be ghosts in there, as well as memories of happier times when he was a child, but it was either go inside, or sleep out in the car with all the boxes. With the wiser of the two options chosen, he slowly turned the key in the lock and the door yielded to him with a complaining creak, as if the hinges were waking with a yawning stretch from a long, deep sleep. The sound also seemed to echo up and down the stairwell behind him.

The main room of Ronnie's old flat was cold and dark, and a fruitless flicking of several light switches proved there to be no electricity. His eyes gradually adjusted to the available light, which was seeping in from the streetlamps outside through the two large and un-curtained bay windows, and soon he could see that the flat, or rather this room, was still partly furnished. Some of the better, newer pieces of furniture had gone, but they'd always been less memorable to him than the old family items that thankfully still remained. Even so, there were many bare, dusty spaces visible; as well as seven-year-old newspapers, from a long-completed packing up process, standing in random piles or loose scattered sheets, all over the floor. He quickly checked the other rooms and found them in a similar state, although there was no bed to be found at all. However, the water was still connected and the loo still flushed with reassuring vigour, just as it always had. It could have been far worse, was the thought he consoled himself with, as he slowly wandered back to the main room.

Dave was thankful that the old sagging sofa was still there, in roughly its old position, and looking much the same as it had when supporting the alluring form of Katie Townsend on that eventful July day back in 1969. He soon began to beat the 1970s dust from the 1950s cushions on what would have to be his bed for the next two nights. In doing so, he noticed a small object projecting out from the back of the settee. He reached down, retrieved it and then went over to the nearest bay window, in order to better illuminate the find. It turned out to be a small pink hairbrush and there was a mat of long blonde hair still trapped within its plastic bristles. Ghosts, he thought, with a single wistful chuckle.

Without undressing, Dave settled down on the old settee for the night. Despite appearances, it was surprisingly comfortable. With his head propped up on one of the threadbare arms, he looked around him. Straight ahead, and against the wall between the two bay windows, was the old family sideboard where it had always been, and resting upside down on top of it the small coffee table with the spindly legs. A faint glint underneath the sideboard, turned out to be a long forgotten whisky bottle; an empty one of course. More ghosts, he concluded, with a tinge of sadness.

Dave propped himself up to double check, but that appeared to be the total of what was left of Ronnie's possessions. The room was otherwise empty, except it seemed, for those ghosts; the echoes and reminders of Ronnie and Katie. Of course, Katie Townsend wasn't dead, or at least he assumed that she wasn't. A quick bit of maths, told him that she would be 22 years' old by now, and 23 in the summer. He imagined her still to be as beautiful as ever and no doubt being pursued by every man she knew, unless she was already married. He further speculated that she had become a model, a fashion designer or even an actress, and then fantasised about her doing the Cadbury's *Flake* advert on telly. He also thought of Ronnie; how could he not? Sleeping as he was in his uncle's old flat, and on the very settee he had perched upon on his fifth birthday, when his uncle had given him that wonderful crane; a toy that was in one of the boxes back out in the car.

There hadn't been a day, during these past seven years, when Dave hadn't thought about his uncle, and the fact that he had died, having been denied access to the arms of the woman he loved. And wasn't it his father, Ronnie's own brother, who had kept them apart, thus driving the distraught man to drink – his uncle's binge drinking on those dark episodes of his didn't really count – and an untimely death? Dave had reproached his father on the subject, in some small way, the day before the funeral, thus earning himself a ban from attending the service at All Saints, and the chance to say a proper goodbye to his beloved uncle. That was why Dave felt that Ronnie was somehow still with him, through each and every day of the last seven years. That was also why he loyally made sure that no one, not least his father, ever said anything remotely negative about the much-missed man.

As for Katie, Dave's parents never mentioned her, apart from his father's occasional over the top references to 'that bloody schoolgirl'; the one who, 'ruined Ronnie's career' and also 'caused his premature death'. Over the years, Len would never discuss her calmly and utterly refused to be drawn on the subject; he had formed an opinion and was determined not to deviate from it. Therefore, Dave was never given the opportunity to mention, in a calm non-confrontational atmosphere, that he had actually met Katie, let alone twice. However, he had been very tempted to, on a number of occasions, especially when his father started on one of his: '*silly young fool…he had every advantage…chances I didn't have*' monologues concerning the unfortunate Ronnie.

Dave would be the first to concede that in all his father's rantings, he had never actually criticised his late brother in a nasty way. His feelings were more of regret that an alternative path had not been taken, or different decisions made. At the end of the day, Ronnie had been his only sibling and Len still loved him every bit as much as Dave did. But it was the differing ways they showed it, the opposing methods by which they expressed their grief at his loss, that really caused the friction between them. Throw in the Katie Townsend factor and it was an utterly untenable situation that saw father and son lock horns on a regular basis.

The tension between himself and his father had finally and inevitably come to an awful head earlier that very evening, Dave recalled, as he adjusted his position on the settee. He then began to run through the explosive events that had occurred only a few hours before.

He and his parents had been contentedly watching one of those 'where are they now' type programmes on the television when, quite unexpectedly, Ronnie had been featured in the second half. They showed brief clips of his final *Opportunity Knocks* appearance and also one of him famously guesting on *The Lulu Show*. There were a few black and white stills of a young Ronnie at various talent competitions, as well as some other less welcome and clandestine views of him with Katie, leaving his London flat, just prior to it all hitting the fan. Almost immediately, his father had started one of his composite: '*Silly young fool/that bloody schoolgirl*' type speeches and unfortunately, Dave had heard it one too many times.

'For God's *sake* Dad, it's almost as if you're *jealous* of Uncle Ronnie,' he dared to suggest, through a petulant grimace.

'David!' his mother interrupted, with a countenance that wasn't so much reproachful as it was a desperate warning to back off.

'You don't know what you're *talking* about, you silly young fool,' Len barked crossly, without making eye contact, as the programme's ending credits rolled.

'Oh, so now *I'm* the silly young fool, am I?' Dave challenged, with a steely stare in his father's direction. 'What are you going to *do* about it then Dad? *I've* got no girlfriend for you to ban me from seeing, but I will go out in the car and kill myself like Uncle Ronnie, if it would *please* you!'

'*David*, that's quite enough,' his mother shouted, with words that were angry, but a face that was fearful.

'How *dare* you suggest that I was responsible for his death,' Len responded, in a tone that was more distressed than angry. 'It was all the fault of that *schoolgirl* ... oh, that shameless trollop *flaunting* herself like that!'

'That schoolgirl, *that* schoolgirl?' Dave bellowed in furious frustration. 'Her name was *Katie* Dad, she was a *person*, …she was a *lovely* person who was kind, loyal, beautiful and…and she and Ronnie *loved* each other! And, she *never* flaunted herself, as you say!'

His mother once more felt she had to intervene in the stag fight.

'*Please* David, you *don't* know what you're talking about,' she warned, unintentionally echoing her husband's words, but with far less bite.

'*Just* a minute, Meg ... it sounds to me like he knows *more* then he's letting on,' his father said with a quizzical look in Dave's direction, leaning forward in his armchair.

'Yes I *do* ... you see, I *met* her!' Dave announced in dramatic fashion. He then went on to explain about his brief encounter with Katie in Ronnie's dressing room back in the spring of 1969.

His father listened impassively, but then afterwards, thought for a while, with his brows furrowing and twitching. Finally, he lifted his head to glare at his son, having passed some sort of intellectual judgement.

'Why the hell didn't you tell us this *before*, you silly young fool? If we'd have *known* Ronnie had got himself a young girlfriend, we might have prevented all that from happening!'

Dave was having none of it.

'How did *I* know how old she was, you stupid old man! I was only twelve *myself*. And how *dare* you...you even *suggest* that it was my fault for not telling you. You're just covering up your *own* guilt. *You're* the one who kept them apart, they were in love and you kept them apart. Because of *you*, Ronnie fled and had that accident. It's all *your* fault Dad; *you killed Uncle Ronnie!*'

There then came all that '*Get out of this house*' type ranting that he'd heard on a number of occasions before as a mere threat. However, this time he realised it was genuinely meant, just as he had really meant his own unequivocal condemnation. And there was no doubt that his father was sincere, as beneath the surface, they were very much alike, and if a son of his had said what he'd just uttered, then he would be out on his ear too.

That had all taken place several hours ago, and now here he was, not only on Uncle Ronnie's sofa, but also holding Katie's hairbrush in his hand. He hadn't told his parents about that second meeting with his uncle's young lover in that very room, and now they would never know.

At that moment, the streetlights blinked out in rapid succession and the room was plunged into complete darkness. Dave closed his eyes and began to think about his immediate future. He had a tolerable job, he had an average car and soon he would have his own passable bed-sit in that old Ridgeway Motel, with a dotty old woman as his landlady. And what is more, he also planned to ask that Vivien out, the young lady he had met at the Young Conservatives; a meeting place and social outlet that had more to do with pragmatism as it did politics. She was attractive, shapely and, if what she'd told him was true, a nurse up at the main Canterbury hospital. And you know what sort of reputation nurses are meant to have, he concluded with glee, as he slowly slipped into sleep. Yes, things were definitely looking up!

*

'I am *not* going to get out ... *huh*, I'm not going *anywhere*!' Dave said, in response to Sheila's manic screams.

This was not bravado; it was damage limitation. Having lost Amanda-Jayne and now seemingly Sheila too, there was absolutely no way he was going to leave behind his plants, his books, his records and all the other accumulated mementos of his life that were contained within that house and garden. Besides which, there was no longer any convenient Herne Bay flat or Chestfield bed-sit for him to go to. There really was no option for him but to dig his heels in and stay put.

'Look Sheila, this is as much my home as it is yours,' he reasoned, with controlled calmness. 'Why can't we just…'

'*Right* … I'll be the one to go then,' she interrupted decisively, before bursting into the hall. Sheila realised that there was no way she could stay there with him any longer, not least because of what Julian had so forcefully declared. Her son had just made it clear that he would not come home while Dave was there, so if her husband would not leave, then it was up to her to go and find a new home for herself; one that Julian would be prepared to come back to.

Dave hurried into the hall after her.

'But *where* will you go?' he asked, with bewildered confusion, whilst blocking her access to the staircase. 'Why don't you stay until we can work something out?'

Even after all that had occurred that day, the idea of being left completely companion less was still a hard one for him to contemplate. Indeed, he was ready to talk Sheila into staying, even after all the horrible things she had said, not least to Amanda-Jayne, and also the delight she seemed to take in reducing the poor girl to floods of uncontrollable tears. Besides which, what would his family think, or work colleagues say, if it were announced that his second marriage had failed as well? And another thing, if it became common knowledge that his wife had left him within days of Tim's death, would that not imply some sort of culpability on his part?

Unfortunately, Sheila was in no mood to stay there in the marital home, even while Dave begged her to reconsider her decision, however much she might enjoy seeing him on his knees. She had to go; she had to get away from him and *then,* perhaps, think things through properly. After all, she reasoned, this was the failure of her second marriage as well. But when the dust had settled, could she ever really forgive him, in spite of all that she'd said, and he done? On the other hand, it was not as if he'd actually slept with Amanda-Jayne, and all that love business could just merely be transitory infatuation, she conceded, looking at the pathetic pleading figure in front of her.

At the end of the day though, for Sheila, it all came down to Julian. He always came first in her eyes, and she had to provide him with a home that he would want to come back to.

'I *can't* stay, Dave … I'm going to pack a few things, and then give Trish and Bob a ring,' she said, both calmly and impassively, as she eased her husband away from the foot of the stairs. 'I'm *sure* they'll be able to put me up for a while.'

Dave watched her climb the stairs, and panic began to set in.

'Would you like me to come up and help you with that?' he offered desperately, thinking he might be able to buy himself some more time to dissuade her from leaving. 'Or can I get you a cup of tea in the meantime?'

'*No,* Dave ... for goodness *sake*, I can do it on my *own*!' she yelled back down at him in frustration from the landing.

He merely peered up meekly and nodded in pathetic acceptance, as she disappeared from view. In his desperation, he thought that if he handled things just right and suddenly became the model husband, she might yet decide to stay, or else be back within a few days. It then occurred to him that while Sheila was gone, if he tidied up the house and did all those jobs she had been nagging him to do, it might show her that he was serious about making it work. Then again, he was fairly confident that Trish and Bob were bound to talk her into coming back, especially if he had a discreet word with Trish first. Although they were primarily Sheila's friends from before she had known him, Dave had become very fond of them both, and especially Trish. She appeared to enjoy flirting with him at dinner parties and even occasionally touching his leg under the table.

Dave was still waiting in the hall, as Sheila came back down with her two bulging bags. They were both calm now after that heated row and also fearful of the future, of having to go through the splitting up of their possessions, a house sale and another divorce. To stay together and somehow manage to patch things up suddenly seemed the less painful option. They could both sense those feelings in each other, as Sheila hesitantly hovered half way down the stairs, and Dave stared up at her from the hall below with child-like pleading eyes. For a brief moment, she actually considered unpacking and staying, but that faithful old maxim; the one she always liked to quote 'you can never go back' repeatedly echoed in her mind. And then there were those maternal responsibilities she had to consider.

Sheila slowly shook her head in reply to the ultimate question, and one that her husband had dared not ask.

'I'm sorry, Dave ... I *won't* be coming back. I'll collect the rest of my things in the next couple of days when you're at work,' she announced, deliberately and painfully hardening her attitude.

'Julian?' he asked, already strongly suspecting the answer.

'Julian!' she confirmed, before resuming her journey down the stairs. 'He has to have a home, you know, somewhere he'll want to come back to.'

Dave quickly stepped forward to block her way at the bottom of the flight.

'But he's 18 and going to university soon,' he appealed, desperately groping for anything that might make her reconsider, 'and *besides*, before today, he and I were really beginning to hit it off!'

'*Ironic*, isn't it?' Sheila commented sadly, with a wistful shrug. 'But I don't think he'll forgive you so easily after this Amanda-Jayne business,' she added by way of an unkind coda.

Dave thought of the rocky relationship with his own father when he was Julian's age, and could think of nothing more to say. He slowly stepped to one side, and then walked over to open the front door for her.

'I'll be putting the house on the market, as soon as I can find the time,' Sheila said starkly, as she crossed the threshold. 'And I'm going to take the car. It's only fair; after all, you're still in the house!'

Dave was really floored by the pair of parting shots his wife had just delivered, but was too stunned to either object or protest. He'd completely run out of energy, and there was no longer the will left within him to fight. All he could do was watch impassively from the open front door, as Sheila drove away through the mixture of sycamore and beech leaves that were blowing across the road from the green. He did not wave.

Dave wandered back into the lounge in a numb daze, and with his body functioning on autopilot. There was too much going on in his head to concentrate on any one particular thought at that moment, so he just let the chaos surge forth unchallenged, as he wandered aimlessly round the room. If there was one single idea he *could* isolate and clarify, then it was that things could not get any worse. There was literally nothing more that could happen to him, or at least nothing that would possibly drag him down even further than the position he was already in.

Calming his mind seemed a desirable goal, so he threw open the drinks cabinet, poured himself a large tumbler of whisky and then dropped down into an armchair. Would the anaesthetic help to ease the cumulative chaotic jumble of thoughts that would just not relent? Would sufficient ingestion of strong spirits dull the emotional pain that had been caused by blow after blow, inflicted upon him in the last 48 hours? He doubted it on both counts, but drank deeply in any case. Dave was then forced to ask himself: was this how Tim had felt towards the end? And would he eventually end up like his friend: a forgotten corpse, discovered almost a full day after his death? Quite frankly, at that moment, Dave had to admit that he did not really care. The first tumbler went down easily, as did the second, and there were more to follow.

Dave woke a number of hours later, having drunk the remainder of the bottle. He did not feel the least bit drunk, nor any less confused or angst-ridden, but now felt utterly sick and, in addition, barely able or willing to move. Nonetheless, he forced himself upstairs and, leaving his clothes in an untidy heap, climbed into the bed; there hopefully to experience the welcome oblivion of further sleep. As he lay there, not only did the nausea gradually fade, but also the chaos in his mind slowly cleared. Unfortunately, all this achieved was to bring into sharp focus what a disastrous day it had been. For him, this really was the worst case scenario possible; he was now completely and utterly alone, as he'd always feared. All his bridges were now burnt and every single positive thought in his mind had been totally expunged. At that moment, there seemed to be no way forward.

As he adjusted his posture and tried to sleep again, dark dangerous thoughts began to haunt him. It began to seem more and more likely that his poor friend had the right idea: when life becomes too hard to bear, why put up with it? Tim had obviously decided that painless and peaceful oblivion was a more attractive option than what his life had brought him: an aggressive estranged wife, a thankless miserable job, a house that was about to be taken away from him and little money with which to buy those few things that made life bearable. Alarmingly, that sorry catalogue could also have been an epitaph for Dave's own life. But there was one thing that Tim had been wrong about, and that was his attitude to the afterlife. His heartfelt conviction that there was only oblivion after corporeal death; an utter nothingness, a complete non-existence was completely wrong. Dave now realised that there was some sort of afterlife; that the human spirit survived our present miserable earthly existence. So for him, the opting-out of our angst-ridden life offered a much more pleasant choice than just the stark end that Tim had envisaged.

Wakefulness slowly gave way to sleep, and those dark thoughts gradually and seamlessly segued into an horrific, yet vivid nightmare. He was an observer at the tragic end of someone's life, but the face of the victim could not clearly be made out. Sometimes it seemed to be Tim, and at others, he was sure it was himself:

Having rifled through the medicine cupboard, in the far corner of the kitchen, Dave/Tim found a full and un-opened bottle of paracetomol. He filled a pint glass with tap water and then walked into the lounge. There was no point in taking alcohol with the tablets, he reasoned; he might be sick and then, wouldn't be able to achieve his objective. Tim/Dave cursed the childproof cap on the medicine bottle and threw it across the room in frustration, once he had managed to wrench the wretched thing off. He began to take the tablets, slowly and methodically. His job with Telecom was not even worth a first thought, let alone a second. And his house, his sanctuary and the vessel for all his worldly goods: it was about to be taken away from him. The people were abandoning him too. Sheila/Alison had deserted him and he knew now she would never be coming back. Things had gone too far! What a failure; he couldn't even hang on to a plain, dumpy, unpleasant and selfish person like her. Dave/Tim lay back on the settee, as a strange sort of tiredness gradually enveloped him. After a while, he could see his childhood, oh those happy days! The last thing he experienced was being bathed in a warm and bright, yet benevolent-feeling light.

The ordeal, for the composite figure in his dream, was now finally over. However, for the soon to wake Dave, the real nightmare was about to begin.

Funerals

The late autumnal sun rose on what, to the vast majority of the village, seemed like just a normal Monday morning. At dawn, there were few people up and about and so, the local wildlife reigned unopposed. A small rabbit scurried underneath the hedge that divided the green from the farmer's field on the other side. She was far too young to remember a time, in the not too distant past, when fertile fields had existed on both sides of that hedgerow. On the green itself, a squirrel clung to the trunk of the massive beech tree, a protected specimen that the early 1980s housing developers had not been able to do away with. The creature studied the branches above him and wondered what magical force had turned the leaves of his home from shiny copper-red to a crisp shrivelled brown. And then, daring to go even closer to the houses, a pair of cretinous wood pigeons fussed round the parking bays, looking for even lower life forms to consume. The brainless birds barely noticed the arrival of the milkman, but both the squirrel and rabbit soon made themselves scarce.

Gradually, one by one, the houses of the close stirred into life, as the shipping forecast, or Chris Evans, blared out of the radio-alarm clocks and lights blinked on in both bedrooms and bathrooms. Eventually, every house was alive with the reluctant rituals of getting ready for the daily grind; every house that is, except one. Then, as front doors slammed in succession, each one of the BMWs, parked in the leaf-strewn bays, blinked and beeped awake, as their respective owners approached. Did any of them notice that Dave and Sheila's house was still both dark and silent? And of their dressing-gowned partners who remained, were any of them aware of the tragedy that had occurred within its walls? The next wave of leavers consisted of the schoolchildren, who wandered zombie-like up to the main road, in order to wait for the crowded school bus. Had any of them been playing on the green yesterday and witnessed the many comings and goings, as the drama in the Darwin household rapidly unfolded?

At about nine o'clock, the human activity around the green died down, and the rabbit and squirrel dared to make a cautious re-appearance. The wood pigeons continued their foraging amongst the fallen leaves, completely unaware that anything had happened. Over the next hour, those leaves that they had disturbed with their beaks and feet were stirred into greater movement by a cool autumnal breeze, which gradually built in intensity. Newly liberated leaves swirled to the ground and joined their fallen comrades on Dave and Sheila's front path. Finally, a small drift built up against the front door, almost as if they knew there was no danger of them being swept away anytime soon.

Dave slowly blinked awake in response to the sunlight that was now streaming in through the un-curtained window. He focused on the light fixture in the centre of the ceiling, and then reached out an arm to touch Sheila. He was shocked to discover that she was not there. Alarmed, he lifted his head from the pillow and instantly triggered the pain and nausea of a typical morning after hangover.

As his mind gradually came into focus, he began to remember, and soon all the turbulent events of the weekend just past, were with him once more. And what a terrible nightmare that was! He had witnessed his own suicide, or was it Tim's? In his confused state, he couldn't decide what had been part of the dream and what had really happened. Where was the dividing line? Obviously, the overdose was imagined, as he was all too alive this morning. But had the rest of his recollections from yesterday also been night terrors? Did he dream that Sheila had destroyed his life, and then walked out on him? No, that was reality; as incredible as it might seem, it had actually happened. Dave screwed his eyes up tight and wondered why he couldn't just return to those first few seconds of the day, when there had been nothing to worry about except focusing his eyes.

With no small amount of effort, he turned to look at the bedside radio alarm clock, which he'd failed to set the evening before. It was a few minutes after 10:00, and he was late for work, but in comparison to recent events, it seemed almost pathetically insignificant. In fact, amongst all that anguish, he felt a smidgen of relief, for the very last thing he could have coped with at the moment was a typical Telecom Monday morning. He thought about phoning them to say he'd be in later, but then asked himself: why the hell should he act responsibly? Let them guess! It then occurred to him to actually ring in sick; he felt ill after all, and besides which he jolly well deserved it, having just suffered a double bereavement. Perhaps he could even get a week's special leave on the grounds that Tiffany got one when her mum died. That prospect cheered him a little, as he dragged himself from the crumpled, chaotic bed, to find that heap of clothes he had left somewhere last night. Dave thought that he'd better have a bath, having missed one yesterday, and the day before. But then again, he reasoned, who the fuck would notice if he didn't bother? So he threw on all of Sunday's clothes from the discarded pile, and then wandered downstairs.

Dave certainly didn't feel like anything to eat at the moment; in fact, tea was all he wanted. That made, he shuffled into the lounge with his mug, went over to the hifi and switched it on. However, after ten minutes of scanning up and down the racks of CDs and LPs, he could not think of a single thing he felt like playing. It was not like there was no choice; his combined collection ran into the thousands, but most of his music had associations with the past, for both people and places. The memory of Amanda-Jayne, in particular, was indelibly stamped on a lot of it. In fact, his entire past, especially the recent past, was certainly something he did not want to think about at that moment. The present wasn't too great either, but that was wholly the fault of the recent past. And as far as the future was concerned, that was a scary concept that he did not really want to dwell on in his present vulnerable state.

Dave switched off the unused stereo and then turned on the television.

'My God, daytime television ... what have I come down to?' he sighed to himself, and concluded that there would be no welcome diverting entertainment from that medium, unless one were senile or simple-minded. He endured about twenty minutes of banality before switching off in disgust.

With the chaos and confusion of the recent past firmly suppressed in his mind, he reluctantly tried to work out what he was going to do with what was left of his life. Yes, it was a frightening thought, but it was, after all, an inescapable one. Despite his nightmare, Dave liked to think he was not the sort to take the coward's way out, as Sheila might have put it, and knew there was no choice but to face up to the future. So, how the hell could he move on and make a new start? Well, one way was to completely dispense with all those things that hitherto had encouraged him to cling to the past; he could dispose of all those reminders of what had gone before. Indeed, he could completely rid himself of all those childhood things that he'd long clung on to like a security blanket: the Dinky toys, the Ladybird books, and that crane. He could have a purge of his record collection too, and discard anything with the remotest associations with people such as Uncle Ronnie, Chloe, Grandad Darwin, Tim or Amanda-Jayne. It would be a case of: out with the old, and in with the new, as they used to say in those optimistic early post-war years. Dave soon laughed out loud at the prospect. Who was he trying to kid? He *liked* the past, or rather, he liked the more long-term past; it helped to define who he was. He also felt comfortable with a life based round a recognisable routine, and what was a routine if not a familiar fragment of the past preserved by repetition. Indeed, even a dull and predictable life based solely on routine was preferable to the uncertainty of a so-called new start.

From the vantage point of his armchair, he looked around the lounge. This house, his house, was a big reminder of the past, both short and long-term, and half of it still belonged to Sheila. Moreover, did she not say yesterday, as a parting shot, that it was going to be put on the market? Wiser men than he would no doubt think that, with the marital home sold, Dave could make a fresh start in a terraced house much closer to the centre of Canterbury. Then, he wouldn't need to replace the car that Sheila had so decisively seized; already being within easy reach of pubs, restaurants, the theatre and heaven help him, work. But he liked the Wellbourne house; it was comfortable and familiar, it was full of his things and right at this moment, it was his sanctuary. He soon began to feel some empathy for his mother, and wondered if this was how it had been for her when she didn't want to leave the house. And was it the present, the future, or other people that she had been scared of? Dave himself, was not so much frightened of the future, as of the changes it inevitably brings. Changed circumstances and changed surroundings were on the cards, and he could not face the idea of that at all. He'd much rather just hide away there in Wellbourne.

The parallels to the last few months of Tim's life had already struck Dave with chilling force, as the previous night's bad dream made clear. And now, here he was, not only dishevelled, stinking and hung over, but also secreted away in a house that his estranged wife was determined to sell at the earliest opportunity. The major difference between Alison and Sheila was that the latter had not taken up with a lot of spiky-haired women. No, his wife's fetishistic preference was a lot more unnatural: she wanted an intimate association with Telecom; her job was her new lover. He then chuckled at the notion; after all, Telecom had fucked him up, so why not her as well!

Dave next considered the possibility that he had been wrong in his judgement of Alison, and perhaps even unfair to her. It was certainly true that much of his opinion of her had come from what Tim had told him, and their few meetings together had been loaded with all those inherent prejudices. Perhaps this 'women's refuge' was just that, as she herself had claimed: a means to escape her unhappy life? But even if it wasn't; even if she wanted to associate closer with her own kind, then a person's sexuality is not what makes them good or bad, he reasoned. And perhaps she also had the right to be somewhat bitter and twisted, having been through the misery of a long and painful marriage break up as well. He soon smiled to himself, to think that he had just been conciliatory about Alison Cross after what she had done – quite maliciously, he assumed – with that note, by including it in the package that Tim's Uncle Stephen had delivered yesterday. But then again, Alison wasn't the one who had written it in the first place; she may have readdressed it to Sheila, but the actual contents were down to him alone.

Not wishing to recall the evil events of yesterday, Dave turned the TV back on and then aimlessly flicked through the channels. But it was still not working as a diversionary tactic, for details of things said and done only 24 hours ago kept on bubbling to the surface. And what was it, that Sheila had said just before she left yesterday? Didn't she say that she would be ringing up and arranging to get some of her things? At the same time, he speculated that his wife was bound to use the opportunity to discuss the selling of the house. But then again, he told himself that she wouldn't be able to do any of that if she couldn't get through to him. Dave sprung up from the chair, ran out of the room, and then took the phone off the hook in both kitchen and hall. I won't answer the door either, he pledged; nor will she be able to get in with her key if I put the security chain across. He did just that, and then rubbed his hands as he smiled in triumph.

Feeling that he'd achieved something, Dave strode confidently back through to the lounge. However, it soon dawned on him that with the telephone receiver off, his family would not be able to contact him either. That thought instantly reminded him of more unfinished business from the recent past, namely Grandad Darwin's funeral. His father, who was making all the arrangements, would surely be calling him today with the details, he thought. If Len couldn't get him at work, then he would automatically ring the home number instead. Dave sighed, did an about turn, and reluctantly went back to replace both receivers.

No sooner had he restored the handset in the hall, than it rang out, causing him to jump out of his skin in fright. He picked it back up with much foreboding, and then mumbled:

'Hello?'

'Ah Dave, at *last* ... it's me!' announced the familiar-sounding caller; it was Sheila. She was matter of fact in her manner, and not hostile in the least. What is more, she straightaway took control of the conversation.

'I rather *thought* you wouldn't be at work today ... umm...in the circumstances. *Look*, why don't I liaise with Darryl Giles and see if I can arrange a week's special leave for you?' she proposed calmly, even kindly.

'Erm...*yes* please!' he agreed, feeling somewhat taken aback by the offer. 'Do you think you can pull it off?'

'I don't anticipate any problem ... you see, at work, it's now widely known that you've just suffered a double bereavement, and besides which, my temporary promotion to managerial grade has finally come through, so I'm the same rank as him, ...well, for the moment at least.'

'Congratulations ... it's what you've always wanted!' he responded, in a somewhat wearisome manner.

'Thank you ... I *am* rather pleased!' she said contentedly, almost as if the breakup of their marriage had never happened. 'Oh, and I don't think that *anyone* at Telecom need know about our...umm, our separation. Don't you agree?' she asked; thus proving that she hadn't entirely forgotten the events of Sunday.

'Err ... yes; *quite*!' Dave said, bewildered as ever by her sense of priority in life. 'There's enough tittle-tattle in my office as it is!'

'*Indeed*... why give that lot something else to gossip about, when they should all be getting on with their work!' she reasoned, in full management mode, before giving out one of her non-humorous chuckles.

Having softened him up with a kind gesture, Sheila was now ready with her devastating denouement.

'And finally, Dave ... just to let you know that the house is now on the market ... it's with the same agent who sold it to us in the *first* place. They've used *exactly* the same details as before, but with a current price of course, and I *knew* you'd be pleased not to have the bother of someone coming up there to measure up and such like!'

Dave could think of nothing to say in response; this was another of those situations in life that he could do nothing about, so there was no point.

'*Oh* ... and *also* to let you know ... I'll be coming up straight after work to pick up some more clothes,' she said, almost by way of an afterthought. 'I've still got my keys so there's no need for you to be in when I arrive!'

'Err ... right-ho...*bye* then!' he mumbled, and then replaced the receiver, before she could unleash any more devastation.

The telephone call having finished, Dave wandered out of the hall and into the kitchen. He told himself that it was kind of Sheila to sort things out for him at work; he'd sooner be miserable at home for a week, than miserable at Telecom. But why did she do it, he wondered? Could it be that she was having second thoughts about the split? He was also encouraged by the fact she had used the word 'separation' in their telephone conversation, which had temporary connotations, as opposed to 'breakup' or 'impending divorce', which were terms that had a permanence about them. However, he quickly dismissed all that as an overly optimistic assessment of the situation, and reminded himself that Sheila had made her intentions perfectly clear by putting the house on the market. With a weary chuckle at his own foolishness, he put the kettle on to make some more tea.

After a couple of hours of doing nothing in particular, the hangover had considerably diminished and was rapidly giving way to hunger. Dave realised he hadn't eaten for 24 hours; his last meal was Sunday breakfast, and that was only toast. He can't have gone that long without food before in his entire life. He was soon searching through the kitchen, opening and shutting the many cupboard doors. There were plenty of packets and tins, so he knew he wouldn't starve, but nothing could be found that would provide instant gratification and he certainly couldn't be bothered to make anything. The freezer was also healthily full, but there again, the same applied; anything he fancied had to be thawed out first.

It was only after a few minutes fruitless searching, that Dave remembered they were going to have a roast for Sunday lunch, and quickly deduced that the components for it should be around somewhere in the kitchen. Then again, he couldn't be sure how far Sheila had got with the preparations before the proverbial shit had hit the fan so comprehensively yesterday. He looked in the fridge, but there was no sign of a chicken, and then noticed the two saucepans on the cooker hot plates. He lifted the lids to discover cooked cabbage in one and cooked sliced carrots in the other. So she *had* got the dinner well underway, he determined with excitement. It was now with a keen air of expectation that he opened the oven door, and was rewarded with the discovery of a roasted chicken and a tray of roast potatoes; all completely cold but fully cooked. The prospect of chicken, bubble and squeak and baked beans soon had his mouth watering.

With the lunchtime menu decided, Dave immediately sprang into action. He found the largest frying pan they possessed, added some oil and put it on the heat. He then sliced up half a dozen of the cold roast potatoes and added some of the cabbage. The carrots would not figure in this meal; he could only eat them with gravy on, or raw in crudités. Baked beans were much more suitable for this leftovers-based lunch; in any case, there was no one around to dictate what he could or could not eat, so he would damn well please himself. Sod it; he could even have a large bowl of Julian's instant mash if he wanted.

With the deft hand of a master butcher, he broke the cold roasted chicken up into pieces and placed them on a plate. On another, he doled out most of the fried bubble and squeak, and then added the baked beans that he'd just heated through.

Dave took the groaning plates, together with the Daddies sauce, through into the lounge on a large tray. He soon proposed to himself that a bottle of claret would go down very well with the choice of cuisine. So, having uncorked it, he positioned himself in front of the telly and then decided that an old video would be nice to watch instead of the news, Australian soaps and chat shows hosted by has-beens. *Oh Mr Porter* seemed appropriate, so he popped it into the machine and then tucked into his sumptuous banquet.

As he gnawed on a chicken bone, in between knocking back mouthfuls of red wine, it dawned on him how much he must look, and probably smell, like Henry VIII at that moment. He soon conceded that it would be more accurate to suppose that he was like one third of King Henry, as he had only got through two wives so far. And there bloody well wouldn't be a third Mrs Darwin, he vowed, recharging his glass. Indeed, he was going to play the field; he intended to shag his way through the young women of Canterbury instead, and not make the mistake of getting serious and actually marrying any of them. And yet, in spite of this aspiration, he would be the first to acknowledge that he loved the comfort and security of a steady relationship and absolutely loathed the dating scene. Moreover, he found the thought of hanging about in pubs or, God forbid, discos, in order to select women that he must try to impress, utterly abhorrent, and also a little frightening too. In fact, he judged the whole single life completely unappealing, so promptly drained another glass of wine and then banished the thought completely from his mind, at least for now.

Still in Tudor king mode, Dave belched loudly and tossed the stripped chicken bone over his shoulder. It was very liberating, but part of him still worried about being chastised for such reckless behaviour. Bollocks, I'll pick it up later he decided and then resumed watching the old film. And the wine was going down well too, as was the bubble and squeak, but he became full long before his plates were empty. However, greed and the pleasure of eating took over and he pressed on. That had always been his problem, and was contributing to that perennial weight problem.

Oh Mr Porter with its plot based on railways and a windmill, was providing him with many uncanny memories of Uncle Ronnie, which in turn, made him think of happier childhood days long ago at Rothermead Farm. This line of thinking, or train of thought – there was no escaping the railway references – inevitably led to Grandad Darwin and, having latched on to his memory, he could not suppress it, no matter how hard he tried. Dave put his tray down on the carpet and quickly drank the last of the claret, before allowing himself to become engulfed in a tidal wave of grief. There was no one there anymore to hear him cry, or else tell him to pull himself together, so he really let go.

After some minutes, Dave had wept himself to near exhaustion and the demanding demon of distress was satisfied for the time being. He was further able to calm himself with the thought that out there, on some idealised plain of existence, the spirits of both Uncle Ronnie and Grandad Darwin could very well be walking together through the fruit laden cherry orchards of an alternate Rothermead Farm.

The video played on unregarded now, as Dave reached in the back of the drinks cabinet to retrieve his anaesthetic of choice: an unopened litre bottle of duty free Grouse whisky, which they had been saving for some long forgotten occasion. Just as he was about to unseal the cap, the telephone rang again.

He tottered into the hall, picked up the receiver and without saying anything, waited for the caller to speak first.

'Dave?' finally came a voice that was unmistakably his father's.

'Oh hello, Dad,' he replied, with a mixture of relief and ominousness, as he recalled the likely reason for the call.

'I tried to ring your personal number at work this morning, but there was no reply!' commented his slightly confused-sounding father.

'*No*, I…err, I took the day off work today!'

'Are you *okay*, son?' asked his father with concern.

'*Yes…you* know, it's just…it's just *circumstances*,' responded Dave, a little guardedly.

'Well, it's *circumstances* I'm ringing you about. The cremation ceremony will take place at 15:00 at Barham, this coming Friday', he announced in grave tones; his voice clearly giving away the stress he was feeling.

'Thanks for letting me know, Dad ... it can't have been easy for you having to make all the arrangements.'

'Yeah…well…Nanna's in no fit state to sort *anything* out at the moment!'

'I can imagine!' Dave conceded with empathy. 'So that's Barham at four o'clock, is it Dad?'

'*No* Dave, it's *three* ... look, are you *sure* you're alright?'

He didn't want to burden his father with any of his other personal troubles, and had no intention of informing him about Sheila, in the unlikely event of her changing her mind. However, with regards to the other one of his major losses, he suddenly felt compelled to tell him, if only to justify the state he was in, and would be for the foreseeable future.

'*No* Dad…actually I'm *not* alright ... Tim, my best friend from work, …umm, he was found dead last week. He ... err, he committed suicide, and I heard about it the same day that Grandad Darwin…the same day *he* passed away.'

'Oh *Dave* ... I just don't know what to say! *Listen* mate, if there's anything we can do…'

'That's very kind of you, Dad,' he quickly intervened, 'but I'm taking a few days off work and ... umm, I prefer to be alone at the moment.'

'Ok son, but you *know* where we are if you change your mind!'

'I really appreciate that…so, see you Friday then, bye.'

In truth, Dave would have loved the comfort and support of his parents and siblings right then, but by ensuring no direct contact with his family, he could delay them finding out about him and Sheila separating, be it on a temporary or permanent basis. However, they would certainly know something was wrong when he turned up at Barham Crematorium on Friday alone. Furthermore, he would have to ask either his father, Ed or Lucy for a lift, as Sheila had taken the car. He wondered if there was any chance they would accept the excuse that Sheila could not get the time off work, based on her track record, but quickly concluded that none of his Telecom working relatives would accept 'the firm' could be that callous. Dave hadn't really wanted to tell his father about Tim either, but Lucy already knew, and sooner or later, she would have said something.

En route back to the lounge, Dave rubbed his distended stomach, and further reflected on the telephone conversation with his father. Overall, he didn't think he'd handled it at all well, and might have given his dad the impression that he was hiding away, drunk and depressed, just like during a typical Uncle Ronnie 'water' episode. Then again, it occurred to him that perhaps he was more like his uncle than he cared to admit. With that prophetic thought, he returned to the new bottle of Grouse, broke the seal and then poured himself a large measure. As he drank heavily of the soothing golden liquid, he pondered on the fact that both Ronnie and himself were deeply flawed human beings, and at the end of the day, leaving all other things aside, this was their most obvious common factor.

Some hours later, Dave awoke on the settee, having just had a dream where, for some reason, Sheila had been shouting at him and repeatedly calling out his name. He slowly sat up somewhat bleary-eyed and put the half full whisky bottle he had been cuddling on the coffee table. That's funny, thought Dave, as his head thumped out a painful rhythm; I'm awake and yet I can still hear Sheila shouting. Confused, he staggered to his feet, and then determined that her voice seemed to be coming from the hall. It wasn't until he'd looked at the time on the video clock, which read 05:32, that he realised it *was* Sheila. Wasting no more time, he ran into the hall, where he could see that the front door was open only as far as the security chain would allow. Moreover, there was a very angry Sheila shouting at him from the resultant gap. With a feeling of trepidation, he released the chain and then let her in.

Having finally gained access to the house, Sheila looked at him with a face like thunder.

'Why the *hell* did you put the security chain across?' she asked, before slowly eyeing him up and down. 'My *God* Dave, you look like shit!'

He just stood there humbled, with his head bowed, and the slump-shouldered posture of a scolded child. He could not think of a suitable reply, nor did he really care anymore about choosing the right words.

'Grandad Darwin's funeral is on Friday,' he mumbled, just as she pushed passed him to go upstairs.

His comment stopped Sheila in her tracks and forced her into a more benevolent mood. She looked at her estranged husband again: this pitiful creature who, quite clearly, could not cope without her, and felt enormously sorry for him.

'Come into the lounge a moment,' she instructed, with a beckoning finger, and Dave followed meekly and obediently behind her. Sheila had only taken three or four steps into the lounge, when something hit her right foot.

'What in heavens name is a *chicken bone* doing on the carpet?' she grumbled, looking down in horror. She then crouched down, retrieved the offending bone, and then held it up with great distaste, between her thumb and forefinger.

'It's ... umm, ...it's part of my lunch ... I must have dropped it', he confessed shamefully, in a very un-Henry VIII like manner.

She sighed deeply, shook her head in resigned fashion, and then noticed the whisky bottle.

'Oh Dave ... *that's* not going to help you!' she said, in superior tones, and with pitying eyes.

'Oh *yes,* it is,' Dave countered, grabbling at the bottle and then clutching it to him, before there could be any chance of it being confiscated.

Sheila merely sighed superiorly once more, before stepping slowly backwards, and then nearly stumbling over his discarded tray.

'For goodness *sake,* Dave ... it's been *one day* and the place is like a tip!' she grumbled crossly, before dropping the chicken bone on to one of the ground-based plates. 'You'll *have* to get your act together if you're going to be showing prospective buyers round!'

'*Me*?' Dave asked incredulously, and with a look of horror etched on his face.

'Yes, you ... *you're* the one living here,' she said, pointing directly at him.

'I'm residing elsewhere now and apart from that, I'm really *far* too busy.' She paused, placed both hands on her hips, and heaved yet another sigh. 'Besides which, this was one of the reasons why I got you that week *off*, now tidy this place up, and for pity's sake, tidy *yourself* up.'

Feeling completely crestfallen, Dave slumped down on the settee. He just couldn't bear the thought that his sanctuary was about to be invaded by a succession of prying, judgemental strangers.

Sheila, who had not sat down, regarded him yet again, as she slowly shook her head. There was just enough compassion for him remaining within her to feel sorry for his recent losses, and enough empathy left to feel just a little of what he was going through at that moment.

'*Look*, would you like me to come with you to the funeral on Friday?' she offered, in more conciliatory tones.

Dave glanced up at her briefly, before resuming his sullen study of the carpet in front of the settee.

'You don't *have* to,' he replied, desperately hoping that she'd meant it.

'What time is it and where?'

'Barham, at 15:00!'

'*Right*, I'll pick you up here at 14:15 on Friday,' she responded and then promptly disappeared to retrieve her things from upstairs.

'Thank you!' he muttered in a muted voice, continuing to stare through his legs; an acknowledgement of gratitude she was unlikely to have heard.

Within minutes, Sheila was back down in the hall with several holdalls tightly packed, and her husband was there to meet her.

'Now *please,* Dave ... do your bit, keep the place clean and tidy, okay?' she gently chided, staring at him in a long-suffering fashion

'Ok.' he nodded glumly and without making eye contact, before slowly wandering back through to the lounge.

'Huh, *bye* then!' Sheila said, with irritated sarcasm, as she watched the shambling, retreating figure.

From the safety and security of the lounge, Dave heard the front door slam, then her car pull away. 'Alone again,' he moaned to himself, before grabbing the Grouse and then putting it back in the drinks cabinet. Next, he bent down, with a weary groan, picked up his lunch tray and then placed it on the coffee table. During that brief manoeuvre, the chicken bone that Sheila had earlier retrieved, rolled off the plate, and then promptly tumbled back on to the floor. With an irritated growl, Dave kicked at the fragment of his meal so that it rolled under one of the armchairs. That's enough tidying for now, he concluded, and flopped down on to the settee to watch the six o'clock news.

The pattern Dave set himself on Monday became the template for a sort of interim routine of television, binge eating and drinking, and of course grieving, which repeated itself for each successive day of that stay at home week. The exception was the whisky bottle, which he left well alone. During all this time, his only contact with the outside world was the daily telephone call he either made to, or received from his parents. Just as he'd done on the Monday, he continuously tried to think positively about the future, but was repeatedly countered by fear of the unknown; an unclear future without either Amanda-Jayne or Sheila, and in a different house as well. As the week progressed, those fears amplified and developed to such an extent, that any future scenario, other than a return to how it had been before that awful Sunday, was completely unacceptable; it was totally out of the question.

By the time Dave went to bed on the Thursday night, there was only one possible acceptable option for the immediate future: he had to get Sheila back at any cost. Of course, he would be the first to admit that their marriage had been far from perfect, but at the end of the day, any relationship was better than no relationship at all. So on Friday morning, he awoke, as a man on a mission. He got up with the alarm at 07:00 – there was no dozing off again – and ran himself a bath, which, even he had to acknowledge, was long overdue. He was quite tempted to keep the quite respectable beard that he'd grown during those hermit-like days, but Sheila was not fond of bearded men, as he'd discovered very early on in their marriage, so off it came, leaving just the usual moustache that he had always worn. On a slightly more worrying note, the bathroom scales showed a gain of half a stone since last weekend, so either they were wrong, or more likely, his recent sedentary lifestyle had taken its toll. Briefly, he considered jogging round the block, but within seconds, laughingly dismissed the notion as the desperation of a madman. That really *would* be a sure-fire way to kill myself, he ruefully decided. The option of having a healthy breakfast, seemed far more preferable, and so he rushed downstairs in his dressing gown for a bowl of sultana bran.

As Dave ate his cereal, he looked around at the vast array of dirty pans, plates and cups that seemed to cover every available surface in the kitchen. It was not dissimilar to the state in which he had found Tim's house; on the last occasion he'd seen him alive. He then suddenly realised with horror that, since telling his father about it on Monday, he hadn't given Tim, or his suicide, a single thought all week. True, on one or two occasions, he had compared his own current, and hopefully temporary, circumstances to those of Tim in his last few months, but that had been more out of self-pity than sympathy for his lost friend. It shamed him to think that he hadn't been grieving in the least for Tim, and that all his tears had been for Grandad Darwin: the man whose funeral would be taking place that very afternoon.

It wasn't long before another rather disturbing thought occurred to Dave. What of Tim's funeral? When would that be? Could it have already taken place? And why hadn't Stephen Cross rung him with the date and time as he'd promised?

Dave then racked his brain and tried to work out if it was at all possible that his friend's funeral had already occurred by that time. His body had been discovered last Thursday, which was just over a week ago; of that much, he was sure. Then, because of the circumstances of his death, he assumed that there would probably have to be a post- mortem. Given that scenario, he concluded that the earliest possible date for the funeral would be that very day, but was probably more likely to take place on the Monday or Tuesday of next week.

Now that Dave had finally thought about Tim, he couldn't get him out of his mind. It would always be a lasting regret of his that he hadn't been able to help his friend, but it occurred to him that there was one last thing he could do for him, and that was to attend his funeral. In fact, obligation aside, he quickly concluded that he would actually like to go to Tim's funeral to say a proper goodbye, and having been denied attending Uncle Ronnie's, he realised how important this was. But there was a problem in the form of Alison Cross; she hated him. And, it was likely that she had been the one to prevent Stephen from advising him about the funeral.

Dave had not fully appreciated how much Tim's estranged wife despised him, until she cunningly engineered the scheme whereby Sheila became aware of the contents of his note to Tim; the one that mentioned his relationship with Amanda-Jayne in the frankest of terms. However, had he really thought about it, and not been so preoccupied with Amanda-Jayne for much of the year, then he would have seen that Alison had good cause *not* to hold him in the highest of esteem. There was that dinner party, back in the spring, where he had spiked her drinks, and she cannot have been too pleased by being publicly vilified in that newspaper article, following Tim's multistorey car park incident in the summer. Dave's so-called journalist friend had exaggerated his role in the whole affair, so he became not only the '*have a go historian*' who saved '*trembling Telecom worker Tim*', but also the man who '*denounced teacher training, modern mother, lesbian Alison*'. However, if he really wanted to go to say a proper goodbye to Tim, he knew he would have to do so in spite of his friend's unforgiving widow. All he had to do was telephone Tim's Uncle Stephen in Faversham for the time and place, on the grounds that – in the absence of an intervention by Allison – he'd likely forgotten to call *him* about it. And surely he reasoned, Alison would not want to make a scene at such a dignified occasion, but then again, he could not be absolutely sure. He decided that the best course of action was to think about it during the rest of the day and then perhaps, phone Stephen Cross in the evening.

With breakfast finally finished, Dave balanced his empty cereal bowl on top of an already precarious pile of dirty dishes and went to leave the kitchen. He then stopped in his tracks and slowly walked back to the sink, remembering that he was a man with a mission. It took a whole hour of hard slog, but after that time, not only was the washing up done, but also everything had been dried and put away as well.

He spent the rest of the morning hoovering, dusting and generally tidying the whole house. Sheila was bound to be impressed, he thought; but at the same time, he recognised it would take more than that to persuade her to come back to him. He would have to meet her halfway, and address her needs too. It soon occurred to him that, maybe, they could have an interim period of, say two weeks, where he could date her again, but they continued to live apart. That would give him a chance to talk his way back into her favour; to try to convince her that Amanda-Jayne had been a stupid one-off mistake, brought on by the stress of Grandad Darwin's illness. He immediately checked himself after that last thought, and recoiled at just how low he'd sunk that he was prepared to use his beloved Grandad's terminal cancer, as the reason for wooing that seventeen-year old girl. Just as he had rubbished Amanda-Jayne herself last weekend, in an effort to extricate himself from any suspicion of proactive involvement with her, so he was now prepared to drag Grandad Darwin into his petty little scheme to convince Sheila to come back to him. Right at that moment, Dave had to admit that he *wasn't* a very nice person. But then again, he also tried to tell himself that if the spirit of Grandad Darwin really was up there somewhere, and also aware of what he'd been thinking, then surely his benevolent relative would forgive him. At the end of the day, nobody wanted to be alone and unloved, and Sheila was now his best and only option for ensuring that this didn't happen.

As the hour of Grandad Darwin's funeral drew closer, Dave became more and more nervous. Because of the sheer number of butterflies in his stomach, there was no room for any lunch, so he just made a cup of tea. Holding his half drunk cup, he pondered on the thought that it had been 15 years since he last went to a funeral, and that one had been his very first. Now there were to be two at roughly the same time; that is, if he could find out where and when Tim's was going to be held. But it was more than just funeral nerves that he was feeling; he was also anxious about seeing Sheila again, because of what was at stake.

With half an hour to go until his lift arrived, Dave went upstairs to get dressed. He did not have a dark suit, so chose a suitable sports jacket and trousers; in fact, it was the sort of thing he would normally wear for work. However, he did have a black tie somewhere, although he hadn't worn it since Nanna Maybury's funeral back in 1976. Funnily enough, it had been Grandad Darwin who'd given him that tie, just prior to the occasion.

*

Dave reached into the back of the funny smelling wardrobe and pulled out a handful of ties. That wardrobe in question was a dark, ugly Edwardian piece, and quite clearly the biggest object in his bed-sit, but it was very useful for keeping all his clothes safe from the damp that seemed to permeate everywhere. As soon as he'd moved into the Ridgeway Motel, other occupants of the bedsits had warned him about the damp problem and how pointless it was to complain about it to Mrs Cottrell, the miserly and eccentric old widow who owned and ran the complex. And yet, in spite of the black mildew on the ceiling, the biting cold, and the fact that his landlady regularly used her master key to snoop in the rooms when she was sure the occupants were out for a while, he thoroughly enjoyed living at that rambling old establishment. He rejoiced in his newfound freedom and best of all, he appreciated being away from home, with its stressful atmosphere and constant rows.

Only six weeks had passed since his father kicked him out, but it seemed so much longer. During this time, he and Vivien had become quite an item. In the old parlance, they were now going steady. Some two years his senior, she was an incredibly attractive girl, with blonde mid-length hair and an hourglass figure. Heads would turn when they were out together, and Dave knew that it was nothing to do with the way *he* looked. And yet, he thought it strange that she hadn't been snapped up months ago, and was not already engaged or even married to some chisel-jawed bloke, with a successful job and a sports car. However, it wasn't long before he began to recognise exactly what the problem was. One evening, quite early on in their relationship, Dave and Vivien had returned to his room at the Ridgeway Motel, following an evening at the cinema in Whitstable. They were enjoying a cuddle on the bed, until she suddenly became distressed when he tried to move into the heavy petting zone. In tears, she felt comfortable enough with him to confess that she had a phobia about sexual intimacy. After her admission, he had held Vivien close and quickly reassured her that he was a very patient man who could wait until she was ready. It was obviously something that no previous boyfriend had ever said to her before and she told a very flattered Dave that he was too good to be true. He was sure that she would eventually respond to his patience, or rather he hoped she would, as he was rather keen to lose his virginity. Unfortunately, over the weeks that followed, nothing much changed in that respect. She did try and please him in her own way and would always happily undress for him. Moreover, he enjoyed caressing her naked body as she lay impassively on the bed; it not only satisfied his voyeuristic desires, but also consolidated them in his mind. And she had no objection to him relieving himself whilst he gently stroked her. However, after about a month of this form of 'love-making', Dave began to feel like some dirty old gynaecologist who was taking advantage of his patient. As before though, tears would result if he ever attempted to stray from this established format. It was a problem he did not know how to resolve, or one he felt could be discussed with anyone.

One other negative aspect concerning those last six weeks at the Ridgeway Motel was that he missed his immediate family, his father excepted of course. Dave had not seen any of them for the entire period in question, although he did make twice weekly calls to his mother from work. However, he had to choose times when he could be sure that his father was not at home. Through those telephone chats, his mum had kept him in touch with what Lucy and Eddie were up to and, likewise, gathered news about their older brother to be passed back to them.

During this time, Dave had continued to maintain close contact with Nanna and Grandad Darwin and had even spent two weekends at Rothermead in the period since leaving home. These were his first stays up at the farm since Uncle Ronnie's death in July 1969. After that terrible tragedy, and the resultant deterioration in the relationship between his father and grandparents, the family had ceased to go up en masse to Rothermead Farm for those wonderful weekends. Day trips there 'for the sake of the grandchildren' had continued intermittently, but it was not the same anymore. What is more, neither Dave nor Lucy got the same thrill, sitting by their parents' caravan in a corner of some remote Kentish field, every other weekend, as they previously had staying in their grandparents' tied cottage. However, now that Dave was independent and had his own car, thanks to Grandad Darwin, he had the freedom to go where he chose, and he was determined to make the most of it.

Dave was delighted that the routine at Rothermead had changed little in the seven years he'd missed being a houseguest. On the other hand, he couldn't help but notice that his grandparents were not getting any younger. Both were now nearly 70, and showing signs, albeit small and well disguised ones, of slowing down a little. Grandad Darwin had reached the official retirement age in 1972, coincidentally the same year in which he'd suffered a debilitating bout of pleurisy, warranting a brief stay in hospital and a number of weeks off work. Lord and Lady Rothermead had definitely wanted him to stay on beyond 65; by their own admission, he was by far the best gardener they'd ever had. However, because of both his age and recent illness, Nanna Darwin had lobbied hard for him to be allowed to retire. At the end of the day though, Grandad, being the stubborn old devil that he was, had wanted to continue working and could not be dissuaded. Finally, a compromise had been reached whereby he carried on with lighter duties, reduced hours and with the promise of help from one of the farm labourers for the heavier tasks. Sadly though, as the years progressed, the hours crept back up, and the promise of help never materialised. Consequently, by 1976, even Grandad Darwin had had enough, and vowed to retire by the end of the year at the latest. His heart's desire was now a bungalow near the sea, with a large plot where he could finally be his own boss and create a garden to please himself.

1976 was not turning out to be a good year for the Dutnells either, especially as far as their employees were concerned. About six months before George Darwin's planned retirement, the groom, Ronald Carter, had suddenly left their employment. There was talk of a massive bust-up with the 'big house', but Nanna Darwin had been unable to establish any definite details, and even the loose-tongued Mrs Cohen was keeping her own counsel. Fortunately, the former groom's daughter Samantha, now a tall, confident twenty-four-year-old, had taken over the position and consequently, the tied cottage. Dave admired this elegant, yet elusive woman, with her long dark wavy hair tied back in an appropriate ponytail, as she led the racehorses from stable block to grazing field. He could not fail to notice her slim but shapely form, accentuated by the light-coloured tight breeches that stretched over her well-toned buttocks as she bent to groom the fine animals in her charge. Dave and Samantha Carter talked as much as he dared and her duties allowed, but she was seven years older than he, and did not display the sort of interest in him as he obviously had in her; she seemed far more interested in her job, or going out riding. Until recently, the latter leisure pursuit had always been one shared with Victoria Dutnell from the 'big house': a close friend of the female head groom. However, on his last visit up to the farm, Nanna Darwin told Dave that 'Miss Victoria' had suddenly gone to live and work in France. At that moment, Dave had wished he could ride too and so be able to replace Victoria on those excursions, but it was a sentiment he didn't ever share with Vivien.

Dear old Alice, Dave's landlady, must have had a field day going through the things in his room during those weekends he spent up at Rothermead Farm. Suzanne, another bed-sit occupant, had heard that Mrs Cottrell had 'gone a bit funny in the head' after her husband John had died in about 1958. It was as a newly married couple in the late 1930s, that John and Alice had bought the rundown farmhouse to the former Ridgeway Farm. Converting and later extending it into a motel was a business venture to exploit the passing trade from the newly constructed coastal road, the Thanet Way. Although the new arterial road was some five hundred yards away, a healthy stream of motorists was ensured by the placement of prominent signs along the broad grass verges of the Thanet Way. The last and largest of these included a white-gloved hand pointing to the right, so that there was no doubt which exit must be taken from the up and coming Chestfield roundabout in order to reach the motel. Ironically, Mr Cottrell had been killed in an accident on that very road and not too far from where Ronnie would later roll his brother's car, with fatal results, some eleven years later. Consequently, Dave had some sympathy for old Alice and didn't really mind her bizarre 'hobby'. However, if he *did* have anything he really did not want her to see, then he took it with him to Rothermead.

Dave stared down at the limited collection of ties that he owned and had spread out on the bed for better inspection. All that reminiscing had not helped him choose one that was suitable to wear for his grandmother's funeral. Poor Nanna Maybury, he reflected; how unfair life could be. She had suffered a minor heart attack at home and then spent a number of weeks in hospital. Sadly, the day before she was due to come home, a blood clot had travelled to her brain and killed her. Naturally, both Grandad Maybury and Meg were distraught and

Dave felt that he wanted to go to the funeral, not only to pay his respects as usual, but also offer some support to his mother, even if it meant encountering his estranged father. Three days ago, he had discussed this problem with Nanna and Grandad Darwin on the telephone and was surprised when they suggested that he should seize the opportunity to bring about a reconciliation with Len. Initially, Dave was not sure about the idea, but had gradually warmed to it. His mind was finally made up when his Grandparents Darwin offered, not only to give him a lift to the crematorium, but also to come to the funeral with him. It was a generous gesture, he thought; after all, they had only met his grandparents Maybury half a dozen odd times at major family occasions, spread out over many years. As it happened, they were going to take the opportunity to combine the funeral trip with a house-hunting expedition in Whitstable and Herne Bay during the morning, have lunch somewhere, and then pick up Dave at Ridgeway Motel at 14:00, an hour before the ceremony was scheduled.

But which tie to wear? He finally chose the most sober looking one, but even that was a joke tie Vivien had recently bought him. True, it was dark blue in colour, but had small anchors printed on it, above each of which was the letter 'W'. Given the current state of their sex life, he wondered if his girlfriend had appreciated the irony of her gift. And if any of his family questioned its meaning, he could always tell them that the symbols represented 'Whitstable Sailing Club'. That decided, he put on the tie, picked up his jacket and then locked the door of his bed-sit. The windowless first floor passage he now found himself in was dark as usual and he felt along the wall whilst cautiously proceeding towards the main staircase. After a few faltering steps, he bumped straight into Alice Cottrell who had obviously been lurking in the gloom.

'Going *out* are you, Mr Darwin?' she asked, in her witch-like squeaky voice, whilst eagerly fingering her bunch of master keys.

'Yes, actually I'm going to my grandmother's funeral,' Dave replied, as he strained to see the diminutive hooked-nosed figure.

'*Oo* ... so you'll be gone a good couple of hours then!' responded a suddenly more upbeat Alice, as she jangled her keys excitedly.

Dave smiled at her, and then went downstairs without replying. Best to keep her guessing, he concluded, as he crossed the crescent shaped gravel drive in front of the old pebble-dashed motel.

Opposite the building and its somewhat neglected grounds, he stood by the ancient unmade track, known locally as 'The Ridgeway', which gave access to it. No doubt, that rutty, pot-holed byway must have given prospective motorists a rather bumpy ride over their last 50 or so yards, as they sought the motel that had been so well advertised on the coastal road. Dave then turned round 180 degrees to face in a northwards direction. From this vantage point, he was able to look across a vast ploughed field, with its nascent corn crop, and then clearly see the Thanet Way, with the railway embankment beyond that. By glancing to the right, he was able to discern the Swalecliffe-Chestfield roundabout and then further round still: the white painted art-deco clock tower of the filling station, where Uncle Ronnie had come to grief some seven years before.

A tooting car horn soon interrupted his reverie and he turned to see Grandad Darwin's new car – a Mark Three Cortina – bumping along The Ridgeway towards him. After the usual round of excessive waving, cheery verbal greeting and familiar shoulder patting, his grandfather turned the car in the gravel driveway of the old motel, and bumped back along the track to the Chestfield Road.

'Did *you* two have a successful morning?' Dave asked of his grandparents, as the car finally moved onto the relative smoothness of a tarmac surface.

It was Nanna Darwin who turned round to reply.

'Mmm, not *too* bad ... we stayed in Whitstable to look this morning, but there was *nothing* we viewed that was absolutely ideal!' she admitted with a stoical smile.

'We drove past the site of Oakenden Nursery, on the way to pick you up, the Dave,' Grandad Darwin remarked, as they gradually picked up speed. 'I must say, they've managed to squeeze a fair few number of houses in there!'

His wife nodded vigorously in agreement.

'*Yes*, it's hard to believe that we once so successfully grew fruit, veg and flowers there ... and you as a little lad used to follow Grandad around everywhere,' she commented, with a backwards glance, and a wistful look on her face.

Living in the neighbourhood again, Dave had already seen the sad state of his old stamping ground, and shared his grandmother's feelings.

'Yes, and it seems so much smaller than it used to when you *lived* there, but the old bungalow, Oakenden proper, is still there ... hemmed in by the new houses,' he said, as memories of those happy pre-school days flooded back.

'Funny thing *is,* old boy,' Grandad said immediately, 'one of those new houses is up for sale, but the plot is *far* too small for what we need.'

By his grandparents mentioning that they'd gone past the nursery site en route to picking him up, Dave instinctively knew that they would have just come from visiting Ronnie's grave, in All Saints churchyard, barely half a mile away from there. They would also have had to negotiate the Chestfield roundabout in order to get to the Ridgeway Motel, and recognised that this cannot have been easy for either of them. Indeed, Grandad Darwin usually avoided the Thanet Way if he could possibly help it.

As the journey to Barham Crematorium continued, the topic of Dave's planned reconciliation with his father inevitably came up.

'Just remember, my old Dave ... you'll be more of a man for being the first to apologise!' his grandfather told him, his familiar bald head nodding in support of the statement.

'Yes, I see!' Dave replied impassively, although he privately realised that it would be hard for him to swallow his pride.

'Len's not a bad person,' Nanna Darwin reinforced, turning her head round briefly. 'You and your father just clash, because you are too much alike.'

'You could be right,' her grandson said politely, although he very much doubted the assertion.

'Families shouldn't fall out with each other ... you never know what might happen,' Grandad Darwin said, his voice trailing off poignantly.

Dave appreciated how hard it was for them to have a conversation about he and his father's falling out, without mentioning Uncle Ronnie. But, the fact remained that neither Nanna nor Grandad Darwin ever mentioned their lost son, at least not in public. He surmised that, even now, the memory of his death was too painful for them to cope with and that their victorian upbringing, particularly as far as Nanna Darwin was concerned, strictly forbade any public display of emotion. It was for the same reason, that Grandad hardly ever mentioned his younger brother, James, who had been in the RAF and was killed in the last war. Therefore, Dave respected their self-imposed taboo and made no mention of why he and his father had fallen out, although he was sure that both Nanna and Grandad Darwin had probably guessed.

Dave was acutely aware of the fact that he was not the only one to have problems with his father. Indeed, Nanna and Grandad Darwin no longer had the relationship with their oldest son that they once enjoyed. Although there had been no complete estrangement between them, relations had become strained almost to breaking point, following Ronnie's untimely death. For some reason, Len got hold of the idea that his parents somehow blamed him for his younger brother's demise. Perhaps something had been said in the heat of the moment, during the first wave of raw grief, immediately following the accident, Dave supposed. Moreover, Ronnie did die whilst in Len's care, and he had previously promised to look after him. It could be that Nanna and Grandad considered that verbal commitment to be some sort of moral contract, and had reacted badly to it being broken. Dave accepted that this was only speculation and if no one in the family would talk about it, then it would forever remain so. He hoped though, that if the planned reconciliation with his own father was successful, it might improve things between Len and *his* parents, but he didn't hold out much hope. Dave knew that there was a lot of resentment boiling away in his father's mind; these were feelings that went back much further than just to Ronnie's sad and premature death.

The new Cortina arrived at Barham before the cortege, just as planned, and Nanna and Grandad Darwin whiled away the time left by admiring the shrubs being grown around the crematorium car park. Dave joined them, but felt rather nervous and fidgeted with his tie.

Not being a huge fan of fidgety fingers, Nanna soon noticed, but then became aware of the tie's bizarre design.

'*There* you are Grandad, you were *right* to have brought along your spare,' she said, tugging at the garment under scrutiny, 'I *told* you he wouldn't have a proper black tie.'

'But this is my *first* funeral,' Dave pleaded in his own defence, before turning the corners of his mouth down.

His grandmother peered at him with a puzzled expression.

'But *surely* you went to… oh no *sorry* ... you *didn't*, did you?' She checked herself with considerable embarrassment and then hurried off to find the spare black tie they'd brought for him.

Dave knew exactly what she had meant, even though her comment was unfinished. She was, of course, referring to Uncle Ronnie's funeral; an occasion that Dave had been forbidden to attend, by his father. The ban had been imposed on him, following an inference that his father had been indirectly responsible for Ronnie's death. It then suddenly occurred to Dave that this might have been one of the reasons why his father had suspected his own parents of sharing the same opinion at the time. After seven years of brooding on the topic, Dave had repeated the very same allegations, though much more blatantly, some six weeks ago, which had been the catalyst for his premature ejection from the family home. Since then, however, during those lonely nights at the Ridgeway Motel, staring up at the black mildew patches on his bed-sit ceiling, he'd had plenty of time to think long and hard about what happened back in the summer of 1969. True, his father's supervision of Ronnie had been too restrictive, but then again, Dave's wayward uncle was a bit of a loose canon; the Rothermead mill incident being a good case in point. However, whatever his methods, Dave was now happy to concede that his father's motives, in keeping Ronnie out of more trouble and thus ward off further press interest, were completely honourable. Perhaps Len Darwin's biggest mistake had been to keep Ronnie and Katie apart. But there again, his son now appreciated that any formal allegations of under-age sex would have been extremely damaging to Ronnie's career. Ironically, Katie had turned 16, the very day that Ronnie died. If only his father had somehow been made aware of that, Dave mused, then the relationship could have been allowed to continue without fear of prosecution. If his uncle had been allowed to see Katie following all those press allegations, and the revelation of her true age, surely she would have been only too keen to mention that her sixteenth birthday was only a few days away. Sadly, there was nothing that anyone could now do to change what had happened. However, Dave accepted that today, the day of Nanna Maybury's funeral, was the ideal time to stop the recriminations and heal those wounds. Perhaps Uncle Ronnie could be laid to rest a second time.

After a few minutes of rummaging in the back of the car, Nanna Darwin came back with her husband's spare narrow-bottomed black tie, and then once more tugged at the broad blue example that was currently hanging around her grandson's neck.

'So what's the significance of the symbols on your tie then, Dave?' she asked, with her head tilted so as to best study it through her bifocals. 'Mmm ... a letter W, and then an anchor ... *werr-anchor*; what *does* that mean?'

'It's Whitstable Sailing Club, Nanna,' Dave replied with a wry grin. From the corner of his eyes though, he noticed that Grandad Darwin was also struggling in vain to withhold a broad smirk.

'Oh I didn't know you liked boats, Dave!' remarked a straight-faced Nanna, as she undid the knot of his patterned tie for him.

'Err no…I only go to the social functions!' he smiled, desperately trying not to look at his grandfather.

'I see ... well, it's quite a nice tie. Perhaps you could get Grandad one,' she proposed, tucking the black tie under his collar. 'As a former navy man, I'm *sure* he'd appreciate it!'

'No bloomin' fear!' her husband responded, before he finally chuckled.

'What…*what*?' questioned a mystified Nanna Darwin, as she glanced between the two now openly giggling men.

Now that Dave was suitably dressed, the three of them wandered slowly down to the small waiting room at the front of the crematorium complex, with its fish tank and plastic flowers. Before long, the short cortege arrived, led by the hearse, followed by the limousine containing Meg and Grandad Maybury. Len brought up the rear in his own car, with Ed and Lucy sitting glumly in the back. Some other more obscure Maybury relatives were also waiting, but Dave only vaguely recognised them and could remember none of their names. However, he was saddened to see that there was no sign of his Great Uncle Martin, Grandad Maybury's estranged brother, or his wife, Great Aunt Poppy. Family estrangements were indeed very destructive, as Grandad Darwin had so wisely reflected earlier.

With all due ceremony, Nanna Maybury's coffin was unloaded and then carried slowly into the crematorium chapel. Dave's family followed the coffin and its bearers, whilst he, and his paternal grandparents tacked on to the end. It was going to be a miserable affair. Grandad Maybury, still obviously ill himself, was sobbing inconsolably and hanging on to Dave's mother for all he was worth. Seeing him like that, it was hard to believe that he would ever get over the loss of his beloved wife. On a more positive note, Ed and Lucy had quickly spotted Dave from the pews opposite and they were soon exchanging furtive little smiles and waves throughout the service; it certainly helped lighten the mood for him. On one occasion, Dave and his father's eyes met, and they both nodded to the other in polite, if somewhat embarrassed acknowledgement. At that moment, Dave knew that their reconciliation was in the bag.

After the brief joyless service, and the curtain had finally closed on Nanna Maybury's life, the family filed out on to the balcony that ran along the side of the chapel, and which overlooked the unspoilt Kentish countryside. Almost straightaway, Dave and Len approached each other and then embraced with a familial spontaneity that needed no words. Very soon, Lucy and Ed were dancing around their older brother, just as Dave had once done with Uncle Ronnie; and pumped him with questions about his bed-sit and new girlfriend. Dave happily obliged and also chilled them with tales of his witch-like landlady. Nanna and Grandad Darwin looked on with delight from a respectable distance. Sadly though, the best they could hope for, and got, from Len was a handshake for him, and a peck on the cheek for her; as well as a few brief yet polite words for the both of them.

As the Darwin family gradually made their way back to the car park, Len invited Dave home for dinner at the weekend, with the option to bring Vivien if he wanted. Dave also extended a reciprocal invitation to his family to come and see his humble room at the Ridgeway Motel. Thus, the sad occasion of Nanna Maybury's funeral, had turned out to be a very positive day for Dave, in that he was not only able to bury the hatchet with his father, but also exorcise his mind of any angst regarding his Uncle Ronnie's death. In some ways, he had finally been allowed to say a proper goodbye to him.

*

Crouching down a little, Dave looked in the bedroom mirror, as he straightened the knot of his re-discovered black tie. It was a bit dusty and slightly creased, but once mostly hidden under the collar of his white shirt, it should look reasonably okay, he reasoned. His stomach was really churning now and any slight thought of Grandad Darwin prompted waves of intense grief that he fought hard to control. However, now was not the time to let go of his emotions, for Sheila would be arriving soon to take him to the funeral service and she always preferred him with his upper lip suitably stiffened. Dave realised that if he stood any chance of convincing her to give him a second chance, he could not be himself today, or even from this day onwards. He would have to become a version of himself that met with her approval. The price would be high, but it would be worth paying. The alternative, a future of change and chaos, was something that, alongside the grief for the loss of his grandfather, he was trying hard not to think about.

The sound of the front door slamming echoed up the stairs and into the bedroom. An alarmed Dave glanced at his watch; Sheila was early. He decided that this was a good sign, although he wasn't exactly sure why. Nevertheless, he scooped up his jacket and bounded down the stairs to meet her. She was not in the hall, so he checked in the other rooms and found her in the kitchen.

On hearing him enter the room, Sheila looked round briefly and then smiled.

'This all looks very presentable,' she said, before easing him to one side, and then pacing through into the lounge. 'Yes, and in here *too*! *Thanks* for tidying up, Dave ... who could *fail* to be impressed?'

'I'm pleased that…*you're* pleased Sheila,' he responded politely. 'And I *must* say you look very nice!'

'Not too casual for a funeral?' she asked, standing in half profile to him and with arms outstretched to the side.

'Not at *all*!' he remarked approvingly, scanning her from tip to toe.

Dave was pleasantly surprised at her appearance, if not a little shocked at his own reaction to it. She was wearing full makeup and her hair seemed a little longer. The skirt of her black two-piece outfit was quite short and her white button up blouse strained over her large bust. And then, as she sat down in one of the armchairs and crossed her legs, she revealed large amounts of bare thigh. Dave couldn't help but notice and felt a sudden and very strong sexual desire for her. How much of that was down to his enforced celibacy throughout that past week, he could not be sure, but it did offer him a further incentive; it gave him another reason to get back with her, and that was regular sex.

Dave would be the first to admit that Sheila rarely denied him those so-called conjugal rights when they were together, although there had been many occasions when she seemed less than keen, and had given the impression that she was only submitting to him for a quiet life. The notable exception was on those weekend mornings when one comes to naturally, as opposed to being shaken from sleep by the alarm. Invariably, Dave would wake up in an aroused state, or quickly became so. Sheila always took umbrage at being wooed from behind by an evidently rampant man, when a quiet uninterrupted doze could be had instead.

'Do you mind?' Sheila asked, pulling a cigarette packet from her handbag, her legs still crossed alluringly.

'Not at *all*, please feel *free*,' Dave responded, with a supportive hand gesture; it was very much against his true feelings, but part of his new policy.

'Well, how have you been?' she asked, exhaling a long stream of processed smoke from her lungs.

'It's been a difficult week!' he replied with a wistful shrug, but also quietly encouraged by her concern. That's another good sign, he thought.

Dave sat back in the armchair opposite his estranged wife and watched her smoke as she carefully looked round the room; it was almost as if she was making a mental inventory of its contents. Nonetheless, he was pleasantly surprised by her conciliatory attitude and wondered if he should either say or do something to encourage the process along. On the other hand, he knew that if he went down on his knees and begged her to come back to him, she would be utterly repelled. His best option was to play along with the idea of a separation for now. But then, when the time was right and she appeared to be weakening, he could engineer the situation so that Sheila believed it had been her idea to reconcile; make her think that it was something that *she* wanted to happen. So, all he had to do was give her cause to think more highly of him, or that she'd been too hasty in her decision to leave last Sunday.

'Listen Sheila, something occurred to me the other day,' he began cautiously, leaning forward in his chair and then linking his hands together, 'and believe me, I've had a lot of time to think this week! Look, just because we're separated, there's no reason for us not to be civilised about it, so why don't we go out for a meal at the weekend, perhaps use it as an occasion to discuss the selling of the house and such like. What do you reckon?'

He looked across at her expectantly. If she agreed, then he could begin the subtle win-back process in the same sort of ambient restaurant atmosphere that worked so well during their original courtship days.

Sheila stubbed out her cigarette and then met his gaze.

'Let me think about it', she responded, before getting up and then smoothing her short skirt down. 'I suppose we'd better be off now ... are you ready?'

'As I'll *ever* be!' Dave sighed, with a sideways grimace, as he got up and then followed her out of the house to the car. Well, at least she didn't say no to my proposal, he reflected; that's got to be a good sign.

Dave didn't say much in the car on the journey over to Barham. All his energies were devoted to damming up the ever-increasing waves of emotion that refused to die down.

As it happened, it was Sheila who finally broke the silence.

'Am I right in assuming that you haven't as yet told your family about the split?' she asked, without taking her eyes off the road.

'Yes that's *right* ... I saw no point in giving them anything *extra* to worry about at the moment,' Dave responded, with a nervous chuckle, but nonetheless pleased that she had enquired. It was another good sign; if they reconciled soon, his parents need never know there had been any trouble in the first place.

'Don't worry,' Sheila re-affirmed, before casting him a brief but knowing smile, ' I'll play the dutiful wife for you today.'

Dave nodded in acknowledgement and then smiled optimistically, as they turned off the A2 and followed the signs for Barham. Unknown to him, his wife's motives were far from being altruistic; she had to protect her reputation, and couldn't be seen to have abandoned a man immediately following a double-bereavement, especially if a future Telecom manager in the shape of Ed Darwin was present.

It wasn't long before the car was passing through the crematorium gates, and then descending the steep sloping drive towards the grim building at the bottom, its tall chimney ominously emitting a visible heat haze, but no smoke. The funeral cortege was only just behind them, so Dave and Sheila quickly left the car and walked briskly over to meet the limousine containing his parents and grandmother. Ed had travelled with Lucy and her family, who had been the first to arrive, and were already waiting there in a huddle, outside the chapel entrance. Other Darwin relatives also began to congregate around the hearse, including Great Aunt Holly, who was Grandad's sister, and a very frail looking

Great Uncle Sydney. With them were their son Robert, his Chinese wife Munha, and their attractive twenty-year-old daughter Connie. Dave could see that Nanna Darwin was composed, but obviously finding her practised emotional control difficult to maintain under these extreme circumstances.

Nanna Maybury's funeral, some 15 years ago, had been a sad affair, but this was infinitely worse. From the very first notes of Grandad's favourite hymn, 'All things bright and beautiful', with its original tune, no one could hold back the tears and only Sheila and the locum vicar sang with any clarity. In fact, Dave was so distraught that he was only vaguely aware of much of the funeral service. Moreover, it felt almost as if he was somewhere outside of his own body. During a quieter moment of prayer, a comforting hand took hold of his. Given the mood he was in, Dave wondered if it might be the spirit of Grandad Darwin reaching out from beyond the grave. However, it soon became clear that the supportive hand was from Sheila. She still cared for him, thank God, he surmised; that definitely was a good sign.

At the end, Dave did not watch those crematorium curtains closing; he couldn't accept the finality of that gesture. Nonetheless, he tried to reassure himself that these were only corporeal matters that were being dealt with today; the spirit of Grandad Darwin, the real Grandad Darwin, was elsewhere, and very much still alive. On the other hand, perhaps some spirits liked to watch their own funerals, and the old boy was there after all, he hypothesised hopefully; but without a well-honed sixth sense, or a medium amongst the mourners, he would never be able to tell.

Once the family had moved out onto the balcony, Dave surveyed the late autumnal landscape. He was glad of the fresh air, as he was nursing the beginnings of a headache: a stress headache presumably. Below in the valley, a blue tractor was ploughing a large field and swarms of native birds were swooping down and congregating in order to rummage in the freshly turned furrows. Immediately beyond the field, there stood an extensive mature coppice that was, by this time, almost completely denuded of all its leaves. About halfway along the fence that divided the field from the wood was a stile, over which two distant figures could now be seen climbing; presumably having just followed a path through the densely packed trees. Dave noticed that the ramblers were making no attempt to either cross or else circumnavigate the vast field, but instead, were standing there together, and seemingly staring back up at the mourners on the crematorium chapel's balcony. Dave squinted his eyes and could just make out that one of them was a young dark haired person, probably a male, and he was in the company of an older man, who was wearing some form of hat. Both people appeared to be carrying some sort of small basket or trug. It was then that the older of the two men raised an arm and vigorously waved in their direction. With an instinctive reaction, Dave waved back, hesitantly, and then turned to Sheila to ask her if she could also see the two far away figures. However, by the time he had re-focused his eyes on that distant woodland stile, the two 'ramblers' had gone; there was no sign of them in either wood or field.

Another funeral was due, so the Darwin family were discreetly ushered away from the balcony, where they had been looking at the displayed bouquets and wreaths , or else just talking in hushed huddles. Nanna Darwin had once more regained her composure and was chatting away to Len, happily arm in arm with him as they slowly walked across to the car park. Dave thought that was such a lovely thing to see. Ed, now towering above everyone else, picked up his nephew Jimmy, just as Uncle Ronnie had once done with Dave, and began to walk slowly back to the waiting cars. Sheila and Dave hung back, and were the last of the family to leave the balcony by the open arch at its western end.

The cortege of the following funeral slowly cruised down the sloping, winding drive to the right of the retreating Darwins, and pulled up outside the main door of the chapel. A crop haired woman, in a denim jacket and red full-length skirt, got out of the first of the two black limousines.

As she noticed this, Sheila's jaw dropped.

'What inappropriate dress for a funeral,' she commented quietly and closely to Dave's ear, as she smoothed down her creased miniskirt.

Her husband was about to agree when he got his first proper look at the woman's face, and then immediately froze to the spot. Oh my God, it's Alison Cross; this cannot be happening, a panicked Dave thought to himself, as his increased heart rate began to make his temples throb.

He slowly turned away from Tim's widow, before either of them could be recognised, and then grabbed Sheila's arm in order to guide her away as speedily and discreetly as he could.

'Oi ... What's going *on* Dave?' she asked both loudly and crossly in response to the unexpected physical intervention by her husband.

Unfortunately, on hearing a voice she recognised, Alison turned to face them, and it was now the turn of her jaw to drop open in astonishment.

'*You've* got a bloody nerve showing up at Tim's funeral,' she barked fiercely, before taking a few strident steps towards Dave.

Straightaway, her alarmed victim held out both his hands in a defensive gesture.

'Alison, *please*, I didn't *know* it was Tim's funeral today ... we've just come away from my grandfather's cremation', he pleaded, with an arm movement towards the sombre clad people in the car park.

Tim's widow stared at Dave through narrowed eyes and then looked over at his dispersing relatives, whose presence seemed to support his claim. Without a word of apology, but seemingly having accepted his explanation, Alison slowly turned away, and the matter might have rested there, but for an unexpected and ill-advised intervention from Dave.

'But having *said* that,' he began, walking forward slightly,

'Tim was my best friend and with your blessing, I would love to show my respects at his funeral service ... you know, say goodbye to him properly'.

Having listened with her back towards him, Alison now turned around, with a face that registered incredulity rather then anger.

'No, you *don't* have my blessing,' she said unambiguously, 'Dave, do you *realise* that your unguarded comments to that newspaper reporter, after Tim's multistorey fiasco, actually lost me my teacher training place?'

'Look, *please* believe me, I *did not* say the things he reported. But, I *beg* you, let's keep our voices down, I don't want to involve my family in this,' he urged, with a suppressive gesture of his down-turned hands.

'*Huh,* you didn't seem to care about the affect on *my* family when you rubbished me to the reporter,' she said, with fuming frustration and flailing arms. 'And I *told* you I *wasn't* gay, so why did you say that I *was?*'

Dave was tired of being on the defensive and wanted to stick up for himself, and yet he desperately needed to put a lid on this conversation, as some of his family had now stepped away from their cars in order to look back at the encounter.

'*Well,* Alison ... perhaps *you* might be interested to know that your returning of that note, cost me my *marriage*!' he countered, in a quiet attempt to shame her into silence.

Straightaway, his opponent's body language and countenance became a lot less confrontational, and she now stared at him almost piteously.

'Then it seems we've *both* lost out then, *doesn't* it Dave?' she retorted with a genuine tinge of sadness in her voice.

They looked impassively at each other; two victims of mutual mistrust and misunderstanding. It was almost as if each of them was wondering if it were possible for them to reach some sort of ceasefire. Sadly, their brief and fragile truce was soon to be shattered by an untimely and most unwelcome contribution from Sheila.

'Oh for goodness sake, this is *really* pathetic!' she snarled impatiently. 'What the hell are you *thinking,* Dave? *I* wouldn't go to Tim's funeral if my life *depended* on it. He just doesn't *deserve* the respect; and as for *that* bitch,' she continued, pointing accusingly at Alison, ' ... *remember,* you've no reason to be talking to her in *any* sort of decent manner, after what *she's* done!'

Quite understandably, Tim's ill-clad widow took immediate umbrage at being insulted by a woman whom she'd tried to help by making her aware of that note.

'So what are you *doing* here then Sheila?' she challenged, with brows furrowed, and hands on hips. 'I thought your marriage was supposed to be over!'

'*It is,* we're separated,' Sheila responded promptly, keen to defend her pride.

By this time, all of the Darwin family were aware of the heated discussion and had gathered around. Likewise, the similarly dressed, but far fewer members of the Cross family had become reluctant spectators to the unsightly spat.

Of all the gathered mourners though, it was Len who could no longer merely observe, for he had heard all of Sheila's recent comments.

'Who *is* this woman son?' he asked, stepping forward and placing a supportive hand on Dave's shoulder. 'And what's all this about you and Sheila separating?'

Before Dave could answer with either half-truths or excuses, Alison, as much wounded by Sheila's unkind remarks as Dave's alleged maliciousness towards her, seized the opportunity to complete her revenge.

'*Ah*, Dave's father ... Mr Darwin *senior* I assume…'

'*Please* Alison, I *beg* you,' Dave interrupted, trying to appeal to any pity she had left within her.

Alison completely ignored the pathetic-looking man's pleas and allowed her grief free rein.

'*Listen* to me, *all* of you ... did you know that your precious Dave has been shagging a teenage girl?' she asked, staring round at the sea of bewildered faces. 'Oh yes, *that's* what split their marriage up ... it was nothing that *I've* done, it was *that*, …it was that…' her voice trailed off into silence; almost as if her more reasonable self had suddenly shaken her back to reality.

Having listened to the brutal allegation, Len quickly judged that the time was now right to withdraw from the altercation, so he and Meg began to lead a confused Nanna Darwin away. Other family members soon followed on; glad to be away from the embarrassing scene.

At the same time, Stephen Cross and a similar-looking man that Dave assumed to be Tim's father, approached Alison from behind and gently but firmly, grabbed both her arms. However, she tried to resist being led away and, in so doing, her more aggressive persona once more took over as she shouted back to the stunned Darwin family.

'*Sheila knows all about it…ask her…go on…ask the fucking bitch*!'

Simultaneously to her emotional ranting, Tim's coffin was being carefully lifted from the hearse. However, Dave was far too distracted to notice; he was still reeling from the nails that Alison had just driven into his own metaphorical coffin.

Once the Cross family had finally disappeared into the chapel, Len came back over to Dave and Sheila.

'This teenage girl business, and…and the separation ... is any of it *true*?' he asked, alternating his anxious gaze between the two of them.

Dave made sure that he was the first of them to respond.

'It's *not* what it *sounds* like Dad, I never even…'

'Yes, essentially it's *all* true,' Sheila cut in, with succinct frankness, and quite oblivious to sparing anyone's feelings.

A shocked and confused Len stared intensely and accusingly at Dave.

'I can't *believe* it ... it's just like Ronnie all over again,' his forlorn father muttered, as he shook his head. He then turned away and slowly walked back to rejoin his wife and mother.

Sheila walked off too, albeit much more briskly, and left Dave standing alone centre-stage: a defeated gladiator who had just been given a universal thumb's down. Right there and then, he realised that all his hopes of a reconciliation with his wife had probably crumbled to nothing. Dust to dust.

After a short while, he ran after her to avoid being stranded at the crematorium, with only the heaven-bound and intermingled warmth of Grandad Darwin's and Tim's heat haze for company.

As the journey home progressed, the cumulative affect of the week's stress, exacerbated by the pent up grief and sudden shock, worsened his already thumping headache and it developed into a blinding red spotted migraine type condition. And all the while, the terrible truth tormented him: he had lost not only his beloved Grandad Darwin, but also any chance of ever getting Sheila back. To make matters worse, if that was at all possible, his recent indiscretion with Amanda-Jayne had been paraded in front of the whole family and he hadn't even been given the opportunity to tell his side of the story.

As they approached the outskirts of Canterbury, Sheila addressed him in a matter of fact way.

'I don't think your idea of a so-called civilised meal out, is at *all* appropriate anymore, do *you*?' she said, almost rhetorically. 'We don't really need to discuss anything *anyway*!'

'But what about the *future*?' Dave asked with head-pounding desperation.

'That's just *it* though, Dave ... we haven't *got* a future to discuss,' she retorted with weary frustration. '*I've* moved out, the house is on the market, and it'll be sold sooner or later. End of story!'

How cold she sounded, Dave thought, through a mist of pain. He also reached the sad conclusion that he'd been deluding himself about having any chance of winning her back in the first place.

'Oh and that reminds me,' Sheila added, as the vehicle negotiated the city's ring road. 'A Mr and Mrs Sanders will be coming round at 10:30 tomorrow morning to view the house ... they seem *very* keen,' she said, without making eye-contact with him. 'I didn't like to worry you about it *before* the funeral. The thing is ... I have to work, so I'm *quite* happy to leave it to you to show them round, *okay*?'

Dave screwed up his eyes and then nodded in reluctant agreement. So now, he was going to lose his house as well, and probably far sooner than even he had hoped. But where would he go? Would either his parents, or Lucy want to take him in? Might Nanna Darwin, or even Ed – once he was settled – be prepared to give him a bed? However, there was a potential problem, if not a pitfall. If his family were going to react badly to the news of his alleged adultery, then he might lose them all as well! There would be nothing left for him, except Telecom. He would be alone, completely and utterly, alone. Those dark, dismal thoughts only made his headache intensify. He just couldn't shake it off, which was strange because, normally, he wasn't a headachy sort of person.

Sheila halted the car outside the house they had once shared and waited for Dave to get out.

'And don't forget ... 10:30 tomorrow ... Mr and Mrs Sanders,' was her parting, utterly businesslike comment.

As she sped off, a billow of disturbed fallen leaves swirled in the air in front of him. Those same leaves, a mixture of sycamore and beech, fluttered around his face, all dead and dried, but he did not flinch. Sheila's car finally disappeared from view and yet Dave could feel no emotion at all, as he slowly turned back towards the house.

The lonely time begins now, he thought, fumbling for his front door keys. This was the final and irreconcilable end of his marriage; it was dead and buried. Ashes to ashes.

As he kicked his shoes off in the hall, Dave was aware of only one thing: the terrible pounding in his head that, even now, was still building in intensity. And was it the headache that was currently blocking his emotions? He didn't know the answer to that, nor did he really care; in fact, there was nothing he cared about at all right at that moment. As Dave allowed his jacket to fall to the floor, he was not aware that he'd left the front door wide open behind him; nor did he notice the many leaves that had begun to drift across the hall carpet.

Zombie-like, he slowly lowered himself down on the second step of the staircase and held his hanging head in both hands, as his temples throbbed with ever-increasing vehemence. Thus positioned, he gradually lost all sense of time and place. Had Sheila been gone for five days or was it only five minutes? It seemed like five years, but at the same time, it also felt like she was still there too. Either way, Dave recognised that he was now entering an interim phase in his life: one of being neither a married man, nor a divorced one. And yet, he wouldn't be perceived any differently by anyone, unless they became aware of the fact; no one would be pointing at him in the street and saying: look, there goes a separated man!

Dave had long been fascinated by the finite period of time, that sense of interim as he called it, between something being decided and it actually being carried out. Usually, apart from the initial decision that a change would be taking place, nothing really happened straightaway to effect that change, but everyone involved knew that it surely would eventually. Their house at Wellbourne had that same sense of interim about it as well now, in that it was neither the marital home, nor yet sold to anyone else, and yet he was still living there as he always had. The condemned Canterbury buildings that he liked to photograph were in an interim phase too. When the demolition order was signed, nothing visually happened to the doomed structure, apart from the fixing of that ominous yellow notice. Sometimes, those buildings stood there for years, and yet, most people didn't become aware of their ultimate fate until the demolition crew finally moved in. An unfortunate man who, having been told by the doctor that his cancer was inoperable, won't just suddenly die there on the spot. His life would continue on as it always had, at least for a while. It's the same when resigning from a job and then working out the notice. In fact, the whole sense of an interim phase was a concept that desperately clung on to what had gone before, whilst ignoring what inevitably was to come, and in that way, it was very much like Dave himself.

The shambling man further pondered on the strange concept of the interim as he plodded into the lounge, each stumbling step feeling like an electric shock in his brain. He reached inside the drinks cupboard and found the litre bottle of whisky that he'd put away at the beginning of the week. Luckily, there was still a good half of it left. Finding a tumbler in the adjacent glass-partitioned unit, he poured out a large measure and quickly knocked it back in one draught. It was then that the similarities between himself and Ronnie once more occurred to him, for had not his uncle once used whisky to dull both his own physical and mental pain?

Following his second drink, it became apparent that neither the abstract thinking, nor the liquor, was helping matters in the least. Therefore, he decided that he simply must take something else for that headache. The paracetomol were in the kitchen medicine cupboard, he recalled, and that seemed so far out of reach, but if this thing was to be zapped, he knew that he'd have to make the effort. With the intense headache as his only companion, Dave shuffled through and found the bottle of pills. And then, with his eyes almost shut, he groped his way back to the lounge and the relative comfort of the settee. Having passed through the hallway on his journeys both to and from the kitchen, he had neither sensed the breeze blowing through the open front door, nor discerned the scurrying leaves that were beginning to cover his abandoned shoes and jacket on the hallway carpet.

Dave hadn't sat back down long before he realised that he'd forgotten to get a glass of water. Oh bollocks, the whisky will do, he muttered to himself, and then poured another glassful. Having mumbled a few more expletives, as the childproof cap was wrestled off, he took two of the tablets with his next mouthful, and then two more for good measure. That'll zap it, he concluded, before taking another mouthful of his so-called anaesthetic.

Putting his whisky tumbler down for a moment, Dave began to fiddle with the paracetomol bottle, and as he did so, one tablet fell out onto the coffee table, leaving a small amount of chalky residue on its shiny surface. He then inverted the small amber glass bottle, and allowed the rest of the pills to rattle out. Dave barely noticed that some of them had rolled onto the floor and settled amongst the beech and sycamore leaves that were beginning to accumulate on the lounge carpet. However, most of the tablets remained on the coffee table and he now began to move them around in various shapes, like draughts on a chequer board.

It was whilst playing with the pills that Dave noticed Sheila's cigarette packet and gold lighter on the corner of that same low table.

'*That* was very forgetful of her,' he said wearily, 'she'll be *gasping* by bedtime!

Now, what are those white things on the surface in front of me? Oh yes, headache pills, *that's* right ... I've got a headache,' he concluded, and then took two more of the tablets with another large mouthful of whisky.

The five-year old Grouse was going down well, and it soon occurred to Dave that, unlike Ronnie, he wasn't drinking it to drown out his emotional pain, because he didn't feel any, but at least, if he got drunk, then that would be feeling *something*! But how could he enjoy being drunk if he still had that damned migraine? So, two more paracetomol should do the trick, he reasoned, or perhaps another two or three.

An indefinable period of whisky drinking and pill taking passed by, but it was a futile effort and he could not rid himself of the pain in his head. It was then that he thought about another concept of the interim, and one that had not occurred to him before now: it was on the subject of suicide. A man jumping off the top of a forty-storey office block had made real his decision to kill himself from the moment he stepped off the ledge, but on the way down, he was still as much alive as he'd been in the lift on his way up. He only actually died when he hit the pavement far below. If you took poison, there was an interim period too, only shorter, in all probability. It didn't work with drowning because someone might pull you out of the water, unless of course, you did it like Virginia Woolf, with no one else about and with huge heavy stones in your overcoat pockets. But what did a suicide victim think during that interim period? Moreover, what had been going through Tim's mind, if anything?

His perception of reality now severely compromised, Dave took a handful of pills and a large draught of whisky, to see if it would help him better understand what Tim had been thinking in those last, lonely moments. Had he hoped God existed after all and that he would go to heaven, or did he welcome the oblivion of nothingness? Dave tried to imagine what heaven would be like, and before long, a series of pleasant prospects passed through his mind. He could enjoy Nanna Maybury's cooking again and also laugh at Uncle Ronnie's jokes. And then he, Ronnie and Grandad Darwin could go for a long walk through the cherry orchards of Rothermead, or across those woods just below Barham Crematorium. After that, perhaps he and Tim could have a long chat with God and ask him if he had ever listened in to their colourful conversations in the cathedral crypt.

He felt very tired now, but the headache still bothered him, although it somehow seemed more distant now; it was a mere echo of pain. However, there was still one small part of him that recognised, on this particular occasion, that this was no nightmare from which he could awake with all that pain gone. Best take some more tablets and try and sleep it off, he concluded; now barely able to see the coffee table in front of him.

The empty whisky tumbler slipped from his hand and fell onto the carpet. A sycamore leaf blew across the room and then lodged itself inside the sticky glass as, back out in the hallway, the front door swung aimlessly on its hinges.

VISITORS

It is amazing what can happen to a person in just a few months. A dreaded period of loneliness, an unwelcome change of lifestyle, or both, can suddenly become a catalyst for new opportunities and chances that never truly presented themselves before. Such was the case with Dave Darwin. As it turned out, he had recovered from his split with Sheila comparatively quickly. In fact, after the dust had settled, they'd become quite good friends. Moreover, with a generous loan from Nanna Darwin, he had bought out her half of the house and continued to live at Wellbourne, surrounded by his beloved treasures. Julian finally went to university a long way away and had vowed never to return to Canterbury, being disillusioned with both Dave and Sheila in equal measures. Dave himself had finally plucked up enough courage to leave Telecom and set himself up as a professional photographer, with further financial backing from his paternal grandmother. He specialised in nature studies, old buildings and, of course, glamour. But best of all though, he was beginning to re-establish a close relationship with Amanda-Jayne. The eighteen-year-old realised that Sheila had been solely responsible for all the upset, and also that none of it would have happened in the first place, had she herself been more 'adult' about the whole relationship with Dave. Her mother, Mrs Roper, had been sectioned for an indefinite period and the house signed over to her daughter. Dave and Amanda-Jayne had been on several dates together and the beautiful youngster was strongly hinting that she was now ready to have a 'proper' relationship with him. She also expressed a desire to become a photographic model and had asked Dave if he would shoot her portfolio. He readily agreed and they soon arranged an evening for the photo session.

That afternoon, Cordelia went round to Amanda-Jayne's house to do her hair and makeup. She advised the would-be model not to wear any bra or pants that day, lest they leave red marks on her skin that would show up in the pictures.

Dave converted a corner of the lounge into a makeshift studio and at seven o'clock as arranged, Amanda-Jayne turned up by taxi. She was wearing a short dress of black crushed velvet, with an off-the-shoulder neckline.

'My God, you look absolutely stunning,' he said, with wide-eyed awe, letting her into the house.

'Thank you ... although imagine what the taxi driver would have thought if he knew I had no knickers on,' she giggled, before kissing Dave slowly on the lips. She then followed him into the lounge, bringing a holdall with her.

'I've brought a selection of basques, swimming costumes and sexy bras to change into,' she said, as her boyfriend poured two glasses of champagne. And as she re-familiarised herself with the surroundings, the young woman made no mention of the dried autumnal leaves that had covered the lounge carpet at least several inches thick.

The session started with Dave shooting some head and shoulder views of her, both smiling, and not smiling, and then drinking from the glass. That Cordelia had certainly done some good work, he observed, squinting through the lens. Finally, he had her sitting cross-legged on a bar stool that he'd provided and then reclining in various ways on the settee.

'Lets spice things up a little,' Amanda-Jayne suggested after a while. She stood up, unpinned her hair, and then shook her head in order to let her hair fall down casually.

'So, what would you like me to change into now then Dave?' she asked, both speaking quietly and fixing him with a knowing stare.

Before he could react in any way, eighteen-year-old had reached behind to unfasten her dress. It fell from her body to the leaf-covered ground in one gliding move and there she stood, completely naked in front of him.

Dave had not seen her in such a state before, but had often imagined what she might look like as nature intended. His eyes hungrily scanned up and down her young slender form, picking out the details of delight: her small yet upright breasts and hardening nipples, her narrow waist, flat stomach and shock of dark pubic hair.

'I want you just the way you are!' he breathed, and then beckoned for her to once more mount the stool.

She struck a series of erotic and yet un-pornographic poses as Dave's camera rapidly clicked away. And then, without being told to, Amanda-Jayne dismounted from the stool and went to lie on the sofa.

'Do you want me like this?' she asked, before spreading her legs wide and then beginning to stroke herself, as the dried and shrivelled beech leaves crunched beneath her body.

Straightaway, Dave stood up from behind the camera, completely incapable of photographing this lovely writhing figure on his settee. Her breathing became more rapid with the continued stroking of her thighs, as she arched her back for their mutual pleasure. And then, she stopped and stood up.

'I must have you inside me now, Dave,' she moaned, before lurching forward and then thrusting the camera equipment to one side as she grabbed for his trouser belt. Having also torn off his tee shirt and boxer shorts, she pushed him down onto the settee before mounting him. And then, with both her hands on his chest, she began thrusting, her breasts quivering with each movement of her body.

I can't believe this is finally happening, Dave rejoiced, as golden sycamore leaves swirled in the air all around them. He then looked up into the face of the woman who was pleasuring herself astride of him. But there was something wrong; it was no longer Amanda-Jayne. Sheila? His lover's breasts were more pendulous now, and her body more squat and plump.

'Playing horsey ... isn't *that* what you want?' Sheila panted, as she thrust harder and also dug her nails into his chest.

But it was Sheila no longer. His lover was now much more slender and smaller breasted. Her long straight blonde hair parted to reveal Katie; the sixteen-year-old temptress from Ronnie's flat.

'You won't tell my mum about this will you?' she pleaded, staring down into his horrified face.

Dave screwed up his eyes in alarm and turned his head away, but a rough hand soon grabbed him by the ear and then pulled his head violently back to facing the front. He opened his eyes, and tried to scream in fright, but no sound came out.

'The young ones are all very well,' remarked a panting and naked Mrs Roper, as she approached her climax, ' ... but there's nothing like an experienced woman ... ooh, yes, yes, *yes*!'

Dave began to struggle now, but her hands continued to push down onto his chest. As the thrusting movement continued, Mrs Roper now seemed to be wearing a nurse's hat, but her face had changed too. He did not know who this woman was.

'*That's* it, nurse ... the pulse is steady now, thank God! You can discontinue the heart-compression,' instructed the doctor with much relief, as he removed the stethoscope from his ears.

The nurse, who had been pressing on to his chest, climbed down from the trolley and then peered closely into the patient's eyes.

'He's definitely coming round too ... Mr Darwin...David, *David* ... can you hear me?'

The prostrate man's eyes blinked rapidly as he tried to separate the fantasy from the reality. Thankfully, the pretty young face he now focused on didn't change into another person; it was quite a relief.

'*Hello* there David ... I thought we were going to lose you for a moment then!' smiled the nurse at close quarters. 'I don't know if you can understand me, but you're being looked after now, and there's *nothing* to worry about!' she added, before slowly moving out of his field of vision.

Dave soon became aware of other people round the settee, but not a settee anymore; it was more like a hospital trolley. What was going on, he asked himself?

It was then that another, much deeper voice came echoing in from the other side of the settee-cum-trolley.

'Okay, now that the patient has stabilised, we can continue on to the ITU,' advised a tall white-coated figure, who seemed to be towering, if not floating above him.

Dave felt his eyelids starting to shut once more. That tall man must be Mr Sanders who's come to look at the house, he proposed to himself, as brown autumnal leaves gradually began to cover him like a soothing blanket.

Dave blinked, slowly opened his eyes and then attempted to focus on the bright light above him. He tried to take a deep breath, but soon began to choke. At the same time, beeping noises to his left suddenly changed in both pitch and intensity.

'*Hold* on a minute, David,' a nurse said, who was now by his side. 'Let me take this out for you,' she added, as her hands approached his face.

He began to retch, but felt relief almost straightaway, as the respirator was pulled from his throat.

'*There* you are, that's better isn't it?' continued the soothing female voice. 'But breathe slowly, as you get used to it by yourself again.'

Instinctively, he knew she had his best interests at heart, and slowly nodded in acknowledgement. He also wanted to ask what the hell was going on, but could only summon up a dry, painful croak.

'You'll be able to speak properly in a few hours,' his unknown angel reassured him, ' ... and when you're up to it, the doctor will come and see you.' She adjusted some dials on an adjacent monitor and then slowly walked away.

A confused Dave lay there and, as all his senses all too slowly returned to him, tried to remember exactly what had happened. Sadly, all he could come up with were questions. What was wrong with him? Why was he here? Had he been run over? He tried hard to concentrate, but could only summon up a vague jumble of images: Sheila, a funeral, draughts on a chequer board and leaves, lots of leaves. Confused, he glanced around him and decided that his surroundings appeared to resemble a film set for *Star Trek: The Next Generation*. No, a hospital; he decided that he was definitely in hospital. But why were there all those dead leaves on the floor? And why did he want to go to sleep once more?

Dave opened his eyes again, and soon realised that he was propped up much more than before, and there also seemed to be less tubes running from his body now. As he focused both his mind and his eyes, Dave became aware of a figure sitting by his bedside to the right, amidst the equipment. It was his father, and he suddenly felt a mixture of pleasure and anxiety.

As soon as Len became aware that his son was awake, he beamed with delight, and then got up to join him at the pillow end of the bed.

'*Hello,* Dave old chap, your mother was here with you before me, but you were asleep and now she's gone to get some tea and talk to the doctor. So how do you *feel*?' he asked, in soft low tones.

'*Confused,* Dad ... to be quite honest,' he replied, with a shallow smile, but pleased to be getting his voice back.

His father slowly nodded in response, and then his countenance became more solemn.

'*Listen* son, I'm not going to reproach you for what you did, or ask you *why* you did it, but I want you to know that your mother and I are *always* going to be here for you. I know we've not always hit it off in the past, but I…' Len broke off, tears clearly welling in his eyes.

'It's *alright,* Dad,' Dave said, as he reached for his father's hand, or as far as the remaining tubes would allow.

His father moved his hand in order to reach his son's and they sat there in silence together, exchanging reassuring glances and small smiles.

'Your mum has looked out a pair of my old pyjamas for you to borrow; we couldn't *find* any up at your place!' he said, followed by a brief close-mouthed smile. 'I've ... err ... I've given them to one of the nurses'.

'Thanks!' he replied, looking down briefly at the white hospital gown he was currently wearing.

Things were gradually coming back to Dave now: Tim's death, Grandad's death, Sheila's support, the note, the row, Amanda-Jayne sobbing, Julian storming out, Sheila leaving, loneliness, Grandad Darwin's funeral, the bad headache, the whisky and the leaves. But why leaves? Thinking harder still, he ran through the latter part of the sequence once again: his headache, Tim's suicide, the whisky and yes, those tablets! Suddenly, he grasped the true meaning behind his father's plaintive words.

'Oh *God* Dad, you *mustn't*…I mean to say, *don't* think that I was trying to *kill* myself, I wasn't…it was just…it was an *accident*!' he asserted with both alarm and urgency.

'*None* of that matters now, Dave,' his father interrupted, whilst rapidly patting his hand. 'Listen ... there's a psychoanalyst, a counsellor here that you can talk to about that. *She'll* sort it out for you; everything will be alright!' he added, in a voice choked with emotion.

Dave swallowed hard and his throat still felt very sore. He was thinking more or less clearly now, and suddenly numerous further questions began to pose themselves. Would he ever be able to persuade his family that the overdose was an accident? And what of the row with Sheila, and Alison's cruel comments at the crematorium. Did his father know the truth about his marriage break up? Was Sheila even aware of the fact that he was in hospital? These were all urgent questions, but ones that would obviously have to wait for now.

A nurse now came over and politely told Len that the visiting time was now over, as the doctor needed to give his son a thorough checking over.

As his father stood up to go, he leaned in, gave Dave a rare kiss on the cheek, and then they both smiled and winked before he turned to leave. However, he'd barely cleared the bed area before pausing, and then turning back.

'Oh, by the *way*, that old school friend of yours, Mrs Holroyd, got in touch with me again, having... erm ... having got no reply at Wellbourne,' he said, clearly being careful in his choice of words. 'I told her that you...err...you'd had an accident and couldn't really *see* anyone at the moment.'

'Thanks for letting me know, Dad,' his son replied politely, at what he considered to be interesting but hardly high priority news, given the circumstances.

Len gave the thumbs-up sign and disappeared through the double doors that were situated almost straight ahead of Dave's bed.

It wasn't long before the doctor was with him; he was a calm but frank man, with a tanned complexion and a shock of blonde hair, whom Dave estimated to be at least five years his junior. After a brief and yet civil preamble, the young doctor explained to him that based on the initial tests, and an earlier examination, he'd probably sustained both liver and kidney damage. However, the outcome would have been far worse, if not fatal, had his wife not discovered him later that same evening. Nevertheless, he reassured the alarmed patient that given enough rest and the proper medication, he could, in all likelihood, make a complete recovery. All in all, he was a very lucky man.

Dave listened politely to the diagnosis and prognosis, but felt an absolute need to set the record straight.

'But I didn't *mean* to do it doctor, the overdose was an *accident*,' he said, managing to lift himself a few inches off the stack of pillows behind him.

The medical man looked at him slightly piteously.

'The thing *is,* Mr Darwin,' he paused, and smiled briefly taking in a deep breath, ' ... the thing *is,* Dave ... my concern is with the body, *not* the mind, but I have a very proficient colleague who will be speaking to you on that very matter, okay?'

There followed a series of bodily check ups, all of which were carried out in silence, except for the odd encouraging murmur from his examiner, and a few 'yes, good' comments thrown in for good measure.

Eventually, having committed his findings to paper, the young doctor stood at the foot of Dave's bed in order to deliver his findings.

'Good news Mr Darwin, the damage to your internal organs doesn't appear to be as severe as I first feared ... you probably *will* make a full recovery. *And* I don't see any reason why you can't be moved to a general ward first thing in the morning!' He then nodded politely and quickly swept from view, to attend his next patient.

'Thank you ... err ... doctor!' Dave said to the swishing white coat tails.

Once he was alone, he tried to make himself comfortable, while beginning to ponder on one specific thing the doctor had mentioned. And it wasn't so much the assurance of a full recovery, as the news that Sheila had come back that afternoon, which he now homed in on. Could it be that she regretted what she'd done? Had she realised how much she'd missed him, and was returning in order to discuss his idea of a meal together? However, it quickly dawned on him that it must have been the cigarettes she'd missed; she must have come back for them. There was no way he was going to find out for sure at the moment, although he had to concede that she had made it pretty clear that a reconciliation was out of the question. Yes, it must have been the cigarettes, he concluded, with reasonable but disappointed assuredness.

Having laid there for a long period of quiet contemplation, Dave was surprised to discover that, in actual fact, there was now a large part of him that no longer wanted Sheila back any more. He remembered his estranged wife's own maxim *'you can never go back'* and for the first time, saw some wisdom in those words. But the inevitable next question now posed itself: what *was* there ahead of him? It was an answer that he could in no way tackle at the moment. However, where the future had once seemed so very bleak, he now saw things in a different context, and began to rejoice in simply being alive. At least he had his life, as well as the love and support of a good family, and following his father's earlier assurance, he now knew that his fear they might abandon him after the crematorium incident, had proved unfounded.

Having been so down in the dumps for so long, Dave was now quite shocked at his own feelings of optimism. But was it the drugs that were making him feel so high, or some newly found sanguinity that he'd managed to conjure up himself? Then again, there was so much else that had gone wrong with his life recently, that Dave sadly concluded that it had to be the medication after all. He sighed deeply, settled back into his pillow and felt low again.

After a few solemn minutes brooding, the nurse interrupted his lonely period of introspection.

'Dave, would you like some ice cream to soothe your throat?' she asked, with the dessert already optimistically in her hands.

'Oh yes *please*!' he smiled, as he took the bowl and plastic spoon.

Hospitals and ice cream. Well I never, he reflected, as the cool confection melted in his mouth. He then worked out that it had been a good 30 years since he'd last associated those things together.

*

David sat up in bed and eagerly ate his bowl of ice cream. It was sweet, cold and welcoming, but despite all that, his throat still hurt him when he swallowed. Having your tonsils out was not the exciting adventure he'd been led to believe it was. The small boy then looked across at Lucy's cot, which was positioned on the other side of the massive bay window to his own berth. They were lucky, for unlike the other four children in the ward, the two young siblings could observe the comings and goings along Northwood Road, which ran past the front of the cottage hospital. The four-and-a-half-year-old could see that Lucy was enjoying her ice cream as well, but it was obviously hurting her to swallow too.

His sister was so young, not yet three, and he desperately hoped that she understood what was happening to them. In fact, the only reason she had been allowed to come in hospital and have her tonsils out so young, was that David would be there to look after her. He was a big boy now, and nearly five; indeed, he had a proper bed, and not a cot like Lucy. Sometimes though, he recalled, it was hard looking after her, especially when her throat hurt more than usual, and she cried for Mummy, but he had plenty of Uncle Ronnie jokes to tell her and could also make funny noises. Invariably, she would soon be grinning back through the bars at him. And, if she still couldn't be pacified, then he would reassure her that Daddy would be along soon, and would have a new comic for each of them, or if it was the evening visit, a comic *and* a tube of Smarties.

Their father came twice a day without fail, on his way to work and on his journey home again. The Whitstable and Tankerton Hospital was conveniently placed halfway between their bungalow 'Damascena' in Ham Shades Lane, and the bus stop in Tankerton High Street. The family had recently bought a three-wheeled car, which was light green, although David assumed their Daddy must have thought it was yellow, as he would often tell Grandad Darwin that he'd purchased a lemon. Perhaps he had meant an unripe lemon. Anyway, the car was broken all through the week they were in hospital having their tonsils out, so Dad was back on the bus.

David looked forward to their father's visits just as much as Lucy did, but he hated him having to go; although not for himself so much, even though he did miss him, but for little Lucy's sake. She never seemed to understand why she couldn't go with him and cried as he left the hospital and continued to cry until he'd disappeared out of sight along Northwood Road. Sadly, their mum had never visited them; on each occasion, Dad came on his own, but that didn't stop Lucy from always asking where she was. David didn't though, as he was used to the fact that she rarely left the house at the moment. There was no doubt in his mind that she desperately loved them both, but this 'agricovia', or whatever it was called, was something that she couldn't help. Grown ups were not infallible, as far as David was concerned; they just had to pretend that they were. In any case, Dad would always reassure them both that mummy was safe at home, she was very near, probably only half a mile away, and was very much looking forward to seeing them both on Friday.

That very morning, when Lucy had asked for mummy, their dad seemed to get quite upset. David wondered if, perhaps, he'd felt embarrassed, because the other little girls and boys parents always came and visited them together. Anyway, when Daddy left this morning, Lucy had wanted to go with him as usual, but David was able to make her laugh with his story of Dad's three-wheeler, even though she'd heard it before. He recalled the Saturday afternoon, a few months ago, when their father had come home with the odd looking car and then taken Nanna Darwin out for a spin in it, quite literally, as it turned out. David had sat in the back as his dad demonstrated how, as he put it, the car would turn on a sixpence. He had then proceeded to spin the car in circles, right in the middle of Pier Avenue. Nanna had screamed for him to stop, but he'd waited until he had gone round five times before doing so. Both children laughed at the story, even though it hurt their throats.

Their dad had not been the only visitor over the last few days. Uncle Ronnie had come to see them the day before yesterday, which was the evening before their operations. He'd bought them some old comics: a *Beano* for David and a *Dandy* for Lucy. These were ones he'd retained from when he was a boy and he had kept them ever so neatly. David had warned him that Lucy didn't treat her books very carefully, but Ronnie didn't seem to mind. He had come down on his scooter from the new house at Rothermead Farm and combined the hospital visit with his driving lesson in Herne Bay. He went there as it was alleged to be easier to pass your test in Herne Bay than anywhere else, apparently. The children's father had tried giving Uncle Ronnie driving lessons in the three-wheeled car, but Len's alarmed reactions to his younger sibling's manoeuvres had made Ronnie even more nervous than his reluctant instructor seemed to be, especially as he always appeared to have his eyes closed. Their uncle made them both laugh when he told them how he'd driven round the Chestfield roundabout too fast, and as a result, had managed it on two wheels too. Laughing at these jokes was especially fun because they were about their dad and he wasn't there to frown at them. Moreover, it hadn't hurt their throats, as they hadn't had their tonsils out then.

That evening, their father visited them as usual and five minutes later, Uncle Ronnie turned up as well. This meant they had two comics each, an old one and a new one. David loved to hear the adult conversations that went on in the various family households, but especially liked those between his father and Uncle Ronnie, and they were certainly talking a lot that evening. Lucy didn't listen; she was happy that her father was within touching distance and so contentedly scrunched up the pages of one of her comics. The first thing the children's father asked Ronnie about was the family's recent move to Rothermead. Until two or three weeks ago, David's Nanna and Grandad Darwin, together with seventeen-year-old Ronnie, had lived at and run Oakenden Nursery, a two-acre smallholding and cottage, sandwiched between Ham Shades Lane and the railway line. The bungalow 'Damascena', where David, Lucy and his parents still lived, was adjacent to the nursery. Ronnie admitted that Grandad Darwin missed being his own boss, but now worked far less hours as head gardener to Lord and Lady Rothermead up at the farm. As far as Ronnie himself was concerned, he liked Rothermead Farm, the garden of the 'big house' and their curious tied cottage, but rather missed the Canterbury, Whitstable and Herne Bay area.

After a short pause, Ronnie excitedly informed Len that, as soon as he could, he was not only going to get a car, but also to acquire his own flat as well. He had seen a couple for sale along Herne Bay seafront, during his driving lessons, and would be viewing one, or both, as soon as possible. Ronnie then somewhat sheepishly admitted that Nanna and Grandad Darwin were financing both ventures, now that they had the money from the sale of Oakenden nursery. He went on to explain to his incredulous older brother that, apparently, by offsetting a certain amount of the capital gained from the sale of the smallholding, their parents were avoiding paying the higher rate of tax on their lump sum. Len acknowledged the sense behind the given explanation, but secretly wondered if it was just another symptom of what he had always perceived to be Nanna and Grandad's favouritism towards their gifted younger son.

Detecting an awkward silence in their conversation, Ronnie asked his older brother if he'd managed to get any buyers for Damascena yet? David's father admitted that there had been some interest and with any luck, his family will have moved back to Canterbury by Christmas. This was all news to David, who now listened more intently, whilst pretending to be engrossed in *The Bash Street Kids*. Len confessed that he was anxious to get away, as he couldn't bear to see the destruction of Oakenden nursery, and dreaded the encroachment of the new houses that were planned to replace it. He told Ronnie how, only the last evening, he had wandered over the former smallholding and was surprised at how quickly the developer, who'd bought the Darwins out, had begun to clear the land. The orchard had already been grubbed up and the 100 foot greenhouse now demolished. Ronnie was very saddened by the news and expressed a wish that he had taken more photographs. David was also upset by the description of Oakenden nursery and wondered why anyone would want to destroy something so special.

Later that same evening, dozing in his hospital bed, young David worried about all the ways in which things in his life were changing. There was no more Oakenden nursery and soon, there would be no more Damascena either. It suddenly occurred to him that the move to Canterbury would also mean a change of schools. What a shame, just when he'd made a nice batch of new friends too! Never mind, he was too tired to worry about that now. He had to get better soon; that was his highest priority for the moment. Indeed, their father had promised a trip to see Nanna and Grandad Darwin at the new cottage at Rothermead Farm, as soon as he and Lucy were back on their feet. And then, there would be the exciting build-up to Christmas, and soon after that, his fifth birthday, with the promise of a special present from Uncle Ronnie. So, in spite of the many changes, there was also much to look forward to, and yet, as he drifted off, David decided that when he grew up, he wanted a steady life with as few changes as possible.

*

There have been so many changes in my life recently, and all of them bad, Dave moaned to himself, as the two porters wheeled his bed into the cavernous lift. It was about 09:00 and he was being moved from intensive care to a general ward. After a brief, yet jerky ride, the lift doors opened once more and they began to mingle with other people in a long corridor that was lined with modernist paintings of varying quality. Although very much stuck in a negative frame of mind with, as he saw, it little to look forward to, he nonetheless tried to home in on something positive. Well, at least he was alive and this move underscored the fact he was out of danger. In fact, the doctor had already confirmed that his liver and kidneys would, in all probability, suffer no long-term damage from the accidental overdose. The word 'accidental' had not actually been uttered by the doctor though; Dave had added that himself. This is what he was now calling that little episode with the drink and the pills, but it would seem that he still had to convince other people of the fact.

Dave soon found himself being positioned near the window of a six-bedded bay, for male patients, in a mixed ward. All the other inmates were older and also looked more poorly than he did, but Dave was not sure if that made him feel better or not. Moreover, unlike where he'd just come from, the so-called general ward seemed to be imbued with the odours of both stale urine and antiseptic, which seemed to assail his nostrils at alternative moments. At least, in this new ward, there seemed to be fewer leaves on the floor than in the ITU.

Having failed to attract the attention of any of the other patients in his shared cell, for the sole purpose of saying 'hi', Dave eased himself round to the left, and then looked out of the Crittall windows. He perceived a row of skeletal trees, all now stripped of their autumnal leaves and soon managed to work out that he must be at the back of the pre-war section of the hospital complex. Those trees, so reminiscent of one of Grandad Darwin's wintry country scenes, marked the route of the disused Elham Valley railway and must have once been part of a line-side hedge, at a time when the last scheduled train had passed through in 1947. Dave always liked the idea that if something had gone, one could still find clues in the landscape or cityscape, to inspire future people to speculate about what might have, at one time, existed there. Fragments of a long ruined church preserved in situ within a later boundary wall, the overgrown rambling rose running freely through the hedges of the former garden to a long demolished country cottage, the rusting chassis and engine block of an old vehicle enveloped by stinging nettles in a forgotten corner of some farmyard; all these things fascinated Dave and he longed to seek out and photograph them, or at least he used to. However, when people were lost to you, there were only your memories and a few snaps to cling to, but they would both inevitably fade in time. It was then that he was very glad of his newfound faith in the human spirit; and was delighted that it hadn't been lost to him like so much else over the last few days. At least now, he was sure that a person's soul would always remain, and live on in some other place; no doubt in circumstances far better than this present, miserable life.

Yesterday, he recalled that the doctor, and indeed his father, had been very keen on him seeing a counsellor, and Dave had reluctantly agreed. At least it would give him a chance to clear up this suicide misunderstanding, or stop them believing he was some sort of attention-seeking wimp who took an overdose as a 'cry for help'. On the other hand, he did not relish the prospect of pouring his heart out to a complete stranger, even if they were qualified in that role. The only people he had really felt comfortable opening up to in the past had been Ronnie and Tim, but they were now both dead. More recently though, he had tried to share his feelings and confidences with Amanda-Jayne and had met with some success, particularly concerning his religious doubts and fears. However, she had been placed too high on a pedestal of his own making to completely fulfil that role. At the end of the day, in the absence of a friendly and carefully pre-selected ear, he would sooner think his problems through himself. He'd much rather go through all the reasons and the options on his own, and then decide on the best way forward. That way, he usually managed to get it right, and if he did sometimes get it wrong, then there was no one other than himself to blame, in spite of how hard he might want to pin it on someone else.

Unknown to her, it was with the battle already mostly lost, that the counsellor came to visit him that morning. She was an attractive Asian woman of indeterminate age, with long straight black hair tied up at the back. Her name was Dr Choudray, but she asked him to call her Meera, at least, that's what he thought she said. Her accent was so heavy that he had great difficulty understanding her. Dave persisted, however, and tried to explain about the misunderstanding over the tablets, but he was getting nothing back from her that he could make out. He didn't like to keep saying he could not understand what she said, or even request to see someone else, for fear of being accused a racist, which indeed he was not. So, in the end, he feigned tiredness and she agreed to come back and see him another day.

Dave soon settled down into the routine of watching the comings and goings of the nurses. He was amused by the nudges and winks of his fellow older patients, and their sucking up to the younger more attractive and shapely nurses. Did they imagine that these girls were anything like their unreal counterparts on the *Benny Hill Show*, with exposed stocking tops and bulging cleavages? Did they really expect those young girls to be sexually attracted by their prostate operations, heart bypass scars or colostomy bags? Dave recalled that his first wife had been a nurse, and Vivien could not have been farther removed from that comedy show cliché.

A stranger now appeared at the far end of the ward to his right, and from the opening that led out into the main corridor. Too early for visitors, Dave speculated, and it was then that he noticed the dog collar. Oh no, the hospital chaplain, he supposed, and, as a result of that speculation, immediately feigned sleep.

After at least five minutes of play acting, Dave opened his eyes a crack to see if the coast was clear, only to find the man sitting by his bedside a couple of feet away to his left. Dave was immediately struck by the chaplain's uncanny resemblance to Dick Emery's comic vicar character – with a large nose, protruding front teeth, and thinning grey-white hair that was slicked back – so his ability to take this man at all seriously, had been severely compromised from the offing. The unannounced visitor soon introduced himself; Dave did not take in his name, but the man already seemed to know his. The chaplain then made it clear that he knew exactly why Dave was in hospital. Moreover, this priest-for-patients had intimate knowledge of, not only the fact he was separated from his wife, but also that he'd recently suffered a double bereavement, one being from suicide.

'*Now* then, David – if I may call you that – I'd like you to know that I'm here if you want...if you *need*, to talk about any of these...issues,' he declared benignly, with an accompanying broad grin.

Dave felt very irritated by this approach, however well intentioned it might be. They were treating him like a failed suicide victim when, in truth, it was an accident. Yes, an accident, he told himself; there was no doubt about that, it was definitely an accident.

'*You've* been doing your homework,' commented a straight-faced Dave, barely able to hide his hostility. Who had been talking to this chaplain? How *dare* they do so without his permission!

'Forgive me,' the chaplain responded, realising that he was causing offence. 'It's just that a person's background, you know, such as recent tragic events can sometimes help me understand their motives,' he reasoned, with delicate Oliver Hardy-style hand gestures.

'Motives for *what*?' Dave barked crossly, now sitting up rigidly in his bed

'Look, David, the *last* thing I want to do is to upset you,' the hospital holy man pleaded; now both visibly and verbally struggling. 'But my understanding is that you...you took a large quantity of alcohol and pills and ... that usually means...'

'Understand *this,* padre ... I did *not* try to commit suicide,' Dave interrupted angrily, pointing accusingly at his alarmed visitor. 'It was an accident ... got that, an *accident*. I don't have any *issues* as you say, and all I want to do is to *get* well, and then *get* out of here. So I would appreciate it if you would kindly *piss off* and leave me in peace!'

The chaplain merely smiled, nodded meekly and then quickly departed as requested. From the very moment that hapless chaplain had turned into the corridor and disappeared, Dave wanted to apologise to him. On the other hand, he tried to justify his rude behaviour by telling himself that all this suicide nonsense needed to be cleared up. My God, next they'll be suggesting that Uncle Ronnie committed suicide, he mused sardonically; now there was an interesting concept.

Dave had not really thought much about Ronnie recently, certainly not since he'd concluded that his former boyhood hero was merely just another flawed human being, like himself, who had fallen for the wrong person and then paid the ultimate price. But could his death be in any way considered suicide, Dave ruminated, as he attempted to pull together all the factors. If one drives a car at over 80 mph, while blind drunk, having just lost a career and reputation; not to mention being kept apart from the love of one's life, is one consciously trying to kill oneself? By the same token, if one ingests large quantities of whisky and paracetomol, having just lost best friend, wife and beloved grandfather, is one likewise, and in some indirect way, trying to do away with oneself? If only I could discuss this with Tim, he thought wistfully; it would be right up his street. That notion made him laugh out loud, and resulted in several of the old boys in adjacent beds glaring at him piteously: the poor mental patient, that pathetic failed suicide victim; the man who was rude to vicars! And how ironic it was, Dave chuckled to himself, that the only person he could have felt confident enough to talk to about suicidal ambiguity, was a man who had recently killed himself and had absolutely meant to do it.

Dave enjoyed his lunch, and ate every bit. So that was another cliché that didn't stand up to scrutiny, he thought; the hospital food was rather good. He had just begun to relax and digest his meal when visiting time came. Dave had no high expectations of there being long queues of people waiting to see him. In fact, he began chuckling to himself again, but this time at the thought of Alison Cross, Mrs Roper, Sheila and Amanda-Jayne, all waiting in line to finish him off, each clutching both whisky and paracetomol bottles. His fellow patients once more exchanged knowing glances and tutted at the poor giggling idiot whom they'd been landed with.

None of those four ladies turned up, nor did he really expect them to, but another one did, in the portly shape of Tiffany from Telecom. Dave considered feigning death, but had already been spotted by her, alive and well. She was clutching a large basket of fruit, wrapped in cellophane and topped off with a hideous yellow bow. Yes indeed, his work colleagues really knew the sort of thing he liked!

'How are you *feeling* now, Dave?' Tiffany asked awkwardly, as she rested his gift on the foot of the bed. She then approached him on the right side of the bed and promptly looked at her watch.

'Well, *actually* I…'

'*I* was in hospital recently!' she interrupted, without waiting for a reply. 'You may remember Dave … I was in here having my ovarian cysts drained! They were able to do it by sticking a tube in my belly button. You can hardly *see* the mark now,' she boasted, before lifting up her sweatshirt up to reveal large quantities of bare flesh. She wouldn't cover herself up again until he'd had a proper look, so, with the greatest of reluctance, he looked.

'Oh yes!' Dave commented , whilst thinking to himself that there had to have been a belly button in there somewhere.

The rest of the conversation was also dominated by Tiffany who, still standing, delighted in updating him on the latest happenings in the office and the miserable lives of his vacuous work colleagues. Dave buried his head deeper into the pillow, but it was no good; he could still hear her voice. The final straw came when she told him, in detail, the finer points of Darryl Giles' new Telecom Initiative Training Strategy. He looked at the fruit basket and in desperation, wondered how quickly one would die from an overdose of mango.

Fortunately, Tiffany finally paused for breath and then glanced at her watch again.

'Oo … look at the time … I'd better be off,' she declared, already beginning to back away. 'Everyone at work sends their best, and we're … umm … we're all looking forward to seeing you back at work soon!'

Whoopee, thought Dave wearily: the only bit of stability I've got left in my life, and it's a loathed job fielding complaints for fucking Telecom!

No sooner had Tiffany beaten her hasty retreat, than the drugs trolley appeared from the corridor end and began to do the rounds. Two nurses were propelling the cumbersome contraption: a short plumpish woman with a bad complexion and a tall, rather good-looking girl, with dark hair and big eyes. Each of them selected a patient in turn, on an apparent arbitrary basis, and then compared his notes to theirs and administered the prescribed drugs. As was typical of the way his day was going, when it came to Dave's turn, he got the shorter of the two nurses.

'Mr David Darwin?' she asked, in a musical tone that implied she thought he was a deaf octogenarian.

'Yes nurse, *that's* me!' he replied, and was handed two white plastic cups: one containing a cocktail of drugs, the other, water. The nurse hovered expectantly, whilst he took them and then rewarded him with a broad smile, once he'd complied.

Well, the first day in the general ward was a bundle of laughs, he concluded after lights out. Three visitors and all of them ghastly: an unintelligible counsellor, an interfering priest and a bore from work, who had obviously drawn the short straw in having to come and visit him anyway. Another day like that and he might be tempted to discharge himself and then go and lie in a pool of his own piss in a shelter in the Westgate gardens, with all of life's other failures.

A weary Dave awoke amidst the hustle and bustle of a typical hospital ward at dawn. The previous night had been both noisy and disturbing. One of his fellow patients had got into difficulties during the small hours. Curtains had been pulled around the bed in question and there was much running about. This morning, he noted that the bed was ominously empty. Dave himself, had developed bad stomach and lower back pains in the night and been given extra medication. Now at breakfast, he felt fine, apart from being rather tired and also having to look at the ugly basket of fruit, on top of his bedside locker.

At about mid-morning, he looked up from his trolley library book, *A Portrait of a Marriage*, to find the hospital chaplain at the foot of his bed.

'Umm ... if you want me to *piss off* again, I will,' he said, before smiling broadly, to indicate that his comment had been meant as humorous.

Dave was completely and instantly disarmed.

'Ah *no*, why don't you sit down?' he offered, with a gesture towards the chair on the left of the bed. 'And I'm sorry for behaving like an utter arsehole yesterday,' conceded the somewhat shame-faced patient.

'And *I* apologise for making assumptions,' added his newly found friend, before lowering himself into the plastic stacker chair. 'And don't worry, I'm not going to ram God down your throat.'

'That's a relief,' Dave remarked in a semi-joking manner. 'As it happens, I'm doing quite well, following my *own* path thanks.'

'Well, let's hope you *get* there,' the chaplain responded, as he glanced briefly at a young nurse who was attending to the patient in the adjacent bed.

'And how did *you* get there?' Dave asked, as he began to warm to the man.

'Through music,' replied the chaplain, with positive succinctness. 'It was the sheer beauty and diversity of music; its power to summon up the deepest emotion, that made me realise there must be an enormous benevolent force responsible, and it sort of snowballed from there!'

'I envy you your clarity,' Dave smiled, finally putting his book down.

'Oh, but don't get me *wrong*, David,' his visitor said, himself visibly relaxing by the minute, 'I constantly struggle with my faith. Life's a bitch, as someone once said, and keeps trying to throw you off course.'

Dave found this attitude extremely refreshing compared to the cradle catholic indifference of his estranged wife, Sheila. He liked this man, he especially liked the way he kept furtively glancing at the nurses, but how should he address him: vicar, chaplain; your holiness? Much simpler to ask him his name, thought Dave.

'Look ... umm ... I know you told me your name yesterday, but ...err, I wasn't very *receptive* to…'

'It's Richard Amery,' the man quickly intervened, 'but most people call me Dick.' Straightaway, Dave began to smile and his visitor soon joined him.

'*Yes*, yes…don't say it…*I* know, Dick Amery!' he conceded, with strenuous nods. 'The *name's* bad enough, but imagine how I felt when I put the dog collar on for the first time and then looked at myself in the mirror!' He paused while they both laughed. '*And* I'm always being asked if *I am* him, or some relation of his,' Dick added, still chuckling heartily; his large white teeth gleaming in the harshly lit hospital ward.

'I know just how you feel,' Dave remarked empathically. 'I've been asked that same question most of my life!'

'Yes, Darwin, of *course*,' observed the humorous holy man. '*So* then, *are* you any relation?'

'What, to *Charles* Darwin: evolution, natural selection and all that? Not as far as I know,' Dave dismissed, with a shallow shrug of the shoulders.

'*No*, I meant *Ronnie* Darwin!' the chaplain beamed; his eyebrows raised in expectation.

'Oh *him*…you're referring to that comedian who ruined his career by getting himself involved with a young girl, and then *killing* himself…aren't you!' Dave commented, his mood gradually darkening.

Slightly taken aback by the negative reaction from his bed-bound companion, Dick Amery narrowed his eyes, but otherwise tried not to let his feelings show. He then decided to say what he was going to say next in any case.

'I *knew* him,' he announced, in a quiet, measured manner, 'and I thought he was a *great* bloke. It was *terrible* what happened to Ronnie, but there but for the grace of God go we *all*, eh?'

'Yes, I suppose that's right,' Dave said, somewhat shame-faced, and only able to glance briefly at his visitor.

Without prompting, the chaplain began to reminisce about the relationship.

'Many years and a full head of hair ago, I accompanied Ronnie on a number of his Kent miner's club gigs. It was the mid 1960s, if I recall correctly, and a time when he was still unsure of his direction, *you* know, when he was both singing *and* telling gags. Well, it was lucky that we met up, as it turned out, what with me being a young semi-professional pianist, who was *also* unsure of his direction in life!'

Having listened to the tale, Dave began to feel some of that old pride slowly re-emerging.

'Actually, I have to confess that Ronnie Darwin *was* my uncle!' he acknowledged at long last, albeit in subdued tones.

Dick nodded, and then smiled as he looked down, but didn't reveal if he had already known that fact, or not.

'Ronnie was a deeply passionate man, not dissimilar to *yourself*, if I dare be so bold,' the chaplain said, peering back up at Dave. 'He felt both the highs and lows of life with equal intensity. I got to know him quite *well* on the old circuit and I never saw him be rude or unkind to *anyone*. And as far as that young lady you mentioned is concerned, I know nothing of her, but I'll tell you *this* David…' he leaned forward to emphasize the point, 'I am *convinced* that your uncle was *not* trying to kill himself ... that car crash was a sad accident, and no more!'

Straightaway, Dave felt much of the weight being taken from his shoulders. It was uncanny; it was almost as if the man could see into his mind.

'And you mustn't be so hard on old Ronnie,' his newfound friend concluded, '*or* on yourself, David. As the old cliché has it: we are *all* only human, unless of course you're John Major, then you're a Thunderbird puppet!'

Dave laughed in response, but not so much that he didn't notice when Dick once more glanced discreetly at the nurse bending over the bed of the adjacent patient; it was almost as if he wanted to reinforce his point regarding humanity, albeit unwittingly. And Dave's sudden upbeat mood wasn't solely down to the chaplain's joke, for it had been a long time since he'd experienced anything even approaching peace of mind. Moreover, he recognised that he felt comfortable in the company of this man of the cloth, and was keen to keep him in conversation.

'Do you ever play *jazz* piano?' he asked, making close eye contact with his companion.

'I *try*,' Dick replied, with a playful grimace, ' ... but I ain't no Thelonious Monk!' He then proceeded to impersonate the stance and hand-chopping style of that famous man. 'In fact, I *still* do the odd jazz gig locally.'

Inspired by the comment, an interesting thought suddenly struck Dave.

'Did you ever know the drummer Tim Cross?' he asked, with rather anxious countenance.

It seemed to be a question that his visitor wasn't expecting, and he could now be seen quickly gathering his thoughts.

'Umm…that was your friend who committed suicide, wasn't it?' he asked rhetorically, and with a little caution. 'No, I'm afraid I *didn't* know him.'

'*Yes*, he committed suicide,' Dave confirmed, with a slow and unhappy nod, '*and* he meant to do it as well!' he paused and sighed deeply before continuing. 'You can't help wondering ... perhaps I could have done *more* to help, but…'

'Now, *listen*,' a stern-faced Dick interrupted, leaning forward in his seat, 'if he was *determined* to go through with it, it's very doubtful that you *could* have done anything to dissuade him.'

'I *suppose* so!' came the meekly, mumbled response.

The benign chaplain sat back up again, and regarded Dave with a hesitant gaze. It was then that he sensed the moment was right to ask the key question.

'We know all about poor Tim, but what about *you,* David? Did *you* mean to go through with it?' he gently asked, placing his left hand on the bedclothes close to Dave's foot.

'I honestly don't know,' Dave replied, without either thinking about, or in any way pre-planning his response. 'But I'm very glad that I'm still here, in *spite* of everything that's happened.'

Dick breathed out audibly through his nose and nodded slowly at the same time.

'Then it sounds to me like you probably *didn't* mean to do it, as you tried to tell Meera Choudray, and no doubt, would have told *me* yesterday if I hadn't gone bumbling in.'

'*Now* who's being too hard on himself,' Dave joked, in immediate response. 'Remember about us all being only human?'

They both laughed loudly and again attracted more disapproving looks from the fellow patients. At the same time, the last of those brown, dead leaves on the floor quietly blew away.

The rest of the morning was taken up with Dave being tortured, that is, by having to endure a thorough going over by the doctor involving much prodding and poking, followed by an enforced long walk up and down the corridor. His lower back: the kidney area, still hurt like hell, as it did when he went to the loo, but the hospital staff were quick to reassure him that it would all soon get better, and that drinking as much water as possible would help. He also noticed that since his long conversation with Dick Amery, the attitude towards him from both doctors and nurses alike had lightened considerably; it had become far less judgemental.

Just before visiting time that afternoon, he had a rather amusing mental image of evil-looking harpies circling round him; the same four characters as yesterday, but now they were pelting him with paracetomol and pouring both scotch and scorn down on his head. However, the smile soon fell from his face, when the visitors bustled in and amongst them, he saw Julian bearing down on him. Anticipating a fight, Dave quickly put his glass of water down and then reached for his buzzer, but it didn't appear to be working. And then again, nothing in life ever goes the way you imagine it; that was a subject about which he could write a book, given recent events.

Julian stood by the right-hand edge of the bed and, straightaway, it was obvious that he was as anxious and nervous as Dave clearly was.

'Err ... *hello* there ... how *are* you...how are you *feeling*?' he asked, blinking rapidly, as he struggled to maintain eye contact with the patient.

'Much *better* thank you ... both mentally and physically,' responded a relieved and more relaxed Dave; if not still a little cautiously.

'Good...good,' Julian replied, nodding slowly and rhythmically.

Now reasonably reassured that there would be no confrontation, the pyjama-clad man gestured towards the chair on the other side of the bed.

'Why don't you sit down,' he suggested, in a manner more friendly than formal.

Julian sat down as bidden, and then with a long intake of breath, dived straight in at the deep end of that shark infested pool, which contained the stormy waters of their past relationship. He explained that when he'd got back to his Dover flat that Sunday afternoon after it had all happened, he thought long and hard about what had occurred, and more importantly why. Unable to make sense of all the disparate pieces, let alone fit them together, he contacted Amanda-Jayne and persuaded her, with great difficulty, to meet him for coffee sometime during the following few days. Between them, they eventually managed to straighten it all out. Julian now realised that Dave and Amanda-Jayne *had* genuinely loved each other, but perhaps had different agendas. The lad had also explained to her that what Dave had written in that infamous letter, was just blokish bravado, and something he might have said himself. For her part, Amanda-Jayne admitted that her desire to reunite with Julian was only a vehicle for her to be closer to Dave once more. In the end, both teenagers managed to part as friends. Ironically, it had been the note to Tim that made Julian realise Dave was just a daft bloke like him, and it became the key to his better understanding of the situation, not to mention, of the man himself.

All that careful thought had also prompted Julian to re-evaluate the whole four-year period, during which he and Dave had shared the house at Wellbourne.

'All those times when you and Mum would have liked to have been alone together, as newlyweds,' he recalled, with obvious regret, 'and I *always* insisted on being there.'

'Believe *me* Julian, there were only a *few* occasions when I would have liked it to have been just her and me,' Dave reassured him, clearly deriving no pleasure in the recollection of those miserable months. '*Most* of the time, I would have been happy if we could have…umm, functioned as a family. Huh, sadly, I got *neither*!'

'I *know*, but I had to be sure that it wasn't *me* who was squeezed out,' explained a frustrated Julian, with emphatic hand gestures. 'You see Dave, I saw you as a threat, especially at the beginning, and it sort of became a habit. Even *now*, I can't help but feel some…some resentment.'

'Look, I *do* begin to see things from your point of view, Julian, *honestly* I do. But like you, I have years of bitterness and…yes… *resentment*, festering away inside me,' Dave confessed, with the same frankness that his erstwhile stepson had just employed. He then immediately softened his attitude in an effort to put them back on to a more conciliatory footing. 'I suppose that road to mutual understanding is a hard one to go down all the way, in one trip, for *both* of us!' he asserted, looking over at his visitor with an understanding smile.

'At least we're *talking*,' Julian observed, with a stoical chuckle and a shrug of the shoulders. The visitor then appeared to become more thoughtful and studied the scuffed floor, whilst resting his elbows on his knees.

'Are you *okay* mate?' asked a genuinely concerned Dave, as he sat forward in his bed.

'Yeah…it's just that I've been recalling that last Sunday again,' Julian admitted, before looking back up to Dave and then addressing him directly. 'The more I think about it, the more I'm forced to acknowledge that Mum's handling of the…of the situation on that day, was cruel…*yes*, it was cruel and shocking. And I know for a *fact* that Amanda-Jayne would agree.'

Dave slowly and thoughtfully nodded in agreement to the lad's assertion.

'I'm *hardly* going to defend your mother's actions,' he commented, with a sympathetic smile. 'But at the end of the day, I suppose we have to acknowledge…*well*, we have to accept the fact that she *is* only human!' His smile soon turned into a chuckle, and Julian began to stare at him with a mystified expression, but it wasn't long before he was able to compose himself. '*Sorry*, old chap, it's only that I can't believe I've just made excuses for Sheila in response to *your* criticism of her!'

To his credit, Julian joined in the laughter, once he'd appreciated the humour behind this further irony.

After the mutual mirth had died down, Dave looked at the young man whom he'd never been able, or even allowed, to call his stepson. But this was a different Julian now: he was quiet, thoughtful and conciliatory; a further development of the new maturity that Dave had detected before it all went pear-shaped that Sunday. He suddenly found himself caring about what would happen to this teenager, the one who had been the principal thorn in his side for so long.

'So, what are *your* plans for the future then, Julian?' he asked, with genuine interest.

'I'm quite happy going on living in the flat at Dover for the time being, even if I *do* share it with two other hairy-arsed blokes who burp and fart all the time and *never* do any of the washing up.' It was now Julian, who chuckled to himself. 'I suppose this summer's experience has also given me an appreciation of having a place of my own, and I'm not afraid to admit that I could probably never go back and live with Mum again full time.'

'I can *quite* understand that,' Dave said, recalling his own turbulent teenage years.

'And don't take this the wrong way,' Julian added, with a wry grin. 'You may be a good bloke *after* all, but I could *never* live in the same house as *you* again either!'

Straightaway, Dave laughed heartily at the remark.

'Yes, the feeling's mutual, you little shit,' he replied in jest, but unwittingly paraphrasing his own words from the past. 'But I tell you *what*, when I get out of here, how about you and I going out for a night out on the piss?'

'Sounds like irresponsible blokish behaviour to me,' smiled Julian in reply, before lifting himself off the plastic chair. 'Give me a call … the number must be at home somewhere!' The lad then shook Dave's hand and briskly departed, giving one final wave before disappearing along the corridor.

Within a few minutes, the teenager unexpectedly hurried back into the ward.

'Dave, I've just seen this amazing looking woman in the corridor,' he announced in an excited manner. 'She was asking one of the nurses where David Darwin's bed was. I interrupted and offered to show her where you were, having just visited you *myself*, but she froze, mumbled something about suddenly remembering an appointment she'd made elsewhere, and then rushed off.'

Dave appeared concerned at the news.

'What did she *look* like, Julian?' he asked, casting anxious glances in the direction of the main corridor.

'Don't worry, it *wasn't* Mrs Roper,' Julian joked, with an accompanying grimace. 'No, your secret admirer is about your age, tall, slim, with sort of light brownish hair and round specs. Very *tasty* for an old bird actually!'

'Okay, thanks for coming back to tell me,' responded a much-relieved Dave. 'I'll let you know if she turns up again, though I'm *sure* it will end up being some Telecom person who couldn't bear the thought of my exclusive company!'

Julian smiled politely and then left the ward for a second time.

For the next half hour, Dave's only thought was about who on earth that mystery woman might be, the one who apparently lost her nerve at the last moment. And then, it suddenly occurred to him that it might be Alison Cross; so perhaps one of those vengeful fantasy harpies was not only coming alive, but also coming after him. Following that rather unsettling thought, Dave kept his eyes firmly fixed on the opening into the corridor, and his thumb placed firmly on the buzzer.

Towards the end of the visiting period, a member of the Cross family *did* turn up, but rather than being the vengeful Alison; it was Stephen Cross, Tim's so-called rich solicitor uncle and the courier of the poisoned package on that fateful Sunday. He was black-suited, white skinned and grey haired; a sort of monochrome man, and this gave him a rather funereal air. Dave looked past him anxiously, to make sure that he was alone, and thankfully it seemed that he was.

'Mr Darwin, I trust you are recovering,' he exclaimed in formal fashion, once he'd drawn level with the bed.

'Yes I *am*, thank you,' Dave replied both slowly and cautiously. 'In fact, I hope to be *out* of here by the end of the week.'

'Well, *that's* a relief,' Stephen responded, in words that were reinforced by a more relaxed demeanour. 'The main reason for my visit, is to assure you that I had *no* prior knowledge of the contents of that packet, when I delivered it to your residence on that particular Sunday. More specifically, I was *completely* unaware of the… umm, the incriminating note.'

'I accept that,' Dave reassured him calmly, now feeling a little more at ease. 'Please, Mr Cross, sit down won't you?' he offered, once more gesturing towards the popular visitor's chair.

'Thank you,' the solicitor acknowledged, looking rather incongruous as he proceeded to perch on top of the plastic seat. 'You see, my niece-in-law, Alison, put that package together when going through the remains of Tim's things, and she was very anxious that I deliver it to your house personally.'

'Now we know *why*!' Dave tutted, with a wide-eyed knowing look.

'Quite!' agreed Stephen succinctly. 'And then, after that terrible scene at the crematorium, I tackled her on why she had said all those awful things to you. It was *then* that I found out about the note, and it soon became clear that malice was her motive for both the packet *and* the unpleasantness at the…err…at the funerals'. He paused to clear his throat and also, gather his thoughts. 'Tim's father, my brother, was never a good handler of life's less welcome throws of the dice, as it were. One *could* say like father…umm… *anyway*, suffice it to say, it should be *him*, here today, explaining all this to you. And yet, it has *always* fallen upon me to sort the excrement out, as the modern parlance would have it.'

Dave smiled in sympathy and looked piteously at the struggling grey haired gentleman who, at that very moment, must have wished he were anywhere else other than there in that hospital ward. The pitying patient imagined him, longing to be sat in some high-backed chair within a hushed room, save for the slow thudding of a long cased clock, and sipping gin and tonic, whilst reading something to broaden his mind; a valuable first edition of course.

Stephen Cross took a deep breath before resuming his difficult and painful explanation.

'Having been made aware of my *own* role in this matter, which I *cannot* excuse, and realising that I'd been made an unwitting pawn in Alison's vengeful scheme, I made a return visit to your Wellbourne abode the day *after* the crematorium catastrophe, and met your… err…I met Mrs Darwin at the property … she was showing some prospective buyers round. And *that* was when I learnt of your…umm, of your unfortunate accident.'

Once again, Dave felt the need to reassure the uncharacteristically flustered Stephen Cross that he fully accepted what he'd said without qualification. Therefore, he summoned up his soothing Telecom voice, the one he used for worried little old ladies who rang the telephone complaints office.

'Listen, Mr Cross, there's *nothing* for you to feel bad about … the unfortunate contents of the note were, at the end of the day, my own fault … after all, I *wrote* the bloomin' thing!'

'Thank you … umm, Dave … I really appreciate your assurance,' he responded, with a rare display of warmth.

'So, what will happen to Alison and the two children now?' Dave asked, after a long pause.

'Ah *yes*, the children…I and Mrs Cross intend to keep in contact with Alison *solely* for the sake of Henry and Phillipa,' he admitted, with his guard now completely down. 'The thing *is* Dave, Muriel and I never *did* have any children, and therefore, no grandchildren, but when they are old enough to be seen alone, well… that may be a different matter.'

Dave appreciated the man's candour, and decided to take advantage of the mood by asking a question he was anxious to hear the answer to.

'And ... err, I hope you don't mind me asking, but how did Tim's funeral go?' he asked, keen not to cause the man any more pain, yet desperate to know himself, having been prevented from participating by the widow in attendance.

'As it turned out, after Alison's outburst, the funeral was a quiet dignified affair,' admitted a brighter looking Stephen, clearly not objecting to, or shrinking from the enquiry. 'Sadly, for *her* that is, *none* of her so-called new women friends showed up to support her; she was very hurt by that! My understanding is that she's already *left* the refuge and gone to stay on some Thanet-based farm with an old school friend. And as far as Henry and Phillipa are concerned, they've gone *with* her, of course. However, I am now holding Tim's share of the money from the house sale, in trust for the two children, until they come of age. Alison's not *happy* about that, but there we are!'

Following an expansive hand gesture, the visitor slowly stood up. '*Anyway* Dave, I must let you rest!' he concluded, rubbing his thighs at the back to restore the circulation.

'Thank you for coming to see me, and also kindly clearing up some concerns I had!' said Dave, as he reached out to shake his visitor's hand.

'And thank *you*, for the self-same reason!' Stephen Cross countered, before reaching inside his jacket, and then slipping Dave his business card. '*There* you are ... please give me a ring if you need someone to handle the divorce ... special rates *will* apply!' With a discreet wink, the man bowed slightly, and then beat a hasty but dignified retreat.

'A solicitor to the last,' Dave chuckled, as his visitor disappeared from view.

The next highlight in the day was the appearance of the drugs trolley, with the same two charges as yesterday. He watched with interest as they began their rounds at the opposite end of the six-berth bay, each of them selecting a patient at random, as before. Dave studied the taller, more attractive of the two nurses and crossed his fingers. 'Please pick me, please pick me', he repeated to himself, straightening up his borrowed pyjama top. The mantra now took him over, and for a while, nothing else mattered. And it was going well too; 'big eyes' was just finishing her second patient, whereas 'spotty' was already attending to her third. By the law of averages, he should be getting 'big eyes', he rejoiced. But that old man was delaying her; he was engaging 'big eyes' in vacuous small talk. 'Come on, *come on*', became his new mantra. 'Spotty' was now finishing off her third patient now, and 'big eyes' was *still* chatting. And then, they both approached the trolley together; both looked at him at the same time, and then exchanged a few words together. 'Come on 'big eyes', pick me, pick me', he begged, in a gruff half-whisper. Sadly, she then returned to the previous patient with a pill she'd forgotten, and a disconsolate Dave flopped back onto his pillow in despair.

Therefore, it was 'spotty' who finally approached his bed.

'You're looking *so* much better today, Mr Darwin,' she beamed, handing him the two plastic cups.

'Yes I *am* thank you!' he replied, with a shame-faced smile. She was so nice *and* the better nurse, and yet he'd actually prayed for her not to exist.

That evening, Dave thought back at what had turned out to be quite a surprising, if not healing day. He had made friends, not only with a comic vicar called Dick Amery, but also with the memory of Uncle Ronnie once again, or at least he had begun to. Furthermore, he and Julian had surprisingly reached something of an understanding. Ironically, with Julian on board, the time had never been more right for a reconciliation with Sheila. The only thing was, he no longer wanted that, or at least was fairly sure that he didn't. Lastly, Stephen Cross had allowed him, as the Americans say, some sort of closure with Tim, but he recognised that the regret, if not the guilt, would be remaining with him for a long time.

The third day on the ward dawned with Dave in a much happier frame of mind. He'd had a peaceful pain-free night; the healing visits of the previous day probably having done as much as the medication to help improve his condition. Most importantly of all though, he was finally rid of the ugly basket of fruit. He had asked one of the nurses to give it to the old boy, at the far end of their bay, who never seemed to get any visitors. However, being in hospital was now getting dull and boring. Having finished the Nigel Nicolson, he had picked up *On the Origin of Species* by Charles Darwin. Dave was surprised to have found it on the hospital library trolley and felt that he had been almost fated to read it, as Tim might have said. Indeed, he was long overdue reading that most famous work of his bearded namesake, and besides which, it had been one of the last books that Tim had read and discussed with him. There were so many reasons to pick it up, how could he not?

Dave was struggling through the first part of the book when Richard Amery paid a visit.

'Third day on the trot ... people will talk,' remarked a smiling Dave, glad of an excuse to put the book down.

'Hi David ... *look*, I have a question for you. Say no, and I won't press you,' he proposed cryptically, before sitting on the edge of the bed. 'I have Sheila with me, or rather back in the office, and she's anxious to see you. Would you consent to a visit?'

Dave looked dubious to say the least.

'Am I allowed to have a bodyguard?' he asked, with an expression that made it obvious he was only half joking.

'No, it's *not* like that, *honestly*,' Dick was quick to reassure him. 'She's perfectly calm and just a little nervous of seeing you, in fact a *lot* nervous ... I would say she's probably *more* anxious than *you* are of seeing *her*!'

Dave sighed deeply, and then nodded his reluctant agreement.

'Okay then, but I won't stand for any more lecturing!' he insisted forcefully.

As soon as the chaplain left, Dave told himself that he'd done the right thing; after all, things did need to be said, practical things concerning the sale of the house and *who* was to have *what* piece of furniture. He put Charles Darwin to one side, finished off his glass of water, and then sat there waiting.

After what seemed like an excessive amount of time, Dick re-appeared with a rather sheepish looking Sheila in tow.

'*Right* then, I'll leave you two alone,' he said nervously, and then in a fruitless effort to try and inject a little humour into the situation, added: 'Remember, no clutching or hitting below the belt'. He walked backwards from them, anxiously rubbing his hands together, and then practically ran out of the ward.

The estranged couple watched the chaplain until he'd disappeared into the corridor, and then slowly turned to face each other.

It was Dave who spoke first.

'I think he's the most nervous one of all,' he observed, in an attempt to break the ice.

'I wouldn't *bet* on that,' Sheila replied, with a half-chuckle, before settling into the well-worn chair.

There then followed an awkward silence, during which both parties twitched and grinned like idiots at each other. Sheila now took her turn to break the silence.

'The Reverend Amery has told me that your overdose was accidental,' she stated, in a quiet low-pitched voice.

'Yes it *was*, in that I had no premeditated notion of actually topping myself,' he confirmed, in a matter of fact manner.

'Oh, thank goodness for *that*,' Sheila sighed, followed by a relieved smile. 'Oh don't get me wrong ... I'm sorry that you've been ill, but if you'd have *meant* to do it and I'd found you dead, then I would *not* have been able to live with myself!'

Dave was glad Sheila felt relief that his overdose was unintentional, but he couldn't get over the implication that if he *had* died as a result of his 'accident', then she *would* have been able to live with herself, just so long as he hadn't meant it. Still, he concluded that there was no point in being confrontational now. Instead, he forced a polite smile.

'Well, I'm *physically* okay now, more or less, but when I get out of here, there'll be a lot of stressful things to sort out, as well you *know*!'

'That's one of the reasons why I needed...why I *wanted* to talk to you face to face,' Sheila replied, in a slow, almost downcast manner. She now reached for his hand, and held it before continuing. 'I talked with Julian last night, or rather he gave me a talking to, and I'm very glad the two of you have reached some sort of understanding. But… we need to talk about *us*…don't we!'

There followed another one of those awkward moments, just like in the hall back at home on that fateful Sunday afternoon, when Sheila was packed and ready to leave. It was one of those occasions when neither party knew what the other truly felt, or might say. Dave's mind began to race: was she going to suggest they try again, now that Julian's restrictive conditions were null and void? If so, how would he gently let her down and say that he now wanted to move on without her? Or if she were contrite enough, would he then melt and agree to a reconciliation? Their future together would be decided in the next few minutes and any decision made would largely depend on what they said to each other.

In the last few weeks Dave, and probably Sheila too, hadn't been able to see the wood for the trees, but now they had both reached a point along the forest path where it forked. The question was: should they go forward together on a mutually chosen route to reconciliation, or take separate paths onward that were never likely to cross again? However, Dave realised that words would not be the sole deciding factor, as far as their future was concerned. There was a more important question of their will; in other words, what they really wanted to happen deep down. But there was also the reality of the situation to consider. True, it would be relatively easy to get back together again, and try to return to that ceasefire: that mutual understanding of the past summer. However, Dave now recognised that such a decision would be delaying the inevitable because, at the end of the day, he didn't love her.

As it happened, Sheila had been thinking along the same lines and was again the first to speak.

'I think we both agree that the marriage is over,' she stated starkly, whilst symbolically pulling her hand away from his.

Blimey, she never pulls her punches, Dave thought to himself, although part of him was a little sorry she hadn't begged him to have her back, so that *he* could have been the one to say that the marriage was over.

'*Yes*, I would have to go along with that,' he calmly responded, with a slow, forlorn nod.

'*Well* then, having established that,' she continued, in a much brighter mood, 'there's no reason why we can't make the split as painless as possible.' She paused and then looked at her husband with a slightly quizzical expression. 'Do you have somewhere to go once the Wellbourne house is sold?'

Dave was instantly taken aback by the enquiry.

'*Come* on now Sheila, I've *hardly* been in a position to…to make any arrangements for…'

'If you *could*,' she quickly interrupted, 'would you be happy continuing to live at, the marital home, as they say?'

Her husband was clearly intrigued, if not a little puzzled by this line of questioning.

'You *know* I couldn't afford to,' he reminded her, 'besides which, you'll want *your* cut, to enable *you* to get a place, surely?'

'Well, fortunately enough, Aunt Theresa's legacy came through just in time for me to be able to use it as a deposit for a terraced house within the city walls, which I'm hoping to buy from a church friend. She's going abroad you see ... I know it seems rather sudden, but I think you'll agree, it's an opportunity worth taking!' Sheila was triumphant in her announcement and clearly enjoying the well-rehearsed benevolence with which she was treating her estranged bed-ridden husband.

Dave however, was still a little confused. He dared to hope that this was good news for him but, nonetheless, needed to clarify exactly what was being proposed.

'Let me get this *straight* then ... are you saying that I can actually stay on at…'

'*Yes*, we can take the house off the market ... you can continue to live there, and buy me out later, say within a *year*? That should give you *more* than enough time to sort out some additional finance!'

This was the first Dave had heard of her Aunt Theresa's death, let alone any sort of legacy, and given the size and location of the old girl's three-storey London house, the amount would have been quite considerable. On the other hand, now was not the time to be checking on Dobbin's dental hygiene.

'I don't know what to *say*…it's, it's *ideal*…*thanks*!' he gabbled gratefully. At the same time though, he thought how clever it had been of Sheila to get him to agree that the marriage was over, *before* mentioning the inheritance, and cleverer still to link it with a generous gesture that would not only be of great benefit to him, but also provide for a more stable future for him. All he had to worry about was the extra money to buy her out, but that could be a concern for tomorrow. How could he possibly make a fuss about Aunt Theresa's money given the circumstances? He knew he couldn't, and besides which, he and the old maiden lady never had really liked each other. Trust the old bag to time her death just right to spite me, he wistfully concluded.

'And as far as our furniture is concerned,' she continued cheerily, 'you can keep most of it at no extra cost. You see, I've also inherited a lot of antiques from the London house. I'll only need one or two bits and bobs from Wellbourne, but we can sort that out later.'

'Yes, that's *fine*!' agreed a totally bewildered Dave. 'Just…umm, just give me a ring sometime.'

'Oh I'm *so* glad we've been able to sort that out so amicably,' Sheila exclaimed, before reaching out and once more squeezing his hand. 'And when the dust has settled, I'd like to think that we could still be friends. We were friends *before* the marriage and I'm sure we could be *after* as well, perhaps even *good* friends.' She stroked his hand several times before slowly pulling hers away.

'I'd like that *too*!' he said, whilst at the same time, registering a little surprise at the intimacy of her touch.

Having completed the arrangements to their mutual satisfaction, Sheila stood up, smoothed her skirt down, and then leaned forward to kiss him on the cheek.

'Let me know when you get out of here,' she requested, before straightening up, waving regally, and then walking out of the bay with a business-like gait.

As soon as Sheila had gone, Dave sank back into the pillows and pondered on what had just occurred. So, at the end of the day, having reached that fork in the woodland path, they'd gone neither to left nor right, but instead, they had turned round and, together, returned back the way they'd come. Shortly, they would leave the dense and restricting wooded thicket that was their marriage and return to the open field, across which any route could be taken. And was Sheila not hinting that she would be glad if their paths crossed again in that more open environment?

Dave consumed his lunch with gusto, buoyed up by the fact that some of his seemingly insurmountable problems were actually being resolved. Not only that, but the quartet of vengeful women, whom he imagined were out for his blood, had been effectively halved. Sheila could no longer be counted amongst their number. His generous benefactor, soon to be ex-wife and future 'good' friend, had deftly handled the arrangements concerning their split and was no longer to be feared. Amanda-Jayne too, had put away her claws and fangs; Julian had seen to that for him. But it was clear to Dave, now more than ever, that he should forget all about his former teenage lover, however painful the process might be. He had reasoned her away in his head once already, and could do it again. And the love he felt in his heart would eventually wither and die, so long as the vital and sustaining nutrients were denied it.

So, as visiting time approached, he imagined there were only two fantasy figures cowering in the corridor; just a pair of monsters under the bed, waiting for the right time to make their move. He recalled that one of them, Alison Cross might have nearly got to him yesterday. From Julian's physical description, it did sound a bit like her. Dave recognised that she had a certain unconventional allure, a kind of hard beauty, but he himself had never actually been attracted to her. But did he really have anything more to fear from either Mrs Roper or Alison Cross? As far as Amanda-Jayne's unhinged mother was concerned, had he not already met her terms and conditions, albeit by default? And as for Tim's wife, now best described as his widow, surely she would be satisfied now that Dave was hospital-bound and his life in ruin? What is more, she had her own guilt to sort out now, according to 'rich' Uncle Stephen. That all seemed very logical, he deduced, and was satisfied that he could now banish all of the harpies from his mind.

But the question remained: who then was this mystery woman; that tall slim one with the light brown hair, and John Lennon-style glasses? He tried to form a mental image of her in his mind, and then suddenly sat up in bed with fright, as he saw the same woman standing in the opening from the main corridor. For a moment, he thought it might be a medication-induced mirage, and checked for leaves on the floor, but there were none. However, she seemed real enough, as she slowly crossed the ward and headed in his direction. The mystery woman certainly wasn't Alison, but as she drew level with his bed, she did seem strangely familiar.

'Mr Darwin?' she asked, in a deep middle class voice.

Dave stared into her face and then nodded cautiously.

'Hello, I'm...umm, I'm Mrs Holroyd,' announced the enigmatic stranger, a little nervously. She then reached out a long slender arm in greeting.

'Hello,' Dave said with a polite smile, and then shook the warm hand that was offered him, noting the single delicate gold chain that was hanging from her wrist. He then beckoned for her to sit on the well-worn visitor's chair to his left.

So, this is the woman who has been trying to get hold of me, Dave thought; the one his father supposed had known him from school. And Julian had been right too, she was very striking; tall, with large round metal spectacles and long, dark blonde hair tied behind her head with a leather clasp. A three quarter-length dress of ethnic design hugged her slender but shapely form, part of which was covered by a long suede jacket. She continuously clutched the strap of a shoulder bag in her left hand, and then proceeded to smooth a few wisps of flyaway hair with her right. There was something else too: an indefinable something; he definitely knew this woman from somewhere in the past.

'So, were we in the same year at the Archbishop's?' he asked, with his best and brightest disarming smile. 'I *know* your face, but I'm ashamed to say I just can't think of a name. I'm sorry ... you'll have to put me out of my misery.'

'I'm not going to make it *that* easy for you, David,' she replied with a wry smile and a twinkle of her eyes, which her specs did little to diminish. And then his enigmatic visitor got up from the chair and sat on the edge of his bed, slipping off her shoulder bag as she did so.

It was obvious to him that his attractive companion had already got over her initial nervousness, and now appeared to be studying his face most intensely.

'Have I got a bogey or something?' he asked, with amused embarrassment.

She laughed and quickly shook her head.

'No, it's just that you remind me so much of...your Uncle Ronnie. We schoolgirls *all* had posters of him back then!'

'I'm surprised you remember him at *all*, especially as he faded away from the limelight so quickly,' Dave remarked, somewhat mystified by her comments. 'Then again, you may also recall all that scandal and disgrace at the time...*Anyway*, I don't have his colouring and I'm...err, stockier than he was, or at least I *usually* am ... I've lost a bit of weight in the last three or four days!'

'Ah, but you have his kind brown eyes and your voices, they're...they're absolutely *identical*,' she said, without breaking her fixed yet fascinated stare.

'You must have been *quite* a fan,' affirmed a most intrigued Dave.

'You *could* say that!' she countered, with a brief, and wistful smile.

He now began to study her face, but with more discretion than she was currently employing. There was definitely a link there with his past, and yet there were elements of her features that were not so recognizable: her massive eyes were so familiar, but they were behind those unfamiliar glasses, that long hair engendered a pleasant memory, but it's colour wasn't quite right; the long neat nose struck a chord, but those delicate laughter lines didn't. Indeed, the visible signs of ageing were gentle and enhanced her beauty, rather than detracting from it, but it wasn't a woman in her late thirties that seemed so familiar.

'D'you know, I'm *sure* you are one of those girls from my year ... one I had a crush on, but never dared ask out. I'm *right*, aren't I?'

'Guess *again* David!' responded his charismatic companion, as she slowly shuffled up the edge of the bed towards him.

He leaned in a little closer too, so that their heads were now only inches apart. Straightaway, his heart began to race with excitement. There was something so familiar about her smell too; something that stirred a memory fragment within his subconscious. Sadly, it was a recollection that came and went in an instant, before he could latch onto it. As a result, Dave shook his head in defeat.

'You seem *so very* familiar to me on several levels, but I'm so sorry ... I just can't remember your name.'

'It's Catherine, with a 'C',' she said calmly, and with a look of keen expectation.

His mind raced again, and the tumblers landed on a very curious combination.

'You're not Catherine Manwood are you? *No* ... she was short and dark and I...'

'It's *me*, David,' she insisted softly, before removing her glasses. 'It's Catherine...Katie...Katie Townsend that was.'

Right there and then, he was transported back to the day they were last alone together; it was her sixteenth birthday, and the day that Ronnie died.

'I...I don't know what to *say*,' Dave gasped, now quite unable to break from *his* gaze into her alluring eyes.

'But are you *pleased* to see me?' she urged in a soft, and yet anxious voice.

He detected from her tone that this was more than the normal casual question posed when old friends meet up again. But he was not sure what to say in reply. In fact, right at that moment, he had more questions than answers. It was then that he became aware of a presence in the corridor; it was the hovering figure of a man. He glanced over briefly, and to his horror, realised that it was his father.

Peering into the ward from the main corridor, Len could see that his son had a visitor. Rather than approach the bed, he stayed where he was and waved, in the hope that he'd be noticed. Luckily, Dave soon looked over, and so Len held up five fingers to indicate how many minutes later he would be returning, and then walked off.

Catherine looked round as the man in the corridor strode away.

'Oh God, was that your *father*, David?' she asked in anxious tones; her face etched in panic.

'Yes it *was*,' Dave replied, 'but he's gone now ... don't worry!'

'I have to *go* now too,' a suddenly agitated Catherine announced, as she slid from the bed onto her feet. 'I'm not ready to meet *him* again just yet,' she confessed, scooping up her shoulder bag, 'but can I call you once you get out of here?'

Staring up into her anxious-looking eyes, Dave hesitated briefly and then nodded with a smile.

'I'm available on the same Wellbourne number. My wife and I are splitting up, but I'll be keeping the house on.'

She seemed more relieved than pleased at his positive response.

'I *will* call you, David; I have *so* many questions, as I'm *sure* you must have too,' she declared, with a brief close-mouthed smile. 'And hopefully, I'll be able to come up with some answers for you as well'. With only a brief backwards glance and a flicker of a smile, Catherine Holroyd left the ward and then promptly walked away in the opposite direction to that which Len had gone.

Dave was stunned and excited in equal measure; what an amazing day it was turning out to be.

It seemed much longer than five minutes before his father returned, but knowing him, Dave could be sure that it would be only a matter of seconds either side in any case.

'Fine looking woman you had visiting you, son,' he commented, immediately on arriving at his son's bedside. He was showing a rare side of his nature, the non-fatherly side, the man with normal men's feelings. 'Was she one of your colleagues from Telecom then, eh?'

Dave smiled up at his father and raised his eyebrows, without committing to either a positive or negative response.

Len nodded his head approvingly, and then drew up the chair closer to Dave's bed-head, before sitting down.

'In *my* day at Telecom, the only women around had better moustaches than *yours*!' he remarked, with a weary skywards tut.

'It isn't *that* much better now,' laughed his son in response, whilst patting his father's arm in fond acknowledgement.

His visitor chuckled briefly, and then sat there with a contented look on his face; that is, until he suddenly remembered something.

'Oh, before I forget, Dave ... Lucy sends her love ... she and the two Jims will try and get in to see you tomorrow before you're released,' he announced, with familial warmth.

'*That'll* be nice!' replied his bed-bound son, with approving nods.

It was then that Len stared at Dave with a narrow-eyed look of mischief. Sitting forward, he reached inside his overcoat and pulled out a flat paper bag.

'Look what *I've* got for you,' he said gleefully, before handing him the gift.

With a sense of eager anticipation, Dave took the bag and peered inside. Within seconds, he had pulled out a copy of the Beano and tube of Smarties. Straightaway, he beamed at his father with delight, before both laughed.

'I just couldn't *resist* it,' his still chuckling father explained. 'Seeing you in the ITU at the beginning of the week, took me back thirty years to when you and your sister had your tonsils out. D'you remember?'

How could he forget his father's unfailing loyalty and love! Those twice-daily visits, without fail, had meant so much to both of them. Suddenly, Dave was a vulnerable four-year-old again. He leant forward and then hugged his father, who happily responded in kind.

'Everything is going to be alright!' his dad assured him instinctively, as the years melted away.

As they embraced in true Darwin fashion, Dave wondered how he could have ever fallen out with this man in the past. Perhaps, this was one of the questions that Catherine would have an answer to, he speculated excitedly.

After what seemed like an eternity, his father finally relaxed his grip.

'*Anyway* old chap, I'd better be going ... I've left your mother with Grandad Maybury and she'll be tearing her hair out by now!' he admitted, with an ominous grimace, before getting to his feet.

'*Thanks* for coming to see me, Dad,' Dave said warmly, maintaining his intense eye contact.

'I'll be bringing your mum tomorrow,' promised his father, as he hovered by the end of the bed. 'Oh, by the way, that reminds me ... she wants to know if you'll come and stay with us this weekend? I think she wants an opportunity to spoil you rotten!' he admitted with an exaggerated wink.

'I'd *love* to, *thanks* Dad!' Dave beamed, as he waved his father goodbye.

On his way out, Len smiled in friendly fashion at the two regular nurses who had appeared on the ward for the afternoon drugs round. As the lumbering trolley slowly made its way towards him – a sort of ice cream van for junkies, he thought – Dave did not mind in the least which of them brought him his drugs. And instead of feverishly monitoring the nurses' progress, he lay back and marvelled at his sudden upturn in fortune. The house was going to be his and his alone, the relationship with his parents had never been stronger, and best of all, the lovely Katie Townsend, now known as Catherine Holroyd, had returned from the past and wanted to spend some time with him.

'It's *pills* time!' came a young cheery voice, which shook him back to the reality of the hospital ward.

Dave raised his head to find the tall, attractive nurse standing at the foot of his bed. He sat up whilst she went back over to the trolley for his cupful of tablets.

On returning, she unhooked his chart and then studied the top page.

'Dave Darwin eh ... any relation?' she asked, her big eyes focused on him for a reply.

How should I respond, thought Dave? He realised that by denying his uncle again, he'd be turning his back on much of his *own* past, as well as Ronnie's. The past was important to him; there was no point in denying it. And now, with Catherine's help, he would have a chance of making some sense of it all.

Dave smiled broadly at the young nurse, as she handed him the two white cups.

'Actually *yes*,' he responded at last, 'Ronnie Darwin was my uncle!'